"It was a massacre."

"I think Aeren is trying to warn us about these other people. He's trying to warn us away from them."

Walter scowled. "Then where are they, these other people? Who are they"?

"Dwarren."

Everyone turned from the bodies back toward the wagons, where Aeren and the other Alvritshai were standing beside the lead wagon, watching them. None of them had heard the group of Alvritshai approach.

"They call themselves the dwarren?" Walter demanded. "They did this? Why? Why would they attack our people?"

Aeren's brow creased in confusion. He motioned toward the wagons, toward the bodies at their feet, toward the arrow that Arten held, and said again, "Dwarren."

"And where are these dwarren?" Arten asked, voice tight. "Where do they live?"

Aeren stared at him solemnly for a long moment, and Colin noticed that his men weren't watching Walter or Arten or anyone else in the group. They were watching the plains.

Then Aeren motioned toward the surrounding grassland, his arm circling, fingers pointing in all directions. "Dwarren."

"I don't understand," Walter said sharply, frustrated.

Arten's gaze had shot toward the plains, his eyes squinted, face intent.

"I think he means," Tom said softly, also turning toward the plains, "that the dwarren are *everywhere*."

And before anyone could react, they heard screams coming from the direction of their own wagons.

BENJAMIN TATE

WELL OF SORROWS

DAW BOOKS, INC.

DONALD A. WOLLHEIM, FOUNDER

375 Hudson Street, New York, NY 10014

ELIZABETH R. WOLLHEIM

SHEILA E. GILBERT

PUBLISHERS

http://www.dawbooks.com

First Paperback Printing, May 2011
1   2   3   4   5   6   7   8   9   10

This book is dedicated
to the loyal folks at DAW Books:
Betsy, Marsha, the Other Josh,
Debra, Peter, the crew at G-Force,
and, of course, my editor,
Sheila Gilbert.

Acknowledgments

A book this size doesn't come into being without some help. I'd like to thank my editor, Sheila Gilbert, for not seizing or having a heart attack when she unpacked (or, these days, downloaded) the manuscript.

But before it even got to that stage, there were some folks who made it a better book by suffering through the first few drafts. My "first reader" has always been Ariel Guzman. He's seen the roughest of the rough and survived. My critique group has seen some pretty hideous stuff as well: Patricia Bray, Tracy, April, Jill, and the token other male, David. All of them give me input when I need it and aren't afraid to smack me down.

And lastly, I want to thank George and the rest of my family—my mother, brothers and sisters, and the new nephew—for all of the support. They also aren't afraid to smack me down, but usually the smackdowns are for things other than writing.

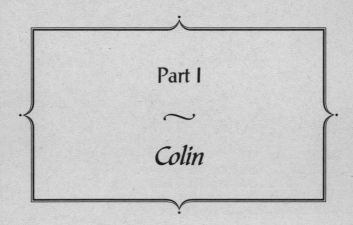

Part I

~

Colin

C OLIN SAW WALTER'S FOOT a moment before it connected with his stomach.

Air gushed from his lungs as the kick landed and he folded in upon himself in the hard-packed dirt of the alley, his arms cradling his gut. Pain exploded from his abdomen, radiating outward into his legs, smothering the aches and pains from all the other blows Walter and his gang had landed earlier. Colin rocked back and forth, tried not to cry out, the pain in his stomach spreading to his thighs, sending tentative spikes into his lower back—

And then, with a sickening sensation—a loose, queasy, tingling sensation—his bladder gave.

Colin's eyes flew wide in horror and he gasped, spittle flecked with blood from where he'd bitten his inner cheek flying from his lips. He felt warmth spread through his underlinen and breeches, and he squeezed his eyes closed tight. Hot tears burned his cheeks; tears he'd managed not to shed as the gang cornered him and began beating him, tears he'd vowed he wouldn't shed again after the last time they'd found him. He fought them as he pulled his knees in even tighter, as he tried to hide the blotch of wetness that now covered the front of his breeches. But he couldn't hide the sharp, pungent stench.

"Diermani's balls," Walter swore, stepping back from Colin with a lurch, one hand covering his mouth as he faked gagging. "The little squatter pissed his pants!"

Walter's three cohorts roared with laughter. One of them stepped forward, planted his feet to either side of

Colin's head, and spat onto Colin's face. Colin flinched as it struck his cheek, tightened the ball he'd made himself into, the tears of shame and pain and ineffectual anger he'd held back now slipping down his nose into the dirt. His breath came in short, hitching gasps. His side cramped with a sudden sharp spasm, and he cried out.

"Stupid shit," the older boy said from above him. It sounded like Brunt, the largest of the gang, Walter's heavy. "Don't you know how to hold your water? You take your breeches down before you piss!"

"Damn refugee," Gregor said from farther away. "Go back to Andover, where you came from. We were here first!"

"Yeah, go back west, back across the Arduon Ocean, back to the Bontari Family and the Court and their goddamned war."

Colin began sobbing. He couldn't stop it, no matter how hard he clenched his teeth. Keeping his eyes tight, he listened as the gang shuffled around, Brunt withdrawing, his feet scuffing the dirt of the alley, kicking it up into Colin's face. Snot clogged Colin's nose, and he began breathing through his mouth in harsh exhalations. He listened to the gang chuckling, listened to see if they were going to kick him more, or punch him, or pinch him as they'd done before. They seemed to have withdrawn.

But they hadn't left.

Someone's foot stamped down hard into the dirt close to Colin's head, and he jerked and cried out. Another burst of laughter, and then a hand clamped onto Colin's upper arm, fingers bruising the skin through his shirt, and wrenched him upright. Colin's eyes flew open as new pain flared in his shoulder, and he found himself inches from Walter's thin face. The thug's gray-green eyes blazed with hatred beneath his dirty, blond hair. His mouth was twisted into a grimace, as if he could barely stand touching Colin.

"Listen, pissant," he hissed. "Portstown belongs to us, to the Carrente Family. We were here first. Our grandfathers crossed the Arduon and settled the damn town, and we don't want any of you refugees here screwing the place up, especially Bontari refugees." He twisted the Bontari Family name with derision, with cold hatred. "So crawl back to your pissant parents in that hovel you refugees have built over in Lean-to and tell them to *get the hell out of our town.*"

He shook Colin to emphasize his words, Colin limp in his grip. He thought Walter was going to kick him again, or knee him in the groin, as he'd done once before—Colin could see the intent in the sudden tightening of the corners of Walter's eyes—but Walter merely snorted in disgust and thrust him to the ground, one of the other thugs giggling. Colin scrambled up onto his elbows, but the gang had retreated to the far end of the alley and now sauntered out into the greater sunlight of the main street. None of them looked back. Rick, the smallest of the bunch but still bigger than Colin, punched Brunt in the arm. Brunt grabbed him around the neck and hauled him down into a chokehold as they rounded the corner, ignoring Rick's shouted, "Hey!"

Once they were gone, Colin sank back and lay flat, wincing at another spasm in his side. He wiped the snot and spit from his face, felt the grit that had stuck to his skin, and let his arm flop back down to his side. He stared up at the blue sky overhead between the edges of the two warehouses to either side and tried to think of nothing.

Instead, he thought of home. Not the makeshift shed in the section of town that locals called Lean-to—no more than a single closed-off room with a dirt floor, a blanket for a door, a crude stone cook pit, and some pallets. He thought of Trent, in Andover, the city across the ocean that he'd called home his entire life. He thought about the house they'd lived in—a real house, with stone floors, a wooden door, and a patch of land enclosed by a low stone wall. When he'd been younger, he'd helped his mother plant gardens while his father was away working for the Family and the carpenter's guild. Tomatoes and peppers and all of the herbs: parsley and oregano and basil. Until age five, when he'd been sent to the school to learn of writing and mathematics and the Codex of Holy Diermani. At nine, he'd begun his apprenticeship in his father's carpenter's guild, even though many of the boys his age had decided to enter the Armory, to serve in the Family's army.

But then his father had come home one day and told them he'd found them room on one of the refugee ships heading to the east, to the New World. Because of the rumblings of a war within the Court, a Feud among the Families.

Colin frowned as he lay in the dirt of the alley, his eyes narrowed in anger. He remembered the day of the departure clearly. He hadn't wanted to leave, hadn't wanted to give up his apprenticeship, his friends, his *life*.

So he'd fled to the guildhall, had been stubbornly sanding down the edges of the Markosan cabinet for Dom Pellum when his father flung open the door to the workroom. Everyone had halted their work when the door cracked against the inner wall—everyone but Colin. The harsh scraping of sand trapped between two planes of wood had been the only sound in the room until the moment his father's hand gripped his shoulder and spun him around.

"Colin Patris Harten, what in bloody Diermani's name do you think you are doing?"

Colin glared up into his father's rage. "I'm finishing Dom Pellum's cabinet."

"No," his father said. "You're coming with me, with your mother."

His father's hand clamped so tightly around Colin's arm that Colin could feel his own fingers tingling. And then his father began to drag him out of the guild.

"No! No, you can't make me!" Colin flung himself backward with all his weight, clawed at his father's hand, dug in his feet, but his father's lean frame was too strong, his grip too tight.

They'd made it to the door, Colin kicking and screaming the entire way, tears beginning to form, when the guildmaster stepped in front of them.

"What are you doing, Tom?"

Colin felt a surge of hope, tasting like sweet apple in the back of his throat.

"I'm taking my son," his father said, voice tight with warning, "and Ana, and we're going to board the *Trader's Luck*."

"Headed for Portstown? With the *Chance* and the *Merry Weather*?"

"Aye."

"That's a Carrente town. Carrente and Bontari have never been allies in the Court. With the coming Feud, are you certain—?"

"I'm a member of the guild. It's a new world, they'll need craftsmen—journeymen—in order to expand. I have my papers. The guildhall will accept me, Bontari or not."

The guildmaster nodded at the defensiveness in Colin's father's voice, although Colin could see the doubt in his gaze as he turned to look down on Colin. "And I take it that Colin doesn't want to go."

It wasn't a question, but Colin's father answered anyway. "No. But he's not yet twelve. He's not of age to make the decision for himself."

Colin stared up into the guildmaster's eyes, pleaded with him with every fiber of his body. The guildmaster's eyebrows drew together in consideration, and he drew in a deep breath, held it—

Then exhaled heavily, shaking his head.

He stepped aside. "He's your son."

The taste of apple turned suddenly sour.

His father stepped forward before the betrayal sank in completely, pulling Colin out into blinding sunlight onto the steps of the guildhall, but then Colin began to struggle again. That's when his father jerked him in front of himself and cuffed him hard on the back of the head. "Stop it, Colin, stop it!"

Colin gasped and froze. Not because his father had struck him—he'd been cuffed on the head before, and not just by his father or mother—but because of the fear he heard in his father's voice. Fear he'd never heard there before; fear he could now see in his father's eyes as he knelt down beside him.

"I know you don't understand this, Colin, but we have to leave. Now. The Families are preparing for a Feud, one that I don't think will be settled in a day or a month or even a year. It's going to rip the Court apart, and I don't want you or your mother to be caught up in it. And it's going to involve all the Families. There won't be anywhere in Andover it won't reach. Which means we can't stay in Andover. The only place left to flee is across the Arduon, to the New World."

Then the city's bells began to toll midday, and his father's haggard glance shot skyward, toward the sun and the drifting clouds, and he swore under his breath.

Standing, he said, "The ship's going to leave soon. We have to hurry."

And they had, running down through the Circle, through the tiered outer Precinct and market, to the shipyard and docks and the vibrant blue waters below. Colin had stumbled along at his father's side at first, but the pace was too slow and after a few blocks his father hoisted him up onto his back. From this vantage, he could see the labyrinthine streets packed with crowds of hundreds as they passed. Sun glinted off the rounded, orange-red clay tiles of roofs, the blinding white buildings, the porticos, walled gardens, and secluded courtyards, all crammed into the steep landscape in haphazard fashion. At the top of the rocky bluff, above Trent, the stone columns of Dom Pellum's estate rose into the blue sky, verandas, colonnades, and stone statues spread out amid the acres of grapes in the vineyards behind. For the first time, Colin noticed the groups of men from the Armory, noticed their brooding eyes as they watched the streets, their armor and pointed helmets glinting in the sun. They were everywhere, especially at the docks, three entire ships flying the Bontari pennant surrounded by them as crates of supplies were unloaded and carted up the terraces to the Dom's estates.

Colin saw his mother on the dock that held the *Trader's Luck* a moment before his father leaned back and shrugged him down from his shoulders.

"Thank Diermani," his mother gasped, crossing herself—forehead, chest, right shoulder, heart—and the fear in her eyes drove the last of Colin's resistance away. But not the resentment. "We have to hurry. The captain has already threatened to leave without us." She snatched Colin's hand and then rushed toward the end of the dock, a satchel flung over one shoulder.

"He doesn't dare," his father growled as he stooped down and hauled two sacks onto his back and lifted a chest containing his tools into his arms, grunting with the weight. "I'm acting as ship's carpenter on the trip."

They hustled to the lowered plank. The captain bellowed, "There you are! Get them down below and your gear stowed. We're leaving. Now!"

His mother had descended the ladder into the hold before him. His father had shoved him from behind, to keep him moving.

And then, with two hundred and twenty other men,

women, and children, on three different ships, they'd fled Trent.

A part of him had hated his father that day. A part of him hated his father still.

His father.

He lurched upright into a seated position in the alley in Portstown, winced at the pain in his stomach and sides, at the bruises he could already feel forming on his arms, chest, and back. But the loose, queasy sensation in his gut had faded, leaving behind a shaking weakness in his legs.

He stared down at his soiled breeches, his dirt-smeared, torn shirt, and felt sick.

His father would kill him.

~

"You may as well come in, Colin. I can see your shadow."

Colin gave a guilty start. He'd been hovering outside of the ramshackle hut they'd claimed in Lean-to, listening to his mother hum softly to herself as she worked. But now he sighed and shoved aside the ragged blanket they were using as a door and entered.

He halted just inside the entrance, not quite able to look at his mother, and waited for the lecture to begin, as it had the last two times.

Instead, his mother simply said, "Oh, Colin. Not again."

The defeat in her voice forced him to look up.

She sat before the circle of stones that made up their fire pit. Wood had been set, ready to be lit, and the tripod braces his father had constructed to hold the pot over the flames were out and waiting. His mother held the pot in her lap, her arms resting on its edges as she sliced a potato to add to the water. The skin around her hazel eyes appeared bruised with exhaustion, her face gaunt. She'd pulled her long black hair back and pinned it to keep it out of her face while she worked.

They stared at each other. Colin felt tears begin to burn his eyes again, but he clamped his jaw tight and forced the sensation back, his gangly body going rigid.

His mother smiled tightly, and then she set the black pot to one side and stood.

"Well, come here," she said, moving toward the table against one wall, where she picked up a cloth and dipped it into water. "We'll get you cleaned up as much as possible before your father gets back. He's down at the docks, looking for work."

Colin could hear the snort in her words. His father had been down to the docks looking for work for the past eight weeks but had found nothing so far. Nothing of significance.

His mother turned, wringing out the cloth, then paused when she noticed the stain on the front of his breeches. Her sudden frown almost brought the tears back, but then she knelt and looked up into his eyes, pressing the damp cloth to his face, wiping away the blood and dirt, and the tracks his earlier tears had made.

"Was it Walter and his cronies?"

"Yes. They caught me on Water Street. They dragged me into an alley."

"And no one saw you?"

Colin didn't answer.

His mother sat back. "People saw you, but no one came to help?"

He nodded.

His mother stood abruptly, threw the cloth back onto the table as she stormed over to the pallets and one of the small chests they'd carried with them all the way from Trent. "Were they townsmen who saw you?" she snapped as she dug through the chest, lifting out clothes and setting them to one side. "Were they from the Carrente Family? Sartori's people?"

"Yes."

She muttered something under her breath, then pushed back from the chest and stalked across the room. "Here. Get out of those breeches and linen and into these. Your father should be here any minute."

Colin moved to the corner of the room and stripped off his soiled breeches and underlinen, his back to his mother. He shoved his feet into the new clothes hurriedly, head ducked and body hunched. He didn't like to be naked in front of his mother any longer than he had to any more. Even the thought made his cheeks burn, his chest and stomach tingle.

He had just cinched the ties of the breeches together when his father stepped into the hovel.

He swore under his breath the minute he saw Colin, his eyes going black. "Walter?"

Before Colin could nod, his mother spat, "Of course it was Walter! Who else would it have been?"

"Any of the goddamned townspeople who were here before us."

"Don't you dare curse in front of Colin." His mother's voice had gone soft and flat; Colin involuntarily took a step backward, edging to the right. He hated it when his parents argued, but his father still stood in the doorway, blocking any exit. "And the townspeople here treated us fine when we arrived. They even gave you a job on the docks after the guild turned you away. A job you'd still have if you hadn't been so arrogant!"

"It was the arrival of the *Breeze*—"

"No!" His mother sliced the air with one hand. "No! You will not blame the loss of your job on the arrival of more refugees from Andover. Yes, more and more of them arrive, practically each day. Yes, they're fleeing Andover and the Feud. And yes, there are others being shipped here as well— prisoners given a second chance, Armory discharged for suspect reasons, and others. But that is *not* why you lost your job. You lost your job because you couldn't stand the fact that you were a guildsman, a carpenter, and you were doing 'menial' labor on the docks because the guild here is Carrente and refused to accept a Bontari Family member into its ranks. You had to let everyone know that the work was beneath you. You had to put on airs. And you wonder why the regular dockworkers turned on you, why they made your life even more miserable. You let them goad you into a fight! Forget the fact that it was the only work available at the moment. Ignore the fact that you have a wife and son to support, that we barely have any funds left from Andover. Forget that—"

But here his mother halted. Colin could see the redness around her eyes, could see the watery tears that she tried to hide by raising a hand to her quivering mouth and turning away. His father had straightened, hands fisted at his sides, but now, staring at her shaking shoulders, he faltered.

"Ana—"

"Don't."

His father shifted up to his mother's back. Reaching for her, he began again. "Ana, I don't know—"

But his mother flinched away before he could touch her, and he stiffened. His hands hovered for a moment, then closed into fists and pulled back in frustrated, impotent anger.

He turned, stared at Colin, his expression tortured, jaw clenched.

Then, without a word, he ducked through the door, the blanket falling back into place with a rustle. His mother sobbed, hunching forward over the lone table in the room.

He *hated* it when they fought. He *hated* it when his mother cried.

Colin slid toward the door and shoved his way out into the late afternoon sunlight, hesitated, trapped between frustrated anger at his father and his mother's sobbing. He glared at the woman sitting outside her own door across from them, at her sympathetic frown, then spun and stormed off into the warren of narrow pathways between the shanties and huts, dodging men and women and children, all of them dressed in what had once been decent clothing but that now looked used and worn, most of them thin, those that had just arrived on ships gaunt or emaciated from the long journey or illness. He ignored them all, ignored the lost look in their eyes, the desperation, a look that had crept into his father's eyes in the last few weeks, a look that had died in his mother's eyes months ago.

Colin dodged a pack of smaller kids, most of them half naked, and wound his way to the center of Lean-to, a small rounded area of land with a large plinth of natural stone thrust up through the packed dirt. The sounds of the refugees from Andover surrounded him—shouts, the barking of a dog, the screams of children, the wailing of babies—all filtered through the sunlight and the stench of too many unwashed bodies pressed too closely together. He considered heading back into Portstown, back to the streets, but the fear of running into Walter and his gang again forced him to turn in the other direction, out toward the plains to the north and east of town.

A breeze gusted in from the ocean as soon as he moved outside the rough but growing boundary of Lean-to, pushing Colin's dark brown hair down into his eyes, bringing with it the taste of seaweed and salt. The ground began a slow incline, so unlike the sharp cliffs and terraced land around Trent, and within moments Colin found himself traipsing through grass, the stalks reaching up beyond his knees, the unripe grain pattering against his thighs. He reached down to run his hands through the grass, but the edges were too sharp, the seed heads too prickly.

He trudged up the crest of land to the north of Portstown and took a moment to stare down at the port, at the narrow docks that struck out into the water, the scattering of wooden buildings that made up the town's center, and the large stone building that belonged to the Proprietor, a low wall surrounding it. A second stone building stood off to one side, almost as large as the Proprietor's house: the church, its small spire topped off with the tilted cross of Holy Diermani. Only a few streets cut between the buildings, one running along the docks, one down to the warehouses to the south—Water Street, where Walter and his gang had caught Colin that afternoon—and three jutting out into the land and the twenty or so buildings that had been erected further inland. Homes and cottages and barns given by the Proprietor to the more prominent people in town continued out beyond where the streets trailed into dust and grass, most of them with small patches of plowed land, early spring crops already growing.

Lean-to had formed over the last few months to the north of the main portion of Portstown. At first nothing more than a few hovels on the bluff overlooking the port, with the influx of hundreds from Andover it had grown into a mass of huts and shacks and tents, all crammed against one another. From this height, Colin could see the section that housed most of the craftsmen, people who'd belonged to a guild in Andover but who weren't part of the Carrente Family or any of its allies. These huts and tents appeared more orderly, with clothes hung out on lines, flapping in the wind, and smoke rising from cook fires. The majority of the tents farther north were ragged, dirtier, barely standing, and haphazardly placed. Most of the prisoners given clemency if they agreed to help settle the New World had ended up there, along with anyone else who had caused problems after arriving in Portstown. People from all over Andover had arrived, representing all of the twelve Families of the Court, from all walks of life.

Except that here in Portstown, here in the New World,

there was no Court, there were no Families. At least, that was what they'd all been led to believe in Andover: that the New World was full of possibility, of riches, of dreams.

Colin snorted. That hadn't been true. There was a Proprietor in every settlement on the new coast. The Proprietor held the power in each of the towns: power sanctioned by one of the Families. The Proprietor of Portstown owned the land for as far as anyone could see, in all directions. He and the townspeople—the men and women who'd founded the town and all of their descendants fifty years back—were beholden to the Proprietor's Family, to the Court, an extension of Andover.

And over the past few months, they'd made it clear that those fleeing the Feud in Andover who were not part of the Carrente Family weren't wanted.

Colin turned his back on the town in disgust and faced east, out across the plains, at the smooth folds in the land covered in grass, dotted here and there with copses of trees or broken chunks of stone like the one in the middle of Lean-to. He struck off farther north, toward where one of those stones cut through the earth in a flat shelf, and sat down, legs crossed beneath him.

He'd found this place within the first week of arriving in Portstown, when the excitement over the new town and the new land had still been fresh, when he'd been trying to forget the death and disease that had plagued the three ships during the trip across the Arduon. He'd come to this rock and simply stared out over the grass that seemed to stretch forever, rustling in the wind, rippling in various shades of green and gold and yellow, dotted with the shadows of scattered clouds.

Now, he leaned back on his arms, stared up into the blue sky, watched the dark circling of a hawk high above, and slowly the tension in his shoulders ebbed. The sun beat down with soothing warmth, and heat radiated up from the rough granite beneath his palms. He closed his eyes, breathed in deeply, smelled the grass, the earth, the stone, listened to the shriek of the hawk above, faint with distance, to the wind as it rustled in the stalks surrounding him. The shame over pissing his breeches drained away, along with the anger at his father and his hatred of Walter and Portstown and the Carrente. All of it faded, even the throbbing of the bruises in his arms and on his chest.

Relaxed, he opened his eyes and gazed into the distance, to where the rumpled land met the sky.

The openness of that world called to him. If he breathed slowly enough, if he grew still enough, he could almost hear it.

～

His father returned to the hut after dark.

Colin sat before the fire. His mother sat on one of the sleeping pallets, Colin's torn shirt in her lap, her needle and thread flashing in the light as she mended it. A pile of assorted clothes sat next to her: shirts and breeches and linens from a few of the other members of Lean-to that also needed repair.

His parents looked at each other a moment after his father ducked through the entrance, his mother pausing in her work. Then Tom's gaze fell on Colin.

He moved toward the fire, reached forward to ruffle Colin's hair, but Colin ducked his head and shifted out of the way.

"Colin, come here."

When Colin didn't move, his father squatted down next to him by the fire with a grunt and held out his hand. "I have something for you."

He still hadn't forgiven his father, but he couldn't help himself. He looked, then frowned.

Tom held what appeared to be a wadded up ball of string.

"What is it?"

His father grinned. "Take it."

As Colin pulled it from his father's hand, Tom settled down beside him. Unraveling the loose ends of the straps, Colin realized it wasn't string, but leather. In its center, a wide rectangular piece was wrapped around a knotted ball. The straps were tied to the rectangular piece through slits. One of the straps had ties on the end; the other ended in the knotted ball.

"It's a sling," his father explained after making himself comfortable. "I made it this afternoon."

"You made him a sling?" his mother asked sharply. "What for?"

"So he can protect himself," his father growled. Then he drew in a shuddering breath and said more calmly, "So he can defend himself from Walter and his gang."

His mother's silence spoke volumes.

"Ana, he needs something he can use to protect himself from those bastards. He needs to be able to fight back."

"He shouldn't need to fight back at all."

"No, he shouldn't. But I don't think anyone in Portstown, least of all the Proprietor, is going to do anything about it. Walter's the Proprietor's son for God's sakes! Colin's almost twelve. I think he can handle a sling. I had one when I was his age. Unless you'd rather I give him a knife to defend himself with?"

His mother's eyes narrowed. "No. I don't want Colin running around with a knife."

"Then the sling will have to do." He hesitated a moment, then added, "I can't do anything about finding work, not at the moment. At least let me try to fix this."

Colin thought his mother would argue more, but she only closed her eyes and shook her head before returning to her mending.

Tom breathed a sigh of relief, barely audible, and the tension in his shoulders eased. He turned to Colin and smiled. The first real smile Colin had seen on his face in months.

"Tomorrow morning, I'll take you out to the plains, and we'll see if I can remember how to use it," he said.

Colin barely slept that night and not because his parents argued in hushed voices from their sleeping pallet not ten paces away, his mother fretting, his father trying to calm her. He curled up in his own pallet, back toward them, the sling clutched in one hand, a tight grin on his face.

In the morning, he was dressed and ready before either of his parents. The bacon fried too slowly, the fire burned too cold, and time dragged, until finally his mother snapped, "Colin, settle down and stop pacing! Your father will take you out as soon as he's finished breakfast. Now, go fill this pot with water before I strangle you!"

Colin froze, then snatched the pot from his mother's hands and tore out of the hut, his mother mumbling, "Holy Diermani preserve us from overexcited children."

"He's almost of age, Ana. He's not a child anymore."

Colin didn't hear his mother's response, already racing through the paths between tents and shanties toward one of the numerous streams that drained down toward the port. He dodged an old woman as she dumped dirty water into his path, leaped over a barking dog as the woman shouted something unintelligible after him, rounded the last corner before the stream—

And plowed into a girl headed in the other direction.

They tumbled to the ground in a mess of arms and legs, buckets and water. Bruises that Colin had forgotten since last night awoke as he struck the ground, and the girl's elbow caught him in the cheek as they landed, the girl crying out. Frigid water sluiced down Colin's shirt from one of the girl's buckets, and for a moment Colin couldn't breathe.

Then he gasped, sucked in a harsh breath and rolled to the side, onto his stomach.

"What in Diermani's eight bloody hells were you doing?" the girl shrieked. "And look what you've done. I just cleaned these buckets!"

Colin heard feet stamping, heard the rattle of a bucket's handle, and then a sudden pause.

"Oh, God." Someone dropped to the dirt beside him and rolled him over. "Are you hurt? You aren't hurt, are you?"

Colin sucked in another breath and winced at the feeling of his shirt plastered to his chest with mud.

"My mother's going to kill me," he muttered.

The girl—slightly taller than him, a year or two older, with short wild brown hair and freckles across her nose—leaned back onto her heels and glared down at him with hard green eyes. "She should, and you'd deserve it, tearing around here like that." Her frown deepened. "You're Colin, the carpenter's son, aren't you?"

He coughed and sat upright. "Yes." He took a closer look at the girl. "Who are you?"

She snorted. "Karen. I was on the *Merry Weather*." Her voice broke, filled with dark inflections. She couldn't hold his gaze, her eyes dropping, darting down and away. More than half the passengers on the *Merry Weather* had died of some kind of wasting sickness on the voyage across the Arduon.

A moment later, she cleared her throat. "Why is your mother going to kill you?"

Colin groaned. "Because this was my last clean shirt."

"That's easy to fix. Take it off."

Colin hesitated, and Karen rolled her eyes.

"Fine, don't take it off. Let your mother see you like that." She scrambled back to her feet, bucket in one hand, and headed toward the stream.

"Wait!" Colin said, grabbing his pot and following her. She'd already retrieved her other bucket and knelt by the stream, one bucket in the water, the second beside her, by the time he caught up.

She looked up at him, then extended one hand. "Well?"

He unbuttoned his shirt, fumbling a little, then handed the shirt over.

Karen gasped at the bruises across his chest and side, a few yellowed and fading, but most blue-black and purple. "How did you get those?"

Colin backed up a quick step when she reached out to touch him, already self-conscious without his shirt on. "Doesn't matter."

She gave him a skeptical look but didn't say anything, turning back to the stream. She plunged his shirt into the water. "This shouldn't be too hard to clean, since the mud is fresh." She began scrubbing the shirt vigorously.

Colin watched her from behind. A breeze gusted from the ocean and all of the little hairs on his arms prickled and stood on end. He shivered.

Karen held up the shirt, frowned at it, then scrubbed it again before declaring it acceptable.

"It's not perfect," she said, holding it out to him, "but it should do." She sluiced out her own buckets, then filled them with water. When she turned back, she added, "You should really learn to clean your own shirts though."

Then she smiled and, buckets in hand, moved off.

Colin stood stock-still, stunned, his shirt held out before him, until the gusting breeze brought him back.

He hastily put the shirt back on, grimacing as the damp

fabric stuck to his skin, then filled his pot and headed back home.

His mother gave him a raised eyebrow when she saw his shirt, but she said nothing. His father didn't even notice.

"Ready to learn the sling?" he asked, as soon as Colin handed the pot of water over to his mother.

"Yes."

"Then grab it and let's head down to the shore."

"The shore?" his mother asked. "I thought you were going to the plains?"

"I changed my mind. We'll practice on the plains eventually, but for now there'll be more stones on the beach."

Colin retrieved his sling from his mother.

"Be careful," she called after them, hands on hips. "Especially you, Tom."

His father grunted as they ducked through the door, and then they were moving down through Lean-to, in the direction of Portstown, but toward the northern end. Most of the people they met nodded to them or raised a hand in greeting. A few of the men called out to his father.

When they reached the edge of Lean-to, a group of three men joined them, most craftsmen Colin recognized from the voyage east on *Trader's Luck*.

"Mornin', Tom. Heading down to the docks?" Paul asked, falling into step beside Colin. Shorter than his father and broader of shoulder, he'd been a smith in Andover with hopes of making master in fewer than the typical twelve years as journeyman here in the New World.

"Not today. I haven't found work on the docks in over a week."

"None of us have," Paul said grimly, and the other two who'd joined them murmured agreement. "They're using those of us in Lean-to less and less, preferring their own men or the crews on the ships, even when it's obvious they could use the help. I don't like it."

Tom frowned. "Neither do I, but what can we do about it?"

Paul traded a look with the others. "We don't know. But if you haven't noticed, it's becoming a little desperate here in Lean-to. Most of us have used up whatever money we brought with us from Andover, and the food is running short. We can't afford anything in the town; they've jacked up their prices, at least for those of us from certain Families. And they don't want to barter with us for goods or services."

"And we can't hunt the game in the forest any more," one of the others mumbled.

His father halted in his tracks. "What?"

Paul nodded. "The Proprietor just issued a new decree. He's claimed the forests to the north and south for himself and the Carrente Family. Anyone caught poaching is to be put in the penance locks in the center of town for two days. Anyone caught twice will be hanged. Or sent back to Andover in chains."

"Which means death for certain." Colin thought the man's name was Sam. "They'll put you in the Armory, send you to the front ranks once the Feud starts in earnest. Most of those here in Lean-to are already criminals, have already been given the choice of the Armory or the New World. If they're sent back from here . . ."

A troubled look crossed his father's face. After a pause, he continued toward Portstown. "Where does he expect us to find fresh meat then?" he asked.

"I don't think the Proprietor expects us to find meat at all," Paul grumbled.

"So what should we do?" Sam asked.

Tom didn't answer for a moment. Then: "Nothing, for now. Except what we've been doing."

"And what about meat? What about food?" the third man snarled. "I didn't come here to starve at the Carrente's hands."

Tom caught his eye and held it. "I'll think of something, Shay."

Paul nodded and broke away, Sam and Shay following, headed toward the docks. Colin's father watched, then turned toward the shore in the other direction, one hand on Colin's shoulder. He squeezed once and smiled. "Nothing to worry about, Colin. Let's find some rocks for that sling."

But Colin heard the lie in his voice, saw it in the troubled look in his eyes.

They moved down from the grass into the sand along the beach, picking up stones as they went. Gulls and other shorebirds banked into the breeze overhead, and waves tumbled and crashed into the strand, foaming white as they drove up onto the beach. Seaweed had collected in clumps, left behind by the tide to dry out in the sun, and sand fleas hopped away in clouds as they passed. Small crabs—too small to be worth catching and eating—crawled among the occasional piece of driftwood. Closer to the water, where the tide was retreating, clams spit jets of water up from where they'd burrowed beneath the sand. The sharp scent of salt filled the air; Colin could taste it when he licked his lips.

Once they'd moved far enough north of the town, they halted.

"Now," his father said, taking the sling from Colin's grip and unwrapping the straps, "the sling is a weapon, not a toy. It can be extremely dangerous, and your mother made me promise that I'd teach you how to use it properly.

"See these ties here? They're used to anchor this end of the sling to your wrist." As he spoke, his father tied the sling to his own wrist. "The strap on this side is meant to dangle between your thumb and first finger, like this. The other strap, the one with the knot tied in the end, is held in the same hand. This forms a small pouch with the rect-angular piece of leather, like a little hammock. To load it, you let the sling dangle down and place the stone in the pocket." His father placed a rounded stone in the pouch. "When you want to release the stone, or whatever it is that you're trying to throw, you let go of the knot." His father let the knot go and the stone dropped down into the sand with a soft thump. His father reached down to retrieve it. "Obviously, you need to get some momentum behind the stone before you release it. You do that by twirling the sling, either to the side if you want to sling it underhand, or if you want more power behind it, overhead."

His father placed the stone back in the sling, then looked at Colin. "So, let's see if I remember how to sling at all. You'd better step back."

Colin took a few quick steps backward, and his father began twirling the sling for an underhanded throw down the beach. The sling picked up speed, his father using his entire arm—

And then suddenly the strap with the knot snapped outward. The stone arched up, a black speck against the light blue of the sky, then fell and kicked up a plume of sand a significant distance away. Tom let out a yelp of laughter, then turned toward Colin. "Not where I was aiming, but . . ." He trailed off into a grin. "Now it's your turn."

Colin leaped forward.

His father tied the sling to his right arm, crossing the cords back and forth in a lattice pattern, then placed the knot in his hand, closing Colin's fist with one hand and squeezing once before letting him go and stepping back. Held at his side, the sling nearly touched the sand; he was a full foot shorter than his father.

"Just spin it at first," his father said. "Get a feel for it."

Colin placed one of the water-smoothed stones from the beach into the pouch, then began twirling the sling, a thrill coursing up his arm and down into his chest, into his gut. He found himself smiling uncontrollably. The weight of the stone, the tension he could feel in the cords around his arm, thrummed in his body, and he began to spin the rock faster.

"Not so fast, Colin," his father said, but Colin didn't need the warning. He could feel the loss of control in his arm, could feel the swing becoming erratic.

He backed off, concentrating, until he regained control. He was using the underhand swing, as his father had done, and he could already feel the strain in his arm and shoulder, muscles he wasn't used to using beginning to burn.

"When you're ready, let the knot go."

Colin waited, focusing on the rock. Then he let the knot loose.

He felt the sling jerk in his arm as the release cord snapped outward. A surge of adrenalin shuddered through his body, cold and warm at the same time—

And then the stone thudded into the sand not two feet from him, spitting up a spume that pattered back down with a hiss.

His father burst out laughing, and he flushed to the roots of his hair, his scalp prickling with the sensation.

He almost turned to run, but his father gasped, "Colin! Colin, wait!" Between chuckles, wiping the tears from his eyes, he clapped a hand to Colin's shoulder and said, "Everyone does that the first time. You need to find where the release point is, that's all. And how to change it so you can hit targets at different distances. It takes practice. Lots and lots of practice." He passed over another stone. "Let's try it again. If you work at it, you can learn to hit just about anything—rabbits, birds, deer. And if you build up your strength, you can even kill with it. But it won't happen overnight.

"Do you think you can keep at it? Truly learn how to use it?"

He looked into his father's eyes, saw the smile there, the pride, and behind it the worry. Worry for his mother, for him. Worry about Portstown and the Proprietor, about their survival here in the New World, on this new coast.

"Yes," Colin said, his hand tightening on the sling's knot. "Yes, I can learn it."

And he meant it. He meant to practice until his arm ached, until he could hit anything within a hundred yards, accurately and repeatedly, standing still or moving.

And then he intended to use the sling on the Proprietor's son.

He intended to hunt Walter down and make him pay.

2

COLIN CROUCHED DOWN IN THE GRASS at the lip of a knoll, his head just above the waving stalks, the knot of his sling clutched in his right hand. The late summer sun beat down on the plains spread out around him, turning the grass gold. Spring had come and gone, most of summer as well. The heat had dried out the ground and the grain had ripened, the seed heads pattering lightly against Colin's face as he stared down onto the flat land below.

Mounds of dirt pockmarked the ground in all directions, the entrances to the burrows beneath like black eyes. An occasional prairie dog poked its head up, chirruped briefly, before vanishing again. But they were relaxing, growing used to Colin's presence. He'd arrived over an hour ago, had settled into position downwind of the burrows for the wait.

One of the prairie dogs slid out from its burrow and stood on its hind legs, nose twitching, tan fur blending into the grasses around it. It scanned the area, turning with quick shifts of its body. It chirruped, went down to all fours, and slid away from the entrance. Three more heads appeared in other burrows, surveying the area, and farther away two more slunk out of their protection into the sun. They called to each other, moving onto the plains warily, at least a third of them standing up and on guard while the rest foraged through the grasses. Clouds passed by, and in the breeze coming from the east Colin could smell a hint of coming rain. But he didn't move. He waited, the prairie dogs edging farther and farther from their burrows. He'd learned the hard way that the little buggers were quick, that with a single chirp of warning from one of the guards, all of them could vanish into safety beneath the earth in the blink of an eye.

One of the prairie dogs inched closer, picking through the grass with his nose and front feet. Colin focused in, clenched his hand around the knot of the sling. His breathing slowed as he watched. The bands of the sling tied around his forearm pressed into muscle as he raised his arm, as he began to gently twirl the stone already placed in the pouch. An overhead throw, because the distance was short.

And because he needed a killing blow.

The motion caught the prairie dog's attention and it stilled, then lifted its head in one swift jerk. At the same instant, one of the guardians emitted a piercing chirp.

Every prairie dog in sight stood up, long bodies rigid, small front feet dangling over the soft lighter fur of their underbellies. All of them turned in his direction.

Colin swore and released the sling, cords snapping out, stone flung.

In puffs of dirt, every prairie dog vanished.

Except one.

Colin released his pent breath with a fierce whoop of triumph and wiped the sweat from his forehead, grinning so hard it hurt. Skidding down the incline, he crouched down next to the body of the prairie dog, noted the splash of blood and matted fur where the stone had struck its head. Exactly where he'd intended.

He sat back on his haunches and smiled. He'd been practicing for months, first on the beach, getting the feel for the sling, for distance, for accuracy. Blocks of driftwood served as targets, set at intervals down the sand, where they remained stationary, then thrown out into the ocean, where he could practice hitting a moving target as the wood bobbed and rocked in the waves. Hours of practice, begun as soon as his chores were finished.

His father had watched him on occasion, had come to throw with him when he could, when he wasn't doing some menial labor in Portstown or helping someone in Lean-to. It had been his idea to send Colin and others out to the plains to hunt for rabbits and fowl and whatever else they could find in this new world that everyone had started to call New Andover. Others from Lean-to were sent down to the beaches to dig for clams or to catch the occasional large crab that had wandered up onto the sand. Still others were sent out in boats into the channel to fish.

Yet over half of those in Lean-to—mostly criminals and miscreants who'd chosen the New World over the Armory in Andover—were doing nothing except seething in discontent and squalor.

Colin had had little success at first on the plains—real animals were harder to hunt than driftwood—but now . . .

Now, he felt ready for his real target.

His smile twisted with anger as his eyes narrowed. His hand clenched on the cords of the sling.

A gust of air, leaden with the weight of rain, pushed against his face. Shoving the anger down, but not the anticipation, Colin closed his eyes and bowed his head, murmuring a quick prayer of thanks to Diermani for the kill, as his mother had taught him, then gathered up the limp body of the prairie dog and placed it into the satchel at his side that contained the two rabbits he'd caught that morning. Shading his eyes, he squinted up at the sun, then stood and scanned the horizon to the east.

"Time to head back," he said to himself.

But he didn't move.

The breeze brushed his hair back from his eyes, the scent of rain stronger now. In the distance, he could see the leading edge of the storm, white clouds at the forefront, darker clouds behind. It would arrive within the hour.

He sighed, removed his sling and stowed it in a separate pocket of the satchel, and headed back to the west, trudging up the incline where he'd waited for the prairie dogs and down the far side. The satchel bounced against his side as he moved, as he picked up his pace.

Half an hour later—the wind gusting at his back with enough force to flatten the grass around him, the clouds beginning to blot out the sun overhead—Colin came upon the outermost farms still close enough to be considered part of Portstown. He paused as he drew alongside the first. The house had yet to be completed, but the barn, twice as large as the house, had been raised the week before in the span of two days. A large tract of land had already been carved out of the grassland, freshly plowed, and if Colin shaded his eyes he could see a team of horses in the distance, digging out another stretch of field. A woman worked in the garden plot nearest the house, a basket tucked in tight to her hip. Two children roughhoused around her.

She stood as soon as she noticed Colin, glared at him, face set with hostility.

Colin spat to one side—a habit his father had picked up in the past months whenever those in Portstown were mentioned—and continued on his way.

He entered Lean-to with the first fat drops of rain pattering down from the sky. Men and women cursed and shot black looks at the clouds, then tucked pots and baskets under their arms, shielding them from the rain as they ducked into huts and tents, flaps falling closed behind them. One woman bellowed, "Come here you little terrors!" and rounded up the last of her four children, ushering them into a shack made from pieces of discarded boat hulls and driftwood.

Colin ducked into his parents' hut to the first grumble of thunder. He squatted and pulled a shutter of wood over the front of the opening before letting the blanket drop, then turned.

And halted. His parents had guests.

"They've shut us out completely!" Paul spat, then took a pull from an aleskin. He shoved it at Sam, who wiped the mouthpiece on his shirt before taking his own pull.

"What is he talking about, Sam?" Colin's mother asked in disgust, motioning Colin toward her where she worked near the fire, taking his satchel.

Colin settled down next to his mother, away from the table where his father, Paul, Sam, and Shay sat on various crates and stools, a game of Crook and Row set out before them. Sam glared at his cards, then threw one before answering, Shay snorting as he picked up the tossed card.

"The Proprietor has banned anyone from Lean-to from the docks. We can no longer seek work there or at the warehouses. It's as if we have the plague!"

"He can't do that."

"Oh, he didn't officially 'ban' us," Paul said, his words slurred with more than derision. "No, no, he's too crafty for that."

Shay played a stretch of four and discarded. "The bastard has sent out the Armory, men just over from Andover, sent by the Family. They've started patrolling the docks."

"I don't understand it," Ana said, knife slicing through the first rabbit with rough jerks as she began gutting and cleaning it. She motioned for Colin to help her. "He should *want* to have refugees flooding the town. He could double its size within months. There'd be more land producing goods, more tradesmen producing wares. Trade would increase. He'd be wallowing in the profits!"

"Portstown has already doubled in size," his father said, as he continued with his own move. "There's a new mill along the river, at least five new merchant houses, two taverns, a granary. But none of that matters. He doesn't need profit, he's already wallowing in it."

"Then what's he looking for?" Paul asked.

"Status."

Everyone at the table turned toward him. Sam frowned. "What do you mean?"

Colin's father paused, caught their intent looks, then set his cards down. "It's all political. I think Sartori sees Portstown as his path into the Court. Look at what he's done with the land since we arrived. He's parceled it out to members of various Families in Andover, to their lesser sons, to those allied strongly with the Carrente Doms and their immediate successors. Last week, he awarded a huge chunk of land to the east to the third son of Dom Umberto, a thousand acres of arable farmland at least."

Paul choked on his ale. "Umberto is part of the Scarrelli Family!"

His father nodded, anger touching his eyes. "Sartori is currying favor with his allies and the Family trading companies, using the land as his collateral. In exchange, he's gaining influence in the Court. That's where the Armory is coming from. His allies are bringing them in to protect their interests here in Portstown. He's never going to award the land to any of us, because we don't have anything that he needs. We can't help him take advantage of the Feud in Andover. Look at all of us here in Lean-to! We're either bonded to one of the rival Families of the Carrentes, or we're miscreants, troublemakers, or criminals shipped here from Andover."

Colin's mother growled, "We came here to escape the Feud."

No one responded. Rain began pounding on the roof of the hut, leaking through near the covered hole where the smoke from the fire could escape. Colin's mother shook her head and set a pot under the drip before returning to the carcasses. They'd finished the two rabbits, had begun working on the prairie dog.

As Colin began cutting it open, careful not to damage the hide, since his mother could use the pelt, he said into the silence, "I saw it."

All of the men turned toward Colin. The knife slipped in his hand, narrowly missing his palm.

"What did you see?" Shay asked.

Colin forced his hands to stop trembling. "I saw the farm, the one given to Umberto's son. On my way back from the plains."

His mother gasped as she took the prairie dog and knife from him. "You were out that far into the plains? I told you to stay close. We don't know what's out there!"

"Ana," his father said, and his mother fell silent with a glower. His father didn't notice, his attention on Colin. "What have they done so far?"

Colin glanced toward Sam and Paul, toward Shay, who'd shifted forward. He didn't like the darkness in their eyes, the intensity, especially in Shay's. Their cards had been forgotten. And the ale.

Thunder growled overhead as Colin said, "They've plowed at least two fields. And the garden."

"What about the house?" Sam asked. "The barn?"

And suddenly Colin understood. They were carpenters and masons and smiths. They could have been hired to help raise the barn, to help build the house.

But they hadn't been. Just as they hadn't been hired to help with the new buildings in Portstown, the mill or the granary.

He swallowed against the sourness in his stomach, against the faint taste of bile in the back of his throat, and said, "The barn is already up. The house isn't finished, but—"

"But it's been started," his father finished for him as all four of them slumped back into their chairs.

Shay slammed his cards down onto the table. "God-damned bloody cursed motherf—"

"Shay Jones!" his mother barked, and Shay leaped to his feet.

"What!" he spat, face livid. "I can't swear? The goddamned Proprietor is sucking our lives away—purposefully!—and I can't bloody curse? What's going to happen? Is the blessed Diermani going to strike me dead where I stand? Is He going to send lightning to crisp me into ash? Because at this point I'd bloody well welcome it!"

"Shay," Colin's father said, and then repeated more harshly. "Shay! Sit down!"

Shay collapsed back into his seat, but the rage on his face didn't change. "What did we cross the bloody Arduon for? Not for this." He motioned toward the rest of the hut, toward all of Lean-to. "Not to live in a shack, begging for menial work on the docks. Not scouring the beaches for crabs or scavenging the plains for rodents, just to eat." Leaning forward, he hissed, "I didn't give up an apprenticeship with one of the finest guilds in Andover for *this*. Something has got to change or, Diermani is my witness, I'll *make* it change."

He hesitated, eyes locked on Tom, then shoved back from the table, the crate he'd been sitting on tilting and tumbling to the ground. He'd ducked out into the storm, the shutter thrown aside, before anyone had even drawn a breath.

No one moved; Sam and Paul sat with stunned looks on their faces, cards held before them. Thunder rumbled.

Then Ana set her butchering knife down and wiped her hands on an already bloody cloth. "Well," she said. "I'd say Shay's a little . . . angry."

"He's not the only one," Sam said, tossing his cards into the center of the table.

Ana hesitated at the warning in Sam's voice, then moved toward the entrance to the hut to replace the shutter.

"A large group of people in Lean-to have gotten tired of waiting," Colin's father said.

"Some of them have already left," Sam added. "The Havensworths gave up and returned to Andover. They used the last of their money for passage. The Colts and the Ferruses both took ship to other settlements along the coast."

"The Wrights packed up and headed inland, to settle their own land," Ana said with a huff.

"And the Wrights haven't been heard from since," Colin's father said meaningfully, watching his mother's back. "I'm not a farmer, Ana. I'm a carpenter. I don't think we'd survive long if I simply packed you and Colin up and headed off into the plains alone. And we don't have any funds left to get passage back to Andover or even down the coast."

After a moment, his father shifted, gaze dropping back to Sam and Paul. "But Shay is right. Sartori is doing everything he can to push us out, to force us to leave, and I'm tired of it. Tired of the restrictions, of the pressure. Of the threats that are becoming more and more overt, like the presence of the Armory. Something needs to change. Soon. If it doesn't . . ."

Paul snorted. "Shay isn't one to waste words when action will do. And he's got plenty of followers. He's been recruiting from the dissidents in Lean-to, the criminals who opted for the New World rather than the Armory in Andover, and there's a lot more of them here than honest folk. There's what? Thirty guildsmen here in Lean-to? There are four times as many of them. It could get ugly."

Ana frowned as she returned, her eyes going to Colin. She hugged him from behind and murmured, "I don't want you going into town, Colin. Not for the next few days."

Colin pulled out of her embrace. "Why not?"

"Because I don't know what Shay might do." When Colin rolled his eyes, she added, "And because I said so! Now, go take this bucket of innards to Nate. He'll make good use of it."

"But it's raining!"

"I don't care," his mother said, voice black, and she held out the bucket. "Now go! And stick to this area of Lean-to, where the craftsmen are!"

Colin sighed in exasperation, but he took the bucket. Because of the warning in his mother's voice and the look he got from his father.

But he didn't intend to stay out of Portstown.

~

The next day, Colin told his mother he was going hunting, but as soon as he left the outskirts of Lean-to, he

cut around the edge of the shacks and tents and headed
toward the town. He carried his satchel, hung over one
shoulder, and his sling was tied to his forearm, the straps
and pouch for the stone bundled up in his hand. He'd worn
a long-sleeve shirt, so that the crisscrossed ties of the sling
would be hidden, the cuff rolled back slightly so that it
wouldn't interfere with his throw. He wanted to be ready.

He entered the town from the north, a flutter of nervousness tightening in his gut as he passed through the
outermost houses. Low stone fences surrounded the town
now, separating the ramshackle Lean-to on the rise above
from the land Sartori had given to some of the more in-
fluential members of the port. The stone walls—fieldstone
mostly, although some had used the water-worn stone
from the shore—marked the boundaries of the different
estates. As Colin came upon a dirt lane, he peered over the
low walls, curious, and tried not to scowl. These were the
houses of the nobility, the tradesmen and lesser nobles, or
those that fancied themselves nobles here in New Andover. The stone walls were broken by iron gates, and carriage houses and stables hid behind the main houses, even
though there were only two carriages in all of Portstown.
Ornamental gardens had been planted inside the walls,
the trees young, barely twice Colin's height, the hedges
trimmed, the rose bushes pruned. Colin saw stable hands
cleaning out the stables, a servant's face appearing briefly
in one window before vanishing, but no one else. Not here.
Most of the regular people in Portstown would be down at
the docks, or in the market in the center of town.

The lanes between the estates ended at the beginning
of Water Street and the docks. Colin slowed as soon as he
stepped onto the new planking of the wharf, his eyes immediately drawn to the Armory guardsmen that stood at
the end of the first dock. Dressed in leather armor, white
shirts with the Carrente Family crest, breeches, and a metal
helm with points to the front and back, they stood out
from the rest of the men that lined the wharf. Two of them
carried swords, sheathed; the third carried a pike. One of
the swordsmen grimaced as Colin moved forward onto
the wharf, pointing with his pipe before puffing on it and
blowing smoke in Colin's direction. Colin frowned, and the
guardsman snickered before turning away.

The docks weren't empty, but they weren't crowded either. A few men were toting crates from a stack at the end of the wharf, a boy younger than Colin sitting watch. Another group moved barrels marked with the Carrente Family sigil onto the back of a wagon, grunting and cursing. On the second dock, workers were readying for the arrival of another ship, although when Colin shaded his eyes and stared out at the dark waves of the ocean he couldn't see anything on the horizon. No ships were berthed in Portstown, but numerous boats were out in the channel between Portstown and the outer banks of the Strand, the stretch of sand that protected the coast from the worst of the storms that came from the sea.

Colin hesitated at the end of the dock, watching the preparations long enough that the Armory guardsmen finally shifted and began drifting in his direction. Before they'd made it halfway to his position, he stepped off the wooden planks of the wharf back onto the dirt road and headed deeper into town.

The buildings closest to the docks were taverns and the mercantiles of the trading companies, with stables or small warehouses in back for storing supplies over short periods of time. Behind these lay the wide town square, the Proprietor's estate on the far side surrounded by another stone wall, higher than those of the lesser nobles. Diermani's church sat to one side, a graveyard in the back. There were more people here: townspeople, women walking in pairs, headed toward the mercantiles, children with dogs in tow, a few men. Colin wove through them, trying not to be seen, ignoring the occasional look of disdain, the furrowed brows, the sniffs and huffs of the women. He'd intended to pass through the square quickly, there and then gone—

But he slowed before the church, halted. He stared up at the steeple and the tilted cross against the clouds and sky, and hesitated.

"It always calms me, even in the worst of times."

Colin ripped his gaze away from Diermani's cross and spun toward the voice, his heart thudding hard in his chest. His hand tightened on the sling, then relaxed as he spotted the priest standing a few steps behind him, watching him solemnly. About the same age as his father, the priest's eyes were dark, his face tanned, but his hair was fair, and a smile touched the corner of his mouth. Dust from the marketplace coated the bottom of his black robe, but the white length of cloth draped over his shoulders was pristine and vibrant in the sun.

Wrinkles creased the priest's brow as he regarded Colin a moment, then cleared. "You're from Lean-to," he said. "That's why I don't recognize you." He hesitated, half turned toward the Proprietor's manse, then halted. Irritation flashed across his face, as if he were angry at himself, and then he smiled. "Would you like to see inside?"

Colin frowned in suspicion, but his heart quickened. Everyone in the guild back in Andover had spoken of the great churches, of the work they'd been commissioned to do inside them, some of the finest that the guild had to offer. No one but a master could take on such an endeavor. His father had been awestruck for weeks after gaining journeyman and being allowed entrance into the cathedral in Trent. "Yes, Patris."

The priest's eyes widened slightly. "So you know a little of the church." He stepped forward, one hand guiding Colin toward the steps and the entrance. "I am a Patris, yes, but here in New Andover we aren't as formal. You can call me Brindisi."

They'd reached the main wooden doors, built of heavy oak. Brindisi opened one side, motioning Colin through, then followed, swinging the door closed behind him. Brindisi stepped forward, but he paused partway into the sanctuary and turned when Colin did not move to follow him. "What's wrong?"

Colin didn't answer. He breathed in the scent of newly worked wood thickened with the heavy taint of oil and some type of incense. A wooden lattice, intricate in detail, separated the entrance from the main sanctuary, where pews formed neat ranks between high, arched windows and heavy banners, all beneath a vaulted ceiling. A huge cross filled the recess behind the altar on the far side of the room, draped with thick folds of white and red cloth, the central beam tall and straight, the crossbeam tilted downward. Below, a long, narrow basin of water gleamed beneath the light of dozens of candles, separated from the pews by another carved railing of wood. Everything had the mark of the carpenter's guild on it, intricate and fine, the pews solid, all of it worked with fine oils to a polished sheen, even the recesses of the windows.

And his father hadn't had anything to do with it. Because his father belonged to the Bontari Family.

Brindisi took a step toward him. "You can enter the sanctuary. Diermani accepts everyone."

He turned a harsh glare on Brindisi. "Even a Bontari?"

Then he turned and fled the heady scent of worked wood, a scent he thought he'd forgotten on the three-month voyage to the New World and the time they'd spent here. He heard Brindisi call for him to wait, but he ignored him, shoving through the door into the bright outer sunlight. He stumbled down the steps, stood blinking as his eyes adjusted, his hand squeezed tight on the sling as anger assailed him. An anger tinged with doubt, with guilt.

He wondered what his mother would think of what he intended to do. His mother, who wore Diermani's tilted cross on a chain around her neck.

He shoved the doubt aside, shot a glare toward Sartori's estate, thought about the Armory on the wharf, of his father's face every time he returned from town with nothing. The scent of wood filled his nostrils. Then he turned and headed farther south, toward the warehouses, toward the end of Water Street.

Toward where he knew Walter and his gang would be.

He saw Walter, Brunt, Gregor, and Rick before they saw him. Even then, fear tingled through his skin, setting the hairs on the backs of his arms on end and settling with an all too familiar queasy feeling in the pit of his stomach. One hand clutching unconsciously to the satchel at his side, he ducked out of sight behind another warehouse. Breath coming fast and harsh, he fought the urge to run, to flee back to Lean-to, back to the quiet of the plains. He thought of how they'd beaten him until he'd pissed his pants, thought about how they'd humiliated him, how they'd driven him from the town too many times since then to count . . . and when his breath had slowed enough that he was no longer panting, when the fear had abated enough that he could loosen the fist that clenched the sling, he shifted to the corner and peered around it to watch.

"Move faster, you slackers!" Walter bellowed, leaning against a cask set to the side of the warehouse door. Behind him, his cronies snickered where they lounged among a stack of empty crates and barrels. "My father wants this cart unloaded and back to the wharf before the next ship arrives."

The leader of the work crew cast Walter a dark glare, but he said, "You heard the little whore's son. Let's get this cart finished, lads."

Walter bristled, face going a stark red, the leader of the crew barely containing a smile as Walter's gang burst out in laughter. One of the crew grinned, then heaved and swung one of the heavy sacks up onto his shoulder with a grunt.

Before he'd gone two steps, Walter shifted away from the cask and caught the man's ankle with his foot.

The man staggered, tried to catch his balance, but Walter jerked his foot from underneath him, and he crashed to the street with a curse. The sack landed with the rip of burlap. Grain hissed from the rent in the sack, spreading across the ground in a smooth fan of gold.

The leader of the crew leaped forward and knelt beside his worker. "What in the seven hells happened?"

"His little royal pissant tripped me," the man growled, wincing as he tried to move his shoulder.

The leader glared at Walter, the tolerant anger he'd shown before now slipping into rage.

"I did no such thing," Walter said. "Your incompetent worker fell. Isn't that right, Brunt?"

Walter's heavy sidled up to Walter's back. "Yup. He fell. Tripped over his own feet."

"The sad sack can't even carry a sack of grain," Rick threw in from behind, then began to giggle.

Colin's shoulders tensed, right between the shoulder blades, and he found himself breathing harder.

The leader stood slowly, the rest of the work crew halting and gathering behind him. He stepped over the fallen man's body. Walter faced the man with confidence, his grin not faltering until the moment the leader's hand snaked out, gripped Walter by the front of his shirt, and hauled him in close.

"I've had enough of your attitude," he said, voice low, but carrying in the sudden deathly silence, "and of you throwing out orders like you're the Proprietor himself. You're nothing but the second son of a privileged landholder. A bastard son at that. You won't amount to anything."

Then he pulled back, hand clenched into a tight fist. Colin felt hope surge up into this throat, almost fell out of his hiding place behind the warehouse—

But then someone muttered, "What's going on here?"

A man emerged from a cross street, accompanied by a contingent of Armory guardsmen dressed like those Colin had seen on the dock. The man was dressed in the fine silks of the nobility—white shirt with ruffles at the neck and down the front, loose sleeves, a blue vest over it with gold-painted buttons and gilt stitching. The tailored brown breeches were tucked into knee-high boots. He wore a powdered wig, the hair stark white in the sunlight, and a hat whose sides were folded up to form a rough triangle.

Everyone in the work crew—and in Walter's gang—froze. The leader of the crew lowered his fist and released Walter's shirt with obvious reluctance before stepping back.

"Nothing, Proprietor Sartori. We've simply had a ... mishap."

Sartori held the leader's gaze a moment, then shot a glance toward Walter. The lines around his eyes and mouth tightened. "Is this true, Walter? Was this an accident?"

Walter tried to flatten the creases in his shirt as he answered. "Yes, sir. An accident."

Sartori drew in a deep breath. "I see. Accidents seem to happen on a regular basis in your vicinity." Walter seemed about to protest, but his father cut him off. "I don't recall sending you here to oversee this shipment."

"You didn't. But I thought with my brother out at the new mill—"

"That you could be helpful. Ah, yes. I understand. Since it appears that this shipment is almost unloaded, perhaps you could be helpful ... elsewhere."

A black look crossed Walter's face, but he hid it from his father by looking toward the ground. "Yes, sir."

Turning toward his gang, he motioned Brunt, Gregor, and Rick down the street, heading directly toward Colin. Behind them, the leader of the crew attempted to apologize, but Sartori waved him silent.

"Clean this up as best you can," the Proprietor said. "Then report to the docks. I'm expecting the arrival of the *Tradewind* today, along with . . . someone of significance to the West Wind Trading Company. I need you there."

And then Colin heard Walter mutter, "Look what I see, boys. A loiterer from Lean-to."

Colin's gaze dropped from Sartori to Walter, now only twenty paces away.

His heart leaped into his throat. Then he spat a curse and dodged behind the cover of the warehouse.

He ran as fast as his legs could carry him, down the length of the warehouse, the tread of Walter's gang close behind. As soon as they were out of sight of his father, Walter began calling out names, taunting Colin as he ran, joined by Brunt and Gregor and Rick. Pulse thudding in his neck, in his chest, Colin cut left at the end of the street, cut right again after that, slipping in the dry grit of the street as he took the corner too fast. Catching himself with his left arm, he rolled, hip hitting the hard-packed earth with a wrench, but he used the momentum to swing back up into a crouch and then leaped forward. It gave him a brief glance of Walter and his gang coming up from behind. But the older boys weren't moving fast, had barely managed to close any distance at all, confident they would catch up.

And after the incident with Sartori, blind and stupid enough to continue following him.

Colin suppressed a grin, then sprinted for the far end of the street.

When Walter and his gang finally rounded the last corner, they found Colin standing in the middle of the back street, feet spread, satchel on the ground to one side, waiting. All four of them ground to a halt, Brunt snorting in derision.

"Looks like the Bontari squatter is begging for a bruising," he muttered.

Colin said nothing, which made Walter frown. He shifted to the front of the group, wary, Brunt to his immediate left, Gregor and Rick to his right, but a step behind. Only Gregor seemed to pick up on Walter's hesitation.

Walter's gaze flicked down toward Colin's satchel, then toward the hand Colin held behind his back. "What do you have in your hand?"

Colin brought his hand forward. A strange prickling sensation coursed through his skin. Fear and excitement and anticipation all mixed together smothered him like a wool blanket, so thick it felt hard to breathe.

"It's something my father gave me," he said.

He let the pouch go, but held onto the knot, felt the cords unravel, felt the sling jerk when it reached the end of the straps, then swing there, a stone already in place.

Gregor sucked in a sharp breath, but Walter and the rest frowned in confusion.

"What is it?" Rick asked.

"It's a sling." Gregor had already taken a step backward, had begun to turn.

Walter's eyes narrowed as he glared at Colin. "He doesn't know how to use it."

Colin smiled. A moment before Gregor broke and ran, he saw a flicker of doubt in Walter's eyes.

Colin wound up and threw without any conscious thought, the tingling sensation surging through his arms, into his fingers.

Gregor was the tallest of the four, the easiest to target, the easiest to hit. The stone struck him in the back of the head before he'd taken three steps and he fell to the ground like a sack of grain, landing with a dull thud, arms and legs loose and gangly, dust rising in a puff.

"Diermani's balls!" Brunt shouted. Rick took a step away from Gregor's body, eyes wide.

Walter didn't even turn to look. His entire face had gone taut with rage.

Colin slipped another stone into the sling, began twirling it by his side.

"Is he dead?" Walter asked.

Rick hesitated, then sidled close enough he could look and still keep Colin in sight. Colin had used an underhanded swing to hit Gregor, not an overhead one, and he hadn't used enough force to kill, but he'd learned that you could never be certain of the outcome when dealing with a sling.

"He's still breathing," Rick said, his voice cracking with relief.

"Good." Walter's eye darkened. "Brunt, take care of the little pissant."

Colin turned his attention to Brunt. Walter's heavy

hesitated, shifted from one foot to another, but then Walter shot him a black glare, and with a roar of anger Brunt charged forward.

Warm terror flooded through Colin as Brunt bore down on him, his arm tightening, the swing increasing. He waited a single breath, two, Brunt closing in with surprising speed, and then let the knot go.

A dark splotch of red bloomed on Brunt's forehead, but Brunt didn't slow. Colin took a startled step backward, reached to place another stone with his opposite hand, knew he wouldn't have enough time to load it, swing, and throw before Brunt hit him—

But then Brunt's legs gave out beneath him. He toppled forward, knees hitting the street first with a sickening crunch, body following gracelessly, a surprised expression cutting through the rage in his eyes. His face slammed into the dirt, then ground forward an inch before coming to a halt.

He didn't move, his arms stretched out by his sides.

Colin gasped and swallowed, wiped the sudden sweat from his face, then grinned at Walter as he placed another stone in the sling. "Now what, Walter? You've lost your heavy, and you've lost your thinker. Who's next?"

Rick bolted for the end of the street, but Colin didn't care. His gaze remained fixed on Walter, on the livid expression on his face, on the cold, hard desperate sensation of satisfaction that coursed through his own body, making him tremble. Stepping around Brunt's limp form, he let the stone fly before Walter had time to move, before the dust from Brunt's landing had even settled to the ground.

And he didn't aim for Walter's head.

Walter screamed, the rage on his face transformed into pure pain as he clutched at his groin and toppled to the ground. The scream bled down into harsh sobbing as Colin advanced, another stone in place, the sling already swinging, even though Colin couldn't remember reloading. A sheet of white rage fell over him, blinded him to everything but Walter, writhing on the ground, everything but the sound of the cords of the sling as he whirled it at his side, everything but the remembered taste of bitter blood in his mouth and the stench of his own urine soaking his breeches.

"That was for my father!" he yelled, moving forward slowly, his voice wild, cracking with emotion. He let the second stone fly, the rock catching Walter hard in the chest. "And that was for my mother!" Walter groaned and rolled away, hands between his legs, body curled into a tight ball, his fine clothes covered with dust and dirt from the street.

Colin had moved too close to use the sling. He circled the Proprietor's son, blood pounding in his ears as he glared down at him. "And this is for me."

He kicked Walter in the stomach, hard, as hard as he could. He wanted to see him piss his pants, wanted him to taste blood, but the arms that protected Walter's balls also protected his gut. The kick landed awkwardly, and with it, all of the intensity of Colin's rage and terror fled. He stood over Walter's body, breathing hard, body flushed, the prickling sensation in his skin feverish now, sticky. He wiped at his nose with one hand, realized that tears streaked his face, hot tears, but he didn't care. The urge— the *need*—to beat Walter unconscious died.

He turned, glanced at Brunt's prone form, at Gregor's, shame mingling with the heat of anger. He'd imagined running away from the encounter triumphant, laughing like a maniac, grinning like a madman.

Instead, he scrubbed the tears and snot from his face with one arm, cast one last glance at Walter where he lay, moaning and rocking back and forth in the dirt—

Then he turned and walked away, head down.

His mother knew something was wrong the moment he pushed through the entrance to the hut. He hadn't expected her to be there, had thought she'd be out to the north of Lean-to, where the refugees had claimed and dug up their own section of land, had planted and now tended their own crops. A plot of ground small enough for Sartori to ignore but enough to provide Lean-to with some fresh vegetables.

"Colin?" she asked, setting the cloth she was stitching down in her lap. "Colin, what's wrong?"

He couldn't look at her. Keeping his eyes on the floor, he stalked over to his pallet, tossed his satchel and sling to one side, and collapsed onto the blanket, lying with his back to the rest of the hut, his arms crossed over his chest, hands hugging his shoulders. He still felt overheated, the skin of his face tight, and his chest ached. So much that it was difficult to breathe.

He stared at the back wall of the hut, at the planks his father had bought when they'd first arrived in Portstown. He closed his eyes and sighed heavily. He felt lost. He didn't know what to think, didn't know how to feel. He knew he shouldn't have led Walter to that back street. He *knew* it.

Yet part of him thrilled at the idea that *it had worked*. Part of him reveled in the bewildered expression on Brunt's face before he collapsed, in the terror on Gregor's when he'd seen the sling.

And he couldn't keep his mouth from twitching into a tight smile when he heard Walter's scream of pain as the first stone caught him in the balls.

Colin shuddered, trapped between the smile and the feverish guilt, then stilled as he heard the rustle of shifting clothes behind him, his mother moving closer, then kneeling at his back.

He flinched when she laid her hand over his.

"Colin, what happened?"

He drew breath to answer . . . but couldn't. Because he knew she'd be angry, after everything she'd taught him about the Codex of Diermani, after everything he'd learned.

But her disappointment in him would be worse.

"Nothing." His voice sounded thick and hoarse, deeper than usual, as if he'd been sobbing uncontrollably for hours. Or as if he'd been shouting. "Nothing happened."

His mother's hand began rubbing his shoulder as she considered this. Colin could feel her thinking, could feel her debating whether to press him.

But then she patted his hand and stood, moving back to her work.

"Your father and the others have gone down to the docks. There's a new ship expected today, and they're hoping to get some work unloading the cargo. As soon as I'm finished here with the stitching, do you think you could run the clothes up to Miriam? She should have a few loaves of bread for us in return."

She spoke as if nothing were wrong, as if nothing had happened. But Colin could feel her eyes on his back, so he nodded.

"Good."

And then she left him alone, working in silence behind him. Slowly, the ache in his chest receded, and he could no longer feel the blood pulsing in his skin, in his throat. He found he could breathe.

When he finally rolled over, arms sluggish, body tired, as if exhausted, he found her watching him, her brow creased slightly in concern.

"All right?" she asked, her voice soft and calm.

He nodded, even though it wasn't. He didn't think it would ever be all right again.

His mother accepted the nod, and somehow that made it worse. She handed over the basket of clothes with a smile, reached to tousle his hair, but then caught herself, a fleeting expression of regret passing through her eyes.

"Don't forget the bread," she said.

Colin ducked out of the hut, paused outside. He squinted up at the afternoon light, the sun almost too bright, then headed off up the slope toward Miriam's, moving slowly.

He hadn't gone twenty paces when Karen fell into step beside him. She smiled when he looked up, then glanced down at the basket of clothing.

"Finally learned to wash your own clothes?" she asked, a teasing note in her voice.

He rolled his eyes. "No. These are for Miriam. My mother mended them."

"Oh." Karen hesitated, then added, "Mind if I join you?"

Colin answered her with a confused look and she laughed.

"I'm headed that way anyway," she said. "We may as well walk together, right?"

Colin shrugged. "I guess." He didn't want to deal with Karen. Not now.

Karen gave him a questioning look. "Is there anything wrong? You seem . . . different somehow."

"Different from what?"

"I don't know. Different from when we crashed into each other by the stream."

Colin blushed. "We've seen each other since then."

"I know," Karen said. "I've seen you watching me."

The blush suddenly deepened, and Colin found he couldn't speak.

Karen grinned. "If it makes you feel any better, I've been watching you as well. Down on the beach, practicing with your sling, and here in Lean-to when you helped your father and his friends build the community oven, and dig the plot for the garden, and any of a hundred other small things. You're pretty good with the sling."

Colin ducked his head, but not because of the compliment. He thought of Walter writhing on the ground instead. "Not that good."

"That's not what my dad says." She eyed him from the side. They'd almost reached Miriam's tent. "You usually bring back at least one kill every time you go hunting. That's something to be proud of."

Colin was about to respond when a voice he recognized—a voice that filled him with dread—barked, "That's him! That's the bastard who attacked me!"

Colin spun, Karen turning beside him. He saw Walter almost instantly, noticed the two guardsmen in the Carrente crest a moment later. Seeing the Armory in the middle of Lean-to, where they'd never dared enter before, sent a shock down through his spine and froze his feet in place. Seeing the pure hatred on Walter's face made his heart shudder.

His only thought was that he'd left his sling back in the hut.

Karen raised a hand to shade her eyes. "What's the Armory doing here?"

Colin didn't answer. Before either of the Armory guardsmen moved, he dropped the basket of clothes and turned to run, but slammed into the chest of one of the guardsmen who'd come up behind them, the man's hand reaching out and closing over Colin's arm as he reeled away.

"Hold on now," the guardsman said, voice hard, like stone. "Where do you think you're going?" Tightening his grip, he pushed Colin forward, heading down between the tents and shacks toward Walter and the others.

"Colin, what's going on?" Karen asked.

"What's going on," one of the guardsmen said as he brushed past her, "is that this little squatter is under arrest."

"What for?" Karen shouted, the outrage in her voice layered beneath the growing fear. She tried to push forward, but the guardsmen shoved her back. People had emerged from the hovels on all sides at the commotion, mostly women and children, all of them with expressions of doubt and disgust, most of them family members of guildsmen.

"For attacking the Proprietor's son and his associates," the last guard said over his shoulder as they shoved their way through the gathering throng.

Colin twisted around in the guardsman's grip. "Tell my father!" The guardsman shook him, forced him to stumble. "Karen, get my father!"

And then he stood before Walter, the Proprietor's son still dirty from their encounter that morning. Hatred burned in Walter's eyes, in the tightly controlled muscles of his face.

Without warning, he punched Colin in the gut, the fluid pain so intense Colin folded over Walter's fist with a gasp, tears coming immediately to his eyes. The denizens of Lean-to cried out in protest, but the voices were muffled, lost in the pounding of blood in Colin's ears.

Walter leaned forward, his other hand on Colin's shoulder. "That was for me," he breathed. He drew back to punch Colin again, but the Armory guardsman behind him grabbed his shoulder and pulled him away.

Walter struggled, but the man holding Colin glared and said softly, "That's enough of that." His grip on Colin's arm had relaxed, but not enough for Colin to even think about escaping.

He motioned to the other guardsmen, and they began wending their way out of Lean-to.

"Where are you taking him?" Karen shouted from behind.

"To Sartori," the guard answered. "To the penance locks!"

Colin twisted around in the guardsman's hand, struggling to see Karen.

His last sight, before the crowd of Lean-to settlers blocked her from view, was of her squatting to retrieve the clothes and the basket from the ground, her eyes a mixed blaze of anger and terror.

3

TOM HARTEN WATCHED from the back of the
crowd of desperate men and women from Lean-to as
the *Tradewind* pulled into port with its sails whuffling in
the wind from the ocean, his arms crossed over his chest. Men
in the rigging and on the deck of the ship called to those on
the docks as the trade ship dropped anchor in the bay. With
a sharp command from Sartori's men, boats were dispatched
from the docks. The *Tradewind*'s hull was too deep for it to
draw up to the docks themselves. Tom knew that Sartori intended for the bay to be dug eventually, deepened so that the
ships with larger hulls could be berthed at the wharf, but for
now, anything that sat too low in the water remained out in
the channel between Portstown and the Strand.

At the thought of Sartori, Tom's eyes skipped over
the boats rowing out to meet the *Tradewind* and picked
the pampered, primped, and vested Proprietor out of the
throngs of dockworkers, tradesmen, and Armory that lined
the wharf. He stood at the end of the longest dock, surrounded by his first son, Sedric, two of the more prominent
merchantmen of Portstown, servants, and a few of the Armory guardsmen. Sartori spoke to the merchants, but they
were far too distant for Tom to pick out any words, even
without the gusting wind blowing in his face.

The rest of the Armory were arranged around the edges
of the wharf and were even now casting black looks in
the direction of Tom and the rest of those from Lean-to,
their hands resting on the pommels of their swords or the
handles of their pikes.

"There's more Armory on guard today than usual," Sam said as he and Paul sidled up to Tom on the right.

Without taking his eyes off the guardsmen, Tom answered, "This is more than just a trade ship bearing supplies. Something else is going on."

"What?" Paul asked.

Tom shrugged. "If I knew, I'd have warned everyone to stay away from the wharf. The Armory doesn't look like they're in a forgiving mood."

Sam shifted nervously, picking up on Tom's unease. "What could warrant such a heavy guard?"

"I don't think it's a what, but a who." Tom motioned toward Sartori with his chin. "Sartori is here in person, along with his son and two of the merchantmen. I think they're waiting to meet someone."

Sam's eyebrows rose. "One of the nobility? One of the significant Family members, rather than the offshoots we've been getting around here all summer?"

"Perhaps." The thought sent a chill through Tom's skin and he shivered. "Where's Shay?" he said suddenly, voice sharp.

"Over there, closer to the main dock."

Tom craned his neck to peer over the restless crowd, catching sight of Shay. He was surrounded by other members of Lean-to . . . but not those from the guilds. These were men from the prison ships, the ruffians and troublemakers who hadn't made an effort to fit into Portstown, their faces scarred, unshaven, their clothes worn and tattered. Shay watched the dock and the boats like a hawk, eyes narrowed, his expression black. Everyone around him fidgeted uneasily, glancing sharply left and right, taking in the guardsmen. Tom scanned the rest of the restless crowd and realized it was mostly composed of men like those near Shay. Angry men. Dangerous men.

Like Shay himself, he suddenly realized.

He frowned, turned to catch Paul and Sam's gazes. "I don't like this. I don't like this at all."

Out in the bay, boats had been lowered from the *Tradewind,* men dropping down to where they rocked in the waves. They broke away, oars plying the waves, and passed the boats that Sartori had sent out for the cargo.

As the lead boat drew nearer, Tom's eyes narrowed.

Someone in a blood red vest and a white wig sat in the middle of the boat. Two much younger gentlemen sat beside him, in brown vests.

"Who is he?" Paul asked.

"One of the West Wind Trading Company's men, based on the color of his vest. Not one of the nobility, but close enough to be within spitting distance." He resisted the urge to actually spit to the side with difficulty. Ana had been after him about it lately. Colin had picked up the habit.

He couldn't help a small smile. Then he nodded to the left. "Let's move closer to the main dock. I want to see this trader."

And he wanted to be closer to Shay and his men.

They stepped out of the main throng of people, now pushing forward as the boat carrying the Company representative reached the dock. Men helped him up from the boat itself, and hands were shaken, introductions made.

When they turned, Sartori motioning for the tradesman to accompany him down the dock, the people of Lean-to surged forward.

"Sartori! Proprietor! We need work! We need food!"

"Please, sir!" a woman cried. "I need to feed my children!"

"Let us help unload the ship!"

Sartori frowned but otherwise ignored everyone. As he neared the end of the dock, he motioned to the Armory men, who pushed forward, those gathered pushing back. As Tom, Paul, and Sam skirted the outer edges, coming up behind the group near Shay and his men, Tom realized he could smell the desperation of the crowd, rank like old sweat, and thicker than usual.

"Fall back!" one of the guardsmen bellowed. "Fall back and let the Proprietor through!"

When no one moved, when the group pushed forward even further instead, the guard growled, hand falling to the pommel of his sword. The rest of the Armory closed in, shoving the people back roughly. A woman cried out, and Tom tensed. More people began pressing in from behind, bodies crushing against him, pushing him forward. He fought back, struggled to keep room between himself and the men in front of him, to keep Shay in sight.

"You have no right!" a man bellowed—one of Shay's men—his voice pleading, cracking with wildness, with an ugliness that began to infect the crowd. "We're people of Andover, we're from Families of the Court! You can't do this to us!"

Sartori had reached the edge of the crowd. "Arten!"

The commander of the Armory unit, grappling with two men trying to push forward simultaneously, barked, "Yes, sir."

"I want this wharf cleared. Now."

"Very well, sir." Broad of shoulder, with a face etched with three long visible scars, Arten shoved the men before him back, hard, the two stumbling into those behind them with startled outcries. They were caught by the crowd, but the Armory commander didn't wait for the angry reaction that would follow.

He drew his sword, raised the blade above his head, and signaled the pikemen forward.

A cold dagger of fear sliced down into Tom's core, a bitter taste flooding his mouth.

"Diermani's balls," Paul gasped. "This is getting out of control."

And then Sam's hand latched onto Tom's arm. "Tom! Shay and his men!"

Tom's gaze snapped toward Shay, toward the large group of men who had shoved their way to the front of the crowd and were now standing at the edge of the wharf, directly in front of the leading Armory guardsmen. A wide swath of empty space stood between those from Lean-to and the cluster of Armory now surrounding Sartori, his son, and the tradesmen and assistants, a space defined by the pikemen and the reach of their pikes, the Armory tightening ranks. He saw Shay motion to men on the other side of Sartori, the Proprietor standing obliviously, arrogantly, behind Arten. He saw Shay's men beginning to surge forward—

And he saw the knife Shay held in one hand, the blades all of his men wielded.

He leaped forward, roared, "No!" but his voice was drowned out in the sudden uproar from the mob. Women screamed, men bellowed in wordless defiance, and Arten and the Armory men shifted stance with a stamp of boots on the wooden planks of the wharf, forming a protective wall of metal and blades around Sartori and his entourage. Pikes were lowered, the hafts settling between the shoulders of the men carrying swords. Tom fought forward, fought toward Shay, everyone in the mob trying to move in a hundred different directions at once, half retreating, half rushing toward the dock, toward the guards. Someone's elbow caught Tom in the ribs. Someone else jabbed him in the small of the back. Sam struggled to his right, the bulkier Paul beside him, his face suffused a startling red with anger.

Then the crowd heaved, like a swell on the ocean, everyone rolling to the side. Those in the front, including Shay's men, staggered into the space between those from Lean-to and those from the Armory. One of Shay's men, knife still at his side, stumbled—

And impaled himself on one of the pikes.

The man gasped, blood forming a bubble on his lips before it burst, speckling his chin, his shirt. A look of shock crossed over the pikeman's face, over the two guardsmen on either side of him.

Arten's face shuttered closed. Tom caught a flicker of horror, of regret, before all of that was smothered by a horrid resignation.

Tom stilled, breathed in the scent of blood mixed with the salt of the ocean, could almost taste it.

Shay's man raised a shaking hand to the shaft jutting out of his chest, to the blood that had begun to soak into his shirt. He looked up at the guardsman who held the pike, eyes pleading, almost confused.

Then he sagged forward, the knife he held in his other hand dropping to the ground beside him, his knees giving way. He fell forward until his knees hit the ground, bearing the pike down with him, then halted, the pike itself holding him upright.

Except for the blood, for the blade jutting out from his back, he could have been praying.

Everyone stilled, breaths drawn and held. Tom used the moment of hesitation to grab the men in front of him by the shoulders and haul them back, stepping into the space between them, sliding forward to within a few paces of Shay, the man's face red with rage.

Then the moment of stillness broke.

In a single heartbeat, the space between Shay's men and

the Armory closed, Shay bellowing, "For the Avezzano! For the Family!" Knives slashed downward; swords were raised. The pikeman kicked the dead man's corpse off of the end of his pike with a jerk. Blades flashed, edges now slicked with blood, and Tom felt himself pulled forward with the tide, the men Shay had seeded throughout the crowd rushing the wharf in outrage, an outrage Tom could feel prickling on his skin, an outrage that sent terror into his gut as the mob overran Sartori and his entourage, guards and all. Screams split the afternoon sunlight, wordless bellows that sounded like battle cries as all of the tensions between those from Lean-to and Portstown finally exploded.

Tom tried to shove back, to retreat, but he was thrust forward. He stumbled into the man before him. The pommel of Arten's sword slammed into the side of the man's neck, and he dropped. Tom staggered into his place, falling to one knee, white-hot pain searing up into his hip as his kneecap dug hard into the dirt. He hissed and jerked backward—

And found Arten's blade trained on his throat.

He froze, muscles locking. His heart halted in his chest for one breath, two, resumed with a shuddering pain. His gaze latched onto Arten's. In their hazel depths, he saw cold, calculated death.

Tom raised both hands, palms outward, empty, and thought of Ana, of Colin.

"I came here for work," he said, voice hoarse, tongue suddenly dry. He swallowed, his throat making a harsh clicking noise. "Nothing more."

The sword didn't waver. Something flickered in Arten's eyes, there and gone.

Then the Armory commander took a single step back, sword still level with Tom's throat, and turned.

Weakness washed down through Tom's legs, trembled in his arms. He lowered his hands to his knee, the riot raging around him, the man Arten had knocked unconscious so casually slumped to the ground before him. Someone shouted a command, the Armory on all sides responding, boots pounding against the wharf, but the sounds were distant, removed.

Sam appeared, knelt down by Tom's side. "Tom, are you all right?"

Tom nodded, still shaky. "I'm fine."

"Then let's get the hell out of here."

He grabbed Tom under the shoulder and hauled him into a standing position, turned and reached behind him to catch Paul's attention. Paul held a knife at the ready with one hand, defensively, the other clutching his upper arm, blood seeping out between his fingers.

"I've got him," Sam said over the tumult around them. "Let's go."

Paul nodded as Sam threw Tom's arm over his shoulder and began shoving out of the riot. When they saw the blood staining Paul's arm, they cursed, the rage in their faces tightening.

They broke through the back of the crowd into the streets of Portstown, near one of the mercantiles. Sam dragged Tom over to the side of the building. They leaned against the wood, gasping, men and women running away from the riot around them, a few running toward it. Three Armory guardsmen pelted past, pikes before them; Paul hid his knife behind his back until they'd gone.

Sam wiped at the sweat on his forehead with one arm. "That turned into one cursed mess." His breath still came in heaves, but he didn't seem to be hurt.

Tom didn't answer. There was no need.

He was just about to shove away from the wall and head back to Lean-to when he heard Ana shout, "Tom!"

He spun and saw Ana and Karen and a small group of others, mostly women, bearing down on him.

He thought instantly of Arten, of the sword leveled at his throat. "Ana, what are you doing here? You shouldn't be here, not now!"

"Oh, God, Tom." Ana charged into him so hard he grunted. His arms closed around her, and he held her a moment, tight, too tight, realized she was trembling. But then she shoved back from him, and he saw the terror in her face, her eyes darting toward the sounds of fighting. "What's going on? What's happening?"

"A riot at the wharf, between the Armory and some of the people from Lean-to."

"Who?"

"Shay and those from the prison ships, the ones who refused to work."

Her lips pressed into a thin line, shoulders straightening, but then the terror broke through even this.

"They've taken him," Karen gasped from behind her, and for the first time Tom noticed the tears that shimmered in her eyes.

Tom shook his head in confusion. "Taken who?"

"Colin," Ana said. She clutched at him, her hands cold as they caught his, her voice unnaturally calm. "Sartori's men have taken Colin. They've arrested him."

"What? What for?"

"They said he attacked Walter," Karen said.

Tom's eyebrows rose, and he couldn't quell a slash of pride, lancing up through his back.

"It's about time," Sam murmured.

Ana shot him a dark look, her expression going defensive and hard, the emotion beneath uglier than anything Tom had ever seen in her before. Then she turned the look on Tom. "You get Colin back, Tom Harten." The ugliness had seeped into her voice, beneath the roughness brought on by tears, by the effort to hold them back. "Get him back, and then by Diermani's Hand you get us the hell out of here."

Then she turned, halted when she saw Karen, saw her tear-streaked face. Placing an arm around the girl's shoulders, she hugged her tight, kissed the top of her head, then tugged her toward Lean-to, the others who had followed her down from their tents and huts trailing behind her.

"We'll make certain she's safe," Sam said, watching them retreat, and Paul nodded agreement, his hand twisting on his knife. They could still hear the clash of weapons near the docks, the sound of metal harsh and vibrant in the sunlight.

Tom didn't say anything, couldn't say anything. The shock, the anger, the fear of what they might do to Colin while they held him, too overwhelming.

As if he understood, Sam patted him on the back, then motioned to Paul.

Tom simply stood, staring after them. He had never intended things to end this way, never intended any of this. Portstown was supposed to have been a haven, an escape from the Feud, a new beginning. And now . . .

Now, all he could hear was the hardness in Ana's voice, the harshness. It settled around his heart like a cold, heavy hand.

As if of its own volition, his hand rose to his chest, to the pendant that hung on a chain about his neck and rested against his skin beneath his shirt. The pendant that signified their vows, that held their mingled blood. He'd worn it so long, hidden from view as such a sacred vow should be, that he barely noticed it anymore. He'd worn it since the day he and Ana had wed in the little church in Trent, since the Patris had used Diermani's power to bind them.

But today . . . today it felt *cold*.

When Sartori and his escort and Company guests finally emerged from the buildings near the docks, Tom had moved to the edge of the square, near the church. A group of Armory appeared at first, thrusting a few of the rougher members from Lean-to, including Shay, before them, their arms tied behind their backs. They led them toward the barracks. Another group emerged behind them. He watched as this group escorted Sartori and the Trade Company representative to the gates of Sartori's estate, the Proprietor stalking through the plaza, head held high, back rigid, face suffused with fury. Sedric and the other merchants must have already broken away. Arten stood outside the gates until everyone had entered, eyes scanning the square. His gaze fell on Tom for a moment, hesitated there, a frown touching his expression, but then he motioned the soldiers in the rear—most of them wounded—toward the barracks, left a few outside on guard, and stepped through the gates. They closed behind him.

Tom felt a momentary surge of anger, but he calmed himself, his hand finding the pendant again. He couldn't afford to do anything stupid, couldn't afford to overreact.

Taking in a deep breath, he closed his eyes, bowed his head, and muttered a short prayer to Diermani, feeling the presence of the church at his back, soothing, comforting. His grip relaxed, and he sighed heavily, scrubbed at his face with one hand, and began to pace.

He waited another hour before approaching the gate. He would have waited longer, but the sun had begun to sink toward the horizon, and with it his apprehension rose.

They had his son. His *son*.

The guards at the gate shifted before he came within twenty paces of the wall, pikes held ready. "Halt where you are," one of them barked. "Don't come any closer."

Tom stopped in his tracks. He choked down the bitterness and anger in the back of his throat and said, "I need to speak with the Proprietor. I need to speak with Sartori."

One of the guards rumbled, "That's not likely today. Now get your ass back to Lean-to, where it belongs."

Tom bristled. "I need to speak with Sartori," he said again, the words hard, edged. "Today. Tonight. I won't leave until I do."

Neither guard said anything. The one on the left—hair peppered with gray, nose broken in at least two places—eyed Tom up and down, then shifted back. Keeping his attention on Tom, he motioned to someone on the other side of the gate, said something Tom couldn't hear, and then settled in to wait.

A short while later, Arten appeared. His eyes narrowed. "Sartori will not be seeing anyone today. Go home." His voice rumbled, deep in his chest, like distant thunder. He began to turn away.

"It's not about the riot," Tom said, taking an involuntary step forward. The two guardsmen outside the gate moved, pikes lowered so fast Tom never saw the adjustment in stance. But he ignored both weapons, ignored the men behind them, focused all of his attention on Arten's retreating back. "It's about my son!"

Arten halted. "Your son?"

"Yes, my son, Colin Harten. He was arrested this afternoon, in Lean-to, before the riot."

Arten's shoulders tightened. Then he turned.

"Do you know what your son did? What he was arrested for?"

"They said he attacked Walter."

Arten took a step forward, a menacing step. "He attacked the Proprietor's son and his friends with a sling. He knocked two of them unconscious."

Tom felt the same thrill of fierce pride spread warmth through his chest, but he forced the emotion down, forced himself to focus on Arten. He took another step forward, raised his empty hands as the guards threatened him. "He was defending himself! He's been attacked by Walter and his friends before. They must have chased him, cornered him, forced him to take action!"

One of the guardsmen snorted but grew still when

Arten glared at him. When the commander of the Armory unit turned back to Tom, his expression was dark, but troubled. He held Tom's gaze steadily, seemed about to dismiss him, to order him back to Lean-to as he'd done before—

But then he nodded. "Let him in."

As those inside the gate began pulling the heavy iron bars inward, those outside fell back, pikes raised, their bases thudding into the ground. Arten motioned Tom forward and preceded him down the crushed stone walkway toward the porch of the Proprietor's house. A small orchard stood off to one side, apples hanging heavy on the branches. A long arbor hung with wisteria and the fat leaves of grapes, a few bunches hanging down into the walkway beneath. Dogwoods spread their branches over the front of the house, their wide white blooms tinged pink as the sun began to set. The shadows of the trees and the wall were long and sharp, the clouds overhead burnished orange.

A stone porch led up to the double doors of the house itself, the pathway—wide enough for carriages—extending around the house to the carriage house and stable behind. As they drew up onto the porch, Tom noted the glass panes in the windows, the unlit oil lanterns that hung on either side of the doorway, and the two Armory guardsmen stationed outside. The doors were made of solid oak, inset with two small glass windows, decorated with subtle but intricate wrought iron hinges and handles. Arten opened one side without acknowledging the guardsmen and stepped aside so that Tom could enter.

Tom halted one step inside the door and drew in a sharp breath.

The interior smelled of wood, of pine and oak and mahogany, cured and stained. Everywhere he looked there were wooden accents: on the casings, on the stairs, on the moldings. Wainscoting banded the walls, and hardwood floors creaked beneath his feet. Wood-paneled doors that slid to the side instead of opening outward on hinges led to rooms to the left and right of the open foyer. Stairs ascended to the second floor straight ahead, another hall running toward the back of the house beneath them. The ceiling stretched above his head. Everything was constructed with simple lines, clean cuts; everything flowed together and melded with the sparse furniture, the simple decorations; and everything felt open and spacious.

Tom reached out to touch the wood, to run his hand along its smooth grain, to feel its texture. His hand trembled. He had not worked wood in so long, had not planed it, sanded it, smoothed it . . .

He felt Arten step up beside him, and his hand dropped back to his side.

"His father had a master brought here from Andover," the commander said. He pointed with his chin toward the room on the left, where someone had lit a lantern against the dusk. "In there."

When Tom entered, he heard someone saying, "—attention has been turned away from New Andover. The heads of the Families, the Doms, are all focused on the Rose, on seizing the land surrounding it, on obtaining it for themselves and learning to manipulate its powers. Whoever does so first will rule the Court. The Families are no longer interested in these lands except for their ability to provide them with resources for the Feud. They want material—ore, wood, food—not land."

"For the moment," Sartori muttered. He stood beside a stone fireplace, the hearth empty. The last of the sunlight filtered in through the windows to the west.

The man in the red vest from the West Wind Trading Company sat in one of the great chairs that littered the sitting room, a teacup and saucer in one hand. He watched Sartori's expression intently as he took a sip from the cup. His face was narrow, his eyes a dark blue, his skin tanned and slightly windburned, most likely from his passage across the Arduon. Tom had seen men from the Companies before, had spoken to them, had dealt with them as a member of the carpenter's guild, and most had been arrogant and effeminate, especially while wearing the powdered white wigs.

This man wasn't. This man reeked of cold, calculated power, even without the four telltale gold buttons across the shoulder of his vest indicating he held Signal rank within the Company.

"Precisely," the Company man said. His cup clinked against the saucer as he set it on the table before him. "Which is why the West Wind Trading Company feels that this is an auspicious time to turn our attention here. We feel there is an opportunity, one not to be missed."

"And that opportunity is?"

"The land of course."

Sartori stilled.

Before he could respond to the Signal's statement, Arten cleared his throat. Sartori glanced his way, noted Tom standing beside him. Anger flashed in his eyes. "What is it? I have business to attend to."

Arten bowed stiffly. "One of the residents of Lean-to has asked to speak to you, on behalf of his son."

Sartori's brow creased in irritation, and he drew breath to spit out a nasty reply, but caught himself, glancing toward his guest. "This can wait until morning."

"Considering the riot this afternoon and that this case concerns your own son, it might be wise to deal with it now, sir."

"This concerns Sedric?"

"No, sir. Walter."

"Ah." A pained expression crossed Sartori's face, and he sighed, waving an impatient hand. "Very well. What has Walter done now?"

Arten straightened, his tone taking on a formal note. "This afternoon, Walter Carrente reported to the Armory that he and his cohorts had been maliciously hunted down and attacked near the warehouses in Portstown by this man's son, Colin Harten." Sartori grunted, but motioned for Arten to continue. "By his report, Colin Harten used a sling to fell two of those in Walter Carrente's group, then used it to stun Walter himself, before viciously punching and kicking him unconscious and fleeing."

Sartori's eyes had grown dark. "And were there witnesses to this attack?"

"Rick Swallow fled the scene at the start of the attack but claims to have watched its conclusion from a distance. He verifies your son's account. He claims they were caught by surprise."

"I see. And what does this man's son say?"

Arten shifted. "I haven't spoken to the boy yet. He was apprehended in Lean-to just before the arrival of the *Tradewind* and is being held in the barracks, awaiting your judgment."

Sartori considered for a moment, turning toward Tom. "And what do you say in your son's defense?"

Tom's stomach clenched, but he held Sartori's gaze. He saw nothing there. No compassion, no warmth. Only annoyance. "My son would never hunt down and beat someone. Not unless he felt trapped. Not unless he were cornered. He was raised beneath Diermani's Hand."

"And my son wasn't?" Sartori snarled.

Tom flinched, then felt his chest tighten with indignation, with a sudden and pure hatred. Of Sartori. Of everything he had made those from Lean-to suffer since their arrival in Portstown.

"My son," he said, voice like flint, "has returned from Portstown over a dozen times bruised and beaten, attacked because he resides in Lean-to, because he is not Carrente, not one of the Family's allies. And the reason he comes from Lean-to—the *only* reason—is because *you* cannot see fit to allow members of rival Families into your guilds here in New Andover. Guildmembers in good standing, with papers to prove it! Even when it's obvious that you want to expand Portstown as quickly as possible, *and that we could help*! I gave him that sling to defend himself, to protect himself from the people of Portstown. He shouldn't have needed it. He should have been protected by the Armory, by the people of this town, by the Carrente Family and the Court. But the Carrente Family has abandoned us. That's why my son attacked your son. And that is why the people of Lean-to attacked you on the docks this afternoon."

"No," Sartori said, his voice hard with anger. "No, the people of Lean-to attacked me this afternoon because they are common criminals, sent here to work off their punishments in New Andover, but who are ungrateful, degenerate slobs who want everything handed to them or fed to them, who don't even appreciate the opportunity they *have* been given."

Tom's eyes narrowed. "You've given us nothing."

"I've left you alone in Lean-to," Sartori said, taking a step forward, voice rising, "when I have every right to send the Armory up onto that hill and clear you all out. And after the attack today, I have every intention of doing just that."

"You can't."

Sartori snorted. "I most certainly can. I am the sole arbi-

ter of the Carrente Family lands in New Andover. I am the
Proprietor of this little section of New Andover. And I now
have evidence that Lean-to is nothing but a pit of political
dissidents, sent here to undermine the Carrente Family and
bring down its assets in the New World."

A growing sense of horror began filling Tom's gut, spreading outward slowly. "We aren't political dissidents! We're
guildmembers. We came here hoping to work for the guilds—"

"No! You were sent by the Avezzano Family to stir up
rebellion, to take down Portstown and Carrente's hold on
the coast!"

Tom stepped back under the fury of Sartori's statement,
realization choking him, making it hard to breathe. "Shay."

"Yes, Shay Jones. Or should we call him by his real
name, Vetralla, member of the Avezzano Family?"

Tom tasted bile at the back of his throat, swallowed its
bitterness. "We didn't know. He told us . . . he told us he
was a guildmember, a shipwright."

"He lied."

Tom reeled beneath the revelation. They'd invited Shay
into their home, had drunk with him, had treated him as
one of their own. But now . . .

Now he saw him in a different light, and it changed
nothing.

He turned back to Sartori, tried to shove Shay aside.
"Some of us have poured our heart and soul into that land,
into those huts and tents. It's all we have left. We aren't
dissidents, aren't political rivals. We only wanted advance-
ment in the guild. There's nothing for us in Andover. We
spent every last resource we had to get here."

Sartori placed his hands behind his back. "Then you
have a problem, don't you? Because I can no longer tolerate such a clearly disruptive element in or near Portstown.
Not after today."

"Where do you expect us to go?"

"Back to Andover. To Trent or Gillem. To any of the
new ports springing up along New Andover's coast, if you
can get their Proprietors to accept you. I don't care. But
you can no longer remain in Portstown."

Tom felt himself harden. "We won't go. *We can't.* We
don't have the means anymore. You'll have to remove us
by force."

Sartori leaned forward slightly. "Then so be it."

Tom thought about the riot on the docks that afternoon, about those from Lean-to facing the Armory with knives, with stones, with their bare hands.

If the Armory fell on Lean-to, it would be a slaughter, even if Shay's cohorts joined them.

The bitter anger turned to nausea as he stared at Sartori's implacable face, as he realized that Sartori was serious, that he'd already made his decision, and nothing Tom could say or do would change it.

"Gentlemen."

Neither Tom nor Sartori turned at the intruding voice, not until the word was repeated, with emphasis.

"*Gentlemen*."

Sartori's gaze broke first. "What is it, Signal Daverren?"

Daverren shifted forward in his chair. "I believe I have a solution to both of your problems, one that does not require violence. If what Tom Harten says is true, and he has been unjustly judged."

"And that would be?" Sartori asked. His tone held a mild warning, but Daverren ignored it.

"It goes back to the opportunity I spoke of before we were interrupted," Daverren said. He reached down to retrieve a wooden cylindrical tube beside the seat. "Do you mind?"

Sartori hesitated but motioned to the table.

Shifting the tray with the tea and cups to one side, Daverren opened the silver end of the cylinder and removed a sheaf of papers, sorting through them until he found the one he was looking for. With a murmured, "Aha," he pulled the parchment out and spread it out on the table, motioning Sartori and Tom forward.

"This is a map of the known world," he said. He pointed to the center of the map, to a large land mass that was divided into different regions using subtle shading. "This is Andover, with each of the Families represented by different colors. And this large stretch of blue is the Arduon Ocean." He traced east from Andover, across the Arduon, until his fingers came to rest on a new coast, the details of the land behind it empty, as if someone had forgotten to draw in the rest of the map. A few towns littered the new coast, represented by dots and scrawled names, the edges of the land itself shaded in colors that matched those used for individual Families from Andover. "New Andover," Daverren said, although it was obvious. "And right here is Portstown." He glanced upward, to Tom, "And Lean-to, of course."

Sartori grunted.

"You'll notice that the coast is shaded to represent the division of the land to the Families as decided by the Court once the new continent was discovered and the first settlements, such as Portstown, were seen to be successful. However, you'll notice that the land behind the coast," he motioned toward the empty area, "has not yet been claimed. Not officially. Proposals were drawn up as to how this land was to be divided, once it was explored, but those proposals have fallen by the wayside in the wake of the discovery of the Rose and its potential."

"Those proposals haven't been forgotten," Sartori said.

Daverren smiled. "No, they have not. But look at what happened with the settlements along the coast. The Court was forced to respect the claims of the towns that had already made a start. If a Family backed a particular group, and that group successfully began a colony on the coast before the Court became involved, the Court ceded the land surrounding that colony to the respective Family. Carrente owns the land around Portstown because your father established the town here, and it thrived."

Sartori leaned back from the map. "You want to lay claim to the inland, while the Families are distracted by the Feud."

"Exactly. The respective Family Trading Companies are already at war. We've been at war since the Companies were first founded. The Rose is a political affair—potentially a religious affair if what I've heard of the powers of the Rose are true—one that the Companies will profit from, true, but at its heart it is not a commercial endeavor. Establishing an early presence in the heartland of New Andover is." Daverren's eyes narrowed. "The West Wind Trading Company wants to stake its claim as early as possible, before any of Carrente's rivals have the chance. And we know that other Companies are interested. The Southern Isles have already gathered an expeditionary force, although it had not yet sailed at the time of my departure."

Sartori held Daverren's gaze for a long moment. "An expedition is dangerous. And expensive. I've already sent groups out into the plains, at significant cost to myself and the Carrente Family. None of those expeditions have returned. None that have traveled a significant distance from the coast. And in order to stake a legitimate claim, the group would have to travel relatively far."

"The West Wind Trading Company is prepared to underwrite the cost of the venture. In fact, I've brought the majority of the necessary resources for an expedition with me, on the *Tradewind*. Wagons, horses, supplies for the establishment of a settlement, a town. My only concern was finding someone to lead the expedition and the people willing to risk it." He turned to Tom. "That's where you come into play, Tom Harten. You and those in Lean-to who are *not* associated with Vetralla or the Avezzano Family."

"I'm not a farmer," Tom said warily. "I know nothing about settling a town."

"No, but you are a craftsman. And I'm willing to bet that there are others in Lean-to with the requisite skills to start a settlement. A successful settlement. The only question is whether you and the others would be willing to risk the open plains, and whatever they hold."

Tom hesitated. He thought about Ana, about Sam and Paul and all of the rest of the guildsmen huddled in Lean-to. "What would we gain from doing this? What are you offering us?"

"Other than survival?" Daverran said, then smiled. It did not reach his eyes. "I'm certain that the Carrente Family would be willing to cede a percentage of the land to the settlers and the guilds. Thirty percent seems reasonable. You'd become landowners, beholden to the Carrente Family, of course, but you'd be free."

Sartori stirred at this, frowning. "There would have to be a Carrente presence in the group, a contingent of Armory." He glared at Tom. "I must protect the Family interests after all."

"Then what's our guarantee that the land would be ours, that the Carrentes won't seize it back after we've established the town?" Tom protested.

"What's my guarantee that you won't seize the land and claim it for your own Family!"

"Gentlemen, please." When neither Tom nor Sartori backed down or spoke, Daverran's eyes flashed. He addressed Tom first. "An expedition of this nature cannot be undertaken without Family approval. The Company would need an official charter, issued by Sartori Carrente, giving us the right to embark on the journey, the right to claim the land we settle in the Carrente Family name. The charter can be written in such a way as to legally cede the land to the guildmembers and the guild."

Before Tom could respond, the Signal shifted his attention to Sartori. "And I believe, given the . . . misunderstanding that occurred because of your association with 'Shay Jones,' that Sartori could be persuaded to decrease the Carrente Armory's presence in the expedition. As a sign of renewed trust and good faith?"

Sartori bristled, then caught and held Daverran's gaze. "And what rights would the Company receive from this . . . venture?"

Daverren smiled. "The trade rights, of course. With exclusive claim to the town and its immediate vicinity for use by the West Wind Trading Company, under the Carrente Family name."

"A percentage of the trade to be extended to the Family."

"Of course."

But Sartori still hesitated.

Daverren shifted closer and lowered his voice. "There is little risk to you or the Family. The risk falls on the Company. And it has the advantage that it will resolve your problem with those in Lean-to without disgracing the Family name. Forcibly removing—or killing—that many guildsmen can only hurt your endeavors in the Court, and at a time such as this . . ."

Sartori winced and turned away, moving toward the fireplace. He stared down into its depths, lamplight flickering on either side of him.

"If the expedition is to go forward," he said grudgingly, "there would have to be a Carrente Family representative in the group, in addition to a . . . minimal Armory contingent."

Daverren relaxed, tension draining from his shoulders. "The Company will have a presence as well. You'll have the appropriate papers drawn up?"

"Yes."

"Good." Daverren began rolling up the map. "We can discuss the particulars later."

"I'll have to discuss it with those in Lean-to," Tom said suddenly. "Those that I can trust. They may not all agree."

"Of course," Daverren said. "But I think you'll find you have little choice."

The Signal made ready to leave, Sartori still deep in thought. When it became clear that the Proprietor had forgotten him, Tom stepped forward, catching Sartori's attention.

"You haven't made a decision about my son."

"Ah, yes, your son." He glanced toward Arten, who stood silently in the background, then frowned. "Is your son of age?"

"Yes, sir. He turned twelve this summer."

"Then I'm sorry. An example needs to be made, to those in Lean-to who may not be as honest as you, to their Families. All of those arrested and currently in confinement will be sentenced tomorrow morning."

"But he wasn't part of the riot!"

Sartori's eyes narrowed. "Nevertheless, he attacked my son, a member of the Carrente Family. He *will* be punished."

With a sharp gesture, he motioned for Arten to escort Tom out, the Armory commander grabbing him by the upper arm. Tom clenched his jaw, but he didn't resist. Arten didn't release him until they stood outside the gates of the estate. Night had fallen, but two lanterns had been lit on the top of the wall above the gates.

"You should accept the offer," Arten said as he let Tom go. "There's nothing for you here in Portstown. There never will be. Not while Sartori is Proprietor."

Without waiting for a response, the commander stepped back through the gates, slipping from the lantern light into the darkness of the yard beyond.

4

"**W**HERE'S COLIN?" ANA DEMANDED the moment Tom ducked through the flap over the door.

A fire blazed in the pit, Sam and Paul on the far side, Ana tightening a bandage over Paul's upper arm. A spot of blood already stained it. A used dressing sat at Ana's feet.

Tom caught Sam's gaze, and Paul's. Sam frowned; Paul spat into the fire.

He couldn't meet his wife's eyes.

"Sartori refused to release him," he said, moving toward the fire, noting the aleskin to one side. He picked it up and took a long, heavy pull before setting it back down, the ale bitter on his tongue.

He caught Ana's expression out of the corner of his eye, but turned away, settling down before the fire, across from Sam.

"What did he say?"

"He said that Colin attacked Walter with the sling, that he beat him."

"I told you not to give him that sling, that it would only lead to trouble." Ana jerked at the bandage and Paul winced. "And what did you say?"

"That Colin must have been provoked."

Ana snorted and stood. "Well then, Tom Harten, you don't know your own son as well as you think."

Tom's shoulders tensed. "What's that supposed to mean?"

"It means that there's more of you and your anger inside of Colin than you can possibly imagine. More of your pride. He's taken his share of beatings from Walter and his gang, but I wouldn't put it past Colin to have started the fight today. What's going to happen to him?"

"I don't know." When Ana didn't respond, he glanced up to where she stood over him, hands on hips, met her gaze directly for the first time. "I don't know! Sartori said he'd pass judgment in the morning. On Colin and all of those they took after the riot."

The anger in Ana's eyes hardened, the muscles of her jaw tensing.

"He arrested people from the riot?" Sam asked.

Tom didn't turn from Ana. "Yes. Shay and a few others."

"And he's lumped Colin in with them?" Paul shook his head. "That's not good. That's not good at all."

Tom felt the urge to punch him.

Ana's hands fell from her hips and she turned away, began rummaging through their few possessions, rattling pots, sorting knives and utensils that didn't need to be sorted.

"We have another problem," Tom said, trying to ignore his wife for the moment.

"What's that?" Sam asked. He stoked the fire with a stick, embers flaring as they rose with the smoke.

"Sartori is going to raze Lean-to. Apparently, Shay's not one of us. He's a member of the Avezzano Family, not a guildmember, and Sartori believes he was sent here to foment a rebellion. He's been using us and the others in Lean-to to cause trouble, like the riot today, but Sartori's had enough. He's going to send in the Armory to clear us out."

Paul leaped to his feet. "He can't do that! We're citizens of Andover! We have rights! We have—"

"Paul!" Sam's voice cut across Paul's rant like a blade, stopping him short, breath drawn in, face red. He motioned for the smith to sit down.

Paul exhaled sharply, mumbled something under his breath, but sat.

Sam turned back to Tom. The small room was silent. Even Ana had stopped moving, although she remained in the shadows.

"I assume you protested," Sam said.

"Yes."

"You told him we had nothing to do with Shay, that we have nowhere else to go?"

"Yes."

"And what did he say?" Ana asked.

Tom shrugged. "He said it was our problem. That we should go back to Andover or find someplace else here on the coast."

Paul cursed loudly, and for once Ana didn't slap him on the back of the head or protest.

"What are we going to do?" Sam said after a long silence.

"I can't go back to Andover," Paul said. "The Armory would snatch me up and send me to the front of the Feud in an instant."

"For being a smith?" Ana asked incredulously.

"No," Paul answered. He caught Tom's gaze. "I was part of the Armory before. The smithing came after. But there was an incident. One of the recruits who joined with me died. I saw it happen. The commander discharged me, with the understanding that I wouldn't speak of it, wouldn't report it to the Family. At the time, I was more than willing to get out; the Armory wasn't for me. The commander's watched me for years. He was elated when I told him I was heading to New Andover. If he saw me back in Trent . . ."

"We can't go back either," Ana said. "We've used all of our coin to survive here in Portstown."

Tom thought he would hear accusation in her words, but he didn't. "There's another option."

"Sartori had another suggestion?"

"No. The West Wind Trading Company's representative."

All of the others frowned.

Tom sighed. "He wants us—the guildmembers in Lean-to and anyone we trust—to lead an expedition onto the plains, to set up a town so that the Carrente Family can lay claim to a large swath of the inland when the Court finally gets around to dividing up the lands here."

"We aren't farmers, Tom. We aren't . . . we aren't settlers, for Diermani's sake!"

Tom shot Paul a glare. "I know that. I told him that. But he doesn't seem to care."

"What about the groups that have already been sent

east?" Sam asked. "Sartori already has people who've settled farther inland."

"According to Daverren, the Signal from the Company, those farmers haven't settled far enough east for it to count. And they're only farms. He wants another town, a place that can trade with Portstown and other towns along the coast once it's established. He's willing to fund the expedition, but he needs people willing to settle it, to make it work."

"He needs people to take the risk," Ana said roughly. "Sartori has tried a settlement before, but none of those people have ever returned, have they?"

No one said anything for a long moment. Then Sam stirred.

"What did you tell him?"

Tom shook his head. "Nothing. But I don't think we have any choice, and Daverren knows it. Sartori isn't going to let us stay here, not after the riot. He's not completely convinced we don't have anything to do with Shay."

Both Sam and Paul grimaced.

"What do you want us to do?" Sam asked, climbing to his feet. Paul followed suit.

"Spread the word. About the trial tomorrow and about the expedition. About Shay. Make certain everyone understands that Sartori is serious about destroying Lean-to."

"What do you think is going to happen to Shay and the others?"

Tom thought about the rage he'd seen on Sartori's face as Arten led him and Daverren back to his estate, and he frowned, troubled. "We'll find out in the morning. But we all know they went to the dock to start a fight."

He'd tried to keep the concern out of his voice, but when Sam and Paul ducked out through the entrance they both looked grim. Tom stood to watch them go, then turned.

To find Ana standing directly behind him. Her hand was clasped to her chest, to the pendant beneath her shirt.

"Tom," she said, and he could hear all the fear he saw in her eyes in that one word, all the worry, the concern, the dread. And all the hatred, of Sartori and Portstown.

And beneath all that, hatred of him. For bringing them to this place. It was thin, and it was buried deep, but it was there. And it hurt.

Because he could think of nothing he could do to make it go away.

~

When Tom and Ana emerged from their home the following morning, the rough blanket sliding off Tom's back as he ducked out into the weak sunlight, they found a group of men, women, and children waiting, mostly guildsmen but a few of the men from the rougher part of Lean-to that they'd befriended. Sam and Paul stood at the forefront. Karen, her father's hand resting protectively on her shoulder, stood behind them. Her father's face looked haggard and drawn, had looked haggard and drawn since the voyage across the Arduon and the loss of his wife and two other children to sickness, but he offered a thin smile and nod of support, his hand tightening, pulling Karen a little closer.

No one said anything, and after a brief moment, casting a quick look at Ana, taking her hand, Tom turned toward Portstown.

The twenty or so that had gathered followed, but along the way they gained more. Men and women stood outside of their huts, waiting. They touched Ana and Tom as they passed, murmured words of support, of encouragement, all in grim voices, before joining the group behind. By the time they left the ragged edges of Lean-to, the group had more than doubled.

The town was shrouded in a faint mist that slowly began to lift as they made their way down the grassy slope to the outskirts of the town proper. They passed through the low stone walls of the estates, down past the wharf and the docks, and turned toward the town's center, toward Sartori's land and the barracks and penance locks to one side.

As they approached, a sound intruded on the morning calm: the sharp report of hammers.

Tom frowned.

When they entered the square, Ana's grip tightened, and she shot Tom a terrified look, halting in her tracks, hand going to her pendant. "They can't," she said, but then she choked on the words, denied them with a shake of her head.

Not certain what she had seen, Tom searched the mist, followed the sound of the construction—

And saw through the lifting fog the Armory, saw the

gallows they had built since last night, which they were finishing now.

A hand closed around his heart, closed and tightened, and for a long moment he couldn't breathe. His vision blurred, narrowed, a yellowish film closing in on both sides. It felt as if he'd been punched in the gut, as if he were reeling from the blow.

He would have stumbled, would have sagged to the ground, his knees weak, but Sam was suddenly at his side. "It can't be for Colin," he said, his voice harsh, angry. "They can't hang him. They'll have another riot on their hands if they do, Diermani curse them."

The hand around Tom's heart loosened. He blinked, steadied himself. Behind, he heard the rest of those gathered grumbling to themselves. A low warning rumble.

Straightening, he squeezed Ana's hand in reassurance, leaned down to kiss her. He could feel her trembling, even though she stood perfectly still, back rigid.

"Colin," she said.

"I won't let anything happen to him. We won't."

She pressed her lips together, nodded.

Tom turned and led the group through the square.

They passed the gate to Sartori's estate and halted where the gallows had been built. The structure was rough, hastily put together, and stood next to the penance locks. As they approached, the Armory finished hammering into place the last of the boards on the narrow platform and climbed down. The guardsman with the broken nose who had halted Tom at Sartori's gates the night before stepped up onto the platform and tossed a rope, noose already tied on one end, over the notch in the support beam that ran horizontally over the trapdoor in the center. He adjusted the height, then tied it off.

Arten, standing back from the platform, nodded his approval, then turned. The commander scanned the crowd from Lean-to, noted their angry looks, their set expressions, before his gaze settled on Tom. He looked exhausted, dark circles beneath his eyes.

"Is there going to be trouble?" he asked. There was no hint of exhaustion in his voice. Behind him, the rest of the Armory guardsmen had formed a rough barrier of pikes between the gallows and the group from Lean-to.

"That depends on Sartori," Tom said.

Arten nodded, as if he'd expected the response.

The mist burned away, sunlight glaring down from across the plains. With it came the people of Portstown, emerging from the streets in pairs and small groups, couples and families, some from the outer farms riding in on horseback. The square separated into two factions before the gallows, those from Lean-to on the left, Portstown on the right. Tom watched them all as they came in, saw some of them drop their gazes as if ashamed, saw others snort in contempt or spit to one side. Most simply refused to look in their direction, and most were taken aback by the gallows and the hangman's noose where it swung in the gusts of wind from the ocean, troubled looks turning the corners of their mouths.

By the time Sartori made his appearance, Sedric and Walter trailing behind him, over a hundred people from Portstown had gathered, including the Patris from the church, and nearly eighty from Lean-to, most the families of guildmembers, but a large enough contingent from Shay's group to cause the Armory to shift forward, hands on pommels. The crowd parted as the Proprietor approached, Sartori taking to the platform without hesitation, as if it had always been there, not erected that morning. Sedric and Walter took their places behind him.

Tom did not see any sign of Signal Daverren, nor any of his assistants.

"People of Portstown," Sartori said, breaking through the low murmur that had drifted through the crowd, "it is with regret that I stand before you to pass judgment this day. As you know, the Carrente Family has seen fit to grant me these lands in New Andover, to grant me the title of Proprietor of Portstown. Unfortunately, one of the duties as Proprietor, in such a wild and unsettled territory such as this, is as Judge. It is my responsibility to see that justice is carried out, that crimes are punished, and it is that role I am to play today.

"As most of you know, there was an incident at the docks yesterday upon the arrival of the *Tradewind*." Sartori signaled Arten, who nodded toward one of the Armory guardsmen. Word passed, and as the Proprietor continued speaking, the barracks doors opened, another escort of guardsmen emerging, leading Shay, three other members of his group, and Colin toward the gallows.

Ana tensed, took an involuntary step forward, but Tom held her back.

"These men were the instigators of the riot that followed," Sartori proclaimed. Voices rose from the people of Portstown. "These men brought blades to the docks and attacked the Armory that were there for protection. Three of the guardsmen died." The growl from Portstown rose, a few cursing.

"How many from Lean-to died?" Ana asked, contempt in her voice.

"At least seven," Sam reported. "Seven associated with the guild anyway. I don't know how many of Shay's men died."

Tom didn't care. His attention was fixed on Sartori, on Colin, who stood next to Shay and the other men, last in line, shorter than the rest by at least a foot, younger by more than a decade. His son searched the crowd desperately, eyes wide and terrified, and finally latched onto his father, onto his mother. He tried to rush forward, but the ropes that bound his hands and feet brought him up short. The guardsman that had followed the prisoners out of the barracks pulled him back into place roughly.

On the platform, Sartori turned toward Shay, toward the entire line of men, including Colin.

"Portstown cannot tolerate such blatant disregard of authority," he said, his voice lowered enough that those from Portstown were forced to quiet in order to hear him. "Because of the needless deaths of the Armory, and the fact that you came to the docks with the intent to do harm, I sentence you to be hanged until dead."

There were gasps from the crowd, a minor uproar from those from Lean-to. Ana turned, gripped Tom's upper arm tight. "Tom."

"I know," he said, and shot a glance toward Sam, toward Paul. Behind, the tumult from Lean-to grew as on the platform two guardsmen shoved Shay forward, over the trapdoor, beneath the noose. He moved stiffly, rigidly, his face blank, as if he hadn't heard anything Sartori had said, as if he couldn't believe any of this was happening.

But that paralysis broke when they dropped the thick

rope over his head and around his neck. He began to struggle, snapped his head left and right, cried out, "No! You can't do this! I'm Avezzano, a member of the Family!" as they cinched the noose tight, writhed as the guardsmen stepped aside. But he couldn't move, his hands still tied tightly behind his back. His breath came in ragged gasps, and sweat broke out on his forehead. In a torn voice, he cried out again, "No!" and then tried to step aside, to leap away from the trapdoor. But his legs were tied together like Colin's, and he tripped and stumbled, fell almost to his knees.

The cord from the noose brought him up short, jerked his head back as he emitted a strangled grunt. His legs pivoted beneath him and he swung back, but it still wasn't enough for his knees to reach the platform.

His face turned a livid red and his eyes bulged as he began to choke. Flesh bunched up under his chin, dragged there by the rope. Harsh sounds, phlegmy and distorted, like a diseased dog choking on its own blood, stretched out over the square as he struggled to get his feet under him, his legs already buckling, already weakening. A woman in the Portstown crowd screamed.

Then Arten barked a curt order, hand chopping down in a succinct, final gesture—

And someone loosed the trapdoor.

Wood slapped against wood as it fell and Shay dropped. But the rope had been pulled taut already. His neck didn't snap. Instead, he lost all hope of finding footing. He kicked at empty air, flailed, jerked back and forth, the hastily constructed gallows creaking, shuddering as he struggled.

His spasms ended, slowly and gracelessly, his face now a bruised and blackened purple, his features contorted, his neck strangely elongated. Dark stains spread over the front and back of his breeches as he pissed and shit himself.

The square had fallen utterly silent except for a few muted sobs and the low sound of the Patris uttering a prayer, crossing himself repeatedly. Women buried their heads in convenient shoulders; children hugged their parents' legs or remained oblivious, playing in the dirt. The men stood, faces blank, bodies rigid.

Ana whispered a prayer, her tone ragged and shocked. Her hand had tightened so hard on Tom's that his fingers had gone numb.

He hadn't liked Shay Jones, had tolerated him because he'd thought he was a member of the guilds, but he would never have wished such an ugly death on him. He swallowed down the taste of bile in the back of his throat, fought back the nausea. Each breath brought with it the smell of salt, of ocean—

And with one gust, the stench of urine and shit.

On the platform, Sartori grimaced and waved the guardsmen forward. They snagged Shay's body, hauled it back onto the platform, removed the noose and carried the corpse to one side as the trapdoor was reset.

The second man spat at Sartori's feet before the noose dropped over his neck. He didn't struggle, didn't even speak, his glare falling over everyone in the crowd, from Portstown and Lean-to alike. Tom hadn't met him, although he knew he'd come from a conscript ship.

Everyone in both groups flinched when the trapdoor was released.

The third man had been a thief. He wept without a sound, struggled only at the last moment, surging forward as Arten gave the command to trigger the trapdoor. He swung back and forth, his neck snapping as the rope pulled taut.

The fourth man collapsed to his knees before they'd even removed the third man from the noose. He begged, pleaded, fell down onto his side. "I wasn't part of the riot!" he screamed as the guardsmen dragged him across the platform, as they jerked him upright. "I wasn't part of Shay's group!"

Sartori simply frowned.

"You have to believe me!" the man roared. "I was there looking for work! I was there to unload the ship!" The noose tightened around his neck and he heaved in a loud, noisy, ragged breath. "I was only looking for work," he mumbled, snot coating his upper lip. His head sagged forward, hair falling down in front of his face—

And then the trapdoor cracked open.

Before the body had stopped swinging, the crowd grew restless, a low unpleasant murmur starting on the Lean-to side, drifting slowly to the Portstown side.

There was only one more prisoner left on the platform. Colin.

"Tom," Ana said, and this time her voice was sharp with warning, cutting deep.

Tom stepped forward, let Ana's hand go, felt Sam and Paul step up behind him, along with a few others from Lean-to. He caught Arten's answering movement from the side, saw Arten's dark frown, hand resting on his sword in warning. But before either of them could do anything, Sartori turned back to the crowd. His face was grim, hard, lines etching the corners of his mouth, his eyes. He looked over everyone gathered, letting his gaze settle finally on Tom.

"Before I handle this last case," he said, and his voice fell into complete silence, into an ominous tension that prickled against Tom's skin, "I have an announcement."

No one in the square moved. Tom felt Arten's presence at his side, like a lodestone, felt every Armory guardsman and every tradesman from Lean-to where they stood, felt Colin's nervous glance as the guardsmen shuffled him forward, as they placed him over the trapdoor.

"As Proprietor of Portstown, I have only the town's well-being in mind. I, and my father before me, have always felt that expansion of the town and the Carrente lands to the east is a necessity for our survival. He, and I, sent expeditions onto the plains in the past, but unfortunately nothing has come of those forays. We don't know why those expeditions failed, but we must make further attempts, or our survival here in New Andover will be in jeopardy.

"To that end, the Carrente Family, along with the West Wind Trading Company, will be sending another expedition to the east, with the intent to establish a new town, one that will be the foundation of our expansion to the east in the future. We have already gathered the necessary materials for this expedition; however we are lacking in the men and women who have the skills to make the settlement a success.

"At the West Wind Trading Company's request, I have extended a proposal to the guildsmen in Lean-to, to Tom Harten in particular." Sartori motioned toward Tom, and everyone's attention shifted, drawn to him, to Sam and Paul and all of the others that stood behind him.

"Tom Harten," Sartori said. "Will you lead this expedition? Will you journey into the plains and start this settlement? The Carrente Family would be in your debt."

Then Sartori lowered his head. Something flickered in his eyes.

And Tom stilled. Because in the Proprietor's gaze he could see what was truly offered, what Sartori truly meant. He'd waited to make the announcement on purpose, waited until Colin stood ready to face judgment, until Colin stood over the trapdoor, the noose dangling over his head. The message was clear.

If Tom said no, Colin would hang.

And he wasn't the only one to see the threat behind the words. The crowd at his back stirred, restless, uneasy. A dark, fluid uneasiness, like deep ocean.

To the side, he saw Arten frown with disapproval, with something deeper.

Discontent.

But the Armory commander didn't move. No one moved, those gathered waiting. To see how he would react, to see what he would do. And he knew that if he said no, if Sartori threatened Colin's life because of it, that those from Lean-to, even the guildsmen, would fight. He could hear it in the dark, swelling murmur behind him, could *feel* it. They hadn't done so for the others, for Shay and his group, but that was because Shay and the others had gone to the docks with knives, had planned on violence.

Colin hadn't. His arrest in Lean-to had been witnessed, and word had spread through the nest of huts and shacks and tents like wildfire.

Tom's eyes narrowed. He glanced toward Colin, looked into his son's eyes, saw the fear there, the stark terror, barely contained, then turned back to Sartori.

For a single, burning moment, he wanted to take advantage of the black emotions of the crowd behind him, wanted to release them, and Sartori and Portstown be damned.

But he knew what Ana would want, knew what she'd do, knew that she would never forgive him. They hadn't discussed the matter of the expedition, had focused on Colin, on trying to get some sleep, on holding each other for comfort to get through the night.

But he didn't need to ask her, didn't even need to turn to look at her. He could feel her at his back.

Drawing a deep breath, everyone around him tensing,

Arten's hand tightening on the pommel of his sword to one side, Tom said, "Yes. I'll lead the expedition to the east."

He was surprised. There was no bitterness in his voice at all.

~

Colin didn't begin to panic until the guardsmen brought him out into the sunlight, harsh after the dimness of the barracks, and he saw his parents standing at the front of the crowd. His father's face was drawn, somehow stark; his mother's was terrified.

And it was that terror that reached down into Colin's gut with a cold hand and brought a shiver of sweat to his skin.

The Armory barracks hadn't been that bad. After seizing him in Lean-to, after allowing Walter that hard punch to the stomach, the Armory had forced Walter aside and led Colin down to the town, stumbling with pain and weak with shock. He hadn't thought beyond his attack on Walter, on his gang. He'd thought that would be the end of it, the end of all of the fighting, that Walter would back off now that he knew Colin would fight back.

That Walter would turn to the Armory had never crossed his mind.

When the guardsmen had thrust him into the cell inside the barracks, he'd worried about what they would do to him. But then someone charged into the room, barking orders, and everyone except a few guardsmen had thrown down their cards or dice, grabbed weapons, and rushed out of the building. Those that remained hadn't been interested in Colin at all, pacing before the tables and cots that filled the majority of the room. They hadn't even looked in his direction.

Nearly an hour later, a group returned, leading Shay and three others, their hands trussed behind their backs. One of the men was bleeding from a cut to his shoulder. Shay looked enraged.

The guards spoke for a moment, glancing in Colin's direction, their new prisoners shuffling beside them. Then one of them opened up the cell, motioned Colin out, and thrust Shay and the rest inside.

"We don't want you in there with the others," the guard

said, leading Colin toward an empty cot at the back of the building.

"What happened?"

"There was a riot at the docks."

Colin's chest tightened, his eyes going wide. "My father was at the docks!"

The guard paused, a strange mixture of emotion crossing his face. Anger and pity and concern. He hadn't shaven recently, the stubble gritty and coarse, brown except for a patch of white at the base of his chin where a scar cut across the flesh. He stared at Colin a moment with hard brown eyes. "What's your father's name?"

"Tom," Colin said, shifting on the cot, trying to see beyond the guard, to where the others were now settling back into place or seeing to their own wounds. They left the wounded prisoner alone, not even bothering to toss him bandages. "Tom Harten. He's a carpenter."

The guard relaxed, smiled tightly. He ruffled Colin's hair, and because Colin was so concerned about his father, he didn't even try to duck away. "Your father's fine. Stay here for tonight. The Proprietor will deal with you—and the others—tomorrow." Before Colin could ask anything more, he turned and rejoined the other guardsmen.

Colin settled onto the cot, lying down, but he didn't think he'd be able to sleep. Not when he didn't know what would happen to him tomorrow morning.

But he woke hours later to the sound of voices, close enough that he didn't open his eyes. He recognized the voice of the guard with the unshaven beard but not the other man's. They stood right over him, barely two feet away. The rest of the barracks was silent except for an occasional snore.

"What do you think, Arten?"

The voice he didn't recognize answered. "I spoke to his father. He thinks his son was defending himself. And we all know what Walter is capable of."

The other guard grunted. "I believe him. He hasn't caused a lick of trouble since we took him in Lean-to. And did you see the bruises on him? I think Walter deserved whatever he got."

Colin heard Arten shift. "You aren't the one passing judgment on him."

The guardsman didn't answer. And after a long moment, the two moved away, their boots heavy on the plank
flooring.

Colin's apprehension faded after that.

Until they woke him the next morning. Until they tied
his hands and feet and led him out into the sunlight and he
saw the newly erected gallows and the fear on his mother's
face.

The terror settled into his stomach like a living thing,
small at first, as he squinted into the light and was shoved
up onto the platform behind Shay and the others. The Proprietor was speaking, but Colin didn't listen. He struggled
with the growing nausea, with the increasing sensation of
something writhing in his gut.

And then they hung Shay.

He almost puked, cold sweat breaking out all over his
skin as Shay flailed, as he struggled; as his face turned
purple and black and finally grew still. Colin's knees grew
weak.

And then the acrid scent of piss and shit hit him, and
he stilled. The nausea didn't fade, the writhing snake in his
stomach didn't halt, but he suddenly found the strength
not to buckle and collapse to the platform. Because he
remembered what Walter had done to him, remembered
pissing his pants, remembered what that shame had felt
like.

Colin glanced to where Walter stood behind his father,
beside his brother and Patris Brindisi, who was muttering one of the litanies under his breath. The guards had
removed Shay's body, had strung up the second rioter, and
as he watched, the trapdoor released.

Walter turned as the body jerked and spun, a thin smile
turning the corners of his mouth. When he saw Colin, the
smile deepened.

Colin frowned, straightened, fought the terror back as
he stared out over the crowd. And for a brief moment he
succeeded, the writhing in his gut abating.

But then the third man wept, and the man who'd stood
beside him the entire time collapsed and screamed, had to
be dragged to the noose.

The screams unnerved him. The sound of the man's
neck breaking sent a wave of tremors through his body,

and he couldn't make the trembling stop. Fresh sweat broke out, prickling across his back, in his armpits, rank with fear.

A guard prodded him forward, forced him to halt over the trapdoor itself. He saw his father step forward from the crowd, heard the Proprietor speaking, but he couldn't make sense of the words. His breath came in ragged gasps, the sounds filling his ears, thudding with the panicked beat of his heart, with the pulse of his disbelief.

They couldn't hang him. Not for something so stupid. They couldn't.

But that wasn't what he saw in his mother's eyes.

He stopped breathing.

And in the sudden silence, in the stillness of his heart, the stillness of the crowd, he heard his father's voice clearly.

"Yes. I'll lead the expedition to the east."

The stillness held for a moment longer, as if the crowd had expected a different answer, and then the Proprietor said, "I thought you might."

Colin's heart shuddered and started beating again. He choked on air.

The Proprietor turned toward him. "Colin Harten, for attacking Walter Carrente, a member of the Carrente Family and my son, I sentence you to a day in the penance locks."

He waved a hand dismissively, and the guard at Colin's back stepped forward, taking him by the shoulder and shoving him toward the edge of the platform, toward the locks that stood in the dirt to one side. He stumbled, numb with a dull sense of relief, then caught Walter's expression.

The Proprietor's son was pissed.

Colin grinned. He couldn't help it.

The grin held until the guardsman sat him down hard on the stump behind the lock and untied his hands as another guard—the unshaven guard, Colin realized—unlocked the top bar and raised it. Taking hold of his hair, the first guardsman shoved Colin forward, bending him at the waist, and seated his neck in the half circle that had been cut into the lower part of the lock. Two other guardsmen grabbed his arms and placed his wrists in the smaller half circles on either side.

And then the top half of the penance lock settled down

over the back of Colin's neck and wrists, the lock snapping into place. It was mildly uncomfortable. The edges of the wood beneath his neck and wrists cut into his flesh slightly, and his back was bent at an awkward angle, but it didn't seem that bad.

The guards stepped back, but they didn't move far. The Proprietor had already left for the docks, and those from Portstown had begun to disperse. Some lingered, a few staring at the gallows, others staring at him with pity or contempt, but they didn't stay long. The priest Brindisi stood to one side with a look of regret.

Nearly all of those from Lean-to remained behind. Straining his neck, Colin could just make out Karen and her father near the front of the crowd. She tried to come forward, but her father held her back, and she bit her lower lip in frustrated concern.

His mother knelt in the dirt before him, brushed the hair back from his face. "Colin." He struggled to twist his head far enough to see her, felt tears burning in his eyes, brought on by the mixed relief and distress in her voice. And because somehow he knew he'd hurt her. Hurt her in a way he'd never hurt her before.

He'd disappointed her.

"I'm sorry," he said, and was surprised when his voice cracked, surprised at how thick and dense it sounded.

"Hush. There's nothing to be sorry about." She kissed his forehead. "I'll bring you something to eat."

"No food," one of the guards said gruffly. "And no water."

His mother shot him a glare. Colin couldn't see it, but he could feel it in the way her hand stilled against his face.

And then his father pulled her back, crouched down on his heels and took Colin's chin in his rough hands, leaning far enough forward that Colin could meet his eyes. "You'll be fine, Colin. It's only a day. Remember that. It's only a day."

Colin couldn't read what else he meant, what he sensed his father was trying to say, but he nodded anyway, blinking back the sudden inexplicable tears.

His father released him and stood. Without saying a word to the rest of those gathered, he put his arm around Colin's mother and led her away, heading back toward

Lean-to. The rest mumbled amongst themselves, shaking their heads or narrowing their eyes at the guards, before breaking away.

Karen was dragged away by her father.

Colin kept his head raised for the first hour, so that the wood didn't cut off his breathing. But his neck and shoulders began to ache, until eventually he couldn't hold his head up any longer, and he slumped forward, turning so his throat wouldn't rest on the lock itself. His wrists began tingling, the lock cutting off the circulation to his fingers. He twisted them in place, the holes large enough he had room to wriggle, and that helped. But the armholes were raised slightly, not quite in line with his neck, and soon he could feel his upper arms tingling with numbness, the sensation gradually seeping down toward his elbows.

The afternoon heat began to settle in. He could feel the lock against the back of his neck, could feel the sweat gathering between his shoulder blades, sliding down the curve of his back, beneath his arms to his chest. It dripped from his forehead, from his nose, slid into his eyes where it stung and touched his lips with salt. Flies buzzed around his head, landed with tickling feet on his hands, on his face, and he couldn't brush them away. A prickling sensation began in his shoulders, the sudden need to *move*, to shift position, to scratch or fidget, spreading from a tingling itch into an incessant urge.

He began to struggle.

A small movement at first. A shifting of the arms that sent sheets of pain up through his elbows and into his wrists. He'd left his arms hanging loose for too long. They'd gone completely numb. The sensation was maddening, and so he shifted his seat on the stump—

And almost screamed, white hot pain flaring in the small of his back. He jerked away from it, his shoulders hitting the lock, rattling the bar over his neck. He hissed as his muscles protested, screaming from his neck all the way down to the base of his spine. He tried to straighten, to relieve the tension there, but was brought up short by the lock.

He cried out, a short, sharp sound.

And then he began to flail. Anger coursed through the frustration, through the stinging of the sweat and the ache

of muscles. Anger at Walter, at the Proprietor, at Portstown, at his father for dragging them across the Diermani-
cursed Arduon to this bloody coast. He gritted his teeth
and thrashed in the lock, jerked back and forth, the wood
creaking, a growl starting low in his throat, catching fire
with the anger and growing, rising into a bellow of rage
as he fought the lock, as it refused to budge. Fresh sweat
plastered his shirt and breeches to his sides, stuck tendrils
of hair to his forehead. He threw himself back and forth,
tortured muscles seizing, cramping, sending white-hot
flares through his calves, his sides, his neck and thighs. Jaw
clenched, the bellow rose into a cracked roar, rose higher
still as he heaved against his constraints—

And then it broke, trailing down into broken sobs as
he collapsed against the lock, heaving, exhausted, sweat
streaming from his chin.

When he'd calmed himself, he heard one of the guards
chuckling, the sound low, barely audible. Colin tensed,
breathing harshly through his nose.

The niggling sensation in his back hadn't gone away.

He struggled with the lock twice more before sunset,
tried to break free, to move, and each time he collapsed at
the end in exhaustion, his roar of hatred dying down into
painful sobs. When the guards laughed the third time, he
didn't even react. He was too tired. His throat was raw, his
mouth dry. It tasted of dirt and sweat, sour with dust.

Night fell, and with it the temperature. The patrol that had
stood around him all day decreased to a single guard. Colin
didn't think he could sleep in such an awkward position, but
around midnight he woke to someone whispering his name.

"Colin. Colin, it's me, Karen."

He moaned, blinked his eyes against the moonlit darkness, tried to shift his head but cried out at the twinge in
his neck. "Karen?" he croaked, the name nothing more
than a wheeze.

"Yes." Her hands touched his face, his cracked lips. She
swore, her hands retreating, returning again with a wet
cloth. She scrubbed at the sweat and dirt that had dried
against his skin, the pressure increasing as she grew angry.

"Guard," he managed in warning, and heard someone
else kneeling down beside Karen, could barely pick out the
second figure in the darkness.

"I found her watching during the day, from the corner of one of the mercantiles," the guard said, and Colin recognized the unshaven guard's voice. "Told her to come back tonight, while I was on duty."

Colin would have wept, but Karen set the cloth aside and produced a skin filled with water. "Here," she said, tipping it up and squeezing it, a stream of water splashing Colin in the face. "Drink."

Colin swallowed as much of the water as he could, greedily, most of it dribbling off his chin to the dusty ground below. He drank as if he hadn't had water in months. It tasted sweet. Cold and wet and delicious.

Until his stomach started to cramp.

"Careful," the guard said, his hand pulling the skin away a moment before Colin puked everything he'd just drunk into the dirt. Spasms shook Colin's body, aches shooting warning pangs through his stomach, back, and shoulders.

When the urge to vomit subsided, the guard said, "Now let him drink again, but slowly this time. And not too much. He won't be able to keep it down otherwise."

Karen wiped Colin's face again, then let him drink again. She took the skin away before he was ready. Satisfied, the guard grunted, then stood. Colin heard him moving away in the dark.

Water sloshed as Karen set the skin aside. He heard her settling back onto her heels. Her voice was further away when she spoke.

"Is it true?"

"Is what true?" he asked, his throat still raw, voice gravelly.

"Did you attack Walter?"

He would have shifted uncomfortably if he hadn't been closed up in the lock. He wanted to lie to her, tell her it was a mistake.

"Yes," he said finally, and hung his head.

He expected her to leave. He expected her to be disappointed with him, as his mother had been.

Instead, she shifted forward, raised his head, and after a careful moment, leaned in and kissed him on the mouth.

It was awkward, and uncomfortable, but it wasn't unpleasant.

When Karen withdrew, Colin blushed. He listened as

she began to gather up the cloth, the waterskin, her motions quick, nervous. She stood.

"I'll see you tomorrow, when they release you," she said.

She hesitated a moment, then left, footsteps receding in the darkness.

He fell back asleep with his cheeks still burning.

And woke hours later, abruptly, when someone punched him on the back of the head, hard. He cried out, jerked back, forgetting that he was trapped in the lock. Wood brought him up short, scraping his wrists, his neck, drawing blood. He spat a curse, one he'd heard his father using on a regular basis. Someone laughed, was joined by a few others. Colin listened carefully, picked out four people in the darkness.

Walter and his gang.

His eyes narrowed and he clenched his jaw.

"Hello, Colin," Walter said, flicking Colin's ear with one finger. Colin flinched, but refused to react in any other way. "This isn't exactly what I had in mind for you when I summoned the Armory. But my father needed something from your father, and, as usual, his needs came first. I wanted something more damaging, perhaps even more permanent, like what the others got."

Colin wondered where the guard had gone, realized that Walter had probably ordered the guard away.

"Oh, well," Walter said, standing with an exaggerated sigh. "It was fun watching you shake in terror on the gallows. However, Brunt and Gregor haven't had their fun yet, so we brought you a little present." He heard Walter retreat, heard fumbling, the rustle of cloth, low anticipatory chuckling.

And then something struck him in the face, a stream of liquid, joined a moment later by another, then two more. He spluttered, tried to pull away, then realized it wasn't water and pressed his lips tight, closed his eyes, ducked his head, and breathed in tight, infuriated heaves through his nose, hands groping the darkness uselessly. The laughter rose with the stench of piss, until all four streams trickled off and died. He shook his head like a wet dog, felt a momentary thrill of satisfaction when Walter and the rest cursed and leaped back out of range. But the satisfaction didn't last.

He thought they'd return again, try something else to humiliate him, but even as he tensed he heard their voices fading into the distance.

The guard returned a short time later but said nothing, even though the reek of urine was obvious.

No one else visited him that night or the next morning. When the time came to release him, his parents were waiting, along with Karen and her father, Sam and Paul, a few others from Lean-to, and Patris Brindisi. The guard who had allowed Karen to help him and the commander of the Armory released the lock, sharing a dark glance when they got close enough to smell the piss, the priest presiding over it all. Colin couldn't stand, his muscles cramping. He cried out and fell to the ground, his mother at his side instantly. His father and Sam finally made a seat by clasping hands, lifting Colin and carrying him from the square back to Lean-to, his arms over their shoulders, escorted by a covey of grumbling supporters.

Once home, his mother washed off the urine, the dust, and cleaned the wounds on his neck and wrists, the water burning the scrapes and cuts. She fed him, slowly, in small doses, and massaged his arms and legs, shoulders and back, until the cramps subsided. Colin moaned and cried out as she did so, and tremors shook his body.

But he did not weep. He buried that urge beneath the anger, beneath the hatred.

He buried the tears deep.

5

NIGHT FOUND COLIN SITTING on the rock
that offered a view of the plains, his satchel and
sling resting on the stone beside him. He'd used
the sling to hunt rabbit and squirrel and prairie dog since
his day in the penance lock three weeks before—had
hunted that evening in the dusk after his father sent him
to warn everyone to prepare, to be at the wagons in the
morning, ready to go—but the intensity of the hunt had
died. He no longer felt the dark thrill of excitement when
he touched the cords or held the smoothness of a stone
in his hand. That thrill had come from the anticipation of
using the sling against Walter, and he had no intention of
doing that again. He hadn't even been down to Portstown
since the Armory had dragged him there and Sartori had
put him in the locks.

He was done with Walter, with Brunt and Gregor and
Rick. In the morning, he'd be on the plains, heading far
away from Portstown, its Proprietor, and his son, passing
beyond the farms, beyond where even he had hunted. The
thought stirred something deep inside him, a prickling in
his chest, a quickening of excitement that tingled against
his skin.

He sat in the moonlight and stared out across the
silvered grass, his knees pulled up to his chin, his arms
wrapped around them. In the distance, he could see the
eight covered wagons, already loaded and ready to go, like
black stones against the plains. A few guards wandered
around them, mostly Armory mixed with a few of the cho-

sen settlers from Lean-to, there to protect the wagons from the dissidents and conscripted prisoners who'd banded with Shay. Crickets chirruped, and something small rustled in the grass nearby. Wind gusted against his face and brought with it the smell of earth, sea salt, and the smoke from the tents in Lean-to. He breathed in those scents, held them, exhaled slowly as he rested his chin against his knees and smiled.

He heard Karen approaching long before she arrived, her dress swishing in the stalks of grass. Resentment stabbed through his exhilaration—he'd come up here to be alone—but that died as she reached the rock. Karen and her father had become part of the main group intent on heading into the plains and establishing the town everyone had started to call Haven. She and Colin had stolen away more than once while their parents and the others argued over what was necessary for the trek and what was not, who to allow into the party and who to leave behind, and how to protect everyone. Those excursions—down to the darkened beach, or more often here, to the edge of the moonlit plains and the flat stone—leaped to the forefront of Colin's mind as she settled down beside him, her legs folded beneath her.

"I thought I'd find you here," she said. She brushed her hair away from her eyes, tucked the strands behind her ear. It had grown long since he'd first stumbled into her at the stream, but it was still wild. In the moonlight, it appeared black, her skin a pale white. "Our parents are discussing—"

"Food," he said, cutting her off. "I know. That's why I left."

"They don't think we have enough, not for as many people as are going."

"We'll have to hunt as we go. The wagons won't be able to move that fast, not without a road to follow. We'll have plenty of time to scout ahead and forage for food." The words were his father's, and he said them with the same curt tone. Beside him, Karen stilled, then shifted position, adjusting her dress as she too pulled her knees up to her chin.

After a long moment of silence, she said, "Aren't you afraid?"

Colin turned toward her, brow furrowed in confusion. "Of what?"

"Of what's out there."

"Oh." He relaxed. "No."

"But it's so open. So . . . empty."

"It will be better than the trip here to Portstown, trapped in the hold of the ship, only coming up on deck an hour every day, crammed in there with all the other people, with goats and chickens. I hated the ship. I hated the ocean. And I hate Portstown."

Karen flinched, and Colin suddenly remembered that she'd lost her mother, brother, and sister on the voyage here. Grimacing, he added, "Besides, it can't be empty. There's got to be something out there."

"What?"

"I don't know, but the other expeditions—the ones the Proprietor sent out before us—went somewhere. Something had to have happened to them."

Karen gave him a look. "That doesn't exactly make me feel any better."

He shrugged. "I think it's exciting. We'll be the first to see it, the first to experience it." He felt the hairs rise on the backs of his arms. "We'll be the first ones there, with no Proprietor to tell us what we can and can't do."

"But the Proprietor *will* be there, or at least a representative of the Family." She gave him a significant look.

He waved it aside. "Doesn't matter. Whoever it is will be outnumbered."

Karen snorted, but didn't argue any further. Instead, she lay her head down on her knees, pulled them in tighter, and sighed. "I hope you're right, Colin." But her voice was still troubled.

Colin's brow creased in slight irritation. "I know I'm right," he said, but quietly, almost to himself. "There's something out there, waiting for me. For us. I can feel it."

Karen didn't say anything. She watched him, the whites of her eyes bright in the moonlight. Her gaze was steady, searching, lips turned down in a slight frown, as if she were trying to come to a decision.

Its intensity made Colin nervous. He glanced toward her, then away, shifting where he sat, pressing his chin into the tops of his knees. The position was vaguely uncomfortable. His legs were too long now to make it comfortable.

A moment before he would have broken and asked her,

"What?" she sighed and looked away. He watched her dig into a pocket of her dress, her hand coming out in a tight fist.

"Colin," she said, then hesitated, ducking her head. Her back straightened, and when she lifted her head again her lips were pressed together.

In a rough voice, she said, "Colin, I want you to have this."

She thrust her fist toward him, opened her fingers.

A pendant sat in the palm of her hand, burning silver in the moonlight, the metal chain that held it trailing through her fingers. It was in the shape of a crescent moon, and in its center lay an oval of hollow glass, empty, without a top or stopper.

A blood vial. An unspoken vow.

Colin froze, panic skittering across his chest. He flushed cold with sweat, glanced up at Karen's open face, eyes wide. "Karen—"

But Karen cut him off, her gaze dropping, her fingers curling around the pendant. "My mother gave it to my sister in Trent. She was older than me, and she expected her to meet someone, to find someone—" She halted, shook her head, grimacing. "But then she died, on the *Merry Weather*. They both died, and it broke my father. He didn't know what to do, didn't know how to handle it. Before we cleaned the bodies and sewed them up in cloth to drop overboard, he took the pendant from my sister's neck and gave it to me. I didn't want to take it, didn't want to even touch it. But he insisted. He was crying and I didn't know what to do. I'd never seen him cry before. So I took it and shoved it into a pocket, and I forgot about it.

"Until I met you."

She reached out and took Colin's hand, and he didn't resist. She rested her closed fist in his palm, but didn't release it.

She caught his gaze, held it with the intensity in her eyes, with the vulnerability he saw there.

"I'm not saying I want you to make the vow," she whispered, and he could feel her hand trembling in his. "Not now. Maybe not ever. But I don't know what we're going to find on the plains, and I wanted you to have this now, before anything happens. After the gallows and the penance locks, after the last three weeks . . . I wanted you to know." She drew in a steadying breath. "Will you take it?"

He could hurt her with a simple action, with a single word. But he found that the panic had receded.

"Yes."

She sighed. A shuddering sigh that brought tears to her eyes, sharp in the pale light. She released the pendant, pressed it into the palm of his hand hard enough he could feel the rounded smoothness of the glass, could feel the sharp metal ends of the crescent moon. And then she sat back onto her heels, scrubbed the tears from her eyes, and laughed. A self-deprecating laugh.

Colin dropped his hand to his lap, uncertain what to do with the pendant, then looked toward Karen, face screwed up. "Would you like me to wear it?"

Karen's breath caught. "If you want."

He held it out to her. She took it back, undid the clasp, then shifted forward on her knees.

Colin scooted around, back to her, and as soon as he saw the pendant fall down before his face, he ducked his head. He felt the chain against his neck, felt Karen's hands brush his skin as she closed the clasp again and sat back.

Turning, he picked the pendant up in his hand, ran his fingers across its cold metal and glass, then slipped it inside his shirt, where its weight rested against his skin.

Karen smiled tentatively, then settled back to the rock beside him.

They sat together staring out into the unknown plains and dark night for another hour without saying a word.

~

"Are the last of the horses ready?" Colin's father shouted from the end of the line.

Colin looked down the wagons, saw the foreman on the end signal with a hand wave, then turned back toward his father, cupped his hands around his mouth, and shouted, "All hitched and ready!"

Three wagons down, his father waved, then ducked between the lead horses out of sight. Colin heard him shouting to someone else, men yelling and whistling on all sides. All the families that had been asked to join the wagon train except two had been assembled. One of those families was still frantically dismantling the tent they'd lived in for the past two months; the other had decided at the last minute to return to Andover instead. Colin could still hear the man apologizing to his father and Sam, his wife standing behind him, a stern look on her face, body rigid with disapproval as she stared at the men loading the last of the supplies. As soon as her husband joined her, she headed toward the remains of Lean-to, her husband following meekly behind.

"Looks like he was whipped with a pussy willow," Sam said as they watched the two retreat. One of the men nearby snickered.

Colin's father merely grunted. "Two less mouths to feed. And two less souls to worry about. I'm certain more will head back to Portstown and Andover once we get started."

The wagons appeared ready. Goats bleated, hitched to the backs with rope, and children shrieked as they chased each other and the dogs everywhere, the dogs yipping and barking. Mothers muttered curses, hurrying to get their last-minute supplies onto the wagon beds, and men laughed, standing in small groups, conversing.

Colin scanned the plains ahead, eyes shaded against the morning sun still low on the horizon, and grinned. His satchel hung at his side, containing only a few rocks and his sling. He'd helped his mother strip everything of use from their hut, including wood from the sides and roof. All they were waiting for now was the Proprietor.

Even as he thought it, he heard Sam's piercing whistle. Abandoning the front of the wagons, where the horses were stamping the ground restlessly with all the heightened activity, Colin slid between the two nearest wagons, hand raised to brush the cured hides that formed their roofs, and emerged on the far side.

Everyone was gathering near the back of the first wagon. Colin saw his father standing in front, but they weren't waiting for the Proprietor. A group of twenty men approached the wagons from the direction of the rougher section of Lean-to, mostly conscripts, their faces hard, eyes black with hatred. The few members of the Armory who'd remained with the wagons headed out to meet them, most of the men from the wagon train, including Colin's father, joining them a moment later.

Colin caught his mother searching for him, her face troubled, but before she found him, he jogged down the slope and joined the group, pushing forward to the front, where his father and the man who led the group were facing each other, both tense, both frowning.

"What do you want, Karl?" his father asked.

The leader of the conscripts smiled, but it didn't touch his eyes above his bristly beard. "So you're going through with it? You're really going to take Sartori up on his offer?" His voice blended disbelief, resentment, and sarcasm.

Colin's father straightened. "Yes."

Karl shook his head. "You know he can't be trusted. He'll take back whatever he promised you eventually."

A few of the settlers shifted uncomfortably, trading glances, but Colin's father didn't waver. "I don't think he will. He needs us. He needs our skills."

"He needs your cooperation," Karl barked, and for the first time Colin noticed that he carried an ax, the weapon hooked through his belt. Most of the men behind him carried weapons as well, mostly knives but a few swords. They all shifted restlessly, the tension on the air increasing as the Armory around Colin responded in kind. Still focused on Colin's father, Karl continued. "You should stay here, join us. We could use you and your men, the materials in those wagons, your skills. Sartori doesn't have the right to force us out."

"Yes, he does," Colin's father said sharply. "He's the Proprietor, named by the charter that was signed and sealed by the Court. This isn't Andover or Trent. There are no judges here, no courts. There's only the Proprietor."

Karl bristled, his lips compressing, arms crossed over his chest beneath his beard. "Then perhaps we need a new Proprietor." The men behind him rumbled agreement.

Colin's father stiffened. "I'm not willing to take that risk, not when my wife or my son may pay the price." He didn't glance toward Colin, but Colin felt his attention on him nonetheless. The guildsmen from Lean-to behind him nodded. "You'll have to find someone else to join your rebellion. You'll get no support here."

Karl grunted, head lowering. "So be it. But if Sartori comes with his Armory . . ." He left the threat unfinished, glancing meaningfully toward the Armory at Tom's back.

When Tom didn't respond, Karl spat to one side and stalked off in the direction of Lean-to, his men parting before him, then closing up behind.

"He's the new Shay," Colin's father said, his stance relaxing as the group moved farther away. "And like Shay, he's going to get himself killed."

He frowned, turned toward Colin, then the rest of those gathered behind him. But before the group could begin to head back toward the wagons, someone shouted and motioned toward Portstown.

A group of Armory guardsmen trudged up the slope from the direction of the town, ahead of another group of ten on horseback, including the Proprietor, Signal Daverren from the West Wind Trading Company, along with one of his assistants in a brown vest, Sedric, Walter, and Patris Brindisi and another priest.

Colin frowned when he saw Walter scowling.

The group that had gathered to meet Karl and his men split, some heading back to the wagons, the rest moving to intercept the Proprietor. Colin spotted his mother headed toward the Proprietor as well and pushed through those gathered to her side. She smiled when she saw him, caught him by the shoulders as he moved to stand in front of her. He realized with a start that he was almost the same height as she.

He'd grown in the last few months.

Then Sartori and his escort drew to a halt before his father. The Proprietor dismounted, followed by all of the rest, and made his way between the Armory to the front. Arten, the commander of the guard, stood beside him on the right, with the Signal, Walter, and Sedric to the left, everyone else behind.

"Tom Harten," Sartori said, nodding in greeting. "Is everything ready?"

"Proprietor, all of the men, women, and children are assembled and our supplies loaded. We were simply waiting for you."

"Good. Then I'll make this quick so you can be on your way. I've brought my contingent of representatives for this endeavor. There will be ten members from the Armory to serve as protection for the group and as escort. Commander Arten has volunteered for this service, along with nine other members of the Armory under his command."

Arten nodded toward Sartori and then toward Tom Harten, while the other guardsmen shifted from Sartori's group to the wagons. They were all dressed in armor and carried swords. And they all held the reins of their horses. Colin was happy to see the unshaven man who'd watched over him while he'd been imprisoned leading his own and Arten's horse. There were a few uncertain whispers from the families gathered around them, but these died down quickly.

"From the West Wind Trading Company," Sartori continued, "Signal Daverren is sending his assistant, Jackson Seytor." Jackson stepped forward, pulling down on his vest as he did so to straighten out the wrinkles. He shook hands with Daverren and Sartori, then turned to Colin's father, nodding before moving to join the Armory guardsmen with his own horse. "Also, Patris Brindisi noticed that your group had no priest. He has convinced one of the Hands of Diermani, Domonic Hansi, to accompany you." The priest beside Brindisi knelt, kissed the Patris' ring in blessing, then rose and bowed to Colin's father before moving to the middle of the group. A few of the men and women smiled at him, touching his robe or murmuring a few words of welcome.

"And lastly, my own representative."

Colin felt his stomach clench even as Sartori turned toward his two sons. His mother's hand tightened on his shoulder in warning as he tensed, his hand dropping toward his satchel and the sling inside.

But Sartori had already continued. "For such an important venture, I cannot send simply anyone. The Family must be represented with someone of significance. And so I choose to send my younger son.

"I choose Walter Carrente."

～

"Did you know?" Colin demanded, glaring out over the grass in front of the wagons to where Walter had mounted and fallen into place behind Arten with a resentful scowl. The supplies for Sartori's group had been thrown into the last wagon, and men were doing last-minute checks on traces and harnesses and horses before climbing up into the seats behind their teams. But Colin's eyes were fixed on Walter, on where he sat stiffly in his saddle, chin lifted, gaze straight ahead. So arrogant, so proud.

Colin snorted, turned toward his mother, and asked again, his voice tighter, denser, "Did you know?"

She shook her head. "No, and neither did your father. We're as surprised as you. We expected him to send a token representative, one of the mercantile men associated with the Family, someone like that. Certainly not one of his own sons." She spoke calmly, but now her face tightened into a frown. "But it doesn't matter, Colin. He's here now. We can't tell Sartori he can't send his own son."

Colin's nostrils flared. "I thought I'd be rid of him."

"He doesn't have the rest of his gang with him. He's alone."

Colin saw his father give the signal to head out, the order passed down the line. Before it reached the last of the wagons, the first two had already started rolling forward, Walter and his escort in front of them. Horses stamped their feet and tossed their heads, and dogs began barking wildly, dashing out ahead of the group into the grass and racing back. Children of all ages raced out with them before being called back sharply by their mothers.

When the wagon next to them lurched into motion, blocking the view of Walter and his group, Colin turned to his mother.

"Just stay out of his way," she said, her voice laced with warning.

Colin spat to one side and saw his mother's frown deepen, but he didn't care. He turned away, caught sight of Sartori's escort as they pulled their mounts around and headed back toward Portstown, then began jogging out ahead of the wagon train as it formed up. He heard his mother sigh in exasperation as he left and caught sight of his father from the side, but he ignored them both. He didn't even stop when he heard Karen call his name, her voice distant, tattered by the wind. He pretended he hadn't heard her.

He passed the lead group, the men who were scouting for the best path for the wagons, and as he moved he took the sling from his satchel, slowing enough to tie the straps to his arm.

When he had drawn far enough away from the wagons

that they wouldn't catch up to him for at least an hour, he
began to hunt.

~

Colin returned to the wagons at midday, two prairie dogs
in his satchel, and found his father waiting. Someone had
forewarned him; he stood on a knoll, arms crossed over his
chest. Colin halted when he saw him, then changed course
to meet him. As he trudged up the slope, the wagons came
into view, trundling down into the shallow fold of land
behind his father.

He stopped a few paces away, noting the creases in his
father's forehead, the set expression on his face.

"Don't ever run off like that again," his father said.

Colin stiffened defensively. "I was hunting—"

"No! Hunting alone while we were in Lean-to was fine.
The land around Portstown had been explored. But once
we pass beyond the last farmstead, once we pass onto
the real plains, you can never hunt alone. We don't know
what's out there, what the dangers will be. And we don't
have that many men. We can't afford to lose anyone."

Colin drew breath to protest, but the seriousness in
his father's voice forced him to stop. This wasn't a lecture,
spoken to a child. His father meant it.

He released the pent up breath. Looking at the ground,
he said grudgingly, "I won't hunt alone."

His father relaxed, but he wasn't finished. "I didn't expect Sartori to give this expedition over to Walter, but he's
part of it now. This isn't Portstown. This isn't even Lean-to.
Officially, Walter is in charge of this expedition. His word
is final; he is, in effect, the Proprietor of the wagon train."

His father glanced toward where Walter rode at the
head of the wagons themselves; they'd begun making their
way up the ridge they stood on. The tension—the sternness
in his expression—suddenly lessened.

"But that's only what's written on paper. We have
nearly eighty people here—thirty men, nearly twenty
women, and twenty-seven children—and none of us will be
inclined to follow his orders if they don't make any sense.
I haven't had a chance to speak to Arten, the commander
of Walter's escort, so I don't know how the Armory will
react if we disagree, whether they'll side with Walter or

with us. But it doesn't matter." And here his father turned back to him. "I don't want Arten to have to make a choice. Walter hasn't caused any problems so far. He's been content to lead the train with his escort, talking with Jackson. But once we reach the last farmstead tomorrow, that will change. So leave him be, Colin. Don't provoke him, don't speak to him, don't even interact with him if you can manage it. Agreed?"

Colin had spent the entire morning venting his anger on the prairie dogs and the defenseless grass. He still shook with rage when he thought of the penance lock, of what Walter and the others had done to him while he was trapped in it, but he didn't need to do anything about that now. He could wait.

So he looked his father in the eye and said, "Agreed."

His father held his gaze a moment, lips pressed together, as if he didn't quite believe him, but then he nodded, his features smoothing out. "Good." He motioned toward Colin's satchel with one hand. "Now, what did you catch?"

They passed the last farmstead deeded by Sartori as the sun began to sink into the horizon the next day. The farmer's wife appeared in the doorway of the small wooden house, wiping her hands on the folds of her dress. Four small children ranging in age from a little over a year all the way up to seven crowded around her legs to watch the wagon train pass. Dust rose on a field behind the barn, and if Colin shaded his eyes, he could see someone turning the soil on a new field.

And then they passed beyond, the farmstead falling behind.

"Looks like we're going to have company," Sam said, and pointed with his chin toward where Arten and one of the other guardsmen had broken away from Walter's escort and were riding toward them.

Colin's father merely grunted. They continued walking, even when Arten and the guardsman arrived and drew the horses up alongside them.

"Walter Carrente would like to know when you intend to stop for the day," Arten said, his tone formal.

"Were those his words?"

Arten's mouth twitched. "I've . . . paraphrased them slightly."

Colin's father grunted. "We'll stop when we hit the river, where we'll restock on fresh water. Also, it makes sense to follow the river upstream. If we're going to settle somewhere, we're going to need a readily available water source. It seems likely we'll find something suitable if we keep to the river's edge."

Arten nodded. "You've thought this out."

"As much as possible, given the time we had to prepare."

Arten looked at Colin's father a long moment, thoughtful. But all he said was, "I'll inform Walter."

They camped on a rise above the river, the wagons forming a rough boundary surrounding the tents that those from Lean-to erected on the grass, even though most chose to sleep on pallets under the open night sky. Fire pits were dug, and whatever had been caught during the day was skinned and cooked. The pelts were set to dry on stakes near the fire. The women organized the meals while the men cared for the horses and inspected the wagons. The priest Domonic blessed the meal and the campsite. Sentries were posted—two of the Armory along with a few men from Lean-to, alternating in two-hour shifts—but the night was cool and quiet.

They followed the river for the next week, sometimes moving far from its banks in order to find safe passage for the wagons but returning to it as evening approached. The novelty of the expedition wore off the second day, and by the end of the sixth, two families had decided to turn back. They departed on the morning of the seventh day, a rough group of nine—four adults and five children—that faded into the distance along the edge of the river with a sack of provisions and whatever belongings they could carry.

"They'll drop half of it before the end of the day," Sam said, shaking his head.

Tom had already turned away, looking at the sky and the clouds scudding across it from the northeast with a frown. "It's going to rain before nightfall. We'd better get moving."

By noon, the clouds had thickened, the wind gusting, but the storm was still distant. The group had paused to ford a stream, Colin splashing through the knee-deep cold water at the side of the wagon, when one of the scouts returned in search of Colin's father. Colin watched from a distance as the scout was intercepted by Arten. An argument ensued, and by the time Colin had gotten the wagon safely to the far side of the stream and jogged over, Walter and Tom had arrived.

"They shouldn't be there," Walter proclaimed, anger in his eyes. The anger increased when he saw Colin arrive, the Proprietor's son shooting him a hate-filled glare, but he focused his attention on Colin's father. "My father hasn't given any land to anyone beyond the Grange estate, and we passed that days ago! This man—and his family—are squatters on Carrente lands!"

"They aren't Carrente lands yet," Tom said, trying to keep his voice level. But Colin could hear the irritation underneath.

Walter growled in annoyance. "I don't even know why I'm arguing with you. Arten, take the Armory and go arrest those squatters."

Arten froze, a flurry of mixed emotions crossing his face before it settled into blandness. In a perfectly reasonable voice, he asked, "And what do you want me to do with them once they're arrested?"

"I don't know, send them back to Portstown."

"With an escort? I don't think the expedition can afford to lose any of its guardsmen at this point." When Walter only glared at him in response, he stiffened. "Tom Harten is right. We're too far out for this land to rightfully belong to the Carrente Family, not without argument. But— Carrente lands or not, squatters or not—there isn't much we can do."

"There is," Tom said, and Arten frowned.

"What?" Walter demanded.

"We can ask the man for information."

Walter scowled in derision, but Tom had already turned away. He saw Colin standing behind him. "Colin, go get Sam and Ian."

At a look from Walter, Arten said, "If you're going to speak to this man, I'll join you."

Once Colin had found Sam and Ian, the five men left a disgusted Walter behind with the rest of the Armory escort and followed the scout, Went, across the plains to the top of a rise that looked down into a flat section of land. A house had been built there, a large section of ground given over to a garden beyond it. A copse of trees clustered at the end of the depression, and a thin stream trickled down its center.

Arten took the lead, heading down the slope, the rest trailing after. Before they'd made it halfway to the small house—not much more than a hut in Lean-to—a dog started barking wildly. A man emerged from the interior of the house, cursing the dog, until he spotted them. A shocked look crossed his face, and he ducked back inside, returning with a sword.

He came out to meet them, his dog at his side, the animal still barking, the growl beneath audible, teeth bared. The man halted three paces from them, his dark eyes flickering across all of their faces. They paused longest on Colin, confusion touching his gaze, before settling on Arten. His tanned skin wrinkled as he squinted. He was broad in the shoulder but not heavily built; what muscle he had came from maintaining his land.

But he held the sword with confidence, an obvious threat, even though the sword wasn't raised, even though his grip seemed casual.

"Hush," he said to the dog, and the dog stopped barking, although it continued to growl, feet planted forward. Its head came up to Colin's waist, and its hair was short, matted, and multicolored, ears pointed, muzzle lean.

"Why are you here?" the man asked. "What do you want?"

Arten didn't respond, so Tom stepped forward. "We aren't here to take your land or take you back to Portstown."

The man's gaze flicked toward Colin's father, but he didn't relax. Nothing in his stance changed at all. "That's good, because I've no intention of giving it up, or going back to town."

"We're part of a wagon train," Sam said, "heading out to settle a new town upriver from Portstown."

"We were hoping you could provide us with a little information," Tom added. "About what we might expect to find."

The man's sword lowered slightly. "Where is this wagon train?" he asked suspiciously.

"Up over the rise. We've been following the river for a week now."

The man grunted. Wind gusted out of the northeast, and Colin turned, saw black clouds on the horizon. They flashed with internal lightning, a low rumble of thunder following.

"Storm's coming," the man said. Behind him, Colin could see a shadow moving in the door of his house. The dog's growl had ground down into nothing, and it now stood straight, its attention on the storm. "You'd better find a place to shelter those wagons."

"What about getting some information?"

The man hesitated, glancing again at Arten. But the commander of the Armory hadn't made a move toward his sword, had kept his arms crossed over his chest for the entire conversation.

The man's sword arm relaxed, and he shrugged. "You can join me and my wife if you want. I'll tell you what I can. But it's not much." Then he turned, heading back to his house. The dog trotted along behind him, all the growling menace gone; it looked back once, as if uncertain whether they should be following its master or not, then caught up with its owner.

"Ian," Tom said, "take Went and head back to the wagons. Tell them to hunker down and prepare for the storm, quick, if they haven't done so already."

"Yes, sir."

Ian began climbing the slope behind, moving fast, Went practically stepping on his heels. The wind picked up even before they disappeared over the top.

"What do you hope to learn?" Arten asked as they moved toward the house. The man had begun shuttering the few windows.

"I don't know. But it looks as though he's been here for a while. He's bound to know something useful."

Arten and the rest entered the house before Colin. A woman stood just inside the door and pulled it closed, latching it with a plank of wood that stretched across the frame. She gave everyone from the wagon train a worried look, tainted with suspicion, her glance shooting toward her husband, who shook his head minutely.

The house was nothing more than a small room, a

rough table set up before the fire pit against one wall, a
bed shoved into a corner along with a few trunks, another
table lined with bowls and knives and chopped vegetables
on the opposite side. A pot boiled over the fire, and the
heady scent of stewed meat and potatoes filled the room.
Pelts were stacked on the dirt floor in another corner—
prairie dog, woodchuck, a few fox, and one wolf. Candles
had been lit, two on the table with the food, a third on the
table before the fire, the light that filtered in from outside
darkening as the storm moved in overhead.

The man pulled a chair out and set it before the table.
"Have a seat," he said, looking directly at Arten.

Arten's eyes narrowed, but he sat, the other man moving away as he approached. Colin's father took one of the
other chairs, Sam the last. Colin found a three-legged stool.

The woman ignored them all, returning to cutting up
the food for the stew.

"You've set yourself up pretty good here," Arten said.

"No thanks to Portstown. Or any of the other towns for
that matter."

"Where are you from, originally?"

"Does it matter?"

Arten shook his head. "No. But if you're that suspicious
of us, why'd you let us in?"

The man hesitated. "Because if you wanted to arrest
us as squatters and haul us back to Portstown for that
bastard's idea of justice, you would have done so already.
There are more of you than there are of us." His gaze
turned toward Colin. "And because you wouldn't have
brought anyone as young as him if that was your intent."

Arten grunted, giving Colin a brief look. "True."

Colin felt a twinge of annoyance and shifted where he
sat.

"That doesn't mean I can't be wary," the man said, and
he touched his sword, within easy reach where he stood
back from the table. His dog sat beside him, attentive.

A burst of violent wind rattled the shutters, set the door
shuddering in its frame, and everyone fidgeted in their
seats. Without warning it began to rain, the downpour
thundering into the grass roof. The fire hissed as some of
the water made its way under the cover that protected the
hole for the smoke, the gusts whistling over the opening.

The candles guttered a moment, but none of them went out. Lightning flared, highlighting the cracks between the wood that made up the house, and thunder rumbled through the ground. Colin could feel it reverberating in his feet, in the frame of his stool.

"My name's Tom Harten," Colin's father said, "and this is Sam, Arten, and my son, Colin."

The man nodded to each. "You can call me Cutter, and this is my wife, Beth."

"How long have you been out here, Cutter?"

For a moment, it seemed Cutter wouldn't answer, but then Beth sighed in exasperation. "Oh, just tell them. You don't have to be so damned suspicious all the time. Not everyone's out to haul you back to Andover!"

Cutter grimaced. "All right, all right. We came to the coast nearly twelve years ago, spent the last ten in this place."

"By yourselves?" Arten asked, clearly impressed.

"We've had the occasional visitor."

"Who?" Sam said, leaning forward in his seat.

"Mostly trappers, or single couples, heading out onto the plains because they can't stand the Proprietors or their taxes and laws and justice. About seven years ago we had a wagon train, like yours I presume."

"Where did they head?"

"No idea where they were going, but they headed east, following the river like you. I'm sure they changed their plans once they hit the Bluff." To one side, Beth snorted, then scooped up a handful of chopped onion, cut around the corner of the table, and dumped it into the stewpot. She stirred it briefly, took a sip of the broth, then returned to her table.

"What bluff?" Sam asked.

Cutter shifted forward, relaxed enough he left his sword behind. His dog settled down on the floor, head resting on its forelegs. "East of here, about a day's walk, there's a jagged wall of rock rising out of the plains, running roughly north and south. It's as if the plains got split and the eastern half got shoved up toward the sky. Once the wagon train hit the Bluff, they must have either turned north or south. If they turned north, they may have made it to the upper plains. The Bluff isn't as steep there, and there are tons of places where the stone cliffs have given way in rockslides. I haven't explored too far south, but it seems to only get steeper and higher the farther south you go. If you're headed east, I'd cut to the north once you hit the cliffs. But I wouldn't head up to the upper plains."

Colin's father frowned. "Why not?"

Cutter sighed, and his wife turned toward them, her face stern. "Tell them."

He waved a hand at her in annoyance. "I was getting there!"

Beth hmphed.

"There's something strange about the Bluff. Well, not the Bluff exactly, that seems perfectly natural, but the area around the Bluff. A heaviness in the air, a tingling. And occasionally the air above the grass ripples, like heat above desert sand. Like the Borangi Desert back in Andover, where they found that Rose. Except this isn't desert, and the ripples occur even when it's not hot out."

"Tell them about the people."

Cutter rolled his eyes. "Beth swears she saw people out there, on the edge of the upper plains, looking down on us."

"Except they weren't really people," Beth added, not turning from peeling and slicing a carrot. Her knife made sharp clunks on the table as she cut. "They seemed too short. And I think they had deer with them. Only the deer seemed too big."

"I think she was just seeing things. Hallucinations, like in the desert."

"Have you ever gone up to the upper plains?" Arten asked.

"No."

"Why not?"

Cutter shrugged. "No need to. I have everything I need right here. Besides, only a few of the people that have gone up there have ever come back down again. Those that have come back don't seem quite the same anymore."

"What did they find up there?"

Cutter shrugged. "Hard to say. More plains like this, according to most. A few have spoken about a lake. A huge lake, the source of the river you're following I presume. And some have mentioned seeing others on the plains up there, but always at a distance. Never near the Bluff."

Lightning sizzled outside, followed by a crash of thunder that shook the entire house. Everyone from Lean-to and Portstown jumped. Colin leaped up from his chair as another one struck, so close it sounded like a pop, the thunder juddering in his teeth, a cold sensation prickling along his skin, making the hairs on his arms and the back of his neck stand on end. In the flare of white-hot light, the flames in the candles dimmed, two of them going out completely. The air reeked of something sharp, acrid, and bitter, something Colin could taste on his tongue, like metal. He fought the urge to spit it out.

"One thing's for certain," Cutter said, staring at them in the deeper darkness, the fire silhouetting him from behind. His eyes appeared white in the flickering shadows. Neither he nor Beth had reacted at all to the lightning and thunder or to the candles going out. "The storms near the Bluff are worse than elsewhere on the plains."

6

"THERE GO OUR PLANS to follow the river."

Tom, eyes shaded to stare across the land through the glare of the late afternoon sun, grimaced, but he didn't respond to Sam's remark. He couldn't. He didn't know what to say. A hollow had opened up in his chest, an emptiness edged with weariness and a hint of despair. But he couldn't let any of those in the wagon train see it. Not at this point. This was the first setback they'd run across so far. He was certain there would be more. And it wasn't as if they hadn't been forewarned.

They'd reached the top of a ridge of land that curved away to the north and south, like a ripple in the earth, as if the Bluff itself were a stone that had been dropped onto the surface of the plains, creating a wave. Tom stood on the ridge with Ana and Sam in stunned awe. Beyond it, the cliff face of the Bluff sliced through the plains, a wall of jagged white and gray rock, striations in the soil clear, juxtaposed against the gold of the grass, the lighter green patches where copses of trees interrupted the plains, and the deep blue of the sky above. Tom had assumed the river would have cut a path through the rock, a chasm or channel. But he could see, even from this distance, that the river fell from the heights in a huge waterfall.

He shared a look with Ana, saw the wonder in her eyes. "I've never seen anything like this in Andover."

"Nothing this large, certainly," she said, breathless.

The wagons had drawn up alongside each other, every-one gawking at the immensity of the stone escarpment.

Tom saw Colin and Karen standing not far away, hands clasped at their side. Even Walter and Jackson stood mute, the Proprietor's son's scowl wiped clean off his face.

Without a word, the wagons headed down the slope, people shaking themselves out of their awe slowly.

They reached the edge of the waterfall two hours later, the Bluff deceptively far away. The roar of that cascading water throbbed around them, mist thrown up in a spume that speckled Tom's skin with tiny droplets even from this distance. It fell into an immense rounded basin, the water in the pool beneath a deep, pristine, almost ethereal blue at the edges, a torrent of white froth and mist near the center where the Falls landed. Those from the wagon train were spread out around the lip of the basin, parents holding their children back from the steep edge, others with their hands lifted toward the sky, letting the spume fall over them. Tom couldn't see any way down to the water's surface from the edge of the basin, short of jumping. A jagged cut in the basin wall allowed the water to escape and run west, forming the river to Portstown, but above . . .

Tom shifted his hand, squinting against the harshness of the light reflecting from the white-gray cliff face. "It's not coming from the top of the Bluff," he said.

"What do you mean?" Sam said.

Tom motioned toward the cliff towering above them, over a thousand hands high, if not more. "The river. It's not flowing over the top of the Bluff, like every other waterfall I've ever seen. There's a hole in the side of the cliff, a tunnel. It's coming from the tunnel's mouth, about two hundred hands down from the top."

Sam raised his own hand to shade his eyes, then swore softly under his breath. "Look at how it's carved a smooth path through the rock, almost perfectly rounded, even at the top." He shook his head, turned to Tom. "So even if we do decide to go to the upper plains, there may not be a river to follow. It may be underground."

Tom let his hand drop, felt the hollowness in his chest expand, but forced it back. He searched those gathered here and near the wagons behind for Arten.

And Walter.

He found them a short distance away. They stood at the edge of the basin as well, Walter staring at the blue waters below. Jackson, the Company assistant, sat in the grass to one side, a wide, flat satchel spread out on the ground before him, weights holding the exposed papers down. Tom had seen him with the satchel open during every break, diligently writing notes, but he hadn't asked what he was doing. Walter and his escort hadn't really interacted with the rest of the wagon train much at all, and after what Walter had done to Colin, after the riot, those from Lean-to had caused on the docks and the hangings that followed, Tom had taken that as a blessing from Diermani.

But that would have to change. If they were going to start a town together, they needed to at least speak to each other. No matter how distasteful Tom might find it.

Sam followed him as he made his way to the small group. Arten saw him approach. "It appears that Cutter was right," he said. "We'll have to make a choice, either north or south."

"There's a third option," Tom said. "We could simply set up Haven here."

"No," Walter said flatly.

Both Tom and Arten shifted, the Armory guardsman frowning.

"Why not?" Sam asked, defensively. "We'd have water, and the land to either side certainly seems arable. We could set up near where the water spills out of the basin. We'd be protected from the worst of the wind from the plains by the Bluff, sheltered from the storms, and we'd have plenty of stone to quarry for the buildings from the cliffs."

Arten nodded as Sam spoke, eyes fixed on the surrounding land. "He's right."

Walter shot him a resentful glare. "No. It won't work. It's not far enough away."

"What do you mean?" Tom asked.

"The new town—"

"Haven," Sam interrupted, voice tight.

Walter's eyes narrowed, but he continued, "*Haven* needs to be far enough from Portstown that the Carrente Family can lay claim to the largest amount of land possible. We're not even two weeks away from Portstown by wagon, which means we're at most a week away on horseback, five days at a hard ride or with a second horse. That's not far enough."

Tom pressed his lips together, surprised. He'd thought

Walter had said no simply to spite them, to take out some of the resentment he felt at being forced to come.

Arten caught his eye, one eyebrow raised. "He's got a point. Sartori and Daverren didn't send us out here simply to settle."

Tom squinted as he considered Arten, then Walter. "Then what do you suggest?"

Walter didn't answer, brow creasing as he hesitated. He'd clearly expected more of an argument. The hesitation made him seem his age—fifteen. "From what you claim that squatter said, the Bluff gets higher to the south. We should probably head north then. If we can cut farther inland, that would be best for the Carrente Family's claim—and the Company—but if not, perhaps we can get a significant portion of land between Portstown and its northern sister port of Rendell."

Tom considered, watching Walter, seeing the arrogant youthfulness in his face, the anger that simmered just beneath the surface, the resentment. But he saw something else as well, an eagerness, hidden beneath all of the darker emotions. For the first time, he wondered what it had been like in Portstown for Walter, to be Sartori's second son—a bastard son—with so much of Sartori's attention on Sedric, on the town itself.

Tom nodded. "I agree. Shall we rest here for a while longer, before we head north along the Bluff?"

Walter frowned, suspicion darkening his expression. Tom wondered how often Sartori had asked his son for an opinion, thought the answer might have been never.

Walter finally said, "Very well. Jackson needs to finish filling in his maps anyway."

Tom ignored the touch of arrogance that colored Walter's voice and glanced toward Jackson, bent over his sheaf of papers. "I'll spread the word," he said, then motioned for Sam to follow him as he left.

"Walter's not as stupid as he looks," Sam said, as soon as they were out of the Proprietor's son's hearing.

Tom shook his head. "No, he isn't. I don't think his father listened to him at all. I don't think he paid any attention to him."

"Perhaps he won't be that bad as Proprietor of Haven."

"Don't forget, he was the one who got Colin arrested,

who got him placed in the locks," Tom said sharply. "He's the one who sent my son home bruised and beaten more times than I can count. And everyone in this wagon train knows that. They won't forget."

"You're the one who asked him what he thought, what he wanted to do."

Tom glanced back toward Walter. "I know. He's an arrogant bastard, but there's some potential there."

"Just be careful mentioning that potential around Colin," Sam said, with a significant look.

Tom frowned. "Tell everyone to stock up on water here. We're heading north."

~

"It's not as high as it was at the Falls," a voice said gruffly.

Tom turned from his scrutiny of the Bluff to see Arten coming up from behind. The commander came on foot, his horse given over to one of the other guardsmen. And he'd abandoned the formal armor he'd worn as the wagon train headed out. His shirt and breeches were still cut better and made with finer cloth than anything those from Lean-to had, but it was better suited to the heat and the rough conditions of travel.

He'd also let his beard grow. Trimmed and perfect, it made his face sharper, more angular. And darker. Tom suddenly realized that Arten hadn't originated from Trent. His features were more southern, from the Hadrian region or the Archipelago.

Tom nodded in greeting as Arten drew up beside him, wiping the sweat from his face with one large hand. "Is Walter calling a break?"

Arten shook his head. "No, we're still moving. But I saw you up here, alone for once. I thought I'd join you."

Tom smiled wryly. "If Sam isn't following me around, then it's my wife, or Colin. Or someone else from Lean-to with a problem they need resolved."

"One of the pitfalls of leadership," Arten said. "It's why I've remained in the Armory. The Family assumed it was a fleeting passion of mine, that I'd grow tired of it and return to them and the Court."

Tom's eyes widened in surprise. "You're a member of the Court?"

Arten smiled. "I could be. I was. But I never developed a taste for it. They sent me to the Armory, hoping I'd come to my senses. When I didn't return to the Family as expected, they had the Armory send me to Trent. When *that* didn't bring me scurrying back, they sent me to Portstown. They figured I'd break under the sheer depravity of it all. Much to their horror, I enjoyed it." He caught Tom's gaze. "There's no pretense here. Or there wasn't, under Sartori's father's hand. Sartori himself . . ." He shook his head regretfully.

"You could have returned to Andover once Sartori took over."

Arten didn't respond at first; he stared out over the plains at the wagons trundling along through the grass. He was silent long enough that Tom began to worry that he'd offended the Armory captain in some way. But then: "I haven't returned to Andover for a different reason."

"The Feud?"

Arten turned toward him, his eyes hard and guarded. "Do you know what the Feud is about?"

"The Rose."

Arten grunted. "And do you know what the Rose is?"

When Tom shook his head, he continued, looking back toward the plains again as he spoke. "A little over twenty years ago, a trade caravan owned by the Taranto Family traveling south through the Borangi Desert stumbled across some ruins once buried in the sands, exposed by the sandstorms that plague the desert. Inside one of the buildings, they found the Rose." He paused, but continued a moment later. "No one knew what it was, but those in the caravan, and those of the Taranto Family who came afterward to see it, knew that it contained power. More power than anything any of the Hands of Diermani wield. Godlike power, although exactly what that power was they didn't know. But the Family members returned to Taranto lands, told the Doms, who kept the discovery hidden for nearly twelve years.

"But nothing in the Court remains secret for long. Our networks of spies are too effective. The fact that they kept it secret for twelve years is staggering and attests to the potential of the Rose itself. They knew that if the other Families found out about it before they could secure their hold on it, the Families would go to war. And they nearly succeeded. However, the existence of the Rose was exposed before they attained that grip. And not only are the Families enraged that the Tarantos kept it hidden, tried to seize it for themselves, but the Hands of Diermani are as well. After all, godlike power should remain within the control of the priests and the guidance of the church. Or so the Patrises believe."

"So now the Families will go to war," Tom said.

Arten glanced toward him. "Now they will Feud. But unlike past conflicts, this will be a holy war as well. The Doms of each Family will be driven by their respective Patrises. And from what I witnessed during the sessions of the Court I attended before I left for Trent, the Hands of Diermani are split on their opinions of how to handle the Rose. Everyone wants its power, Dom and Patris alike; and everyone wants control of the land surrounding it, the desert that is in the center of Andover, the center of nearly all of the Families' lands. The desert that has remained unclaimed and uncontested for hundreds of years.

"This Feud, if it begins, will last for decades. Blood will be shed. Families will fall. All in the name of Holy Diermani."

Tom turned back to his survey of the cliffs, silent for a long moment. "You could have remained in Portstown. You would have been safe from the Feud there."

Arten shook his head, smiled bitterly. "The New World won't be safe from the Feud. The war will affect everyone, everywhere. It already has. You've experienced it, with Sartori's prejudice against your family and those in Lean-to."

"Is that why you volunteered to join the wagon train?"

Arten didn't answer at first. One hand rested on the pommel of the sword strapped around his waist, the other on his hip as he stared out at the Bluff, eyes squeezed tight against the glare of the sun off of the stone. "I didn't like the way Sartori handled the refugees from Andover or the prisoners. And after the hanging—" He looked Tom directly in the eye. "I didn't want to be part of that, of what it could become. Neither did any of the other guardsmen who came with me."

"And what about Walter?"

Arten glanced toward the Proprietor's son, to where he rode with a few of the guardsmen and Jackson Seytor. "I'm surprised. Not that Sartori would send him on this expedition; Walter was always an embarrassment, always getting into trouble, creating scenes. This was the perfect opportunity for him to rid himself of his bastard son."

Tom thought he heard a touch of derision in the commander's voice, but he couldn't be certain. "Then what are you surprised by?"

"Walter. By how he's handled it. I expected him to sulk, as he has, but I assumed he'd return to his old ways after that. To bullying everyone around him, as he did in Portstown, as he did to your son."

Tom considered for a moment. "He doesn't have his usual audience anymore. Brunt, Gregor, and Rick."

Arten grunted, shook his head. "Nor his father. Putting him in nominal charge of this expedition may have been the best thing his father ever did for him, even if that wasn't his father's intent."

"'Nominal' charge?"

Arten smiled. "I think you'll find the Armory will follow Walter's orders only so long as those orders make sense and are to the benefit of everyone involved. I'll give him a chance to be a Proprietor, to be something other than his father, but if he falters—"

Before Tom could find a suitable response, Arten tensed, his hand tightening on the pommel of his sword, his smile vanishing. "Something's wrong," he said.

Tom heard one of the horses below scream. The sound was muted, coming from a distance. As he spun, orienting on the sound, he saw one of the horses hitched to a wagon rear, feet kicking the air, its teammate doing the same, both thundering back down to the ground before lurching forward, still harnessed to the wagon. The wagon shuddered as it was yanked forward, the man in front yelling, pulling on the reins hard. Those walking around the wagon scattered, a few harsh cries and screams piercing the relative quiet.

And then the wagon foundered. Its front end jumped into the air, as if it had hit a ridge of stone hidden beneath the grass. The frenzied horse stumbled, feet collapsing beneath it, and with a wrench the entire wagon began to tilt.

It slammed into earth, dirt and grass plowing upward from the impact, the second horse dragged to the side and over by the hitch, feet kicking the air. A hideous shriek cut across the plains—a horse in pain—and then the wagon ground to a halt. The driver was thrown clear, his body like a rag doll, limbs loose and wild.

Tom stood stunned, the second horse still kicking the air, now on its side, the wagon shuddering with its movements. The entire event had happened in the space of a few heartbeats, yet it had seemed so slow at this distance, so quiet, all of the sounds dulled.

But as he watched, he thought he saw the air around the wagon shimmering, a vague distortion, there and then gone. He blinked and wiped the sweat from his forehead with the back of his arm, but it didn't reappear.

He and Arten shared a grim look, then began jogging toward the wagon.

Below, the wagons behind the one that had foundered turned toward it; those in front halted. The people who had scattered when the horses first reared now rushed to the animals, toward where the hide covering of the wagon had been torn from its supports. Chests and trunks and bundled goods lay scattered in a rough arc around the back of the wagon, but the men who arrived at the wagon first went to see to the horses. They were worth more than all the wagon's contents combined.

Someone broke from the group as it gathered and raced toward Tom and Arten.

"I believe that's your son," Arten said.

Colin met them halfway to the wagons, gasping as he ground to a halt.

"What is it? What's happened?" Tom spat.

"One of the wagons . . . The horses went wild . . . The wagon . . ."

"I can see that," Tom snapped. "What spooked them?"

Colin shook his head, catching his breath. "I don't know. But Paul's hurt."

Tom thought about the rag doll figure he'd seen fly from the front of the wagon as it rolled and felt ropes tighten around his chest. He pushed away from Colin, heard Arten's feet pounding the ground behind him, but his eyes were on the wagon. Men had climbed into the traces, were calming the horse that lay on its side, still kicking, nostrils flared, head thrashing, as they tried to cut it out of the tangled reins and harness. Its teammate lay beneath it, not moving.

The women had gathered on the grass to one side of the wagon.

"Let me through," Tom shouted as he pushed the thought of the loss of the horse from his mind and slowed. The women parted, and Tom saw Ana and the priest, Domonic, kneeling at Paul's head, another woman standing to one side, Paul's arm cradled in both hands. Paul's rounded face was ashen, his lips almost blue, his eyes watery and wide, breath coming in short, harsh gasps.

Before Tom could speak, Ana said, "Ready?"

Paul swallowed and nodded.

And then the woman kneeling on Paul's opposite side pulled the smith's strangely angled arm out straight and *wrenched*.

There was a sickening sound from Paul's shoulder, like gristle being chewed, followed by a tortuous click that sent shudders into Tom's gut.

Paul roared, his body arching up from the grass as Ana, Domonic, and two other women tried to hold him down. The woman who'd pulled his shoulder back into its socket was thrust backward, stumbled and fell with an undignified oomph.

Paul's roar died down into barely controlled panting. Tears and sweat streaked his face, and he appeared even paler than he had when Tom arrived. His arm lay curled against his chest, held there gingerly.

"Careful," Ana said as the other woman picked herself up and brushed stalks of grass from her dress.

"It's fine," Paul murmured in a weak voice, repeating it over and over. "It's fine, it's fine. I'm fine."

"Is he going to be all right?" Tom asked.

"Ah, it bloody fucking *hurts!*"

Ana glanced up, her expression black with anger and disgust. "He's fine."

Tom turned toward the wagon, cast one last look at Paul as Domonic gently helped him to sit upright and Ana held out a skin of water, then stepped over the smith's legs.

"Sam! What happened?"

Sam spun. "We're not sure, but we've lost one of the horses. Korbin's checking out the wagon now." One of the men cried out in triumph as a tie snapped beneath his knife. The entire wagon lurched as the surviving horse rolled away from the traces that had held it on its side, stumbling to its feet. Men surrounded it, hands raised to calm it down, its eyes white. It snorted, danced back and forth, trying to escape its wranglers, but Tom could see it calming even as he watched.

Sam must have seen it as well; he turned his back to the wagon. "How's Paul?"

"He'll be fine." The tension in Sam's shoulders relaxed. "Where's Korbin?"

"On the other side of the wagon, looking at the undercarriage."

Tom rounded the wagon, careful to steer away from the spooked horse. He found Korbin leaning over one of the wagon's wheels. Korbin was a full hand shorter than Tom, thin, and younger by nearly ten years. A wheelwright, he'd come to New Andover on the same ship as Tom with his new and newly pregnant wife, Lyda.

Tom took in the splintered wood of the wheel, the cracked spokes, and grimaced. "What's the damage, Korbin?"

The young man glanced toward Tom, pushed his glasses farther up onto his nose, then sighed as he stood up straight. "Wheel's broken, but that's easy to fix. I made certain replacements were packed. The real problem is going to be sorting out the traces and the damage to the axle and tongue."

"How long to fix it, do you think?"

Korbin shrugged. "A few hours at least."

The sound of thundering hooves approached, and Tom turned to see Walter, Jackson, and the escort of guardsmen pulling up near the overturned wagon, clods of dirt and grass thrown up by the horses' feet. Walter's horse pranced as he maneuvered it closer to the group crowded around the wagon's base.

"What happened?" he asked.

"Something spooked the horses," Tom said. "They bolted and overturned the wagon."

"It was the air that spooked them."

Both Walter and Tom shifted their attention to Paul as he rounded the back of the wagon, Ana and Arten at his side. Ana had put his arm in a sling made from someone's apron to keep it immobile, but Paul still winced as he walked. Some color had returned to his face, but he appeared haggard, his clothes stained with mud and grass from the fall.

"What do you mean it was the air that spooked them?" Walter asked, the words twisted with derision.

Paul frowned at his tone. "It was the air. Just before the horses reared up and bolted, I felt the air get heavy, as if someone had laid a blanket across my shoulders. It became harder to breathe, and the hairs on my arms prickled." A few of those around the wagon nodded in agreement. "I was about to whistle for a halt."

Walter snorted. But many of the men and women who had been near the wagon before the horses bolted were mumbling to themselves.

Tom thought about the distortion he'd seen from the ridge. He caught Arten looking at him and wondered if the commander had seen it. Cutter had said something about the air as well. He almost mentioned it, but after a glance at the uneasiness in everyone around the wagon, he decided to keep quiet, at least for now. He wouldn't be able to later. Rumors would spread, and someone would remember Cutter's story; they hadn't tried to keep anything the squatter had said quiet.

"Repair the wagon as best you can," Walter finally snapped. "We'll rest here." He scanned those gathered, then tugged the reins of his horse, the animal dancing to the side before heading back toward the front of the wagon train, the rest of Walter's escort following behind.

"What should we do about the dead horse?" one of the men asked.

Tom grimaced. Korbin had already gone back to work on the wagon.

"Butcher it. We may need the meat."

⁓

Colin found Karen sitting on a small stool, milking the goats. He shuddered.

"What was that for?" Karen asked. "Am I that hideous? I know the sun's been harsh, but . . ."

Colin smiled. "No. It was for the goats. I don't like

them, their bristly hair, their skeletal faces . . . but most
especially their awful, yellow, hourglass eyes. They aren't
natural." He shuddered again.

Karen laughed, still milking as she glanced at the goat in
question. It ripped some of the grass free beneath its feet
where it was tied to the back of the wagon and chewed
contentedly, ears flicking away flies. "They are rather ugly,
aren't they?" she finally said, then shrugged. "But they're
easier to bring along than cows."

As Colin settled down to the grass behind her, the goat
turning to watch, bits sticking out of its mouth in all directions, she asked, "What's going on with the wagon?"

"Korbin is almost finished. They're trying to figure out
how to rig it so a single horse can pull it. They thought
about using some of the guardsmen's horses, but they
aren't workhorses. They're a few hands shorter, and they
don't think they'd have the endurance. So some of the supplies are being redistributed to other wagons to decrease
the weight, and Korbin is altering the hitch and harness. We
should be moving again shortly."

"Good. I'm tired of waiting. We've been sitting here
for three hours already." She tilted her head, squeezing
a last few drops of milk from the goat's udder, then sat
back, one arm reaching to massage the opposite shoulder.
Shoving the goat aside, she picked up the half-full bucket
and turned to where Colin stood, brushing grass from his
breeches.

Before he knew what had happened, she'd backed him
up against the wagon and kissed him. Her free hand fell
against his chest, where the crescent moon pendant rested
against his skin. He could hear children playing on the
plains somewhere close by, tossing a stuffed leather ball
about, their laughter ragged with the wind. A twinge of
worry pulled in his chest that someone would see them,
that they'd be caught, but here in the wagon train this was
as private a moment as they were likely to get until nightfall, so he let the worry slip away.

When Karen finally backed off, he said, "You smell like
goat."

She slapped his upper arm, harder than he'd expected,
but she couldn't hide her grin.

Someone cleared his throat, and both he and Karen

spun, guilt already burning up Colin's neck. But when he saw Walter, he froze. The anger that he'd buried so deep during the night in the penance lock, that he'd buried again after his mother told him to stay away from the Proprietor's son on the trek, flared up. He'd managed not to run into Walter for the entire journey so far, at least alone. His father had always been present, Colin in the background, so that they didn't have to interact. But now the anger burned, suffused his skin with a tingling hatred, and it took everything he had to control it, to remain rigid and motionless, hands squeezed tight.

Karen took a small step forward, placing herself between the two, but to one side. Her eyes were narrowed, her face set. She didn't seem embarrassed at all, merely angry. "What do you want, Walter?"

Walter's gaze didn't leave Colin's face. Colin couldn't read what he saw there, it was too controlled. Even his voice was bland.

"Korbin says the wagon is ready. We're leaving."

"Good." When Walter didn't move, she said tightly, "Was there something else?"

Walter's eyes shifted toward Karen, glanced up and down, taking in her rumpled dress, her bare feet, the bucket of goat's milk, then returned to her face. He almost smirked, but something he saw in Karen's face stopped him. He frowned instead, the tension in his shoulders relaxing. "No. Nothing else."

He began moving away. Colin watched him, jaw clenched, breathing through his nose. Before he rounded the end of the wagon, he shot Colin and Karen a thoughtful look . . . and then he was gone.

Karen turned toward Colin, sighed in exasperation when she saw his face, his clenched fists and tightened jaw. "Ignore him, Colin. He's not worth it."

"I didn't like the way he looked at us when he left."

"So what? It was just a look. Now come on, I want to ditch this milk before we get started."

~

"What do you think, Arten? Can we make it?"

"Yes, we can," Walter answered, voice heavy. He shifted with impatience.

Tom ignored the Proprietor's son and turned to the commander of the Armory. To the east, the shortened cliffs of the Bluff—over a thousand hands high at the Falls, a mere seven hundred hands high here—were broken by a huge landslide. Tons of stone had slipped free and crashed down when the cliffs had given way at some point in the past, and now a scree of rock and dirt and brush formed a rough pathway from the rumpled valley below to the heights above, a mound of dirt that narrowed to a crack in the Bluff itself about a hundred hands down from the top before opening up again on the far side, forming a cusp to the heights.

Arten shook his head uncertainly. "It's hard to say. It's definitely the best option we've seen for reaching the upper plains since the Falls. The only option, truthfully."

"What have the scouts reported about the Bluff farther north?"

"It continues, with minor rockfalls and a steady decrease in height, but they haven't seen any evidence that the Bluff itself ends anytime soon." He caught Tom's gaze. "If we're going to make it to the upper plains, this will have to be it."

Tom sighed, scanned the rockfall again.

He didn't like it. It was too steep, especially near the top, near the mouth of the slide, where the Bluff cupped it to either side, the collapse forming a fairly large indentation in the facade of the cliff. The wagons would never make it.

"If we go slow," Korbin said from behind him, "and have the wagons switch back and forth across the length of the scree, I think we'll be fine. But it will take most of today to scale it."

Walter stepped forward, fists clenched. But he kept his voice calm, controlled. "We need to reach those heights. For the Family. For the Company. We need to lay claim to that land before anyone else."

Tom bowed his head, closed his eyes, and swallowed the gritty taste of grass and dust in the back of his throat.

"You heard the Proprietor," he said. "Secure everything loose inside the wagons, tie everything down. The slide is mostly rock. It's going to be rough."

Everyone who'd gathered to argue and listen in dispersed, a sense of excitement passing through them in a low murmur. They'd been following the Bluff for ten days, the scenery barely changing. There'd been no viable location to set up a settlement—no rivers, no lakes, only narrow streams and creeks, all meandering southward toward the river they'd left behind. They'd run out of the dry flatbread, and most of the smoked meats, and while small game was in abundance, Tom had grown tired of the taste of rabbit and fowl. They needed to find a major water source and some larger game soon, and the reports from the scouts searching northward weren't promising.

"What do you think?" Arten asked, stepping up to Tom's side.

Tom shook his head. "It's a risk. I'd rather set up the town down here, but we don't have the water resource we'd need, nor the wood. We've only seen copses, the trees too young to be used for anything useful. So if Korbin thinks we can make it to the top with the wagons . . ."

Arten grunted. "Let's see how stable the rockslide is first. We can always stop and continue north."

"I'm not so certain of that." Tom nodded toward where Walter and Jackson stood at the base of the slide itself, the first wagon already starting to crawl up the slope along its base, angled sharply to the north; it was too steep to head directly up the side. The wagon rocked as it was pulled over the rough stone. One of the guardsmen led the wagon, cutting through any tangled undergrowth in the way. "Walter's intent on getting to the upper plains. He's been searching for a way up since we left the Falls."

"And he's right." When Tom raised his eyebrows in question, the commander added, "To the Court, the difference between having a settlement down here or up there is significant. The Bluff is a boundary, and the Carrente Family position will be stronger if Walter can establish a town, or even an outpost, on the far side."

The wagon had reached the edge of the slide, and both men watched in silence as its driver and the group of men around it turned it so it could head back toward them, a little higher up the scree. Tom drew in a sharp breath when a few rocks gave way beneath one wheel, the stone clattering down the short distance to the grass, but the horses didn't falter.

Once the leader was on its way, a ragged cheer erupted

from the rest of the men and women still on the ground, and the second wagon started out.

"I'll feel better about it once we're all safely at the top of the Bluff," Tom said, then searched for Ana. He found her at the third wagon, with Korbin and his wife, Lyda. He headed toward her, smiling as Ana reached out to touch Lyda's growing stomach; Arten moved away, toward Walter and Jackson and the rest of the Armory.

"Has he started kicking yet?" Ana asked.

"Not yet," Lyda said, her voice soft, her face radiant in the sun, a glow that Tom had seen in Ana's face when she was pregnant with Colin, a vibrance that had shown through no matter how sweaty, grimy, or dirty Ana's hair and face had been.

Lyda's hair was lighter than Ana's, her face rounder, skin smoother. But Tom thought the differences had more to do with the difference in their ages.

"Hmm," Ana said wryly, then smiled. "It won't be long now though." It was the first smile he'd seen on her face that wasn't tainted with anger or weariness or regret since they'd left Trent. A pure smile, touching her eyes, trembling in her hands.

When she drew away from Lyda, one hand going to her chest and the hidden pendant there, Tom took her other hand and kissed it.

She gave him a questioning look, but he shook his head. The wagon beside them gave a lurch and started forward, Korbin and Lyda moving to follow. "He's a lucky man," Tom said.

"I was worried about her when they told us they intended to come with the wagons," Ana said. "I thought they'd head back to Andover, since they were expecting a child."

"Why were you worried?"

They started after the wagon, walking hand in hand, watching where they stepped.

Ana glanced ahead, to make certain that Lyda and Korbin wouldn't overhear. "She seemed a little ... soft. Delicate. I wasn't certain she'd be able to handle the walking or the work. But she's handling it better than some of the others."

Tom nodded. Ahead, the wagon had reached the first

turn, Korbin overseeing the change in direction. The wheelwright shouted for help.

Tom squeezed Ana's hand. "I'd better go be useful," he said, then jogged forward. As he put his shoulder to the side of the wagon and shoved hard, he saw Ana rejoin Lyda, both cutting up ahead of the horses. And then sweat ran down into his eyes, and he focused his attention on getting the damn wagon to move.

Afternoon grew steadily into evening, and the wagons zigzagged their way up the slide, each pass getting shorter as the rockfall narrowed. The first wagon passed the neck of the slide an hour before sunset, struggling up the last section into the bowl that had sunk into the upper plains beyond, where the ground was flatter and less rugged. They reached the top of the Bluff moments later, whistles and cheers echoing down the scree from above. Tom paused to stare up at the men waving from the heights and smiled, relief coursing through him. All down the trail, people clapped and whistled in response, the excited conversation that had died down after the first hour of climbing returning with laughter and claps on the back. Dogs barked, tails wagging, and goats bleated.

"I told you it was possible," Korbin said, and Tom turned, gave him a grin. Korbin smiled in return, pushed his glasses up onto his nose.

Behind him, Tom saw the ground beneath the back wheel of the wagon slip.

"Watch out!" he barked and surged forward, rock and dirt cascading away from the wheel in a small avalanche. The wagon began to tilt as he brushed past Korbin—

Then his shoulder slammed into the corner of the wagon, his feet sliding in the dirt. For a moment, he thought the ground beneath him would give way, that his weight would set the entire slope tumbling down to the plains below, but his boots found solid stone and held.

The weight of the wagon began digging into his shoulder. He gasped, sweat already sliding down into his eyes, down his back. He heard shouts as men began converging on the wagon from all sides. Korbin dodged in behind him, sending another cascade of dirt down the hill, loosening Tom's footing briefly, and then the wheelwright added his strength to Tom's.

"Henri!" Tom bellowed. "Get the damn wagon moving! We can't hold it forever!"

He heard Henri curse the horses, heard the whip snap, the wagon shuddering, gouging deeper into his shoulder, but it didn't move. Someone scrambled next to Korbin from the far side, near the front wheel, another avalanche of stone rattling down the slide. Tom blinked the sweat from his eyes, stared down the steep slope toward the wagons below, saw men surging up the fall toward them, stumbling on the rocks—

And with no warning at all, the stone beneath Tom's feet gave way. He spat a curse as he kicked, feet digging into earth and stone, and then he was falling.

He heard Ana scream, "Tom!" her voice cracking with fear, and then his shoulder slammed into the rockfall, pain shooting up into his shoulder from his elbow as he spun and rolled, stone sliding with him. He didn't cry out, didn't have time. He ground to a halt a short way below and to the side of where Korbin and another man—young, no more than seventeen—were frantically trying to hold the wagon upright.

But the wagon began to tilt, to slide downward toward him as the ground for ten hands to either side suddenly gave way. The rear wheel crunched into the ground and splintered, the entire wagon shuddering as it struck. The weight inside the wagon shifted, slammed into the downhill side, cracking the side of the wagon, pushing it outward. Tom heard Henri roar, heard the horses shriek as the twisting wagon wrenched to the side and began to overturn.

The ground beneath Korbin and the younger man slid away, dragging them both downward, pulling them away from the wagon's edge. Korbin hit hard, spun in the loose dirt, his glasses jarred from his face, sunlight glinting on the rounded glass, on the frames—

And then the full weight of the toppled wagon crushed his chest.

He never made a sound.

The younger man beside him screamed—an animalistic, terrifying scream that shuddered down into Tom's bones. The wagon rolled, already beginning to break up, and slammed into the younger man's legs. Supports snapped,

wood cracking with sharp reports, and then the wagon
rolled over Korbin and the other man completely, dragging Henri and the two shrieking horses with it. It tipped,
ground into the slope, starting a huge avalanche of stone
and debris, disintegrating as it rolled, horses kicking, a
cloud of dust rising in its wake. Men and women scrambled
to get out of its way farther downslope.

The wagon below it didn't have a chance.

The disintegrating wagon crashed into it halfway down,
tipping it over as if it were made of paper. The animal hide
covering imploded as it skidded, wheels snapping beneath
it, and then it and its team of horses joined the mass of
tumbling wood, stone, supplies, and bodies on their way to
the plains below.

Tom lay on his side against the stone of the rockfall,
stunned, hand clutched to his arm where pain still shot
from elbow to shoulder. He watched, gasping, as the dust
rose, as the wagons reached the base of the slope and
crashed into the grass. He listened to the clatter of stone
as the slide settled, listened to the distant splintering of
wood as the wagons struck and came to rest, but all of
these sounds were muted, barely piercing the thunderous
beating of his heart.

And then he heard more rocks clattering behind him,
felt pebbles pelting his back. He jerked to the side, expecting to see the ground above him giving way again, but then
Ana skidded to a halt beside him. "Tom! Tom, are you all
right!"

Tom hissed and bit back a blistering curse as she
touched his arm. "Don't touch it," he yelled, laying his
head back against the stone. For a moment, his vision wavered, filmed over with a vibrant pulsing yellow. He grew
lightheaded, but he gasped, closed his eyes, and fought it
back.

"Thank Diermani," Ana whispered, her hands covering
his body, feeling for more wounds, searching for blood,
although she kept clear of his arm. Her voice shook with
relief, the terror he'd first heard there buried beneath. He
heard her muttering a prayer, her movements frantic, and
then she seemed to relax. "Nothing but the arm," she said,
and now he could hear the tears.

He opened his eyes, saw her bowed head, one hand

raised to her face to shield it. She was shuddering, barely holding herself together.

People shouted, bounded down the slope to either side. He caught a glimpse of Lyda, her face blank, yet intent, and he suddenly lurched up into a sitting position.

"Lyda!" he shouted in warning. He could hear the sickening crunch as the wagon crushed Korbin's chest, could see the smear of blood it had left behind—

And then Lyda screamed. A high, piercing scream that reverberated in Tom's skull, that sank claws into his gut, that tightened his chest with juddering grief. She screamed until she ran out of breath, choking on it, then she sucked in air and screamed again, the sound thicker now with phlegm, harsher.

At his side, Ana jerked, her hand falling away from her face. Her reddened eyes searched the slope below, where Tom could see Sam trying to hold Lyda back from Korbin's body. It had come to rest in the sliding debris nearly thirty hands downslope. His chest was unnaturally flat, caved in and bloody. His head angled downhill, face upturned to the sky. The priest, Domonic, was leaning down next to him, but he was obviously dead.

"Holy Diermani," Ana said, voice raw. Her expression smoothed from terrified relief into a grim, hardened calm.

Without a word, she stood, folds of her dress held in one hand, and began picking her way down toward Lyda and the body. Tom watched her a moment, then struggled to his feet. Lyda broke free from Sam, her screams faltering, and stumbled to the ground beside Korbin's head, stones shifting away at the movement. Her hands shook as she reached down, as she cupped his face, then traced his features, his forehead, his jaw, his mouth. Her entire body shuddered, back arched as she bent over him, her forehead dropping to meet his, arms cradling his head. No one near her made a move. Sam stood back. Domonic sat back on his heels, caught Tom's gaze with his own and shook his head, his face stricken. No one moved except Ana. They stood, some heads bowed, others tilted toward the darkening sky, all of them silent.

When Ana finally reached Lyda's side, her arms falling across the woman's shoulders, Tom glanced to the ground.

There, not three paces away, Korbin's glasses lay against a rock, sunset flaring in one shattered lens.

7

THE GROUP BURIED KORBIN, Henri, and the driver of the second wagon at the top of the Bluff the next day, a good distance away from where the land had collapsed and formed the rockslide. Two children had also been riding inside the second wagon, and they were buried next to the men. One of the mothers wept openly. The other mother, older than the first, simply stood next to the grave, one of her other children, a boy, resting on her hip, a second clinging to her leg. She stared, stoic and unmoved, out over the plains, her movements desultory, her face blank.

Its lifelessness sent a shudder through Tom, and he shifted his glance toward the fathers, both of them standing at their wives' sides, heads bowed, faces grim. The younger looked haunted, eyes a little too wide.

"—as we give this mortal flesh back to the earth," Domonic murmured, "as we give the light of their souls back into Diermani's Hand, into his keeping forever."

Tom turned toward Domonic as the Hand of Diermani finished the litany and transitioned into a prayer. Tom glanced around those gathered, taking in Lyda's reddened eyes, her hand resting protectively on the swell of her stomach, the Armory, their clothes sweaty from dragging whatever was salvageable from the wreckage of the wagons and from digging the graves, and Walter, the future Proprietor, glaring down at the gaping holes in the ground, his face angry and pinched, as if the dead men had somehow sabotaged the attempt to climb the Bluff.

Tom felt his stomach turn. Walter had ordered the attempt, practically demanded it. He'd known that someone might die during the ascent, but he wasn't going to take responsibility for those deaths. Tom could see it in his eyes.

"Aldiem patrus," Domonic murmured, reaching down to grasp a handful of dirt from the heap beside him. At each of the other four graves, men scooped up their own handfuls, all except Korbin's grave. There, Lyda took the dirt in hand, Ana at her side to steady her. *"Diermani arctum verbatis."*

Domonic tossed the dirt into the open grave, all the rest doing the same, everyone murmuring Domonic's last words under their breath as they did so. The young mother broke out into fresh sobs, as her husband brushed the dirt from his trembling hands.

Then everyone stepped back, distancing themselves from the dead, and those designated to inter the remains slid forward with shovels, filling in the graves as quickly, yet as solemnly, as possible. Most signed themselves with Diermani's tilted cross, mouthing their own additional prayers wordlessly, heads bowed. Only a few didn't participate in the rituals at all, not speaking or signing themselves.

As soon as the dead were buried, Tom moved toward Walter. He gripped the young man's shoulder as he said, "You couldn't have known that would happen—"

Walter twisted out of his grip roughly, irritation flickering across his face. "Of course I couldn't have known," he spat. "We needed to get to the top of the Bluff. For the Company. For the Family." He looked directly at Tom and Tom silently willed the bastard to keep quiet. With a dismissive wave, Walter said, "It was worth the risk, worth the deaths."

Tom tensed, knowing that Lyda and the others had heard. He could feel the resentment building from behind, prickling along his back.

Unaware, Walter turned to glare out over the plains. "We still have half of the day left to travel," he said curtly. "We should get started."

The resentment escalated, murmurs rising. Tom said through a clenched jaw, "Where should we head?"

Walter glanced toward Jackson, who nodded. "Southeast. I want to see if we can return and find the river."

"Very well," Tom said, and turned toward the others. "Let's head out."

He should have said something to placate those that had heard Walter's words, to ease the resentment. Everyone was still on edge, emotions sharp and brittle.

But he didn't.

Those gathered broke for the remaining wagons, dispersing slowly. Ana moved to join him, leaving Lyda in Sam's hands.

"How's Tobin?" Tom asked.

"Considering both of his legs were crushed by the wagon, he's doing fine. We've loaded him into the back of Paul's wagon. I've done what I can to ease him, to clean the wounds and set them, but we'll have to wait and see. If they become infected, we may have to cut them off."

Tom grimaced. "I didn't hear him moaning during the burial."

"He passed out about an hour ago, thank Diermani." She shuddered, leaning into Tom's side, arms wrapping around his waist. Around them, the drivers had climbed into their seats, the wagons beginning to move forward, Walter and the Armory taking the lead.

"I don't like it up here," Ana said.

Tom scanned the horizon, frowning. The plains up here looked no different from those beneath the Bluff. In the distance to the east and north he could see hills, the faint purple shadows of mountains; to the south, nothing but more grassland. "Why?"

Ana shuddered again, tightening her hold. "Can't you feel it? There's a weight up here, as if the air is heavier. And it's harder to breathe. Like what Paul said happened to the wagon earlier, when he was thrown. Except here it isn't just in one spot, it's everywhere. I noticed it as soon as we reached the top of the Bluff."

Tom drew in a deep breath, let it out slowly ... and felt the skin across his shoulders crawl. He'd noticed the shortness of breath but had shrugged it off, attributing it to the exertion of the climb. But Ana was right; there was a denseness to the air, as if something were pressing down on him from above. He felt heavier here.

And it felt as if someone were watching.

He scanned the horizon again but saw nothing. He frowned, thinking about Cutter and Beth.

"It's just the change in elevation," he said, hearing the falseness in his own voice.

Ana snorted.

~

"What are they?" Sam asked.

Nate answered gruffly, "Dinner."

Those nearest to Nate turned toward him. Tom grinned.

"We'll never be able to keep up with them on foot," Arten said. "We'll have to use the horses, try to drive them toward the hunters."

"You'll never take them with swords," Nate said. "At least not easily. They look fast."

"Bows. We'll have to take them down with arrows."

All the men and most of the women had gathered at the edge of the hillock overlooking the grassland to the east, where hundreds upon hundreds of animals grazed in a herd larger than anything Colin had ever seen before. The animals were like deer—tawny, thin-legged, lean of body and neck—but unlike the deer from Andover, two long pointed horns sprouted from the males' heads, near the ears. And these deer were smaller than those from Andover by a few hands, with white chests and faint streaks of white lining their sides.

Colin's father turned toward everyone assembled. "Anyone who's experienced with a bow, get your weapons and report back here. Paul, start unhitching the horses. We'll use the Armory's mounts to drive the beasts toward the archers, but the workhorses can be used to hem them in. Everyone else, stick close to the wagons. Get the children inside the wagon beds. We don't know how these horned deer will react."

People began scattering, men rushing to the wagons to begin removing the workhorses from their harnesses, women herding the children to wagons, lifting them up and into the shade of the hides. Arten and the rest of the Armory made for their own horses, handing their swords off to younger men. A smaller group began pulling bows and quivers from the wagons, stringing the bows with smooth motions, settling the quivers across their shoulders so the arrows were in easy reach. Excitement coursed through the expedition, everyone talking, the dogs tearing out across the plains, pausing to stare at the distant deer, ears perked up, before reluctantly racing back when their owners shouted or whistled.

Those who were to be part of the hunt started gathering near Tom. Colin felt the exhilaration prickling against his skin. When Karen touched him, a tingling sensation raced up his arm, and he jumped.

Karen grinned. She nodded toward where the men were gathering. "You'd better get over there, or you'll be stuck here watching the little ones."

Colin grimaced. "I can't use the bow, and there aren't enough horses for me to ride."

"But you have your sling, and they'll need men to help drive the animals. You can shout, can't you?"

Colin straightened. He doubted he could take one of the strange deer down with his sling, but that didn't mean he couldn't try.

Grinning madly, he sprinted for the wagon where he'd tossed his satchel, retrieved his sling, and tied it on as quickly as possible, eyes on the men. Karen rolled her eyes and shook her head, as if asking Diermani to explain the stupidity of men. Colin ignored her.

Sling secured, stones thrust into his pockets, Colin dashed toward the group of men, arriving just as Arten barked an order and those on horseback spun their mounts and took off toward the plains at a trot.

His father gave him a curt nod, then addressed the group that remained, all on foot, most carrying bows. "All right. Arten and the others will drive the animals toward the fold in the land over there." He pointed toward where a depression in the land narrowed down to a small gap between two banks of earth. "We'll set the archers on the banks. You can shoot down into the depression. The rest of you need to line up to either side. Try to get them to funnel down into the opening. We don't want them rushing up the banks and overwhelming the archers."

"How do we do that?" someone asked. "We aren't on horseback."

"Grab something to wave or flail about, make noise, yell and shout. Anything you think may startle them and get them moving in the right direction."

The men nodded and then broke for the banks and the gap between them, spreading out. A few ran back to the wagons, returning with long sticks, one bringing a length of bright cloth, another a blanket. Others simply removed their shirts, wrapping the sleeves around their hands so they could wave the material overhead.

Colin jogged across the rough ground, stalks of grass lashing his legs as he moved. He watched the herd of animals, saw Arten and the group of horses break apart, the workhorses spreading out to form a wedge pointed toward the dip in the land where Colin and the rest were settling into position. Arten and the Armory banked away, cutting around the herd. Some of the animals—singletons that roamed on the outside edges of the main group, like scouts—raised their heads, watching the horses as they circled around behind the herd, their gently curving horns sweeping back over their bodies. The plains were dotted with shifting shadows as scattered clouds moved overhead, and far to the north, black storm clouds darkened the horizon, moving east. They flashed an ethereal purple as lightning struck inside their depths, but the herd and the expedition were too distant to hear thunder. A thick slash of gray cut down from the dark clouds to the plains, where it was raining. The storm was moving away from them though, and after the storm at Cutter's and the few showers they'd experienced since reaching the Bluff, Colin felt a mild relief. He'd grown accustomed to the strange heaviness in the air over the past few days, but when it was raining, especially when there was lightning, the air seemed to sizzle, to shift and flow around him like water.

Colin shuddered, and thoughts of Cutter suddenly made him wonder where Walter was. He scanned those nearest to the depression in the ground, then turned toward the wagons.

Walter and Jackson were both standing in front of the wagons, hands raised to shade their eyes from the sun as they watched the activity, the two isolated from the rest of the members of the expedition by a significant distance. Jackson pulled something from his satchel, then sat down in the grass, scribbling madly. Walter pulled a waterskin out and drank, his gaze turning from where Arten and the others had begun to cut into the herd toward where Colin and the rest waited.

He caught sight of Colin and lowered his waterskin with a grimace, as if the water had suddenly taken on a bitter taste.

Colin jerked his attention back to the hunt, the muscles in his shoulders tensing. He spat to one side, but the acridness in the back of his throat, like bile, didn't go away. His hand kneaded the leather pocket of his sling, the ties biting into his forearm as he flexed the muscles, and he forced himself to stop with effort.

On the plains, a purple arc of lightning flashed from cloud to cloud in the far off storm, and a whistle pierced the air. Arten's group cut sharply to the left, angling into the herd of beasts. As soon as they shifted direction, the sentinel deer snorted and stamped their feet.

Nearly every head in the herd rose, ears and tails flicking.

Arten's group didn't falter. They bore down on the herd fast, the hooves of their horses a low, grumbling thunder.

Before they'd covered half the distance to the herd, the lead animals bolted. The herd hesitated half a breath, maybe less, and then every creature in it turned and sprinted away from the horses.

Directly toward where the workhorses stood.

One of the men waiting in the depression began to whoop and holler, and Colin turned to glare at him, saw the man nearest motion him to be quiet. The noise of Arten's group was drowned out in the sudden thunder of thousands of hooves as the strange deer picked up momentum, charging toward Colin's position, their sleek forms bounding forward, leaping hidden stones, small ridges, heads laid back and straining forward. Colin tensed, slid a rock from his pocket into the sling, held it ready as the deer closed in on the wedge of workhorses.

At the last moment, something startled the deer in front—movement from one of the workhorses, or the wild barking of the dogs who'd been tied up at the wagons—and with a flash of their white tails, the charging herd banked, streaked hides glistening. Arten cut sharply to the right, trying to cut them off, but the majority of the herd rumbled past the mouth of the funnel, tearing their way out toward the center of the plains.

But not all of them. A large group at the rear of the herd

split off, thundering through the wedge of workhorses. The riders began shouting, slapping their horses' flanks, the deer shying away from the sounds, bolting toward the other side of the wedge, where the second line whooped and roared, sending them back. Panicked, the deer raced down the center, heading straight for the safety of the gap in the two banks, down into the depression where Colin and the rest stood. Everyone was yelling, bellowing at the top of their lungs, swinging their shirts or their blankets overhead, slapping their sticks into the ground or their hands to their thighs. Colin cupped one hand over his mouth and shouted out nonsense words, then began laughing, his heart pounding in his chest, an echoing roar to the sound of the hooves, to the feel of their movement through his feet, the ground around him shaking. The strange deer skittered away from the noise, and he began swinging the sling overhead, still laughing, tried to pick out a single deer in the mass of bodies, found it impossible with all of them moving so fast, the tans and whites blending into each other. He realized their colorations were a form of protection, that he *couldn't* pick out individuals in the crowd—

And then the first arrows shot down into the depression. The deer had made it to the gap, were within the archers' range. He couldn't hear the twang of the bowstrings above the roar of the herd—

But he heard the first animal scream. A raw, terrified sound that made him wince back, that made his stomach twist inside him. The sound was repeated as more arrows struck into the heart of the herd. Colin cringed beneath the sound, felt it grating along his spine, and he let the swing of his sling lapse.

Then he smelled blood.

Before he could react, the entire herd shifted. Near their center, where the arrows had struck, the herd shuddered as individual deer twisted and bolted every which way, trying to escape. They veered away from the scent, from the screams of their brethren dying, chaos erupting as some stumbled in their fright, falling in their haste. With an action too swift to follow, Colin saw the main group of animals split, turning at what Colin thought would be an impossible angle—impossible for a horse anyway—

And suddenly half the captured herd was headed directly toward him. The lead animals were beyond panic, beyond reason, their large brown eyes rimmed white, their mouths flecked with foam, their hides slicked with sweat.

Colin choked on his own spit. Reflexively, he raised the sling again, whipped it around once, twice, then let the ball of the sling free, felt the cords snap as the stone flew. Eyes widening, he saw the stone vanish into the onrushing stampede. He couldn't tell if it struck one of the deer or not. They didn't slow, didn't even flinch from the motion.

He roared as they bore down on him. At the last moment, he covered his face and head with both arms and dropped down into a crouch, making himself as small a target as possible. He heard the animals thunder past, felt their bodies to either side, wind pulling at his shirt, his hair, his sling, the ground beneath him shuddering. He risked a quick glance, saw one of the animals leap over him as if he were a stone, dirt and sod raining down on his arms. Another and another leaped from the grass as the entire herd streaked past, flashes of brown and white, nothing more, their musky scent strong, almost overwhelming.

And as suddenly as they were on him, they were gone.

He shot upward, heart shuddering, and turned to see the group racing toward the wagons. Walter and Jackson saw them coming, bolted toward the nearest wagon, Jackson leaving his satchel and notebooks on the ground behind. Shouts rose, and women ducked behind wagons, some tossing children before them. Walter ducked under the bed of a wagon, Jackson on his heels, and then the hundreds of deer were on them, swirling around the wagons like water around stone, re-forming into a dense group on the far side.

Colin watched as they turned to the south once they were past the wagons. He stepped forward, intent on those around the wagon, until he saw Karen, staring off after the animals. He gave a whoop of excitement, unable to contain himself, unable to stop grinning, his arms tingling; then he turned to look into the depression behind.

Four animals were down, three dead, the fourth still moving, although its horrible screams had died down into pitiable huffing grunts. One of the men approached it carefully, wary of the strange but deadly looking horns, a wicked dagger in one hand, a look of distaste on his face.

Colin watched as he seized one of the long, pointed horns in one hand, wrenched the animal's head to the side so the horns were out of the way, and slit the deer's throat. On the far side of the depression, the other half of the group of deer that had been caught in the wedge had angled southward as well, heading back toward the main herd, now a dark splotch on the plains, like a shadow. Arten and the workhorses were galloping toward the kills. Men on all sides were yipping and calling out in elation, everyone converging on the bodies, on the scent of blood.

Then someone roared, "Look!"

The warning in the voice sliced through the elation like a blade.

Colin spun and saw someone pointing toward the northeast. His gaze flicked in that direction, focused on the black-purple storm in the distance first. He frowned in annoyance, ready to call out in derision that it was just a storm—

And then his eyes settled on one of the hillocks between them and the storm, the highest hillock.

There, in full sunlight, easily visible, stood a group of men.

~

"Who are they?" someone asked as Colin scrambled up the slope to join his father and most of the men as they gathered on the far bank. The rest remained below, beginning the processing of the strange deer. The scent of blood became thick and cloying in the heavy air, to the point where Colin began breathing through his mouth so he wouldn't have to smell it.

"I don't know," his father responded. "People from one of the previous expeditions?"

"Something's wrong with them," Sam said, his eyes squinted. "They're . . . too big to be men, too tall."

"How can you tell at this distance?"

Sam shrugged. "I can't. But something about them isn't quite right."

"Didn't Cutter and Beth say that the people they saw were shorter?"

"Yes."

No one said anything to that, but Tom frowned. "How many are there?"

"I can see five ... no, six. There's someone standing mostly below the hillock they're on."

"It looks like one of the men in front is carrying some kind of spear," Colin said. "He's got it angled out away from his body. And now he's pointing it toward us."

The men around him shifted nervously.

Arten had pulled his group of horses up about a hundred paces away, facing the unknown figures, but now he spun his horse about and trotted up to Tom, dismounting smoothly. "Send some of the men back to get our swords and any other weapons they can carry."

Tom's brow creased. "They're too far away to do anything. We don't even know if they're a threat."

"The other wagon trains never returned, right?"

Tom turned to order a group back to the wagons to retrieve the swords.

"We've gotten rather lax with the sentries and other defenses," Arten continued, terse and all business. "I'll double the Armory in the guard at night. You might want to do the same with the men from Lean-to." He considered for a moment, not taking his eyes off of the distant group. Then he swore. "I guess it was too much to assume that this land would be completely uninhabited."

"Tom," Sam said, his voice layered with warning. He'd shifted his gaze back to the wagons, where the men were gathering the weapons, their motions a little panicked. He motioned to where Walter and Jackson were climbing the bank. "Here comes Walter."

Walter arrived before Tom could answer. Most of the others from the expedition drifted away, shooting Walter and Jackson dark glances.

"Who are they?" Walter demanded.

"We don't know. They're too distant to make out clearly."

"Then send someone out to meet them! If they're from another Company, if they think they're going to lay claim to this land—"

Arten broke through the beginning tirade, his voice calm but hard. "I don't think they're from another Company. I don't even think they're men."

That brought Walter up short. He glared at Arten uncertainly, to see whether he was serious, then snapped his fingers at Jackson. "Jackson, the spyglass."

Jackson slid a cylindrical case from behind his back, the strap across one shoulder, and opened it, withdrawing another compact cylinder, handing it over without a word. The Company representative's face was set, jaw slightly clenched, lips pressed together. He glanced toward Colin as Walter took the spyglass, his eyes a deep green. He held Colin's gaze a moment, then turned away dismissively, running one hand through his dirty blond hair before shifting his attention back to Walter, who had extended the spyglass and raised it to one eye.

Walter's body suddenly stiffened.

After a moment, he lowered the spyglass.

"May I?" Tom asked, one hand held out.

Walter considered briefly, then handed over the spyglass without a word.

Tom raised it to his eye, frowned as he peered through it, adjusting it slightly.

And then he grew still as well.

He lowered the glass slowly, eyes flashing toward Arten. "They look somewhat like us, but they certainly aren't from Andover. Set as many guardsmen as you want. We'll circle the wagons around the kills. It will take time to butcher the animals and prepare the meat and hides. We'll camp here tonight, set up some defenses in case those . . . people decide to come closer."

Walter bristled. "I'm the Proprietor. I'll decide where we'll camp and what we'll do."

Colin's father met Walter's gaze, his eyes full of withheld fury. "You lost those rights back at the Bluff, at the burial."

As he spoke, one of the men still watching the distance gasped.

Everyone turned sharply, the Armory reaching toward weapons that they didn't have yet, the rest drawing knives or daggers.

"They're gone," the man who'd gasped said with a swallow. "They were there one moment, and then the next . . ."

Uneasy murmurs arose, the group unconsciously pulling in tighter to one another. Colin suppressed a frustrated shudder. He'd desperately wanted to look through the spyglass, had willed his father to hand it to him, but now it didn't matter.

Instead, his father handed the spyglass back to Jackson.

"You can't do this," Walter spat. "This is my expedition, given to me by my father—"

"This isn't Portstown," Tom said, anger creeping into his voice. Anger Colin realized he'd held for days, since they'd left the Bluff. He turned to Arten, ignoring Walter. "Circle the wagons and set up the defenses."

"No," Walter said. "We'll butcher the animals, but we'll move on after that. Arten, go tell the others."

Arten didn't move.

Walter spun. "Do it! You work for the Carrente Family! You work for me!"

Arten shook his head. "Not any more. Not since we left Carrente lands."

Walter turned, caught the black expressions on everyone's faces, all except Jackson's. Rage filled his eyes, smothering the shocked disbelief. He drew himself upright, fuming.

His gaze fell on Colin, jaw clenched, a moment before he stormed down the bank, back toward the wagons. Frowning, Jackson followed.

Colin's father let out a long, heavy sigh.

"It needed to be done," Arten said as the men carrying the Armory's swords and other assorted weapons arrived. "The rest of the expedition would never follow him, not after what he said at the Bluff."

"I know. But I was hoping he'd change."

Arten snorted, strapping his sword around his waist. "No one changes. Not that drastically anyway."

Colin had finished passing out some of the cooked deer meat to the guards on sentry duty and was headed back toward the camp when Walter found him. He never even saw the Proprietor's son or Jackson. Darkness had settled, the last of the light fading from the sky to the west. As he stepped into the shadows thrown by the wagons and the campfires of the expedition inside their protective circle, a hand reached around his neck from behind and clamped tight to his mouth, fingers digging in with bruising force. An arm reached across his chest from the opposite side, jerking him backward, bringing him up tight against his assailant's chest a moment before their two bodies hit the side of the wagon. Colin's eyes flew wide, thoughts of the strange men they'd seen on the plains flaring bright into his mind—

And then, in a hoarse whisper right next to his ear, breath hot against his neck, he heard Walter mutter, "So your father thinks he owns this little wagon train, does he?"

All of Colin's fear—all of the prickling terror that had flooded down through his arms and legs and gut, making them fluid and rubbery—vanished. The rage that he'd buried, that had sat locked inside since his day in the penance lock, burned forth, searing through his chest.

He lashed out, kicking, body writhing beneath Walter's hold, realizing as he did so that he wasn't as small as he used to be, that he and Walter were nearly the same height now. Walter cursed, his grip tightening, fingers digging even deeper into Colin's cheek, into his side. Still kicking, Colin reached up and back with his hands, went for Walter's face, for his hair. He felt Walter's head jerk backward, heard it thud into the side of the wagon, but Walter's grip didn't loosen. Instead, he hissed, "Punch him! Punch him, you pissant Company bastard!"

He sensed more than saw Jackson move, the shadows too deep—

And then the fist landed in his stomach, awkwardly, but with enough force to double Colin over, Walter dragged down with him before the Proprietor's son caught his balance and jerked him back upright.

"Again!" Walter barked. "Harder!"

The second blow drove the wind from him. He gasped, breathed in and out through his nose, nostrils flaring, as Walter chuckled.

Before he'd recovered, Walter spun and shoved him face first into the wagon. The Proprietor's son leaned hard into his back. One of Colin's arms was trapped between his chest and the wagon at a painful angle. Colin slammed his other hand into the side of the wagon, tried to push himself away, but Walter had his full weight behind him.

"You'd better hope that your father wises up, or I'm going to make your life miserable," Walter said through clenched teeth.

"I'm not afraid of you anymore, Walter," Colin gasped.

He grunted. "We'll see. I don't have my father holding me back anymore. I'll find some way to hurt you. And out here . . . no one's safe out here."

Then he pushed back, the pressure against Colin gone.

Colin spun, back against the wagon, but he couldn't see anything except the flicker of firelight from behind the wagons and the stars and moonlight farther out on the plains. In the lee of the wagon, there was nothing.

He thought he was alone until another voice, soft and low, said, "Your father must realize that the Company will never accept this."

Colin sucked in a sharp breath, the Company representative's cold, implacable voice slicing through his rage with a thin blade of fear. But then he heard the rustle of grass as Jackson retreated, and the silence of the night descended again.

When he stepped into the reach of the firelight, where his mother had set up camp inside the circle of wagons, other fires scattered around to either side, he'd managed to stop trembling. He found his father, Sam, Paul, Lyda, Karen, and her father joking and laughing together, his mother stirring the pot and checking on the skewers of meat set over the flames. The scent of the charred, sizzling meat was strong. Someone nearby had pulled out a fiddle, and low music floated out over the group. A few tents had been erected, children and some of those that would stand guard later already bedded down.

His mother stood as he halted. "I see you've decided to return to camp," she said, and then her smile faltered. "What's wrong, Colin? What happened?"

He glanced toward his father, toward Karen. "Nothing."

His mother sighed. "Well, they've finished with the butchering, but we could use more water." She reached down to retrieve a bucket from the ground and held it out to Colin expectantly. "The stream's on the other side of the gap."

Colin almost refused to take the bucket—his stomach hurt from Jackson's punches, and he'd barely managed to control his rage—but then he stepped forward, snagged its handle, and headed off in the direction of the gap without a word.

Behind, he heard Paul resume his interrupted story,

the rest bursting into laughter, and then he passed beyond hearing.

Preoccupied with thoughts of Walter, he made his way down between the two banks, nodded to the guards on duty, then paused to listen for the sound of the stream. Water gurgled over stones off to the right, so he headed in that direction, one hand massaging the ache in his abdomen.

He found the stream, black with glints of white and silver in the weak moonlight. Kneeling, he dipped the bucket into the frigid water, listening to the sounds of the fiddle in the distance, faint because of the intervening bank. He hummed along with it, his anger abating, the bucket almost full, then glanced up.

A figure crouched on the opposite side of the stream, three paces away.

He jerked back with a grunt, yanking the bucket up out of the water. He overbalanced, sat down hard on the grass embankment, water sloshing onto his shoes, and then he scrambled backward, his throat closed so tight he could hardly breathe, his heartbeat thundering in his ears. His arm hit a hole hidden in the grass and he collapsed onto his side, his scramble halted, but he rolled onto his back, bucket held up before him like a weapon, water spilling onto his chest.

"Don't move!" he ordered. "Don't move or I'll—"

He choked on his anger as he realized it wasn't Walter or Jackson. It wasn't anyone from the expedition at all.

The man on the other side of the water didn't react, except to tilt his head to one side, chin slightly forward, brow wrinkling. His face was narrow and thin, his skin pale in the moonlight, paler than anyone in the expedition. His eyes were dark, his hair darker, but Colin couldn't tell what color they were, not in the scant light.

Heart still shuddering in his chest, Colin swallowed and sat up, gathering his feet beneath him while still holding the bucket out before him, defensively now.

The man watched silently. He was dressed in a fine material that Colin didn't recognize, his shirt strangely patterned, the torso a swirl of lines and colors, all muted in the moonlight, the sleeves a single color and long, covering his arms. His breeches were tanned leather, supple, his boots made of the same material, but hardened. He carried a bow, unstrung and longer than any of the bows Colin had ever seen, the curved wood held in one hand, reaching up to twice the man's height while crouched. Colin could see lettering carved into the side of the bow near the grip. A compact quiver was slung over one shoulder, and a sheathed short sword and pouch were secured to his waist.

A glint of gold or silver drew Colin's eye to the man's fingers. He wore a band of metal around two fingers on one hand and another thicker band around his wrist. There were markings on the bracelet and rings.

Colin met the man's eyes and frowned. "Who are you?" he asked. He thought about the guards on duty at the gap, a swift sprint away. But something in the man's subtle movements, in the considering tilt of his head and the dangerous, casual way he held the bow, told him he'd never make it more than a few paces.

The man straightened and said something in a language Colin didn't understand, certainly not Andovan. His voice was harsher than Colin expected, rougher, but the words had a smooth cadence.

When the man finished speaking, he frowned, waiting expectantly.

Colin shook his head. "I don't understand you."

The man scowled, glanced out toward the plains, out into the darkness. His motions were a strange combination of short, sharp gestures and fluid movements. Colin suddenly wondered where the rest of the man's group was. They'd seen at least six figures on the horizon. How close were they? Did they intend to attack the wagons?

He felt his heart quickening again and shifted backward.

The strange man's head jerked toward him, hand falling to the hilt of the short sword at his side, and Colin froze. He licked his lips, his mouth suddenly dry. Sweat prickled his skin, on his forehead and back, in his armpits.

They held still, regarding each other. The bucket began to tremble, Colin's arm tiring. He saw the man's hand tighten on his sword hilt as the bucket began to shake, but Colin couldn't hold it up any longer.

He let it sag to the ground, released his death grip on its handle, and flexed his fingers, wincing at the pain.

The man watched silently. Then he relaxed, a thin smile touching the corners of his mouth. His hand fell away from the short sword.

He said something else, the words still incomprehensible. His eyebrows rose as he waited for a response, then fell as he sighed.

Shifting, he pointed to himself and said, "Aeren." Then he pointed to Colin. "Name?"

Colin gaped in surprise, stunned into silence.

The man—Aeren—frowned, seemed to think about what he'd said, then said again, putting a slightly different emphasis on the word, as if he weren't certain he'd pronouncing it correctly, "Name?"

"Colin," Colin stuttered. "My name is Colin."

Aeren nodded. "Colin." He said it carefully, almost reverentially, then ruined the image by muttering something under his breath in his own language.

"How do you know my language?" Colin asked.

Aeren's brow creased, and he tilted his head again. Then he shook it. "Where go?" He waved a hand into the darkness. "Where?"

Colin pointed. "South and east."

Aeren followed his finger, his frown darkening, deepening. He turned back, the motion sharp again. "No." He stood, and as he did so Colin realized he was tall—at least a hand taller than Colin—although the bow he now held in both hands, its point on the ground, still reached over his head. Colin wondered if he'd mistaken the bow for a spear earlier. "No," Aeren repeated. "Meet here." He motioned to the ground on the other side of the stream. "Meet here. Sun." He gestured toward the horizon, his motions easy to read.

"Meet you here in the morning," Colin said.

Aeren regarded him for a long moment, the lines of his face intent.

Then he turned and vanished into the night.

8

PANIC SPREAD THROUGH the wagons when Colin returned to tell his father of the meeting with Aeren at the stream. Everyone gathered closer to the center of the wagons, where the grass was stained red with deer blood. Tensions escalated, and arguments broke out. Arten and Tom sent more men to the edges of the camp, many men volunteering to help out, Walter hovering at the edges of the group, scowling, as the orders were issued. More wood was thrown on the central fire—wood they couldn't afford to spare, not when the plains had so few trees—but one woman demanded it in a shrill voice, and Tom finally conceded. Many sought the solace of Diermani's Hand, Domonic.

But nothing happened. When the night remained silent, the initial panic faded, reduced to a general murmur, a tightening of shoulders and furtive glances out into the night. As they relaxed, the people began to disperse back to their wagons and tents.

"They wouldn't have warned us if they intended to attack," Arten said. He surveyed those still gathered around the fire. "The additional sentries are useless."

Tom nodded. "I know. But they're also harmless. And they make the rest of the group feel more relaxed, more protected. Besides, how many of the men on duty would be able to sleep now?"

Arten snorted. "Given what we've seen so far and what Colin reported," he said, looking toward him as he spoke, "they can take out any number of us from the darkness with their bows, and we wouldn't be able to do anything about it. Our fire makes us easy targets."

Colin shifted uncomfortably at that, his gaze darting toward the darkness beyond the nearest wagons. The hairs on the back of his neck stirred and he shivered, then shrugged the sensation of being watched aside.

The rest of the night passed slowly. Colin tried to sleep, but he woke constantly with sudden starts until it was close enough to dawn that he finally rose.

He found his father, mother, and Arten seated around the fire. As he approached, he heard his mother ask, "Are you certain Colin should be included?"

Colin slowed as his father sighed.

"No, but they made contact with him. I think he should be there in case there was a reason they chose to speak to him and not any of the others."

"I don't like it," his mother said, and rubbed her upper arms with her hands, as if she were suddenly cold. "I don't like it here on the upper plains. Maybe we shouldn't be here. Maybe this is their land, whoever they are, and we're trespassing."

"We haven't seen any roads anywhere," Arten said, "and no signs of a city or even a village."

"That doesn't mean we aren't intruding somehow."

Arten didn't have an answer, so Colin stepped into the fringe of the firelight, his feet making noise in the grass. All three of them turned, Arten's hand dropping to his sword, then relaxing as Colin settled down before the fire next to Arten, opposite his mother and father.

"You're going to include me in the group?" Colin asked

His mother frowned, but it was his father who answered. "Yes. We've decided it will be you, me, Arten, and Walter."

Colin grimaced. "Why Walter?"

"Because his name's on the town's charter." He met Colin's gaze. "He may not make the decisions, but he's still the Proprietor."

Colin thought about that a moment, then shifted back to Aeren and the meeting. "I don't think they intend to hurt us," he said. "He could have killed me at the stream. I didn't even notice him when I approached, he was just there." He ignored his mother's shudder.

"So what do you think they want?" Arten asked.

Colin frowned. "I don't know. He asked where we were headed and seemed upset when I showed him."

"You told them where we were headed?" a bitter, derisive voice asked sharply.

Colin leaped up and turned to where Walter and Jackson stood at the fringe of the firelight. One hand dove into his pocket for a stone, but his sling was still bundled up in his satchel. He clenched his jaw and fought the urge to chuck the stone at Walter regardless. If his mother hadn't been there, along with Arten and his father . . .

"That's enough, Walter," Arten said, with a note of warning.

"He gave away our only advantage," Walter spat, taking one step closer to the fire.

"Yes, he did," Colin's father agreed, and Colin felt a harsh pain in his chest, his hand closing hard on the stone. He dropped his gaze to the grass, his eyes stinging, a bitter taste flooding his mouth as his father continued. "But it wasn't much of an advantage. They may have been watching us for days, may already know where we're headed."

Walter glared at Tom, his jaw working. Around them the rest of the wagon party had begun to stir, to wake and gather. He cast a contemptuous glance at Colin, scowled, and turned away.

Arten stood, followed by Tom. "Shall we head to the bank, see if they're there?" the commander of the Armory asked.

In answer, Walter stalked away from the fire.

Arten and Tom traded a look.

They followed him to the top of the embankment near the gap, coming up on the sentries on duty, one of them turning.

"Report," Walter said, his face flushing red when the sentry looked toward Tom and received a nod before answering.

"Still too dark to see anything. We thought we heard some movement a little while ago, but we haven't heard anything since."

Tom looked toward the horizon to the east, where the sky was just beginning to lighten above the jagged peaks of distant mountains. He scanned the growing number of people behind them. Most of the men had gathered, and a significant number of the women, their faces tight and grim. All of the children had been separated and hidden in the backs of the wagons. Colin noticed Karen weaving her way through the people toward him and took her hand when she reached his side.

And then they waited. People shifted nervously, whispered among themselves, a few coughing quietly. Gazes drifted toward the horizon, toward the hollow behind them where the wagons had halted, toward the plains hidden by darkness.

Colin saw the mist on the plains first, a thin layer that had settled in the hollows, only the highest banks and hillocks visible above it. He'd never seen the mist in the morning; it had always burned off before the wagons began moving, before the majority of the people had even risen for the day. But in the gray light—the mist white, the hillocks and banks dark, almost black, the hills and mountains in the distance more pronounced as the sky turned a soft yellow, the few clouds on the horizon now a muted gold—the plains were beautiful.

Someone gasped, and all along the embankment the men with swords shifted, clothes rustling, hands falling to weapons. Arten straightened to Colin's left, but the only reaction from Walter on seeing those waiting below was to narrow his eyes. Karen's hand tightened on Colin's, and he gave a reassuring nod.

Below, beneath the bank but on the far side of the stream, the group of men they'd seen from afar the day before stood silently, staring up at those gathered. Aeren stood in the front, his bow still unstrung, planted in the ground before him more like a staff or spear. Five others stood behind him. They were dressed like Aeren, in shirts with curved patterns on them, hide breeches and boots. As the sunlight strengthened, Colin could see that they all bore the same features—pale skin, dark eyes and dark hair, all in varying shades. Three of those behind Aeren had markings on their faces, three slashes on one side like claw marks, as if they'd painted their cheeks with mud. All of them carried bows, shorter in length than Aeren's, and short swords. And all of them were taller than Aeren by at least a hand.

Only when he saw the other men's faces did Colin

realize that Aeren was the youngest of the group. And he was the only one with a band of gold around his wrist and markings on his bow.

The two groups took stock of one another in silence. Two of Aeren's men eyed those in Walter's group with swords, their faces intent. One of those with the claw marks on his face leaned forward slightly to whisper something in Aeren's ear. Aeren listened, frowned slightly, then shook his head.

The man with the claw markings leaned back, unhappy.

None of Aeren's men seemed concerned that they were outnumbered. Those who weren't starkly serious were curious instead, their gazes flickering over all of those from the wagons that they could see.

When the men on the bank began to fidget nervously, Arten stepped to Colin's father's side and said softly, "We should approach them."

Tom nodded.

Colin released Karen's hand and moved forward, following in his father's tracks as he, Walter, and Arten moved down the slope to the edge of the stream, to almost exactly the same spot where Colin had encountered Aeren the night before. Aeren lifted his head as they approached, his eyes following Colin at first, then shifting to his father, who was in the lead. The rest of Aeren's men shifted position, the motions subtle, their stances no longer quite so casual, and Colin felt the tension between the two groups climb.

They halted at the edge of the gurgling water.

For a long moment, no one moved, the silence awkward. Aeren's head lowered, his eyes narrowed. Colin felt the mood shifting, from open curiosity to something more dangerous, more hostile.

Colin's father caught his gaze, motioned him forward with a frown and a tilt of his head. Colin stepped forward, to his father's side. Sweat broke out on his back, even in the cool morning air, and his stomach twisted sickeningly, but he nodded toward Aeren and the other strange men.

"The one in front is Aeren," he murmured.

His father nodded. "Introduce us."

Colin drew in a steadying breath, all of the strange men's attention fixing on him as he did so. "Aeren, this is my father, Tom."

"Tom," Aeren said, pronouncing the name as carefully as he had Colin's the night before. Colin's father nodded, but Aeren had already turned toward Arten and Walter. He looked at Colin expectantly.

"This is Arten—"

"Ar-ten."

"—and Walter." He said the name curtly, his anger tingeing his voice.

Aeren frowned. "Walter."

Then he turned back toward Colin's father and gave him a deep bow from the waist, the gesture strangely formal. When he rose, he motioned them across the stream. "Come," he said, indicating a section of ground where the grass had been trampled down in a circular pattern, the edges of the circle clearly defined. "Sit."

Tom hesitated, then stepped across the stream using the stones that weren't submerged beneath the water, settling to the ground on the far side, near the center of the circle, opposite where Aeren sat, legs crossed. As Colin knelt in the grass, he noticed that it hadn't been trampled down but laid in a distinctive pattern, almost as if the stalks had been woven together.

When everyone had settled, only two of Aeren's followers still standing at the edge of the circle of grass, Aeren motioned for a pouch from the man who'd leaned forward to murmur in his ear. Opening it, he withdrew two bowls, one wide and shallow, the other small and deep, and two packages that appeared to be wrapped in long, wide leaves, the outermost leaves charred. He unwrapped one of the packages, sniffed at the haunch of meat inside, nose wrinkling, then proceeded to draw a wicked-looking knife from a sheath at the small of his back.

Arten instantly tensed, hand falling to his sword, over an inch of the blade appearing in the strengthening sunlight. On the opposite side of the circle, Aeren's guards barked a warning, drew their short swords in a flash of motion that stunned Colin, so fast that he saw only a flare of light as sunlight struck against metal. Aeren stilled, his expression annoyed.

No one moved.

Aeren murmured something under his breath.

Neither of his guards looked pleased, but they resheathed their swords. Slowly. They didn't take their hands from the hilts, however.

Aeren set the meat down into the shallow bowl. His knife never wavered. Without taking his eyes off of Arten, he lowered the long knife to the meat and began to cut it into thin slices.

Arten released the hilt of his sword, letting it slide back into its sheath.

Only then did Aeren look down at what he was doing. All of the meat sliced, including the second package, he sheathed his knife, reached back into the pouch, and produced a drinking skin. Pulling out the stopper, he drained it into the deeper bowl, then set the skin and the leaves used to wrap and cook the meat aside.

Standing, he picked up the bowl of meat and moved to the center of the circle of grass. He motioned Tom to do the same, and when he stood opposite him, he said something in his own language, the words formal, and then presented Tom with the bowl of meat.

He took the bowl uncertainly, and at Aeren's insistence he picked up a thin slice and passed the bowl around to the others. Colin took a slice last, then returned the bowl to Aeren, who smiled and passed the bowl among his own group until everyone had his own piece.

Then he said something more in his own language and bit into his slice.

Colin waited until his father took a bite before he tried his own. It smelled spicy, with some type of chopped green herb he didn't recognize coating the outside edges. It tasted even spicier, salty and peppery, with something hotter kicking in at the back of his throat after he started chewing. There was a citrus taste to it as well, like lemon. The meat itself was wild and gamy in flavor, and he guessed it was one of the deer, like those they'd killed yesterday.

He heard someone choking and glanced up to see Walter coughing into his hand, looking as if he wanted to spit the food out. Arten glared at him, and he grimaced, forced himself to continue chewing, and swallowed with effort.

Aeren's followers glanced at each other, troubled, but no one said anything.

Aeren stepped back to retrieve the other bowl. As with the meat, he said something over it, like a benediction or prayer, and then presented it to Tom. This time, his father took it without hesitation and sipped, his face carefully neutral. He passed the bowl to Arten next, and Aeren nodded, watching as it was passed around.

Colin was last again, the dark red liquid some kind of wine, drier and more tart than he was used to. It made the inside of his mouth pucker.

The wine made the rounds of Aeren's group, and then Aeren motioned everyone to sit back down, taking his own place on the other side of the circle.

The formalities over, Aeren's expression grew stern. He considered Colin and the rest seated before him, glanced at all of those up on the bank, Karen and Colin's mother at the front, behind the line of sentries, then looked hard at Colin's father. "Where go?"

His father shifted, then pointed. "South and east."

Aeren shook his head. "No." He motioned toward the group on the bank, mimed all of them turning around and heading back the way they'd come. "Go."

Tom frowned and leaned back, shaking his head. "We can't go back. There's nothing for us back there. We want to go to the south and east."

"No!" Aeren said more emphatically. He said something sharp in his own language. "No go southandeast!"

"We can't go back," his father repeated, patiently. "Why do you want us to go back? And how do you know Andovan?"

Frustrated, Aeren waved toward the northwest. "Go! Go!"

When Tom only continued to shake his head, Aeren snorted in disgust. Behind him, one of the other men said something, and he stilled, listening.

As they spoke, Arten leaned forward. "I think they're trying to warn us of something."

"They aren't doing a very good job of it," Tom responded. "And even if they are, we can't afford to go back at this point. We've come too far."

"It's obvious they don't know our language well," Arten said. "We'll have to be patient. They're trying to tell us something. And as Colin says, I don't think they intend to harm us."

Opposite them, Aeren finished the argument with his guard and turned back to Tom, who'd straightened. Seeing the stiffened back, Aeren sighed.

Carefully, he folded the leaves that had been used to wrap the meat and placed them, the bowls, and the wine-skin into the pouch, handing it off to one of the guards. He motioned to Colin and the rest, to those on the embankment behind them, and then said, "Come." When no one moved, his expression darkened. "Come," he said more forcefully, indicating a direction almost directly south of them. Part of his group had already stood and headed off ahead of him, spreading out in a wide line. Most of them didn't seem all that concerned with making certain the people from Portstown were following them, their attention turned outward, as if they'd already forgotten they'd met the group. Only Aeren and one other stayed behind, inside the circle.

Tom hesitated a long moment, frowning, eyes locked on Aeren, then stood, brushing off his breeches before heading back toward the camp.

"What are you doing?" Walter demanded. He'd remained quiet for the entire exchange.

Without turning, Tom said, "I'm going to order the rest of the wagons loaded. He obviously wants to show all of us something, and I intend to see what it is."

~

"Why are you helping them? They obviously don't want to listen, like the last group."

Aeren didn't turn to his Protector but kept his eyes on the strange group of brown-skinned people as they made their way back to their wagons and cook fires. The one called Walter was already speaking to the group's leader, Tom, arguing with him. He found their language harsh, their names strange . . . but intriguing. Their beasts called horses—so large, so powerful—frightened him, their clothes coarsely woven and cut, and their customs savage, without proper form and structure, but still . . .

"I'm helping them because they do not understand."

"You are helping them because you are curious. They are primitives, wandering into a land they know nothing about. We should leave them to the dwarren."

Aeren turned to his Protector then, frowning at Eraeth's scowl. "This is not your Trial," he said defensively, even though he knew the Protector was partially correct:

He was curious. He'd approached Colin because they'd appeared to be the same age. And because Colin did not carry a weapon.

"No, it is not. But I am your Protector. I—and the Phalanx—are here to protect you. From the dangers of the plains, from the risks of the Trial . . . from yourself."

Aeren stiffened, his shoulders straightening in indignation. "I am not the child my father assigned you to protect twenty years ago!" The words came out harsher than he intended, petulant and not fitting for the son of a House Lord, even a second son. He saw the instant disapproval in Eraeth's eyes, in the lips pressed tightly together.

He turned away from that look, caught his breath and held it to calm himself, then said, "This is my Trial, Eraeth. Are you now an acolyte, part of the mystical Order? Who are you to say that they," he nodded toward where the strangers were preparing their wagons for travel, "are not part of the Trial? Do you know Aielan's will?"

Eraeth stepped forward, so that Aeren could see him out of the corner of his eye. "No, I do not know Aielan's will, but I fail to see how they could be part of your Trial. You have already passed. You've faced the dangers of the plains and the dwarren. You have seen the Confluence, have drunk its rose-tinged waters, have gathered those waters—the Blood of Aielan—as your proof."

"But I have not yet returned home."

"All the more reason to leave these strangers to the dwarren. This is not our land. This has nothing to do with the Alvritshai."

"Not now," Aeren agreed, "but they continue to appear on the plains. Eventually, they will head northward. We should learn as much about them as we can."

Eraeth merely grunted, although it was tainted with grudging agreement.

They remained silent for a long moment, the air between them tense, shouts from the strange group rising from the hollow where they'd taken refuge for the night. Eraeth had been his Protector for twenty years, had taught him the nuances of being a member of a House, had trained him in the art of the sword, the bow—all the arts of the Phalanx guard.

But everything would change now, with his passage

through the Trial. He would no longer be Eraeth's student; he would be a full member of the House, the Protector's master.

And neither of them had figured out exactly what that meant yet.

~

"What is it?" Karen asked, falling in beside Colin as soon as Walter, his father, and Arten reached the top of the bank. Tom barked out some orders a moment before Walter would have done the same. Everyone on the bank hesitated, uncertain, glancing back down at the circle where Aeren and his guard waited, the pattern woven into the grass clear now that the sun had risen completely, a swirl of lines like the patterns on their shirts. But when Tom clapped his hands and repeated the orders, prodding the nearest sentry into motion, the rest of the group began to move toward the wagons.

Colin led Karen toward the campfire from the night before and began scrambling to load up the pots and kettles, dismantling the spit. Karen stooped to help.

"I don't know," Colin said. "They tried to get us to turn back. Now I think they want to show us something. They want us to follow them."

"Where?"

Colin shrugged. "Somewhere south of here."

Trying to handle too many pots at once, Karen dropped a few with a rattle and cursed. On all sides, men and women were running to and fro, tossing supplies into the backs of the wagons, where the older children were shoving them into place. The younger ones were trying to see what everyone was doing and to catch sight of the strange men, their attention focused on the embankment. Some of the men were hitching the horses.

Someone rushed forward and doused the coals of the fire with a bucket of water, steam rising with a harsh hiss. Colin and Karen handed off the last of the supplies from their wagon, and then Colin searched for his father. He wanted to be at the front of the wagon train, near Aeren.

"Come on," he said, catching sight of his father near the lead wagon. He was talking to Arten and Walter, surveying the mad rush to pack and head out.

"—were heading southeast anyway," his father was saying as they approached. "Why shouldn't we see what they want to show us?"

"Because we don't know what their intentions are!" Walter answered. "What if they're leading us to the rest of their people? We have the advantage of numbers now. We might not if they take us to one of their villages or towns."

Colin's father glanced toward Walter and said grudgingly, "You have a point. But then why would they try to get us to turn back?"

"So they wouldn't have to deal with us at all! But since we refused to turn back—"

"I don't think they live on the plains," Arten cut in, and all of them turned toward him.

Walter snorted. "Why not?"

Arten shrugged. "Their clothes, their swords. Their breeches make sense, but their shirts aren't made for the plains, and their boots are too high. Half of us don't even wear shoes anymore, they're too painful. It's easier to go barefoot. And their swords make no sense at all. We haven't killed anything with the swords since we headed out."

"But they have bows," Colin's father said.

Arten nodded. "Which makes sense if they intend to be here for a short time. They'd need them to hunt with. But if they lived here permanently, they wouldn't need the swords at all."

Sam appeared out of nowhere, breath short. "We're ready to leave. Paul's stowing the last few things into Tobin's wagon, with Ana's help, but they'll be done by the time their wagon has to start moving."

Tom nodded and turned to Walter. "We'll follow them, but we'll be cautious. I don't see any reason not to trust them at this point. They know the plains better than we do."

Walter didn't argue any further, storming away to where Jackson waited with their horses.

Tom put two fingers in the corners of his mouth and whistled, the sound piercing the commotion of the rest of the wagon train. "Let's move out!" he shouted, motioning with one hand over his head. Men climbed up into their seats and snapped the reins, and the lead wagon creaked forward, heading toward the gap between the two banks.

"I think we should stick close to Aeren," Tom said to them all, then turned to Colin. "He seems to have bonded with you, possibly because he's younger than the rest of his group. Hell, you two may even be the same age, I can't tell. But see what you can find out about him and his people."

Colin nodded.

They passed through the gap and found Aeren and his guard waiting on the far side. The rest of Aeren's group had vanished into the plains.

"We're ready," Tom said as they approached the two strange men.

Aeren nodded, watching the first wagon as it began to ford the stream, wheels splashing through the water. He eyed the horses intently, not without a little fear, and Colin realized he hadn't seen anything like horses here in New Andover. The closest animal had been the deer.

But then Aeren motioned toward the south. "Suren," he said, in his own language.

"Suren," Colin's father repeated as they began walking in that direction.

Aeren grinned and nodded, then pointed north, east, west, and south, as he said, "Nuren, est, ost, ai suren."

Tom followed suit. "Nuren, est, ust—"

"Ost."

"—ost, and suren?"

When Aeren smiled, Tom repeated the directions in Andovan, Aeren frowning seriously as he listened, repeating the words as they both pointed, the directions getting more complicated as they started doing southeast, northwest, southwest, and northeast. Aeren's guardian scowled until Aeren threw him a dark look. Everyone else smiled or chuckled.

"Eraeth," Aeren said, pointing to his guardian, who scowled again, pointedly ignoring Aeren. Colin saw Aeren's mouth twitch. Then Aeren motioned to Karen, his eyebrow raised.

"Karen," Colin said. "Her name is Karen."

Aeren paused and gave Karen another of the formal bows, almost the same he'd given Tom but slightly different. He said something in his own language, and even though no one except Eraeth could understand him, Karen lifted her head higher and blushed.

They traveled through the morning, pausing to rest on occasion, Aeren pointing out animals and plants and flowers as they went, speaking mostly to Colin and Karen, trading the names of each object in the two languages. At one point, Aeren began quizzing them all, and Colin discovered that Karen was more adept at remembering the new language. The strange deer were called gaezels by the Alvritshai, the name of Aeren's people. Colin couldn't determine exactly where the Alvritshai were from, but after numerous attempts he thought they came from a range of mountains to the north. At least, Aeren kept pointing to the mountains to the east, making jagged up and down motions with his hands, then shaking his head when Colin or Karen pointed east and saying nuren instead.

Eraeth listened to all of this disapprovingly, keeping his eyes on Arten and Tom. Sam had drifted away to help one of the wagons when it got stuck in a low spot.

Toward midafternoon, both Aeren and Eraeth grew quieter, Eraeth speaking to Aeren in a low voice, as if trying to convince him of something. Aeren kept shaking his head but otherwise didn't argue with him. Until at one point he grew exasperated and said something short and curt, raising his arm across his chest, his hand in a fist near his shoulder. The band of gold around his wrist gleamed in the steady sunlight.

After that, Eraeth kept silent, his face studiously blank.

It was after this altercation that Walter and Jackson approached the group, drawing their horses up sharply. Both of the Alvritshai stepped back, distancing themselves from the animals, their eyes slightly wider than usual, although they showed no other signs of fear.

Walter ignored the two of them completely. "Jackson says that, according to his map and calculations, we should be nearing the river that leads to Portstown, assuming it kept the same general course. He estimates the Bluff and Falls are about two, maybe three, days travel to the west."

Colin's father raised a hand to his eyes to shade them from the sun and scanned the horizon. "I don't see anything."

"What about that?" Arten pointed toward the southeast, where a darker line appeared on the plains, blending into the heat waves on the horizon.

At Aeren's quizzical expression, Colin tried to explain the river. Eraeth snorted and said something in Alvritshai, and Aeren motioned them forward, but not toward the darker spot Arten had seen. They continued south, the dark line spreading, until they were close enough to see that it was a low ridge where the plains were interrupted by a line of trees and brush cutting its way almost directly east. As they drew closer, Colin heard a strange rustling, then realized it was the leaves of the trees brushing against each other in the breeze. He hadn't heard the sound in so long, he barely recognized it.

"I don't see the river," Walter said, standing up in his stirrups.

"Do you feel that?" Arten said.

Everyone stopped at the edge of where the grass grew thicker and greener, the verge of the thin line of trees.

"What?" Karen asked.

"In your feet. The ground feels like it's trembling."

Colin focused on his feet and thought he could feel a faint trembling in the earth. He stepped forward, moving in among the trees themselves, and the sensation increased. When he stood in the middle of the copse, he knelt, then lay flat against the earth and pressed his ear to the ground, closing his eyes.

Through the shuddering earth, he could hear a dull roar. He frowned, pressing harder into the earth, heard a few of the others approaching as he strained to figure out what the sound was—

And then he jerked his head away from the ground.

"What is it?" his father asked.

Colin looked up at them in wonder. "It's the river. It's underground, beneath the trees. You can hear it, like the sound of the Falls, only muted by the earth."

Tom and Karen both dropped to the ground and copied Colin, listening to the grumbling sound of an unfathomable amount of water roaring through an underground chamber, more water moving faster than Colin could imagine. Walter looked as if he wanted to hear it as well, but he refused to dismount from his horse, sitting up straight in the saddle, towering over all of them. Both his and Jackson's horse were fidgeting, feet dancing as they tried to shy away from the trembling ground.

"Do you think it travels underground from here to the Falls?" Arten asked.

Tom had climbed back to his feet. "Remember how it shot out of the Bluff? And we haven't seen any significant water sources on the upper plains at all, mostly streams and small creeks and runoff from the storms." He stared down at the ground, hands on his hips, then turned to Arten. "If all the major water sources are underground, we're going to have one hell of a time finding a place to settle Haven."

Aeren stepped into the grim silence that followed and motioned toward the east. His expression was grim as well, although he couldn't have understood what Tom had said. Eraeth kept close to Aeren's side as they followed him through the thicket of trees, wider than Colin had expected, the river rumbling beneath them, the trees marking its edges. As they moved, a few more of Aeren's guard appeared, startling Karen and Walter both as they emerged from the thicket as if from thin air, their steps silent, their forms fading into the background when they stood still. Colin listened to Walter cursing as the branches of the trees dragged at him, but he still refused to dismount, choosing to duck beneath them, leaning forward, almost hugging his mount's neck.

The trees thinned. Colin pushed through the last of the branches, into scrub brush, and found himself staring out across another expanse of plains, almost exactly like those on the other side of the trees.

He sighed in disappointment. He'd hoped for something different.

Aeren pointed toward something just to the east, a small group of dark objects sitting in the grass near the verge of trees.

Everyone shifted forward, a few with eyes shaded. Colin squinted, felt Karen moving up beside him. He could see five distinct shapes in the grass, rectangular, blackened, low to the ground. He frowned, not recognizing them—

And then Karen gasped under her breath, "They're wagons!" And suddenly the shapes came into focus, harsh and visceral. A cold fear seeped into his chest, spreading out to his arms, down into his gut.

"What is it?" Walter asked.

"It's one of the previous expeditions," Tom said, his voice strangely flat and remote. "It's what's left of their wagons."

Shock settled over everyone as they stared out at the abandoned wagons, the words sinking in slowly.

And then Walter spun his horse toward Aeren, who was suddenly surrounded by Eraeth and the other Alvritshai who had emerged from the forest as they approached. Their bows were strung and pulled, arrows steady, although Colin didn't know when they'd strung them. They were pointed toward his father, toward Arten and Walter, the commander's hand already on his sword. But when he saw the arrows trained on him, he froze, eyes blazing.

"Who did this?" Walter spat, not in a roar but in a hiss. He kicked his horse forward a menacing step, completely ignoring Aeren's guards. "Who did this?" he demanded again. "Did you do this? Did you?"

"Don't be stupid, Walter."

Colin felt a hot surge of satisfaction pierce the coldness of the fear in his chest at his father's voice, flat and even.

Walter spun on Tom. "What did you say to me?"

"I said, don't be stupid. They wouldn't have led us here to see this if they'd done it themselves. They would have killed us back where we met. So sit down and keep quiet, before you get us all killed."

"Yes, Walter," Jackson added, looking pointedly toward Aeren's guards. "Sit down and shut up."

Walter stiffened, his glare never leaving Tom's face, but he sat back in the saddle. The muscles in his jaw flexed. "I'm the Proprietor here," he insisted, his tone sullen.

Tom's eyes darkened. "Then act like it." Without waiting for a response, he turned to Arten. "We need to check out those wagons, see if we can determine what happened."

"What about them?" Arten asked, nodding toward the Alvritshai. Aeren stood in their midst, his bow the only one not strung. He watched everyone in the group carefully, all trace of the smiling man they'd spent the day traveling and trading languages with gone. His guardsmen had not relaxed, not even when Walter backed down, and Arten's hand had not shifted from his sword hilt.

"I don't think we have to worry about them." Tom turned his attention on Aeren. "We're going down there," he said, motioning toward the wagons.

Aeren nodded, said something in his own language. His guards relaxed, their bows dropping, some of the tension in their strings easing. But they did not remove the arrows; they kept them pointed toward the ground, ready for use.

Arten waited until everyone else had headed toward the wagons, Walter making a point of riding out in front first, before easing away from the Alvritshai and following.

The first thing Colin noticed as he and Karen approached the wagons was that they were nothing but burned out husks. Charred wood stood out against the green and yellow of the grasses, pieces torn from the sides of the wagon completely overgrown by the grass itself. Karen's hand found his as they came up on the first wagon, the rest of the group spreading out, Arten and Tom heading toward the center of the grouping, Walter and Jackson circling around to the other side. The wagons were spaced as if they'd been hit while traveling.

"What do you think happened?" Karen said, as she reached out a tentative hand toward the side of the wagon, brushed her fingers against the charred wood. Her hand came away black with soot, cinders crumbling off and falling to the ground, flakes catching in the breeze and drifting away.

"They were hit while moving," Colin said. "It looks like they were trying to run away. Look at the wheel. It's shattered, like when the horses bolted on the lower plains and Paul's wagon hit the stone and flipped." He pointed toward the broken wheel, the wagon canted in that direction. The smell of char and soot was strong, even though the wagons had been sitting out exposed for what must have been months.

Colin stood, glanced into the back of the wagon as Karen drifted away, noticed that most of the supplies were still inside, although charred almost beyond recognition. Something might be salvageable though. The hide cover was gone, although a few of the supports that had held it still remained, also blackened by fire.

"Oh, Diermani help us," Karen gasped, her breath choked.

He circled around toward the front of the wagon, toward Karen. "What is it?" he asked as he approached and saw Karen looking at the ground. Her hand covered her mouth as she took shallow breaths.

And then the breeze shifted and he caught the rancid smell of rotten meat. He gagged, even though it wasn't that strong, one hand covering his own mouth.

"The horses," Karen said, voice thin.

The team of horses that had pulled the wagon lay in the grass, hidden by its stalks. They were still tied to the tongue, their bodies half cooked by the fire. The blackened skin had pulled away, exposing their yellowed teeth, and holes gaped in their sides where animals had gnawed at their hides, chunks of flesh torn free. But they'd been on the plains for a while, the rancid smell more a lingering memory, the bodies themselves more gruesome than anything else.

Colin sucked in a breath to steady himself, then crouched down close to the dead horse to look it over closely. "Get me a stick," he said.

"From where?" Karen said, moving away.

"The line of trees over the river if you have to."

Karen snorted. He heard her rooting through the back of the wagon, then return.

"What about this?"

She held out the end of a hoe, the metal and part of the handle still intact. The top of the handle had been burned to ash.

He grunted, grabbed the end of the handle, greasy soot coating his hand, then used the metal part of the hoe to prod something from the flaking hide of the horse. It took a moment to work it free, but once it fell out, he pulled it toward him, then reached down to pick it up.

Karen leaned forward as he brought it up into the sunlight.

"It's the head of a spear," Colin said.

Karen stood up. "So they were attacked, and they tried to run, but—"

"They didn't make it."

They considered this in silence, broken a moment later by Karen. "So who attacked them?"

They both turned toward Aeren and the Alvritshai. Uneasiness settled into Colin's stomach, roiled there.

"Let's show this to my father," he said, standing.

They moved toward where his father and Arten were inspecting one of the other wagons. Within twenty steps, he felt something soft give beneath his foot and glanced down.

Karen shrieked and leaped back, but Colin only stared, withdrawing his foot hastily.

He'd stepped on an arm, the impression of his shoe clear in what remained of the man's flesh. The man's body was mercifully facedown, a ragged hole in his back where a spear had killed him, then been jerked free. The body was shrunken, the flesh collapsed in upon itself, and like the bodies of the horses, the predators of the plains had been at it. One of the man's legs was completely missing, torn free and dragged off somewhere to be eaten.

The man had clearly been running from the wagon—abandoned after it had caught fire or when it had hit the stone and the wheel had shattered—and had been killed as he fled.

Colin shuddered, then grabbed Karen's arm and led her away, although she'd already recovered from the initial shock. They jogged up to where his father and Arten were kneeling down at the back of a second wagon.

"We found a body," Colin said.

His father looked up. "So have we." Then he reached down and turned the body on the ground beneath the wagon over.

It wasn't one of the people from the wagon train. It wasn't even Andovan. The body was short, perhaps a hand or two shorter than Colin. It would have been stocky—broad of shoulder and chest, with short legs and arms—except that it was as mauled and decomposed as the body Colin and Karen had found. The fact that the face was caved in on one side, crushed by a heavy, blunt object, didn't help matters. But even so they could see that the man's skin had been a dusky brown shade, like dirt, and that he'd worn a closely shaven beard, trimmed on the edges, the length bound and twisted into small braids and tied off with beads. His hair was a tawny brown, a few locks braided and tied with beads and small feathers. He wore a shirt of woven cloth, soft where it wasn't stiff with caked dirt and blood and soot, but his breeches were made of a different material, something tougher than the shirt. He didn't wear shoes.

In one hand, he held the end of a spear, the haft splintered where it had been broken. Numerous pouches were belted to his waist, along with a sheathed knife, the blade small, in proportion with the rest of his body. His nose was pierced, as well as one ear, a thin silver chain running from one to the other so that it draped down across his cheek.

"I think he tried to climb up into the back of the wagon and got clubbed by someone inside," Tom said.

Arten nodded. "These must be the people that Beth saw looking down from the upper plains. They're shorter than the Alvritshai."

"And they look more vicious," Karen said, frowning down at the man's face. "Look at the scars on his face."

"Definitely a fighter," Arten agreed. "A warrior."

"Did you find one of them as well?" Colin's father asked.

Colin shook his head. "No. We found one of the people from Andover. He'd taken a spear in the back." He handed over the burned spear point. "They killed the horses with spears as well. I got this from the horse's body."

"They ambushed them," Arten said, glancing up, looking out over the rest of the wagons they could see. One of the blackened hulks was flipped onto its side, its contents strewn about and hidden by the grass. "They forced them to run, but there were others waiting."

Walter's horse came charging around the end of the wagon, and he pulled it up short, turning back. "We found the rest of the group," he growled, "the rest of the wagon train. They've been slaughtered."

The bodies—men, women, and children—were all lying in a heap in front of the lead wagon, along with the bodies of a few horses, two cows, and three dogs. Arten stared down at them, his expression blank. Walter and Jackson were pacing their horses behind him.

"It was a massacre," Tom said, and for the first time since they'd come down to the wagons, Colin heard anger in his voice.

Arten nodded, then reached down and retrieved an arrow from one of the corpses, working the arrowhead free from the body with care. He held it up to the sunlight, inspected the fletching, the point. "They rounded them up and then killed them with arrows. But it wasn't the Alvritshai. The arrows are too short for their bows, and the fletching and arrowheads are different." He lowered the arrow and turned to Tom. "I think Aeren is trying to warn us about these other people. He's trying to warn us away from them."

Walter scowled. "Then where are they, these other people? Who are they?"

"Dwarren."

Everyone turned from the bodies back toward the wagons, where Aeren and the other Alvritshai were standing beside the lead wagon, watching them. Their arrows had been put away, although Colin noticed their bows were still strung.

None of them had heard the group of Alvritshai approach.

"They call themselves the dwarren?" Walter demanded. "They did this? Why? Why would they attack our people?"

Aeren's brow creased in confusion. He motioned toward the wagons, toward the bodies at their feet, toward the arrow that Arten still held, and said again, "Dwarren."

"And where are these dwarren?" Arten asked, voice tight. "Where do they live? How come we haven't seen any of them yet?"

Aeren stared at him solemnly for a long moment, and Colin noticed that his men weren't watching Walter or Arten or anyone else in the group. They were watching the plains.

Then Aeren motioned toward the surrounding grassland, his arm circling, fingers pointing in all directions. "Dwarren."

"I don't understand," Walter said sharply, frustrated.

Arten's gaze had shot toward the plains, his eyes squinted, face intent.

"I think he means," Tom said softly, also turning toward the plains, "that the dwarren are *everywhere.*"

And before anyone could react, they heard screams coming from the direction of their own wagons.

9

TOM TORE THROUGH THE BRANCHES of the line of trees over the river, his heart thundering in his chest, his breath harsh, his lungs aching. Something raked across his face, slicing open his cheek, the pain stinging; but he didn't stop, didn't even stumble. All he could think about was Ana.

And the corpses of the previous expedition, lying discarded on the plains, forgotten.

He leaped over a bent sapling, heard Arten and the rest plowing through the trees on either side. As soon as they'd heard the scream, Arten and Tom had bolted for the tree line, Aeren and the Alvritshai spinning in that direction, their arrows suddenly nocked and raised. Colin and Karen had stood stunned, Walter and Jackson as well, but then both the Proprietor and the Company man had kicked their horses into motion, surging toward the trees, outdistancing Tom and Arten in a heartbeat. Tom had heard Colin shout, knew that he and Karen were charging after them and silently willed Colin to stay with the burned out wagons. But he knew Colin wouldn't, knew Karen wouldn't stay behind either. Part of him cursed them for their youth, but another part surged with pride.

He crashed through the edge of the trees and stumbled out into the brush and grass at its edge, his breath tearing at his lungs. Arten spilled from the trees to the right, his sword already drawn, the Alvritshai emerging smoothly farther away. Clutching the sudden sharp pain in his side, Tom swallowed and spun to the left.

Walter and Jackson were galloping toward their wagons, their horses' hooves throwing up clods of dirt in their wake. And beyond them—

Tom's heart faltered in his chest. From fear, but also from startled shock.

The wagon train was under attack. A group of the short, vicious-looking men that Aeren had called the dwarren launched a rain of arrows and spears toward where the wagons had tried to circle for protection, maybe twenty of the dwarren in all. But it took a moment for Tom to grasp what was actually happening, for him to sort out the chaos.

Because the dwarren weren't attacking on foot. They were riding the gaezels. As if they were horses.

He turned to see Arten gazing toward the scene with wild eyes. Before either of them shook themselves out of it, Colin and Karen burst from the tree line.

"What's happening?" Colin shouted. "What's going on?"

"The dwarren are attacking the wagon train," Arten said, Colin's appearance snapping him out of his shock. He strode toward Tom, reached down and drew a knife from a sheath in his boot and handed it to him. "Here. I don't have another one for you, Colin."

Colin—breath rasping in his chest, eyes fixed on the group of dwarren astride their gaezels—fumbled in a pocket, drawing out the tightly wound sling Tom had given him what seemed like an eternity ago. "That's all right," he said. "I have this."

"And I have this," Karen said, opening her hand to reveal a small but sharp knife used for eating.

Behind them all, the Alvritshai had halted, were hesitating, Aeren watching Tom, Arten, and Colin, waiting to see what they would do. Aeren's escort kept their eyes on the fight at the wagons, faces taut. Their bodies strained forward, but they held themselves in check.

A man cried out, and Tom spun back, saw someone fall to the ground, a spear jutting from his chest.

He took Arten's knife grimly. "Karen, stay close to Colin. And Colin, for Diermani's sake, and your mother's, stay as far back from the fighting as you can."

Without waiting for a response, he and Arten ran forward, toward the front of the fighting. The dwarren had made another pass and were now circling back, pulling their gaezels sharply to the left, using the beasts' horns as reins, the deer snorting. They were fast, turned tight, tighter than horses. Tom saw Walter and Jackson lunging after them with the much larger horses, swords gleaming in the sunlight. They were joined by three other men on horseback, Armory it looked like. Two women had rushed out to the grass in front of the haphazardly circled wagons as soon as the dwarren banked away, were dragging the man Tom had seen fall back behind the wagons, one on each arm, the spear jutting from his chest rocking back and forth as they moved the body. He could see Lyda gazing out of the back of one of the wagons, eyes wide in terror, hand on her swollen stomach, her other arm around one of the children, three more terrified faces cowering behind her—

And then he saw Paul, the bulky smith roaring something unintelligible after the dwarren's backs, a heavy ax thrust into the air.

"Paul!" Tom shouted, veering toward the smith.

Three more men took up the roar on either side of him, one of them bellowing, "Come back, you bloody bastards!"

"Paul!"

The smith turned, his face red with rage. "Tom! We thought—"

"What happened?" Tom gasped, coming to a halt.

"They came out of nowhere, as if they just popped up out of the grass, like fucking prairie dogs. We didn't have any warning at all. Thank Diermani we'd already begun to draw the wagons into a circle to make camp. Sam saw them just before they hit us with the first pass. They're riding those fucking deer!"

"I saw." Tom swallowed, trying to catch his breath. He scanned the men nearest, the rest of the Armory, others from Lean-to with swords or pikes or knives. A few were brandishing hoes and spades, one an ax like Paul's.

"They're fast," one of the men said. "Those deer can outrun our horses."

He motioned to the plains, where Tom could see that the dwarren had outdistanced Walter and his cavalry.

He frowned. Walter had led the horses too far out.

Even as he thought it, the dwarren suddenly turned, swinging around, heading back toward the wagons, leav-

ing Walter and his men behind as their gaezels picked up
speed.

Someone swore, the words bitter.

"They're coming back," Arten barked. He spun. "Get
as many of the horses behind the wagons as possible! Find
cover! We can't fight them with swords, not when they're
using spears and arrows."

Men scrambled, a few breaking away to unhitch the
exposed horses, not bothering to undo the harness, simply
cutting it free, trying to calm the horses as they worked.
One of the horses panicked and bolted as it was freed, men
yelling and cursing, one of the younger men racing after it.
Tom shoved the nearest men toward the wagons, including
the priest Domonic, yelled at those inside who were leaning out to see to get back. He saw Colin and Karen duck
behind the closest wagon, Colin scooping something up
from the ground, and felt a surge of relief, but he had yet
to see Ana. Heart in his throat, the sound of the gaezels'
hooves growing louder, he waved the rest of the men behind the wagons as well, then turned.

In time to see the horse that had bolted and the man
who'd raced after it fall, both riddled with dwarren arrows. The ground shook as the dwarren converged. Tom
watched the lead dwarren as he brought the gaezel in for a
sweep across the length of the wagons, parallel to the trees
above the river, saw the man's face contorted with rage, the
braided locks of his black and gray beard bouncing against
his chest as he raised his spear. His eyes were gray in color
but black with hate. Three chains fell across his cheek from
pierced nose to ear, gold in the light, and he wore armor, a
leather vest across his thick chest, scored with marks from
previous battles.

The dwarren saw Tom. He kicked the gaezel he rode
hard, driving it forward. Tom stepped back, felt the shadow
of the wagon at his side fall across him. The dwarren warrior's face twisted into a sneer and he leaned back, spear
arm extended, the muscles in his arm flexing—

Then he threw.

Tom felt hands grab his shirt and haul him behind the
wagon, the spear whistling as it cut through the air and
sank into the ground just inside the makeshift camp, near
where a group of men who'd rescued the horses were

trying to tether them to one of the wagons closest to the trees. And then the dwarren were thundering past. A rough shout rang out, the voice deep, almost a growl, in a language that was not Andovan nor Alvritshai, but more guttural and harsh, and Tom heard the gaezels being pulled to a halt.

"They're dismounting!" Domonic barked, pointing beneath the wagon.

Tom crouched down, saw the lithe legs of the gaezels milling about thirty paces from the wagons. "Wait!" Tom barked to the men who were already readying to charge out onto the grass. "They aren't all dismounting, only a few of them."

Low murmurs arose, tight with fear.

Tom glanced over toward the next wagon and saw Arten huddled with another group of men, looked over his shoulder and saw Colin and Karen with a few others on the other side. He didn't see the Alvritshai anywhere, wasn't even certain they'd followed them in their mad dash for the wagons.

"What are they doing?" Domonic whispered.

Tom ducked back down to peer under the wagon. The few dwarren who'd dismounted were walking around near the edge of the rest of the gaezels. He couldn't see above the men's waists, but occasionally a box on a chain swung into view, sort of like a lantern, then was raised, as if those still astride the gaezels were taking something from it.

Tom frowned. A breeze gusted beneath the wagon, and he caught the faint scent of smoke.

He thought suddenly of the wagons that Acren had shown them, and he sucked in a sharp breath.

Before he could turn, he heard a crack as something struck the side of a wagon and shattered. Liquid splattered down from the bottom of the wagon—

Followed by the unmistakable whomph of flames catching in oil.

"They're firing the wagons!" he shouted, stepping back from the edge of the wagon he huddled against, thinking of Lyda's face and all of the children huddled around her as he'd charged toward the wagons earlier. "Get out of the wagons! Get everyone out now!"

He began working frantically at the ties that held the

hides to the strakes, using the knife Arten had given him. He could hear those inside begin to move around restlessly, crying out. The scent of smoke became suddenly sharper, a thin trail marring the blue sky overhead.

More cracks and thuds as more arrows struck, and Tom swore, cursing the leather thongs that held the hides tight, so tight his blade couldn't get up underneath them. His fingers cramped and he licked his lips, tasted blood from the slash across his cheek. Sweat broke out across his chest, his back.

Inside the wagon, someone screamed, and the suddenly restless sounds became a panic. The wagon shook. Someone cried out, trying to keep the children calm, a woman's voice.

"Don't come out the back!" Tom barked. "They're waiting—"

But someone leaned out of the back of the wagon. Tom felt the wagon shift as they moved, heard the sickening chunk of an arrow hitting flesh. A body—a woman's body, Clara, her face stark, eyes dead, facing Tom almost accusingly—hit the ground with a horrifying rustling sound, and the wagon shifted back.

Fresh screams escaped from the wagon, and everyone inside rushed away from the back entrance. Tom's dagger slid beneath the first set of ties, cut through them with a jerk, and he cried out as wisps of smoke escaped through the opening.

"Arten!" he bellowed, his voice cracking. He gasped in desperation as he moved frantically to the next set of ties. All around, understanding dawned and men leaped forward with their own knives, began sawing at the hide, not bothering with the ties. "Arten! Sam! Anyone!"

"Those of you with weapons," Arten bellowed, "come with me! We'll have to charge them, give those inside the wagons a chance to get out."

Tom didn't turn, heard feet gathering behind him, heard Arten barking orders, dividing the men up, and then he heard all of them roar, saw them charging out from behind the wagons out of the corner of his eyes, an acrid taste filling his mouth as he heard the sudden twang of more than a few bowstrings, the screams that followed, breaking the roar of the charge—

Followed instantly by another roar coming from the other direction and the thundering of horses' hooves.

Walter, he thought, grinning in spite of himself, in spite of all the pain that Walter had put him and his family through.

The hide was tough. As he sliced through it, a small hand suddenly emerged through the hole and grabbed his wrist. He cried out, startled, then gasped, "We're coming!" and shook the hand free. He continued to whisper, "We're coming, we're coming," under his breath as he worked. To his right, men shouted in triumph, and he risked a quick glance, saw children spilling out of a hole in the nearest wagon along with white-gray smoke. The women inside practically threw them out, motions controlled but still frantic.

And then the last of the hide succumbed to his knife and he ripped the flap aside, a small boy already half outside, his face streaked with tears, eyes wide open in terror. His shirt rucked up to his arm as it caught on the edge of the wagon, tore as he slid free and fell to the ground, and then a girl's face appeared, coughing harshly. Domonic was suddenly at Tom's side, reaching forward to haul the girl out and the next, more openings appearing on either side, the smoke coming out thicker and blacker as they worked. Tom shot a glance under the wagon, saw a scramble of feet—men, dwarren, horses, and gaezels—heard shouts and commands, roars of pain. Someone fell, hand clutching an arrow embedded in his shoulder, and then Tom grabbed the nearest man and hauled him close. "Take the hide! Hold it!"

As soon as the man took the flap, Tom darted to the edge of the wagon and looked out onto the fight before the wagons.

As he watched, Walter swung his sword in a loose arc, more brute force than skill, and cut into the spear the dwarren used to block the blow. Both maneuvered their animals around, the gaezel dancing out of the much larger horse's way. Walter pressed his horse's advantage, swinging again and again, the haft of the dwarren's spear shattering on the last blow, Walter's sword cutting down into the dwarren's forearm. The man roared, blood flowing down his arm to his elbow, and kicked his gaezel away from the battle.

Walter wheeled his mount toward where Arten and a group of the expedition's men were surrounded, the dwarren circling their gaezels around the group, continuously moving. Arten watched warily for an opening, while the others tried to cut into the dwarren's flanks. Walter charged the dwarren line, Jackson and the three other Armory men on horses already engaged with the outskirts of the group.

As soon as Walter struck, the dwarren turning to meet his charge, Arten ducked in behind them and cut two of the dwarren down from behind. One of the animals screamed—the same haunting, grating scream they'd made when Tom's group had hunted them before—as Arten's sword cut a gash in its side. It bolted for the plains, a few of its brethren following suit with snorts. The rest of the men with Arten closed in.

But they were outnumbered, even with the dwarren they'd already killed, even with Walter and the others on horseback. Only those from the Armory were true fighters. The rest were farmers or tradesmen, unskilled with weapons, even Walter and Jackson.

Tom shot a glance to either side behind the wagons, but everyone was occupied trying to get the last of the women out of the burning wagons, even Colin, Karen still sawing at the hides on her side with her thin eating knife. Black smoke gusted into Tom's face and he coughed, covered his mouth with one hand, and turned back—

To see a dwarren raise his spear at Arten's back. The commander's attention was on the dwarren before him, fending off that man's thrusts. He couldn't see the dwarren behind him.

Tom drew breath to shout a warning—

And three arrows sprouted in the dwarren's chest with three distinct hissing thunks.

The dwarren fell back off of his gaezel with a stunned look on his face. Arten stabbed his sword forward and pierced the dwarren he fought through the chest, the blade sliding out freely as he stepped back, and then he turned, glanced down at the dead dwarren who'd been ready to spear him from behind, then up.

Tom followed his gaze.

On the far side of the burning wagons, Aeren and the rest

of the Alvritshai stood, firing into the fight, their targets the dwarren, their faces calm and intent. Aeren nodded toward Arten, the gesture somehow formal, and then turned, drawing an arrow from his quiver and sighting along it into the melee, releasing it with no change at all in his expression. Dwarren fell right and left, and with a roaring command, the gray-eyed dwarren that Tom had watched lead the charge, who had thrown his spear at Tom as he came, broke away from the fighting, the rest of the dwarren following suit. They streamed out onto the plains on their gaezels, half of their number left behind either dead or dying. Walter and the others on horseback charged after them for a moment, before finally slowing and turning back.

Tom watched long enough to be certain that the dwarren weren't returning, then spun back toward the wagons. Pillars of smoke rose into the air, one of the wagons already a total loss, but the other two—

"Sam! Paul! Get some blankets or buckets of water! We need to get these fires put out." He suddenly remembered the sound of liquid splashing. "Wait! Not water. They used some type of oil to help the fire catch and spread. Use sand or dirt instead!"

He heard Sam shouting, and everyone began scrambling, beating at the flames. Some of the women rushed to help. As soon as he felt the situation was under control, Tom turned back toward the plains.

The area in front of the wagons was littered with bodies—dwarren, gaezels, one horse, and a few men from the wagon train. He found Arten kneeling at the side of one of the fallen men, the one that had taken an arrow to his shoulder, now propped up against one of the dead gaezels. The man's breath came in short, hot, huffing gasps, punctuated by moans as Arten prodded the area around the wound. His shirt was soaked with blood, from the wound down across his chest to beneath his arm. His face was pale. He turned pleading eyes on Tom as he approached.

Arten sat back. "The arrow's in deep, Brant, but it missed the lung. I'm afraid that if we try to pull it out, it will catch on your ribs, or worse."

"So what should we do?" Tom asked, crouching down beside the commander.

"Here." Arten placed his hand up under Brant's armpit, below where the arrow had pierced his chest. "Feel right here, where my hand is."

He withdrew his hand, and Tom slid his in where it had been. Blood coated his fingers, but he ignored it as he felt where Arten had indicated, frowning. "What am I—"

But then he halted.

He could feel something hard beneath his fingers, beneath Brant's skin. He pushed it, barely even moved it, but Brant hissed and jerked away, the end of the arrow wobbling. His hiss became a harsh cough that he tried to control, the arrow shaking with every movement.

"That's the tip of the arrow," Arten explained, and Tom shuddered, his stomach turning. He could still feel it beneath his fingers. "Brant must have twisted away when the arrow was fired. It hit him in the chest, at an angle, missing anything vital, but lodging there beneath his armpit."

"How do we get it out?"

"We'll have to push it all the way through."

Tom's breath caught. Brant's did the same.

"You can't just pull it out?" Brant gasped weakly. "Or cut it out?"

"The dwarren arrowheads are shaped with points on the back, like barbs, so that they'll do almost as much damage on the way out as on the way in, especially if they're jerked free. We could try to withdraw it, but we'd have to go slow, and we might hit something more vital on the way out. A good chunk of the shaft is still inside you as well. We might not cut in the right place for us to pull the shaft out without angling it and doing more damage. It needs to come straight out. The best option is to push it through."

Brant sagged back, looked up into the blue sky. He muttered a prayer under his breath, winced in pain, then glanced toward Tom, pleading.

Tom shook his head. "It's up to you, Brant. We can do it either way."

He struggled with himself a moment, then sighed. "Do it. Push it through."

Arten didn't give him a chance to change his mind. "Get some clean rags, some wine, a stick for him to bite on, and some water."

Tom lurched to his feet, trotted toward the wagons,

noting that the fires had been put out on two of them, that the third had burned out of control. Someone had shifted the rest of the wagons away from the one that still burned.

Aeren and the Alvritshai were standing off to one side, three of them surveying the plains, watching, bows ready, the others talking to Aeren in animated voices, arguing with him. Tom wondered what they were arguing about—

Then he spotted Ana. She was climbing out of one of the wagons in the back, the one that held Tobin. "Ana!" he said, turning to head toward her.

"Tom! Thank Holy Diermani!" She crossed herself, hand clutching the pendant beneath the shirt on her chest, and then Tom was there, kissing her. It was a brief kiss, fierce and not perfunctory.

"Arten needs some rags, water, wine, and a stick," Tom said as soon as it broke. "He needs to remove an arrow from Brant's shoulder."

"Where's Colin? And Karen?" she asked, rummaging in the back of the wagon.

"They're fine. What about Tobin?"

"He was in one of the wagons in the back. He's still feverish, and he tried to get up to help, but he's too weak to do more than exhaust himself. Did you see Miriam?" When Tom shook his head, she continued, while handing him rags, a thin dowel, and a skin of wine. "She heaved the kids out of the burning wagon—the one we lost—then started throwing out whatever supplies from inside she could get her hands on. She stayed inside a little too long and got burned."

"How bad?"

"Not bad enough to fret over. She's more concerned about the hair she singed off." She rolled her eyes. "Now go. I'll send someone with a bucket of water."

Tom hesitated, the shock of everything that had happened starting to seep in. He felt his body trembling, tasted bile at the back of his throat because he knew that there were more than a few people dead. He'd seen their bodies on the grass.

Ana gripped his arm, her face stern. "Tom. We don't have time. Brant doesn't have time."

Tom sucked in a large breath, noisily, swallowed the acrid taste in his mouth, and turned without a word. As he jogged across the remains of the camp between the wagons, horses whinnying and snorting, people dashing to and fro, or sitting stunned on the grass, he saw Walter on horseback, grouped together with six other men—three Armory men and three others—also mounted.

And armed.

Walter saw Tom coming, said something, his face black with hatred, with purpose. The rest nodded.

Then they spun their horses and charged out across the plains, toward where the dwarren had fled.

"Walter!" Tom roared, lurching forward, but Walter ignored him. "Walter, goddamn it!"

He halted, juggled the rags and wine in his hand, then spat another curse under his breath. Walter and the others were nothing but figures in the distance.

"Tom!"

He turned toward Arten, dashed forward and spilled the supplies near Brant's side.

"Where are Walter and the others going?" Arten asked.

"I don't know," Tom spat, furious. "They didn't confer with me before they left."

Arten grunted. "Give me the dowel." He took the rounded chunk of wood and placed it between Brant's teeth. "Bite down on this. It will keep you from biting your tongue off."

Brant nodded. Arten had already ripped the wounded man's shirt free, exposing the wound, the shaft of the arrow still protruding from it.

"What do you want me to do?" Tom asked.

"Hold him. I'm going to have to break the fletching off the arrow in order to push it through, and it's impossible to do that without moving the arrow. He's going to struggle."

Tom placed his hands on Brant's chest. As he did, one of the older children rushed forward with a bucket of water, the contents sloshing over the side as he dropped it to the ground near Arten, then stepped back and crouched down so he could watch.

Arten took the arrow in both hands, Brant hissing through the stick in his mouth. "On three," he said, catching Tom's gaze in warning. And then, without counting, he snapped the shaft of the arrow.

Brant screamed and bucked, throwing Tom off his body and into the grass. Tom heard Arten curse as he scrambled back to Brant's side, grabbing hold of the younger man again. Brant twisted beneath Tom's and Arten's grip, body arched as he tried to roll away from the pain in his shoulder, but then he collapsed back, his scream dying back down into harsh pants. Sweat and tears streaked his face, and his skin had turned a ghastly white. He'd bitten so hard into the dowel there were indentations in the wood. Fresh blood welled from his wound, thick and viscous. His skin felt hot and feverish beneath Tom's hands.

"Now," Arten said, his voice unnaturally calm to Tom's ears, "we need to push it through. Ron, hold down Brant's legs." The commander didn't even look as Ron slid in beside Tom and gripped Brant's legs. Instead, he looked directly at Brant himself. "I'll push it through as fast as I can, but you need to hold still. Once it's out, I'll have to clean the wound and dress it."

Brant nodded, his breath harsh as he drew it in and out through his nostrils. Tears still welled from his eyes, and sweat plastered his hair to his scalp.

Arten nodded in return, and both Tom and Ron leaned into Brant's shoulder and legs.

"Here we go," Arten said.

He took hold of the shaft of the arrow and pushed.

Brant growled, whimpered, bit down hard on the dowel, and caught Tom with wide, haunted, pleading eyes. Tom stared into them, into their warm hazel depths, and grimly held on as Brant began to shudder. The whimpering growl grew, escalating toward a scream, and Tom saw Brant's eyes begin to dart around in desperation, saw them squeeze shut, then flare open as Arten did something that interrupted Brant's growl with a moaning bark of pure pain—

Then he saw consciousness flicker in Brant's eyes, saw it struggle to remain and then die.

Brant's body slumped to the ground, and as it did, Arten slid the splintered end of the arrow free of the fresh wound beneath Brant's armpit. Blood gushed from both cuts, but Arten had already set the arrowhead aside, the wood stained black. He began cleaning the wounds with the wine and water, using the rags to stanch the flow. He held the rags tight, pushing with his weight, and after a long moment withdrew them.

When new blood welled up through the cuts, he cursed.

"I'm not a doctor," Arten said, pressing the rags down hard again. "But if we can't get the blood flow to stop—"

He didn't need to finish.

Ron suddenly gasped and lurched back, tripping over his own feet and falling to the ground. Tom spun, half standing, then halted.

Aeren stood a few paces away, Eraeth and another of the Alvritshai flanking him. He stared down at Brant, then held something toward Tom, murmuring in his own language. Tom hesitated, then stood and accepted what Aeren offered.

A small, clear, glass vial filled with what looked like pinkish water.

Tom looked at Aeren in consternation, but the Alvritshai motioned toward Brant, mimicked pouring the water over Brant's wounds.

Tom returned to Arten's side. "He wants us to pour this over the wound," he said, as he began to remove the cork from the top of the bottle. It was sealed with wax, so he used the knife Arten had given him earlier to break it.

"And you're going to use it?"

"We don't have a choice. The blood isn't stopping, and they haven't given us any reason to distrust them so far."

Arten didn't respond, but he did pull the rags back from the wound and let Tom dribble some of the liquid onto the cuts.

Nothing happened at first, the pinkish water mixing with the blood, diluting it. Arten shifted, ready to start pressing the already saturated rags against the wounds again, but Tom halted him. "Look. It's stopping."

The flow of blood had grown sluggish. Tom poured a little more of the fluid onto the wounds, held his breath, then exhaled as the bleeding stopped completely. Both wounds were still there, on the chest and beneath Brant's armpit, but they had clotted, and no new blood flowed from them.

Arten dipped his hand in the water from the bucket so he could wash the excess blood away from Brant's wounds, but Aeren said something, clearly a warning, and he stopped.

"Maybe the water will wash away whatever this pink stuff is," Tom said. He sat back, stared down at Brant's slack face. "Bind it. And take him to Ana."

Then he stood, noted with a troubled turn of his stomach that the rest of the Alvritshai were gone, then stepped toward Aeren and his two guards. "Thank you for this." He motioned with the small bottle, tried to hand it back. There was still liquid in the bottom of it.

Eraeth frowned, said something with scorn in it, as if he'd been insulted, but Aeren shook his head. He pushed Tom's hand back, closing Tom's fingers around the bottle. "Keep."

Tom nodded, and Aeren turned to survey the surrounding grass.

Where the dead lay.

Tom swallowed, gaze flicking from body to body. Flies were already gathering, buzzing in small clumps around the drying blood, the gaping wounds. He felt sick, skin flushed, as he counted nine men dead. Ten, counting the young man who'd foolishly raced after the escaping horse.

No. Eleven. The man he'd seen impaled by the spear before he'd even arrived at the wagons had been dragged into their circle by two of the women.

And then there was Clara.

He closed his eyes, bowed his head a moment to steady himself, then turned his face to the sky so he could feel the sunlight on his face. He breathed in the scent of smoke, of blood, of death, but also the grass, the earth, the trees.

He opened his eyes when he heard horses pounding toward them, and he saw Walter and the rest returning, driving their mounts hard. The anger that rose when he heard them stilled when he saw the panic on Walter's face.

"Get everyone on the wagons," Walter barked, his mount skidding to a halt before Tom and Aeren, the other riders not stopping, heading toward the wagons, shouting for everyone to move. "We have to get out of here. Now. As fast as possible."

"What is it? What did you find?"

"The dwarren." He flicked the reins in his hands, his horse skittish. Walter's gaze darted across the open plains, searching, not resting on any one location. "That was only a scouting party," he said. "They have an army, headed this way. And from what we saw, they could come at us from anywhere."

"How?" Tom asked, his anger touching his voice. Behind him, he could hear the others driving the rest of the wagon train into panicked motion.

Walter held his gaze, his face as serious as Tom had ever seen it. "Because they live underground."

Tom frowned. "Show me."

~

"We must leave them. You have done enough. They can fend for themselves."

"As the others did?" Aeren glared at Eraeth. His Protector's flat but forceful statements infuriated him. "No. You saw what happened to the other wagons, what the dwarren did to them."

"You approached this group against my advice. You tried to warn them back, to get them to return to the lands below the Escarpment, where there is relative safety from the dwarren and the plains. And when they would not listen, you led them to the burned wagons and the dead in hopes that they would return then."

"The warning came too late!" Aeren spat. He stepped away from Eraeth and his other guardsman, ignored the look that passed between the two. He watched the settlers instead, the group of men racing about, gathering together a small scouting group while the rest prepared the wagons for travel. Women were salvaging what they could from the burned wagon and gathering up the wounded, loading the man that had taken an arrow in his shoulder into the back of one, some of the smaller children in the others. He had never seen so many children at once. Alvritshai children were rare and precious. They certainly would not have been allowed onto the plains at such a young age. The robed one, who appeared to be an acolyte of some kind, moved among them all, parents and children alike, comforting them, leading some in short prayers while they clutched the strange pendant he wore. A few were gathering up the dead, laying them together to one side.

Aeren felt something dig into his chest at the sight of the bodies. "It came too late," he repeated.

Eraeth moved to his side. "Yes, and you ordered us to help defend them against the dwarren scouts. But if there are scouts, then the army will not be far behind. You know they cannot defend themselves against the dwarren armies, even with our help. And it is doubtful they will be able to outrun them."

"Except that the dwarren army isn't interested in them." Aeren turned to Eraeth, saw his Protector scowl. "The dwarren scouts weren't looking for these people, they were looking for their own kind. We've stumbled into one of their tribal wars. If we can determine where the other dwarren tribes are coming from, perhaps we can elude them."

Eraeth's eyes narrowed. "You are correct. The dwarren are not interested in the human wagons. That does not mean we should risk our lives—Alvritshai lives—for these . . . these savages!"

Aeren's brow creased at the venom in Eraeth's words. He held his Protector's gaze, then asked, "When will the other Phalanx members return with news of the other dwarren's whereabouts?"

Eraeth hesitated. "Not for some time."

"Then we have time to help them further."

Anger flared in Eraeth's eyes. "No. You have risked yourself and the rest of your Phalanx already by simply contacting these people, let alone aiding them against the dwarren. And now you have given them the Blood of Aielan, the proof of the success of your Trial, all to save one man's life? A man you did not even know! You have more than satisfied your obligation to these people. I refuse to allow you to continue. You will rejoin the House contingent waiting to the north and return to Alvritshai lands with us. Immediately."

Shock coursed through Aeren at the tone in his Protector's voice, even as Eraeth turned away, toward the other Phalanx guardsman. He'd spoken to him as if he were a child. No, as if he were a *student*.

But he was no longer Eraeth's student.

"Protector!"

His voice cracked across the grass, loud enough and forceful enough that even the group of humans paused in their activity. Eraeth stilled, back stiff, then turned.

Aeren closed the distance between them in two short steps, stared hard into Eraeth's eyes. "I have passed the Trial. I am now a full member of the House, with all of the rank and privileges and responsibilities that such entails.

And whether you like it or not, these people are our responsibility. It began when we shared our food and wine with them. Or had you forgotten? We entered a bond with them then, and I intend to see that bond fulfilled, for the honor of my House."

Eraeth held his gaze, unflinching, although the anger and defiance in his stance had abated. Something else flickered there instead—pride, regret.

Resignation.

He let out a low breath, then nodded. "Very well."

The tension in Aeren's shoulders relaxed, and he found himself trembling. He caught the other Phalanx guardsman's gaze, then turned toward the group of humans. Tom had stepped forward, concern on his face, but Aeren motioned him away. Tom hesitated, then returned to the group of men ready to mount their horses.

"We will help them," Aeren said, "for as long as we possibly can."

~

Like fucking prairie dogs.

Paul's words came back to Tom as he lay on a ridge of ground, Walter, Arten, and another Armory guardsman to the side. Eraeth had crawled up to the ridge with them, but Aeren and the other Alvritshai were behind, hidden from sight in the depression behind the ridge, along with the horses. Tom hadn't thought the Alvritshai would be able to keep up with the horses on foot—and they hadn't, but they hadn't been that far behind them either.

Below, in a large, flattened portion of the prairie, a hole gaped in the ground, a cavernous opening that slid into the ground in a gentle incline so wide it could hold at least three wagons side by side. The opening was shaded by a huge multicolored tent, the material bent and twisted around thick poles driven into the ground, the entire edifice practical but at the same time strangely artistic. The curves of the tent, which billowed out in the wind from the plains like sails, flowed from one stretch of cloth to another, the colors blending into one another, shades of tawny gold and muted blues and greens. They all seemed to flow to a vivid red center.

The large tent was surrounded by hundreds of smaller

tents. They spread out from the central tent in a haphazard fashion, as if they weren't permanent structures, although none of them were set up before the entrance to the burrow.

The entire tent city teemed with dwarren and gaezels. Men charged back and forth from the entrance to where nearly a thousand others had gathered on the plains before the burrow, divided into ranks of twenty. Most of these divisions were on foot, but a few were mounted on gaezels or held the fleet animals in check to one side.

As Tom watched, a sickening pit opening up in his stomach, a few more divisions emerged from the burrow and formed up near the back of the group.

"Diermani's balls," the Armory guardsman said to one side, his voice low. "There's more than a thousand of them now." At Arten's glance, he added, "There were only a few hundred when we were here before."

"Did they see you?" Arten asked.

"I don't know. We charged up the ridge, following their trail in the grass, but as soon as we saw them we turned and headed back."

"Saw," Eraeth said, succinctly and with conviction.

Tom and Arten turned toward him.

Arten grunted. "It doesn't matter. Their scouts know we're there. And it looks like they're headed in our direction. Let's hope Paul and Sam managed to get the wagons loaded and headed out, although I'm not sure where we can run." He frowned. "I don't see any wagons. Or women."

Eraeth grunted and motioned to the gathered force, the air, the tents, and the ground. "Dwarren above, wagons below."

"They supply the army from belowground?" When Eraeth nodded, Arten said, "Then they must have more entrances like this."

"So what do we do?"

Arten turned to look at Tom, his face grim. "We run, and hope that they don't find us."

Eraeth slid back from the ridge, moving to Aeren's side. Aeren listened to what he had to say, then instantly turned to the other Alvritshai guard and gave him orders. The other guard tore out across the plains, heading in a straight line, but not toward the Andovan wagons. Instead, he angled slightly away from them, east and north.

"Where's he going?" Arten asked.

Tom wondered the same thing. He began slipping down off the ridge, the rest following. That hollow pit in his stomach had expanded, and he found he couldn't focus on anything. He kept thinking about Ana, about Colin. He'd dragged them to Portstown, had forced them to stay, then drafted them into this expedition onto the godforsaken plains.

"Where are you going?" Arten asked, as Tom slid into the saddle of his horse.

"Back to the wagons," he said, and heard the roughness in his voice, the rawness. "Back to my family. It's the only chance we've got."

He spun the mount and kicked him toward the east, toward the heat-blurred horizon, not waiting for the others.

10

COLIN HALTED AND TURNED at the shouts, Karen doing the same beside him, edging a little closer as the wagon they trailed continued on ahead. Neck craning, he saw horses tearing toward the wagons through the grasses of the plains. Something caught at his throat, made it hard to breathe, and he reached for Karen's hand.

"He's there," Karen said, her voice strained as she entangled his fingers with her own. "They're all there."

Colin didn't relax until his father charged past them, heading toward the front of the wagons, where Sam and Paul steered the wagon train east. Arten and the others sped by on their own horses a moment later, none of them sparing anyone in the wagon train a glance. They were followed by Aeren and Eraeth on foot.

All their expressions were grim.

Colin felt the pressure around his throat tighten. "They look worried," he said, catching Karen's gaze. Her eyes were slightly widened. She glanced back toward the west, where the riders had come from, and bit her lower lip.

"Whatever it is," she said, turning back, "we'll outrun it."

Colin nodded, even though he heard the doubt in her voice beneath the forced conviction.

One of the Armory guardsmen, still on horseback, suddenly skidded his mount to a halt beside the still-moving wagon. "We have to pick up the pace," he gasped. "We need to move!"

He made to turn away, but Colin halted him with a shout. "Why? What is it?"

"The dwarren," the guard said, irritated. "Hundreds of them, headed this way. A war party. So get these wagons moving!"

Before Colin could respond, he kicked his horse, the animal leaping forward with a snort, head lowered as it charged toward the next wagon.

"Help me," Karen said, and Colin turned to see her herding the children nearest to them toward the back of the wagon. "Get them up inside. We'll want to push the wagons as fast as possible, and we don't want the children to slow us down."

Colin hefted a little boy up from beneath the armpits, the boy instantly bawling. He handed him off to the boy's older sister, already inside the wagon.

"Where's our mom?" the girl asked, voice trembling.

"I don't know, Lissa," Karen said. "I'll try to find her. Just take care of your brother for the moment, please?"

Lissa nodded seriously, hugging her wailing brother closer, her eyes as wide as saucers.

As soon as Karen hoisted the last kid in, Colin slapped the wagon's back and shouted toward the driver. The wagon lurched forward, trundling over the rough ground, bouncing and rattling. One of the kids cried out as they were thrown from their perch, but then all of them hunkered down beside the supplies. Colin and Karen broke into a trot at the wagon's back. Colin could see Lissa's terrified face over the back of the wagon, her eyes watching him, almost pleading. He swallowed against the bitterness in his own throat and looked away. He could think of nothing to say to her, nothing that would make things better.

They ran, the entire wagon train moving far too slowly across the open plains. The initial surge of adrenalin and fear pushed them through the evening hours, but then it began to wear off. Wagons began to lag, people to falter. The Armory rode back and forth along the train, urging everyone forward, but as darkness settled, clouds beginning to move overhead, obscuring the emerging moon and stars, even the Armory began to flag. Lightning flickered in the distance, the ethereal purple lightning of the plains, but they heard no thunder. The storm was moving toward them though. Colin could taste it on the wind, metallic and cold.

When one of the wagon wheels cracked, the driver plowing into a stone he couldn't see in the darkness, Colin's father reluctantly called a halt, and the wagons broke and made camp for the night. Tensions were high, men and women snapping at each other as food was prepared, as Paul and the others worked late into the night repairing the wagon wheel, cursing everything and everyone in sight. Colin and Karen settled down near one of the wagons on the grass, both ordered to try to sleep by Colin's mother as she bustled from one end of the camp to the other. They stared up into the black, featureless sky, listening to activity on all sides—the cursing, the pounding of tools, the sharp cry of a child hushed harshly by a woman's voice— until Colin heard Karen shift in the darkness, rolling onto her side, elbow propped on the ground.

"Are you scared?" she whispered.

Colin almost lied to her, the words instinctive. But then he thought of the gallows, of the horror of watching the wagon crash down the Bluff, of the terror of hearing the dwarren attacking, of fumbling with the ties on the wagons and smelling the smoke as the people inside cried out and scrabbled at the hides that trapped them.

"Yes," he murmured and was shocked to hear exactly how scared he was in the roughness of his voice. He could feel his heart beating, faster than usual, and he couldn't seem to make it slow down.

He jumped when he felt Karen's hand come to rest on his chest, as if she could hear his heart as well. But then he realized she'd laid her hand over the pendant she'd given him, the vow.

His heart faltered.

"Colin," she started to say, and Colin heard the question in her voice.

Before she continued, he said, without hesitation, "Yes." He didn't know when they'd have time to make the vow, but he knew he wanted it. They'd need Domonic to bind their blood together in the vial of the vow, to marry them in Diermani's eyes. As a priest, he was the only one in the wagon train who could do it, the only one who had the power.

Karen was silent a long moment. He thought she was crying, but he wasn't certain until she laid her head down on his chest and he felt the tears seeping through his shirt. He raised a hand tentatively to her head, and as he stroked her hair she nestled in closer. He could feel her trembling, could feel her silent sobs.

Eventually, he felt her grow still, heard her breathing slow. He began to drift off himself, but his mother's and father's voices drew him back.

"We'll never be able to outrun them, Tom!" His mother's voice was bitter, hard, but practical. "Not if they truly want to catch us. We're being slowed down by the wagons, by those on foot. The dwarren have gaezels. And if what you say is true, they don't have to worry about lugging around all of their supplies."

"What do you expect me to do, Ana? We can't just stop and hope to hold them off. Look at how many died when it was just a scouting party attacking us! Eleven men! Eleven! And this certainly isn't a scouting party following us now."

"What do the Alvritshai say? They seem rather calm about all of this."

Colin's father snorted. "They tried to warn us away, remember? They told us to head back west as soon as they found us. But no, we were too stubborn to listen to them."

"Walter is."

Colin tensed at the accusatory note in his mother's voice, felt the same taint of hatred in his own chest. Karen stirred in her sleep as if troubled, then settled.

Colin's father was silent a moment. Then: "It wasn't Walter's fault. And it wasn't the Alvritshai's fault either. None of us wanted to go back. We got ourselves into this mess because none of us has anything left to go back to in Portstown."

Colin heard his mother sigh.

"What do they say now? Do they know what's going on? Are the dwarren coming after us, as they did the previous wagon train? Gathering over a thousand men seems a little extreme to take out those of us that are left." Bitterness had entered her voice again, and it made Colin shiver. He didn't think they knew anyone could hear them. Their voices were soft, but unguarded. And he hadn't moved since they'd arrived, hadn't even opened his eyes.

Colin's father didn't say anything for long enough that Colin thought his parents had drifted asleep. But then: "If I understand Aeren, there's more than one group of dwarren. This group isn't really after us. Apparently, the groups are at war, and we've accidentally stumbled into the middle of an upcoming battle. We're trapped between three forces—the dwarren we saw to the west, another group coming up from the south, from across the underground river, and a third coming down from the northeast. From what Aeren says, the dwarren have been fighting each other—and the Alvritshai—for years."

"There are more Alvritshai out there?"

"Apparently Aeren is leading a small scouting party of his own, some kind of trial. He's sent the others back to warn the rest of the main group to the north."

"Why didn't he go himself? Why didn't he just abandon us?"

"Eraeth's been trying to convince him to do just that, but I think he feels responsible for us. He led us to the previous wagon train, right into the middle of the upcoming battle. He intended for us to see the burned out wagons and turn back west, but he didn't know the dwarren were gathering, didn't expect to run into their scouting party. He's made some type of vow to get us out if he can."

Before Colin's mother could respond, a low grumbling roll of thunder came from the northeast. The grass rustled as both his parents shifted position, and then his father swore.

"The storm's going to pass right over us," he said. "It's going to slow us down even more."

"But if the dwarren are fighting their own people, or they're gathering to fight the Alvritshai, they probably don't care about us," Colin's mother said. "We should be able to escape them."

"Not if we can't get out of their way. And right now, according to Aeren, we're caught neatly in the middle of them all. Our only chance is to head east, as fast as possible."

As if in answer, lightning flared, bright enough and close enough that Colin could see it through his eyelids. Thunder followed, but not closely. The storm was still distant.

"We'll have to move as soon as the wagon wheel is repaired," Colin's father said when the thunder had growled down into silence. "If we hope to have any chance of escaping, we'll have to travel all night, storm or not."

Colin heard his mother shift, knew she had stood by the sound of her voice. "I'll spread the word. You go check on the repairs."

He must have dozed after they moved off, because the next thing he knew, his mother was shaking him and Karen awake, and the storm was almost on top of them.

"Get as many of the kids into the wagon as possible and then head out!" she shouted over the wind. "Stay close to the wagon!" In a flash of lightning, he saw his mother's face, the lines of age he'd never seen there before stark, the gray in her hair he'd never noticed glowing silver as the wind blew it into her eyes and she pulled it aside in annoyance. The resultant crack of thunder shuddered in Colin's skin as he scrambled to his feet, Karen beside him. And then darkness descended, so complete he couldn't see his mother anymore, could barely see Karen's face though she was standing right beside him, her hand closed about his upper arm.

"What about the storm?" Karen yelled. "Shouldn't we wait it out?"

"There's no time! We'll have to weather through it!" Ana replied. Her voice came out of the night, torn by the wind, but they both knew she'd moved on to the next wagon.

Without a word, they stumbled to the back of the wagon, where two others were throwing supplies and children into the back, the older kids already inside shoving the supplies out of the way as fast as possible, the middle kids trying to quiet the younger ones, all of their faces suffused with fear in each flare of light from the storm. Lightning sizzled and crackled around them on all sides, thunder shuddered through the ground at their feet, and the wind tore at the flaps of the wagons, at the hides, at loose clothing and hair. Colin began heaving boxes and crates and pots into the wagon, while Karen helped with the kids. The only illumination besides the lightning was a single lantern sheltered inside the wagon, held by a boy who couldn't have been more than eight. At every crack of thunder, every flare of unnatural light, the lantern's flame seemed to dim, almost guttering out twice. The boy held the lantern as far from his body as he could.

And then the last of the wagon was packed, and suddenly a guardsman was there, on horseback. Seeing everything was ready, he bellowed to the driver, "Go! Move out!" and then he turned to peer out into the storm, into the jagged purplish lightning as it pummeled the plains. Colin saw three other wagons, saw the fourth already headed out, but they were all instantly lost as soon as the lightning ended.

"How are we going to stay together?" he shouted toward the guardsman.

The man gave him a sidelong look as the wagon began to move. "We're not even going to try. We'll head east, or as close to east as possible in this storm, and regroup once it's passed." He turned his attention to everyone, raised his voice to a shout. "Stay close to the wagon! If you lose it in the darkness, you may never find any of us again!" Then he spun his horse and trotted toward the front of the wagon.

"Colin," Karen said, her voice sharp with warning. She grabbed his arm and pulled him closer to the wagon, already beginning to fade out of sight. The rest of the women and men in their group edged closer to the wagon as well, some of them linking arms and hands, a few keeping hold of the back of the wagon itself.

They'd only moved a short distance when, with a warning splatter of light mist in their faces, it began to rain.

"Oh, great," Karen said, before she hunched her shoulders and bowed her head.

Colin was instantly drenched in the downpour, spluttering as the frigid water sluiced down his back. Holding Karen a little tighter, he plowed forward, keeping the wagon close to his left side.

They struggled through the storm, the lightning making the surrounding landscape harsh and ethereal, the grasses thrashing in the wind and rain, swirling like the ocean. During the first hour, Colin saw two of the wagons close by, but after that the worst of the lightning moved farther west, and any sign of the other groups in the wagon train vanished into the darkness. They were enfolded by torrential rain, by darkness, by the receding sound of thunder and the occasional crack of a strike nearby. Once he thought he saw the vibrant orange glow of a lantern's light out in the grass, but the image was fleeting, lost in the sheets of rain before he could turn and focus on it. And once he thought he heard shouting, close, but the wind tore the sounds away.

He lost track of time, his feet stumbling over each other, over stones and ridges of land he couldn't see, but he kept close to the wagon, reached out and brushed its side to make certain it was still there, even though he could hear the occasional creak of the wheels as they moved. At one point, the guardsman appeared out of nowhere, his horse snorting and stamping, and he shouted, "Have you seen Peg? Either of you?" When both Colin and Karen shouted no, he swore and rode past them. Colin heard him asking the rest of the group, catching only a word here and there, the rest torn away by the wind. He traded a grim look with Karen, and they trudged on. If Peg was lost, there was no hope of finding her until after the storm ended.

And they couldn't stop. Not with the dwarren behind them.

When the storm finally broke, the rain fading to a drizzle, then halting entirely, it was already midmorning, the light a pale, thin gray as clouds scudded by overhead. Colin glanced up into that sky, clothes soaked with chill water, hair plastered to his face, then turned toward Karen, shivering slightly at his side as she moved forward, but still holding tight to his arm. Her face was blank, her head bent, eyes on the grass that had been beaten flat by the rain.

He shook her gently. She turned exhausted eyes on him, her face white.

"It's over," he said.

The words took a moment to sink in, and then her steady footsteps faltered and she halted. She looked up into the sky, where patches of blue sky had begun to peek through as the clouds began to tatter.

She smiled. It was a weary smile, haggard and torn from lack of sleep, but it was still beautiful.

The guardsman galloped up from where the wagon had drawn to a halt at the top of a knoll. "Look for the other wagons. We need to regroup as quickly as possible. And keep an eye out for Peg. She got separated from the wagon during the storm."

Colin nodded as the guardsman moved on, then turned to scan the horizon. To the east, the plains sloped down from the ridge they stood on, the land rumpled, before hitting a flat area edged with darkness. In the vague light, it took Colin a moment to realize that the dark stain on the plains wasn't a shadow but a forest of trees, what looked like pines, the dark green, needled branches blowing in the wind. The forest stretched into the distance, both to the east and curving around to the south where the plains broke into low hills.

Movement caught his attention, and he tore his gaze away from the trees. "I see one of the wagons," he shouted.

"Where?" the Armory guardsman asked, and Colin pointed as he brought his horse up to Colin's side.

"There. Between us and the forest. They just rose up out of that dip."

The guardsman sighed with relief, a sound that didn't carry far at all.

"There are two more to the north," Karen said. "They're already headed toward us."

Colin turned away from the east and the darkness of the forest, caught sight of the two wagons Karen had spotted—

And then someone behind them muttered, "Holy Diermani protect us. Look!"

Everyone spun to where one of the women in the group pointed to the west. The storm still raged on the horizon, the black clouds lit from within by lightning above, rain and the cloud's darker shadow completely obscuring the plains below.

But as Colin watched, as the storm receded, something emerged from that shadow.

The dwarren. Thousands of them. Headed straight for the wagons. Fast.

The guardsman swore, and Colin felt his stomach clench tight.

"Barte!" the guardsman spat. The driver of the wagon leaned out from the side. "Get the damn wagon moving! Head toward the two wagons to the north! The dwarren are right behind us!"

Barte's pudgy face turned toward the west, his eyes going wide as he caught sight of the dwarren army, and then he vanished, the wagon shaking as he dropped back into his seat. Colin heard him shout at the horses, and the wagon rolled forward, but slowly. Far too slowly. The horses had been worked almost to their limit.

The guardsman watched the wagon begin ambling down the far side of the ridge, glanced toward the other two wagons, then back toward the dwarren, and he swore again, more vehemently.

"Someone's riding hard toward us from the other two wagons," Karen said. She frowned as she squinted into the distance. "I think it's your father, Colin. And Walter. The Alvritshai are right behind them on foot. I don't see Arten."

The guardsman kneed his horse and took off toward the figures, surging out ahead of them, his horse's hooves kicking up clods of dirt behind him. Frowning, Colin grabbed Karen's hand and said, "Come on."

They ran forward, slipping in the wet grass on the steep slope, but they outpaced the wagon and the rest of those walking beside it. Ahead, the guardsman and the others met. The guardsman shook his head, pointed back over the ridge. Everyone turned in that direction, including the Alvritshai, faces grim, and then Colin and Karen were close enough to catch the conversation.

"—we can't," his father was saying. "The reason we're headed toward you is there's another dwarren force to the north. They're converging here."

"What about the Alvritshai?" Walter spat, his face dark. But even though his words were harsh, there was a look of desperation around his eyes.

Tom frowned. "They're farther to the north, out of the dwarren's path."

For the first time, Colin noticed that Aeren and Eraeth had been joined by two other Alvritshai, both with bows strung and ready, their focus on the plains.

Looking at Aeren, whose gaze held his, the skin around his eyes tight with concern, Colin said, "Maybe we should join them. Maybe they can protect us."

But his father was already shaking his head. "We can't. We'll never make it in time; the dwarren are too close. We'll have to go east, take refuge in the forest, hope that the dwarren are more concerned with their own fight than with us."

Aeren suddenly stepped forward, his gaze flicking back and forth between Colin and his father. "No. No trees."

"Why not?"

Aeren turned his full attention on Tom with an intensity Colin hadn't seen there before, even during their formal first meeting, when they'd shared food and drink. "No trees. Sukrael there."

At the word sukrael, the other Alvritshai shifted, unsettled.

"Sukrael?"

Aeren motioned with his hands. "Sukrael," he said in frustration, in impatience, then pointed to the ground. "Sukrael!"

Everyone looked to where Aeren pointed in confusion.

"He's pointing to your shadow," Karen said, hesitantly.

"What the hell does that mean?" Walter asked. Behind him, the two wagons they'd been escorting topped the rise and trundled down toward them.

"It doesn't matter," Tom said, his back straightening as he saw his wife at the head of the wagons, her eyes wide with fear. "We're out of time."

He began to turn, but Aeren's hand suddenly latched onto his arm, held him in place, even though he sat on a horse. The other Alvritshai sucked in a sharp, stunned breath, their faces openly shocked, and Colin suddenly realized that none of the Alvritshai had ever touched any of them, had never gotten close enough except to hand over food. Now, Eraeth and the others took an uncertain step away from Aeren.

"No trees."

The words hung in the tense air. The guardsman's hand had fallen to his sword's hilt. The other Alvritshai—those with bows nocked—had shifted, their shock at Aeren's action gone now, their focus on the guardsman. The tableau held, Tom staring down into Aeren's face. Colin couldn't see what his father saw, but he'd heard the warning in Aeren's voice, could see the cold, rigid tension emanating from the Alvritshai's body.

And then Ana barked, "Tom! They're right behind us!"

Tom slid out of Aeren's grasp, and in a harsh voice, tinged with apology, he said, "We have no choice."

He broke his gaze with Aeren, spun toward the two

wagons. "Sam! Paul! Head toward the forest! The dwarren are right behind Colin's group as well! The forest is our only chance!"

The wagons turned instantly, Ana pivoting to wave everyone on foot in that direction. People moaned, all of them looking as exhausted as Colin felt, wet and weary, but edged with fear.

The guardsman yanked his horse's reins hard. "Barte!" he shouted. "Head west, head toward the forest!" But Barte couldn't hear him. With a muttered curse, he sped off, his horse leaping forward as he dug in his heels.

Eraeth snorted, said something obviously derisive to Aeren's back. Aeren's face darkened, and he called something heated in reply, not even turning, something that made Eraeth bow his head in shame.

Tom turned, brow furrowed. Then he nodded in Aeren's direction, ignoring the cold look Eraeth cast him. "Thank you. For everything."

Aeren nodded in return.

Colin felt his father's gaze fall on him, and something stabbed deep down into his gut at the despair he saw there. He'd never seen a look like that on his father's face before. Not even in Portstown.

"Colin," he said, his horse shifting closer, sensing its rider's tension. "Stay with the others. Help them as best you can."

It seemed he would say something more, but he shook his head instead. Then he and Walter spun their horses and rejoined the wagons. Overhead, the clouds began to clear completely, the gray sunlight strengthening to a late summer yellow, vibrant on the rain-washed grass all around. Colin felt it against his skin, felt it touch his hair, but he discovered it didn't warm him. It should have, but it didn't. Coldness had seeped into him—from the rain, the storm, the nightlong trek through the darkness—a coldness that penetrated deep, to his very bones. A coldness he'd seen in his father's eyes.

Aeren looked toward him, stepped close and grabbed his shoulders, locked eyes with him. "No trees," he said, adamantly, his hands tightening. And then, softly, sadly, "No trees."

"No trees," Colin repeated.

Aeren let his hands drop from Colin's shoulders, reluctantly.

At his side, Karen shifted. "Colin." One word. But Colin heard the terror in it, the need to move, to run.

"Let's go," he said, grabbing Karen's hand, but refusing to look in her eyes. He didn't want her to see what he'd seen in his father's eyes, didn't want her to feel as cold as he did.

They ran, back toward Barte and the wagon, now angled toward the dark line of the forest to their left, still shuddering down the slope of the ridge, the others scattered around it, all of them running, sprinting toward the safety of the forest. Colin glanced back over his shoulder, saw the Alvritshai standing alone on the plains, Eraeth trying to get Aeren to move, Aeren watching them retreat stoically, his expression troubled.

And then more movement caught his eye. Farther out on the plains, farther east, he saw the fifth wagon as it crested another ridge, silhouetted against the cloud-driven sky a moment before it plunged down the side of the slope toward them. Colin's heart leaped, and he skidded to a halt and cried out. A wordless shout, cut off as Karen's hand was wrenched from his own and they both stumbled to the grass.

"Colin!" Karen gasped, her breath harsh from running.

Colin ignored her, cupped his hands around his mouth as he bellowed, "The other wagon!" Ahead of them, the guardsman pulled his mount to a halt, frowning back at him, and Colin shouted, "It's the other wagon!" as he turned and pointed.

The Alvritshai had vanished.

The sudden elation over seeing the other wagon died on Colin's lips.

"Diermani's balls," he whispered to himself.

To the north, on the ridge to the right of the fifth wagon, the dwarren were spilling down the slope, riding their gaezels hard. A sudden cacophony of noise erupted from the dwarren as they spotted the wagon, a battle cry ripped from a thousand throats, threaded through with a sudden frenzy of drums, with the thunder of a thousand gaezel hooves and hundreds of dwarren feet pounding into the grassland as they charged. Colin couldn't see any

difference between this group of dwarren and the ones
they'd run into near the underground river, not at this
distance, but it didn't matter. The group of dwarren that
had attacked them appeared on the ridge to the southeast,
raising their own battle cry and they charged down into the
dip, the wagon trapped between them.

At his side, Karen gasped and scrambled to her feet. She
tugged on his shoulder. "Colin, we have to go." But Colin
didn't move, rooted to the spot in horror. He watched as
the driver of the wagon realized the dwarren were close,
watched as he lashed the horses, trying to get them to
run faster. Those on foot were scattered to the sides and
behind, running as fast as they possibly could, a few of the
men out in front of the wagon itself. One of the women
stumbled and fell, her shout faint with distance, almost lost
in the thundering charge of the dwarren armies—

And then, like an ocean wave, the dwarren army to
the north struck, the charging gaezels overrunning the
wagon, smothering them, the people on foot lost instantly,
trampled beneath a thousand hooves. The wagon remained
in sight for another breath, but then the driver was pulled
from his seat, the horses themselves cut down and dragged
beneath the horrendous tide of dwarren. The hides that
covered the wagon shuddered and jerked as the dwarren
surged around it, and then gave way, the faint screams of
children piercing the general roar on the plains.

Colin gasped, clutched at his chest as a searing ache
exploded there. He almost fell to his knees, but Karen's
hand suddenly latched onto his upper arm, fingers digging
into flesh.

In a voice that allowed no argument, she said, "Time to
go, Colin."

Colin stumbled as they began to run, staggered, but
caught himself, Karen ending up a few steps ahead of him.
Pain shot through his legs at the sudden exertion, but he
forced more speed from them as the battle cries of both
groups of dwarren escalated, gathering force and momentum, then breaking as behind him the two forces of charging gaezels met. The earth seemed to tremble beneath his
feet, the very air to shudder, but he couldn't tell for certain.
He was moving too fast, the chill air rushing against his
face, blotting out most of the sounds of the battle behind,

his feet thudding into the earth, legs lashed by the grass. Karen began to outdistance him, and he saw the guardsman and the rest of those from the wagon charging toward the forest ahead, his father, Walter, and the other two wagons already close to the trees. The fourth wagon, closer to the forest, had halted and turned, lurching toward them from the right. He felt a pressure against his back, felt certain that the dwarren themselves were riding hard behind him, were close enough that any second he'd be overrun, smothered by their sheer numbers, like those who'd been with the fifth wagon. Tears streamed from his eyes, and air burned in his lungs. A sharp stitch began to burrow its way into his side—

And suddenly he realized the wagons ahead had halted, had turned so their sides faced outward protectively, the sharp line of the forest at their backs. Men were scrambling to get weapons, women yanking the children out of the wagon beds and ushering them behind the incomplete circle, near the forest. Colin saw Karen slow, come to a gasping halt, leaning against one of the wagons. He tried to slow down himself, his heart thundering in his chest . . . and tripped.

He spilled to the ground, hitting hard with one shoulder, his face smashing into the grass. He tasted damp stalks and dirt, spat them out as he rolled, coming to a stop near one of the wagon's wheels.

He lay for a moment in the wet grass, felt the sun beating down on his back, then rolled to one side.

"Colin! Are you all right?"

Colin blinked up into Karen's terrified face and nodded. "I'm fine," he coughed, out of breath, his throat raw. He lurched into a sitting position, the stitch in his side flaring. "I need my sling."

"Maybe not." Karen motioned toward the plains. "The dwarren started to follow us, but they've halted."

A twinge of shame made Colin wince. He'd thought the dwarren were right at his back, thought he'd felt their breath against his neck.

But then he noticed the group of dwarren. They'd stopped over a thousand paces away, the main group milling about behind the leaders in the front, as if reluctant to come any farther forward. The leaders stared at the

wagons for a long moment, discussed something among
themselves—

And then they motioned to the dwarren in their group,
spun their mounts, and charged back toward the battle raging on the plains behind them.

Colin frowned. He saw his father, Walter, Jackson, and
Arten standing off to one side, their faces creased with
worry, with confusion. The rest of the men and guardsmen
stood in front of the wagons with weapons ready. They
were all tense, all grim.

The dwarren retreat didn't make any sense. Those from
the wagons had no hope of holding them off. The dwarren
could overrun the wagons in a matter of moments.

Unless—

No trees.

Colin's eyes widened in realization.

He spun toward Karen. "They're not approaching the
forest." Karen's brow creased, still confused. "They're not
coming close to the forest. There must be something in the
forest! In the trees!"

And as Colin saw comprehension dawn on Karen's face,
someone screamed.

Colin's first thought was of his mother.

He scrambled to his feet, but before he could take a
single step toward the side of the wagons facing the woods,
the piercing scream broke, cut cleanly from the air, followed immediately by the panicked cries of children and
more screams.

"The forest!" Arten barked, his sword waving toward
the backs of the wagons.

Colin grabbed Karen's hand and lurched toward the
space between the two nearest wagons.

They stumbled into chaos. Children were screaming,
fleeing the edge of the forest, tears coursing down their
faces. One of the youngest boys collided with Colin before
slipping around him, the rest banking away as Colin's father and the others emerged between the other wagons.
Colin couldn't see what had spooked them—

But then one of the guardsmen shouted, "Look!"

His eyes snapped toward where the guard pointed, saw
the terrified women herding the children away from a
crumpled body on the ground. The woman lay facedown

in the grass. Someone had thrown a black blanket over her shoulders, although where they'd found a black blanket in the mad rush to escape the dwarren Colin couldn't fathom.

At his side, Karen gasped, and Colin suddenly realized it wasn't a blanket.

The black form rose from the woman's body, moving fluidly, like water, like silken cloth, an intangible swath of darkness that reared upward with insidious grace. Before Colin could react, could even suck in a shocked breath, it leaped from the crumpled form on the ground toward the retreating women, lashed out—

And one of the women dropped, collapsed like a sack of grain. The shadow fell on her with a visceral shriek, like a predator onto prey.

"Holy Diermani," one of the guardsmen whispered. "What is that thing?"

The children had seen it, and fresh screams broke out, those retreating breaking apart, all semblance of order lost. Arten began barking orders, men surging forward, hustling the women and children behind them, until someone shouted, "There's more than one of them!"

Karen's hand clamped down hard on Colin's shoulder, spun him slightly. He tore his gaze away from the blackness feeding off of the fallen woman, centered it on the forest.

Beneath the trees, the forest was dark with shadow. *And those shadows were moving.*

The horses—still tethered to their wagons—whickered nervously and danced back, one rearing, hooves kicking the air, eyes white as it shrieked, a hideous sound that Colin felt in his bones. As the last of the women and children passed the line of men, one of the shadows slipped free of the confines of the forest, slid out into the vibrant sunlight. It flowed outward toward one of the tethered horses, moving fast, the men closest gasping and skittering back, the entire group shifting as children whimpered and someone sobbed. The shadow hesitated a moment as the horse yanked hard at the reins that held it in place, so hard the wood of the tongue of the wagon creaked—

Then the Shadow flowed forward, covered the horse from neck to shoulder, latching itself onto the horse's form, sinking deeper into the horse's flesh as if it were insubstantial. The horse shuddered and stilled. Its eyes rolled and its lips pulled back, baring teeth. It snorted once, then collapsed to its knees and rolled to the ground, dead, its head twisting as the reins held it upright, its neck contorting to an unnatural angle.

The Shadow rose up from its body, a malevolent shroud, glistening and throbbing.

Then it turned. Colin sensed it focus on those closest, on Colin and everyone huddled on this side of the wagon, and he felt a cold dread sink into his chest.

Paul charged. Everyone gasped. Colin's father shouted, "No!" The smith swung his ax, grunting with the effort, his face suffused with a mixture of rage and fear.

It should have cleaved the Shadow in two. Instead, the ax passed through the Shadow as if it weren't there.

The swing pulled Paul off-balance. He stumbled, cried out in surprise—

And then the Shadow lashed out, a tendril passing through Paul's outstretched arm.

Paul screamed, the ax dropping from his grip. He jerked the arm toward his chest, cradled it as if it had been broken, his breath sucked in sharply. Sam bellowed, "Watch out!" and rushed forward, caught by Tom before he could take two steps. Paul looked up in time to see the Shadow rear above him, and Colin saw utter fear register on his face—

And then the Shadow descended, falling like a shroud, smothering him. In less than a heartbeat, Paul's body crumpled to the ground.

Colin found he couldn't breathe, that his arms and legs had gone numb. He could hear his heartbeat, could taste something sour on his tongue, could smell his own rank sweat, but he couldn't *move*, couldn't *think*.

Everything was happening too fast. Far, far too fast.

Fresh screams broke out, and Colin tore his gaze away from Paul's body as more Shadows emerged from the forest, surging forward toward the line of men and the women and children huddled at the base of the wagon. The nearest guardsman swung his blade, more reflex than thought, but like Paul he staggered as his sword passed cleanly through the Shadow in the lead. In the next instant the black creature had swept through his arm and leg. He cried out and fell to the ground, his sword slipping free of his grip as he rolled to escape the next slash of the Shadow. But it ignored him, heading toward the women and children near the wagons, heading toward the group closest to Colin.

It sprang, and the children scattered, screaming as it lashed out in all directions in a strangely graceful, violent dance. Two bodies fell to the ground, skin blanched white. A boy struggled away on his elbows, his legs dragging behind him, tears streaming down his contorted face. And still more Shadows emerged from the forest, gliding out into the sunlight and striking at the sudden chaos that raged on all sides. Colin stood rigid, Karen's hand clutched tight, unable to move. He heard names being called out, orders barked, heard someone bellow desperately, "Nothing stops them!" while before him more bodies fell to the ground. Colin could barely breathe, the sound of his heart pulsing in his ears, overwhelming the screams, drowning them out. The sour taste in his mouth turned bitter and dry, as if his tongue were coated with ash. He watched in silence as Lyda ran past, shrieking, her hair streaming out behind her, her hand on her swollen belly, a slew of the black Shadows trailing her. He watched as she stumbled, watched her roll onto her back, still shrieking, her face twisted into pure terror, watched as the Shadows converged on her like carrion birds to dead flesh. She rolled to her side and clawed at the ground, dragging herself away, but the Shadows were too swift, pouncing on her, feeding off of her, off of the unborn child inside her, their actions far more frenzied than they were with the others, far more greedy, more gluttonous. Her fingers dug at the earth as her screams broke down into tortuous sobs, as tears streaked her face, and then a Shadow lashed out, almost impatiently, its form passing through her neck, and with a gasp her head fell to the ground and her struggles ceased.

Colin choked, his stomach seizing, his chest tightening, bile rising up sharp and acrid in the back of his throat. He struggled to draw air into his lungs, but he couldn't, struggled to swallow the bitterness and nausea and horror—

Until a hand clamped onto his shoulder, the grip so hard he winced, the paralysis shuddering in his chest beneath the wave of pain. He sucked in air, felt something tear in his throat, and deeper, in his lungs, and coughed as he staggered and turned.

"Colin! Karen!" his father barked, his voice rougher than usual, higher in pitch. He shook him, shook Karen as well, her eyes wide and shocked. "You have to get out of here. We can't stop them. We can't even hurt them. You have to run! Both of you! Back to the plains!"

"But what about—"

Before he could finish, his father's grip tightened. Leaning forward, his voice black, he growled, "Run, goddamn you!" And then he shoved them both, hard, shoved them back toward the space between the wagons, back toward the plains and the dwarren's battle. Colin tripped, landed hard on his ass, Karen's hand tearing free from his, but his father had already turned. He scanned the chaos before him, face tight, then shouted, "Ana!" and dashed off to the left.

Colin lurched to his feet, took off after his father, but within two steps he was brought up short by Karen as she grabbed his arm, spun him around. "Where are you going? You heard your father. We have to get out of here!"

"I have to help him. I have to find my mother."

"But he told you to get out!"

"The dwarren are out there! There's nowhere to go." Karen bit her lower lip, wavering, so he drew in a sharp breath and added, "What about your father?"

Her eyes darkened, angry and concerned at the same time. "You bastard," she whispered. Then she spun, searching those nearest, trying to see past them. "Over here."

They stumbled away, one of the Armory guardsmen staggering in front of them, a Shadow reaching for the man's chest. Colin dodged, slipped to his knees in the grass, Karen keeping him upright, shot a glance left and right, searching for his mother, for a glimpse of either of their fathers—

And caught sight of Walter instead.

The Proprietor of Haven stood with his back to one of the wagons, his sword leveled before him, the blade twitching back and forth among three different Shadows. A fourth Shadow writhed on the ground, feeding off Jackson, the Company's representative staring up into the sunlight, eyes glazed with death, skin white, yet still beaded with sweat. Walter hissed as one of the Shadows feinted with a tendril of darkness, his sword jerking toward the black shape. He wiped sweat from his face with the back of one arm, the gesture short and rough and desperate, then barked as another Shadow slid closer, this one from the opposite side. His sword swung toward the second Shadow, hovered point first, trembling there, while his gaze followed the movements of the third.

Colin frowned. The Shadows were playing with him, like cats who'd trapped a mouse in a dusty corner of an alley. They didn't seem as frenzied as when they'd first attacked, and the ones surrounding Walter glistened with a fluid gold color.

And then Walter noticed them, his eyes settling on Colin with a flare of hope. "Colin!" His voice was tight and thick and shook with fear. "Colin, help me!"

One of the Shadows slipped closer, and Walter growled a warning, his sword swinging toward the new threat as another Shadow edged forward, almost imperceptibly. The fourth one—the one feeding on Jackson—began to rise, shimmering with a patina of gold in the light. It moved sluggishly, but with more intent, as if it had been sated.

Colin didn't move. He could feel Karen at his side, slightly behind.

"Colin!" Walter yelled, and Colin jerked. No fear this time in Walter's voice. It was threaded with demand, with arrogance. The voice of a Proprietor.

Colin thought about the alley, about the beatings, about the day Walter had kicked him hard enough that he'd pissed his own pants. He thought about the arrest, the gallows, the day spent in the pillory, unable to move, unable to even scratch an itch, thirsty and hungry, covered in blood from his own struggles and the spit of the other townspeople. He thought about the look on Walter's face as he left him in the alley, about the satisfied smirk he'd given him on the gallows, and he heard Walter's laughter as he pissed on him from the darkness while he was in the penance locks.

A cold rage settled over Colin, the same rage he'd felt as his mother cleaned his wounds after the locks, as she cleaned the piss from his body. A rage Colin had shoved deep down inside himself, that had simmered next to his heart since he'd been released from the pillory, seething as they crossed the plains, as they climbed the Bluff, as they hunted and camped and struggled to survive.

Colin let that hate out now, let it course down his arms, tingling with heat, prickling his skin. He let it show in his eyes, his back straightening.

Walter stilled, his eyes widening slightly, his sword dropping a few inches toward the ground.

With a surge of satisfaction, Colin spat to one side and turned his back, turned toward Karen. He caught a flicker of motion as one of the Shadows leaped, heard Walter curse, saw the so-called Proprietor duck down and roll beneath the underside of the wagon out of the corner of his eye, the Shadows a flicker of black movement behind him, and then he dismissed Walter completely from his mind.

Karen eyed him with a faint frown. "We need to find our parents. *Now*."

The space between the wagons and the trees was littered with bodies, with Shadows and shrieking forms. He saw Sam swinging wildly with a whip, two women at his back, saw another group of men make a break for the open plains behind, saw three children huddling in the grass beneath one of the wagons and recognized Lissa's face as she raised her head and stared out at the chaos, her younger brother's body held protectively to her chest, his face buried in her arms so he wouldn't be able to see. Colin headed toward the kids, had made it halfway to them, dodging feeding Shadows as he went, when Karen pulled him up short with a frantic, "Dad!"

Colin spun around. Karen's father stood protectively over three others, a mother and her two children, their backs to the last wagon, a sword held uselessly before him. His face was lined in fury, with pure and unadulterated rage, the most alive and intense Colin had seen the man since he'd met Karen and her father in Lean-to. All the sorrow, all the grief over losing his wife and two children on the passage across the Arduon Ocean, had been transformed into one goal, one purpose: keep the Shadows at bay.

And the Shadows were playing with him, as they'd played with Walter. Nearly all of them were now, their initial frenzy gone. They moved with purpose, with intent, with a cold intelligence.

Karen's shout distracted her father. He turned, yelled, "Karen!"

And the Shadows struck.

Karen's hand wrenched from Colin's. He cried out, tried to catch her, to hold her back. He heard her scream, "Dad!" again as she charged forward, her hair streaming out behind her, her dress flapping around her feet.

Colin leaped after her, his heart thundering in his chest, his skin flushed with sudden prickling heat. Not enough to smother the coldness, but it burned in his arms, his legs, his lungs. Nothing mattered but Karen and her father, nothing but the Shadows that had drawn back, their glistening darkness—so like cloth—shuddering outward as they readied to attack. All sound dampened except for his breath and the pulse of blood in his ears. Everything faded except for the brilliant patch of sunlight before the wagon.

Karen's father drew himself up, back straight, as the Shadows streamed forward, smooth and deadly. He didn't even use the sword. He tried to block the Shadows with his own body, his own life. The Shadows slid through his chest and pulled themselves up over his torso even as Colin saw the life in his eyes dim, as his body began to fall.

"No!" Karen screamed, and stumbled, reaching for her father, ignoring the Shadow that had bypassed him and those he protected, that was converging on her. Colin felt his heart shudder in his chest, felt the metal and glass of the vow burning against the skin beneath his shirt, felt a spurt of adrenaline shove him the last short space between them as a roar built in his throat.

He threw himself at Karen, the roar escaping. A roar of denial, of hatred, of anger and fury and determination.

A moment before he struck her, before his arms wrapped around her and pulled her down, he saw a tendril from one of the Shadows lash out, saw it connect, felt its bitter coldness as it passed over his shoulder.

Then he and Karen were rolling, his roar choked off as they struck the ground. Pain tore through his shoulder and he gasped, but he held Karen tight, tried to protect her as they tumbled, arms flailing wildly. They struck the wheel of the wagon. Wood cracked, and Colin's shoulder twisted even more, pain shooting down his back, his entire arm going numb, tingling viciously, but he ignored it all, not even crying out. He struggled with Karen's body, with the limp arms tangled with his own, with the folds of her dress.

Rolling onto his back, his shoulders propped against the broken wheel, legs straight before him, her body over his, he shifted her toward him, fumbled for her face.

"Karen," he gasped, and tasted blood on his lips, felt where he'd bitten the inside of his mouth. "Karen! It's all right. It's all right. I couldn't save your father, but—"

His hands found her face, touched the skin there. Skin still slick with sweat but cold, so very cold. Like ice.

His breath caught, and something squeezed his chest hard, tightened like iron, like the slats of the penance locks. Tightened and wouldn't let go. Beneath, something hard and bitter and fluid began to build, began to press outward, constrained by the locks.

He tried to swallow and couldn't. His mouth was suddenly full of saliva, the back of his throat thick with phlegm, with the taste of blood, and still he couldn't swallow, his throat working, a strange heat seething up his neck and into his face, burning in the skin beneath his eyes, prickling in his hair. He shoved the sensations away, shoved down hard on the pressure in his chest. His hand brushed Karen's hair away from her brow, and he moved, so that her face rolled toward him, the motions careful, gentle.

"Karen?" he choked out, the name barely audible, almost lost in the pounding of blood in his ears, in his head. He reached for Karen's cheek, his hand trembling, reached to touch her forehead above her dusky dead eyes, reached for the freckles that brushed her skin, even though he could feel the Shadows closing in around him, around them both. He traced the contours of her nose, touched the corner of her mouth, her too pale lips.

And then the pressure inside became too much. The penance locks broke.

He screamed and clutched her body close, felt the vow's pendant crushed between them, felt its heat burning into his skin. He screamed into the blackness of the Shadows that loomed before him, the sunlight bright around them—a sunlight far, far too bright for the death taking place all around him, far, far too golden. He screamed into the face of the sukrael as the pain inside him surged outward, as it coursed along his arms and through his body, as it shuddered through his chest in waves. He shoved the hatred and grief away, toward the closest Shadow, the one reaching toward him with a tendril of darkest night, glistening with flecks of gold. A tendril that bled cold, that bled death.

And the Shadow hesitated.

Colin's scream grew ragged and then broke.

He stared up at the Shadow before him—at the sukrael—stared up into its cold, considering darkness—

And then he pulled Karen's limp body even closer, leaned forward over it, his head bowed down over hers, her face hidden in his shoulder. He could smell her hair, like freshly cut hay, like sunlight, like a breeze from the sea.

"I should have run faster," he whispered into Karen's ear, her hair tickling his face, catching in his mouth. "I should never have let go." His face twisted into a soundless sob, and he squeezed his eyes shut, tears slick against his skin, tasting of salt.

The Shadows hesitated, then closed in. But not in a frenzy. He felt the first tendril slide through his arm, touching, tasting, testing. For what, he didn't know, but they did not swarm over him as they had the others. They'd already fed. They needed him for something else. He shuddered, the ice of its touch sinking deep, the entire limb tingling, frigid, then going mercifully numb. He pulled Karen closer still with his other arm, buried his face in her shoulder, and felt one of the tendrils slide smoothly into his twisted shoulder, flicker deeper into his chest, sampling him. He gasped as the cold touched his lungs, as air froze deep inside him, and he felt the Shadows respond with an ecstatic shiver. They savored his grief, savored his pain, reveled in his soul, in his life, in his warmth. The gold against their black forms shifted in patterns, as if they were speaking to each other, arguing, coming to a decision.

Without looking, he felt them rear above him, felt them tense to smother him, their ethereal forms blocking out the sun.

But the Shadows halted. Another shiver passed through them. Gold glistened in hatred and contempt and rage.

And then they withdrew.

Colin lifted his head from Karen's shoulder, his face smeared with tears, with snot. It required more effort than he thought it would, because where the Shadows had tasted him, the coldness had sunk in deep. But in the space between the forest and the circled wagons, all of the Shadows were fleeing, slipping back into the forest, back beneath the trees, leaving dozens of bodies behind in the grass. He could see where Sam had fallen, could see Lissa's crumpled form beside that of her brother beneath one of the wagons, could see the bodies of the horses, still trapped in their harnesses.

None of the bodies were moving. Except for the faint roar of battle from the dwarren somewhere farther out on the plains, there was no sound. Here, near the wagons, it was unnaturally silent, unnaturally still.

The last of the Shadows vanished beneath the trees. A wisp of darkness in the sunlight, and then nothing.

Colin sat, quiet and motionless. The pressure in his chest was gone, leaving behind a vast, empty hollowness, as if he were a shell, scoured clean. Tears streamed down his face, and his chest burned with cold, part of it numbed by the Shadow's touch, that numbness seeping inward, spreading. He couldn't feel his arm or shoulder at all.

He stared out over the bodies, over the trampled grass, a few upright stalks shuddering in a breeze he couldn't feel. He stared at the trembling stalks, tears dripping from his chin. He breathed in the scent of hay, of upturned earth, and the acridness of pine.

He decided he'd sit there until the numbness claimed him completely.

Lights appeared in the forest. They flickered between the trees, pale at first, hidden within the shadows. But then they burst out into the sunlight, burning a harsh white, a dozen of them, perhaps more. He couldn't keep track of them. They flared out over the bodies, spun above them, circled the wagons and the dead horses, paused over Lyda and her swollen belly, over the children. They ducked between the wagons, beneath them, found Lissa and her brother and the other boy that had hidden with them. They checked inside the wagons as well.

And they spoke. Like the rustle of leaves in a gust of wind. Soft and ephemeral, yet tense with indignation, with horror, with despair.

. . . too late, too late . . .

. . . sooner, should have come sooner . . .

... we didn't know, didn't know ...

... all dead, all dead ...

Colin let his head fall back against the wagon wheel with a thump. He couldn't hold it up any longer, didn't want to. The coldness from the Shadows had penetrated deeper into his chest, into the muscles on one side of his neck. He could feel it touching his heart, could feel it seeping into his other lung, reaching for his throat. His breath became shallow. He struggled to draw in air as he stared up into the pale blue sky, at the wisps of clouds that drifted by.

One of the white lights flared into view above him, its light so harsh he squinted.

... one still lives! ...

The light was joined by another, and another. They dove closer, and he turned his head away, closed his eyes.

... barely, barely ... he's been touched by the others, but not killed ... why? ... why was he touched, not killed? ...

... they plan something ...

... touched too deep, too deep ... he won't survive ...

... no ... we can save him ...

... how? ...

... the Lifeblood ... the Well ...

Through squinted eyes, Colin saw the lights retreat slightly. Their voices receded, but their light flared, brighter and brighter. Others gathered as the lights argued, until one of the lights flared so brightly that Colin winced, even with his eyes mostly closed.

... enough! ... there is no time to argue ... he will die ...

... we can't ... he is the one who will pay, not us ...

... he is our responsibility ... we allowed this to happen ...

... we must save him if we can ...

The lights returned to hover above him.

... it won't matter ... he'll never make it to the Well ...

One of the lights flared in irritation, in warning, and the rest backed off slightly.

The light that remained drifted closer.

... stand ... you must stand and walk ...

Colin sighed, felt the weight of Karen's body against him, so heavy, heavier than he thought possible, holding him down. He felt the vow cutting painfully into his skin. His throat closed shut, and he shook his head in denial, tried to say, "No," but no sound came out.

. . . you must . . .

"No," he managed, his voice rough. He looked down at Karen's body, her face still hidden in his shoulder.

The light flared brighter in annoyance.

. . . you'll die . . .

He shot a glare at the light. "Let me die!"

The light considered this in silence. Then it dipped lower, so close that Colin could feel its light against his face, tingling in his skin, the fine hairs on his arms standing on end. A shiver coursed through him, and he drew in an involuntary gasp of air. He smelled earth, damp and moist. And leaves.

. . . would she have wanted you to die? . . .

Colin stilled, the indrawn breath caught in his throat, lodged there. He stared past the light, past the bodies, into the distance.

He heard his father screaming into his face, *Run, goddamn you*!

A fresh wave of grief sliced through him, and he swallowed it down, biting back a sob with a choked gasp. He glanced down at Karen's body, squeezed it tight again as he fought back more tears, and then let her roll away, so he could see her face.

It hurt more than he thought he could bear. He leaned forward and kissed her forehead, tasted her dried sweat, ignored the unnatural chill of her skin. He struggled for something to say, but nothing came, and so he whispered hoarsely, "I'm sorry."

And then he struggled out from beneath her body, the arm touched by the Shadows completely dead and useless, a limp weight at his side. Fresh tears started, refused to be held back, and he cried out as circulation returned to his legs. With a broken sob, he managed to shove Karen's body off of him completely, something in his chest tearing as he crawled away on his knees. He collapsed into the grass, uncertain he'd be able to move any farther, but the light grew insistent, a whisper of sound in the background, urging him forward, and so he shoved himself up with his good arm, pulled himself upright, staggered to his feet.

He didn't look back. Tears blurred his eyes as the lights led him beneath the cover of the trees, into the shadow of the forest, into its cool heart. He stumbled along behind them, listened to their encouragement, and the farther he walked—brushing against the bark of tree trunks, catching in limbs, tripping over fallen branches, his dead arm a hindrance—the deeper the Shadow's coldness seeped into his chest. His breath grew ragged and sharp as that coldness crept into his throat and down across his breastbone. Fingers of ice dug deep into his other lung, began to close about his heart. It became harder and harder to breathe, and he panicked. He'd thought the coldness would seep over him completely, as if he were going to sleep, but the deeper it clawed, the more he realized that he'd suffocate first, and so he lurched forward, moved faster, the lights themselves becoming frenzied, speeding ahead and then dancing impatiently.

. . . not far now, not far . . .

Colin began to wheeze, his breaths coming in strained whistles, and his heart began to stutter, to shudder, as the ice sank deeper. He gasped, collapsed to his knees, and saw the light that had spoken to him earlier flare before him, saw that the trees had given way to the amorphous shapes of white buildings, hidden in the gloom, that the ground beneath was patched with stone, like cobblestones. But all of that was peripheral.

. . . get up! . . . almost there! . . .

He clawed at his throat, sucked in another thin breath of air, and flung himself forward, tripping at the top of a set of stairs, then falling and rolling down their length before coming up hard against a lip of stone. Not white stone, like the buildings, but rough stone, rounded like river stone, with all the colors of the earth.

. . . drink! . . . drink now or the Shadows will take you! . . .

Colin reached for the edge of the stone, pulled himself up, his breath lost completely, his lungs no longer working, his entire chest a pit of numbness, of bitter cold, all except for his heart. He could no longer feel the base of his throat. He dragged himself up the stone wall, hung over its edge and realized that it held a wide pool of utterly clear water; but he didn't pause to reflect on its clarity, on its stillness. He dipped his good hand into it and cupped it to his mouth, swallowed it greedily, felt it spilling down his neck, staining his shirt, burning against the harshness of the vow. He drank as much of it as he could before the frigid claw at his heart squeezed tight, before the struggle to breathe sapped his strength, and then he sank onto his back on the edge of the well.

He stared up into the sunlight above, into the blue sky that seemed so distant. He strained for another breath, but his chest would not work.

The claw around his chest squeezed hard, and he felt his heart stop.

Darkness closed in at the edges of his vision, crept in slowly. He gazed into the deep sky as it began to recede, growing brighter, the gold deeper, its edges fine and brittle. As the darkness closed in tighter, as the muscles in his good arm and his legs relaxed and he sagged down against the river stone beneath him, two of the lights drifted into his sight.

. . . were we in time? . . . will he live? . . .

And then the sky, the lights, and the golden sun went black.

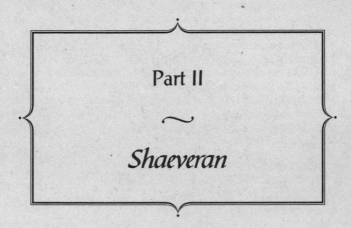

Part II

~

Shaeveran

11

COLIN WOKE WITH A START, eyes flaring wide, a moan escaping his lips, the sound torn with grief. He choked it off, coughed into the darkness of his room, then raised an aged hand to rub at his face. He wiped away the tears that wet his skin and sighed—a tired sigh, a weary sigh—and his hand closed over the crescent-shaped pendant on his chest.

He'd been dreaming again. The same dream he'd had these last long years, since he'd drunk from the Well, since he'd choked down the cold, sweet waters of the Lifeblood.

How many years now? He couldn't remember. Too many. And yet apparently not enough. Not if he could still wake with the feel of tears drying on his skin. Although he knew why the dreams had returned recently, knew why they seemed so fresh.

He grimaced and sat up on his cot, moving slowly, letting the pendant go. His feet touched the cool white marble of the floor, and he shivered, the sensation running down into his arms, tingling in his fingers. He shrugged, stretched the muscles in his back, wriggled his toes, and then stood, leaning on the cot for support as he yawned and reached for the robe tossed on the chair beside the bed.

He stilled when he saw the black mark on his arm, felt the familiar frisson of fear, followed immediately by anger. He pulled his arm back and covered the mark with one hand, rubbing the skin over his wrist, as if he could massage the mark away. But when he withdrew his hand, it remained. Like a bruise, but deeper, darker. The discoloration was *beneath* his skin, not on the surface, and it swirled like oil, as if black blood had pooled there, pulsing with his heartbeat.

And it had grown, was now nearly the size of his thumb. Seven years ago it had only been the size of a grain of sand. He'd almost dismissed it as a mole or freckle, but when he showed it to Osserin and the rest of the Faelehgre . . .

He grunted, reached again for the robe, the motion laced with anger. He pulled the robe up over his head, settled the folds with a disgruntled jerk—

And his stomach clenched with pain.

He paused, closed his eyes, and pressed one hand against his side as the pain intensified. Through the cloth of his robe, he could feel his aged skin grow hot, as if with a fever. But then the pain peaked and faded.

He let his held breath out in a sigh and straightened, massaging his side as the heat in his skin dissipated. The pain hadn't been this bad since those first few years in the forest, when he'd begun experimenting with the water and its effects, with its powers. He'd gone almost a year without going to the Well then, to see how long he could last without drinking it, how long he could suffer through the pain. A year.

He'd have to go much longer than that this time.

He frowned at the thought. How long *had* it been since he'd been to the Well? Two months? Three? More?

He didn't know. The days blurred into one another in the forest, weeks and months passing without notice. But it didn't matter. Not anymore, not now that the black mark had made its appearance. The Faelehgre had warned him that this would happen, that eventually the Well would claim him. He hadn't believed them, even when the first pains had begun. He'd ignored them, ignored all of their warnings. He'd stayed, certain that they were wrong, that he'd be able to resist, that he could remain here, within the forest, near the Well, unchanged. Or if not unchanged, at least *human*.

Then the black mark had appeared.

He had to leave. Now. But leaving was proving to be difficult. He didn't *want* to go.

And the Well was more powerful than he'd thought.

Troubled, he reached for the cedar staff that leaned

against the end of the bed. His fingers closed about the worn wood near the grip, and he unconsciously reached out and touched the remnant life-force that imbued the staff, felt it twine around his own. The scent of cedar overwhelmed him, and he closed his eyes and breathed in deeply, drew the scent into his lungs. For a moment, he literally *felt* the tree that had sacrificed part of itself to form the staff, felt the wind brushing through its needles, the roughness of its bark, the musky earth that fed its tangle of roots . . .

Then the sensation faded.

He exhaled with a huff, scanned the confines of the room he had claimed for his own decades ago here among the Faelehgre ruins, running through what he'd need to bring with him. He moved to the corner and dug through layers of discarded clothing; he tossed most of it aside but chose a few pieces to take with him. He'd wear the robes if he could, but he packed a shirt and breeches, sandals, boots, stowing it all in a satchel he could sling across his back; he'd need them once he reached the Escarpment and the edge of human lands. He'd take the staff, of course, and his sling, but what else?

Standing, he surveyed the room, spotted the bowl he used to hold tinder, the flint beside it. A lantern he'd salvaged from the wagons after the Shadows attacked so long ago sat next to them. He shoved the bowl and flint into the pack, then began sorting through the rest of his supplies. Most of it he'd had no use for in the forest, although he hadn't known it at the time. But some of it could be used for trade—pots and pans, brooches and other jewelry. He'd need some coin once he passed beyond the plains and dwarren lands. Everything had come from the chests and crates stacked in the wagons. He'd taken nothing from the bodies of those the Shadows had killed except the vial of pink-tinged water he'd found in his father's pocket. He wrapped this in cloth and stowed it away.

Then he ran across the knife.

He paused, setting the bolt of cloth that had covered the blade aside distractedly. He reached for the knife, hesitated a moment, then picked it up. It was meant for eating, its blade no longer than his fingers, although the edge was sharp and would cut flesh easily. He knew. After he'd awakened in the forest, near the Well—after he came to realize that he'd been saved but that everyone else had perished—he hadn't wanted to live. So he'd slid the knife into his heart, had felt the warmth of his heart's blood spill over his hands when he pulled it free with a shuddering gasp and then collapsed. He'd heard Osserin cry out in shock, had smiled as the Faelehgre's light hovered over him, the Faelehgre yelling, *You fool! You utter fool!* He'd gathered the encroaching darkness to him willingly, succumbing to it with a grateful sigh.

And then he'd woken up, leaves blowing into his face, the bloody knife half fallen out of his grasp. The ground around him had been saturated with his blood. His shirt had been matted to his body, a rent in the fabric above his heart where he'd shoved the knife through it. Blood had coated the inside of his mouth and he'd rolled to spit it out—

To discover that his chest hurt. A pain so deep he'd gagged, then curled up into a fetal position and shuddered with its intensity. There wasn't a mark on his skin, but he could feel the wound deep inside, a wound that hadn't completely healed yet, a wound that should have been fatal.

It's the Lifeblood, Osserin had explained as he healed. *When you drank from the Well, the Lifeblood saved you from the Shadow's touch and in the process it . . . changed you.*

Colin turned the blade over in his hands in his room, then slid it into his pack as well. He hadn't tried to kill himself since that day, didn't intend to try again. That had been a dark moment, not even two weeks after he'd drunk from the Well. A moment of utter despair.

And it had been the first sign that the Lifeblood hadn't simply saved him from the Shadows. It had altered him in some fundamental way.

He thought of the black mark on his wrist and grimaced. "And it's changing me still."

Slinging the pack over his shoulder, he scanned the room, but he saw nothing else he needed, nothing he wanted. Grabbing an empty flask and the lantern, he turned and left without looking back.

There was still one more item left to collect.

He passed through the darkness of a few other interior rooms before stepping into the dawn. The air was crisp, sharp with autumn, the pervasive smell of pine and cedar underneath. Mist hung between the trees and what remained of the rounded grayish-white buildings that had once formed Terra'nor, the central city of the Faelehgre when they had ruled the forest depths, when they had been flesh and blood beings. The ruins were surprisingly intact—a consequence of the proximity of the Well—but there were signs that the abandoned buildings were crumbling here and there. Colin could see where a pedestal that had once supported a statue was now half subsumed by the earth. Drifts of leaves and pine needles had mostly covered the paved white roadways between the buildings, and here and there one of the balustrades of a balcony in one of the myriad towers had shattered. Few of the glass windows or doorways remained intact, although in his explorations over the years he had found one or two, the glass itself nearly flawless, without the typical bubbles and imperfections he'd seen in Portstown and Trent—

Colin stilled, his earlier troubled frown returning. He hadn't thought about Portstown, let alone Trent, in ages. He'd tried hard to forget Portstown—Sartori and Walter and all the rest—had succeeded for years on end. Yet now he woke from an age-old dream, one he hadn't had in a long time, one that he wished he could forget. And he saw Portstown in the ruins he'd called home for decades.

Uneasiness crawled across his skin, and the muscles in his shoulders tightened. He drew the staff closer, his eyes darting around the sunken plaza before him, searching the mist tinged with the first signs of sunlight, the shadows of the open doorways and windows of the buildings.

Trees rustled in the breeze, and the mist began to lift.

His uneasiness grew. He suddenly wanted to talk to one of the Faelehgre—Osserin or Tessera. Now.

As if he'd reached out and called to him, Osserin's voice exploded in his mind.

Colin! The sukrael! They're at the Well!

Colin was moving before Osserin had finished, uneasiness transformed into motion. The mask of age—a physical affectation—sloughed away. Wrinkled skin tightened, slack muscles firmed. A slight limp in his right leg straightened, and the tweaks and twinges of old muscles dissipated. The weariness brought on by the weight of years was shrugged aside, shed like bothersome clothing. In the space of a heartbeat, he grew young, at least twenty years younger, if not more, a nearly unconscious transformation. A reflex.

Where are they coming from? And where are the rest of the Faelehgre? He couldn't stop the anger from entering his voice, the acidic bite that always appeared when he thought of the Shadows.

The south. We went to investigate a disturbance at the edge of the forest.

And you left the Well unguarded?

Colin felt Osserin's annoyance. *We can't guard the Well at all times. There aren't enough of us. You know this. We've had this argument before.*

Colin snorted. *So there's no one at the Well right now? No one at all?*

It's unprotected.

Colin growled and picked up his pace.

His room wasn't far from the Well, but far enough. He sprinted down pathways lined with dirt and needles, past standing stone columns, past a wide-based, cracked fountain in the center of an oval plaza. He dodged through the rounded door of a low building, through its empty inner rooms and out the far side, satchel jouncing against his back, then raced down gentle steps to what had once been a marketplace. Sunlight burst through the layer of fog and lit the main roadway through the city a gleaming, vibrant white as he sped down its length, the buildings on either side growing taller, the spires more intricate and magnificent. Then the buildings fell away, abruptly, the roadway opening out into an oval amphitheater, gentle white steps sloping downward toward the rough stone edges of the Well itself.

He sucked in a sharp breath and drew up short at the edge of the highest step, using his staff to steady himself. He could sense the Well now, a physical force pressing against every layer of his skin, tingling there. It pulsed in his blood, shivered through his gut, tickled his lungs with every breath he took. A cool sensation, smooth and fluid, smelling of dried leaves and dark earth.

His stomach cramped in reaction, in anticipation. The breath he'd drawn hissed out at the pain, but he shoved the ache aside while repressing an ecstatic shudder, surveyed the theater, the trees to either side, the boundaries of the Well beneath. The wide stone steps—ones he'd barely seen so many years before when the Faelehgre had led him here, ones he'd stumbled down, at the edge of asphyxiation—descended gradually, narrowing until they reached the lip of the Well and terminated. There, the waters of the Well stretched outward in a wide, placid circle, the surface perfectly smooth and untroubled, the depths clear. Over a hundred hands across, the Well seized Colin's attention, and he involuntarily took a step down. The hand holding the lantern spasmed and lifted, reached toward the water, and for a moment he literally felt the grit of the ancient stone that held its waters on his fingers.

But he caught himself, his outstretched hand tightening into a white-knuckled fist. He forced it back to his side. He wasn't here to drink. He never intended to drink from the Well again. He was here to protect.

He tore his gaze away from the water. To either side of the white steps, where the city ended, the forest took over, encircling the Well with a thick border of tall, ancient trees. The largest trees he'd ever seen before entering the forest, their boles nearly forty hands around at the base, their tops towering over even the highest of the Faelehgre's spires. The heart of the forest.

And that heart was rustling now, agitated. Colin could feel its anger.

He shifted down the steps, moving slowly, eyes darting back and forth, watching for movements beneath the trees, searching for the Shadows. They'd attack from the forest. They couldn't move over the white stone of the city, couldn't move over water, but the stone steps of the theater ended at the Well. There wasn't even a lip of the white stone around the Well itself. Not even the Faelehgre, at the height of their power, when Terra'nor had been a vibrant, flourishing city and one of the trade hubs of the plains, had been that possessive of the Lifeblood.

When he reached the Well, he set his satchel, the flask, and the lantern aside, then dropped a hand to the stone that contained it and caressed it without thought, his eyes on the forest. With a frisson of shock he remembered crashing into this stone—rough, unworked, and dense. He felt it scraping against his skin through his clothing as he crawled over it, his vision fading, his chest numbed with the Shadow's touch. Then he'd drunk the water, felt the stone's coldness against his skin as he collapsed onto his back, as he stared up into the sky and let the darkness take him . . .

Something in the forest moved, and he jerked his hand from the stone and settled it onto the staff.

The trees shuddered.

On the opposite side of the Well, a figure emerged from the forest. The same height as Colin, it stepped from the trees and halted, sheathed in the glistening black of the Shadows, as if clothed in them. They writhed over the figure from head to toe, an occasional section of blackness flaring away from the form, as if the Shadows themselves were flapping in a nonexistent wind.

Colin's stance altered. His eyes narrowed; his muscles hardened. He took the staff into both hands and balanced it defensively before him without thought.

Osserin, he sent, *it's one of the Wraiths.*

He felt the Faelehgre pause. Then, with renewed urgency: *We're coming.*

Colin regarded the Wraith across the smooth surface of the Well in silence. He could feel the figure's presence, could taste the Shadows that cloaked it. A sour taste, tainting the air with a visceral enmity, with a hatred that made Colin's nostrils flare.

He'd been battling the Wraiths since he first arrived; he knew there were at least six of them. The Faelehgre said the first one had appeared nearly twenty years before the wagons carrying Colin and the others had arrived on the outskirts of the forest. They didn't know what they were, but they knew that they'd been created somehow by the Shadows. They carried the sukrael's taint.

The Wraith reached forward and dipped a hand into the Well, ripples spreading outward as it disturbed the surface and drew the water toward its mouth to drink.

Colin barked out a wordless denial, a sound of pure rage, and leaped off the lip of the Well to the ground and into the edge of the forest. Weaving around the tangled roots of the huge trees, he sped along the curve of the Well, the rage inside growing into a growl. An old rage. Not directed at the sacrilege of the Shadows touching the water, of their taint on the Lifeblood, or their creation of the Wraiths, but at what they had done so many years before to the wagon train, at the death and destruction they had wrought. He could hear the men and women and children of the wagon train screaming in the depths of his growl, could hear their cries of pain and outrage.

The Wraith didn't react, reaching again toward the water with both hands, liquid spilling from its arm in rivulets as it cupped it to its face, the Shadows around it writhing in a frenzy, as if the wind they felt had increased to a gale. It reached a third time to the water as Colin raced around the last leg, and then it turned, the motion slow and measured, unconcerned—

It was the only warning Colin got.

Its total disregard for his approach registered a moment before the Shadows that had been lying in wait struck.

Colin's roar of outrage broke off with a shocked gasp as he brought up the forest staff a moment before the Shadow's tendril would have passed through his neck. The tendril struck the wood, struck the essence it had been imbued with, and drove Colin off his feet and into the edge of the Well. Stone bit into his side, and a frigid numbness passed down through his arm, tingling with fear and the Shadow's power. But the Shadow hadn't touched him, its blow deflected by the staff, a gift of the forest, and there was no time to collect himself. He rolled away from the stone wall, out of the Shadow's path as it came after him, and he brought his staff up hard into the Shadow's middle. The staff snagged in the seething blackness, and with a quick motion Colin flicked it up and back, flinging the Shadow out over the water of the Well. It shrieked as Colin spun. He didn't need to see the Shadow trying to coalesce over the water, didn't need to see its struggle as it tried to hold its form and failed, sinking into the surface. He'd seen it all before, and not just over the water of the Well. Any water with some depth to it would work. He'd discovered that during the years he'd spent actively searching out and killing as many of the Shadows as he could.

Which is how he knew that there were at least two more of them behind him. They hissed as their counterpart's grating shriek died and drew up short when Colin brandished the staff.

"Ha!" he barked, his gaze flicking over the two no more than three paces away, just out of reach, then toward the three others he could see back in the depths of the forest. The feral grin that had started forming on his lips, died.

Two he could handle easily, three with some effort. But five . . .

He caught movement out of the corner of his eye. The Wraith had shifted. Finished at the Well, it regarded Colin, silent as a statue, only the Shadows that cloaked it moving in the warmth of the sunlight.

Colin jerked his attention back toward the forest as two of the three moved forward to join the two closest to him. He swore, hands gripping the staff tighter as the fifth shifted forward as well, his gaze flicking back and forth between the Wraith and the Shadows.

And realization struck.

An ambush. The Wraith had been the lure.

This was why he'd ceased hunting the Shadows before, why he'd finally allowed the Faelehgre to convince him to set the rage that drove him all of those years aside. Because they were intelligent. They learned from their mistakes, had gotten smarter, harder to find, harder to catch.

Now they'd changed tactics as well. They were actively hunting him in return. But why now? He'd stopped stalking them at least twenty years ago.

The uneasiness he'd felt when he had woken that morning returned. Something had changed. Something significant.

Before he could ponder it further, the Wraith turned away and within three steps vanished into the darkness beneath the forest.

As if it were a signal, the five Shadows sprang forward.

Colin caught the first two Shadows in a sweep and flung them aside, pivoting on one foot as the other three closed in. He blocked out their shrieks, tried to block out the memories of the wagon train under attack, then darted away from them. He had no chance of holding them off with the staff alone, not all five of them. His only chance was to reach the white stone of the city, where they couldn't travel.

Breath already burning in his lungs from the sprint to reach the Wraith, he jumped over a tangle of roots, skidded on the soft soil on the far side, and swore as he caught his balance. He felt his body shift into a younger form, one more suited to an all-out sprint, and he adjusted his grip on the staff as it grew longer and more unwieldy in comparison. He vaulted over a fallen trunk covered in moss, risked a glance behind, and felt fear grip his heart. Three were behind him, closing fast. The two others—

He cried out as one of them appeared ahead, waiting. He caught a flicker of black motion to his left, the direction they expected him to dodge, but instead he used the staff to vault onto the lip of the Well to the right. He swung the staff hard into the one lying in wait, felt its dark folds get caught, felt its weight as he grunted and dragged it in a wide arc behind him, hoping to toss it into the Well; but the end of the staff struck the bole of a tree, the force of the blow shuddering up the length of wood into Colin's arms. He bit off another curse and sprinted down the arc of the Well, not pausing to shake the Shadow free. The staff jerked as he ran, the Shadow fighting to disentangle itself, and then suddenly it tore free. Colin let loose a bark of laughter as the white stone of the amphitheater appeared ahead.

Something bitterly cold swept through his leg, numbing it instantly.

He cried out, stumbled. For a terrifying moment, he thought he'd tip into the water of the Well. He didn't know what would happen if he fell in—whether it would behave like normal water or if he'd simply sink into its bottomless depths—but he didn't want to find out. Twisting as he fell, he threw his weight to the right.

His shoulder slammed into the stone, and his other arm flailed, catching at the surface of the Well, the splash soaking into his robes. Then he tucked and rolled off the edge, landing hard in the pine-scented dirt. His legs tangled in the staff, but he held on tight, back slamming to a stop in the dirt, his head rebounding off an exposed root. His teeth bit down hard on his tongue, and he tasted blood.

Dazed, he stared up into the too bright sunlight overhead, up through the branches of the huge conifers of the forest. The numbness in his leg became a fiery tingle, as if the blood were returning to it, slowly, only a thousand times worse. A throbbing ache awoke in his bruised shoulder.

And then a Shadow loomed up over him, blocking out the sunlight.

He reacted without thought, shoving the end of his staff upward in a warding motion. Not a sweep, not a move at all, just an attempt to thrust the Shadow away. He felt the Shadow's frigid presence mere inches from his fingers, the chill he'd felt years before at the wagons biting deep into his hands—

And Osserin blazed into sight, his white light flaring as bright as Colin had ever seen it. The Shadow hissed and flickered away, Osserin charging after, the Faelehgre's rage palpable, throbbing in the air. More of the Faelehgre appeared, and with their fiery light they drove the Shadows away.

Colin rested his head against the root and listened to the Shadows shriek as they retreated. The burning tingle in his leg increased, and he grimaced as he tried to move it. When it became unbearable, he halted and stared up into the sunlight. He knew the tingling would fade and his leg would return to normal, but it would take days.

He didn't have days. If he didn't leave today, he wasn't certain he'd be able to leave at all. Ever.

Osserin returned, drifting to a halt above Colin, his light still pulsing with anger, though none of it touched his voice. *The Shadows touched you?*

"I'll be fine." He sighed and lifted himself up into a seated position, his head spinning. After feeling the lump and trace of blood where he'd hit his head, he began massaging his bruised shoulder. "It was a trap. They used the Wraith to lure me off the white stone of the city into the woods, where the Shadows were waiting for me."

Osserin had stilled. *A trap? Are you certain?*

Colin shot the Faelehgre a glare. "Yes. I'm certain."

Osserin pulsed, the flashes erratic. *They've never been so . . . direct before.*

"No, they haven't. I've been attacked before, by the Wraiths and the Shadows, but it was always while I was traveling in the forest or when I was hunting them years ago. But typically they were attacks made by one of the

Wraiths or a few Shadows. None of those attacks were this coordinated, felt this planned." Colin began climbing to his feet, using the staff for support, hissing whenever his Shadow-touched leg moved. He tried to keep his weight off it, but he found it nearly impossible, even with the staff. "Something's changed," he managed through shortened breaths. "Something's given them a direction, a purpose. And something is driving them."

What?

"I don't know." He began making his way back to the white stone of the amphitheater, automatically moving closer to the Well as he did so.

They've grown restless. Restless with hunger, with their confinement here in the forest, here around Terra'nor. They're tired of foraging off the life-force here within the forest, within the range of the Well. They crave more.

"When did they start becoming restless?"

After the dwarren arrived and intruded into the Well's influence. They feasted then, as they had not done for centuries. But the dwarren grew wary and eventually learned the edges of the Shadows' reach. Yet the Shadows can see them on the plains. They want to feast again.

"But you told me that the dwarren have been here for hundreds of years."

And the sukrael have been searching for a way to break the Well's hold on them for those hundred years. But they will fail. The Well's hold cannot be broken.

Colin climbed up onto the lowest steps of white stone and moved to where his satchel lay with the lantern and flask. He sank down onto the stone wall of the Well. "What if that's what has changed? What if they've found a way?"

Osserin stilled in contemplation. *What binds the Shadows here binds the Faelehgre as well. If they had found a way to break its hold, we would know. And they would not still be here, near Terra'nor. They would have already set themselves upon the world.*

Colin shuddered at the timbre of Osserin's voice, at the sorrow and horror it held, but he said nothing.

Osserin moved to hover over the lantern. Colin saw him still. *You're leaving.*

"I have to." Colin jerked the sleeve of his robe back, exposed the black mark on his skin, presented it to Osserin.

"Unless you think I should stay," he said bitterly. "Perhaps I should. To help you with the Shadows, with the Wraiths."

The Faelehgre edged forward, then glided back.

It's grown.

"Yes."

Then you can't stay, even to help with the Shadows and Wraiths. We can handle them.

Colin pulled his sleeve back down. "Then I'm leaving. Today." He reached down and picked up the flask, twisted the top free. He returned to the water's edge, almost reached down and drew a handful of it out of habit so he could drink, but he halted mid-motion. Shaking his head, he dipped the flask into the water.

The Lifeblood tingled against his skin, and he shuddered, felt the pain in his gut, a pain he knew he could slake, but he focused on the flask. Bubbles rose to the surface of the Well as the last of the air escaped, then he withdrew it and held it up to the light.

Clear, like water. No hint that it was anything else.

Unless you'd already drunk some of it.

His nostrils flared. He could *smell* it: fresh loam, dried leaves, snow.

When he turned, he felt Osserin watching him, and he bristled. "I don't intend to use it," he said. "It's . . . a precaution."

A precaution.

"Yes." Colin shoved the flask inside his satchel, making certain it was protected by layers of cloth so that it wouldn't break. "In case the pain becomes too great."

With the Lifeblood present, the pain will always be too great.

Colin sent the Faelehgre an annoyed glare, adjusting the pack on his shoulder. "Perhaps." Taking up his staff, he paused.

Now that he was prepared to leave, he found his anger fading.

He stared out over the ruins of the city, over the white towers, the amphitheater, the road and buildings. He could imagine what the city had looked like before the Well destroyed the Faelehgre as a people. Osserin had told him enough stories over the years. The white stone had glowed in the moonlight, the streets filled with music, with life. The dark-skinned Faelehgre had danced along those streets in clothes of every hue, had serenaded each other beneath the balustrades and beside the pools and fountains, moon-flowers tucked in their hair.

The ancient trees stirred, the wind sighing in their branches, and Colin drew in a deep breath. He could smell the acrid scent of their needles, the coolness of the Lifeblood, the bitterness of bark and leaves and the vividness of the ferns and other undergrowth. But the music he could almost hear from the past faded.

"I've been here so long, I can't imagine leaving," he finally said. His voice sounded small, vulnerable, as if he were twelve again.

Osserin drifted closer. *But you must, or the Well will claim you. As it claimed us.*

Colin hefted the pack into a more comfortable position, then gathered up his staff before looking directly at the Faelehgre's light.

"Let's go."

~

They emerged from the edge of the forest into late afternoon sunlight, and Colin paused and raised a hand to shade his eyes, blinking at the brightness. He'd shifted back to his aged form again, shedding the youthfulness he'd assumed to escape the Shadows. The plains spread out before him, wide and open, and he felt himself cringe back from them, from the vast emptiness of the sky.

"I've been inside the forest too long," he murmured.

Osserin didn't respond. He seemed to be waiting, expectant.

Colin scanned the horizon, breathing in the scent of late autumn grass and heat. And something else. A taint on the breeze, of smoke and—

He turned and caught sight of a black cloud of carrion birds wheeling in the distance between columns of thinning smoke. Thousands of them, rising and settling with sickening grace.

He frowned. "What happened?"

Osserin shifted forward, out over the grasses in the direction of the smoke. *A battle. A large one. It's the disturbance we abandoned the Well to investigate this morning.*

"A battle between whom?"

It took place outside the Well's influence. We couldn't get close enough to see.

Colin grunted. "I'll check it out. After." He watched the flock of carrion birds a moment more, then turned away, searching the nearer grasses for the shepherd's hook.

He spotted it almost instantly, and his breath caught, his throat tightening. As it did every time he came here, every time he traveled through the forest to this place, to where the hopes and dreams of all of those who were part of the wagon train out of Lean-to and Portstown ended. The wagons had vanished long ago. He'd scavenged as much as he could of the supplies that first year, taking whatever he thought he'd need to survive in the forest, before he knew how much the Lifeblood had changed him. The rest had been looted by the dwarren or had simply rotted and decayed and been claimed by the grass.

But not all. He'd used some of the metal from the wheels and the wagons' hitches to fashion a shepherd's hook, and he'd planted it where the wagons used to be, had sunk it deep into the earth to mark the location, years after most traces of what had happened there had vanished, after he realized that if he didn't do *something*, all traces would be lost completely.

Initially, he'd come to this place every year with a lantern taken from the wagons, lit it, and placed it on the shepherd's hook. To remember. But after ten years he'd turned his grief outward, turned his rage onto the Shadows. By then he'd learned enough of how the Well had changed him that he could hunt them, learned enough from the Faelehgre and the forest to kill them. That pursuit had consumed him for nearly twenty years. He'd forgotten about the lantern, the shepherd's hook. He'd forgotten himself. When the Faelehgre finally convinced him that his hunting was merely making the Shadows stronger, more dangerous, he'd sunk into listlessness, wandering the forest, the ruins of Terra'nor, letting its cool depths enfold him. Only when Osserin began following him, began relating the history of the Faelehgre—how they'd built Terra'nor near the Well, how they'd built their entire culture around its power, worshiping it, reveling in it, using it—did he reawaken.

He began to learn then. Of Terra'nor and its fall, how

the power of the Well had slowly begun to corrupt the Faelehgre, how it began to distort their bodies, changing them. Of how the Faelehgre had refused to leave until it was too late, until the Well had changed them enough that they could no longer leave. And of how it had continued to change them, the corporeal bodies of the Faelehgre finally fading and splitting into the Shadows and the Lights.

And once he'd learned of the Faelehgre and the Shadows, he turned to the plains, exploring their reaches, although never moving too far from the forest. He'd watched the dwarren and their tribal wars from afar, watched the humans continue to attempt to settle on dwarren lands, watched the Alvritshai attempt to as well. The plains had become a battlefield, blood spilled across its length. He'd watched it all.

Until seven years ago, when he'd finally noticed that the black spot on his arm—a mere sliver of darkness then—wasn't a freckle.

Suddenly, he knew his time in the forest was running out. Unless he wanted to become like the Faelehgre and the Shadows: trapped.

It was then that he'd recalled the shepherd's hook, had begun returning every year with the lantern.

"How long have I been here, Osserin?" he rasped. He felt tears burning at the edges of his eyes already, heard them in his voice, but he choked them back. "How long since I drank from the Well?"

Sixty-seven years.

Colin's breath stopped, his eyes widening. The tears that had threatened dried up. "Sixty-se—" he began, but the word caught in his throat.

He swallowed. "How is that possible?" he breathed.

Because you willed it, Osserin said, and Colin heard the edge in his voice. *Because the Lifeblood made it possible.*

Before Colin could respond, the Faelehgre moved toward the hook, hovering close to the ground at first, as if looking for traces of the wagons, of the bodies, of the deaths. When he neared the hook, he spun around it, halting near the top.

Colin struggled a moment longer, then exhaled heavily. Staff in hand, the lantern banging against it as he moved, he trudged forward, the weight of the years he hadn't real-

ized had passed—not consciously—making the trek more
difficult. His leg screamed in tingling agony, but he ignored
it, pulling up beneath the S-shaped curve of the hook. Setting the lantern on the ground, he pulled the hollow bowl,
tinder, and flint from the pockets of his robe, and using
some of the surrounding dried grass, he got a flame started
in the bowl. Blowing on it to keep it lit, he opened the
glass door of the lantern and set the small bowl inside. It
wouldn't burn long, but he'd run out of oil from the wagons
ages ago.

Then he closed the lantern and hobbled backward,
pocketing the flint. He stared at the flames until he was
satisfied they would continue to burn, then looked around
at the surrounding grass.

You don't need to relive—

"I *need* to remember," he said, cutting Osserin off,
angry. Then, in a softer voice: "I want to remember. I don't
want to forget her."

Osserin flickered, troubled, but said nothing.

Colin bowed his head, took a few deep, steadying
breaths, eyes closed, trying to relax himself.

Then he opened his eyes . . . and *sank*.

Around him, the world stilled, the grasses stirred by
the breeze halting in mid-motion. Sound died, the quiet
so profound that Colin shifted uncomfortably. He felt the
stillness—the utter absence of motion—pressing against
his skin, felt it resisting him, trying to shove him forward,
back into his proper place, the sensation prickling, the
hairs on the back of his neck stirring. He had never liked
this initial quiet, this absence of life in the world around
him—knew that if he remained in this limbo too long he
wouldn't be able to breathe—and so he shoved against the
pressure, thrust himself backward through its resistance.

And crossed a barrier, thrust himself through it . . .
pushed himself beyond.

The sun dipped down toward the horizon as if it were
setting . . . but to the east. He slogged backward without
moving, the effort like trying to walk on sand. Night fell, but
in reverse, as midmorning pressed into dawn, and still he
shoved, pushed farther backward, moving faster and faster,
the amount of effort required increasing. The sun rose in the
west, set in the east, rose and set, again and again, picking up

speed until it was only a flicker, a blink between light and dark, light and dark, and still he forged backward.

On the plains before him, in the stuttering blinks of light, the grasses turned from dried dead stalks to lush greens with heavy heads of grain, then shrank into slender sprouts before vanishing, replaced by brief fields of snow—a rare occurrence this far south of the mountains—and then back to a swath of dried yellow. Colin watched the seasons pass again and again, in reverse, then frowned and shoved harder, speeding up the process until there was no distinction between light and dark, only sunlight. Birds appeared, a flicker, nothing more, soaring in the sky. A fox, a grouse, passing by the shepherd's hook, their appearance so brief Colin didn't have time to gasp. Farther out, he caught a stutter of wagons, the passing of an army of men, a shadow of darkness as a herd of gaezels spun by.

He pushed harder, sank himself into the past, forced himself down roads already traveled, and the farther he went, the greater the pressure against his skin, the greater the resistance. The prickling became an itch, the hairs on his arms shivering, stirring, vibrating. A sound arose, deep and throaty, resonating in his chest, as if the world were moaning, but he forged back farther, shoved harder, grunted with the effort it took, and the moaning increased.

Then, on the ground before him, within the space between heartbeats, the remnants of decayed wagons appeared.

His heart lurched and he gasped, the press into the past slowing, losing momentum. He staggered under its weight, fell to his hands and his good knee, his Shadow-touched leg stretched awkwardly behind him, the staff pressed into the grass and earth beneath his hand. His satchel slipped from his back and hung beneath him. But he was too close to let the pressure thrust him back to the present. He remained where he was and shoved harder, a cry escaping him as the decayed wagons rose from the concealing grasses, as the bodies rose with them, as if being pushed upward out of the earth, as if it were rejecting them, denying them—

And suddenly the wagons were whole, the bodies complete. White lights flared from the forest and then vanished, and with another gasp Colin stopped shoving against the tides of time, letting his head drop.

The world settled, shuddering as it did so. The moaning halted, and normal sounds returned, normal textures and scents. Pine, trampled grass, upturned earth. Horse musk and the stench of fear. The sun beat down on his back, warming his skin from the chill of the passage, and wind tugged at his robes, drying his sweat. Far off, the sounds of a battle raged on the plains, a battle they'd attempted to flee.

Colin closed his eyes, drew in a deep breath, steadied himself . . .

And looked up.

Karen's father lay where he'd fallen, where the Shadows had taken him, the sword he'd tried to use lying useless in the grass beside him. Other bodies lay scattered around the wagon where he and Karen had stood last, and Colin knew there were more behind him. Many more, including his mother and father, both of them on the far side of the wagons, as if they'd been caught trying to flee to the plains. He'd come here, like this, many times, had searched out everyone. Not all of those who had made it this far from Portstown had died here. Some had managed to run outside the Shadow's reach; some, like Walter, had been chased into the forest; some he'd never been able to find. But everyone of significance was here. His family, his friends.

His chosen.

He pulled himself up, *dragged* himself upright with the staff, adjusting the satchel, and moved to the edge of the wagon, so that he stood over his own crumpled form. He watched as his younger self stared out over the plains, face smeared with tears and dirt and snot, eyes vacant. Empty of everything, body and soul. Karen lay slack in his arms, her dead body across his chest, her head rolled back, throat exposed. Her skin glowed a pale white in the sunlight, the freckles across her nose dark in contrast, her mouth slightly open, her green eyes eerily vivid.

Colin knelt down beside himself, the position awkward with his deadened leg. He reached out a hand, wanting to touch her, to close her eyes, her mouth, to trace the line of her jaw and brush the wild brown hair from her brow one more time. And he *could* touch her, could press his hands against her flesh. He was present—it wasn't simply a dream; Osserin had assured him of that—but it wasn't the same. It was a strange half-presence. He wasn't really there, no matter how much he felt the wind gust against his face, or how visceral the scent of grass or the sounds of the far-off battle. He could feel everything, could sense it, but he couldn't change any of it. As soon as he thrust himself past that barrier to come here, nothing could be changed.

And yet every time he came, he tried. Partly because Osserin had said that there were some who could touch the past, could manipulate it. But mostly because he couldn't help himself.

His past self's chest hitched, his gaze drifting from the plains upward to the sky, and he withdrew his hand where it hovered over Karen's face. He watched himself. But unlike all the times before this, the ache in his chest—beneath where the pendant burned against his skin beneath his robes, the blood vow still empty, never claimed— that ache didn't crush him. It didn't rise into his throat and cut off his breath, didn't fill his chest and suffocate him. He felt it, a fist of pain, hard and unforgiving, but it remained contained.

He stood and stepped back from himself, from Karen, a moment before the Faelehgre sped from the forest and began their first frenzied searching of the bodies around the wagons. They flitted from one lifeless figure to the next, their agitation growing. He could hear them clearly now, unlike the echoing half-voices he'd heard back then— another consequence of drinking the Lifeblood according to Osserin. They hovered over Lyda's body, over the womb that would never bear a child, and Colin swallowed back the same sick nausea he'd felt back then over the Shadow's gluttonous feeding. They slipped inside the backs of the wagons, where Colin knew they'd find Tobin's body. He'd never had a chance to escape with his broken legs. They hovered longest over the children—Lissa and her brother, Ron, all the rest—their despair palpable.

And then they discovered that he was still alive.

As the argument over whether or not to save him erupted, Colin wandered away from himself, from Karen, and knelt beside Sam's body. The mason had died attempting to protect a group of women, had fallen facedown into the grass, his sword beneath him. He desperately wanted to turn Sam's body over so that he could see the sun, look at the sky, but he couldn't.

Instead, he stood and wandered among the rest of the fallen: Miriam, the burns from when the dwarren fired the wagons still etched on her skin; Brant, his shoulder bound from where the dwarren arrow had been removed; Barte, the wagon driver; Domonic; and Jackson, the West Wind Trading Company's representative. Walter had escaped the wagons, but the sukrael had caught him in the forest. Colin had gone back once and watched as they fell on Walter, as they smothered him. They'd been sated by then, had tortured Walter as they'd started torturing Colin, but the Faelehgre had not arrived to save him as they had Colin.

Last, he found his parents. Arten, the Armory guardsman, lay a short distance away. Arten had tried to hold the Shadows off as Colin's parents and a few others fled, but the gesture had been useless. The sukrael had cut him down and sped onward without pausing.

His father lay on his side. He'd stumbled when the sukrael took out his leg, had reached for Colin's mother as they fell on him. His arm was still outstretched. Colin's mother had made it another few steps, had crumpled to the ground, half curled, her own arm reaching back, her other hand clutching at Diermani's tilted cross and the vow beneath her shirt.

Crouching down, Colin laid his hand on his mother's shoulder. The hard fist of pressure in his chest throbbed once, twice, then stilled.

Closing his eyes, Colin crossed himself—head, chest, shoulder, side—and murmured a half-remembered prayer to Holy Diermani, then kissed the back of her hand.

You've never done that before.

Colin hadn't felt Osserin join him in the past, but he didn't start in surprise. He didn't even flinch. Instead, he twisted where he crouched and repeated the gesture and prayer for his father, even though his father hadn't believed in Diermani as devoutly as his mother had. Then he stood.

Why now? Osserin asked.

"Because . . ." he began. Fumbling, he said, "Because it felt right. My mother deserved it. My father . . . because of her. And because I'm leaving."

You've never been particularly religious.

Colin smiled, his expression wry. "I wasn't back then

either, to my mother's dismay." The smile faded. "But it had its place. It still has its place."

Osserin said nothing, and after a moment, both of them turned to where the dwarren still fought on the plains before the wagons. The battle had shifted, ranging farther to the south and east, leaving only dead and wounded behind. Carrion birds were already gathering.

The birds reminded Colin of the battle he had yet to investigate in the present.

Always, there are battles on these plains. Always, there is blood.

Colin watched the battle that had trapped the wagon train play out before him. "Why?"

Osserin stirred, shifted forward as if to get a closer look. *We don't know. It's been this way for hundreds of years, since the dwarren came. And now, with the introduction of the Alvritshai and of man, it's become worse. Much worse. You've seen them. Alvritshai fighting dwarren. Dwarren fighting men. Men fighting Alvritshai. Even dwarren against dwarren, men against men.*

On the plains, the dwarren battle shifted, edging farther from the forest, from the wagons and the Faelehgre.

"It's senseless. Useless."

It's the way of man. And dwarren and, to a lesser extent, Alvritshai. It was the way of the Faelehgre once. It still is.

As Colin turned away, troubled, he caught sight of the swirling black spot on his forearm and shuddered.

Are you finished here? Osserin asked.

Colin considered, then nodded. "Yes. I'm done."

And with that, he let the pressure of time still pushing against him carry him forward, felt Osserin traveling with him. The plain blurred, time slipping away so fast he couldn't distinguish anything in its passage, and then it slowed, settling him back into the present. The wagons had vanished, long gone, the bodies with them, including the bodies of the dwarren and their gaezels. They were replaced with the columns of smoke he'd seen when he first emerged from the forest and the clouds of birds rising and settling like a black fog. The battle itself had played out beyond the nearest ridgeline.

Colin watched the smoke a long moment, frowning, thinking of the dwarren battle in the past, of what Osserin had said.

Always, there is battle on these plains. Always, there is blood.

"I'll be back shortly," he said. Without waiting for a response, he trudged forward, through wet grass, the stalks brushing past his knees. By the time he'd reached the top of the hill, his robes were soaked and cumbersome, tangling with his legs.

But the battlefield beyond pushed all of those petty concerns aside.

"Holy Diermani, save us all," he whispered, and unconsciously crossed himself again.

The field of dead encompassed the breadth of the plains in sight, bodies fallen near and far, horses and gaezels, men and dwarren. Hundreds of them, thousands, impaled on pikes, pierced by spears, riddled with arrows. Armor glinted in the sunlight, much more extensive armor than he remembered any of the Armory guardsmen using in Portstown, heavier, and more protective. The columns of smoke rose from burning supply wagons. Everywhere he looked the carrion birds flocked, their black feathers glistening in the sunlight, their harsh cries echoing across the distance. They hovered close, dozens trying to settle, disturbing those already gorging themselves, others rising as they were shoved out of the way.

And then the wind shifted, blew toward Colin, and the stench of death—of blood and smoke and scorched earth—doubled him over. He gagged, fell to his knees, and retched into the grass, heaving even when there was nothing left to purge.

When it ended, he rose slowly, wiped his mouth as clean as possible with his sleeve and spat to one side. His stomach continued to roil as he climbed back to his feet. Leaning heavily on his staff, he pushed forward, down the edge of the hill. Carrion crows took reluctant flight as he approached, their protests raucous, only to settle back again as he passed, watching him warily. He ignored them all, focused on the bodies, on the death.

He saw men and dwarren both, covered in blood, the earth soaked in it, churned to mud by the passage of the horses and the army. A man with blond hair—his eyes wide and empty, staring up at the sun—lay alone, his chest gaping where a spear had punched into his heart. A few paces beyond, bodies were stacked one on top of the other, thrown there haphazardly, arms and legs askew. An arrow had taken an older man in the throat, one hand still clutching the shaft loosely; another had been slashed as if with a dagger. A few had been trampled into the earth, their faces squashed into the mud, already half buried. Row after row, body after body, arms severed, legs crushed, heads caved in on one side.

And scattered among the men were the bodies of the dwarren. Like the dwarren Colin remembered, they wore long tangled beards, braided with beads in complex patterns. Most had pierced noses and ears with fine chains running from nostril to lobe, a sign of their status in the tribe and their standing in the army. They wore armor, heavier than Colin remembered, like the men, but some of them carried swords and axes; they'd used only spears and arrows when they'd attacked the wagons. He recognized a few of the tribes by the bands of iron around their wrists or farther up on their forearms: Thousand Springs Clan . . . and Silver Grass.

Colin continued deeper into the field, trying to breathe through his mouth, the stench increasing, the bodies growing denser. Horses and gaezels, men and dwarren. They grew thicker, until he was forced to halt because moving forward meant he'd have to step on the dead.

He scanned the near distance, the carrion crows still flocking, their shadow passing over him now, blotting out the sun. "Bold bastards," he murmured to himself.

Not ten paces away, one dropped from the sky next to another. The one already on the ground flapped its wings and gave a harsh cry of protest, but the other advanced, hopping over the bodies. With a last squawk, the first retreated, taking sudden wing, and the victor settled in to feast. It turned its black gaze on Colin a moment. Then its head darted downward, and after two quick stabs of its beak, it rose, something clutched in its mouth.

An eye.

Colin cried out in outrage, stumbled forward, slipped on the dead and fell as the crow lurched into the sky, wings flapping, its prize held tight. Struggling where he'd fallen, Colin spat a useless curse, his stomach churning again, the taste of vomit still fresh.

And then he looked down.

He'd landed on the bodies of men, their clothes still damp with blood, their flesh soft beneath his hands, the armor chill. But the man he'd fallen on wasn't really a man. He was just a boy, twelve, with dark hair, a few lighter strands catching the occasional sunlight. His mouth was set in a determined look, gone slack with death, his eyes empty, face rounded. His nose had been broken sometime in the past, but other than that . . .

Other than that, it could have been Colin himself. The Colin he had just seen clutching Karen's body to his chest.

A shudder passed through Colin's body, and something gripped his throat. He didn't lurch upward, didn't scramble back. The boy's face, so like his own, held him transfixed, breath caught.

And in that still moment, he realized he'd been asleep, that he'd forced himself into an unnatural slumber in the forest. He'd hidden there from the world, from his parents' deaths, from Karen's. He'd willed himself into nonexistence, living off the Well, off the Lifeblood, smothering himself in his grief, just as Osserin and the other Faelehgre had said.

He needed to wake up. If he didn't, the Lifeblood would claim him. The spot on his wrist would only be the beginning. He'd die, as surely as this boy had died here on the battlefield, a sword lodged in his side. And he realized he didn't want to die, he didn't want to sleep anymore.

He turned at the sound of a banner flapping in the breeze, the motion startling him out of his paralysis. He glanced once more at the boy's face, reached to close his eyes and murmur a prayer over him, then climbed carefully to his feet, making certain to place the end of his staff on ground and not flesh. The banner flapped again, a stylized shield on a background divided in half diagonally, one side red, the other yellow, a banner he didn't recognize. He hadn't traveled outside dwarren territory on his excursions, had only made it to the Escarpment—what they had once called the Bluff—and the edge of human lands. Frowning, he searched for more banners, looking for the colors on the overshirts and surplices, the sigils stitched into shirts or etched into shields. He found numerous tilted crosses and references to Diermani—clasped hands, fire, white candles—but he didn't recognize anything else. No Family crests, no stylized symbols from the Court.

When the stench became too great, the feeding of the crows too much, he retreated back to the hill, passing back out through the ranks of dead. He paused, scanned the scope of the death, then returned to where Osserin waited at the edge of the forest, the lantern he'd lit in memory of Karen, his parents, and all the rest still burning in the shepherd's hook. Dusk had fallen, the few clouds in the sky orange and gold over the sighing of the trees.

What did you find? Osserin asked.

"A battlefield," Colin reported, his voice muted. "Hundreds of dead. Thousands. I didn't recognize any of the humans' banners except those of the church."

It has been over sixty years. The world changes.

Colin grunted.

Who fought in the battle?

Colin shrugged, troubled. "Men and dwarren. I didn't see any of the Alvritshai."

The Alvritshai are less willing to fight. They live longer, and they do not like to risk their children's lives. They respect life more because it is so difficult for them to bear children. That is why they halted their expansion southward from their northern mountain reaches and the foothills and forests beneath. The dwarren made the expansion onto the plains too costly for them. But the Alvritshai have fought here before. And they will again.

Colin thought about what he'd just seen, all the faces, all the blood, particularly the face of the boy, and grimaced, sick to his stomach. He could still taste the vomit in his mouth.

He glanced back toward the plains, to where the smoke had thinned to wisps and the black cloud of birds had increased.

After a long moment, Osserin asked, *What will you do? Where will you go?*

"I don't know. Portstown, I guess."

Then safe travels.

And Osserin began drifting away.

Colin watched the Faelehgre's retreating light with mild shock. "Farewell to you too," he murmured.

You'll return, Osserin said before passing out of sight beneath the trees.

Colin snorted, then shifted uncomfortably. He almost glanced down at the black mark on his arm, then realized he didn't need to. He could *feel* it, a shadow beneath his skin, a taint.

Then he adjusted the satchel and headed away from the forest.

Toward the plains. Toward the Escarpment and the human lands beyond.

12

SIX WEEKS LATER, he stood at the edge of the main road leading down to Portstown, shocked into immobility.

"How could I have missed all this?" He drew in a deep breath, tears burning at the corners of his eyes, and let it out in a heavy sigh. What lay before him had no resemblance whatsoever to the town that he'd left behind so many years before.

Where the port used to be—the docks where the riot broke out, the gallows where Sartori had threatened to hang him in order to gain his father's cooperation for the expedition to the east—he could see building after building, smoke rising from the chimneys of most, black and sooty, the stone used in their construction old and gray, leeched of life. Warehouses and stockyards, he guessed, where most of the dirty, hard work got done. The buildings blocked the shoreline, but he could see the masts and rigging of ships lined up and down the waterfront, ships larger than any he'd seen before, judging by the number of masts and the complexity of the rigging.

The buildings farther south, near where the river drained into the bay, were newer. The road led down through estates and residential buildings to this section, and even from this distance Colin could tell that he'd find the marketplace there. He could see gaps between the buildings for fountains and plazas, and piercing through the rooftops here and there were the spires of churches, some topped by Diermani's tilted cross, others by winged

statues or simple poles, banners flapping in the breeze
from the ocean. Across the inlet, he could see the swath
of sand that protected the town from storm surges, what
they'd called the Strand.

But the thick wall of stone and the buildings to the
north of the town drew Colin's attention most. Behind
the defensive wall, he could see the square towers of a
large building, a manse of some sort, although twice the
size of anything he'd seen before, and the angled rooftops
of a few smaller buildings, including another church. The
manse stood where Lean-to would have been, on the hill
overlooking the town.

As Colin watched, the gates of the outer wall opened,
and a large force of men on horseback emerged, standards
flying. Guardsmen, what Colin would have called the
Armory in the Portstown of his time, but what he'd heard
others refer to as the Legion since he'd reached the first
human outpost of Farpoint at the top of the Escarpment,
where he'd traded for coin and information. His eyes narrowed as the group descended from the walled manse
down into the city proper, heading toward the ships. The
banners catching the wind were half red, half yellow, the
field cut diagonally. He couldn't make out the symbol in
the center, but he'd be willing to wager it was a shield.

The same banner he'd seen on the battlefield outside
the forest.

The guardsmen vanished among the buildings, and
Colin turned back to his study of the city. His hand massaged the grip on his staff with nervous tension, and he
could feel a tightness at the base of his back, in the center
of his shoulders.

"What am I doing here?" he whispered to himself.

He didn't know. He'd expected Portstown to be similar
to what he remembered, not . . . *this*.

He glanced around at the people passing on the road,
a cart loaded down with late autumn squash, a man on
horseback with an escort of uniformed guardsmen. No one
had noticed him. No one had even looked in his direction,
not even the few men and boys traveling on foot.

Loneliness settled on his shoulders, the weight of over
sixty years of isolation suddenly too great a burden. His
shoulders slumped. He didn't belong here. Portstown had

changed too much. But if not here, and not within the forest, then where?

As if in answer, his stomach seized. Fear lanced through him as he clamped his hand to his side, the heat already building. Before he'd left, he'd thought the pain of withdrawal from the Well and the influence of the Lifeblood had been bad but tolerable. He'd discovered otherwise on the plains when the first seizure hit. It had begun like this, a cramp, followed by the searing heat. He'd stumbled to the grass, lips pressed tight, as the pain increased, the heat seeping outward through his side into his chest, into his left arm and his legs, until it had become too much to bear, and he'd collapsed to the ground, seizures wracking his body.

When the seizure had finally faded, he'd lain in the grass, staring up at the sky, muscles trembling, too weak to move. Not even when a brown plains snake slid over his body, split tongue tasting his sweat in the air a moment before moving on. He'd lain there for nearly a day, unable to move, wondering if the dwarren would find him and what they would do to him if they did. But finally the weakness had passed, and he'd struggled to his feet.

He'd almost drunk from his stash of Lifeblood then. The vial had been in his shaking hands, open and halfway to his mouth, before the unclaimed vow slipped from beneath the neck of his robe and glinted in the sunlight. As tremors coursed through his body, he'd forced himself to put the vial away, the smell of the Lifeblood—earth and leaves and snow—so sharp and tempting that he actually moaned.

He'd had two more seizures before reaching Farpoint and human lands, then another on the trek from the Escarpment here. He'd been able to stumble off the road and out of sight for the last one.

But now, as the heat intensified enough to drive him to one knee, leaning on his staff for support, he could hear the people around him. The creak of the farmer's cart and the clop of the horses' hooves sharpened as he fought back the pain. He gasped as it threatened to escalate and break into another seizure, but before it crested, he felt the heat beginning to ebb. He brought his hand away from his side and held onto the staff, resting his forehead against it. Sweat made his grip slick, but as the pain receded, he used the staff to pull himself back onto his feet.

One of the uniformed guardsmen watched him with concern, but Colin motioned that he was fine. He massaged his side, wondering if the lack of a seizure meant he was getting better, if the pull of the Well was lessening.

Then his stomach growled.

A thin smile quirked his lips, but it didn't linger.

"Food," he said to himself, then sighed again. "Food first and then . . ."

He stilled, then shrugged and headed down the gravel road into the city proper.

~

He found himself drawn to the older part of the city. He wanted to see if there was anything left of the Portstown he knew. The imperative had even overridden his stomach.

He went to the shipyards first, but there was no sign of the wide plank docks where the riot had broken out between the Armory and Shay and his men. Instead, he stood on a long cobbled street before a massive stone wall, the street and wall itself built out into the water. He placed his hands against the damp stone, felt its chill in his fingers, then let his hand drop. Glancing up, he could see the spits of ships jutting out over the top of the wall. Based on their height, he guessed that the ocean itself lay directly on the far side of the wall, that if the stone were to break, seawater would pour into the street and flood the lower wharf.

He shuddered, then stepped into shadow as a door in the wall twenty paces away opened suddenly; men and women dressed in vests and coats in a style Colin didn't recognize stepped out onto the cobbles. Their undershirts were a vibrant white, stark against the dirt that coated the buildings, but no one seemed to notice the grime. Carriages were waiting for some of them, the horses stamping the stone impatiently, heads rattling their traces. Others branched away in various directions. Those with the finer clothes were followed by men and women dressed more conservatively, in clothes Colin found more familiar: shirts and breeches, patched and stained in places. Once the carriages pulled away, their drivers tch-ing the horses into motion, the yard workers in even rougher clothing, most without shirts, began unloading the cargo, wagons arriving to take the carriages' places, hauling the crates and barrels away into the city.

Colin turned to look down the stretch of the street and saw numerous doorways all along its length; he shook his head. "Far larger than the wharf from my day," he murmured, then turned his attention inland. He didn't know how the streets were set up, didn't even know if he was close to where the wharf he remembered had been, so he chose a street at random.

As soon as he entered the inner reaches of the wharf, he adjusted his pack and hugged the walls of the buildings, wary of the number of people. He made it down to the next street, and then he drew to a halt.

The closeness—of the people, of the buildings—and the sheer volume and activity began to close in on him, crushing him. His chest tightened, and his breath began to quicken. Desperation pulled at his shoulders, until he finally glanced up, into the sky, into its blueness, its openness high above. He drew that openness into his lungs, tasted the odor of the city along with it, and wrinkled his nose.

It reminded him of the rougher part of Lean-to, where Shay and the conscripts had stayed, only the stench was a hundred times worse. But it calmed him.

He turned back to the street and watched the crowd as they bustled here and there, entering taverns and shops. Then he reentered the flow, passing a bakery, the smells of fresh bread making his stomach growl yet again, but he didn't stop. He turned at the next corner, bumped into someone and apologized without looking up. He caught a few people staring at him strangely, brows creased, and he realized that no one else wore anything remotely close to robes, but he ignored them. He'd brought a shirt and breeches, but he'd never changed; he wasn't comfortable in them anymore. He caught a few other stares, more predatory, and he tugged his pack closer, shifting his grip on the staff. He had nothing that they'd want, but he knew that didn't mean anything.

And then the buildings fell away, abruptly, like the Faelehgre buildings that had surrounded the Well. The street emptied out into a small square, a rectangular area filled with grass and trees protected by a low wrought-iron fence. From the sides of the square streets branched off in every direction between yet more buildings, and to the right—

Colin sighed, an ache in his heart easing.

The church he remembered from Portstown, the church he'd halted in front of before hunting down Walter and his cronies with his sling, stood alone, as if carved out of the facade of the surrounding city. He smiled at the memory and moved across the street and around the park. The wooden fence had been replaced by iron, and the stone of the building had aged, but otherwise it was exactly as he remembered it. He could even see a few headstones in the graveyard behind it.

Without thought, he passed through the open gate and ascended the stone steps. The vestibule was as he remembered it, with the intricate latticework of wood separating the entry from the sanctuary itself, but the smells had changed. Dust hung in the air, scented with old wood and decades of burned tallow and smoke and incense. Pews lined the walkway leading to the altar, the tilted cross still draped with white and red cloth at the far end. Colin moved down the aisle, glancing toward the stained-glass windows now darkened with layers of soot and age. He halted at the railing before the altar, the wood floor creaking beneath his weight, and stared up at the cross.

He thought about his mother and father, about everyone in the wagon expedition who had died outside the forest, and he signed himself. "May Holy Diermani protect you all. You deserved a better burial than I gave you." And as he stood there, he thought of Patris Brindisi, who'd offered him sanctuary on that day so long ago. He wondered whether, if he'd accepted that offer, everything would have been different. He might never have attacked Walter and been arrested. His father might never have been forced into leading the expedition onto the plains.

Karen might have lived.

His hand rose to clasp the unclaimed vow that hung around his neck.

"Have you come seeking solace?"

Colin spun, half expecting to see Brindisi, but it was another priest, young, the white shawl of a Hand draped around his neck. He thought of Domonic and smiled tightly. "No. I don't think solace will ever be mine. I came for the . . . memories."

Without waiting for a response, he moved down the

central aisle, past the Hand of Diermani, back out into the sunlight. He hesitated on the steps of the church, his hand falling away from the vow, and turned toward where the Proprietor's manse had been.

The building still stood, surrounded by a stone wall, a few trees visible inside. But when he approached the gate, a metal placard next to it stated that it was a mercantile house. Peering through the iron gates, he could see that changes had been made to the facade and windows, and a new stable had been built off to one side. Where the old stable had been now stood a large warehouse.

He stepped back from the gate and oriented himself again.

"The church, Sartori's manse—" he spun in place and pointed with his staff "—the gallows."

There were no gallows there now, only a solid row of buildings.

He wandered across the square and stopped before a tavern, on the ground where Sartori had threatened to hang him. Someone brushed past him, opened the door, and sounds spilled out—the clank of glassware, the raucous noise of voices. The scent of roasting meat hit him like a slingstone to the gut. Before he entered the tavern, he glanced up at the sign posted over the door: The Hangman's Noose.

He shivered as he stepped into the tavern's interior.

The first burst of noise almost made him retreat, but he straightened his shoulders and made his way to a far corner table, half-hidden in shadows. The reek of spilled ale and old sweat and the scent of cooked meat dominated the room full of tables and chairs. A bar stood against the back wall, most of the patrons around it, although a few were gathered near the hearth, where a man sat on a stool telling tales.

Colin hadn't been seated for more than a few heartbeats when a young boy, no more than twelve, appeared at its edge dressed in a serving apron.

"What can I git fur ya, oldster?"

He stared at Colin with lively brown eyes, his light hair tousled and wild, his shirt stained with grease.

Colin frowned and leaned his staff against the wall. He fished a coin from his pack, aware that the boy watched him closely, then set it on the table, making certain he kept his hand on it. "Whatever food this will pay for."

The boy nodded and slipped away. Colin folded the coin back into his hand and turned his attention to the storyteller.

"...They met at the Escarpment, all three armies come together at last—King Maarten's Legion, the Alvritshai White Phalanx, and the dwarren Riders." A low grumble rolled through those listening, a rumble of hatred and anticipated anger. The storyteller nodded, his face grim. "Yes. You know the story, you know the betrayal." He paused, let their anger simmer, then contin-ued with a frown.

"The three forces met, the Alvritshai coming from the north, the dwarren from the east, and the Legion from the south. It was to be a decisive battle, a final battle! For un-known to the dwarren, Maarten had met with the Tamaell of the Alvritshai in secret and forged an alliance, one that would bind the Alvritshai to the colonies, and would allow us to finally seize control of the edge of the plains and drive the dwarren back. Back into their burrows and tent cities in the deep plains." Those around the storyteller grumbled some more.

"It was with this alliance in place that the Legion took the field. King Maarten led them to the edge of the hill overlooking the flat, his heir, Stephan, his trusted advisers, and his councilmen beside him, banners snapping in the winds blowing from the plains. He came with three thou-sand men, with two hundred horses, and the hope of the Provinces in his heart.

"Across the flat, the Alvritshai's White Phalanx al-ready waited, pennons flying, all of the Houses rep-resented, nearly two thousand strong. When Maarten crested the hill, Tamaell Fedorem flashed the signal indicating that all was ready, that all was well, a sign that the alliance still stood. Everyone on the ridge saw it, and as the sun finally pulled away from the horizon, they heard the thundering approach of the Riders. A thousand gaezel—more!—dwarren astride their backs, emerged from the eastern plains, a storm of dust rising behind them to cloud the sky, golden in the sun's light. They charged the flat, as if they intended to fling themselves off of the cliffs of the Escarpment to the west, but at the last moment they swerved, the gaezels turning in a sharp, smooth curve back on themselves, the dwarren erupting in a cacophonous battle roar. Swinging around, their cry echoing across the breadth of the plains, they came to a halt, their line curved to face both the Legion and the Alvritshai's Phalanx, their ranks falling silent.

"The men in the Legion shifted at this display, disturbed, but the King did not quail. With a nod of his head, a message was passed down the line, colored flags flashing in the brightening morning. The men stirred again, readying their weapons, tightening the clasps of armor, of shield, testing the strings of bows. Horns blew across the field from the Alvritshai, but Maarten kept his eyes on the dwarren, on their shifting ranks of gaezels. He caught the eye of his nearest adviser, and at his nod of readiness, he drew his sword. Steel flashed in the light, and the Legion fell silent behind him, hushed, waiting for the signal."

As if mimicking the storyteller's words, his small audience fell silent. Most were leaning forward in their seats, alcohol-hazed eyes wide, shoulders tensed. The storyteller looked over them all, his arms outstretched, as if holding the entire battlefield, armies and all, before him, a satisfied smile on his face.

"And then," he whispered, a chair creaking as he paused and someone leaned farther forward, "as the Alvritshai horns blew, as they'd agreed upon at their secret meeting, Maarten dropped his sword."

The men surrounding the storyteller sighed, settling back. But Colin noted that not all of those in the tavern were enthralled. Some sat far back and snorted at the reaction of the others, lifting tankards to their lips. Others merely shook their heads.

"The King's army charged down the hill onto the flat, heading directly for the dwarren, letting out a battle cry of their own to rival the Riders. And simultaneously, the Alvritshai Phalanx, their long white pennons flaring out behind them, charged from the north. The dwarren didn't wait for either army. The gaezels, heads bent forward, wicked horns down, met them on the flat. It's said the clash of their weapons when they struck could be heard a day's walk distant. It's said the ground itself trembled. It's said the sun vanished from the sky, lost behind the black cloud of dust that rose from the tread of thousands of feet. And I believe it, for it was a meeting of the three races, with the best of their men, their bravest warriors.

"And it was a trap." At this, everyone in the tavern growled, and the storyteller smiled grimly. "Not the trap you think. No. Not yet. A different trap, set up by King Maarten and Tamaell Fedorem to lure the dwarren Riders to the edge of the Escarpment." The storyteller's smile faded, his eyes darkening with anger. "But it was indeed a trap for King Maarten as well, although none knew it except the traitorous Alvritshai."

The storyteller spat this last remark, and everyone in the room burst out with their own curses, some literally spitting to the side.

"Maarten rode down onto the flat and fought like a madman, his blade bloodied in instants, his surcoat stained," the storyteller continued, rising from his seat as his voice rose, his arms miming sword thrusts and parries, not letting the riled patrons settle back down. "He roared as he drove into the dwarren ranks, slicing at the dwarren warriors, at their horned mounts, cutting flesh and sinew, severing arms and heads with mighty strokes, threshing a path through them as if they were grain and he a scythe. His men called out challenges behind him, some falling to blade and spear, those that followed pressing forward to take their place. Archers filled the skies with arrows until they blotted out the sun as effectively as the dust, and the dwarren ... the dwarren fell, crushed between the two forces—Maarten and the Legion on one side, the Alvritshai White Phalanx on the other. Bodies littered the field, were trampled as the armies pressed together. For a moment it appeared that the dwarren might hold, but then their wardrums shuddered through the air, signaling a retreat.

"Maarten heard the order, but he'd be damned if the dwarren escaped him. He intended this battle to be the last. He intended the ages-long war among the three races to end, here, now, at the Escarpment, and so he spun his horse. But he was trapped at the forefront of the fray, his men so eager to fight that they'd blocked his retreat. So he bellowed to his son, Stephan, the heir to the throne of the eastern ports, his command heard over the clash of the battle, 'They cannot be allowed to retreat! Stop them! This ends here!'

"And young Stephan heard him. Not yet eighteen, still he brandished his sword, already slick with blood, and called, 'Fellow Legion, follow me!' He charged his steed to the eastern flank, even as the dwarren began to break away, as their gaezels began their unnaturally swift turns to head back to the vastness and safety of the plains. Hundreds followed the heir, but he fell on the first of the retreating dwarren himself, and he held them. He held them back so that the rest of his force could arrive to support him. He held them, and then he held the line. No! He advanced the line! He pushed the dwarren back into the Legion's main force, back into the Alvritshai Phalanx. Desperation caused the dwarren to hold for long moments, their retreat severed, but then their lines began to waver. Taking advantage, Stephan shoved them farther back. Harried on the east by Stephan, on the north by the Alvritshai, and the south by the King, the only available escape for the dwarren was the west ... where the cliffs of the Escarpment waited.

"And that was where the combined armies forced the dwarren. They herded them like cattle, and as they were driven to the edge, the lower plains shadowed far below, the dwarren became frenzied. Step by slow step, they gave ground, their gaezels going mad, lethal horns skewering man and dwarren and Alvritshai indiscriminately, and still they were pressed back, Stephan and Maarten and Fedorem closing ranks. Step by slow step, the cursed dwarren—who'd hounded our every step onto the plains, who'd slaughtered entire trading parties, who'd returned the severed heads of the delegations sent to negotiate trade pacts between the races—*those* cursed dwarren were driven back, and back, and back ...

"Until they were driven off the edge of the Escarpment, to fall to their deaths below."

The entire room sighed with intense satisfaction, only faintly tinged with horror. Colin shuddered, the hatred of the dwarren in the room almost tangible. An unwavering hatred that crawled across his skin, as black as the spot on his arm, as sickening.

And yet he understood that hatred, felt it himself, in his bones. Because of what the dwarren had done to the wagon trains, his own and the one they'd found near the underground river. They'd slaughtered everyone in that wagon train, herded them together and killed them—men, women, and children—with no mercy. They'd burned the wagons to the ground. They would have done the same to Colin's group, would have succeeded if the Shadows hadn't gotten to them first.

He found his hand gripping the coin so hard the edges bit into his palm and he forced himself to relax. At the hearth, the storyteller let the vindictive murmurs rise, but he interrupted them before they could reach their height.

"But that wasn't the end. Not the end that Maarten envisioned anyway. Oh, no. Because even as the two forces—Alvritshai and men—stood at the cliffs, staring down into the shadow of the bluff, where the dwarren Riders lay in bloody, broken heaps, even as Maarten drew back from the edge and turned toward Tamaell Fedorem with a triumphant smile, the Alvritshai betrayed him.

"Fedorem's escort, his most trusted advisers, his closest lords, leaped forward, daggers raised. Stephan cried out, his shout heard across the battlefield, as the Alvritshai fell on the King. The heir tried to kick his steed forward, but he was restrained by his own men, even as a cry of outrage rose from the Legion. Before they could react, the Alvritshai Phalanx let loose a rain of arrows, cutting down hundreds in a single volley, catching the Legion unprepared. The group nearest to Maarten charged the attackers, and then both armies were engulfed in a melee—not a battle but a brawl—as the Legion tried to retrieve their fallen King's body. Stephan tried to join them yet again, but he was hauled to safety by his own advisers, pulled off his horse out of sight of the Alvritshai archers and dragged to the back of the Legion as they retreated, Maarten's body in tow.

"It was a black day, a bitter day for the Provinces. We lost our King to betrayal, to the *Alvritshai*." He whispered the name like a curse. "But it was a triumphant day as well, for the entire coast. For at his death, Maarten claimed the defeat of the dwarren Riders in his name, for his lineage."

"But not the defeat of the dwarren," the man nearest to

Colin murmured, his voice no more than a whisper, so low that Colin doubted anyone else had heard.

Silence reigned in the tavern but for the faint sounds of tankards being raised in salute and a few quiet and respectful murmurs or prayers.

Then the young boy reappeared and laid a plank of meat and cheese and roasted onion down in front of Colin, along with a tankard of ale as well. "Too bad 'tisn't all true," he huffed, softly enough that Colin almost didn't hear him.

"What do you mean?"

The boy eyed him warily. "'Tisn't all true, least not how my grandda tells it."

Colin frowned. "And how would your grandda know?"

The boy snorted. "He wuz there! Right there, in tha King's own men at tha end o' tha attack. He says 'twasn't all of the Alvritshai that attacked, only sum o' them, that Fedorem seemed as shocked as any o' them. He says a few a tha lords e'en tried to stop it—Lord Vaersoom and Lord Aeren. But 'twas too late by then. Tha armies wuz already brawlin'."

Colin stilled. "Did you say Aeren?"

"Lord Aeren," the boy said, nodding. "And Lord Vaersoom. There's a group of tha white-skinned bastards in tha city right now, jus come in on a ship."

Colin thought about the group of guardsmen he'd seen emerge from the walled manse, headed toward the wharf.

"Is Aer—Lord Aeren among them?"

The boy shrugged in irritation. "Could be, could be not. Not likely to come here." Then he tucked one hand beneath his arm and held out the other expectantly, eyes wide.

Colin grunted and handed over the coin, and the boy was gone in the blink of an eye. He turned his attention back to the storyteller, but the crowd had tired of histories and were rowdily demanding a ribald song of mirth and mayhem, so he began to eat.

"Aeren," he murmured, letting the bursts of laughter from the other patrons roll over him as he thought about the plains, about the Alvritshai he'd met so long ago. He might have written the boy's story off as nonsense—a grandfather's interpretation of the battle, told to impress his grandson—except he'd seen the slightly contemptuous faces of the other men in the tavern. The older men, the ones with scars on their faces and the habits of fighting men, their movements careful, stances too casual, even here, relaxed with drink. Those around the hearth were younger, quick to judge and eager to accept.

He wondered if the Aeren from the tale was the same Aeren he'd met so long ago on the plains.

There was one way to find out.

~

Colin eased a little closer to the main thoroughfare where the delegation from the Alvritshai was rumored to pass on their way to their ship at the harbor. He'd missed the initial procession to the Governor's estate, the manse he'd seen from the ridge when he'd first viewed the city, and no one from the delegation had been spotted outside the walls of the estate since.

A wise decision, Colin thought, glancing around at those gathered on both sides of the street. Most had come to gawk at the foreigners, at their strange skin and wild clothes, some with their children in tow. "Careful of their eyes," an old man in the alley next to Colin hissed. "If they catch your gaze, they'll suck out your soul!"

A middle-aged woman scoffed. "Don't be ridiculous. They just hold you with their eyes; it's the knife to the gut when you can't move that takes your soul!"

Colin's brow creased in irritation. He pushed his staff forward between two younger men—their faces taut and angry, arms crossed over their chests—and slid in between them. He now stood at the mouth of the side street, barely more than an alley, but it was enough for him to see down the thoroughfare if he craned his neck. He hadn't managed to find out from the citizens of Portstown if Lord Aeren was part of the group; they only knew it was an Alvritshai delegation, come to see the Governor to discuss trade agreements.

Colin settled back slightly. Provinces, Governors, and Kings. He'd learned enough in the past few hours to know that shortly after the wagon group had headed east— within a year if he'd pieced all of the information together correctly—outright war had broken out in Andover, the

Feud over the Rose and its powers coming to a head, and the Proprietors of the colonies had been drawn into it. But by then the refugees from the war had grown desperate. Small groups had risen up against the Proprietors, groups like those in Lean-to, led by men like Shay and Karl and composed mostly of criminals and political dissidents, only with four or five times the number of members by then. The Court thought they could crush the rebellions. But the war for the Rose had sapped their resources. The Proprietors found themselves abandoned, the Court's attention completely on their own lands in Andover, on preserving their standing in the Court itself while still pursuing their bid for the Rose.

The "minor" rebellions became a full-fledged revolution. The Proprietors attempted to pull together to defend their lands, but they'd allowed too many refugees into their towns. And this time the dissidents and rabble-rousers had the support of the laborers and craftsmen and merchants. The Proprietors had counted on their Armory to protect them, but in the end ...

In the end, the Armory wasn't as loyal as the Proprietors believed.

The Proprietors fell, or vanished. No one knew what had happened to Sartori, which Colin found ... disappointing. He could go back and find out, *sink* back, but he satisfied himself with knowing that he'd been removed, most likely killed by Karl and the men who'd led the revolt.

Ahead, on the thoroughfare, a ripple passed through the crowd. Colin straightened, pushing away from the stone of the building at his back. He would have stepped forward, but the two men he'd passed to reach the position pressed forward instead, shoving people aside, their faces intent. They kept their attention on the street, where the crowd had begun to sigh with passing whispers of awe and wonder, but they pushed farther down the block, joining two other men at the next corner.

Colin frowned as he saw something pass from one of the men's hands to another, something narrow and thin.

The crowd ahead parted as the Legion forced a path through the center of the street. The guardsmen were there to hold the press of people back, except that as the horses of the delegation appeared, those in the crowd, full of whispers and murmurs a moment before, fell silent and withdrew. Not in fear, but respect. It left the members of the Legion uncomfortable, alone in the space between the citizens of Portstown and the delegation itself. Their hands fell to the hilts of their swords for reassurance, their eyes on the crowd, flicking from face to face.

When the delegation came into full view, Colin caught his breath.

These were not the Alvritshai he remembered from the plains. Aeren and his escort had been rough, deadly, exotic, but practical. He remembered their intensity, their curiosity, and their profound respect for the people in the wagon train.

These Alvritshai were also intense. But they radiated a stiff formality and an intangible aloofness. The rough practical clothing from the plains had been replaced with soft, colorful silks sewn with severe lines, emphasizing the Alvritshai's angular features, their tense postures, heads held high, eyes gazing down from the elevated height of their mounts. The expressions on the guardsmen in front were close to sneers, mouths drawn down in distaste, and they kept their eyes forward, not deigning to look to either side. Colin thought of what the old man and woman had said about their eyes and wondered if the Alvritshai knew what the common people thought—

But then he saw the Alvritshai lords the guardsmen protected.

Colin let his held breath out with a sigh, felt his heart falter with relief.

It was Aeren. Older than on the plains, taller and hardened somehow, more mature, but not as old as Colin had expected, not as worn. He kept his eyes forward as well, not looking to either side, but his expression was set, registering neither distaste nor scorn. It was merely . . . regretful, as if he were enduring what must be endured. He was dressed in a deep blue tunic, slashed along the torso, with a vibrant red fabric beneath. He wore the same band of gold on his forearm Colin remembered from the plains, although it couldn't be the same one. This one appeared larger and contained more writing.

Another lord rode next to him, dressed in a warm maroon with gold accents—buttons and braided cords. Behind the two lords rode personal guardsmen, and with a start Colin recognized Eraeth. The guardsman had aged more than Aeren, with new scars on his face. But if Aeren had been at the battle the storyteller had related at the Hangman's Noose, then no doubt Eraeth had been there as well.

But it was Aeren who caught Colin's attention, who held it. Because since he'd left the forest, he had found nothing familiar, aside from the church. That lack had settled into his bones, an ache that he hadn't even recognized until he saw the Alvritshai lord.

He stepped forward, only half aware of what he'd done, not certain what he intended to do—

And out of the corner of his eye he caught a flash of movement, motion where the crowd should have been still.

It happened fast. The four men Colin had noticed earlier broke through the edge of the crowd. He heard one of them bellow, "Traitorous bastards!" saw the flicker of knives, the deadlier glint of sunlight on a crossbow—a bolt, the slim shaft he'd seen being passed from hand to hand had been a crossbow bolt—and then the snick of the release, the bolt flying too fast for the eye to see.

Someone in the Alvritshai entourage roared, a sound of shock and pain and rage. The thick scent of blood punched through the stench of sea salt, sweat, and smoke from the city.

The crowd broke, screams rising, the Alvritshai Phalanx a flicker of fluid movement, no longer aloof, no longer pretentious, the Legion sent to protect them hesitating. Aeren and those in the Alvritshai party were lost from sight as the Alvritshai pulled the lords from their horses and surrounded them, but he could see the four men as they charged the Alvritshai line. They launched themselves into defending Alvritshai guardsmen as the Legion reacted, but slowly, almost leisurely. Another crossbow bolt sped into the fray, and an Alvritshai guardsman fell. The three men with knives clawed at the edges of the wall of bodies surrounding the lords, too close for the Alvritshai to draw their long, thin blades.

And then an Alvritshai guard pulled a dagger and stabbed it deep into the side of one of the attacking men. The man reared back, his scream setting the hairs on Colin's arms on end. With a vicious twist, the Alvritshai withdrew the blade, blood flying, and as the body fell, the leader of the attacking group swore in frustration.

As if it were an order, the attackers broke off and fled, two heading toward the street one block away, the other bolting down the thoroughfare in the opposite direction.

Colin hesitated a moment—enough to see that the Legion hadn't yet moved to follow, the men looking to their commander; enough to see that the Alvritshai were focused on protecting the lords—

And then Colin spun, dodged into the street at his back that ran parallel to the one the attackers had taken. Rage burned in his lungs, lay thick on his tongue. The Legion had expected the attack, had barely moved to halt it, and were now allowing the culprits to escape. They *intended* to let the men escape.

But Colin could still smell the blood. Possibly Aeren's blood. He hadn't seen Aeren fall, couldn't tell who within the group had been struck, but it didn't matter. He'd seen the expression on the Legion commander's face, the same expression he'd seen on Walter's face as the Proprietor's son beat him senseless in the dirt streets of Portstown, the same expression he'd seen on Sartori's face when the Proprietor blackmailed his father into accepting the lead role in the expedition east: a grim satisfaction and the knowledge that there would be no consequences.

Colin shoved forward through the fleeing people, *pushing*, aware that the crowd moved too slowly as he rounded the corner and cut left onto the cross street, rage driving him. He burst into the next intersection, turned to see the two fleeing men charging toward him, also moving slowly, too slowly, as if they were running through mud. Colin ground to a halt, felt a familiar pressure shove him from behind, and staggered as the world settled . . .

And realized everyone hadn't been moving slowly. No. The entire *world* had slowed. *He'd* slowed it, reached out without thought and forced it to slow in order to get to the intersection ahead of the attackers.

The implications of what he'd done stunned him. But there was no time for thought. The two men were almost on him, shock registering on their faces a moment before Colin's staff lashed out. He drove it hard into the leader's groin, and the man folded over with a strangled grunt; then he pulled it back and pivoted the other end so it connected with the second man's head.

They fell like sacks of potatoes, the leader groaning, curled into a tight ball. The other simply crumpled, unconscious, his knife striking the cobbles with a brittle clang.

Colin drew up straight, gasping, his heart thundering in his chest, blood pounding in his neck, rage tingling along his arms. He wiped sweat from his face, coughed as he tried to swallow and breathe at the same time, then leaned heavily on his staff. A few stragglers from the crowd streamed past on either side, giving Colin and the bodies a wide berth, but he ignored their sharp gestures and fierce whispers.

At the end of the street, where it intersected with the thoroughfare, members of the Alvritshai Phalanx suddenly appeared. They poured between the buildings, swords drawn, faces black with intent, the Legion a step behind.

They halted when they saw Colin standing over the bodies.

Someone stepped to the forefront of the Alvritshai—Eraeth—and said something in the Alvritshai language that Colin didn't catch. He held his blade before him, his eyes locked on Colin's, and for a moment—no more than a breath—Colin felt a thrill of fear as he considered the possibility that what the old man and woman had said was true about Alvritshai eyes.

But then he realized there was no recognition in Eraeth's gaze, and the moment broke.

"What happened here?" the commander of the Legion barked, moving forward to stand a few paces ahead, but to one side, of Eraeth.

Colin tried to answer but couldn't. He still hadn't caught his breath.

The commander's eyes flicked from Colin to the surrounding citizens, trapped against the side of the street, none of them daring to move. Not with both the Legion and the Phalanx present.

"He stopped them," a woman finally said, nodding toward Colin. When the commander's gaze fell on her, she hesitated, then straightened, her shoulders back, and took a small step forward. "He came from the cross street there—like a blur, so fast I barely saw him—but then he

was there, and he struck them both before they even had a
chance to raise their knives."

A few of the surrounding people nodded, murmuring to
one another. The commander glared until they fell silent.
The woman stepped back, her head bent but with a defiant
look in her eyes, and then the commander stepped up to
the two men on the ground. He stared at them a long moment, then shoved the leader over onto his back with his
foot, the man still clutching his balls. The Legionnaire gave
a snort of disgust.

Behind him, Eraeth lowered his blade. But he stiffened
again as someone else pushed through the Alvritshai at
his back.

Aeren. Unharmed.

Colin sagged in relief.

"What has happened here?" Aeren said, his Andovan
precise, with only a hint of an accent.

The commander glared at Colin, then turned with a thin
smile. "It appears that one of Portstown's good citizens has
kept the attackers from escaping."

"How fortunate," Aeren said. Colin thought the Alvritshai lord would add something else—he could see the intent
in the narrowing of the lord's eyes—but instead Aeren
asked, "What do you intend to do with them?"

"Kill them," Eraeth said, his voice flat, his eyes on the
two men lying on the ground.

Aeren raised a hand in warning.

The commander's smile vanished. "That's not how
things are done here in Portstown. In any of the Provinces.
We aren't barbaric. They will be arrested and tried before
a judge."

The Alvritshai bristled, Eraeth drawing a sharp breath
to respond, but Aeren's glance kept him silent.

"Very well," Aeren said. "I leave them to your ...
judges." His gaze shifted to Colin, took in his staff, his robe,
glanced off his face—

And snapped back again. His brows narrowed, and he
frowned.

Colin stepped forward, managed a weak, "Aeren—"

Then his stomach seized. Not with hunger but with the
full force of the Lifeblood.

Colin cried out, a sound of denial and pain, both arms

clutching his sides as he sank to his knees. He clenched his teeth, fought against the searing heat, against the sudden taste of blood in his mouth, against the narrowing vision, tried to keep himself upright and conscious . . .

But the pain overwhelmed him, so much worse than when he'd left the forest weeks before. He felt the cobbles scrape against his cheek as he collapsed, heard the shuffle of feet as he was surrounded, heard a babble of voices, both Alvritshai and Andovan, as the pain increased. He groaned, felt hands against his face, his chest, as they rolled him onto his back, heard the commander bark, "What's happening?" from a distance. "Is he sick? Is it contagious?"

"Seizure," Eraeth answered, his voice still flat, without a fleck of emotion, but he stood closer than the commander. Practically on top of him.

More voices, an argument, but Colin couldn't follow it. A wave of heat and pain shoved the world away. Then:

"We'll take him to the infirmary," the commander said, grudgingly.

"No!" Aeren this time, not Eraeth. "We'll take him with us."

"Like hell you will," the commander spat. "He's a citizen of the Provinces!"

"He's helped to subdue the men who threatened to take my life," Aeren said, his voice taking on an edge. "I will not harm him. The honor of my House demands that I see to his welfare."

Colin didn't hear the commander's response, only the sudden rise in volume as they argued. The taste of blood filled his mouth, its scent swelling and smothering his senses. He struggled against it, fought the expanding film of yellow over his vision, the sudden muted ringing in his ears that blocked out all sound—

Then the heat became too great, and everything went black.

13

THE SHIP ROLLED BENEATH HIM, and Colin clutched the wooden support, the press of the other refugees from Trent close around him. The sour-sick stench of vomit filled the dark hold, and he tried not to gag as he breathed through his mouth. Not ten paces away, he heard someone heaving up his minimal breakfast, and he blocked out the sound, closing his eyes and tucking his head down between his shoulders, cowering against the support. Someone nearby wept, and a baby cried—had cried nonstop for the last two days, sick with colic—its mother shushing it.

Overhead, on deck, the sound of running boots thudded into the hold as the ship lurched to port. Everyone cried out as they were thrown to the side.

Then a hand fell on Colin's shoulder. He looked up, even though it was too dark to see any faces, and felt his mother's breath against his neck as she spoke. "It'll be all right, Colin. It's just a storm. It'll be over soon enough."

She pulled him close, hugged his body tight to hers, nestling him under her arm. He didn't let go of the wooden support, not completely, but he did bury his head against her chest. He could smell her sweat, the reek of the potatoes she'd been peeling for the cook for the captain's dinner, the collected grime from unwashed clothes; he could smell *her*.

He wanted to stay here, in her arms, in her warmth.

The ship lurched again, and suddenly there was another hand, on his other arm.

"Colin," a girl whispered, tugging at him, trying to gain his attention.

He pulled away, clutched tighter to his mother. She smiled down at him—he could *feel* it—tousled his hair—

And the girl tugged harder. "Colin! Colin, listen to me!"

Colin growled and turned his head to snarl, "What?"

It was Karen.

A cold, cold hand sank deep into his gut.

Karen shouldn't be here. Karen shouldn't be on this ship. He hadn't even known her yet.

With a look of pity and patience, Karen said, "You can't stay here, Colin."

Confused but with a growing awareness that this couldn't be happening, that Karen was dead, that his *mother* was dead, he whispered, "Why not?"

"You have to wake up. There are things you need to do."

"But . . . but," he stammered, aware now that he could taste blood in his mouth, warm and metallic. The visceral sensations of the ship were receding—the smell of vomit, the warmth of his mother's body, the splinters biting into his hands.

Karen receded as well.

"What do I need to do?" he shouted into the burgeoning darkness, but the words were mumbled, the blood thick on his tongue.

He woke with a jolt and spat blood to one side of the bed he lay in, moaning as a tendril of the spit drooled down from his mouth. He wiped it away, his body aching, his head pounding, then lay back on the bed again.

He smelled leaves and earth and snow.

After a moment, he realized that the rolling sensation of the ship from the dream had not ended.

His eyes flew open and he turned onto his side—

And found three Alvritshai watching him from the opposite end of the narrow room. Aeren, Eraeth, and a guardsman Colin didn't know. They stood just inside the narrow doorway. Colin could see a ship's corridor outside, and with a quick glance he determined that the room they held him in contained five more bunks, two above him and three across an aisle. Lanterns burned, swinging at the motion of the ship, and he could hear the thud of numerous feet around him.

Eraeth said something in Alvritshai. Colin caught a few words he recognized, but not enough to translate it. He'd learned more dwarren than Alvritshai in his time in the forest.

"Speak Andovan, Protector," Aeren said, and when Eraeth sneered, he added, "as a courtesy to our guest."

Eraeth's sneer vanished, his eyes going flat. "I told you he would wake soon."

Aeren nodded. His eyes didn't leave Colin's face. "Yes. You were correct to summon me."

Eraeth snorted. "I do not know why you wanted to bring him with us. He's nothing more than a commoner, and he stinks."

"I brought him because he stopped those who attacked us, those who killed one of the Phalanx and nearly killed Lord Barak. He stopped them even when it was obvious the Legion's commander would have allowed them to escape. I brought him because he appeared sick, and the honor of Rhyssal House demanded it, but also because I felt that the Legion's commander intended him harm." Aeren stepped forward, a frown touching his lips. "And I brought him because he seems . . . familiar."

Both Eraeth and the other guard stiffened when Aeren moved, their gazes falling on Colin as if they expected him to leap up with bared sword at any moment. Colin didn't have a sword, didn't even have his staff or satchel, although the satchel must be close if he could smell the Lifeblood. He hadn't dared move since he'd caught sight of the three Alvritshai; he'd seen how fast they could move when there was need.

Now Aeren tilted his head slightly, his attention focusing completely on Colin while the two guardsmen shifted farther into the room. "Who are you?"

Colin cleared his mouth of blood-tainted saliva and swallowed. Then, in a hoarse voice, he said, "Colin. My name is Colin."

Aeren's eyes narrowed as he thought. Colin could see his mind racing, reaching back, then back farther, memory tugging at him.

And then his eyes widened. He swore, in Alvritshai, but the flavor of the words was clear.

Eraeth asked him something, and he responded in a

hushed voice. Eraeth said something, realized that Colin couldn't understand, and repeated himself in Andovan. "Impossible!"

Colin eased up onto his elbow, swung his legs off the edge of the bunk, aware of the Alvritshai's swords. And aware that doubt had settled into Aeren's gaze.

"I survived the attacks by the dwarren and the Shadows . . . the sukrael," he said, "but only with the help of the Faelehgre."

"The Faelehgre?"

"The lights in the forest. The ones that burn with a pure white fire. They've lived there with the Shadows for hundreds upon hundreds of years."

Aeren's eyes narrowed. "The antruel. The Guardians." Both Eraeth and the other guardsman shifted nervously.

Colin thought about the Faelehgre, of the Well. "They call themselves the Faelehgre."

Aeren nodded. But he hadn't relaxed. Neither had Eraeth. "And how did these . . . Faelehgre help you?"

Colin shifted uncomfortably, dropped his head, the memories rising up so fast, so vividly. He breathed in deeply to steady himself, smelled the grass of the plains, the clean wetness of the storm that had passed. "Most of the wagons managed to escape the dwarren battle," he began, his voice low. "We halted at the edge of the forest. The dwarren followed us, but they refused to come to within a hundred paces of the edge of the trees. We thought we were safe. But then the Shadows attacked. The sukrael."

"We warned you," Eraeth said, voice tight with contempt.

Colin looked up, anger rising in his chest. "Where else could we go?" he asked bitterly. "After the fight near the underground river, fleeing across the plains, the storm. . . ." He shook his head. "Even if we had followed you, we wouldn't have been able to go far. We were exhausted. We would have slowed you down, even without the wagons." He remembered how fast the Alvritshai warriors had moved back then, how fast they could run, nearly keeping up with the horses.

Eraeth grunted, still dismissive, still suspicious. But Aeren intervened before he could say anything more. "How did you escape the sukrael?"

"I . . . didn't."

Aeren's brow creased in confusion.

Pain filled Colin's chest, cold with the memory of the Shadow's touch, but he forced himself to continue. "The sukrael attacked the wagons, and everything went to hell. Karen and I tried to find our parents, but everyone was running back and forth, and the Shadows were everywhere, falling on everyone, taking the horses, the Armory . . . nothing could stop them, not swords or axes. When we finally found Karen's father, he'd been cornered near a wagon. I watched him fall, tried to hold Karen back. But she broke free." His throat closed up but he forced himself to swallow. The emotions weren't as raw here, away from the forest, away from the plains, but they were still strong enough to make breathing difficult.

He glanced up, met Aeren's pained look, Eraeth's narrowed, his mouth turned down in a frown. "I stayed with her, held her. I couldn't move. Too drained—from the run, from the intensity of the dwarren battle, from the horror of what was happening around me. So I simply sat there and let the Shadows touch me."

Eraeth hissed, the sound so unnatural that Colin started. Then the Protector muttered something under his breath, lips drawn back from his teeth as he reached for his sword, but he didn't draw it. The effort *not* to draw it was clear in the tension on his face. "No one survives the touch of the sukrael," he said sharply.

Colin felt his anger escalate. "I wouldn't have. I wanted to die. But the Shadows didn't take me right away, like the others. They'd been sated. So they tested me instead, touched me, searching for something. But then the Faeleghre came, and the Shadows fled. They saved me, led me to the Lifeblood, and—" He halted, about to say the Faelehgre had *forced* him to drink the waters; but that wasn't true. "—they had me drink from the Well. That's what saved me from the Shadows' touch, but it changed me as well." He hesitated, then shoved back the cuff of his robe, exposing the black mark on his skin.

Eraeth stilled, his body going rigid, but the other guardsman wasn't as controlled. He stepped back, eyes wide with fear, and hissed, "Shaeveran," warding himself.

Eraeth barked something in Alvritshai, the guardsman

arguing with him a moment, until Aeren finally cut them both off with a gesture.

Colin covered the mark again. The other guardsman whispered something to Aeren, his glance shooting toward his lord. Aeren's lips pursed.

"He says you've drunk from one of the sarenavriell, from a—" He paused, brow creasing as he translated the Alvritshai word, "—from a 'Well of Sorrows.' He says that you are cursed."

"Well of Sorrows." Colin barked bitter laughter. He thought of all those who'd died in the wagon train, of his parents, Arten, and Karen. "That's appropriate."

Eraeth's suspicious gaze hadn't wavered. "It could be a trick," he said tightly. "He may not be the boy we met on the plains. He may have assumed the identity to get close to you."

Aeren frowned. "Very few knew of the wagon train on the plains: you and the rest of the Phalanx present for that portion of my Trial, but no one else. Are you saying I cannot trust my own House guard?"

Eraeth's lips peeled back from his lips in a silent snarl, but then he relaxed, the snarl vanishing. He shot Colin a black look. "Of course you can trust your guard."

Aeren nodded, accepting the emotionless words without comment. He regarded Colin a long moment, the silence thick, his face unreadable, his gaze intense. Colin shifted nervously beneath that gaze, the rolling of the ship beginning to make him nauseous again. Then he straightened.

"I can prove that I'm the boy you met on the plains," he said suddenly.

Before any of the Alvritshai could respond, he concentrated. His age fell away, the wrinkles of the fifty-year-old man smoothing, muscles tightening. He took himself all the way back to twelve, the age when he and Aeren had first met.

As soon as he started to change, the guardsman Colin didn't know whispered something long and complicated. Colin could taste his fear. Eraeth's blade slid from its sheath, and with a fluid grace he stepped in front of Aeren. The Alvritshai lord didn't protest, his own eyes wide. Fear tightened the skin at the corners of his eyes, pressed his lips into a thin line.

"Stop," he said, and waved his hand. When Colin only frowned, he repeated in a harsher tone, "Stop!"

Colin returned to the older version of himself. He could feel the tension in Aeren now, the lord fidgeting, as if he wanted to pace, which the confines of the cabin on the ship didn't allow. He shot a hard gaze at Eraeth, then turned back to Colin.

"Do *not* allow anyone else to see you ... change," he said, his voice soft but dangerous. He waited until Colin had nodded agreement before continuing, relaxing only slightly. "Is this a consequence of the sarenavriell?"

"Yes. I can become any age I want, up to my true age."

"And can you shift into other forms? Can you make yourself look like Eraeth, or myself?"

"No."

"I see. And were there ... any other consequences?"

"I have seizures, like the one you saw." At the look of concern that flashed in Aeren's eyes, Colin ran a hand across his mouth, as if there were blood still there, then grimaced. "There's nothing you can do for me. If it happens again, let it run its course." He didn't explain that the seizures had gotten worse since he'd left the Well's influence or that he'd only coughed up blood once before, on the plains.

Aeren regarded him a long moment, then nodded, as if he'd reached a decision. He said something low to Eraeth, the Protector's expression darkening, but he stepped outside the room, returning with Colin's staff and satchel. He handed them off to Aeren.

Kneeling down, Aeren set the staff aside and reached into the satchel. Colin felt his heart leap into his throat, thinking of the flask of Lifeblood, hoping that neither Aeren nor Eraeth had tasted it or even opened it, but Aeren didn't remove the flask. He drew out the small vial of pink-tinged water instead.

From his crouch, turning the vial over in one hand, Aeren asked, "Do you know what this is?" He looked up, met Colin's gaze. "It's water from a ruanavriell. It has the power to heal. Not completely, but enough to halt blood loss, to seal a wound long enough for it to heal on its own." He closed the vial in a fist. "Where did you get this?"

Colin swallowed, felt sweat break out on his forehead and upper lip. Aeren had given the question a weight that Colin didn't understand. But he sensed that of all of the questions that Aeren and Eraeth had asked, the answer to this one was the most important.

"I don't know where it came from," he said. "But I found it on my father's body."

Aeren's eyes narrowed as he considered. Then, abruptly, he stood, and Colin felt nearly all of the tension drain out of the room. Only Eraeth still remained wary.

"The vial is marked with a sigil," Aeren said. "My own House sigil. Only someone from my House could have given this to you—or your father—and at present, I am the only remaining member of my House." He grimaced, and Colin heard the pain and grief he tried to keep hidden. "I gave such a vial to your father, before the dwarren attack, to help him heal someone's shoulder. I see no other way you could have possession of this . . . unless what you say is true."

Eraeth drew breath as if to protest, but Aeren stiffened. Eraeth's jaw clenched, his eyes darkening as he glowered at Colin. Aeren stepped forward and handed Colin his staff and satchel.

"You may move about the ship with one of my guards as escort if you wish. We are headed toward Corsair, where I intend to meet with the King. I realize that you more than likely were not headed to Corsair when we took you on board. Once we arrive, I will make arrangements for you to be returned to Portstown, if that is your wish. Now that I know you are . . . well."

"I had only arrived in Portstown the day of the attack in the thoroughfare," Colin said. He shrugged. "I have nowhere to go."

Aeren hesitated, and behind him, Colin saw Eraeth make a warning gesture, one his lord couldn't see. "Then you should remain with my party, at least for the moment," Aeren said. Eraeth swore silently, flashing Colin a vicious glare. The guard's hand dropped, clenched slightly into a fist. Aeren's gaze fell on Colin's robes. "You should change into the shirt and breeches in your pack. Those will suffice until I can have suitable clothes prepared."

When Colin nodded agreement, Aeren glanced down

at the vial of pink-tinted water he still held in his hand. He started to hand the vial back to Colin, but stopped.

"There is one other thing, Colin," he began hesitantly.

"What?"

Aeren looked up. "During the attack in Portstown, the lord accompanying me, Lord Barak, was mortally wounded by the attacker's crossbow bolt. We have stabilized him, but our healer does not feel that he will survive the journey back to our own lands, and there is no one within the Provinces who would be willing to help heal . . . one of our kind." He said it with the barest hint of bitterness, but even that faded as he continued. "The Alvritshai are not welcome along the coast, and the hatred is not entirely undeserved. The attack in Portstown was not unexpected." His hand closed over the vial again, and he straightened. The guardsman behind him shifted nervously, his gaze falling to the rolling floor. Even Eraeth shifted uncomfortably.

"The waters of the ruanavriell are rare, collected only by members of the Evant during their Trials, as proof that they have, in fact, seen the Confluence and tasted its waters. It is not the Alvritshai custom to ask for gifts—"

And suddenly Colin understood. "Take it." He smiled and pushed Aeren's closed fist toward him, both guards stiffening until he withdrew his hand. "My father would have wanted you to have it back."

Aeren frowned at Colin a long moment, then bowed, the gesture formal, reminding Colin with a lurch of his heart of their first meeting on the plains. "Thank you. I—and Lord Barak—are in your debt."

Then he rose and turned to Eraeth, motioning toward the door. The other guardsman stepped back against the wall to let them pass, Eraeth murmuring a soft command in Alvritshai; Colin assumed he'd been assigned to watch over him.

At the entrance to the cabin, Aeren turned back. "We will be arriving in Corsair tomorrow."

And then he left, leaving Colin alone with the attendant guardsman.

Colin opened the satchel and rummaged through the clothes, surprised they'd left him the knife he'd used to try to kill himself, but shuddering with relief when he found the cloth-wrapped bundle that contained the Lifeblood.

~

Colin visited the deck of the Alvritshai ship twice over the course of the next day, but he did not see Aeren or Eraeth. The guardsmen assigned to escort him changed sometime during the night, but they did not speak to him. While he was on deck the following morning, he heard a pair of them whispering about him in their own language. The only word he caught was "shaeveran," and he frowned, wondering what it meant, recalling that that was what the previous guard had muttered when he exposed the black mark on his forearm.

He kept the mark hidden after that, the sleeve of his shirt fully extended.

He was in his cabin the following afternoon when one of the guardsmen appeared and motioned him to gather his things and come up on deck. The first thing he noticed as he stepped out into the late afternoon sunlight was that the ship's crew had become more active, rushing from post to post, securing ropes and tying down sails. He saw why almost immediately.

The ship had entered a sea lane. At least ten other ships of varying sizes surrounded them, and land filled the horizon to port. They'd crossed the strait while Colin was below with the help of a stiff western wind, and now the prow of the ship was pointed toward the mouth of an inlet that broke through the rocky coastline. The ocean crashed against crags of rock to either side, sending up sheets of spray taller than the deck of the Alvritshai ship; and as they drew nearer, Colin could feel the currents beneath shuddering through the hull, the deck vibrating beneath his feet.

"Look," Aeren said, pointing toward the top of the promontory to the north of the inlet, where a large castle stood above the pounding waves, unlike anything Colin had seen back in Andover or in the New World. A single tower of pale stone pierced upward from a building made of the same stone as the cliffs. While the main palace looked like the walls of a fortress, the tower was oddly delicate, a light shining steadily from its peak. "The palace. The lighthouse is called the Needle. It was designed by King Maarten, the current King's father. Probably the Province's greatest King so far."

Then the ship passed into the inlet, rocky crags closing in on both sides, close enough that Colin took an involuntary step backward, sucking in a sharp breath. Before he could swear, the sides of the inlet fell away, and the riptides of the narrow opening smoothed out. The wind died down to gusts, the inlet protected by the surrounding land.

The Alvritshai captain steered the ship into a seething hubbub of ships and boats. They wound through the chaotic order of the ship lanes, skiffs and smaller boats appearing as they neared the docks. Those standing on the decks of the passing ships eyed the Alvritshai with fear and suspicion, and Colin realized that Aeren and the rest of the Alvritshai had tensed, their eyes forward, looking to where the ship would make port. Only the ship's crew remained in motion, stepping quickly to follow snapped orders as the sails were furled and tied.

Colin was about to ask what was wrong when a new ship broke away from the docks, heading toward the Alvritshai's courier. Even Colin could tell it wasn't a trader. It was built for speed.

Aeren issued orders tersely, and the crew rushed to raise a set of flags.

"What is it?" Colin asked.

Aeren shook his head, his eyes on the approaching ship.

As soon as they were within hailing distance, someone on the ship bellowed, "You can't dock in Corsair!"

Eraeth moved up to the railing, hand waving toward the flags that now snapped above. "We've come to speak with King Stephan. There are Lords of the Evant on board."

"I don't care if the fucking Tamaell is on board," the man shouted over the water. "You can't bring that ship into the docks! Drop anchor in the harbor and wait. If you attempt to leave, you will be boarded!"

Eraeth growled, but another ship had joined the first. Farther out, Colin spotted two more covering the mouth of the inlet, on patrol. They'd skimmed through the inlet so fast he hadn't seen them, too intent on catching sight of the city beyond.

Aeren ordered, "Do it," in Alvritshai—words Colin actually understood—and Eraeth grunted, then motioned toward the captain of the courier. The ship began to slow, the nervousness on deck doubling as the anchor dropped.

As soon as the ship had settled into place, a boat dropped from the edge of the patrol ship, and six of the Corsair's crew climbed on board. They rowed toward the Alvritshai ship, members of the Alvritshai crew tossing down a rope ladder so they could climb aboard. All the men were part of the Legion, dressed in light armor, armed with swords. The Alvritshai Phalanx had withdrawn from the end of the rope ladder, leaving the crew to hold it steady as the humans climbed up.

The Legion clustered in a tight knot. Then the same man who'd ordered them to anchor stepped forward with a deep-seated frown. "Who's in charge of this vessel?"

Colin expected Eraeth to step forward, as he had to answer the hail, but Aeren did.

"I am Aeren Goadri Rhyssal, Lord of House Rhyssal of the Alvritshai Evant."

The Legionnaire hesitated a moment, eyes narrowing at Aeren, then gathered himself. "You dare to enter Corsair's harbor and attempt to dock without waiting for an escort?"

Colin saw Eraeth tense, saw Aeren stiffen as well.

"I did not realize that an escort was required at Corsair. We've come from Portstown. The last I heard, Alvritshai ships flying the trade colors were welcome in the ports of the Provinces."

"Not anymore," the Legionnaire huffed, "by order of the King. 'All foreign vessels entering the Port of Corsair must be accompanied by an escorting Provincial vessel until it is determined that such vessel is not a threat to the port or city, at which point it will be allowed to dock.'"

"When was this new policy put into effect?"

"Three days ago. Now, what is your business here in Corsair?"

"I am here to speak to the King."

"About what?"

"Matters of state."

"Ahuh." The Legionnaire looked over Aeren, Eraeth, and the rest, his gaze pausing briefly on Colin. He frowned. "And who are you?"

Eraeth muttered something in furious indignation, and Aeren's shoulders stiffened. "That," he said, "is my adviser from Portstown."

The man grunted. "We'll need to search the vessel."

Murmurs passed through the Phalanx and the crew, the ship's captain stepping forward to Aeren's side, but the lord held up his hand. The grumbling settled, although it did not dissipate.

"I do not believe that you have that right," Aeren said, his voice tight, and the Legionnaire shifted awkwardly. "But very well. You should know that Barak Oriall Nuant, Lord of House Nuant, was wounded while in Portstown and is currently recovering in the captain's cabin. As long as you do not disturb him unduly, the ship is yours."

The Legionnaire nodded, then motioned to the rest of his men. Four of them broke away, descending into the hold, while the fifth remained on deck with the commander. The two groups—Alvritshai and human—eyed each other warily, until the four men returned.

They conferred quietly with their commander, then stepped back.

Straightening, the commander said, "Everything appears to be in order. You may dock, and a small group will be allowed up to the palace. Everyone else must remain on the ship. Follow us to your berth."

"An Alvritshai representative should already be waiting to meet us at the docks, a member of my House."

The commander nodded. "Very well. Welcome to Corsair."

He turned and his group descended to the waiting boat. As they rowed back to their own ship, Aeren motioned for the captain to weigh anchor and prepare to dock.

Lines were tossed from the pier, and the two patrol ships broke away as they slid into their berth. Dockhands tied them down and a plank was dropped, Aeren moving down it to join another Alvritshai and a small escort of Phalanx in Aeren's Rhyssal House colors waiting below. Eraeth nudged Colin to follow, Aeren's chosen escort from the ship closing in around them. Two carriages were waiting at the far end of the pier, along with a group of the Legion.

Aeren and the Alvritshai Colin didn't recognize were deep in conversation by the time they arrived. As soon as they paused, Eraeth broke in with a sharp question.

Aeren glanced around the harbor, watching the ships as they wove in and out among each other. From this distance,

Colin could see a distinct difference between the Alvritshai ship and those from Corsair. It sat deeper in the water, its lines sleeker and more subtle, appearing elongated next to Corsair's ships, which were rough and practical, built for a single purpose and nothing more. Aeren's courier was more refined.

Colin's attention shifted to the town. Larger than Portstown—larger even than Colin's memories of Trent back in Andover—Corsair stretched out across both sides of the inlet. Warehouses, taverns, and shops crowded the docks on the northern side, a haphazard mass of roads, alleys, and buildings that sloped upward from the water to the ridge of land stretching across the horizon, leading out to the promontory where the palace and Needle stood. Like Portstown, the buildings were mostly wooden, although nearly all of the churches and what Colin assumed were mercantiles were stone. The architecture was again utilitarian, plain and simple, unlike the varied and more artistic structures he remembered from Trent. The distinction between the rebellious Provinces and their original homeland in Andover was clear. The streets were thronged with people, horses, carts, and wagons, the greatest activity on the docks, the raucous sounds and smells of the wharf reminding him of Trent. The city had spilled over to the southern part of the inlet as well, the buildings newer and only trailing halfway up the rocky shore.

Turning back, Colin heard Aeren say in Andovan, "Tell them, Dharel."

Dharel sent Aeren a questioning look, looking askance at Colin. He began to speak in Alvritshai, but Aeren cut him off, saying, "Consider him Rhyssal-aein."

Colin frowned as he felt a sudden shift in all of the Alvritshai present, Eraeth included. Before, on the ship and the dock, they'd treated him as if he were an extra set of baggage, including the guards. Now, he could feel their attention on him. The Phalanx had become *aware* of him, not as something to be stepped over or around but as a physical presence.

Dharel frowned but drew himself upright. "Ten days ago, a group of ships from Andover arrived, four ships in all, only three of them traders. The fourth carried representatives from the Andovan Court. Four days after they arrived, during a meeting with the King, Stephan had them all escorted out of the audience chambers by the Legion. They were confined to their rooms within the Needle under constant watch after that. Word reached the Andovan ships docked at the wharf the next day, and a riot broke out in the shipyards that night, begun by a confrontation between members of the Legion and the Andovan Armory in one of the taverns. Tensions escalated. The Armory warned all the Andovan citizens in the port to be ready to leave the city on short notice. Another riot broke out on the docks as everyone from across the Arduon Ocean tried to find passage on any available ship headed in that direction. The Armory blockaded the docks where the traders were berthed, and the Legion was called in to quell the riot. Somehow, in the confusion, fighting broke out between the Armory and Legion. Thirty people were killed, and each side is blaming the other."

"I don't see any ships flying Andovan colors in the harbor," Eraeth said.

Dharel nodded grimly. "After the second riot, the King went to speak to the Andovan representatives, but he came out of their chambers in a rage and ordered the Legion to escort them down to their ships. He then gave anyone from Andover one day to find passage back to Andover or face arrest."

"On what charge?"

"Spying. Most of the Andovan ships at port—including the envoy from the Court—left at the next tide, holds packed with passengers. The next day, King Stephan had any remaining Andovan ships at the docks boarded, the crews arrested, and everything in their holds confiscated." Dharel hesitated, then added, "All the captains of the ships were hung, their ships taken into the middle of the inlet and burned."

A few of the Alvritshai nodded in respect. Colin remembered Eraeth's demand that they kill the men he'd caught in the street and the obvious Alvritshai disdain for the human concept of a judge. He didn't know what all of the factors at play here were, but he shuddered at the image of the gallows that appeared in his head, complete with the gut-wrenching stench of piss and shit.

"What did the Andovans say to the King?" Aeren asked. "What set off all of this . . . rage?"

Dharel grimaced. "They want the Provinces back. They want to reclaim the land they lost while they were fighting their Feud for the last sixty years. The representatives on the ships were here to demand that the King hand those lands back to the Court. Immediately."

Aeren didn't move. His expression remained flat and unreadable.

Eraeth frowned. "What does this mean?"

Aeren paced slowly away from them, then turned back, a troubled look flickering through his eyes, there and then gone. "I don't know. I don't know what it means for what I intend, and I don't know what it means for the Alvritshai. I have never been able to predict the human Kings, even after nearly sixty years of careful study."

He turned to Colin. "What do you think it means? What do you think the King will do?"

Colin almost snorted, then thought about Portstown and Lean-to, about the tensions that existed even then between Andover and the group of conscripts, criminals, and guildsmen that would become the Provinces. "He'll fight them to keep the coast. And the Legion will back him up. I think the entire coast will back him."

Eraeth swore in Alvritshai under his breath. "It seems this coast is made for war," he said to Aeren.

"The plains as well," the lord answered.

Colin shifted. "What are you here for? Why did you come to Corsair?"

Eraeth stiffened, glaring at him, but Aeren moved back toward the group. "For the last sixty years, there has been nothing but conflict on the plains between the Alvritshai, the dwarren, and the Provinces. That conflict escalated until the confrontation at the Escarpment. It should have ended there. A pact had been made to end it. But a ... mistake was made, a flawed decision, one that led to a misunderstanding, and the pact was broken. The conflict remained. It has simmered for the past thirty years. Thirty years of stifled trade, of petty bickering and skirmishes across all borders. Thousands have died because of it, including my family—my father, followed by my elder brother. I am the last of my House. Aureon, my brother, died at the battle at the Escarpment. I held his body in my arms. His blood stained my skin for days afterward." Eraeth's jaw clenched as his lord spoke, his hand tightening on the pommel of his sword, and the surrounding guards stirred.

Aeren looked up into Colin's eyes, and he saw the Alvritshai's pain there. "I want this conflict to end. I want to finally be able to wash my brother's blood clean from my hands."

Silence stretched, until the tension in Aeren's shoulders finally eased. "It has to stop. The plains have drunk too much blood. It needs to end."

Colin almost asked how it could end, after going on for so long, but Aeren turned toward Dharel. "Take us to the palace."

~

The door to the audience chamber in the palace at Corsair opened, and an officious man with a blunt nose entered. He stepped past the two Alvritshai guards, pointedly ignoring them, scanned the room as if looking for missing items, then finally let his gaze sweep across Eraeth, Dharel, and Colin. He gave a small frown when he saw Colin, but he turned to Aeren and said, "The King is willing to see you now."

"Very well."

The man spun and led them out of the room, down one of the Needle's wide marble-floored corridors lined with huge urns and potted plants and tapestries. Servants and guardsmen passed them in the hall, and they left a wake of half-whispered comments and backward glances behind them. Colin tried to keep his attention fixed forward, but he caught glimpses through open doors into side rooms. Like the audience chamber they'd just left, they were spacious, the walls covered in polished wood, the ceilings vaulted, with niches for statues or artwork on nearly every wall. The audience chamber had held tables and chairs arranged beneath bookcases lined with books and assorted glass objects and small figurines. But as they moved, Colin saw other rooms with long dining tables or walls covered in artwork and huge chandeliers. The sheer size of the rooms overwhelmed him.

When they reached the center of the building, the officious man stopped before two large, paneled, wooden doors. Legionnaires stood stiffly outside, carrying pikes and halberds, in full armor.

The man didn't consult anyone, didn't even turn to see if Aeren and the others were following. He shoved the heavy door open and stepped into the inner room.

Colin had seen the official meeting rooms of the Court in Trent. Wide and spacious, they were usually open to the elements, paved in slabs of white marble, with numerous thin columns supporting a lattice-worked roof that could be covered with canvas in the event of rain. Sunlight would glance off the occasional small fountain or other central piece of artwork symbolizing the Family and its power. But the focus of the meeting rooms in Trent were the raised daises, usually with three or four seats, the largest reserved for the Family's Dom, the remaining seats for the visiting Dom or their representatives.

The meeting hall in the Needle was nothing like that.

It was long and narrow, the floor made of flagstone, the walls of intricately paneled wood and skilled carvings. Banners hung on most of the walls, framed by the carvings, and when Colin recognized the diagonally cut field of red and yellow, a shield in the center, he realized the banners represented the Provinces. He counted six altogether, three on each side, and at the far end of the hall—

Colin's step faltered. The King waited at the far end of the hall, standing behind a large desk. Behind him, a much larger banner took up almost the entire wall, a single field of yellow, a sheaf of wheat in black in the center. Aides and guardsmen stood to either side of him, but a pace back. As they drew nearer, Colin saw the dark look on the King's face. He was leaning slightly forward, his fingers steepled on the desk. Dressed in shirt and breeches, he still radiated a sense of power, as if he wore armor instead. Broad shouldered, eyes gray like the flagstone, he glared at them as they approached.

Aeren came to a halt before the desk, and the officious man stepped to one side. Colin's gaze flicked over the aides, noted the papers that lay in neat stacks to either side of the space before the King, the ink bottle, the feathers of numerous quills, and the chunks of sealing wax. There were no decorative weapons, no personal mementos of any kind.

Then his gaze fell on the guards and halted on the man standing to the King's right in full dress armor. Obviously part of the Legion, high ranking. The man eyed all of them with suspicion, his gaze traveling over the members of the Phalanx first, judging them, weighing their potential danger.

Then his gaze fell on Colin. Creases appeared in his forehead as he realized that Colin was not Alvritshai and yet wore Alvritshai clothing. Aeren had ordered Dharel to find something appropriate as they rode to the palace. It had been too late for an audience with the King the night before, but Dharel had arrived with Colin's new clothes—in the Rhyssal House colors—that morning, before they were summoned to the audience chamber.

Now Colin's hands tightened reflexively under the commander's scrutiny, trying to grip the staff he almost always carried. He'd been forced to leave it back in Aeren's appointed rooms.

Leaning forward, the commander murmured something to his King. His eyes never left Colin's, and the King's never left Aeren. The King's jaw clenched as he finished and stepped back.

"I have already dealt with one group of foreign visitors this past week," King Stephan said, the menace in his low, cold voice unmistakable. "I had not expected to deal with another. What is it that you want, Lord Aeren Goadri Rhyssal? What is it that the Alvritshai want?"

Aeren tensed ... and then visibly forced himself to relax. "I come as an emissary. I come as a seeker of peace."

Stephan barked laughter, pushing himself away from the desk so he could pace behind it. "As you came to my father so many years ago?" he spat. "Is that your idea of peace? To cozen us into a treaty, to dazzle us with your offers of trade and wealth and good fortune so that you can betray us on the battlefield, so that you can murder our King?" Stephan shouted the last, his voice ringing in the enclosed hall, loud enough that some of his aides winced and cringed, looking down at the floor.

Aeren didn't react. When the echoes faded, he said, "No."

Stephan snorted, still pacing back and forth, his arms crossed over his chest. He no longer looked at Aeren but glared down at the floor.

Aeren drew a deep breath and let it out slowly. "I come now as a representative of the Alvritshai, to plead for the

Alvritshai . . . but not at the Alvritshai's behest. The Evant is not aware of my true purpose here on the coast. They believe I am here to forge trade agreements for my own House, attempts that they scorn as a waste of time, doomed to failure."

Stephan halted. "And the Tamaell Fedorem?"

Aeren shook his head. "He is not aware of my true purpose either."

Stephan shot Aeren a disconcertingly intense glare, but Aeren did not flinch. "You seem sincere. But you seemed sincere before, when you were dealing with my father."

"I was sincere then. I am sincere now."

"And yet you bring spies!" Stephan spat, hand jerking toward Colin.

Aeren frowned. "Colin is not a spy. He aided Lord Barak and myself in Portstown and was wounded in the process. The honor of my House demanded that I care for him. He has since agreed to remain with my party."

The commander's eyes darkened, his mouth turning down in a frown, but Aeren had already shifted his attention back to Stephan.

"If what you say regarding the Evant is true, then your presence here is meaningless. The Evant and Tamaell Fedorem," Stephan's face twisted into a sneer, "will not recognize any agreement we reach here. You have no official authority."

"I have no official authority, but that does not mean I have no power," Aeren said. And Colin heard a subtle change in the Alvritshai's voice, a smooth modulation that deepened it, made it throb. Aeren took a small step closer to the King's desk, one hand reaching out to touch the finely crafted, polished oak. "I am a member of the Evant, King Stephan. My House has been a member for more than four generations, and we Alvritshai live a long time. I did not come here to draft a peace treaty. I did not come to discuss terms and make concessions and seek compromises. I came because it is my opinion that neither one of us—the Alvritshai nor the Provinces—can afford to continue waging this petty war. Too many resources are being wasted. Too many lives are being lost. It is my hope that, like your father, you will agree with me. If that is the case," Aeren said, cutting off the King's response without raising his voice, doing the opposite in fact, speaking softer, slower, "if that is the case, then I will return to the Evant, to Tamaell Fedorem, and I will walk every path before me, offer everything I have to Aielan's Light, to convince the Tamaell and the other Houses to come to you with a formal offer of peace and *I will force them to honor it.*"

Aeren's voice shook, fury buried deep beneath the words themselves. A fury aimed at the Evant and the Houses, at Tamaell Fedorem. The room fell silent beneath the force of that fury, beneath the raw emotion that it exposed. Colin felt it like a hard knot in his chest; he realized he did not dare breathe for fear of breaking the silence.

In that silence, he noticed that Eraeth had turned to his lord, a troubled frown on his face.

Then Stephan chuckled, the sound killing the silence with a shudder. Colin felt the hard knot in his chest give and exhaled with relief, the sound harsh.

"I see now why my father fell for your Alvritshai tricks," Stephan said, his voice bitter. "Do all of the Lords of the Evant have such powers of persuasion?" He paused for a moment, then waved his hand. "It doesn't matter. I am not my father. I will not be swayed by the smooth words of liars. And I will not be lured onto a field of battle so that I can be murdered by your hand."

No one spoke for a long moment until Aeren stirred.

"Not all of the Lords of the Evant on the field of battle that day at the Escarpment knew of the betrayal the others intended," he said.

It took a moment for Aeren's words to register, but when they did, Stephan's face blackened with fury, as if actually naming the battle had brought all of the emotions from that fateful day that they had both been skirting to the forefront.

"Get out," he spat, shoving away from the desk, barely in control of himself, his hands shaking, his face livid. "Get out of Corsair, now, before I have you escorted out on the point of a sword."

The Legion commander had already stalked forward before Stephan had finished, the other guards in the room on his heels. Aeren wasn't inclined to linger, turning to where his own guardsmen had tensed to give a small shake of his head. They were herded to the door, the officious man closing it behind them with a murderous look. Just before the door closed, Colin saw the King standing with his back to the desk, staring up at the yellow and black banner on the wall behind him.

"Move!" the commander ordered harshly. He motioned them down the corridor, back toward their rooms in the eastern wing of the castle. His guards flanked them, servants and aides already in the hall pressing themselves up against the wall or dodging into open doorways to get out of their way, even though Aeren moved at a casual pace.

As soon as they reached the door to their assigned chambers, the Legion commander said, "You have twenty minutes to pack. We'll escort you to the port after that."

Aeren turned. "That won't be necessary. Only Lord Barak and his retinue will be using the courier to depart. I've made arrangements to travel back north by land."

The Legionnaire's brow creased with suspicion. "Then we'll escort you to the edge of the city. Twenty minutes."

Aeren nodded. "Very well. We'll be ready in ten."

He swung the door closed in the commander's face.

He immediately barked orders in Alvritshai, and Dharel and the guards scattered, pulling clothes and supplies— papers, ink bottles, various odds and ends—and putting them into trunks and cases, hurried but not rushed.

Eraeth said something terse, and Aeren gave him a nasty look. "No, it did not go as I expected."

"How did you expect it to go?" Colin asked. When Aeren gave him the same look, he added, "I heard about what happened at the Escarpment while I was in Portstown. At least, the Province version of what happened."

"I know what the humans believe happened. I didn't expect Stephan to simply agree out of hand."

Colin frowned. "What did happen at the Escarpment?"

Aeren sighed, shook his head, and moved to the table in the corner he'd been using as a desk, beginning to sort and stack papers, placing them in a leather satchel. "I don't know. I wasn't at the forefront of the battle at the time of the betrayal. I was ... elsewhere." He paused and stared down at his hands a long moment, then shuddered and looked up. "From what I've gathered through the Evant, there was a betrayal at the Escarpment, one that has set the Alvritshai and the Provinces against each other for decades. I'd hoped that enough time had passed for the grief over his father's death to have abated. Obviously, I was mistaken."

"It didn't help that you came immediately after the Andovans arrived and made their own demands," Eraeth said.

The door to their chambers opened. The Legion commander stepped into the room. A small detachment of Legion stood behind him in the hall, at least three times their original escort from the King's chambers.

Aeren ignored both him and the Legion guardsman. "Dharel, send someone down to the courier, along with whatever supplies we won't need, and tell them to take Lord Barak to Caercaern. We'll meet up with them there."

Dharel nodded, motioning to the rest of the Alvritshai Phalanx. The guardsmen began toting the small trunks and cases out into the hall under the Legionnaires' careful watch. One of them handed Colin his staff and satchel.

Aeren turned his attention on Colin. "Will you come with us, Rhyssal-aein?"

Colin hesitated, catching Eraeth's eye. But while the Alvritshai Protector still scowled, it wasn't as heartfelt as it had been before on the ship and the docks.

"Of course," he said.

Aeren's shoulders sagged in relief before he turned toward the Legion commander, his voice darkening. "Then it's time to leave Corsair behind."

∼

Colin looked back as Aeren's entourage—all on horseback, the White Phalanx riding to the front, the sides, and slightly behind—clopped down the flagstone-paved eastern road out of Corsair. The waters of the inlet glittered with the late evening sunlight, a turgid deep blue, cut by the activity of the boats and ships from both sides of the city. Birds wheeled and shrieked in the air over the water, gulls and terns and cormorants. Smoke rose from numerous chimneys, settling in a thin layer at a uniform height. On the promontory, the Needle pierced the pale clouds that scudded across the sky, just beginning to show the pink-orange accents of the setting sun.

But it wasn't the city or the palace that caught Colin's attention. It was the Legion commander and the rest of the Legion he'd gathered, standing at the edge of the city, watching them depart. As he watched, the Legionnaire barked commands to those around him and cast one last baleful glance back, his eyes meeting Colin's. A shock ran through Colin, tingling in his fingers, causing him to catch his breath—

And then the Legion commander cantered back into the city, lost among the buildings within the space of a heartbeat.

Most of the Legion remained behind.

Ahead, one of the Alvritshai removed a white banner from a satchel and unfolded it so that the black bundle of wheat could be seen, raising it on a standard whose base rested in a cup on the saddle. It declared that they were traveling under the King's protection, and in theory it would keep the Legion and other Province citizens from attacking them on sight.

"He'll send scouts to follow us," Eraeth said, bringing his mount up close to Colin's. His tone carried a sneer. "I wouldn't be surprised if he followed us himself."

Colin shifted uncomfortably in the saddle. He hadn't ridden since the wagon train, over sixty years before; he could already feel aches in muscles he'd long forgotten. Frowning more at the saddle than at Eraeth, Colin said, "Wouldn't you?"

Eraeth looked toward him, straightening as if affronted. "Of course."

Colin expected Eraeth to retreat with a backward scowl. Instead, he glanced back toward Corsair, toward the Needle, then cast a troubled frown toward Aeren.

The lord of the Rhyssal House rode near the front, his back stiff, head held high, looking straight ahead. He hadn't spoken to Eraeth or any of his own Phalanx since the palace Colin suddenly realized.

Colin looked at Eraeth out of the corner of his eye, saw the wrinkles of concern near his eyes, the tightening of the skin in the Alvritshai's pale face.

"What does Rhyssal-aein mean?" he asked suddenly.

Eraeth broke off the scrutiny of his lord. He hesitated, then said shortly, "Friend of Rhyssal."

"What does that mean?"

Eraeth's mouth twisted with derision, but then he

seemed to reconsider, focusing on Colin as he settled back into his saddle. His tone was clipped, but serious. "To the Alvritshai, it means that you are under the protection of the Rhyssal House, that those of the House are to protect you from harm, that Aeren has taken responsibility for you and has extended that responsibility to everyone in the House." He paused, then added, "It also means that you are a representative of the Rhyssal House. Everything that you do, everything that you say, every gesture and emotion, will reflect on the House."

Colin thought back to the wharf, when they'd arrived in Corsair. "That's why the guards changed their stance on the docks then, when we first arrived?"

"Yes." Eraeth glared at Aeren's back. "The Phalanx is bound to protect you now." And under his breath, "At least until he comes to his senses."

Colin ignored him even though he knew it had been meant to be heard. Instead, he glanced around at the surrounding land. Fields lined the roadway to either side, interspersed with farmhouses, barns, storage sheds for grain, and the earthen mounds of potato cellars. The ground appeared rocky, which accounted for the paved road, now made out of carefully fitted granite rather than the flagstone used near the city. The rough, low walls separating the fields were made of the same stone, as were the buildings. Everywhere he looked, workers halted their harvesting and watched the Alvritshai group pass, dogs barking in wild abandon. A pack of children followed them for a long stretch, until one of the mothers called them back with a few harsh words, taking her own son by the ear when he got close enough. Colin smiled.

"And what does shaeveran mean?" he asked. "I've heard the Phalanx calling me that since we were on the courier ship."

Eraeth regarded him a long moment. His face was set, probably the first serious look the Protector had given him that wasn't twisted with a slight scowl or sneer.

Then he turned away and said, "It means shadow. You've been touched by the sukrael, marked by them. They call you Shadow because of it."

Colin's gaze dropped to his arm, to where the black mark lay hidden beneath the sleeve of his silk shirt, and his stomach clenched. A tremor passed through his arms, and for a brief moment, the scent of earth, leaves, and snow nearly overpowered him. He could feel the vial of Lifeblood in the satchel strapped to his horse's side, but he resisted reaching for it.

The effort sent a shudder through his body. He'd thought it would get easier the farther away from the Well he traveled, but it hadn't. Osserin had been right: The presence of the Lifeblood made it worse. Yet he couldn't force himself to pour the Lifeblood out.

Up ahead, Aeren had slowed, the Phalanx at point drawing to a halt. Colin glanced around, saw that the farmland had given way to low hills dotted with patches of trees and grass. The road had become a hard-packed gravel track with low walls on either side, striking out hard toward the north and the city of Rendell in the next Province. But it looked as though Aeren intended to cut away to the east.

"Where are we going?" Colin asked.

Eraeth grunted and shot him a dark look, back to his usual disapproving glare, then nudged his horse forward to speak to Aeren.

Colin sighed.

An hour later, the group angled sharply east, heading deep into the plains.

~

"Should we continue following them?"

On horseback, on a tree-lined ridge distant enough that he doubted the Alvritshai would notice him, Legion Commander Tanner Dain lowered the spyglass he had held to his eye with an angry frown. He'd led the group of scouts sent to keep an eye on the Alvritshai lord and his party as they left the Provinces, and his initial rage at their audacity—asking for peace after murdering King Maarten at the Escarpment and bringing an obvious spy before the King—had lessened, tinged heavily with grudging respect. Mostly because the Alvritshai had done exactly as they said they would: headed north and east, to the plains. They hadn't stopped to speak with anyone, and as far as his scouts had been able to find out, there wasn't an army of Alvritshai waiting to meet up with them anywhere close by.

All the intelligence he'd managed to gather had indicated that this Lord Aeren and his group on the courier ship had come to the Provinces alone, for exactly the purposes they'd stated—the prospect of trade with the Governors.

That didn't mean he had to like it.

"No," he finally said, then sighed. "No, leave them. They've left the Provinces, as they said they would."

A small part of his mind began to wonder. Could Lord Aeren's offer of potential peace be sincere?

Tanner's brow creased in annoyance, and he shoved the nagging thought aside.

"What should we do then?"

Tanner dragged his eyes away from the receding figures of the Alvritshai and the lone human in their midst—nothing more than dark shapes on the gold of the grass now—and faced his captain, pulling his mount around in the process. The horse snorted and shook its head, stamping the ground between the trees once, as if impatient to get moving. Tanner suddenly felt the same impatience itching between his shoulders.

"We head back to Corsair to report to the King. We have more important issues to deal with than the Alvritshai."

"Like what?" his captain asked, casting a heated glance in the direction of the Alvritshai party. For the first time, Tanner noted the gray streaks in the captain's hair, registered the man's age. He'd likely been at the Escarpment. A young man then, perhaps barely fifteen. He might have experienced the Alvritshai betrayal firsthand, might have lost friends to the battle fought afterward, as they tried to retreat.

"Like the Andovans," Tanner said sharply, his tone catching the man's attention. "They're a more imminent threat than the Alvritshai at the moment."

And with that, he shoved the Alvritshai from his mind and kicked his horse toward Corsair, his thoughts turning west, toward the Andovans and the protection of the coast.

14

"DRIFTER!" COLIN CALLED SHARPLY.
Eraeth, standing about twenty paces distant, spun, his sword half drawn before he realized that Colin pointed toward one of the strange rippling distortions. Colin had seen one a few days out onto the plains after leaving the Well to return to Portstown. But that had been distant and looked no larger than a man; it had been far enough away that he could shrug it off as heat haze, although he was certain it wasn't.

This one was much closer and much larger—big enough to swallow the entire group of Alvritshai with Colin, even with them scattered apart as they were during the rest period.

Eraeth snorted in derision and slipped his sword back into place with a snick. But Colin noticed he didn't relax.

Neither did any of the other Alvritshai who'd looked up. They all tracked the distortion's slow, steady progress as it slid by. The grass beneath the translucent ripples bent downward beneath it, pressed flat at the drifter's base. Waves spread outward from it, as if it were a stone thrown into water.

When it became apparent that it wouldn't drift close enough to them to be a concern, Eraeth turned back to his horse, lifting up one of the animal's hooves to check for damage. He slipped a small tool, like a miniature pick, from a pouch and began cleaning.

Colin shifted closer, his own horse still drinking heavily from the stream that bubbled up from the earth near the base of a small hillock. Sources of water were scarce on the plains, since most of it was hidden underground, so when they found a stream aboveground, they always stopped to refill their waterskins. The Alvritshai seemed to know where the streams were located and had hidden caches of food stored at various places on the plains—mostly dried, smoked gaezel, spiced, like what Aeren had offered his father and the rest of the greeting party when they'd first met on the plains. Once, they'd even halted in the middle of a flat and dug down into the earth until water gurgled to the surface and formed a small pool. Eating was formal, almost ritualistic, even here on the plains, as it had been during their meeting over sixty years before. Nearly everything the Alvritshai did was ritualistic, stiff and formal, and yet Colin found himself settling into the rhythms as the days passed.

"What is it?" Colin asked.

Eraeth looked up with a glare. He'd been much more scathing and vicious since they entered the plains; Colin suspected that it was because Aeren refused to tell the Protector where they were going and why, although neither Aeren nor Eraeth had confirmed this. Aeren had barely spoken to either of them, keeping to himself during the breaks, withdrawn and distant, his mood bleak and troubled. The same mood had infected the rest of the Alvritshai, Eraeth in particular.

"What is what?" Eraeth snarled.

"That," Colin said, exasperated. "The Drifter. What is it? Where does it come from? What does it do?"

Eraeth rolled his eyes, finished cleaning out the collected dirt and grass from his horse's hoof, then released the horse, murmuring something in the animal's ear before patting it on the flank. Its ear pricked back, and it snuffled softly before reaching for the grass.

"We call it an occumaen, a 'breath of heaven.' They appear on the plains, travel a ways, and then they vanish. And they are extremely dangerous."

Colin thought about the horses being spooked in the wagon train, before the disastrous attempt to climb the Bluff. "But where do they come from?"

Eraeth's face twisted into an irritated grimace, ready to shove Colin's question to one side as unimportant, when someone else spoke.

"The Scripts claim that the occumaen come from Aielan, that they are here to seek out those she wishes to speak to and take them to her. Many people have vanished in the presence of one of the occumaen. There are legends that entire armies have been lost to them."

Both Colin and Eraeth turned toward Aeren. The Alvritshai lord's face was still fixed, mouth drawn downward, but it was the first time in the past week that he'd interjected anything into a conversation. Eraeth straightened, a look of hope flashing through his eyes.

"If that's the case, why don't the Alvritshai rush toward them? Why do you keep back? You obviously worship Aielan, and her . . . Light."

Aeren smiled slightly. "Would you rush to meet this Diermani you pray to?"

Colin frowned, thought about the day of the wagon attack, of the Shadows touching him, of the cold death they'd offered. He'd had a chance to seek out Diermani then, but when the Faelehgre offered him an alternative, he'd taken it. Even though he hadn't fully understood the consequences of his choice. "No," he said softly. "No, I wouldn't. I didn't."

Aeren nodded, his ironic smile softening. "Faith is a strange thing. We worship Aeilan, we pray to her Light, hope that in the end we shall find it . . . but until that end is inevitable, we shun it. At all costs. And yet without faith. . . ." He didn't finish, turning to face Eraeth. "We must all have faith. In Aielan, in Diermani—" a quick flick of his glance and a respectful bow of his head toward Colin, "—in ourselves, and, most important, in each other. It is all that we have, in the end."

Eraeth stiffened, as if Aeren had offered up a formal reprimand. Then, he bowed his head.

Aeren moved off. When he was far enough away, Eraeth said in a low voice, "He was once an acolyte in the Order, training to be a follower of Aeilan. It was a common calling for second sons of the Houses, and it suited him. He had risen fairly high within the acolytes' ranks and in the esteem of Lotaern, the Order's leader, before the death of his father forced him to return to his House." Eraeth turned toward Colin, a strange mixture of pain, regret, and hostility in his eyes, as if somehow the death of Aeren's father were Colin's fault.

And at that moment, Colin's stomach seized, the heat flaring up his side and into his chest, the pain piercing into his abdomen. He gasped, clutched at his gut, tried to remain standing, but the strength drained out of his legs. He fell, writhing on the grass as the heat expanded until it felt as if it were consuming him from the inside out. Hissing between clenched teeth, he rolled to the side and pressed his face into the earth, breathed in the scent of grain overlaid with the hideously enticing scent of leaves and snow. The sharp tincture of blood flooded the back of his throat, and with a nearly soundless cry he began scrabbling for his satchel. The pain was too great, the heat eating him up inside. He needed the vial, needed the Lifeblood to soothe it. His fingers found the ties, jerked them open as his arm spasmed, and then he rooted through the contents blindly, still curled over the pain in his stomach. Vaguely he heard shouts, but then his hand closed over the cloth containing the vial.

He snatched his hand free of the satchel, let the bag fall, and pulled the vial out of its protective cloth. His entire body trembled now, although the heat had begun to recede. He held the vial up to the sunlight, could practically taste the clear liquid inside already, reached to open it—

And a hand—a pale-skinned, Alvritshai hand—latched onto his arm and held it. He cried out, his voice cracking with frustrated anger, and glared up at Eraeth, who'd crouched down next to him in the grass.

"Let go." The words came out in a growl, between clenched teeth.

"What is it?" Eraeth asked, his voice hard.

Colin tried to break Eraeth's hold, but the Alvritshai was stronger than he looked. He shot a glance toward the nearest of the Phalanx as they gathered around, at Aeren, who stood a few paces back, his brow creased in confusion, but none of them moved forward to help him. So he turned his attention back to Eraeth. "It will help with the seizure. It will stop the pain."

Confusion flickered across Eraeth's face, and his grip on Colin's arm eased.

But then Aeren spoke. He'd moved forward so that he stood behind Eraeth. "Is it from the sarenavriell? Is it from the Well?"

Colin didn't have to answer. Aeren nodded and frowned, a look of pity crossing his face.

He turned to Eraeth. "Let him have it. He is shaeveran. He knows the consequences of using it."

Colin shuddered at the weight in Aeren's words as Eraeth released him. He snatched the vial close to his chest, his body still shaking. Eraeth stared down at him a long moment, his expression unreadable. Then he stood and turned away.

"Wait," Colin said. He tasted the blood in the back of his throat, swallowed it.

Eraeth paused but didn't turn. Everyone else hesitated, even Aeren, the lord looking back.

Colin thought about Osserin's last words as he left the forest. *You'll return.*

This was why. He'd taken the Lifeblood with him. He'd felt it every step of the way across the plains, tasted it in the back of his throat after every seizure, yearned for it. Its presence exacerbated the withdrawal symptoms, might even have made them worse. He needed to get rid of it, but he couldn't. The thought of pouring it out on the ground made his bones ache. And he wasn't certain he wouldn't need it eventually. If the Well had claimed him completely, he'd need the Lifeblood to survive. But he needed distance from it. It was too tempting.

"Take it," he said, the words rough, barely more than a whisper. He held the vial out toward Eraeth, and when the Protector turned but didn't move, he thrust it toward him and growled, "Take it! Before I change my mind!"

No one moved. Eraeth's brow furrowed. "Why me?"

"Because you hate me," Colin spat. "Because you won't give it back to me if I ask, no matter how much pain I'm in."

Eraeth's eyes narrowed, but after a moment he stepped forward and took the vial, staring at it a moment before tucking it into a fold in his shirt near his belt. He looked directly into Colin's eyes and said, "You are a strange man."

Before anyone else could speak, one of the Alvritshai guardsmen on watch gave a piercing whistle and cry. He shouted something in Alvritshai, pointing toward the southeast with the tip of his bow.

Eraeth tensed, hand falling to his sword, but Aeren merely sighed.

At Eraeth's questioning glance—not as harsh as those he'd given his lord the past week—Aeren said, "It's the dwarren we've come here to meet."

~

"You should have warned me of whom we were to meet," Eraeth said tightly in Alvritshai. His hand gripped the hilt of his sword as the dwarren appeared on the flat of the plains below. Dust rose, thrown up by the dwarren's gaezels, and Eraeth felt sweat break out between his shoulder blades, his lips pressed together. "There are more dwarren than there are of us," he hissed, his voice low so that the other Alvritshai couldn't hear. He scanned the hillock where they'd halted and noted how vulnerable it was, and then his eyes flashed over the rest of the Phalanx. Messages were passed in silent hand signals, the others spreading out, clasps on blades loosened. Bows were strung by the few that carried them, but no arrows were drawn. Yet.

Satisfied with the Alvritshai, he caught the look on Colin's face—a cold and pure hatred, the anger tightening the human's skin near the eyes. It made the human look . . . hard and unforgiving. He'd recovered enough from the seizure to join them, his staff angled forward and to one side, feet slightly apart, balanced and ready.

The change startled Eraeth, enough that he took a moment to reevaluate the man Aeren had insisted on bringing along. He'd thought the human was soft and worthless, as well as cursed, but the way he held the staff indicated he knew how to use it. He'd brought down the two assassins in Portstown but had collapsed immediately afterward, so Eraeth had assumed he was weak. Colin's reliance on the vial of water from the sarenavriell supported that . . . except that he'd given the vial up, had handed it to Eraeth, not Aeren. And Colin's presence at the meeting with King Stephan had only antagonized the King. Not that it mattered. The King of the Provinces would never agree to a peace with the Alvritshai, not after the betrayal at the Escarpment and the death of his father.

Eraeth felt a surge of anger and a pang of regret. The Lords of the Evant who had participated in the betrayal that day had deceived more than the humans. They'd defied the will of the Tamaell and the other lords. They'd betrayed the Alvritshai people as a whole.

Yet Tamaell Fedorem had done nothing to punish those Lords. Nothing.

The thought left a bitter taste in Eraeth's mouth and led to other thoughts that he knew he could not voice, not even to Aeren, even when he could see the same thoughts in Aeren's eyes. Such as whether or not Fedorem had known of the lords' intentions before they'd reached the Escarpment. And if he had known, why he'd done nothing to stop them.

The obvious answer—that Fedorem had planned the betrayal all along—nauseated Eraeth with shame.

The dwarren drums rumbled across the distance, and Eraeth tore his gaze away from Colin to see the large contingent of dwarren and gaezels pulling to a halt over a hundred paces distant. The dwarren in the lead glared at them from his position, then motioned to the others beside him, not taking his eyes off Aeren. The rest of the dwarren scattered, a group of warriors spreading out in a thin line. Eraeth watched as scouts slipped from their mounts and took off at a run, vanishing in the grasses in the space of a breath. Another group behind began unloading bundles and packs from an array of baggage animals. Sheets of blue-green cloth were unfolded, and poles were erected, the wood looking freshly cut. There must be a copse or thicket nearby, probably in another area where the water breached the surface. The dwarren knew the plains better than the Alvritshai.

A moment later, Aeren released a pent up breath in a slow, careful sigh. "Look," he said, nodding toward where the poles had been positioned. The unfurled sheets of cloth were being wound around them in an intricate pattern, numerous lengths folded and woven in and out as the dwarren walked back and forth around the central poles, almost like a dance. "It's to be a formal meeting. We'll have to give them time to set up the tent and arrange the interior. Once they're satisfied, they'll come to us."

"How many of the Alvritshai will they allow inside the tent?"

Aeren turned to consider the size of the tent. "Four, no more."

"I assume you'll insist that the human join us." Eraeth tried to keep the derision out of his voice, knew he hadn't succeeded.

Aeren smiled. "No. Colin will remain in the camp. I'll want you there, of course, and two others. Dharel, perhaps. And Auvant. They can bring the cattan blades, but no other weapons. And they are not to draw except on my order."

Eraeth stiffened at his lord's tone, but nodded.

Aeren must have seen the disagreement in Eraeth's face. He turned his full attention on him. "After what happened in Corsair, I want nothing to interfere with the possibility of an agreement with the dwarren here. Nothing."

Eraeth heard the same intensity in Aeren's voice as in the audience chamber in Corsair, the same driving force. His lord's voice throbbed with it.

"Very well," he said, nodding again, without the stiffness of disapproval, without even a trace of it in his voice.

Aeren relaxed imperceptibly, his attention returning to the industrious dwarren. They were tying off the last lengths of the tent, the edges trailing outward from the central spire. After a moment, Eraeth realized it was set up like a reverse whirlpool, the center of the tent the vortex. And like a whirlpool, he felt a sense of power surrounding it, a density of motion, of force.

"Have the others set up a more permanent camp here, near the stream," Aeren continued. "And set sentries to keep watch."

"And then what?"

Aeren turned toward him. "And then we wait."

～

The dwarren came for them at dusk, the bright orange of the clouds fading when the sentries called out in harsh warning. The rest of the Phalanx came instantly alert, after the tension of the dwarren arrival had eased through hours of boredom. They'd caught glimpses of the dwarren scouts at a distance, but other than that there had been no movement or activity.

Toward evening, Eraeth had watched Colin wander out to where the occumaen had drifted by earlier; the human had knelt down in the grass to inspect it, lifting his head to gaze off into the distance.

When he'd returned, Eraeth had asked, "What did you find?"

Colin had shrugged. "Crushed grass. But the stalks in the center of the path had been sliced off, as if cut with a scythe. I couldn't find the heads of the grain anywhere."

Eraeth hadn't responded.

Now Aeren rose, and Eraeth motioned Dharel and Auvant forward. At the top of the hillock, the sentry stepped back as two dwarren appeared on foot, both at least a foot shorter than Colin, one carrying a ceremonial spear, strings of feathers and beads trailing down from the head. The spear carrier wore the leather armor the dwarren had used before the humans introduced metal armor. Symbols and letters were burned into the armor, reaching all the way around to the back. Thick bands of metal covered both of the dwarren's forearms in silver. A gold band enclosed his upper right arm. More beads were woven into his gray-streaked beard, and the skin around his eyes was marked with ash.

The other dwarren was younger, dressed in less ceremonial armor. Only one of his forearms had a band encircling it. He regarded the approaching Alvritshai with wariness, his eyes never resting long on one individual.

"A Rider," Aeren said under this breath, nodding toward the younger dwarren, "sent to protect the clan's shaman."

Eraeth nodded, but they were too close to respond.

He could see the shaman's face now, lit by the fading sun behind them, their shadows falling across the two dwarren. Tanned a dark brown by the sun, wrinkled with age, his eyes were sharp and cold, his mouth set in a slight frown. He kept his attention focused on Aeren after a brief glance at the accompanying Phalanx. Eraeth turned his attention to the Rider, the more dangerous of the two, as Aeren and the shaman began to speak.

In the distance, where darkness had already fallen far out over the plains, a flash of purple lightning lit the sky.

"You summoned the Thousand Springs Clan?" The shaman's voice was deep and guttural, the Alvritshai words thick with accent, almost incomprehensible. But he did speak Alvritshai.

Aeren nodded his head formally, in the manner of a lord

addressing a fellow member of the Evant. "I requested a meeting with Clan Chief Garius, yes."

The shaman's eyes narrowed, and the Rider tensed. "You summon the clan chief, you summon the clan." Both Dharel and Auvant stiffened at his tone of affront.

Aeren hesitated, then nodded again, more carefully, keeping his head down as he spoke. "I intended no insult to the clan."

The shaman grunted and considered Aeren a long moment; then he turned and gave the Rider a short barked command in dwarren. The Rider frowned, but the shaman had already stepped away and now regarded the occasional flicker of purplish-blue lightning on the horizon as he stumped down the hill, using the spear as a walking stick. The beads rattled against the haft as he moved, and he called back over his shoulder, "Come! Clan Chief Garius awaits!"

The Rider gave them all an unhappy look, then followed the shaman, not waiting for the Alvritshai.

They entered the dwarren camp, passed the sentries, and headed straight for the tent erected earlier. Numerous other tents surrounded it now, smaller, not as complex in construction or as varied in color. Practical tents, made for quick setup and dismantling, but sturdy nonetheless. Even in the deepening darkness, Eraeth could see that. The entire camp itself was practical: central fires, placed so they wouldn't interfere with the sentries' night vision, the tents arranged in circles around key locations. Dwarren sat around the fires, eating, drinking, telling stories and laughing. A few were throwing what looked like small bones in some type of intense game, and he counted at least three dwarren men stitching cloth with needle and thread. A dozen Riders in all, which left nearly another dozen on sentry duty, scouting, or watching over the gaezels. He saw no dwarren women, which didn't surprise him. He'd never seen any dwarren women aboveground.

None of the Riders in the camp seemed concerned about the Alvritshai; Eraeth's skin prickled at the slight.

The shaman halted at the edge of the tent to allow them to catch up. Eraeth didn't see an opening and frowned as the shaman removed a rattle—made from the tail of one of the deadly brown plain snakes—shook it once up, down, left, and right, connecting the four imaginary points with a wide circle, then bowed deeply at the waist, arm extended, and said, "Ilacqua and the People of the Thousand Springs welcome you to the meeting hall of Clan Chief Garius. May you drink long from the Sacred Waters and may you find whatever it is that you seek."

He stayed bent over, as if waiting, and Aeren shot Eraeth a troubled look. No one moved.

The shaman shook the rattle in irritation, without looking up, and Eraeth realized he was pointing with it.

He glanced to the side, and saw that if they followed the sheet of blue-green cloth, it would spiral them into the interior of the tent.

He touched Aeren's shoulder, motioned to the right, and saw Aeren's uncertainty fade. His lord stepped forward and entered the curve of the tent's arm, Eraeth a pace behind, the other two Alvritshai Phalanx following. They came up against a flap of green cloth. Aeren pushed it aside gently and ducked down to enter.

The first thing that struck Eraeth, as the smooth green cloth slid off his back and he stood, was the smoke. It hung in a pungent cloud, sickly sweet—not unpleasant but strong, invading his nostrils and overpowering almost every other sense. He stifled a cough, heard either Dharel or Auvant choke on it. He found if he relaxed and breathed in deeply, he could breathe normally. Eyes watering slightly, he glared around the small chamber and noticed the metal-worked braziers that emitted the smoke at four locations around the circular room, set on low tables made of finely worked wood. Another low, round table sat in the center, surrounded by numerous pillows. A wide, shallow bowl full of fruit sat in the middle of the table, and directly above it, near the apex of the tent, hung a fifth brazier.

Garius sat on the opposite side of the table, near one of three other entrances to the chamber. Another dwarren sat next to him. The clan chief was younger than the shaman and sat cross-legged, his arms crossed over his chest so that the two gold bands on his upper arms were visible in the braziers' soft light; but like the shaman he wore lighter, more comfortable armor, although with fewer symbols scorched into it.

Garius gave them a moment to adjust, then motioned to the pillows scattered around the table. "Sit."

Like the shaman, his voice was deep, but smoother, his Alvritshai more fluid.

Aeren sat down opposite Garius, so Eraeth sat opposite the other dwarren. He motioned for Dharel and Auvant to remain standing, backs to the sides of the tent. It gave them a slight advantage if the meeting turned ugly. He could feel the tension in the air, from Garius, but more from his companion. The younger dwarren sat stiffly, his darker eyes glaring at the Alvritshai with undisguised hatred. Letting his gaze flicker back and forth between the two, Eraeth realized that the younger dwarren must be Garius' son. He could see the resemblance in the rounded face, the hair, but particularly around the eyes. Garius' were brown, his son's darker, but the bone structure was the same.

"You wished to speak to the clan?" Garius rumbled.

"Yes."

"Why?"

Aeren drew a deep breath, then let it out slowly. Eraeth thought his lord would be direct, as he'd been with King Stephan. But instead, Aeren asked, "How many of your clan have died this past year? How many in the past five years? The past ten?"

Garius shifted where he sat, the creases in his face deepening as he frowned. He hadn't expected the questions, had expected something else entirely. "Too many," he finally answered.

"Too many of the Alvritshai have been lost as well. And for what? The plains?"

Garius' chin came up. "For our home!" he exclaimed. "You are the ones invading our lands! You and the humans, sending out raiding parties, crossing our borders with your wagon trains, with your Phalanx, stealing our water and our herds, killing the members of the clan when we try to defend ourselves. You are the ones killing us. We were here before you. We have always been here. We are simply protecting what is ours!"

Aeren let him speak, didn't flinch at the words, didn't react when Garius' son bristled, hands falling to his thighs, although not touching the hilts of the two knives sheathed at his waist. He let Garius finish, gave him a moment to catch his breath, then he nodded in agreement. "You're right."

Both Garius and his son looked stunned, and Aeren took advantage of the pause.

"We crossed your borders with our parties, with our Phalanx, and we raided your herds and drank of your water. And we've killed each other, over and over again, for nearly a hundred years. And I came to ask you a simple question: why?"

Garius frowned.

"Do you know why we crossed your borders, why we came to your plains? Because we had to. The Alvritshai have lived in the northern reaches for generations, in the Hauttaeren Mountains, underground, like you. There and in the surrounding hills and forests. We would have stayed there, except for the ice."

"Ice?" Garius murmured.

Eraeth shifted uneasily, tried to lock gazes with Aeren, to warn him to be careful, not to reveal too much about the Alvritshai. But Aeren was focused completely on Garius.

"Yes, the ice. The region to the north of the Hauttaeren was once arable land, even though the growing season was short. The Alvritshai farmed there and to the south of the mountains. We worked the land, built cities there. The winters were always harsh, but we could retreat into the halls of the Hauttaeren for the worst months and return after the thaws.

"But in the last two hundred years, the winters have worsened. The growing season in the north has vanished completely, the ground now covered with snow and ice the entire year. It happened slowly, the ground free for six months, then four, then two. Now it is locked solid. We were forced to retreat to the Hauttaeren permanently, abandoning the cities to the north. But the halls couldn't contain us all, and the forests to the south couldn't produce enough to support all of us. So we headed south, onto the plains."

"Onto our lands," Garius' son growled. His father shot him a black look. He spoke Alvritshai, but not as smoothly as his father, the words clipped and broken.

"Onto your lands, yes," Aeren said, unruffled by the boy's outburst. "We didn't know that at the time, of course. You live underground. There is little evidence of your existence aboveground, especially here, in the northern reaches of the plains. We didn't know. And by the time we found out, we were already desperate. We *needed* the land, needed those crops. If we couldn't harvest them, we would starve. So when your Riders first appeared, we thought they'd come to steal from *us,* to take what was *ours,* and so we fought back." Aeren's voice had hardened. "No one stopped to ask whether we had encroached on your lands. No one stopped to talk. I'm not certain it would have mattered then if we had, since we didn't speak a common language, and because the situation for us was so dire. But we know about each other now, know *of* each other, know a little of each other's culture. It's time to stop." Aeren sucked in a breath and repeated in the dwarren tongue, leaning slightly forward, "It's time to stop and *talk.*"

Garius didn't move, although his eyes widened slightly as Aeren spoke the thick, guttural dwarren. Eraeth could barely follow it, even though Aeren had forced him to learn it, along with Andovan. Unlike the humans, who seemed more than willing to talk in any given situation, even when words were useless, the dwarren weren't as open or forthcoming, so the Alvritshai's grasp of the language was tenuous. But they knew some, and that fact clearly surprised the clan chief and his son.

Garius sighed unexpectedly, shoulders slumping, his arms dropping from their defiant position across his chest. He glanced toward his son, mouth pressed tight as he saw the fixed angry expression there, then bowed his head, eyes closed.

Eraeth swore silently to himself as the clan chief lifted his head, let his hand fall close to the hilt of his cattan.

"The Lands ... the plains ... are sacred to us. They are a gift of the gods, given to the dwarren to protect, to preserve. We believe the clans were created and left here to guard them and everything that they contain—the sky above, the grass, the earth below, the forests, and the waters that feed them all, the waters that give them life, that give *us* life. And we have guarded these Lands, protected them, for generation upon generation."

"How?" Eraeth asked, his voice taut. He saw Aeren tense, but continued. "How have you protected the grassland, when all that the Alvritshai have seen since we came here are the clans warring with each other?"

Garius' eyes flared with anger. "The clans do not always agree on how the gods intended the Lands to be protected, and so we war. We have seen the same conflicts among the humans and among the Alvritshai. But that is not the point."

He turned back to Aeren, the anger seeping into his voice, darkening it. "When the Alvritshai came to the Lands, they did not seek out the People and ask for the use of the Lands. They did not honor the gods and their great gift. *You* did not honor the gods. Instead, you defiled the Lands, built houses and towns and cities upon its earth, plowed its fields and sowed it with grain, all without the gods' blessing, without the permission of the dwarren left to preserve it." His breath heaved with indignation, with suppressed fury, but with effort he managed to control himself. "That is why the dwarren have fought against you, why we continue to fight. Your presence here—on this grass, on this earth—is a desecration of the Lands."

Eraeth drew breath to protest, his own anger rising—at the arrogance of the dwarren, at their self-importance— but Aeren laid a hand on his shoulder to quiet him.

"Does our situation mean nothing to you then? Thousands of Alvritshai would have perished in the winters that followed our abandonment of the northern reaches. Do your gods have no mercy? No patience for the ignorant?"

A troubled look passed over Garius' angry face, but his son spat something in dwarren, spoken so fast that Eraeth could not catch it, although it was obviously derogatory.

"Hush, Shea, you do not know of what you speak. You are not yet a member of the Gathering, and you are not a shaman. Do not presume to know our will, or the gods." The words were soft, but the reprimand behind them bit. Shea flinched and bowed his head in angry discontent.

Garius considered Aeren with an intent frown, the smoke from the braziers drifting in heavy tendrils between them. No one moved, and Eraeth felt sweat break out against his skin. The tent had grown hot.

Garius finally spoke.

"Ilacqua is merciful, especially to the ignorant . . . and the foolhardy." This last was directed toward Shea, whose head dipped slightly lower. "I cannot say what he or any of the other gods would say regarding what you have revealed. I am not a shaman and would never presume to know the gods' will. But I am a member of the Gathering, and we have noticed that winter comes earlier every year, that occasionally there is snow on the plains where there was never snow before." He lifted his chin. "What would you have me say to the Gathering?"

Aeren's hand fell away from Eraeth's shoulder. "Tell them what I have said here, about why the Alvritshai are on the plains and why we have fought so hard to retain what we have taken. Tell them that we were ignorant of your ways. And tell them . . . tell them that if there is a chance for peace between us, the Alvritshai are willing to ask the dwarren for permission to use the Lands, that we will vow to protect them as the dwarren would."

Garius stirred, his eyes going wide. Even Shea's head rose. "The Alvritshai would be willing to do this?"

Aeren hesitated, then nodded. "If it will mean peace between us, then yes. I will convince the Tamaell—our chief—that it is necessary for the skirmishes to end."

Eraeth turned to look at his lord. Aeren had said it as if it would be simple, as if he could simply walk into the halls of the Evant and ask.

Garius' entire posture changed. The doubt that had tightened his shoulders and back, that lined his face, eased.

"If this is true, if your chief, this Tamaell, would vow to protect the Lands as the gods demand . . ." He glanced toward Shea, then back toward Aeren. "I cannot say what the Gathering will say, but know this, Lord Aeren of the Alvritshai. I wish my son to grow old, spawn many children, and die on these Lands without the threat of war, no matter that he desires only to prove himself on the battlefield so that his blood may feed the grasses." A look of scandalized horror crossed Shea's face, but his father ignored him completely, leaning forward through the haze of smoke. "I have lost many in these battles—friends and family alike, and sons. I'd guess that you have lost as many, if not more. This war is wicked, destroying the plains. The gods are not happy. The shamans know this; that is why the storms have grown worse, and the air itself shimmers and cracks. They are omens."

The occumaen, Eraeth thought. He's speaking of the occumaen. And the unnatural lightning.

Garuis sat back, considering Aeren, one hand stroking

his beard, tangling in the beads braided there. It was the first relaxed gesture Eraeth had seen the chieftain use since they'd arrived.

He grunted, as if reaching a decision. "I will call a Gathering. I will speak to the other chieftains, to the People of the Lands. If they agree, I will bring them to this flat in one month. This I swear, in blood, before the gods' eyes." He pulled a thin knife, all of the Phalanx tensing. But it wasn't a fighting knife. He placed the short flattened blade against the soft outer pad of his palm and made a small knick, enough to draw blood. With the thumb of the hand holding the knife, he smeared the blood across his palm, spat on it, and held it out to Aeren.

Eraeth saw Aeren still. He could sense the distaste in his lord, but Aeren reached forward and clasped Garius' hand tightly.

Garius' grip tightened for a moment, not allowing Aeren to withdraw, and he caught the lord's eyes. "If your chief would have peace between us, he will be here."

He released his grip, leaning back, his arms crossed over his chest again. "Now go."

Eraeth rose with Aeren, the lord bowing toward the chief of the People of the Thousand Springs. A formal bow, one that would be given to another Lord of the Evant. Then they left, passing back through the entrance, around the curved arm of the tent and out into the night.

Darkness shrouded the entire camp, broken by the fires and the stars above. As he came out into the cool night air, Eraeth stumbled, a wave of dizziness sweeping over him, brought on by the heat of the tent and the dense smoke. He gasped, sucked in a cleansing breath, the cold shocking his lungs, heard the others doing the same.

The shaman stood to one side, watching them through narrowed eyes. But when the storm they had seen upon entering the tent flared to the east—closer now, enough that they could hear an answering rumble of thunder—he turned back to study it. The rest of the dwarren ignored them completely.

"That was . . . interesting," Aeren said as they began to move through the circles of tents back to their own camp.

Eraeth didn't hear any sarcasm in his voice. "I did not like his son, Shea."

Aeren shrugged. "He is young. He does not trust us, and he has yet to learn how to be . . . diplomatic. You and he are much alike."

Eraeth snorted. "I am not young."

Aeren smiled. "No, you are not. And for that you are forgiven much." They passed through the dwarren sentries and walked up the hillock in silence, turning near the top, where Eraeth gave the sentry on duty there a nod that all was well. The Phalanx guardsman relaxed.

Behind them, the dwarren camp lay among the black grass, the campfires burning in rounded glares of light, the tent where they had met with the chieftain glowing blue-green with the light of the braziers inside. The storm lit the sky to the east with flashes of blue and purple and set Eraeth's skin tingling with its nearness.

"But we found what we came for," Aeren said, and as Eraeth turned to look at him, his face was lit with the glow of purple lightning. Eraeth saw weariness there, and pain, along with satisfaction. "Now all we need to do is convince the Tamaell and the Evant."

~

"You're listening to them?" Shea barked as soon as the Al-vritshai warriors left the tent. He jumped to his feet, paced the confines of the tent. "You trust them? Remember what was done to our People at the Cut!"

"I will take their words to the Gathering and the rest of the clan chiefs, yes," Garius said, his voice coming out in a low growl. He watched his son pace, saw the pent up anger in each step, the frustration in his clenched hands. Garius nearly reached out to grab his son's arm and force him to stop, but he crossed his arms over his chest instead.

He'd been young once himself.

The smoke from the braziers—representing the four gods of the Winds, with the fifth overhead representing Ilacqua, so that he could oversee all that transpired in the tent—hung thick and heavy, swirling around his son's movements. Garius drew the cleansing yetope smoke deep into his lungs, held it, then exhaled slowly before continuing.

"I do not trust them, Shea. But a decision like this cannot be made by a single clan chief. It may affect all of the clans, so it must go to the Gathering." He let his voice harden. "You know this. And you know why we must at least listen."

"Because of the Cut," Shea sneered.

Garius slammed one fist down on the table in the center of the tent, the bowl of untouched fruit jumping with a rattle. "Yes, because of the Cut! Over two thousand Riders were killed at the Cut, massacred by the Alvritshai and human forces, including your grandfather and three of your uncles—my father and brothers! I would have been there, would have *died* there, if I'd been old enough to wear my first band. None of the Riders who left the Lands to meet the Alvritshai and the humans survived, not clan chief nor first-banded. It decimated our ranks. Enough Riders remained to keep the human incursions at bay, but barely. If they had come in force within ten years of that day . . ."

"When they did come we fought them back—"

"*I* fought them back," Garius interrupted. "You were nothing but a kernel of grain in Ilacqua's eye."

"We should fight them now!"

Shea halted near one of the braziers, and they glared at each other. Garius' anger flared in his blood, but staring at his son, at the tension in his shoulders, at the clench of his jaw, he faltered.

Shea looked too much like his older brother, Jasu.

"Jasu," Garius said tightly, and saw Shea wince. "I don't fight them because of Jasu."

"What do you mean? What does my brother have to do with it?"

"Everything!" Garius snapped. He suddenly couldn't sit anymore. He rose and began to pace, taking Shea's place. "He has everything to do with it. When he received his first band and became a Rider, I was proud, as any father would be. He could join me, could help me protect the Lands, help drive off the humans and the Alvritshai in Ilacqua's name. And he did, riding the plains, joined later by your older brothers, arriving back at the Thousand Springs warren victorious, welcomed by your mother and sisters, by the entire clan." His pacing slowed and he looked toward Shea. "And then he died."

Shea frowned, but he said nothing, his brow still creased in irritation.

"You weren't there—you were barely waist-high! You don't remember. The humans had built an outpost on Silver Grass Clan lands. Thousand Springs joined them in the attack, but the outpost had been fortified with the Legion. Your brother fell in the initial charge, and I brought his body home with me.

"I could barely enter the warren. I knew what this would do to your mother. But when we rode into the city through the tunnels and I saw her waiting at our cleft, I realized she already knew. I don't know how, but she had already wept; her eyes were red but dry. But the pain on her face, pain that she hid for the sake of the clan, for *my* sake as clan chief—" Garius broke off, his voice cracking. He held his arms before him, as if he still carried Jasu's body, as if he were crossing the threshold of the tunnel into the cavernous main room of the warren even now. For a moment, he could see the entrances of the cliffside clefts rising in tiers on all sides, could hear the roar of the river crashing into the central pool of the cavern, all of it lit with a thousand lanterns, decorated with garlands of straw and wheat to celebrate their return . . .

It threatened to overwhelm him, the grief crushing. He clenched his jaw, forced the emotion down, and glared at Shea, one hand squeezed into a tight fist. He could see that Shea didn't understand, realized that he'd never understand until he had a wife and sons of his own.

He needed to give Shea a reason he could understand.

He swallowed, lowered his arms, and started again. "There are barely ten thousand dwarren left in the clan, when once there were twice that," he said gruffly. "Four thousand of us are Riders. The other clans fare no better. All told there are maybe thirty thousand Riders left to protect the Lands, less than a hundred thousand of the People. Once we were a thriving race, but now we are dwindling. Already our numbers approach those of the Alvritshai, who guard their lives and the lives of their children with such reverence. That is why the Alvritshai have not attacked us recently, because their own survival is threatened. They've lost too many of their children to the fight. The humans have outnumbered us for years, and they are reckless with their lives, as we once were with our own.

"We cannot be reckless any longer. We cannot throw

our lives away on the plains. Your need to fight—and that of your generation—will destroy the People completely."

Shea regarded him for a long moment in silence, his jaw clenched tight. When he finally spoke, he said, "The need to fight—the urge to avenge those of us who have died, like Jasu—was trained into us by you."

He left, ducking out through the cloth covering the western entrance.

Garius stood stunned. His gaze fell on his fists, knuckles white, and he forced them to open. The yepote smoke in the tent had dissipated, three of the braziers burned out. He breathed in deeply, then sighed heavily.

When he emerged from the tent, he saw no sign of Shea; the camp was mostly dark. The storm still rumbled off in the distance, and a few cook fires still burned, mostly dampened coals.

"The sky is troubled."

Garius turned and picked out the figure of the shaman standing with his ceremonial spear, his back to the tent. He moved to the shaman's side and stared out at the flickers of lightning far distant. "What do you see, Oudan? Should we listen to the Alvritshai?"

Oudan snorted, then waved his spear out toward the darkened plains. "The Land is troubled. We see it in the sky—" he pointed toward the storm "—and feel it in the shimmering air. We taste it in the food we eat, the water we drink. Even the gaezels sense it. We have lived in our warrens for thousands of years, slept in our clefts, and honored and protected the Land and our gods. But the gods are restless.

"Perhaps it is time for the People to change."

15

THE FOLLOWING DAY, the dwarren tore down their tents, loaded up their gaezels, and headed back into the plains, east and south.

Colin watched them from the top of the hillock while the rest of the Alvritshai gathered together their loosely scattered gear, saddled the horses, and prepared to leave. He'd managed to get close enough to verify that these dwarren were from the Thousand Springs Clan, the dwarren who had fought the humans and left such carnage on the battlefield outside the forest. He frowned as the sound of their drums faded and the group of figures vanished over a fold in the land. He could still see a thin trace of dust in the air from their passage, faint against the blue of the sky.

"You hate them."

Colin started and turned to find Eraeth standing behind him. "Why do you say that?" Colin asked.

Eraeth grinned, not a pleasant expression. "You tensed the moment you knew the dwarren were approaching and haven't relaxed since. And now, even as they depart, you're gripping your staff so hard your knuckles are white."

Colin glanced down in annoyance, tried to make his hands relax, but couldn't.

Not able to meet Eraeth's gaze, he watched the horizon. "They killed Karen, my mother and father, my friends." He could hear the defensiveness in his own voice, could hear the hatred, and realized he didn't care. He'd seen and heard the same hatred in Eraeth since the dwarren had arrived,

But he winced when Aeren spoke from behind him. "That's not true. They didn't kill your parents, your friends, or your beloved. The sukrael did."

"We would never have run into the sukrael if not for them," Colin snapped.

"True. But that was an unfortunate consequence. It was not the dwarren's plan—"

"Not their plan?" Colin exclaimed, turning toward Aeren incredulously. "What about the wagon train before us? The dwarren found them, rounded them up, and slaughtered them. And they would have done the same to us. They trapped us against the forest, and if the sukrael didn't get us, the dwarren did when we tried to escape into the plains. I *know.* I went back and *watched it happen.*"

Aeren frowned, his brow creasing, but he said nothing.

Colin snorted. "What did they want?"

Aeren hesitated. "It wasn't what they wanted, it was what I wanted from them."

"And that was?"

"Peace. As with the humans. With you. I want peace, so that the Alvritshai no longer have to fight. So that the Alvritshai no longer have to die."

Colin stared at the Alvritshai lord intently for a long time, struggling with his hatred of the dwarren, with the emotions seeing them here had dredged up. He searched Aeren's face, but he saw nothing familiar.

"How can you?" he finally asked. "After what the dwarren have done to the Alvritshai all these years, after what you know they've done to the humans. How can you approach them and ask for peace and mean it?"

Aeren shifted where he stood, and for the first time Colin saw anger in his eyes. "You do not understand how sacred the Alvritshai hold life, how precious it is in Aielan's eyes. We live longer than the dwarren, longer even than you humans, but we are not as ... prolific as you are. Children between those who bond are rare. The fact that my mother bore two healthy sons for the House was ... miraculous. Most of those bonded only bear one child, if that. But now, because of this war, my father and brother are dead. I am the only living member of my House left. And I have not yet bonded. There is no heir to the Rhyssal seat."

Behind him, Eraeth stirred, looking toward his lord, a

pained expression in his stoic stance. But he said nothing as Aeren continued.

"Those deaths—my brother, my father—and the sheer number of Alvritshai lives lost since that first excursion onto the plains, since that first misunderstanding between Alvritshai and dwarren, have finally overwhelmed my hatred. I'm hoping they have overwhelmed the Tamaell and the Evant as well. I had hoped they had overwhelmed the human King, but unfortunately, King Stephan's pain is more recent, more personal. His pain comes from a betrayal, not battle. Not so for the dwarren."

"More dwarren died at the Escarpment than all of the Alvritshai or humans combined. They were slaughtered there."

Aeren nodded. "Yes. The war has finally taken its toll on the dwarren, as it has for the Alvrishai. Their aggression has lessened over the past thirty years. Which is why I am hopeful that the dwarren will be willing to discuss peace."

Behind him, one of the other Alvritshai whistled. He didn't turn, although both he and Eraeth straightened.

"The dwarren have agreed to a meeting, here, in one month. I have little time to convince the Tamaell that peace between the Alvritshai and the dwarren is a necessity. We're leaving, and we'll have to travel fast."

"He'll have to ride," Eraeth said to Aeren. "We can travel on foot. We'll switch out the horses so that they can rest. It will slow us down, but . . ."

Colin stiffened at Eraeth's tone. He thought about what he'd done at Portstown to catch up to the attackers and said abruptly, "I can keep up. On foot." At Eraeth's and Aeren's skeptical look, he added, "*If* you allow me to use the Lifeblood's powers." And he let himself shift, growing younger for a brief moment.

Aeren frowned, then glanced down toward the rest of the Phalanx escort.

"It will shake them," Eraeth said in warning. "They know he has been touched by the sukrael, that he has drunk from the sarenavriell, but most don't give the account much credence. If they see it, with their own eyes . . ."

Aeren thought for a long moment, glancing toward the sky, where the sun had already shifted toward midmorning. "They'll have to adjust. If we're to reach Caercaern and have any chance of convincing the Evant and the Tamaell to return here for the meeting, there can be no delays." He looked Colin in the eyes. "Do whatever you have to do to keep up, Shaeveran. If you fall behind, we will leave you."

He turned, and Eraeth whistled to the rest of the group. They formed up, all of their packs secured on the backs of the horses, only their weapons—cattans and bows—in hand. Eraeth barked orders in Alvritshai, and within the space of a few heartbeats the Phalanx scouts vanished onto the plains, the rest bringing the horses up to a trot, then a sprint behind them. Colin waited at the top of the hillock long enough to pick out the direction the Alvritshai were headed, then he reached out and *pushed*.

⁓

Colin cursed himself as he slipped through the grasses of the plains, staff in hand, satchel across his back. The world around him moved at an infinitesimal rate, birds barely flapped their wings in the sky, the grasses standing nearly still. The first day he'd found it disconcerting—he'd never realized how much the grass had moved before, even without a wind—but this wasn't just the lack of wind, this was lack of movement. *Any* movement. At least, movement significant enough to register on the eye. Sound was dulled here as well, and smell. He could catch only the faintest of scents: a touch of broken grass stalks, the ripeness of grain heading toward decay, a whiff of the tail end of autumn, with a hint of winter to it. But he'd found he didn't have to move as fast as he'd first thought he would. The Alvritshai were moving as fast as possible, but he could keep up with them by simply walking fast.

And that fact is what made him curse. He could have crossed the plains easily in a few days, reached Portstown in a week, if he'd known he could travel this way. But he hadn't known. It hadn't occurred to him. But he'd spent the last day experimenting. He couldn't pick objects up while time was slowed, or move them—they were fixed in place once the world slowed—but he could hold them and *then* slow time, carrying them with him to the new location. But if he slowed time too far, if he thrust through that barrier he'd felt while traveling back to see Karen and the wagon train after the attack, then when he dropped the object, it returned to natural time. It shifted location, but he couldn't leave it behind, in the past. As long as he stayed on this side of the barrier though ...

Off to the side, he caught a ripple on the otherwise still plains, and he drew to a halt at the edge of a small stream. The plains had grown more rumpled, with higher hills and deeper flats. To the east, a forest stretched into the distance, its edge growing closer. During the last break, Era-eth had said it was the same forest that held the Faelehgre and the sukrael, although they were much farther north.

Between his position and the forest, he could see one of the distortions he called Drifters. He'd seen dozens of them since he'd left the forest, but none of the Drifters had been this close. And here, with the world slowed, the Drifter looked ... different.

He glanced back to where he knew the Alvritshai were. Aeren had said they'd reach the first Alvritshai outpost that afternoon, at a rough division where the plains ended and the first few stands of forest began, marking the end of dwarren lands and the edge of Alvritshai territory. It would be another few days before they reached Caercaern and the halls of the Alvritshai.

But Colin knew he could catch up if he fell behind.

He moved closer to the Drifter, careful not to come into contact with any of its outstretched ripples. The Drifter coruscated with light, shifting though all of the various colors at its edges and through its arms but melding into an intense white as the light reached its center. The center itself was clear, and as he drew closer, he realized that he could see through it.

What he saw on the far side wasn't what he expected. Grass, yes, as if the plains continued on through the eye of coruscating light. But this grass wasn't lit with afternoon sunlight. Instead, it was silvered with faint moonlight, as if it were night on the far side.

One of the arms of the Drifter reached out, as if sensing him, and he pulled back. It brushed by where he'd stood a moment before and passed on, almost like the antennae on an insect.

Frowning, Colin searched the grass and found a stone, releasing his hold on time so he could pick it up. He turned, the Drifted no longer coruscating with color, merely a ripple of distortion, like heat waves, although he could still see the moonlit plains on the far side. It was moving slowly toward him. Stepping forward, he tossed the stone at the eye in the Drifter's center. It passed through, landing with a thud and rustle of grass as it rolled into the moonlight.

"It's a doorway," he murmured to himself. He considered for a moment, then slowed time. The Drifter shifted from clear ripples to coruscating colors again, but stopped drifting forward.

He prodded the stone with his staff through the distortion, then shifted position, keeping track of the rippling arms of the Drifter. If he stooped over, he could step through the eye himself, but the thought made him shudder. He couldn't see anything of significance on the far side, nothing to place where the doorway led. The features in the background—the shape of the land itself, the hills and depressions—seemed to match where he stood, although the forest appeared much closer. It was simply night there.

Then he caught the scent. A familiar scent. But here, with time slowed, the scent was *strong*. An earthen scent, of leaves and mulch and trees.

The Lifeblood. So strong he could taste it, as if he'd placed dried leaves in his mouth. It struck his gut hard, an ache shuddering out through his bones. Since he'd given Eraeth the vial of Lifeblood, the pull of the Well had eased and he'd had fewer and less severe seizures, but now the craving returned, harsh and powerful. He fought it back, forced himself to focus, to inhale deeply. Because there was something else as well, another scent intertwined with the Lifeblood. He concentrated, but he couldn't place it, even though he felt he should, as if he'd smelled it before. Like roses, sweet and clean.

He stood for a long moment in deep thought. He thought about what Aeren had said, that the Drifters had swallowed entire armies. He suddenly remembered Peg vanishing during the storm as they fled the dwarren.

But it didn't explain where the distortions were coming from. Nor why they were appearing more frequently now than when Colin's family had first headed out onto the plains.

He shrugged, turning away from the distortion, and as he did so, he heard a faint whisper.

. . . Colin . . .

He stilled, spinning slightly, like the needle of a compass, until he faced the forest on the far side of the distortion. *Osserin?*

The Faelehgre didn't respond, although Colin thought he heard . . . something.

Without looking back, Colin headed toward the far woods, slipping around the distortion and leaving it behind. A hundred paces farther on, he felt the faint edges of the Lifeblood's influence slip through him and he hissed in response, repressing a shiver. He could taste its coolness against his tongue, could feel it filling him, tingling through his skin, worse than when he'd smelled it near the Drifter. The fine hairs on his arm and on the back of his neck stood on end, and for a brief moment he shuddered at the thought that he had ever left its embrace.

Then his stomach cramped. He gasped, found himself on his knees, one hand on his staff holding him upright, the other fisted in the grass and earth, the dried blades cutting into his palms and fingers. He focused on the slivered pain, so thin and sharp, and fought back the duller, wider ache in his gut.

Trembling, he rose and pushed on toward the forest. He hadn't thought he'd react so strongly to the Well, now that he'd been away from it for so long. And he knew he was only at the edge of its influence. He could feel its power growing as he moved closer.

Except he was too far north to be within its influence at all.

. . . Colin . . .

I can hear you, Osserin. I'm headed toward the forest.

A wash of relief, and as if the Faelehgre had focused in on his voice he heard the reply clearly. *We've been trying to contact you since you left. We'd given up, but then we sensed you close to the forest. We've been calling for you for the last day.*

Colin stepped under the branches of the forest and sank into their shadows, the dulled scent of pine filling his senses. He moved deeper into the forest, feeling it close in around him, sunlight lancing down through breaks, dust caught in the shafts seemingly motionless.

Where are you?

Here, Osserin sent and Colin focused in on the direction of his voice. *Here, by the Well.*

And then Osserin wove out of the forest, flickering in agitation. A few other Faelehgre hovered around him, darting here and there in agitation.

"What's wrong?" Colin asked. "What's happened? I didn't think the influence of the Lifeblood spread this far north."

It doesn't. It shouldn't. But look.

Osserin streaked away, the others following. Colin forged after them, picking his way over tangled roots and the fallen trunks of trees, using his staff as a crutch. He reached the crest of a ridge, began making his way down the far side, then glanced up and halted in shock.

The ridge was the edge of a shallow bowl, earth sloping down toward a basin. In the center of the basin sat a ring of river stone, rounded and smooth, like the lip of the Well at the center of the Faelehgre's ancient city.

"Another Well," Colin murmured. Except this Well pulsed with a faint blue light.

He stumbled the last few steps and leaned forward over the lip of the Well, down into its depths, toward the blue light. He couldn't see any of the Lifeblood—the Well appeared empty—but he could *smell* it, could feel it throbbing in his skin.

It's filling slowly, Osserin whispered. *We think that's why the radius of our own Well increased, why we can travel here now. We think it has something to do with the disappearance of the Wraiths.*

Colin shoved back from the Well. "Tell me what happened."

Osserin hovered uncertainly for a moment, as if he didn't know where to start, but then his light dimmed and he settled closer to the ground.

It began a few days after you left. Or so we think. We can't be certain. But that was the first sign that something was different. We sent out some of the Faelehgre to scout. What they found was not that something had changed, but that something was missing. The Wraiths were no longer in the forest, were no longer anywhere within the Well's influence.

"None of them?"

None. All six of them were gone.

Colin felt something crawl up his back, the flesh of his spine prickling, the sensation creeping up into his shoulders and spreading out along his arms.

"What about the Shadows, the sukrael? Where are they?"

Still inside the forest. They're still trapped by the Lifeblood, as we are. But you and the Wraiths. . . . We never considered whether or not the Wraiths could leave the forest. They never have before, so we thought they were trapped like us, like the Shadows. But they're not. They're like you. They're touched by the Lifeblood, but not yet caught.

"Where did they go?"

We don't know. We can't follow them, and we can't track them. We tried to contact you as soon as we realized that they'd left. We thought that perhaps they'd gone after you, especially since they left almost immediately after you did.

Which was strange. But maybe his departure hadn't been a factor. Maybe it had been a coincidence. Or maybe his leaving the forest had forced the Wraiths to act.

"If they aren't coming after me, then where would they go?"

Osserin flared in anger. *Again, we don't know. But a few weeks after you left, something else happened. The Well itself . . . flashed.*

"What do you mean?"

Colin could sense the Faelehgre's frustration. *The air around the Well began to hum, to vibrate, so we gathered at the edge of the Well itself, on the amphitheater's steps. And then the sukrael appeared in the forest on the far side, hundreds of them. They came out of the forest, as if drawn to the sound, and they were . . . dancing, weaving in and out among the trees, cavorting with each other. The hum escalated, and everything around the Well grew still. The Shadows halted, the trees quieted. Even we grew silent. Because we could feel the buildup of power, could feel it throbbing on the air.*

And then a white light pulsed up through the water from deep below, from the Well's source, and spread outward, rustling in the trees, shoving all of us back toward the city, the Shadows back into the trees. A few of the Shadows shrieked, and one of the nearer buildings cracked, the foundation splitting.

But that was it. We stayed at the Well. The Shadows stayed as well, for a time, and then, as if by signal, they fled into the forest again.

When we went to investigate, we found that the influence of the Well had expanded. We could travel farther in all directions, out onto the plains, to the north, south, and east as well, deeper into the forest.

The same thing has happened twice more, the Lifeblood pulsing, and each time the extent of the Well's influence grows. We've only been able to reach this far north within the last few days. And then Yssero sensed you at the edge of our reach yesterday. We've been calling to you since then, hoping you'd hear and come to us so we could warn you.

Colin had settled back onto the stone of the Well as Osserin spoke. "Has this ever happened before?" he asked.

Not as far as any of us remember. And the Faelehgre have long memories.

He narrowed his gaze at Osserin in suspicion. "What do you think the Wraiths are doing?" When Osserin hesitated, he added, "Osserin?"

In a flash and dimming of light that was almost as audible as a sigh, Osserin said, *We think the Wraiths are attempting to . . . free the Shadows.*

That same prickling sensation coursed up Colin's back, only this time it continued to spread, sinking into the pit of his stomach with a nauseous heat, into his lungs with a tingling cold.

"Can they do that?" he asked, almost breathless.

We've spent hundreds of years trying to find a way to escape the Well. We couldn't, because we can't move beyond the Well's influence, and we found no way to break the Well or alter its power from within. The Shadows are in the same situation. When you came, when you drank from the Well, there was much discussion about sending you out to find a way to free us. But in the end, we decided that couldn't be done because freeing us would also mean freeing the Shadows. And that is too much to set upon the world. Not for what was our own mistake.

We never considered that perhaps the Shadows were trying to find a way to free themselves as well. We know that

*they are intelligent. After all they were once an embodiment
of us, were once part of us, separated from us by the Lifeblood. They are the remnants of our bodies, while we are
the remnants of our souls. That is why they feed. They are
searching for the life-force that their bodies once held. But
we did not realize how intelligent they are.*

Colin heard something in Osserin's voice, something
dark, that made his skin break out in a light sweat. "What
do you think they've done?"

Osserin hesitated. Then: *We think that when the dwarren
first arrived here in the forest, the Shadows tasted true life-
force for the first time in centuries. They feasted, but when
the dwarren grew wary of the forest, they realized that in
order to continue feeding, they needed to find a way to break
the Well's influence.*

"You said that couldn't be done."

Osserin flared in annoyance. *Exactly. When the Faelehgre realized this, we stopped searching. Our drive to be free
waned. It had never been as strong as that of the Shadows
in any case. But the Shadows continued searching. And after
the dwarren appeared, they realized that, if they couldn't
break the Well's influence, then perhaps they could extend it.*

"How?"

Osserin dipped toward the second Well. *With this. Somehow, the Shadows learned of this second Well. A dead Well,
one empty of the Lifeblood. They realized that if they could
reawaken it, if they could bring it back to life...*

"Then their realm of influence would expand," Colin
breathed.

Osserin pulsed in agreement. *Yes. But the second Well
was outside their influence. They couldn't touch it, couldn't
activate it themselves. They needed someone else, someone
who could travel outside the restrictions of the Lifeblood.
So they created the Wraiths.*

"How?"

Osserin flickered with uncertainty. *We aren't certain, but
think back to the attack on your group. You said that the
Shadows attacked in a frenzy, that they gorged themselves
on the people in your wagon train, feeding frantically. They
had not fed in a long time, and there were so many of you.*

*But then you said that their attacks changed, that they
began to taunt you. The frenzy died, as if they had been*

sated. *When you remained with Karen, they did not fall on you like they did the others. You said they "tasted" you.*

Colin's mouth had gone dry and he clutched at the stone of the Well, the memory of that day still sharp. "Yes."

We think that they were testing you. Osserin drifted closer. *We think that they were trying to decide whether you could be made into a Wraith.*

Colin shuddered and his fingers scraped against the rough stone of the Well as he tried to dig into it. He lowered his head. "You're saying that all of the Wraiths are ... victims of the Shadows. That they were all once people, that they have been ... poisoned in some way by the Shadows."

By the Shadows and the Lifeblood. The first Wraiths, created before the appearance of humans on the plains, were short, about the same height as—

"The dwarren. They were dwarren." Colin thought about all of the Wraiths he had seen since he'd drunk from the Well. They were always cloaked in the Shadows, so that their features were never clear, but now that he knew.... "They have Alvritshai and human Wraiths now."

And the Wraiths or the Shadows figured out how to re-awaken this Well.

Colin stared down into the soft blue glow beneath him. "If there was a second Well, then there must be others. The Wraiths must be searching for them."

If they find them, if they reawaken them, then their influence and that of the Shadows will increase. Already the influence has expanded enough to intersect with dwarren lands ... and Alvritshai. Osserin drifted closer. *The Wraiths have to be stopped. The Shadows cannot be allowed to prey upon the world.*

Colin gave Osserin a sardonic look. "And you want me to stop them. How do you expect me to do that? You don't know where they are, and I don't know how to find them."

Osserin considered for a moment, then said, *We think they're moving northward.*

Colin frowned. "Why?"

Because the influence of the Lifeblood isn't expanding in all directions at the same rate. The first pulse spread it out circularly, like a widening pool, but the second and third only increased the Well's influence to the north and east. When we explored the new region, we found this Well. When this one was reawakened, it intersected with the radius of influence from our own Well. And as it fills, its radius increases.

"And none of the Faelehgre knew of this Well?"

Osserin wavered. *None. The Faelehgre traded with people to the south, east, and west. We did not reach this far north.*

Colin turned to stare down into the pulsing blue light of the Well behind him. "You don't know where any of the other Wells are either, do you?"

Osserin's light appeared to wince. *No. You have to warn the Alvritshai of the Wraiths and the Shadows. Part of their lands are within Shadow territory now. We'll try to protect them as much as possible, but we can't be everywhere at once. The area is simply too large now.*

"You should keep searching for the Wraiths as well, and the locations of any more Wells. I'll do the same."

~

"Aielan's Light, where is he?" Eraeth demanded. "We're almost at the outpost."

Aeren frowned at Eraeth. "For your supposed hatred of the humans and everything they do, you've certainly taken to their penchant for blasphemy."

"I knew we couldn't trust him," Eraeth mumbled under his breath, ignoring Aeren's comment completely, still scanning the horizon.

They'd reached the last of the plains, the edge of the lands the Alvritshai had claimed from the dwarren. The land rose abruptly into hills, scattered with trees and brush and dense thickets of thorn and sedge. The scattering of trees continued, the hills steadily growing steeper, then thickened into copses and eventually forest. Rearing up in the near distance were the jagged northern mountains, what the Alvritshai called the Hauttaeren and the humans called the Teeth.

"He's followed us since Corsair," Aeren said. "I doubt he has abandoned us now."

Eraeth growled and turned to his lord, stiffening slightly, his tone becoming formal. "I've been watching for him since we left the dwarren. He isn't invisible when he travels. There's a shadow, a darkness, that you can catch out of the corner of your eye. I saw it numerous times those first two days, and most of this morning. He's been keeping close now that we're nearing the outposts. But I haven't seen him since this afternoon. He's gone, and I would like to know where. Especially now that I know he can bypass the Phalanx sentries whenever he feels like it." He straightened, faced Aeren completely. "You should be concerned about that as well."

"I am concerned," Aeren said, "but not for the same reason. There may be others out there with this . . . ability. And if Colin can bypass our sentries, then so can they. Those are the men you should be worried about, not Colin." He scanned the horizon, searching for the flicker of shadow Eraeth had mentioned. Because he'd noticed the shadow as well. Nothing tangible enough to track, to follow with the eye, but if Colin passed through his peripheral vision . . .

"I'm more concerned that something has happened to him," Aeren said. "Have you noticed he isn't keeping as old of an appearance as when we first met him in Portstown?"

Eraeth's lips twitched into a sneer, then smoothed. "Should we wait for him?" he asked, completely formal now.

Aeren suppressed a sigh. "No. We'll move on to the outpost, and then directly to Caercaern. If Colin can slip by our sentries, he should have no problem with the outposts."

"We won't be traveling to Rhyssal?"

"There isn't time if we're to convince the Tamaell to meet with the dwarren."

"And have you figured out how you're going to do that?"

Aeren didn't answer, catching Eraeth's gaze instead. Lines of concern appeared at the edges of the Phalanx's eyes, but he said nothing. "Let's move," Aeren said, stepping away from the plains into the edge of the heavier scrub to the north.

They reached the outpost an hour later, Eraeth approaching the lone building nestled in the branches of the trees above to announce them, although Aeren knew that the Phalanx that manned the outpost had likely seen the party nearly fifteen minutes before as they climbed the lower hills and entered the verge of the higher forests. One of the Phalanx had removed the Rhyssal House banner and attached it to a pole to declare themselves once they'd come within shouting distance of the outpost.

When Eraeth turned to look back, Aeren moved forward, escorted by the rest of the Phalanx in his party. The caitan of the outpost who'd been speaking to Eraeth bowed formally at the waist as he approached. "Lord Aeren," he said, rising slowly. He wore Ionaen House colors: Peloroun's black and orange. "Aielan's Light upon you."

"And you," Aeren answered, then asked, "What news?"

The caitan shrugged. "Nothing of note here beneath the Hauttaeren."

"And elsewhere?"

"Nothing from the plains, but there has been activity on the coast."

"What kind of activity?"

"Lord Barak returned with news of war between the Provinces and Andover. The Andovans have attacked numerous ports along the coast. The human Governors have been able to repel all such attacks so far, although there are rumors that the Andovans have yet to bring their main fleets across the Arduon."

"Have the attacks affected any of our own ports yet?"

"The Andovans have yet to venture that far up the coast. They seem to be relegating their attacks to the areas south of Sedaeren and the Claw."

"It would be stupid to antagonize us by attacking Alvritshai ports," Eraeth said.

The caitan snorted. "When have the humans ever shown such intelligence?"

Everyone in Aeren's party stilled. Such prejudiced comments were not allowed in the Rhyssal House, by any of its members, including the Phalanx.

But this was not his House lands, and these were not his Phalanx. Each lord kept their own army, trained it and supplied it using their own House resources, its members loyal to the House's lord and the Tamaell.

The silence held until the caitan shifted awkwardly, uncertain how he had offended Aeren. He fell back on protocol. "Will you be passing through to your own House lands?"

Aeren shook his head and answered coldly. "No. I will be traveling to Caercaern on urgent business. I have my own Phalanx. There will be no need of an escort." The caitan nodded, glancing over the group and frowning. There were fewer of the Phalanx in attendance than most of the other lords used in their own escorts. "Are any of the lords currently seeing the Tamaell?"

"Lord Barak, Jydell, and Khalaek are in attendance."

More than Aeren expected. "Have word sent to the remaining lords that their presence is required in Caercaern. Immediately."

The caitan nodded, motioning to members of the Phalanx behind him.

Then they left the outpost behind and entered Ionaen House lands.

Aeren saw the flicker of shadow out of the corner of his eye a moment before Colin appeared before him.

Eraeth's cattan snicked from its sheath, blade pointed at Colin's chest, before Aeren had even had time to lean back.

"Where have you been?" Eraeth demanded, his voice like stone. On all sides, the rest of the Phalanx rose from their positions around the way station beside the road where they'd stopped to rest the horses and eat their midmorning meal.

Aeren glared at Eraeth in annoyance. "If he'd wanted to kill me, I'd already be dead," he said calmly, in Alvritshai, "and there would have been nothing you could have done to stop him."

Eraeth grimaced, his blade lowering, even as he sent Colin—standing perfectly still—an angry look. "He would make a perfect assassin," he growled, a certain amount of respect in his voice. The rest of the Phalanx went back to their tasks.

Aeren nodded. "Thankfully, he is not."

Then he turned to Colin and said in Andovan, "I assume something has happened."

Relaxing slightly, Colin nodded. "Something has happened, although I don't think it has anything to do with your plans." He told them about the Well, the disappearance of the Wraiths, and the expansion of the sukrael's range in Alvritshai lands. He shuddered as he spoke, and Aeren saw something dark and haunted flicker through Colin's eyes, the same haunted look he'd seen on the ship when he'd woken from the seizure, the same desperation he'd noted at odd moments since. But that initial look had been worn, old in some way, as if it were a wound that he'd learned simply to accept. This wound was new and fresh, still bleeding. Aeren could see it in Colin's hold on the staff, in the way he unconsciously massaged the wrist of his right hand.

Colin swallowed as he finished and met Aeren's gaze. "If the Well's influence is spreading northward, then the Alvritshai will be the first affected by the presence of the sukrael."

"It will affect the dwarren as well."

"What are the Wraiths?" Eraeth demanded.

Colin shrugged. "They were part of the forest when I arrived, there when I awoke. They must have been people who wandered into the Well's influence."

"Or were driven there," Eraeth said.

Aeren nodded slowly. "If they were created to awaken the Wells, so that the sukrael would have a larger hunting ground, then in order to find the Wraiths, we need to find the Wells." An unpleasant pit had opened in his stomach, and a dry, sour taste filled his mouth. He shifted his attention to Eraeth. "We'll have to inform the Order."

Eraeth winced.

"What's the Order?" Colin asked.

"The Order of Aielan," Aeren answered. "Its acolytes are the keepers of the Scripts, the holders of the ancient texts and their knowledge. They interpret Aielan's will, and they lead us all to Aielan's Light. And most of their members have certain ... talents."

"Like Diermani's priests in the church."

Aeren smiled, the expression taut. "Yes and no. Like your priests, the acolytes have power. Nothing like what you have shown, but power nonetheless. But unlike your churches, the Order has direct political influence. In effect, they are a ninth House, except that they have no direct role to play in the Evant. But they can control it, if they desire, simply by manipulating those among the lords who are faithful. Your church does not have that power, at least not in the Provinces, although I've heard your church holds tremendous power in Andover across the ocean. It was a driving force behind the Feud that has torn Andover apart for the last sixty years." As he spoke, he motioned for Eraeth and the rest of the Phalanx to gather the horses. "I do not think this news of the sukrael will affect the main reason that we go to Caercaern, but it will complicate matters. The acolytes are the only ones who would know of the whereabouts of any of the Wells—their locations may appear in the Scripts—but if we approach them, they will become involved. In everything."

And that was what Aeren dreaded. He'd dealt with the Order before, had been an acolyte until his father had been killed on the plains. Forced to return to the House lands and assume the role of ascension beneath his brother, Aureon, he still considered himself one of the devout followers of Aielan's Light. But he'd never appreciated their manipulation of the members of the Evant. Lotaern, the Chosen, leader of the Order, had been disappointed when Aeren left the Order. But Aeren was wise enough to realize that his return to the Rhyssal House gave Lotaern influence over Aeren and his House in the Evant, influence the Chosen would not hesitate to use. He'd seen it in Lotaern's eyes the last time they'd met as Chosen and acolyte.

He would have to approach Lotaern about the Shadows and the Wells as soon as possible, to warn him of the possibility of attack from the sukrael if nothing else, and the potential aid of the antruel—the Faelehgre. But perhaps he could enlist Lotaern's aid in approaching the Evant about the dwarren. Influence was a dual-edged blade.

Eraeth signaled that the Phalanx was ready and Aeren turned to Colin. "You should stay with us, now that we're within Alvritshai lands. Ride if necessary, although we'll be moving more slowly than on the plains. And keep the colors of the Rhyssal House you wear visible at all times. Few humans have traveled among the Alvritshai, fewer still across our holdings. And when we reach Caercaern . . ."

"Don't draw attention to myself," Colin finished.

Aeren nodded, then heard Eraeth mutter in Alvritshai under his breath, "That's going to be impossible."

And they moved, swiftly, past wide, flattened valleys and farmland claimed from the dwarren decades past. The acreage was broken up by mounds of earth with low walls of stone on top for irrigation and a complex system of stone aqueducts that brought snowmelt down from the mountains to the lowlands. The fields were mostly barren, only dead vines and vegetation left after the harvest. Late winter grains were being scythed and mounded to dry in some. The air held a frigid bite, settling in the evenings and growing colder through the night, a taste of the coming winter. They passed through towns, the buildings a blend of wood and stone, tiered, with curved, wooden-shingled rooflines up to the base of the next floor, rising at least three levels in height, the largest up to six tiers high. Chimes dangled down from the apex of some, rung at intervals throughout the day. Aeren couldn't help comparing his own homeland to that of the humans, and he found the Provinces lacking. Alvritshai towns were cleaner, the architecture richer, the structures more pleasing to the eye. Hidden gardens and gurgling fountains were everywhere, with stone bridges crossing the streams and aqueducts at regular intervals, everything integrated into the surrounding land.

As they traveled, more and more roadways met their own, all paved, all in better repair than anything the humans had constructed. Handheld carts and baskets used by those in the outlying regions yielded to wagons and the occasional horse-drawn carriage. The Alvritshai clothing became more exotic than the rough uniforms worn by those working the fields. Men wore silken shirts and tunics, the cuts severe but with loose folds; women wore silken blouses with slim leather vests on top, a few with skirts, but most with more practical silken pants. Some wore conical hats woven from the reeds found near most of the streams. They passed through increasingly larger towns, Colin drawing attention everywhere they went, people pausing and pointing, murmuring with heads lowered and hands covering their mouths. They were stopped on more than one occasion by Ionaen Phalanx, the House guards questioning Eraeth and Aeren extensively while frowning and keeping their eyes fixed on Colin, but none of the Phalanx dared detain a Lord of the Evant.

As they neared Caercaern, Aeren motioned for the Phalanx to mount. He stared up through the edge of the thick trees to the mountains that towered above. They blazed in the sunlight, and he tasted the snow on the air, realized his breath came in plumes before him. He shivered, the roadway mostly in shadow.

Then they cantered around a twist in the road, and Caercaern came into view. "Welcome to Caercaern," he murmured, and heard Colin gasp.

Caercaern rose up out of the trees, a colossal work of stone, tiered like the buildings below, cascades of water running down the mountain to either side. The first tier consisted of a wall built out from the stone face of the mountain; the road leveled off at the wall's base, running nearly its full length before reaching the gate. Each tier above it acted as another wall, with gates at various positions as they ascended, no two in a direct line. Banners snapped in the wind, and Alvritshai were visible on the walls and rooftops and the bridges and streets that they could see from this vantage.

"All the buildings that you see, the roads and courtyards, squares and temples, all of it is a facade," Aeren said as they approached the gates. "The real Caercaern is hidden beneath the mountain. There are enough halls and fountains and pools beneath the stone to house all the Alvritshai for years if necessary."

"What do you think?" Dharel asked.

"It's . . . huge." Aeren watched the human struggle for a moment, then shake his head. "I thought the Faelehgre city was exotic, but it's a frail beauty, made of white stone and narrow towers. And its beauty is fading, collapsing inward. But this . . ."

Aeren smiled. "Look behind you."

Colin turned and gasped again. The entire valley spread out beneath the mountain fortress, hills and trees undulating away, covered in a thin layer of mist. A few towers stood out in the distance, on hilltops and promontories, and the occasional town or city peeked up from the rumpled blanket of forest. Much farther away, the duller browns and yellows of the cultivated fields interrupted the greenery.

The group drew to a halt at the gates, Eraeth and Aeren nudging their horses forward to speak to the waiting sen-

tries. A caitan of the Resue House Phalanx—also called
the White Phalanx—stepped forward to greet them, and
Aeren frowned, a shiver of dread coursing through his
body. Resue was the Tamaell's House.

The Phalanx caitan bowed formally. "Word of your arrival has already reached Tamaell Fedorem's ears," he said
as he rose, "as well as that of your . . . guest." The caitan's
eyes flicked toward Colin, conspicuous on his mount because of his shorter stature and darker skin, even though
he wore the Rhyssal House colors. "He requests your presence in his private gardens."

Aeren scanned the caitan's accompanying Phalanx, all
dressed in the white and red colors of House Resue, all
standing at formal attention, faces rigid, revealing nothing.
"I intended to visit my own House chambers, to wash the
dust of the road from my face," he said, "and to prepare."

The caitan shifted, although his features did not change.
"The Tamaell wishes to see you immediately. You may
honor your House with your presence later."

"Very well." Aeren bowed his head to the caitan. "My
Protector will accompany me. The rest of my Phalanx will
retire to my rooms, along with my guest."

The caitan returned the nod, then motioned to the
members of the Tamaell's Phalanx that accompanied him.
They formed up around Aeren's group, taking positions
of honor, rather than a more formal escort, and Aeren
relaxed slightly. A few remained with the caitan.

He shared a glance with Eraeth as the escort led the
others away.

They were led through the sunlit streets of the first
three tiers up into the enclosed fourth tier, the Tamaell's
public chambers. The halls were immaculate, leaves
and vines threading up the stone columns set into the
walls, murals and friezes around every corner, the ceiling painted to resemble the sky, pale blue, with clouds
lining the horizon, the blue fading into a soft, brilliant
yellow like the sun at intersecting corridors. Members of
the White Phalanx, the Tamaell's House guards, moved
about among aides and couriers in House Resue colors,
mingling with Phalanx bearing a few other House colors.
Audience chambers, dining halls, and other rooms opened
off to either side, filled with chairs and tables, plants

and statues, all placed with elegant care, yet somehow ostentatious.

They ascended to the fifth tier. Aeren had only been into these upper rooms a few times. This was the Tamaell's private tier, and it was significantly different. The walls were a flat polished white stone, the support columns rectangular but without detailed carvings. A few statues and urns and delicately pruned trees were placed in artful locations, lit by angled slants of sunlight from hidden windows. The ceilings were again painted in skyscapes, but the streaming cloud formations all swept inward, toward a central location, the outermost edges the pale white of horizon, shifting from a faint green to a deep blue, then to pale yellow—as if the clouds were tinged with the light of sunset—then deepening to pink and a burnished orange. Near the center of the array of rooms, the orange shifted into a shimmering gold, as if the central chambers were lit by the sun itself.

Spread throughout the chambers, stationed at corners and outside the Tamaell's private doors, were pairs of White Phalanx, their gazes flickering over Aeren and Eraeth with cold appraisal, noting weapons and faces, even though they were accompanied by one of their own caitans.

They drew near the central chambers, close enough that Aeren thought the Tamaell had changed his mind and intended to meet with them in his own private rooms, but at the last moment the caitan turned into a side corridor, and within twenty paces they stepped out onto a wide, walled garden, a series of steps leading down to stone paths and a lush carpet of grass. A cascade of water from the mountain heights above splashed down from the rock face and spilled into a clear pool near the garden's edge, a stream winding through the sculpted trees and shrubs and flowers before escaping through a hidden grate on the far side.

The Tamaell stood in a small grotto to the left, and Aeren was startled to see the Tamaea Moiran, his wife, kneeling in the grass beside him, calmly trimming one of the shrubs with careful, precise snips of a pair of pruning shears. Both were dressed in the white and red of the Resue House, but the style was casual, not the formal dress of the Evant. He frowned when he noticed Lord Khalaek sitting to one side, his attention on the Tamaell, whose gaze rested on the hazy distance.

"—what we have seen," Lord Khalaek said, turning as the caitan led Aeren and Eraeth down the wide steps to the grass beneath, his eyes narrowing as he focused on Aeren, "what Lord Waerren has seen, I should say, is a decrease in the activity along the Province bordering his House lands. He claims that the Legion has pulled back from the border. Not completely—they've left a small force behind in the major cities—but for the most part the Legion has retreated to the port cities. An increase in the number of ships being built has been noted as well, although of course these new ships are not expected to be complete until next year at the earliest."

"And Lord Waerren believes this is due to the recent attacks on the human Provinces by the Andovans?" Tamaell Fedorem asked.

The caitan halted a short distance from where the Tamaell, the Tamaea, and Lord Khalaek had gathered and waited to be recognized. Khalaek's black eyes had not left Aeren since he entered, but Aeren ignored him, focusing on the Tamaell, who still stood with his back to him.

The Tamaea had stood as they approached, and now she dismissed the caitan with a smooth motion of her hand, then bowed toward Aeren. "It is good to see you safely returned, Lord Aeren," she said, and as she raised her head, something flashed through her gray eyes—a flicker of caution or warning, hidden swiftly behind her vibrant smile. She stepped forward to grip both of his shoulders and formally greet him with a kiss to each cheek. Before drawing back, her face turned away so that neither Khalaek nor Fedorem could see, she breathed, "Tread lightly," so softly that Aeren felt the words against his skin more than heard them.

Leaning back, she scanned him up and down, noting the dust and dirt on his clothes with a raised eyebrow and frown. "After Lord Barak returned and informed us of what had happened in Portstown, we were concerned. Where have you been? He said you'd traveled by land from Corsair. Whatever for?"

"That," Tamaell Fedorem said, "is precisely the question I would like answered."

The Tamaell had turned from his perusal of the city. He regarded Aeren with cold green eyes, his face completely expressionless, his posture at odds with the relaxed setting, shoulders stiff, hands clasped behind his back. He looked older than Aeren remembered, his skin paler, yet darkened beneath his eyes, haggard with lack of sleep.

But not dulled. Aeren could see the hardness beneath the weariness, could hear it in his voice when he spoke.

"I thought this venture to the Provinces by you and Lord Barak was to begin talks about trade agreements."

"It was," Aeren said, aware that Lord Khalaek sat to one side. "And we succeeded to some degree. I'm certain he's reported that a few of the Governors have signed tentative agreements that will need to be formalized before the Evant." The Tamaell had begun to relax, but he stiffened again as Aeren continued. "But there was another purpose to the trip as well. I went to Corsair in the hopes of opening a dialogue with King Stephan."

"A dialogue concerning . . . what?"

The Tamaell's voice was flat, without inflection.

"The possibility of an alliance between the Provinces and the Evant, between humans and Alvritshai."

Absolute silence fell on the small garden, interrupted only by the rush of the water from the falls behind the tower. Aeren kept his eyes locked on the Tamaell; he saw irritation crease his forehead, his lips twitch, before shifting into a frown.

"And how did King Stephan react to this proposal?" the Tamaell asked softly.

"He was . . . enraged."

Khalaek snorted, but Aeren noted that the Tamaell's shoulders sagged as if he were disappointed, even as he turned slightly away.

"Did you expect anything less?" Khalaek said. "The humans are reckless, ruled by emotion, quick to anger, King Stephan the worst among them."

"Because we slaughtered his father under the pretense of an alliance," Aeren snapped, his anger rising sharp and unexpected at the derisive tone in Khalaek's voice. He reined it in swiftly, his hands clenching at his sides. He felt Eraeth at his back, knew that his Protector had slid forward in mute warning in an attempt to restrain him, but the gesture wasn't necessary. He hadn't traveled so far to lose everything now because of his hatred of one lord, because of his hatred of that lord's betrayal at the Escarpment.

Khalaek watched him with a cold, knowing smile, and Aeren realized the lord was trying to provoke him.

"That still does not explain why you returned by land," the Tamaell interjected, and Aeren dragged his attention away from Khalaek, back to the Tamaell.

"When my attempt in Corsair failed," he said, "I traveled to the plains and met with one of the dwarren chiefs, Garius of the Thousand Springs Clan. If we cannot find peace with the humans, perhaps we can with the dwarren."

"And?"

The Tamaell had shifted forward again, all his attention focused on Aeren. Behind him, he could see the Tamaea, her hand raised, the shears poised to snip a branch from the small topiary shrub. But she'd frozen in mid-motion, her face locked in a frown.

To the side, Khalaek had stood, his stance defensive, as if he were about to be attacked.

Aeren drew a tense breath, then said, "He's summoned the Gathering. They intend to meet with us, with the Tamaell and the Evant, in three weeks."

16

"IT IS ... AN OPPORTUNITY."

Moiran spoke carefully as she moved across the bedchamber toward the window, afraid to let herself hope. She pushed the heavy curtains aside so that she could look out over the city, to where the sun set on the horizon. Sharp orange light spilled into the room, changing to a burnished gold before it began to fade as the sun vanished.

Behind her, she heard Fedorem grunt.

She closed her eyes, then sighed and turned.

Fedorem had settled into the chair behind the desk shoved into one corner. Candles had been lit throughout the room, giving the translucent drapes on the bed an ethereal glow. Wardrobes flanked the bed, and in the corner opposite Fedorem's desk, chairs were arranged around a low table for intimate conversations. That corner was Moiran's. An abstract glass sculpture in deep red shot with streaks of yellow sat in the center of the table, but it was rarely used.

As Fedorem reached for a stack of papers, Moiran frowned.

The desk was a recent addition to the room, brought in a few months after Fedorem had returned from the Escarpment. She had fought placing the desk here. She'd wanted this room to be theirs and only theirs, a sanctuary for both of them, without the taint of the Evant and the other lords upon it. But the Evant tainted everything.

Even Fedorem.

She let the curtains fall back into place, shutting out the darkness.

"What do you intend to do about Lord Aeren?" she asked. "About this meeting with the dwarren?"

Fedorem glanced up from his papers. "What business is that of the Tamaea?"

Moiran snorted, moving into the room. "Anything that may affect the stewardship of the House or my role as head of the Ilvaeran—the body that controls all of the economic resources of the Houses—is the business of the Tamaea. Peace with the dwarren could affect both. But more importantly, it's the Tamaea's business when it affects her Tamaell."

His eyebrows rose, but not in annoyance. "And has it affected the Tamaell?"

"Yes, it has."

"How so?"

A hard pressure seized Moiran's chest, the hope surging up from her heart unwanted. She shoved it back down forcefully.

"It's changed you, my Tamaell," she said, searching his face. "It's drained you."

He stiffened, and she could sense his withdrawal, could feel him pulling away.

"Have you looked at yourself lately?" she asked. She moved to his side, took the papers from him, and caught hold of his hands. "Have you seen yourself? You aren't sick, but you aren't well." She hesitated, but he hadn't retreated, hadn't withdrawn from her as he'd done so often in the last thirty years.

"It's the Escarpment," she said, the words thick, rushing up and out from the pressure in her chest. She felt his hands tense beneath hers, begin to pull back, but she tightened her grip and continued, relentless. "That's where it started, there and the months before. You made a mistake, and ever since you returned from that battle, it has eaten at you, destroyed you from within. You need to acknowledge what you did, begin to make amends, and this is your opportuni—"

"Enough!"

The word cracked through the room, but Moiran didn't flinch.

Instead, her jaw clenched and her eyes narrowed.

Fedorem saw and sighed wearily. "Enough, Moiran. We've been over this before. I will not speak of what happened at the Escarpment. It has passed."

"But it hasn't passed," Moiran said, surprised at how rough her voice sounded, how torn. She could hear tears she had never allowed herself to shed beneath the words, fought against them, overrode them with anger. "It will never pass, not when you refuse to speak of it. Not when you refuse to acknowledge what happened. Lord Aeren is trying to move beyond what happened at the Escarpment. He's trying to correct it. You—" The words stuck in her throat, but she forced them out, tasting their bitterness. "You've buried it, ignored it, and look what it has done to you! You've become tainted by it! Controlled by it!"

Fedorem jerked his hands free from hers. "It does not control me."

"Ha!" Moiran stepped back. "The event may not control you, but those who participated in it do."

Fedorem's eyes narrowed. "What do you mean?"

"Can you be so blind?" she asked softly. "After all these years of manipulating the Lords of the Evant, can you not see how you are being manipulated in turn?"

Fedorem flinched, a gesture Moiran saw in his eyes, more than in any motion of his body. And with that one gesture, she realized that he knew, had known, and had allowed it to happen.

"Aielan's Light," she whispered, her voice thready. All her anger had vanished. She felt hollow, even the hardness in her chest gone. "You knew."

She turned away and moved across the room toward her own wardrobe, opening its doors and riffling through the clothes that hung there, not seeing them, the material rough against her skin. Her hands tingled, as if numbed, and she realized her entire body trembled.

"Who in the Evant is manipulating me?" Fedorem asked, his voice following her, laced with warning, yet somehow distant.

When she didn't answer, she heard him rise from his desk, his papers forgotten, heard him cross the room and felt his presence behind her. She started when he put his hands on her shoulders.

"Who do you believe is manipulating me?" he asked again, softer. But she could feel the tension in his grip.

She broke free and turned to face him. "Lord Khalaek," she spat viciously. "Lord Khalaek is manipulating you. He's been doing so since the betrayal of the human King at the Escarpment, the betrayal that you have condoned through your silence. By not denouncing the uprising of some of your own lords, members of your own Evant, there on the battlefield, you have given those lords your tacit support. You have given those lords power. And because Lord Khalaek is at the center of those lords, you have implicitly given him power. The other lords, like Aeren, don't know what to think, and because they are outnumbered by Khalaek and his supporters, they dare not approach you or oppose you. You are the Tamaell! You could have halted his rise in the Evant over the last thirty years. All you had to do was admit that your support of Khalaek back then was a mistake. But no. Lord Khalaek is using your stubbornness and your own mistake to control you. *And you're letting him do it.*" She glared at him, not letting her gaze falter, knowing that there were tears in her eyes and hating them, knowing that the corners of her mouth trembled, even though her lips were pressed tight together. "He's trying to seize the Evant, Fedorem. How often does he come here to Caercaern? How often is he here, in the fifth tier, in our personal chambers, our private garden?"

Fedorem's hands lowered slowly, but she could see him considering what she'd said, could see him thinking.

"It has torn the Evant apart, my Tamaell," Moiran added. "It is tearing *us* apart."

And the tight frown that creased his brow gave her hope.

"Fedorem has called for a meeting of the Evant in two days," Aeren said, then glanced up from the announcement to catch Eraeth's gaze. His Protector raised one eyebrow in surprise. "All of the lords have been summoned, by the Tamaell himself."

"Sooner than expected."

"Yes. And the official summons is unexpected as well. Especially after seeing Lord Khalaek in the gardens last night." Aeren frowned, troubled, as he let the paper an-nouncing the meeting fall to his desk. He settled into the chair, heard it creak beneath him as he stared at the litter of parchment, the sleek feather quill and bottle of ink, without really seeing them.

Eraeth grunted. "What does it mean?"

"It means we will have to meet with the Lords of the Evant individually before the general meeting in two days. We have to convince them that it's in their best interests to hear the dwarren out, regardless of what Lord Khalaek may be saying to the contrary."

"Lord Barak will support you."

Aeren nodded. "Without question. He is of the same mind as I regarding trade and the hostilities on the plains. But neither of us has as much power within the Evant as we'd like . . . or as we used to."

Eraeth said nothing, but Aeren had already heard his thoughts on the descent of his House within the Evant. Part of it was due to the fact that Aeren had not yet bonded and produced an heir, and part of it was that Aeren himself was not as ruthless and ambitious as most of the other lords, especially Khalaek. His brother Aureon had been both. No one had expected Aeren to ascend to lord of the House. Which was why he'd become an acolyte in the Order.

But even that wasn't the real reason his House had fallen within the Evant.

"It all comes back to the Escarpment," he said with a sigh. When Eraeth merely raised one eyebrow in question, he continued. "Since the betrayal of the human King at the Escarpment, Lord Khalaek and his supporters—Lords Peloroun, Waerren, and Jydell—have ascended in the Evant, with the support of the Tamaell."

"The Tamaell has never officially shown support for any of those lords."

Aeren smiled slightly. Eraeth's voice had taken on the same tone he'd used as Aeren's tutor when he was younger. "Not aloud, no. Unspoken support. And his unspoken support, along with those four lords, gives Khalaek the majority in the Evant." His smile faded. "He should have denounced Khalaek and the other lords who attacked King Maarten at the Escarpment the moment it occurred. The battle had ended. An alliance had been made."

"Unless the Tamaell knew of the betrayal beforehand, unless he intended to betray the King all along."

Aeren frowned heavily. "That is the real question, isn't it? Did the Tamaell intend the betrayal or not? Was he part of the plan?" He met Eraeth's steady gaze. "I wish I'd been there with the lords at the end. I wish I'd seen how it played out. Then I would know. But I was . . . elsewhere."

Eraeth said nothing to the roughness in Aeren's voice. "And none of the other lords know, those who were there?"

Aeren shook his head. "None who are willing to challenge the Tamaell and Khalaek openly, and none who are willing to speak bluntly in private. They are afraid of Khalaek and the power he has gained, power given to him by the Tamaell with his unspoken support."

"So who do you need to convince to help you in the Evant with the dwarren?"

Aeren stood, suddenly restless, the memories of the battle at the Escarpment unsettling him. "Not Khalaek, obviously. And I've done what I can with the Tamaell already."

"Peloroun? Waerren and Jydell?"

"Peloroun will follow Khalaek's lead. Waerren as well. But Jydell . . . he has shown some independence recently within the Evant."

"Which only leaves Vaersoom."

"I'll speak to him as well. But his lands border the dwarren lands. He has faced more attacks from the dwarren in the past thirty years than anyone else, has suffered more losses."

"But he doesn't support Khalaek outright."

Aeren grunted in agreement. He moved away from his desk, from the notes and correspondence of the Evant and the running of his House.

The room was meant as a meeting room, and it was where Aeren conducted most of the business of Rhyssal House while he was in Caercaern. Ornamental carpets covered the stone floors, and tapestries and a large map filled what little wall space remained between the numerous shelves full of books and artifacts—dwarren, Alvritshai, and human—that he'd collected through the years. But tucked against one wall, in its own little alcove, rested a small table, the Rhyssal House banner hanging above. Blue cloth covered the table in rumpled folds, and on top—

On it lay the memories of his family.

His hands brushed lightly over his mother's brooch, silver with a white inlay of marbled stone. He touched his father's knife, ran his finger along the flat of the blade, then skipped over to his second brother's cattan. Fingers closed over the hilt, and he picked it up, pulled the sheath free in one smooth motion, the metal humming. A familiar tension pulled his shoulders taut as he remembered holding his brother's body at the Escarpment, Aureon still clutching this blade, even as he coughed up blood from the wound in his chest. Aeren had tried to stanch the flow, had tried to save him . . .

His knuckles turned white where they gripped the leather-wrapped handle, and with a slow, deliberate motion, he resheathed the blade and set it back in its place. He grabbed the silver-chained necklace resting beside it, closing the white-gold pendant in the shape of flames inside his fist before turning.

"Get Colin," Aeren said. "It's time to pay our respects to Aielan and the Light. We're going to the Sanctuary."

~

Aeren slid the white-gold flame pendant—symbol of the Order and a signal indicating his standing within the Order—over his neck outside the huge Sanctuary doors. Made entirely of banded wood, the doors glowed in the late morning sunlight, the iron gates that were closed at night already flung open, black against the white-gray of the temple walls to either side. The steps before the doors were littered with small offerings—flowers and shallow bowls of wine mostly—but the wide open plaza itself was empty. Dociern, the second sounding of the chimes, had occurred a short time before, and those who would gather for the third would not arrive for hours.

Pendant settled, Aeren hesitated.

"You believe him," Eraeth said, eyes flickering toward Colin, standing to one side, gaping at the temple. They were speaking Alvritshai.

"Yes. And I believe it is something the Evant does not have the power to handle."

Aeren moved to the Sanctuary doors and knocked. Eraeth caught Colin's arm and drew him near. The two accompanying Phalanx flanked them.

After a long moment, the massive wooden doors eased open, moving smoothly, effortlessly, without sound. A frowning acolyte peered out, his gaze flickering over Aeren. "The terciern service will not begin gathering for another—" he began automatically, in a slightly irritated voice.

And then his gaze grazed the pendant on Aeren's chest. He sucked in a sharp breath, nearly choked on it.

"I need to speak to Lotaern, the Chosen," Aeren said. "Immediately. Tell him it regards the Order, not the Evant."

The words startled the acolyte, who bowed in apology to Aeren. "I will find Lotaern and relay the message."

He stepped back, pushing the door open wider as he did so, and Aeren passed through the vestibule and into the sanctuary proper. As soon as the rounded room opened up before him, lit with a thousand burning candles, the scent of tallow and incense and smoke and oil settling over him like a cloak, he felt the tension slough from his shoulders. He breathed in the heavy scents and released them with a long sigh, bowing his head at the edge of the room, at the edge of its heat, letting the chamber's silence and calm seep through him.

Then, lifting his head, he moved toward the center of the room with purpose, to where a shallow basin stood on a low pedestal. Flames burned in the basin, roiling upward, but low. During a ceremony—one of the numerous feasts, or the bonding of a lord and lady—the basin would fill with flame, tendrils of it spilling over its edges. And during a major festival—a solstice or one of the celestial events such as an alignment or an eclipse—the fires would burn white, burn with Aielan's Light. The floor was stained with soot around the basin's lip, and with slow reverence, Aeren moved to this ring of shadowed darkness and knelt, bowing his head.

He found his center, pulled himself to it as he had been trained to do as one of the Order's acolytes so many years before, and then he pulled in all of the sensations of the chamber—the smells, the soft whuffling of flames, the echoes of the tread of feet trapped in the domed space above—drew all of it in and used it to soothe the ache in his chest. An ache he'd lived with for more years than he could count, an ache that had become unbearable after the loss of his brother.

He heard the acolyte return, his sandals scraping against the stone floor, hurried, and so he murmured a prayer of thanks to Aielan, traced a finger in the greasy ash-gray soot on the floor, smudging it along one cheek. Then he stood, turning to face the acolyte as he arrived.

The acolyte bowed, again in apology. "Forgive me for disturbing you, but Lotaern said to show you to his chambers immediately."

"You have disturbed nothing. Lead the way."

The acolyte drew them out of the main sanctuary into the familiar corridors beyond. They passed a dining hall where acolytes were already preparing for the afternoon meal, a bustling kitchen, a smaller chamber mimicking the outer one for individual prayer by the acolytes themselves, and numerous personal chambers where the acolytes lived. Found by the members of the Order, as they traveled Alvritshai lands or worked in the smaller temples scattered throughout nearly all the cities and towns, the acolytes were from all levels of Alvritshai society. Each had displayed a talent, power given to them by Aielan, or had volunteered to serve the Order like Aeren, but only those who had studied and passed through Aielan's Light could bear the pendant Aeren wore about his neck. As they walked, as he relived a thousand memories from his time here as an acolyte, he found his hand gripping the pendant.

He would have remained here, if given a choice. Few managed to pass through Aielan's Light unscathed. Most did not even take the risk, preferring to remain acolytes. But Aeren had needed to prove something—to Lotaern and to himself—before returning to the duties forced upon him by his House. So he'd faced Aielan's Light, hidden deep within the halls and tunnels of the Sanctuary beneath the mountain.

They drew up before a large door, and here the acolyte knocked hesitantly. A gruff voice bellowed for them to enter, and the acolyte pulled the door open and motioned Aeren and the others through before vanishing down the corridor without looking back.

Aeren hesitated a moment. He'd spoken to Lotaern on many previous occasions, during the Sanctuary's official ceremonies, but those meetings had occurred in the outer chamber or in one of the rooms reserved for meetings close to it. He'd never met with Lotaern here.

As he stepped over the threshold, the scent of earth and green foliage and some type of flower overwhelmed him. Every available surface of the inner room was covered with plants. They sat on tables, on pedestals, hung from the huge wooden crossbeams that supported the ceiling, and climbed trellises and lattices secured to the walls, reaching toward the sunlight that streamed in from the windows high overhead. A few of the trees bore round fruit—small oranges and bright yellow lemons.

"Come in," Lotaern barked from the opposite side of the room, where a worktable had been shoved against the wall. He hovered over a small shrub, tsking as he turned over leaf after leaf with a troubled frown. Grumbling to himself, he moved the plant to one side and turned his attention to Aeren. His gaze skimmed over the others but halted as it fell on Colin. His brow furrowed.

"Now," he said, "to what do I owe the honor of this unofficial visit from one of my more promising acolytes?"

Aeren motioned toward the still open doorway. "May I?"

Lotaern's eyes narrowed, but he nodded. As one of the Phalanx moved to close the door, then remained there to guard it, Aeren met Lotaern's dark gaze squarely and said, "I come because of the sarenavriell . . . and the sukrael."

Lotaern's body went rigid, and all emotion drained from his face. "The sarenavriell."

"And the sukrael," Aeren repeated. He realized he'd shifted his stance slightly, that Eraeth and the other Phalanx had done so as well, on guard now, wary. Because Lotaern had not reacted the way Aeren thought he would. "You aren't surprised."

Lotaern didn't move. "I *am* surprised. I did not expect you to come here and mention the sarenavriell. I assumed this would concern the Evant and the summons sent by the Tamaell. Obviously, it regards your recent return and whatever news you have brought with you."

"And yet," Aeren repeated, "you aren't surprised."

Lotaern said nothing, still motionless, eyes unreadable. And then he smiled. A grim smile. "You read me too easily, Lord Aeren. Not many within the Evant can do that."

Aeren bowed his head. "You honor me."

Lotaern snorted. "I'm not certain I meant it as a compliment." He turned away as Aeren raised his head. "What have you come to ask me about the sarenavriell?"

"I do not come to ask. I'm here to warn you."

Lotaern's hand fell to the desk. "Warn me of what?"

Aeren didn't understand Lotaern's reaction. He could feel the tension in the air, could hear it in Lotaern's troubled voice. Something else was going on here, something that Aeren knew nothing about. He shared a glance with Eraeth, saw the uncertain shake of his head.

Lotaern turned back, his expression hard. "Warn me of what?"

Aeren drew his shoulders back. "While I crossed the plains on my return from the Provinces, I learned that the extent of the sarenavriell has increased."

"How do you know this? Were you attacked by the sukrael?"

"No. We were told so by this man, this human." Lotaern's gaze fell on Colin and Aeren watched as the human drew himself up to his full height, his eyes darkening as Lotaern appraised him and, with a sniff, dismissed him.

"And you believe him." A statement, but laced with condescension.

Aeren felt a flash of irritation. "I believe him, yes."

"Why?"

Aeren answered carefully. "When I first met him on the plains, during my Trial, he was a boy." Lotaern's eyebrows rose in surprise, and he shot Colin another considering look. "I befriended him and all of those on the wagon train, including his father, believing that they were a sign, of significance to my Trial. They had just come onto the plains, did not know of its dangers—the dwarren, the storms, the occumaen."

"More of a danger now than back then," Lotaern muttered, then apologized for his interruption with a wave of his hand. "Please continue."

"I tried to warn them away, but it was difficult. We did not speak the same language. They refused to turn back, even when we showed them the burned wagons and slaughtered bodies of a previous party that had run into the dwarren. By this time, we had ventured far into dwarren territory, and we had been noticed. Their wagon train was attacked, but only by a scouting party. When the dwarren were driven away, they returned to their tent city, where an army of dwarren had already been gathered.

"The wagon train was caught between three clans and the sukrael's forest. My attempts to warn them of the sukrael were futile. They took refuge near the forest and were attacked by the sukrael. Colin claims to have been found by the antruel, the Guardians of the forest, people he calls the Faelehgre. He says they led him to the sarenavriell, that they had him drink its waters."

A deep frown etched lines of disbelief into Lotaern's face. "I don't believe it."

"How else do you explain his presence? It has been over sixty years since my Trial, and yet here he stands, looking no older than thirty."

"Tell him of his . . . abilities," Eraeth murmured softly.

"What abilities?" Lotaern snapped.

Aeren sighed, head bowed, before looking up. "He can alter his appearance so that he is young or old at whim. And he can travel swiftly, faster than any of us. I have no other explanation for these abilities except the sarenavriell."

Lotaern turned back to Colin, drifted forward. He drew up close to the human, glared down at him, at least a foot taller, then he leaned forward, so close Colin shifted back slightly before halting himself with clenched jaw and curled fists.

Lotaern sniffed at Colin's neck, a long indrawn breath, and held it, eyes closed.

Colin sent Aeren a confused, angry glance, but Aeren shook his head.

When Lotaern drew back again, the glare had been replaced by a thoughtful expression. "He smells of the forest. The deep forest. He smells of the Lifeblood." He hesitated, eyes narrowed, then snatched up Colin's arm, pulling the sleeve back roughly, exposing the black mark. Aeren was shocked to discover the mark had grown, tendrils extending away from the wrist toward the elbow.

Lotaern grunted, then let Colin's hand go. In Andovan, he said, "Become young. Show me what you looked like when you and Aeren first met."

Colin's eyes widened in surprise, Aeren guessed because of Lotaern's fluent Andovan, but then they narrowed in anger. One hand covered the mark on his arm. "You sniffed me!"

Lotaern ignored him. "Convince me that you have touched the sarenavriell."

Colin snorted, but then he shifted. Skin tightened and muscles toned, until the boy Aeren remembered from their first encounter stood in the center of the room, back rigid, his gaze not wavering from Lotaern's, whose eyes had widened. The rest of the Phalanx in the room shifted in discomfort. There were no gasps, no sharply indrawn breaths. The Phalanx had already heard of or seen Colin's powers, and Lotaern was too much of a lord in his own right to react.

"Can you hold this form? Can you become younger? Older?"

"I can become any age I want up to my own current age and stay there for as long as I want."

In Alvritshai, Aeren interjected, "He was older when we met in Portstown. He seems to be growing younger the longer he stays with us."

Lotaern nodded. His disbelief had faded completely, and he now had a scholarly look. "He claims that the Well's influence has widened?" he asked Aeren.

"He claims more. He says that the sukrael have created something he calls Wraiths and that those Wraiths have left the forest. The Faelehgre told him this. They also told him that there are other sarenavriell, dormant ones, and that somehow they are being reawakened."

Lotaern's gaze had hardened. "And has he seen these . . . dormant Wells?"

"He has seen one of the newly reawakened ones."

"Where?"

"In the northern part of the forest, not that far from the Licaeta House borders."

Lotaern grunted as if struck and spun away from both Aeren and Colin. From the side, Aeren could see the Chosen pinching his lower lip between his fingers, head bowed, brow creased in furious thought.

"Forgive me, Chosen, but it appears that you knew something of this already."

"And?" Lotaern let his hand drop, the lines of concern smoothing from his face. He became a lord, letting nothing show.

Aeren felt his irritation spike. "I came to you with this knowledge so that something could be done."

The Chosen sighed heavily and began pacing, moving to the far side of the desk. "You put me in an awkward position, Lord Aeren. The Chosen's purpose is to guard the secrets of the Scripts, and to advise the Evant in the event that something ... unnatural occurs. The Order was established for this purpose. What you have revealed is one of those secrets, one that every acolyte of a certain rank is sworn to protect, one that *I* have sworn to protect. I cannot reveal such a secret on a whim, and certainly not on the word of a single human."

"But the sukrael—"

"I was not finished," Lotaern said. He came to a halt behind the desk, pressed his hands into its polished surface and leaned forward, catching all of them with his gaze. "I would not believe you, or this human, except for two things. The first is that I have already been approached by the Tamaell and Lord Vaersoom from House Licaeta over an ... incident on Licaeta lands. One of the outposts was attacked over a week ago, the Phalanx members all killed, at their posts, without a mark on their bodies. None of those on duty survived. In addition, a few surrounding Alvritshai villages and towns, those nearest the forest, were also attacked. The few who survived by fleeing report the very shadows themselves came to life to destroy them."

"The sukrael."

Lotaern nodded grimly. "Lord Vaersoom discounted the initial stories, believing that the villagers were lying, that there must be some other, more mundane explanation, that perhaps it was the dwarren raiding the borderlands as they have for the past hundred years. But he traveled to one of the towns himself, saw the bodies. Like the Phalanx at the outpost, they were found strewn about the town, dead, without a mark on them. Most had fallen while in the act of harvesting later winter wheat from the fields, their scythes still in their hands."

Aeren glanced toward Eraeth, saw his Protector's lips

pressed into a thin line. "We'd hoped to arrive in time to warn you."

Lotaern pushed back from his table. "You have. Before your arrival, I had only suspicions based on vague reports from villagers and the more concrete reports from Lord Vaersoom on the aftermath. You've confirmed those suspicions."

"And did any of these villagers report on these other creatures, the ones Colin calls Wraiths?"

"No. They spoke only of shadows. No figures."

"So what can we do to protect Licaeta?"

Lotaern grimaced. "I'm not certain. We've never had to battle the sukrael directly before. But there are references to them in the Scripts. I have acolytes researching those references already, but now that we have confirmation, I will double our efforts. I'm afraid that for the moment, the only option is to pull the Alvritshai away from the area of the sukrael's influence. Does this human, Colin, know how far northward their range extends?"

Aeren turned to ask, but before he could speak Colin said, "I know a little Alvritshai. I didn't waste all of my time in the forest sunk in grief. He's asking about the Shadows."

"Yes," Aeren said in Andovan, wondering how much of the conversation Colin could follow. "He wants to know if you know the extent of the sukrael's range. They've already attacked Alvritshai outposts and villages. And do you know a way to defend against them?"

"I don't now what their range is, but I do know it's expanding. The Well that I found, the one the Wraiths have awakened, it's filling slowly, and as it fills, its range increases. As for killing the sukrael . . . if you can get them over water, deep water and especially running water, they can't hold their form."

Lotaern nodded, frowning in thought. "Our research has pointed to water as a defense on more than one occasion. Perhaps the aqueducts will be useful. I will inform Lord Vaersoom."

Aeren waited a moment, then said, "You mentioned a second reason?"

Lotaern smiled grimly. "Yes. The second is the fact that nearly a month ago, one of my acolytes came to me with a rather bizarre request. He wished to do research on the Scripts, personal research."

"On what?" Aeren said, stepping forward toward the desk.

"On the sarenavriell. I agreed to give him access to the Scripts, to allow him to do his research. It is not unheard of, especially when an acolyte has ambition. And this acolyte does. But this request felt ... odd. So I watched him as he did his research, and when he left the Scriptorium, I perused the texts he'd used, noted the passages he'd copied, the maps he'd drawn. Would you care to guess where his interest in the sarenavriell lay? Not on their power, not on their uses, nor the lore surrounding them, but rather—"

"On their location," Aeren finished.

"Precisely. He's been researching where the sarenavriell are, attempting to find where they have been hidden. Some of them are known, such as the one in the forest. Most have been lost. But according to the passages this acolyte referred to, one was hidden in the northern forests."

"This acolyte," Eraeth said, his voice harsh. "What is his name? What House does he belong to?"

Lotaern gave him a placid look. "Acolytes rescind their House ties when they enter the Order. They are connected to no House, are beholden to no lord."

Eraeth snorted, but before he could respond, Aeren broke in. "We both know that House ties are not so easily broken, no matter what vows are involved." He touched the band around his wrist and the two lord's rings on his fingers. His House had not been forgotten once he entered the Sanctuary.

Lotaern tapped his fingers on the desk. "True. And given what's been happening in the Evant lately ..." He began walking back toward the table against the far wall, where more plants waited. "I expect to be kept apprised of any actions that you take, and to be told of any information that you gather."

"Of course," Aeren said, bowing his head. He could feel where his hand gripped the hilt of his cattan. He didn't know when his hand had drifted to it, but when Lotaern finally spoke, back to them all, he realized he'd already guessed what House the acolyte belonged to.

"The acolyte's name is Benedine," Lotaern said, "and he's originally from House Duvoraen. Lord Khalaek's House."

~

"He's left the Sanctuary," Eraeth reported, and Colin watched his face twist into a vicious grin as he crumpled the small note that the Alvritshai boy on the street had handed him in passing.

"Who?" Aeren said, in Andovan, since that's what Eraeth had used.

"Benedine. The acolyte."

Aeren grunted, but he remained focused on the plaza ahead and the hundreds of Alvritshai that lined it. They were headed toward the Hall of the Evant, a huge ornate building at the end of the marketplace. Colin could see the thick arched colonnades that surrounded the circular building within, beyond the mass of people, carts, and small tents that had been set up in the plaza itself. Sunlight beat down, but it didn't take the bite of winter out of the air, nor the metallic sharpness of snow. The marketplace was a cacophony of noise, most of which Colin couldn't understand, since it was all in Alvritshai. He could pick out phrases and words here and there, but he couldn't follow entire conversations.

"Dharel is following him," Eraeth said. He almost reached out to halt Aeren as they forged their way toward the Hall, restraining himself with effort.

Aeren glanced over his shoulder and caught his Protector's expression. "The Evant intends to meet in three hours," he said.

"We will return before the meeting begins."

Acren frowned. "Very well."

Eraeth bowed from the waist, gave orders to the rest of Aeren's Phalanx, then gripped Colin's arm and dragged him away into the crowd, heading back toward the plaza's entrance and the streets beyond with a grim glint of anticipation in his eyes.

Halfway back to the street, Colin jerked his arm out of the Protector's grip. "I'm coming," he protested. "You don't have to drag me."

Eraeth drew up short, his eyes narrowing. Colin felt

himself shiver at the raw intensity in Eraeth's gaze, at the dangerous heat to it—

But then that heat cooled, and the tension in Eraeth's shoulders relaxed. "I apologize. But we'll have to move quickly if we're to be of any use following the acolyte."

Colin nodded in return, tugging his shirt back into place, smoothing the folds where Eraeth had gripped his arm. "Lead the way. I can keep up."

Eraeth frowned at the not so subtle reminder. "Stay close. You'll draw attention, and you're safe only as long as you're with me. Most of the people in Caercaern have lost family to the wars with the Provinces." Without waiting for a response, he turned and headed toward the street.

They moved out of the plaza and turned to the right, staying close to the buildings, passing the open doors and windows of businesses, winding past carts laden with produce and wares, one full of straw, another some type of melon. Colin definitely drew attention, mostly shock, titters of laugher, and a few angry glares, but not as much as he'd drawn outside the city, closer to the plains. As they neared the ramp and the gates leading down to the first tier, Colin saw the flash of Rhyssal House colors on one side. Before he could point it out, Eraeth saw it as well and cut sharply to the left.

It was one of the Phalanx in Dharel's group. The guard tucked the cloth he'd used to catch Eraeth's attention back into a pocket. He wasn't dressed in the typical House colors or in the Phalanx's usual garb. Instead, he wore the flatter, looser clothing of the people in the street, all whites and grays and duns.

Eraeth spoke to him briefly, words too clipped for Colin to follow, then turned a hardened gaze back down the street they'd just traversed.

"What is it?" Colin asked. His breath came in shallow gasps. Eraeth had been moving fast.

Eraeth shot him a glance before returning to his scan of the crowd. "The acolyte is already here, in the second tier." He turned back to the Phalanx guard, said something in Alvritshai, then nodded. "The acolyte headed toward the courtyard."

On the far side of the street, a large wrought iron gate stood half-open between two other shops, the bright green of plants on both sides inside the entrance. Sunlight lanced down on the interior, suggesting a large open space.

They slid from the main flow of the crowd, to the right of the courtyard's entrance. Dharel stood at the corner, back against the building, one foot resting against its side. Every now and then, he'd turn and peer into the courtyard beyond, a passing glance, as if he were bored. When he caught sight of Eraeth and Colin, he straightened. "He's inside, in the shadows of the far corner, near the fountain. There's hardly anyone in the courtyard at the moment. I couldn't enter without being noticed."

Eraeth scanned the inner courtyard with one glance, no more than a breath long, then turned to Colin with a grim look. "There aren't many places to hide. It's an open courtyard, a fountain in the far corner, a few potted plants near the walls, a portico against the back wall. The portico is mostly in the shade, so I can't see Benedine or if anyone is there with him." His gaze fell on Colin. "Can you do it?"

"Let's find out," Colin said, lacing the words with irritation. Before Eraeth could respond—but not before Colin saw his eyes begin to darken with a sharp reply—Colin let the world slow. The street stilled. People halted in midstep, one man in midfall, the contents of the basket he carried already spilling onto the stone walkway. Colin slid around them all and walked through the open gate and into the courtyard, shivering at the silence.

The courtyard was set up exactly as Eraeth had described. Colin headed straight toward the fountain and the shadows of the portico.

He found the acolyte in the shade of the roof, his back toward Colin. Another Alvritshai faced him, hand raised to accept a folded piece of paper from Benedine, mouth open. His eyes were hard, face etched with angry warning. Dressed like Dharel and the rest, in commoner's clothing, Colin thought he was actually a member of the Phalanx or a high-ranking member of a House, based on his arrogant posture and the dark hair tied back behind his head. It wasn't as long as it should be for a commoner.

Colin scanned for a good place to hide so that he could watch or overhear the conversation, but there wasn't anything beneath the portico except a set of closed doors along the back wall, beneath the roof. Cursing, he stepped back out into the edged sunlight and considered the colonnades.

They were thin, no thicker than his body. But perhaps . . .

He positioned himself behind one, standing sideways to minimize his profile, sucked in a deep breath, then let time slip back into motion—

And spat silent curses. The men were speaking Alvritshai. He could only understand a few words they said. He nearly stilled everything again to retreat back to Eraeth, but he halted as the unknown man barked at Benedine, something about a map and the sarenavriell and forests, his voice low but carrying well, even with the gurgling of the fountain to one side. Colin heard the crinkle of paper. He didn't think the acolyte replied.

A long pause. Colin felt sweat beading on his forehead as he waited, tense; he almost raised a hand to wipe it off but realized that would be seen and stopped himself.

Then the unknown man spoke again, a question, urgent and forceful.

A scuffling of feet, and the acolyte responded, his uncertainty obvious.

The other man berated him, but then his irritation vanished. He sighed heavily, murmured something so low that Colin strained to hear its tenor and tone over the fountain. Out of the corner of his eye, he caught the movement of an arm, as if someone had raised their hand to pat someone on the back or grip their shoulder—

And then he saw the acolyte, heading toward the open courtyard.

He stilled time with a gasp, lurching back from Benedine's sight, even though he knew the acolyte couldn't see him. Berating himself, he turned back to the acolyte and the unknown Alvritshai. The meeting was over, and Benedine had headed back to the street. The acolyte couldn't see the look the other man had given his turned back as he left. A calculated look, so cold that Colin shuddered.

But the unknown man still held the paper in one hand.

And it was unfolded.

Colin skirted to the man's side so he could see the contents of the note. Most of it was written in Alvritshai and was unreadable, but the rest . . .

Looking at the man with the note one more time,

memorizing the features of his face, the dark eyes, the heavy brow and angular cheekbones, Colin retreated back across the courtyard, positioning himself between Eraeth and Dharel before letting time flow again.

"I couldn't understand everything that they said," Colin said in irritation.

All three of the Phalanx members—Eraeth, Dharel, and the man who'd found them near the gates—flinched. All of their hands dropped to their cattans reflexively, but only the unnamed guard actually drew the blade, a few finger's worth of metal showing in the sunlight before he caught himself.

"Why?" Eraeth asked.

"Because they were speaking Alvritshai," Colin said dryly.

He felt gratified when Eraeth's eyebrows rose as he realized their mistake, but then the Protector growled, "You'll have to learn to speak it. Fluently. And write it."

Dharel hissed, and they all fell silent.

"What is it?" Eraeth asked, slipping back to the corner near the gate.

"I think Shaeveran may have been spotted. Benedine has stopped."

Colin edged far enough out into the street so that he could see the inside of the courtyard. Benedine had circled the colonnade Colin had stood behind. He scanned the shade beneath the portico, said something to the man he'd met, and turned back to the sunlight, his brow creased, mouth set in a tight frown.

As his gaze swung to scan the plaza, Eraeth and Dharel withdrew, and Colin stepped to the side, out of view.

Eraeth grinned smugly. "He won't find anything. He probably caught a flicker of your shadow. Now, what happened? You were there too long to have just retreated."

"He met with someone beneath the portico. I didn't recognize him. Benedine gave him a piece of paper, a map of some kind."

"A map of what?"

"I couldn't tell. But it had mountains on it, a few rivers. I couldn't read any of the markings on it. But they did mention the Wells."

Eraeth growled again, but before he could say anything,

Dharel pulled away from the courtyard's entrance and said, "He's coming."

Without a word, Eraeth caught Colin's arm and steered him toward the street, entering the flow of the passersby smoothly. Colin sighed and almost jerked his arm free again, but Benedine appeared, and Eraeth relaxed his grip. They angled across the street, coming to a halt on the far side before a meat market, the smell of blood strong.

"Do you want us to continue following him?" Dharel asked.

Benedine glanced in both directions, searching, the frown still twisting his mouth, but then he headed back toward the gate and the Sanctuary.

Eraeth nodded. "Go. Let me know if he does anything other than sit in the Sanctuary."

Dharel grinned, then bled into the crowd. In a matter of a heartbeat, he and the other Phalanx guardsman were lost from sight.

Eraeth turned back to Colin. "We need to reach the Hall and report to Aeren."

～

It took them another hour to reach the Hall, the marketplace thronged with too many people hawking wares, even with most of them falling back or shifting out of the way once they spotted Colin and realized, despite his clothing, that he wasn't Alvritshai. Women ducked their heads and averted their eyes, but not before Colin could catch a flash of emotion—fear, hatred, surprise. One spat on the stone before him, and Eraeth barked something in Alvritshai that made her bow down in supplication, although it wasn't heartfelt. Men glared openly, their anger barely controlled. The children merely gawked.

They broke through into an open area around the circular colonnades, the Hall tucked away beneath their tall forms. This close, the stonework of the Hall was magnificent, etched and chiseled into myriad reliefs—Alvritshai working the earth with hoe or gathering wheat with scythes and rakes; lords surrounding the Tamaell in a coronation ceremony; Alvritshai bowed down before a huge basin of fire, members of the Order in the background, hands reaching for the sky. Birds of a variety that Colin had never seen, brown with startling flashes of black and swatches of red, flitted among the nooks and crannies of the stonework.

Eraeth headed directly toward the Hall's entrance, heavy stone double doors, both flung open to the sunlight. He nodded in passing to the Phalanx inside the foyer, a pair for each House of the Evant, then pushed through a set of polished wooden inner doors.

The Hall within was huge, circular arrays of seats surrounding a large open area. The arch of the circle broke on the opposite side from the entrance, where one large throne flanked by two smaller seats sat on a raised platform lined with folds of a heavy, rich, red fabric, accented in white.

The platform was empty, but the floor was not. Lords and their advisers and escorting Phalanx mingled in a loose throng, the rumble of numerous conversations filling the Hall, the colors of their clothing a bright splash in the pale whites and grays of the stonework and the stark white of the marble floor. Eraeth paused at the top of the stairs descending down to the main floor as he searched those gathered for Rhyssal colors. He tugged Colin's sleeve, nodding to the left. "Aeren is there."

They moved down the steps. When they reached Aeren's side, Eraeth edged behind the Alvritshai Aeren was speaking to and caught his attention. A moment later, Aeren broke off his conversation, and Eraeth pulled him to one side.

"What happened?" Aeren asked. He kept his attention focused on Eraeth, but his eyes roamed the room.

"The acolyte met with someone in the courtyard on Brae."

"Who?"

Eraeth shook his head, lips pursed. "We don't know. Only Colin saw him."

"What did he look like?" Aeren asked, his gaze flicking toward Colin.

"He had dark hair, almost black, and he wore common clothing. But I don't think he was a commoner."

"Why not?"

"Because his hair wasn't long enough. He'd tied it back, but it still seemed too short. Longer than either yours or Eraeth's, though."

"Most of the lords don't wear their hair as short as I do," Aeren said, "nor do their assistants and aides." His gaze fixed on someone on the floor, and he asked, "Is that him?" with a barely perceptible nod. "The man in black and gold."

Colin tried to turn casually and noticed that many of the surrounding Alvritshai were looking at him from the corners of their eyes. Sweat broke out on his back, and his skin prickled. He found the man Aeren had pointed out. Dark hair, cropped shorter than a commoner. But this man's face was narrower, sharper, giving it a predatory look.

The man in black and gold moved and caught Colin's gaze. Ice cascaded through Colin's arms, and with effort he tore his eyes away, but not before he saw the corner of the man's mouth turn upward in a frigid half-smile.

"Who is that?"

Aeren smiled tightly. "That's Lord Khalaek," he said blandly, "my rival in the Evant, the one most likely to oppose my proposal today. He arrived a mere fifteen minutes before you did, which is unusual. Is he the man who met with Benedine?"

Colin shook his head. "No. He has black eyes. The man who met Benedine had dark eyes, but they were brown. And Khalaek's face is too narrow."

Aeren sighed in disappointment. "It's too much to expect Khalaek to be meeting with a lowly acolyte directly." His eyes suddenly narrowed, his brows coming together in a deep frown, eyes locked on the entrance to the Halls.

Both Colin and Eraeth turned to see Lotaern, along with four acolytes, descending the steps.

"What's he doing here?" Eraeth asked, his voice sharp. The lull in the surrounding conversation that had occurred when Lotaern arrived ended, and the volume suddenly rose higher. "The Order has no power in the Evant, no representation."

Aeren didn't answer, moving swiftly across the marble floor among the rest of the gathered lords and aides to speak with the Chosen at the bottom of the steps. Eraeth and Colin trailed behind. When they caught up, Aeren broke off his conversation with Lotaern and turned immediately to Eraeth. "He was summoned by the Tamaell and asked to attend. It must be because of the sukrael and the attacks in Licaeta." Aeren's gaze darted around the Hall, then fell on Colin. "What else happened at this meeting?"

Colin shrugged, feeling his hands clenching in frustration. "Nothing. I couldn't understand much of what they were saying. The acolyte passed the other man a piece of paper. It was written in Alvritshai, but looked like some type of map."

"You didn't take the note?"

Colin's eyes narrowed. "I couldn't. That's not how it works. I'm there, I can see things and move around, but I can't move anything else while I'm there. I can take things with me and leave them, but when I let go of them they return to their proper time. They simply change position."

"Their proper time?" Eraeth asked.

"It's as if time has slowed. If I concentrate and push hard enough, I can even go backward and visit an event that has already occurred. But I can't change it in any way. Trust me, I've tried." Eraeth drew breath to ask a question, but Colin anticipated him. "I can't go forward and see what will happen either. I've tried that as well."

Eraeth let his breath out in a sigh.

"Interesting," Aeren said, "and potentially useful." He turned back to the Chosen and spoke in a hushed voice, Lotaern's gaze falling heavily on Colin, enough to make him shift uncomfortably. Colin had sensed the Chosen's curiosity about him since their initial meeting in the Lotaern's rooms. He thought that curiosity had faded, but now, with Lotaern's eyes boring into him . . .

The sharp rap of metal against stone rang out through the hall, echoing in the vaulted ceiling. All conversation ceased, and Colin turned to see an escort of the White Phalanx accented in red and white now surrounding the raised platform containing the throne and flanking seats. Two guardsmen standing at the corners of the platform carried what looked like large metal pikes, which they raised in unison and drove into the marble at their feet, calling the room to order.

Eraeth grabbed Colin's sleeve to catch his attention, and they followed Aeren to where a section of the circular seating had been draped with cloth of blue and red. Everyone in the Hall moved to their prescribed area as one of the White Phalanx near the platform stepped forward and cleared his throat. As he spoke, Eraeth leaned to the side and translated for Colin.

"This session of the Evant, under the Ascension of House Resue, with all of the Lords of the Houses of the Evant in attendance, and under the auspicious and blessed eye of the Order of Aielan—" here the attendant bowed toward Lotaern, who nodded in acknowledgment as a murmur rose among the lords "—is hereby called to order." The two Phalanx with the pikes slammed them into the floor twice more. "Tamaell Fedorem, Tamaea Moiran, and Tamaell Presumptive Thaedoren," the attendant announced. Then he dropped to one knee, back bent, head bowed, hands resting on the upthrust knee.

Colin saw Aeren's back straighten as the three Alvritshai entered the room, emerging from some hidden doorway behind the platform, the Tamaell first, followed by the Tamaea and the Tamaell Presumptive. Beside him, Eraeth's breath caught, and Colin scanned the room, noticed the same shocked wariness on the faces of most of the lords in attendance.

"What is it?" Colin whispered to Eraeth.

"The Tamaell's heir hasn't been called to a session of the Evant for nearly twenty years. He shouldn't even be in Caercaern. He's part of the White Phalanx, one of their caitans, and he's been carrying out duties along the dwarren border since a falling out with his father. Each House has its own Phalanx and guards its own borders, but the White Phalanx augments those forces and shares the burden since the Tamaell's House does not border either the human or the dwarren lands. Since their argument, Thaedoren has elected to remain on the border. The Tamaell must have recalled him."

"Recalled him in secret," Aeren added without turning, his voice drifting back to them. "It doesn't appear that any of the other lords knew of it."

Colin drew breath to ask what it meant, but at that moment, the Tamaea and the Tamaell Presumptive both took their seats at a gesture from the Tamaell. The attendant who had announced him rose and moved swiftly back into the line of Phalanx beneath the platform, all of the guardsmen now standing at attention.

Then the Tamaell began to speak, his deep voice filling the room. After a moment, Colin realized that Eraeth had no intention of translating the entire session, but he tugged on Eraeth's sleeve and asked, "What's he saying?"

Eraeth looked down on him with an annoyed glare, then said, "He's introducing Aeren as the reason for the summons. In a moment, he's going to hand it over to him. I won't be able to translate with everyone's eyes on him, so shut up."

Before Colin could react, the Tamaell motioned toward Aeren and then settled back onto his throne. Aeren hesitated a moment, head bowed, then rose and stepped out into the central oval.

When he finally spoke, his gaze circling the gathered lords, catching all of their attention, his voice was steady, slow, and purposeful. Colin saw the tension at the corners of his eyes and felt the same power vibrating throughout the chamber that he'd heard in the King's chambers at Corsair. He struggled to understand what Aeren said, determined that he spoke of the dwarren and assumed it was about the meeting on the plains, but his grasp on Alvritshai was too tenuous. Yet he felt the earnestness behind the words, the conviction.

Colin glanced toward Eraeth, but the Protector was focused entirely on Aeren and on how the other lords were reacting. He sighed and settled back, began taking in the lords and their retinues.

The Chosen of the Order had been seated on the far side of the circle, opposite the Tamaell. He kept his attention on Aeren, but occasionally an attendant would approach and after a discreet pause, or when Aeren had turned slightly away, the Chosen would accept a note, or lean back to receive a whispered message. Often, he would simply nod, or his glance would shoot toward one of the other lords with a frown or small gesture with one hand. Only once did he actually murmur in return, the messenger scurrying back.

Colin followed this messenger with his eyes and grunted to himself when he realized the messenger had come from Lord Khalaek. The lord received the response with a dark, worried frown and glanced toward Lotaern, but the Chosen ignored him. Disgusted, Khalaek's hand formed into a fist, his glance skipping toward two of the other lords, ones that Colin didn't know, before settling on the Tamaell.

Colin didn't know what was going on, but Khalaek appeared troubled.

He'd begun to turn away when a slight movement behind Khalaek caught his eye.

Someone had entered the room late and now shifted forward through the seats to join Khalaek's retinue. He moved slowly so as not to draw attention to himself, like the messengers, but unlike the messengers, he came from the height of the room, not from those seated around the central circle of the hall.

Colin shifted forward and scanned the room, but neither Eraeth nor Aeren had noticed the new arrival. He turned back in time to see the man slip closer to Khalaek, standing back, waiting patiently to be acknowledged, something held in one hand. His face was turned away, but when Khalaek finally noticed him and leaned back, the man turned and faced Colin directly.

Brown eyes. Angular features. Short hair, but not short enough to be a member of the Phalanx, not long enough to be a commoner.

Colin gasped, the sound cutting through the growing conversation on the floor as more and more lords rose to question Aeren. Aeren cut off, turning toward Colin with a raised eyebrow, but Eraeth spun with a glare, one hand clamping down hard on Colin's shoulder as he hissed for silence. Colin waved an apology, not daring to look in Khalaek's direction.

When Aeren turned back to address the Evant again, Colin yanked on Eraeth's sleeve hard enough that the Protector growled.

"It's him," Colin said. "The man who met Benedine."

Eraeth straightened. "Where?"

"He came in after Aeren started speaking and handed Lord Khalaek a note."

"The note he got from Benedine?"

"I think so, but I can't tell from here. Should I—?" He made a fluttering gesture with his hand, but Eraeth's eyes widened slightly in horror.

"Not here!"

Colin frowned in disgust, but then his gaze fell on

Lotaern. The Chosen was watching him with that same concentrated interest he'd shown before. The other lords may have turned their attention back to Aeren, but not Lotaern.

"Keep an eye on him as best you can," Eraeth said, his own gaze flicking toward Khalaek's location, but not lingering long. "I'll inform Aeren." He shifted forward, so that he stood beside the seat designated for Aeren, unobtrusive, but far enough forward to catch Aeren's attention.

Colin settled in to watch the man who'd met with Benedine, conscious of Lotaern's continued interest as a prickling of the hairs on the back of his neck.

~

"—find it distasteful that you would presume to begin talks with the dwarren, let alone the humans, without first seeking the advice and counsel of the Evant," Lord Peloroun stated. His words were civil, but the tone was bitter. "What of those of us who have lands bordering along the plains? What of our losses over the last hundred years? Do we not have a say in whether peace should be sought with them?"

Aeren didn't respond at first, waiting to see if Peloroun's tirade would continue, but the lord shook his head in disgust and returned to his seat. Out of the corner of his eye, Aeren could see Lord Jydell and Lord Waerren nodding slightly. None of the issues brought up against his proposal so far had been unexpected, but the resistance he felt from the Evant was greater than he'd anticipated. Yet it wasn't the lords that bothered him.

It was the Tamaell . . . and the presence of Lotaern. Fedorem had said nothing since he'd called the session into order and handed the proceedings over to Aeren. He sat in silence, even as the lords attacked him, the Tamaea and the Tamaell Presumptive to either side. Aeren risked a quick glance at the three, not certain what the presence of the Tamaea and the Presumptive indicated, but all three were watching him, waiting for him to respond. The Tamaea frowned slightly, but otherwise there was no sign of what any of them were thinking.

As for Lotaern . . .

He shook his head and turned fully toward Lord Peloroun. "I realize that the majority of the burden placed on the Alvritshai regarding the dwarren has fallen on you and those with lands along the plains, Lord Peloroun, but what I have to offer—what the dwarren seem willing to accept—is a release of that burden from you altogether. Would it not be beneficial to all concerned if the tension along the border eased? How many resources do you and Lords Jydell, Waerren, and Khalaek expend on guarding the border, resources that could be used for something productive, such as farming or the expansion of the irrigation canals?"

"But what of our losses?" Lord Peloroun growled. "What of the destruction the dwarren have caused? What of the loss of life, of family and kin, killed during the raids?"

"You would rather risk the lives of those who remain by continuing to fight, when there is a chance to end it?" Aeren let some of his own pain color his voice. "You are not the only one who has lost family to the dwarren. Do not presume to claim a greater pain than the rest of us—"

He would have continued, but a sharp gasp interrupted him. He cut off and turned to see Colin, eyes wide, Eraeth's hand clamped onto his shoulder. The human caught Aeren's gaze and held it, but then waved his hand in mute frustration. As Aeren turned away, he saw Eraeth speaking to him. Aeren turned back to Peloroun, his voice hardening.

"As I was saying, we have all suffered. I, for one, am tired of it."

"But some of us are not," Peloroun said, leaning forward. "Some of us have lost *sons* to the dwarren and are not so ready to forgive."

"Some of us have lost our entire family to the dwarren," Aeren countered.

Peloroun rose at the challenge in Aeren's tone but before he could say anything, Tamaell Fedorem stood and said, "Enough."

The word sliced through the tension in the room as smoothly as a blade, and everyone's attention turned toward the platform. Aeren noticed that Eraeth had stood and moved to the edge of the Evant's inner circle and made his way to his Protector's side to clear the floor. When Eraeth drew breath to speak, he waved him to silence.

Tamaell Fedorem waited until he had everyone's attention, the room falling utterly silent, then stepped forward to the edge of the platform, his face impassive.

"As Lord Aeren has pointed out, we have all suffered from this prolonged war with the dwarren and the humans. We have all lost loved ones as well as friends. We are not here to dispute that. And we are not here to determine who has suffered more or less than the others. Such a thing cannot be determined, no matter how long we spend in this room arguing over it.

"What we are here to discuss, and what we are here to decide, is whether or not it is time to seek peace with the dwarren. Lord Aeren has provided us with . . . an opportunity." Fedorem smiled tightly and turned to the Tamaea, who bowed her head. "We have been at odds with the dwarren for nearly two hundred years, the war fluctuating, with intense periods of battle and long years of tension and general unrest. During these years, many decisions were made, all with the good of the Alvritshai in mind, even though in retrospect not all of those decisions were . . . wise."

A low murmur arose, although it died quickly. Aeren shot a glance at Eraeth, eyes raised in question, but his Protector shrugged. He wondered if the Tamaell's words refered to the decisions made at the battle at the Escarpment, but there was no way to tell. If they had . . .

If they had, then perhaps there was hope after all.

And as if he were answering that hope, the Tamaell continued. "We have lived in a period of general stability in the last thirty years, since the Escarpment. Mistakes were made then that cannot be easily rectified, but Lord Aeren has given us a chance to start. I think it is time to start." He cast his gaze out over the Evant, catching each and every lord's eye.

"There are those who will disagree with me. There are those who feel that what the dwarren have done in the past cannot be so easily forgiven. But I am not willing to let this opportunity pass by. Because of this, I will be traveling to meet with the dwarren, accompanied by the Tamaea and the Tamaell Presumptive. In addition, I would ask that the Chosen of the Order be part of my escort, as well as Lord Aeren and any of the remaining Lords of the Evant who wish to take part. I will not require this of any of you, and those who chose to remain behind will not be censured in any way.

"But it is time for these skirmishes—these raids and this war—to come to an end. It is time that I begin to rectify the mistakes I have made in the past. If the dwarren are willing, if they are sincere in their offer, then it *will* come to an end."

The Tamaell let the silence that followed his announcement hang for a long moment, the lords stunned. Then he turned to Aeren.

"I assume that you will agree to accompany me, Lord Aeren?"

Aeren pulled himself out of shocked immobility and bowed formally. "Of course, Tamaell."

Fedorem nodded once, then turned to Lotaern. "And you, Chosen?"

"Aielan has always and shall always support peace. May her Light guide us all in this."

In the end, all protests and disagreements were set aside as all of the lords, including Khalaek, agreed to take part in the meeting on the plains.

"Then it is agreed," Tamaell Fedorem said. "We shall meet with the dwarren and their Gathering in two weeks time. Gather your escorts. We will depart in two days."

17

"KHALAEK AGREED TO COME too easily," Eraeth said in Andovan, so that Colin could understand.

"Especially considering that the Tamaell all but declared that his support of Khalaek and the others over the last thirty years has been a mistake," Aeren said.

"He still has not answered the real question," Lotaern muttered as he handed off orders for supplies to be gathered for the envoy to waiting acolytes, then turned his attention toward Colin, Aeren, and Eraeth. They'd gathered in his offices in the Sanctuary, the plants shoved to the side, the room bustling with activity. They were departing tomorrow at dociern, the second chiming. "He didn't say what his mistake back at the Escarpment was. Did he plan the betrayal of King Maarten, along with Khalaek and the others? Or did he simply take advantage of the opportunity at the time and claim the betrayal as his own?"

When neither Aeren nor Eraeth answered, the silence unsettled, Lotaern grunted and continued. "But I agree. Khalaek agreed too quickly, and because he agreed Lord Peloroun and Lord Waerren agreed to come as well. And now you claim that Benedine's actions are indeed connected to him?"

"So it would seem. The Phalanx followed Benedine to a courtyard on Brae. There, Benedine met with a man that Colin identified as one of Lord Khalaek's aides."

Lotaern swore. As he did, the hairs on Colin's arms prickled, standing on end. He felt something brush past

him, like a gust of wind, and he turned toward the open
door to the Chosen's office with a frown, a shiver coursing
through him. He tasted dry leaves in his mouth, smelled
damp earth. "What was that?" he asked sharply.

"What was what?" Aeren asked.

"I felt something, like a breeze. And I can smell leaves
and earth."

Eraeth had moved to the door, hand on his cattan, but
he turned back now. "I don't see anything."

"It must have been a draft," Lotaern said. "And we *are*
surrounded by plants."

Everyone looked at Colin, but the scent of leaves and
earth was fading now, so he settled back into his seat. Eraeth returned to his position behind Aeren.

"I don't understand the connection between Benedine,
Khalaek, and the awakening of the sarenavriell," Lotaern
said. "It doesn't make any sense. What is his connection
to the Wells? Why does he want to know where they are
located?"

"I don't think he cares about the sarenavriell. His goal
has always been control of the Evant. He wants to become
the Tamaell."

"The Wraiths." All three Alvritshai turned to Colin,
and he shifted under their scrutiny. "Khalaek may not care
about the sarenavriell, but the Wraiths do. If Khalaek is
looking for the locations of the remaining Wells, then he
must be doing it for the Wraiths."

"That," Lotaern said, his voice heavy and dark, "is not
a pleasant thought, and violates at least a dozen of the
Order's tenants."

"Nevertheless." Aeren had lowered his head in
thought, then looked at Colin. "You said the antruel—the
Faelehgre—thought the Wraiths were moving north." Colin
nodded and Aeren turned back to Lotaern. "Khalaek's
lands are north of the forest, to the west of Lord Vaersoom
and Licaeta. It's possible his lands were also attacked by
the sukrael, and when he arrived to investigate—"

"He found the Wraiths." Lotaern drew in a deep breath,
although it did little to break the lines of anger that
creased his face. "If this is true, then the Wraiths must be
offering him something that will help him gain the Evant.
But what?"

Aeren shrugged. "I don't know. I can't think of anything that would warrant the risk of releasing the sukrael."

"Perhaps you misjudge Khalaek's ambition," Eraeth said bluntly.

Aeren frowned.

Lotaern stirred and rose from behind his desk, his eyes narrowed in anger. "I think it's time we spoke to Benedine about his . . . actions. He may know why Khalaek is interested in the sarenavriell and whether he's working with the Wraiths."

They followed Lotaern out of his personal rooms and into the corridors of the Sanctuary. Lotaern waved acolytes away as they made their way past the common areas and into the dormitories. Most took one look at the Chosen's face and backed off.

"I've had Benedine's activities here in the Sanctuary monitored since you arrived back in Caercaern," Lotaern said as they arrived before one of the small dormitory rooms. "He keeps to himself mostly," Lotaern said as he knocked. When no one responded, he frowned and pushed the door open, stepping through. "His main activity is research and—"

Lotaern halted, two steps inside the small room beyond. Colin heard his voice catch, saw his hand tighten on the handle of the door—

And then the stench of blood hit Colin hard. He gagged, stumbled backward into Eraeth, heard Aeren suck in a sharp breath, hand raised to cover his mouth, and then Eraeth shoved past them all. The Chosen shook himself, then stepped back out into the hall.

"Aielan's Light," Aeren gasped, breathing through his mouth. "What is it?"

"Karvel!" Lotaern barked, then called something to an acolyte farther down the hall. The acolyte leaped to retrieve a lantern, rushing toward them. He began to ask something in Alvritshai.

He didn't finish, the stench of blood and shit hitting him as he reached the doorway. He bent over, began to retch. Lotaern snatched the lantern from him, then stepped up behind Eraeth, raising the light high, his face a stoic mask, devoid of emotion. Colin and Aeren moved in behind him.

The room contained a rough cot, a single stool, and a

small table with a few sheets of parchment, a tome, and a bottle of ink. A feather quill lay broken to one side. The tome and parchment and most of the table were coated with what looked like spilled ink.

Except it wasn't ink. It was blood.

It saturated the blanket on the cot, dripped from its edge onto the floor, had formed a pool that continued to spread along the stones. Splatters of it streaked the walls in grisly patterns. Colin had never seen so much blood, and he felt his stomach clenching at the shock of it, at its dark, viscous color, its stench, the taste of it on the air.

Then Eraeth took a step into the room, and Colin saw what had caught his attention.

Benedine's body lay in the center of the room, mostly obscured from view by the table and stool. But what he could see of the body made Colin's stomach turn again. He tasted bile, acidic and thick, and he swallowed, hard, trembling as it burned his throat. The acolyte's body had been slashed open with too many cuts to count, so many his clothes were nothing but tatters, the skin beneath not much different. He lay facedown, his back lacerated, the backs of his legs, his calves, shredded. His throat had been slit, his head to one side, his eyes wide, mouth open. Blood streaked the pale contours of his face, had matted in his hair and pooled in the hollow of his back. The stone beneath him had been stained black with it.

"How did this happen?" Lotaern muttered. Then he turned on Karvel and roared, "Find Tallin, or any member of the Flame. Now!"

Karvel, face still pasty white, staggered to his feet and rushed off, even though Loatern had spoken in Andovan. Lotaern turned back to the room, where Eraeth had knelt down next to the body. He touched the pool of blood, rubbed it between his fingers with a grimace, then stood.

"The blood hasn't had time to congeal yet. This happened recently."

"Who did this?" Lotaern growled.

Colin suddenly remembered the look on Khalaek's aide's face in the courtyard as he watched Benedine leave: cold and heartless.

"Khalaek," Aeren said. "He must not need Benedine's help any longer."

"Impossible. How did he gain access to the Sanctuary? I have acolytes guarding all of the entrances!"

Two acolytes dressed in the same robes as the others, but with a white patch of flames in the centers of their chests, charged down the corridor, faces tense. Colin was surprised to see they carried swords and saw Aeren and Eraeth trade a shocked look as well. These men did not act like acolytes. Their actions were tight, controlled, and dangerous, as if they were members of the Phalanx.

Lotaern stepped away from the room and met them. A heated discussion in Alvritshai ensued, one of the acolytes stepping into Benedine's room, inspecting the body, then returning, his face grim. When Lotaern finally turned back to them, he didn't look any happier. "They say Benedine worked in the archives all morning and retired to his rooms less than an hour ago. I don't understand. Who could have entered the Sanctuary, killed Benedine, and left, without being noticed?"

Colin thought of the taste of leaves and earth. "Maybe it wasn't a person," he said softly.

Lotaern, Aeren, and Eraeth stilled.

"What do you mean?" Eraeth asked.

"The Wraiths," Aeren answered.

"Here? In Caercaern?" Lotaern spat, his eyes darkening. "In the Sanctuary?"

Colin heard the doubt in his voice, saw it in Aeren and Eraeth's eyes as well. He drew a steadying breath, regretted it as another wave of nausea swept through him at the smell of the blood, then said, "I can find out."

All three Alvritshai stilled. Even the two members of the Flame, the acolytes who were not acolytes, traded a glance and shifted uncomfortably at the sudden stillness.

"How?" Lotaern asked.

Colin glanced toward Aeren, who merely nodded. "I can travel back to the moment he was killed. I can see who killed him."

Lotaern's eyes widened, flickered toward Aeren a moment, then back. "Then do it."

Colin closed his eyes and drew into himself, straightened . . . and then *pushed*. Time slowed, and he approached the barrier that separated the present from the past. Gathering himself, he shoved through it, his skin tingling as it ruptured around him, and then he waded backward into the past. The acolyte guards retreated, and as Lotaern and Eraeth stepped away from the doorway, Colin slid inside, stepping around the body, even as Lotaern shut the door, closing Colin in with Benedine's body. He tried not to shudder as he moved to the far side of the room, and then he pushed again. Hard.

And sank back into time too fast. The room blurred, a smear of sudden, violent movement that made him queasy. When he finally stabilized it, he found Benedine sitting at his desk, quill in hand, as he worked on the tome before him.

He kept time stationary for a moment, to catch his equilibrium, then moved around to see what Benedine was working on. The tome was yellow with age, the pages stiff, the text written in a tight scrawl with long, nearly vertical letters, interspersed with amazingly detailed pictures. Benedine had copied a few phrases from the book onto his sheet of parchment and was turning the page, his brow creased in concentration.

Unable to read the Alvritshai words, Colin allowed time to resume and stepped back.

Benedine flipped the page and sighed heavily before leaning forward to read. One hand rose to knead his forehead.

Colin smelled the Wraith before he saw it, the same scent he'd caught while they'd been speaking in Lotaern's rooms—leaves and earth: the Lifeblood.

A moment later, the door to Benedine's room opened.

Colin caught a flicker of darkness, of shadow, but nothing more. He doubted Benedine had seen even that. Even as the acolyte spun, the door closed, with another smear of shadow.

Face pinched in confusion, Benedine began to rise. He'd only made it halfway up when the Wraith appeared at his side, completely visible for half a breath. No longer draped in the cloak of the Shadows, he wore a dark gray shirt and muddied breeches, a cloak with a hood pulled up over his head, obscuring his face, and boots. He carried a dagger. And he was human.

In that single half-breath, the Wraith slashed along Benedine's arm, then vanished. Benedine cried out, stumbled forward over his desk, the quill snapping in his hand as he tried to catch himself, the stool he'd been sitting on rattling to the floor behind him. The Wraith flickered into view on his other side, slashed at him again, this time across the face, blood flying in a smooth arc to splatter agains the wall. Gasping, Benedine shoved away from the desk, half turned, but the Wraith was there, cutting into his arm, vanishing, reappearing two steps away to cut again. Benedine cried out at every cut, spinning around, bewildered, unable to follow the flickering movements of the Wraith. Blood flew in every direction, the cuts getting deeper and deeper. Benedine tried to make it to the door with a strangled scream, but the Wraith slashed the back of his calf, and he stumbled to his hands and knees. Slices appeared all along his back, his sides, the Wraith no more than a blur, and as Benedine arched back, arms raised to ward off his tormentor, the Wraith appeared behind him.

Colin stepped forward, even though he knew he couldn't change anything, knew he couldn't stop it.

Gripping the acolyte's head, yanking it backward, the Wraith cut Benedine's throat. Blood fountained down over the acolyte's shredded robes, drenching the bed, splattering onto the floor. Even as Colin gagged, the stench overpowering, the Wraith thrust Benedine's body forward and stepped toward the door. Colin's knees grew weak, the shock of the violence—all happening in the space of a dozen heartbeats—hitting him hard. He lost his hold on time, felt it shove him forward, the aftermath of the attack as the Wraith departed a smear of action, and then he fell to his hands and knees and vomited onto the acolyte's stone floor.

He heard Lotaern gasp, heard the acolyte guardsmen cry out, and then Aeren said, "In here!"

They crowded the doorway to Benedine's chambers, all staring at Colin in shock. All except Aeren and Eraeth.

"Well?" Eraeth asked.

Colin spat out the sour taste in his mouth, swallowed, then pulled himself upright. One hand had landed in Benedine's blood, and with a grimace he wiped it off on a clean edge of Benedine's blanket. "It was a Wraith," he said. "I couldn't see his face, but he moved like I do. And he reeked of the Lifeblood."

"Could you identify the Wraith?" Lotaern asked. "Was it one of Khalaek's men?"

"No. He wore a hood and kept his face concealed. But he wasn't one of Khalaek's men. He was human."

Lotaern swore, glanced toward the carnage in Benedine's room, then asked, "What should we do?"

Aeren frowned. "We need to find out what Benedine found in the Scripts regarding the sarenavriell, what it was that Khalaek wanted. Without Benedine, we have no way to connect the Wraiths to Khalaek. We have nothing."

Lotaern turned to Colin. "Can you go back to see what he was researching?"

Colin shook his head, one hand falling to his stomach and the vague heat and pain there. He still trembled, shaken by the Wraith's cruelty. Like that of the Shadows. "Not right now. I'm still too weak. Unless . . ." He trailed off, catching Eraeth's eye. He could smell the vial of Lifeblood on the Protector. If he drank that . . .

"No," Eraeth said, frowning. When Colin began to protest, his eyes hardened and he repeated more forcefully, "No."

"And we're leaving with the Tamaell tomorrow," Aeren said. "We'll have to discover what Benedine found another way."

Colin turned to Lotaern. "He was reading that book when he died."

Lotaern moved to the desk. The parchment Benedine had been writing on was destroyed, soaked in blood, but the Chosen gingerly lifted the edge of the book to look at the cover, then set it back down. "This wasn't part of his research. This was for daily study as an acolyte. It tells us nothing. Which means we still don't know what Khalaek intends."

Aeren regarded Lotaern for a long moment, then turned away, motioning Eraeth and Colin to follow. "Find what Benedine found," he said.

"And where are you going?"

"To finish preparations for the meeting with the dwarren."

~

Garius reached down and tugged on one of the gaezel's horns, and the animal snorted and angled slightly right, thundering through the grasses of the plains, reaching a slight rise and charging down into the dip beyond. Hot wind blasted his face, catching his beard as he leaned forward into it. He could hear the beads tied into his braids clicking together, beads that signified all his accomplishments throughout life: his marriage, the births of his sons and daughters, his feats in battle. Behind, the thunder of the hundred other Thousand Springs Riders, including Shea, was a distant rumble. They'd been riding hard for two days. They were almost at the designated meeting place for the Gathering: the warren of the Shadow Moon Clan.

He'd returned to his own city immediately after the meeting with the Alvritshai and had barely spent an hour seeing to the needs of his wife, Tamannen, and of his sons and daughters and extended family. Shea watched and scowled the entire time as he explained what had happened and what needed to be done. Then he'd donned the mantle of clan chief and, with Shea and the rest of the Riders as escort, descended from the height of the cleft to the central chamber of the warren. There, beside the central pool and the cascade of the river, he'd ordered the great drum brought forth and a signal sent through the tunnels to the other dwarren cities and their clan chiefs.

The Riders he'd selected for the journey mounted even as the first hollow boom of the great drum echoed through the city's cavern, its voice deep and hollow, vibrating in Garius' bones. Aimed at the wide mouth of the largest tunnel leading out of the city, its slow rhythm called a Gathering of the clans a ten-day hence at the Shadow Moon Clan's city, a message that would be heard and relayed by drum throughout the warrens. Shadow Moon wasn't the most central of the clans on the plains, but it was close enough to the designated meeting place with the Alvritshai to give the clan chiefs time to gather, discuss the situation, chose a Cochen—a Gathering leader—and then arrive on time if it was decided to meet with the Alvritshai.

Assuming all the clan chiefs heard the drum message in time.

Ahead, Garius caught sight of the outermost scouts of Shadow Moon. One of them stood and signaled that they'd been recognized and could proceed without stopping. Garius thundered past them, and minutes later the outer tent city rose into view.

Swirls of cloth wrapped around poles and stakes emerged from the plains in a confusion of colors and shapes. Some pierced straight up to the sky, those nearest the gaping hole of the entrance to the warren the highest. Others jutted out to the sides at odd angles, the fabric stretched taut here, falling in soft folds there, the entire array of cloth and pole and ties giving the sense of movement, the blues and greens blending together to give the impression of water, flowing free aboveground, without constraints, without boundaries. A river without banks, dwarren walking free among its eddies and currents. The tents filled the entire length of the shallow valley.

Garius headed his group toward the center of the vortex of cloth along the main approach to the warren, dwarren carrying trade goods and leading wagons and pack gaezels scrambling to get out of the way. Once, only the Riders would have appeared aboveground near the main entrance to the warren, to protect the most exposed portal to the underground tunnels beneath. The women and those protecting them and the clan's shamans would ascend through the network of much smaller hidden entrances near the communal fields scattered throughout the plains.

But the introduction of the Alvritshai and then the humans onto the plains had changed everything. The dwarren had been forced to live aboveground more and more, the threat from both foreign races too great. It became inefficient to keep supplies and resources below, and once the Riders shifted to the surface, so did the women and the trade. Within a decade, the tent cities gained limited permanence, and from there they only grew.

Garius ignored the tents and the people and angled his gaezel toward the dark depths of the entrance instead. The well-trampled ramp sloped downward, and he ducked his head as he passed through into the shade beneath. Riders lined both sides within, most standing near a double line of giant pillars embedded in the walls on either side, supporting arches overhead embellished with ancient stonework. The stone between the successive arches was rough and unworked, rigged to collapse and seal the warren if the dwarren destroyed the pillars. But this defense passed by in the space of a heartbeat, Garius not slowing his descent into the massive tunnel. The sound of Shea and the rest of his Riders increased behind him and echoed out ahead. Tunnels branched off to either side, much smaller in diameter, intersections lit with metal-worked stands containing wide flat bowls of burning oil. The walls were lined with stone, buttressed with supports at regular intervals, the stone shifting in color until it had run the entire spectrum found on the plains, including the vivid reds from the desert near the Painted Sands Clan to the east. As above, fellow Riders and dwarren transporting goods dodged out of their way as the roar of Garius' gaezel reached them.

Then the worked stone ended, the walls and floor abruptly white and smooth, no supports visible. This was the stone of the Ancients, the ones who came before, the ones who gave the Lands to the People, to guard and protect. The rounded edges of the tunnel above became sharp rectangular angles, although the tunnels were still lit with the basins of oil.

When the stands of flame began appearing closer together, Garius pulled back on the gaezel's horns and slowed.

Moments later, the Ancients' tunnel ended, opening up into the true city of Shadow Moon, a rounded room that could enclose the entire tent city above. Like that of Thousand Springs, the wide floor swept away to a massive pool, the river cascading down from the circular opening high above, wider than the tunnel they'd just left, frothing in the pool before spilling over its edge into another channel and funneling down into a second circular tunnel. The open holes of the dwarren's clefts surrounded the walls on all sides, some lit from within by lantern light, but more than half of them dark and empty when once they were crowded, teeming with families. Dwarren scrambled from level to level in the lowest tiers, using stairs cut into the stone walls, but most of the dwarren were on the floor, the wide plaza choked with blankets spread with wares as women bartered for goods and children dodged and cavorted around them, laughing and screaming as they played. Garius saw earthen bowls painted with geometric designs, woven blankets with depictions of Ilacqua and the

Four Winds, spears and bows, fabric, produce, and butchered animals, all offered up for the women's examination. The chamber echoed with a dull throb from the rushing water and the noise of the marketplace, dampened by the immensity of the cavern.

Garius' attention was caught by the waiting Riders at the far side of the thoroughfare ending near the great pool. Mannet, clan chief of Shadow Moon, stood with three other clan chiefs, including Harticur from the Red Sea Clan—the most powerful clan at the moment—each with his own shaman and at least four of his own Riders. It appeared that the clan chief from Painted Sands, Adammern, had arrived shortly before Garius. His mounts had been herded to one side. Only two clans were not present: Broken Waters and Claw Lake.

Garius frowned as he led his group toward the others. Broken Waters was the clan farthest from Shadow Moon, so it wasn't unexpected they had not yet arrived, but Claw Lake lay adjacent to Shadow Moon. Its clan should have been one of the first to arrive.

Pulling his gaezel to a halt, Garius dismounted, heard the rest of his group doing the same behind him. Smoothing the tangles of his beard, he stepped toward the other clan chiefs and felt his son and Oudan, his shaman, falling into step behind him.

Mannet broke off his conversation with the others as Garius approached. "Garius, Chief of the Thousand Springs Clan, the People of Shadow Moon welcome you."

Garius nodded in return. "May Ilacqua blaze down upon you and the Four Winds keep your granaries full."

Mannet grunted. "And yours." Pleasantries complete, his face darkened. "Why have you called a Gathering? We are nearing the end of harvest and must prepare for the Tesinthe and the blessing of the Lands for renewal."

Behind him, the chiefs from Silver Grass and Painted Sands grumbled in agreement. Sipa stood as far from Mannet as possible and shot the clan chief a hostile glare. Their clans had warred for generations across the boundary of the Tiquano River. Both Harticur and Adammern were separated for a similar reason. Garius could feel the tension on the air, although all the clan chiefs were respecting the sanctity of the Gathering.

He suddenly realized that getting them to agree to meet with the Alvritshai and to choose one of their group to be the Cochen might be harder than he'd thought. He needed to make them understand the seriousness of the request for this Gathering, serious enough that they needed to set aside their conflicts.

Running his fingers through the beads in his beard, he drew himself upright and in a deep voice said, "This discussion requires the use of the keeva, and the presence of our shamans."

Mannet's eyes widened, and a growling murmur rumbled through the rest of the group. Use of the keeva and the presence of the shamans meant the words would be heard directly by the gods, the actions of the clan chiefs judged by them. It was used only for the most powerful ceremonies and rites or to commune with the gods before the clan chief made crucial decisions.

"Hochen!" Mannet barked, and his shaman—older than Oudan by at least ten years—shuffled forward, the plains snake tails on his spear rattling as he moved. He glared at Garius with a flattened, wrinkled face. "Prepare the keeva."

Hochen smacked his lips together, mumbled something incomprehensible, then began shuffling off toward the wide doorway of the ritual chamber at the base of the tiered clefts near the cascade. Oudan and the rest of the shamans moved to help, some already beginning the blessing and the litany that would seal the oval chamber from evil spirits and prying ears and open it up to the gods.

~

"I've left a small group of acolytes behind in the archives attempting to reconstruct the research that Benedine has been doing for the past few months, but it will be difficult."

Aeren paused in the act of slicing a piece of gaezel meat and stared at Lotaern, who sat across from him at the low, portable table set up on the grass of the plains. They'd traveled with the Alvritshai envoy the full length of Lord Peloroun's lands and were about to enter the land that the dwarren claimed as their own. Aeren hadn't had an opportunity to speak to Lotaern since they'd departed Caercaern, the Chosen of the Order having first dined with nearly all of the other lords who outranked Aeren, starting with the Tamaell. Aeren could have insisted, but he didn't want to draw any attention to how closely he'd been working with Lotaern recently.

Setting his knife aside, Aeren dipped his hands into a tiny bowl of water and dried them on a towel set to one side. "Why is that?"

"Because following Benedine's logic—what thought led to which reference, what material he looked at first—is nearly impossible. He looked at hundreds of texts, including the Scripts, but most of those lead to dead ends. We don't know which of those texts were important, and finding them will take time."

Aeren nodded. "I see."

Lotaern gave him a strange look. "You've been rather quiet. What is it that concerns you?"

Aeren caught Lotaern's eye and thought back to the day the envoy had departed Caercaern. All the lords had gathered in the plaza before the Sanctuary before dociern, as the Tamaell had requested. Only the Chosen and his acolytes had yet to arrive. When the bells of the Sanctuary began to chime, everyone on the plaza turned toward the doors to the Sanctuary, which had already begun to open. But unlike a typical dociern ceremony, the acolytes who emerged didn't begin drifting among those gathered to offer up blessings and prayers or give alms and accept donations. Instead, the Chosen of the Order stepped out into the sunlight in robes of vivid white. Four files of acolytes marched out behind him, dressed in light armor, every footfall in sync, moving in precise columns that lined up behind Lotaern in formation. Two of the acolyte warriors carried tall banners, a white flame against a blue background, signifying Aielan's Light. They fell into place on either side of Lotaern. Behind the Chosen, more acolytes emerged, this time leading a slew of horses and two wagons. One of them led a white horse to Lotaern's side and handed over the reins.

The spectacle had drawn a murmur from the gathered Alvritshai, from the lords and the Phalanx. Aeren hadn't realized the Order had their own warriors. The Order *shouldn't* have warriors. Were they simply for show? Or could they actually wield the cattans they carried?

Aeren drew a deep breath, then let it out slowly. "I did not realize that the Order had trained warriors. It didn't when I was an acolyte."

Lotaern stilled for a moment, then set his own knife down and finished chewing before answering. "There is nothing in the Scripts that forbids it. In fact, there are references to the Order having its own army, the Order of the Flame, brethren who felt that Aielan and her Light must be defended at all costs."

"And is that what these acolytes—this Order of the Flame—are for? Defense?"

"Yes. For the defense of Aielan and the Order, to help protect us against those who would oppose the Light. And against those creatures like the sukrael and the Wraiths who abhor the Light, who may seek to destroy it."

Aeren met Lotaern's gaze. "You must have begun training the members of the Order of the Flame years ago to have them prepared at the level I have seen on this march. Training that began long before the sukrael or the Wraiths were an issue."

Lotaern's eyes narrowed. "I would have thought that you, of all of the lords in the Evant, would be supportive of the Order and the Flame."

"I do support the Order," Aeren said, "but I am also Lord of House Rhyssal. The Order was never intended to have its own Phalanx. It's how the balance of power between the Evant and the Order remains stable. It's how the Tamaell retains his power and keeps the Order separate from the Evant. The Order was never intended to be a rival to the Evant, the Chosen a rival to the Tamaell. It is intended to serve the people, to offer them solace and guidance in their everyday lives and to give them hope in times of strife. I cannot be the only lord in this envoy who has expressed concern over this."

"No, you are not. But I believe that you will find the Flame useful before all this is done. They are skilled at more than swordplay. They have other talents. And I do not intend to oppose the Tamaell or use the Flame against any of the Houses. But the world is changing. The arrival of the humans was only the beginning. Now we have the sukrael, the antruel, the Wraiths ... I do not see an end to the changes in sight. The Order is simply preparing."

Aeren didn't answer, the tension between them thick.
He knew that some within the Order had power like that
which Colin displayed, although not as great. He wanted
to ask how Lotaern had trained his contingent of warrior
acolytes without anyone in the Evant learning of it, but he
already knew. He'd been in the depths of the Sanctuary
himself when he'd gone to pass through Aielan's Light
to earn his pendant. He'd seen the empty chambers deep
within the mountain where the Alvritshai had once lived.
Lotaern could have trained an army ten times this size
within those halls, and no one outside the Order would
have known.

The thought sent fingers of unease prickling along his
arms.

But Lotaern's small force—a hundred and twenty acolytes altogether—was the least of Aeren's concerns at the
moment, and it was not the main source of the tension and
unease that had preoccupied him since they'd reached the
edge of Alvritshai lands.

Aeren glanced out toward the falling darkness and
the rest of the entourage heading to the plains. Nearby,
Eraeth and Colin sat beside one of the many fires lit for
cooking and for the coming night, Eraeth drilling Colin in
the Alvritshai language, using the light to show him the
corresponding words on scraps of parchment. A few of
the Rhyssal Phalanx had gathered around to watch and
were tossing in their own contributions. Ever since the trek
across the plains and the meeting with the dwarren, the
Phalanx had taken Colin under the Rhyssal wings, more
than even declaring him Rhyssal-aein warranted. They'd
begun training him with the knife he carried in his bag,
spending hours after the convoy halted, sparring until the
light faded. Beyond them, the convoy stretched out into
the distance along a swath of trampled and wheel-rutted
grass, so large he could barely discern Tamaell Fedorem's
banners at the head of the column. They were arranged
according to their power in the Evant, the Tamaell at the
front, followed by Lords Khalaek and Peloroun, Waerren
and Jydell, Vaersoom and Aeren, and finally Barak.

The size of the group had grown since they'd departed
Caercaern.

"I find it troublesome that Lord Peloroun added over

one hundred of his own House Phalanx to his escort when we reached his estate," he finally said. "I could have let that pass without comment, could have accepted it as a mere precaution on his part. He has dealt with the dwarren on more occasions than nearly any of the rest of the lords. And as he said at the Evant, he has suffered more of their attacks. But then, at the border—"

Lotaern shifted at the change in conversation, then nodded in understanding. "At the border, we were joined by no less than one thousand of the Phalanx, composed of members of the Houses Duvoraen, Ionaen, and Redlien."

"Precisely." Aeren turned to gaze out over the hundreds of fires that now lit the night. "What began as a simple envoy has begun to feel more like an army. An army marching to war." He paused, then turned to face Lotaern directly. "There are now nearly two thousand Phalanx in this envoy, five hundred of them the White Phalanx. When we left Caercaern, the entire envoy contained only four hundred. It's begun to feel like a repetition of the Escarpment."

Lotaern caught the undercurrent in Aeren's tone and poured a glass of wine, forehead creased in thought. "You think this is a ploy, a means to get all the dwarren clan chiefs together in one place so that we can finish them off in one crushing defeat. You think Tamaell Fedorem intends another betrayal."

"That's exactly what I fear." The words were more bitter than he'd intended, loud enough that Eraeth glanced over with a frown. "But I can't tell. He had me convinced he intended peace with the humans at the Escarpment. Why shouldn't he do the same again?"

"He doesn't have the army gathered here that he had at the Escarpment."

"Near enough. But he doesn't need such a large army now. We're only meeting with the dwarren. They aren't expecting a battle, certainly not a battle of the extent we saw at the Escarpment, with all three races present."

"True." Lotaern traced the edge of his glass with one finger, brow creased with concern. "Whether or not we have enough of a force to handle the dwarren depends on how many of the dwarren are present at the meeting." He glanced up at Aeren. "Do you know how many dwarren will be there?"

"At least as many as there are Alvritshai in this current . . . convoy. The clan chief I spoke to intended to bring all the dwarren clans together for the meeting. There are seven. If each chief brings his own force and escort—and knowing the dwarren, each chief will attempt to bring an escort larger than any of the other chiefs—it's likely there will be more dwarren at the meeting than we have Alvritshai at the moment."

Lotaern shifted. "You know that the Tamaell and I have not gotten along well together, even before the Escarpment, but we have always treated each other with the respect that our positions deserve. I did not sense any deceit in him during our own meal at the beginning of this journey. Perhaps there is nothing to worry about."

Aeren grunted. "I had no worries at the Escarpment. Forgive me if I find it difficult to set aside my worries now."

Lotaern didn't respond, and they sat in silence for a long moment, the occasional exasperated sigh audible from Eraeth as Colin mispronounced a word or phrase. Aeren smiled when Colin bit back, Eraeth stiffening, both refusing to give ground.

"He is an interesting human," Lotaern murmured.

"Is he?" Aeren kept his eyes on Colin. He remembered following the humans' wagons as they made their slow trek east, remembered the first meeting at the small creek, where he'd exchanged the ceremonial offerings to Aielan with Colin and his father and the others. But it had always been Colin that intrigued him. "Eraeth tried to warn me away, but there was something about the human boy that drew me."

Lotaern's eyebrows rose. "Perhaps it was Aielan's will that guided you."

Aeren reached down to touch the pendant hidden beneath his shirt. "Perhaps. It's certainly been fortuitous. For all of us. We wouldn't be aware of the Wells and the Wraiths otherwise."

Lotaern stirred. "About the Wraiths . . ."

Aeren turned from watching Colin and Eraeth. "What?"

"We need to know where the Wells are located, and I'm not certain that those I left behind will find their locations in the Scripts in time, even knowing where Benedine has already looked. This boy speaks to the Faelehgre who guard the sarenavriell. He may be able to learn something more from them."

Aeren turned to face the Chosen, saw Lotaern recoil slightly from the look on his face. "When Colin returned from speaking to the Faelehgre the first time, the black mark on his arm had grown. Somehow, the sarenavriell hurts him. I've seen the haunted look in his eyes, the tension in his body when he speaks of it. And yet, as soon as the convoy reached the plains, he offered to go back, offered to see if the Faelehgre have found out anything more. He's already been to the forest and back once, and the Faelehgre have learned nothing new, except that the Shadows continue to hunt on their new hunting grounds and that the new Well continues to fill. They have not seen the Wraiths at all.

"I will not ask him to return again. He may return on his own, and he will inform us if there is news, but I refuse to allow him to hurt himself at my request."

~

Moiran sat astride her horse, back stiff, as the army of Alvritshai lords and their entourages made their slow but steady crawl across the plains. Her position was near the front of the column, before the Tamaell's wagons but not part of the Tamaell's lead group.

Her eyes drifted toward Fedorem, where he rode his own steed at the front, surrounded by four Lords of the Evant, a covey of attendants, pages, messengers, and a slew of House banners, all vying for height and the wind that gusted across the plains.

Games! She thought, her mouth twisting in distaste. *Games played by men with more ambition than common sense.*

She nearly grunted, her disgust with the lords and their manipulations rising. But then a group of the lords shifted their horses, and she caught sight of Thaedoren.

The tightness in her shoulders relaxed, and she released her pent up breath in a long sigh.

Thaedoren's arrival in Caercaern had shocked her. Fedorem had not told her he'd sent for their firstborn son, had not sought her counsel since that night in Caercaern, when she'd confronted him over the Escarpment and Lord Kha-

laek. So when she'd come in from tending her gardens and
found Thaedoren speaking stiffly with Fedorem, dressed in
his Phalanx colors . . . Only when she'd felt the tension in
the room, seen the hardness on Thaedoren's face, the way
he'd clenched his jaw, had the shock dissipated.

She'd dropped her pruning shears and gloves and em-
braced him. Thaedoren had stiffened in her embrace at
first, his breath tight and controlled, but then he'd relaxed,
pushing her back gently, allowing her to gather herself together, to wipe the tears from her eyes.

"I've had Thaedoren transferred back to Caercaern,"
Fedorem had said from behind her, and she'd heard the
disapproval in his voice over her display of emotion. "This
meeting of the Evant is too important for him to miss."

She could sense Thaedoren's confusion. What had been
merely a strained relationship between father and son,
due to disagreements on how to control the Evant, had
degenerated into public vocal arguments after the Escarpment. Thaedoren had always been more forthright than his
father. And more honorable. He'd viewed the betrayal of
the human King as a stain upon the Resue House, upon the
Alvritshai in general. Fedorem had ordered him to the border with the Phalanx. Thaedoren had been more than willing to leave and had taken his brother, Daedelan, with him.

It was one of the issues that had driven a wedge between Moiran and Fedorem in those years following his
return from the battle. His actions within the Evant, with
Khalaek, had done the rest.

"It's good to have you back," she'd said, her voice calm,
with no trace of the roil of emotion—elation, hope, and
fear—she felt inside. Why had he recalled Thaedoren?
Why now? Fedorem must have a reason. He did nothing
without purpose.

She still had no answers when, a day later, Fedorem
had requested her presence at the Evant. The request had
prompted more questions, and now, a week onto the plains,
with two days lost to one of the violent, unnatural storms
slowing their progress, she still had no answers. Fedorem
remained stubbornly silent, barely speaking to her when
the army halted for the night. He spoke to Thaedoren, the
two retreating to Fedorem's tents.

The sudden change ... troubled her. His actions were too close to those he'd taken before the Escarpment.

Moiran shifted in her saddle. Her horse snorted, picking up on her unease, and she quieted it by stroking its neck. To the side, one of her attendants looked at her with a questioning frown, but she shook her head, her brow creasing in irritation.

Ahead, one of the attendants surrounding Fedorem suddenly cried out in warning. Instantly, Fedorem was surrounded by the White Phalanx. The lords leaped into defensive positions, all of them facing west. The Phalanx set to guard Moiran reacted as well, closing up around her and her attendant, a few more taking charge of the wagon behind her.

Moiran ignored them and rose slightly in her saddle as the column ground to a halt, commands and warnings shouted down the line. She raised one hand to shade her eyes, shivering as the chill wind sneaked down through the nape of her shirt.

"What is it?" her attendant asked, bringing her mount up close to Moiran's. Her tone was breathless with fear, yet tinged with excitement.

"I can't see—" Moiran cut off as someone on horseback charged up over a distant ridge. They were moving fast, and as they drew near, Moiran could see the lather on the horse's sides. "It's a rider, coming in fast."

A horn blew from Fedorem's position, and everyone relaxed, Moiran's attendant heaving a sigh of relief.

"It's one of our scouts," the closest Phalanx muttered. "Nothing to worry about."

"He wouldn't have pushed his horse so hard if there were nothing to worry about," Moiran said without turning.

The guardsman and her attendant frowned at each other.

The scout pulled up sharply in front of the lords and their forest of banners, then literally fell from his horse. A few of those nearest cried out. Lord Aeren and Lord Jydell dismounted and rushed to the scout's side, helping him to rise. As they did so, the horse the scout had ridden heaved a shuddering sigh and collapsed to its knees, its tongue protruding from its mouth. Someone rushed toward it with a pail of water, but before it could drink, it leaned drunkenly to one side and fell.

Moiran's attendant gasped again and whispered, "What happened?"

Moiran looked at her. "He rode the horse to death." She couldn't keep the condescension from her voice, and the girl winced.

More men rushed to the horse, but Moiran kept her eyes on the scout. With Lord Aeren's help, Jydell trailing behind, he staggered toward where Moiran could see Fedorem through the crowd of bodies. She swore as she lost sight of the scout and Fedorem altogether.

She glanced at the Phalanx guard, considered ordering him to go find out what had happened, then shrugged the thought aside with disgust. He wouldn't leave his post, not even at an order from the Tamaea.

The group surrounding Fedorem suddenly grew agitated, and she heard the Tamaell bellow, "Quiet!" The voices fell into low murmurs, but they still shifted back and forth.

The strain in the air was palpable, and Moiran edged her horse farther forward, trying to hear something—anything—to catch a glimpse of the scout, of Fedorem, of—

Her Phalanx bodyguard sidled his mount in front of her, cutting her off. She gave him a dark look and drew breath to berate him, but he said coldly, "Whatever it is, it's obviously the business of the Evant, not the Tamaea."

She could have insisted that it didn't matter, that Fedorem would tell her, or Thaedoren, or that her role as head of the Ilvaeran and the steward of the House gave her the right to know, but she choked the words back. Because they would have been a lie. The Ilvaeran—commonly called the Lady's Evant—might control the economic resources of each of the Houses, but it had little to do with the current meeting with the dwarren. And before the Escarpment, Fedorem had told her everything, or nearly everything. But since then . . .

Fedorem emerged from the tangle of lords and attendants on foot and bellowed, "We'll halt here for the night."

Murmurs rose from those nearest as the orders were passed down the line, both by word of mouth and by horn. Servants burst into sudden activity, wagons directed to either side of the path they'd made through the grasslands, spreading out, cooks hauling food and wares from trunks and compartments, others scattering to the nearest visible copses of the trees in search of firewood to supplement what they'd brought with them, the Phalanx themselves settling shifts for sentries, assigned scouts darting away onto the plains. Moiran normally would have watched the setting up of camp intently, since her duties as lady of the House and as head of the Ilvaeran included making certain the convoy had supplies, but instead she observed Fedorem. The Tamaell watched his men intently, Thaedoren emerging from the group with the weary scout in tow as the lords scattered, most with pensive expressions or deep frowns on their faces. As soon as Thaedoren appeared, Moiran nudged her horse around her bodyguard and approached Fedorem, ignoring the Phalanx's protests.

"What happened?" she demanded.

Fedorem's face set, his jaw clenched, chin lifted slightly as he turned away.

Moiran felt herself stiffen, her hands clutching the reins tighter. "Why are we stopping? What news did the scout bring?" Then, in a softer, more dangerous voice: "Don't tell me it isn't important. He wouldn't have ridden his horse to death if it weren't."

Out of the corner of her eye, she saw Thaedoren cast his father a questioning look. "Father?"

Without turning, Fedorem said harshly, "No. We haven't discussed it yet." Then he turned to face Moiran, stance stern and solid, like stone. But Moiran saw the touch of worry in his eyes, a hint of fear. "Thaedoren and I will be in the council's tent. We'll be eating there as well, will likely remain there most of the night."

Then he spun and motioned to Thaedoren and the scout, heading toward where the tent was even now being erected.

Moiran gripped her reins even harder. She forced herself to calm, suppressed a scream of frustration, then turned and spat, "Games!" under her breath.

"My Tamaea?" her attendant asked timidly.

Moiran hadn't even realized the girl had followed her. She couldn't even remember her name . . . Fae? Faeren?

But a thought suddenly struck her, and her shoulders

relaxed, a slight smile touching her lips. Easing her horse forward, toward her own tents, she motioned the attendant closer. "I have something I need you to attend to," she said.

"Yes, Tamaea."

Moiran felt the guardsman fall into position behind her, just out of earshot, and her smile widened.

~

Aeren halted at the edge of the Tamaea's—and the Tamaell's—range of tents and frowned into the darkness. The late afternoon and evening had been a flurry of activity as the convoy settled in after the arrival of the scout and the unexpected halt. Messengers had run between all of the lords' encampments. Aeren himself had sent some of those messages in an attempt to gather as much information as possible. But he'd learned only what the other lords knew, which was nothing more than what he'd overheard the scout reveal after his arrival, before Fedorem had cut the scout's report short and called the halt.

And then Faeren had arrived and delivered her message: *Tamaea Moiran Resue requests the presence of Lord Aeren Goadri Rhyssal, to dine in the Tamaea's tents in the absence of the Tamaell Fedorem Resue.*

Without moving, he scanned the fires scattered throughout the Tamaell's enclave, his gaze lingering on those near the council tent. He could see light flickering inside, but he could not see any shapes or figures moving about.

Aeren's gaze drifted to the Tamaea's tent, and his frown deepened. "What do you want, Tamaea?" he whispered to himself.

In the distance, someone laughed, the sound jarring in the openness of the plains, the stillness of the night. Aeren breathed in the chill air, tasted winter on it, then stared up briefly at the brittle stars overhead, the sliver of moon.

He stepped across the imaginary boundary between the rest of the camp and the Tamaell's domain and moved swiftly toward the Tamaea's tents. One of the Phalanx stiffened as he approached, then recognized him and let him pass without a word.

The two Phalanx outside the tent did not.

"The Tamaea requested my presence for dinner tonight," he said.

The taller of the two nodded. "I'll inform the Tamaea you have arrived."

As he waited, Aeren realized he could see his breath on the air, a faint plume, visible only because of the nearness of a fire. He shivered.

The Phalanx guard returned. "You may enter. The food has already been served."

Aeren nodded, then ducked down through the entrance of the tent.

He smelled spices a moment before slipping through a second opening deeper inside the tent—sage and parsley, nearly smothered by the scent of spiced venison. When he stood, the apprehension he'd felt in coming here surged.

The Tamaea sat before a single small table with two settings, bowls of food of various sizes spread out on either side, steam rising from most. Another low table sat to one side, a decanter of wine and two glasses already set out, along with a tray of cheese and grapes. The floor was littered with pillows, a large pillow serving as a seat. Lanterns lit the room, the flames creating a soft light.

"Welcome, Lord Aeren," the Tamaea said, her mouth quirking in a slight smile. "Please join me."

Suddenly wary, Aeren moved to the pillow opposite the Tamaea, settling himself slowly, legs crossed. "I did not realize this was a . . . private dinner," he said.

The Tamaea reached for the wine, pouring two glasses as she said, "As private as the Tamaea can make it." She passed Aeren's glass to him and raised hers, one eyebrow tilted upward, "To . . . alliances."

Aeren stilled, eyes narrowing, then raised his own glass. "To peaceful alliances."

The Tamaea nodded, then sipped her wine before setting it aside and turning to the food, taking a small portion from each bowl before passing them to Aeren. Her motions were smooth and practiced, even though a servant typically served at dinner.

She spoke as she worked.

"It's been an interesting few weeks. Your arrival and the news you brought, the meeting of the Evant and the assembly of the army—"

"Envoy," Aeren interrupted, without thinking.

The Tamaea froze, a skewer of meat half-raised toward

her plate, her eyes on him. They held steady for a moment, then dropped as she set the skewer down slowly and handed him the bowl. "I'd hoped that this could be an open discussion. One where we could share information, without any dissembling." She locked eyes with him, the smile no longer present, her expression hard and serious, her hands in her lap. "This is not an envoy. Not anymore. Not since we were joined by the Phalanx at the border. This is an army. Both of us know this."

Silence settled. A silence Aeren felt against his skin, tingling. A silence intensified by the Tamaea's unwavering gaze.

Aeren set the bowl of skewered meat down with a sigh. "I'd hoped that this would be an end to the conflict with the dwarren. I'd hoped . . . many things. But you are correct, Tamaea. This is an army."

She didn't move. "The scout."

Aeren nodded. He glanced down at the food on his plate, no longer hungry.

"What news did he bring?"

"The Tamaell has not told you?"

"The Tamaell has chosen not to inform me."

He could leave. He knew that. He was a Lord of the Evant, and the Tamaea need not concern herself with the dealings of the Evant, of the lords and the Tamaell.

But Aeren knew that the Tamaell had something planned, Khalaek as well. He had Lotaern as an ally, and Lord Barak. Perhaps the Tamaea knew more than she thought.

He hesitated a moment more, staring into the Tamaea's eyes, then said quietly, "To alliances then."

The decision made, he felt as though a weight was lifted from his shoulders.

The Tamaea relaxed as well, her posture softening. "What news did the scout bring?" she repeated.

"He brought news that the human army—the Legion—has gathered on the border with over five thousand men, led by King Stephan. And approximately four days ago, they entered the plains, moving to intercept us."

The Tamaea's body froze, the only movement a slight widening of her eyes. For a moment, she didn't even breathe.

Then she let out her breath in a low sigh, nearly a moan. "It's the Escarpment all over again."

Aeren frowned, taking a bit of meat from a skewer, chewing it thoughtfully. "Yes . . . and no."

"What do you mean?" the Tamaea snapped. "All three races, coming together with armies at their backs, two of them under an ostensible agreement of peace—" She choked on her words, shook her head in frustration, turning to stare at the side of the tent. Aeren watched as tears glistened in her eyes, the only crack in the armor of rage she'd laid over herself. But no tears fell. She held them back, her entire body trembling with the effort.

Aeren let her grapple with the anger in silence, nibbling at his food. But he watched.

And sooner than expected, the hard edges of rage in her face softened, her eyes widening with dawning horror.

She turned to him and whispered, "What has Fedorem done? What has he planned?"

Aeren pushed his plate aside and looked at her. "I don't know." Her eyes narrowed in suspicion, but he forged on. "None of the Evant knows, as far as I can discern."

"Not even Khalaek?" The bitterness and hatred in her voice made him smile.

"Not even Khalaek." He hesitated. "I believe Khalaek is playing his own game."

"Khalaek is always playing his own game. What do you think it is this time?" When Aeren didn't answer immediately, she asked, "Does it have anything to do with your human friend?"

Aeren felt his face go blank, unintentionally, a reaction learned on the floor of the Evant. "Yes and no."

"You are too fond of that answer."

Aeren smiled. "I have not shared this with any other Lords of the Evant, not even with the Tamaell. Mostly because neither Lotaern nor I know exactly what is happening. But it seems to be connected to Lord Khalaek."

"Lotaern knows?"

"It has to do with the sarenavriell."

The Tamaea's eyebrows rose, but she nodded for him to continue.

And he did. He told her of the warning brought to him by Colin from the Faelehgre. He told her of Benedine and his research, of his meeting with one of Khalaek's attendants, of his death. He told her of the awakening of the Wells and what little he knew of Colin's powers. He told her everything, including Colin's return to the forest to check up on the Faelehgre and their progress and that Colin had volunteered to return again when they'd halted unexpectedly today.

She accepted it all in silence, staring down at her hands. When he was done, she looked up, her eyes more troubled than before, somehow deeper and darker. "And you have not told the Tamaell?"

He shook his head with a frustrated snort and shrugged. "Lotaern has informed the Tamaell of the awakening of the sarenavriell and the reason for the attacks on the eastern Houses by the sukrael. As for the link between that and Khalaek . . . what is there to tell? We have no proof of anything. And then—" He cut himself off.

"And then what?" She stared at him in confusion, and in her eyes he saw sudden comprehension. "You think the Tamaell may be involved somehow." The realization was followed immediately by anger. "Fedorem would never conspire with Khalaek—"

"Wouldn't he? What happened at the Escarpment, then? Can you say without doubt that he did not conspire with Khalaek to bring about Maarten's death?"

That brought the Tamaea up short. He could see her struggling with words, trying to come to her husband's defense, to the Tamaell's defense . . .

But in the end, she sagged with defeat. "No. I cannot say that without doubt." Her voice hardened. "But I *do not* believe that Fedorem is conspiring with Khalaek. And especially not with the sukrael or these . . . these Wraiths. I *refuse* to believe it."

She said it with such vehemence that Aeren felt himself relaxing. He hadn't known how the Tamaea would react to the implied deceit.

"Even if Fedorem isn't dealing with the Wraiths, Khalaek is. And neither Lotaern nor I have any idea why."

The Tamaea pursed her lips in thought. "Everything Khalaek has done since he ascended in his House has been to bring him closer to the Tamaell. He wants to rule the Evant."

"He wants to rule the Alvritshai," Aeren countered.

"Is there a difference?"

Aeren didn't answer. "What do you think the Tamaell will do about the Legion?"

It was not a question he would normally have asked the Tamaea. She was not a lord, was not part of the Evant. But the fact that she had called him here, the fact that she understood immediately what the presence of the Legion meant . . .

She watched him silently for a long moment, but he could not read her expression. All of her thoughts were hidden.

Like a lord.

"I think," she said, then paused, drawing in a deep breath, letting it out with a weary sigh. "I think he cannot afford to ignore the presence of the Legion."

Aeren nodded and found himself regarding the Tamaea with new eyes. "He can't," he said, and shifted so he could rise, gathering himself to depart. The Tamaea did not stop him. "He won't."

"Then we are headed toward war. Again."

Aeren felt a flare of anger. "It would appear so." He turned toward the tent's opening.

"What about the dwarren? Will he still seek out the dwarren?"

Aeren paused, one hand on the soft material of the flap, holding it back.

In the corridor outside, he saw a flicker of movement, a blurred shadow, nothing more.

He flung the flap back completely, his heart pounding in his chest, his hand falling to the hilt of his cattan, the tent shaking with the force of his movement.

"What is it?" the Tamaea gasped behind him, surging to her feet.

Aeren ignored her, didn't even turn. He scanned the narrow corridor beyond, the folds of cloth undulating in the light and shadows thrown by the lanterns of the room where they'd dined. But he saw nothing, no figures, no shapes. Nothing.

"Shaeveran?" he asked. His voice cracked with tension.

The Tamaea moved up behind him, stared out into the darkness of the tent around him.

"It's nothing," he said. "I thought I saw ..."

"What?"

"A shadow," he said, forcing himself to release the grip on his sheathed blade. He turned to give the Tamaea a reassuring smile but was startled to find her holding a thin knife defensively in one hand. Not one of the knives from the table. This was a fighting knife, one used for close personal combat.

He caught her gaze and saw the challenge in her eyes. She wanted him to ask about the knife, a weapon that no one would expect the Tamaea to possess, let alone know how to use.

Instead, he repeated, "It must have been a shadow."

Disappointment flashed in her eyes, but she nodded. "Very well." Aeren found himself reassessing her yet again. She didn't believe him, but she didn't push him either, moving away from the entrance of the tent. She set the thin blade on the edge of the table containing the remains of their meal. "Let us hope that when it comes to the Legion—and King Stephan—that the Tamaell acts with ... discretion."

Rising from his kneeling position, Aeren said, "Yes. Let's hope."

It was not a hope he believed in.

～

Two days later, Aeren and Eraeth were interrupted by the approach of one of the Tamaell's pages. He halted a respectful distance away after catching their attention.

Aeren felt his chest tighten. "It appears the Tamaell has finally made a decision," he murmured, low enough so only Eraeth could hear.

Eraeth grunted as Aeren motioned the page forward.

"The Tamaell requests your presence," the page said with a short but precise bow of his head and shoulders, then added, "immediately."

Aeren shared a look with Eraeth, and the bands around his chest tightened further. "Gather an escort, Protector. No more than four."

Aeren and his escort halted outside of the council tent less than an hour later as the sun began its descent to the west. There, black clouds could be seen, the tattered fringes scudding toward the encampment. On all sides of the Tamaell's tents, men were hustling to break down and pack away supplies, their actions frantic, and Aeren heard word being spread that the army would head out again within the hour. Servants were cursing, members of the Phalanx as well as they stumbled over them in their own preparations.

Aeren's unease grew, but a moment later the page exited the council tent and said, "The Tamaell and the Tamaell Presumptive are waiting inside."

He found the Tamaell and the Tamaell Presumptive sitting on mounds of pillows surrounding a large rectangular board of polished wood, a map spread over its length, held down with small lead obelisks at the four corners. Numerous other lead figures were strewn out over the map, and as Aeren moved into the room at a gesture from the Tamaell, he realized that the map depicted the entire length and breadth of the plains. Hills and valleys were shown, including the Escarpment. Settlements were denoted with black markings, human, dwarren, and the few Alvritshai villages established on the plains. Water sources were marked in blue, the forests in green. The rest of the map—the grassland—was shaded in various golds and yellows and browns.

The map was beautiful ...

Except for the large black masses of lead figures in three separate locations across the plains.

With one quick glance, Aeren felt his heart shudder and closed his eyes, bowing his head slightly. He sent a small prayer to Aielan, then opened his eyes and met the Tamaell's gaze.

"I see you understand the situation," the Tamaell said, his voice heavy.

"Yes, Tamaell. I believe I do."

The Tamaell nodded and motioned for Aeren to take a seat beside him, opposite the Tamaell Presumptive. Eraeth settled in opposite the Tamaell.

"King Stephan has left me no choice," the Tamaell began. He pointed to the board as he spoke, moving from each massed group of figures to the other. "He's gathered a large force of his Legion here, by our last accounting, and is headed toward the plains. I did not expect him to move, not when he is being pressed on the coast by the continued attacks of the Andovans in their attempt to reclaim their lost colonies. But those attacks *are* affecting Stephan's army. He has not been able to gather as many of the Legion to him as he probably wanted, but he has certainly gathered more than enough to be a threat to us."

"More than we have here in the envoy," Eraeth murmured.

The Tamaell nodded, his expression grim. "Yes." He turned his attention to the group that represented the dwarren, a frown creasing his forehead. "According to the scouts who have managed to get close to the dwarren gathering, there are more dwarren coming to the meeting than expected as well. Again, their force is larger than our own, around three thousand."

"Which means it's a true Gathering," Aeren said. "For that many dwarren to be gathered together at once, there must be at least three clans represented, if not more. This means that the dwarren are serious about seeking peace. They could never have gathered that many clans together otherwise."

"Unless they intend to simply overwhelm us," the Tamaell Presumptive said.

Aeren turned to him, noticed how young he appeared. But not vulnerable. The time spent with the Phalanx on the borders had given the Tamaell Presumptive an edge, a hardness that Aeren did not remember seeing in him before he'd left. "The dwarren have never been able to work together before this."

"Except at the Escarpment. And they were slaughtered there. Do you think that has been forgotten?" The Tamaell Presumptive shifted forward, his eyes narrowing. "I think it more likely that they remember, perhaps too well, and they—all of them—see a chance for reprisal."

Aeren thought back to Garius and their meeting in the dwarren clan chief's tent. He did not think Garius intended vengeance.

However, he could not say the same for Garius' son, Shea.

"The dwarren are not that devious," he said instead. "They are not a subtle race."

The Tamaell replied. "No, they are not. But their intentions are irrelevant. I cannot ignore the presence of the Legion. Not this close, and not with those numbers."

Aeren bowed his head. "You've ordered the envoy to intercept the Legion."

"There is no other option." Aeren couldn't ignore the note of warning in the Tamaell's voice.

"And what of the dwarren? Will we simply leave them?"

The Tamaell frowned, although Aeren couldn't determine whether it was in annoyance or offense. "We will not ignore them either." He shifted, reaching forward to retrieve a new set of lead figures from a flat, narrow box at the edge of the map table. "Unknown to any but Lords Khalaek, Jydell, and Waerren, I've had a force of two thousand mixed Alvritshai House Phalanx gathering on the edge of Alvritshai lands here," he said, placing the figures on the map. "I've sent orders that they are to move immediately, in the hope that they can join with the envoy . . . here." He pointed to a spot on the map and purposefully met Aeren's gaze.

Aeren froze, his body rigid, all the hope he'd held out for the meeting with the dwarren stilled. "The Escarpment."

The Tamaell drew back: "Yes."

In his mind's eye, Aeren could see the movement of the armies, could see them gathering, amassing as they moved toward the break in the land called the Escarpment. For a moment, he thought he could feel the earth shuddering beneath him with the tread of their feet, thought he could hear the clank and rattle and groan as the wagons moved. He smelled the sweat of their bodies, tasted the blood that would be spilled.

"All to come together there," he whispered, barely aware he spoke the thought out loud. "There, on that grass, on that soil. Again."

The words held in the silence for a long moment, somehow potent, throbbing with intensity.

But then the Tamaell leaned forward. "Not all," he said. "You and the Tamaell Presumptive will go to meet with the dwarren as planned. To extend to them my apologies."

18

"**N**O! LEAVE THE CURSED wagon behind!" Servants scrambled, the tents already nothing but lumps of canvas on the grass, rolled up haphazardly and chucked into a stack waiting to be packed. Everything else in the army was being packed and thrown onto wagons as well, but Aeren noticed a few troubled glances among his own servants. He rarely barked orders, or spoke impatiently. They knew something had happened. But all they'd heard was that the army was moving, and they didn't understand why their lord had suddenly decided to split the Rhyssal escort, loading only essentials on the horses, leaving the wagon and everything he wouldn't need for the next ten days with the army.

"Remind me again why we aren't taking the wagon to meet with the dwarren?" Eraeth murmured blandly, as if he were bored.

Aeren frowned in irritation. "Because the Tamaell ordered me to escort the Tamaell Presumptive to the meeting with the dwarren, but he didn't say it had to be at a leisurely pace. I intend to get there as fast as possible, let Thaedoren give the dwarren the Tamaell's regrets," Aeren couldn't keep the bitterness from his voice, "and then catch up to the Tamaell's army as soon as possible. I'll drive the horses into the ground if I have to."

"I see."

Aeren shot his Protector a glare, but Eraeth didn't see it, his face set in a hard frown of concentration.

"Have you informed the Tamaea of what you intend? She may be able to slow the Tamaell down and give you more time."

Aeren considered, then cursed himself. The Tamaell's decision had riled him too much. He wasn't *thinking,* only reacting.

He sauntered to the edge of the main convoy, Eraeth following, then raised a hand to shade his eyes from the sunlight, pretending to scan the horizon. He focused on the head of the army, too distant to pick out individuals. But he could pick out the Tamaea's banner and the small group of figures beneath it.

"She's already waiting for the army to depart. Any message I send would be seen," he said.

"What about Shaeveran? Send him."

Colin had returned from the forest and his meeting with the Faelehgre the night before with no additional news. The Faelehgre hadn't seen any of the Wraiths since the expansion of their territory, and they still had no way to track them using the Wells.

Aeren sighed. "She's in the open. He'd be seen the moment he arrived."

But mention of Colin reminded him of someone else. "Send a message to Lotaern," he said abruptly. "Tell him I need to speak to him. Now."

Eraeth didn't wait to summon a page; he took off himself.

Twenty minutes later, the Chosen of the Order stalked through the remains of the Rhyssal House encampment, escorted by three acolytes and Eraeth.

"What's so important that I must break away from the Order's preparations to depart?" he growled as he came to a stop, his gaze raking the encampment. "This is not an opportune time for a friendly chat. The Tamaell—"

"Has issued orders. I know. But it seems that I am not going to accompany the rest of the convoy on its journey."

That halted Lotaern's rage in its tracks. "What do you mean?"

Aeren motioned him forward and the two stepped away from their escorts, out toward the plains. Lotaern kept up the pretense of indignant anger. "What's happened? I heard you had a private meeting with the Tamaell."

"I did. He intends to take the army to intercept the Legion. The threat they represent is too great to ignore."

"Where is he sending you?"

"To meet with the dwarren. I'm to escort the Tamaell Presumptive so he may extend the Tamaell's apologies for not attending."

"Which means all of your efforts to reach a peace agreement were for naught."

"Yes. But I'm hoping to keep the Tamaell from making the same mistake he made at the Escarpment thirty years ago."

"How?"

"I intend to meet with the dwarren and then return to the army before it reaches the Legion."

Lotaern snorted, then glanced around at the encampment, noting the wagon and the frenzy of activity as the Phalanx and the servants argued over what supplies went where. "You won't make it," he finally said. "Even reducing your weight by half and forcing everyone to ride."

"I know. Which is why I need help."

Lotaern's eyes narrowed skeptically. "I'm the Chosen of the Order, not Aielan herself."

"I need you to warn the Tamaea. Tell her to slow the army down as much as she can."

Lotaern's eyebrows rose. "An interesting ally." Aeren could see him considering the Tamaea's potential. "I'll contact her and relay the message."

~

As soon as the Tamaell sounded the horn to depart, the large convoy lurching into staggered motion, Aeren turned to the Tamaell Presumptive standing beside him. He didn't know Thaedoren well, but what Aeren had seen of him in the council tent had set him on his guard. He remembered him as a boisterous child, tearing around the halls of the Tamaell's quarters or the streets and levels of the city. Then later, as an impetuous young man who defied his father whenever possible, sometimes publicly.

The Alvritshai who stood beside him now, hands holding the reins of an impatient horse, was no boy. He held himself with the confidence of a lord, carried himself like one of the Phalanx. His eyes were steady and completely unreadable.

Aeren saw much of the Tamaell in him and little of the Tamaea.

He frowned. "I would prefer to depart as soon as possible and move swiftly."

Thaedoren's gaze—centered on the convoy, the distance between Aeren's party and the larger group growing—shifted toward Aeren, then back. A slight frown touched the corners of his eyes, his mouth. "Very well."

Aeren nodded to Eraeth, waiting to one side, and the Protector waved Aeren's party into motion. All of the men—the twenty Phalanx from the Rhyssal House, Colin, a few servants, and the ten White Phalanx that formed Thaedoren's personal guard—immediately began to mount.

As Aeren moved to his own horse, brought forward by Eraeth, Thaedoren said, "You hope to return to the army before it reaches the Legion."

His gaze locked on Aeren and held this time, still unreadable.

"Yes."

"My father said you would not be happy with our decision."

Aeren let the anger he held inside flare for a moment. "I worked hard to arrange this meeting with the dwarren," he said. He pushed off from the ground and slid into the saddle, controlling the horse with a few sharp tugs on the reins. "If there's any chance at all to salvage something from it, I will."

He turned his horse away, toward Eraeth, not giving Thaedoren a chance to respond. "Let's move."

~

Nine days later, the small party crested a rise in the plains, the depression where Aeren had first met with Garius below.

It was empty, the ground bare.

Aeren felt his heart shudder, even though he'd known the dwarren would not have arrived yet and would not have camped at the prescribed meeting place itself if they had. They'd ridden hard, as fast as Aeren could push the horses without compromising them, and managed to arrive a few days early. Thaedoren had said nothing, hadn't hindered Aeren in any way, giving command of the party over to him without question, although he kept himself close, his influence felt at all times.

Now, the Tamaell Presumptive said, "Look," and pointed toward the south.

There, on the horizon, a bank of dust angled away to the east, blown by the wind. Aeren squinted into the distance. "How far away are they?"

"Two days at the most," Thaedoren said, without hesitation. He turned and barked orders to make camp, motioning to a place near where Aeren and the others had camped the first time they'd come here, close to the spring. When he turned back, he said, with the granite voice of the Tamaell, "We'll wait for them here, as they expect."

As the young Presumptive nudged his horse around and headed down off the rise, Aeren watched his receding back intently. Eraeth passed Thaedoren on his way toward Aeren on foot, the two exchanging a brief, formal nod.

Aeren dismounted as Eraeth arrived and handed over the reins of his horse.

"You aren't happy," his Protector said in greeting.

Aeren snorted. "I'm not. The Tamaell Presumptive has ordered us to wait for the dwarren to arrive."

"We did arrive early. And the dwarren are close."

When Aeren didn't answer, Eraeth stepped up to his side, staring down at Thaedoren as he merged with the rest of the Phalanx and servants setting up the camp. As they watched, he ordered a group of servants to dismantle what they'd erected of a tent and begin setting it up in a different location, closer to the spring.

"What do you think of him?" Aeren asked. "Now that he's returned. Now that we've traveled a small distance with him."

Eraeth scowled. "He's easy to anger. And he doesn't listen well."

"What Tamaell hasn't been easy to anger?" Aeren countered with a small smile. "He'll learn to listen. I think, in the end, he will be stronger than his father."

"He already has the respect of the Phalanx. The Tamaell sending him to the border was a bold move."

"We both know the Tamaell didn't send him to the border to gain the Phalanx's respect."

Eraeth tactfully didn't respond, a frown darkening his face, one hand rubbing the nose of Aeren's mount when it nudged him from the side. "Will he be wiser than the Tamaell?"

Aeren stirred and glanced toward his Protector, eyebrow raised. "He asked intelligent questions about my preparations for this meeting, about what I thought we can expect. But we'll find out when we meet with the dwarren."

~

"I think," the Tamaell Presumptive said, hesitating before turning to Aeren, tightening his hold on the reins of his mount, "I think the dwarren meant it when they requested this meeting."

Aeren tried not to react to the look of surprise in the Tamaell Presumptive's eyes. "They meant it. Do you think I would have asked the Tamaell to come here otherwise?"

Thaedoren didn't respond, but his expression clearly said he thought Aeren had brought the Tamaell and the Evant out here for nothing. But he'd spent the last thirty years on the border, dealing with dwarren raids. As he turned away, steadying his horse, Aeren could see him reevaluating the situation, his gaze flickering over the meeting tent in the flat below and the dwarren that had amassed beyond.

Aeren shared a look with Eraeth on his other side, then turned back to face the dwarren. He didn't know what Thaedoren had expected or what he'd intended to do, but the confusion on the young lord's face gave him hope.

The dwarren had assembled on the far side of the flat as before, the blue-green cloth of the meeting tent ruffling in a slight wind. Banners had been set into the ground on the dwarren's side, the long triangular pennants rippling, showing the symbols of the dwarren clans, one banner for each. Aeren presumed that the dwarren gathered behind each banner represented that particular clan. One of the banners stood higher than the others, in the center—Harticur's banner, the head of all of the clans, called the Cochen. He could see the clan chiefs and their escorts gathered at the front of each group, all on gaezels, waiting. Harticur sat with four Riders, each of the other chiefs with two. The sun blazed down, glinting on dwarren armor and armbands, although it couldn't warm the winter-chilled air.

In the far distance, one of the plains storms rolled southward. Aeren could hear the distant thunder.

"What are they waiting for?" Thaedoren asked. He fidgeted in his seat, jerking the reins yet again.

Aeren drew breath to answer, but one of the dwarren suddenly stepped from between the gathered ranks and marched out into the flat, carrying a feathered and beaded spear. "That," Aeren said.

"Who is it?"

"One of their shaman. He'll bring everyone to the tents, including us, once he feels it is safe."

Thaedoren's brow creased in irritation, jaw tightening, but he said nothing and simply watched.

The shaman circled the meeting tent once, and then again. He stopped at each of the four entrances, chanted and gestured with his spear, then flung something into the wind with a strangely familiar gesture, one that Aeren didn't recognize until Eraeth grunted and said in surprise, "He's sowing seeds."

After a lengthy pause, the shaman staring out at the passing storm to the east, he nodded as if satisfied, even though his ancient face was set into a black frown. In a strangely informal motion, he gestured for the clan chiefs to approach.

The gaezels leaped forward, Harticur in the lead, the other clan chiefs falling in behind, a huge cry rising from the rest of the dwarren as they sped past the banners, circling around the tent as the cries from the dwarren increased. The shaman watched in silence, although Aeren would have sworn he saw the old man roll his eyes in disgust, and then Harticur and the rest brought their gaezels to a halt in a small group before him, dismounting as the dwarren shouts trailed off.

Harticur approached the shaman, the other clan chiefs and Riders hanging back. Aeren picked out Garius, noticed that one of his Riders was his son, Shea. He didn't recognize any of the other clan chiefs, but he'd never met with any of them personally. Garius ruled the lands closest to the Alvritshai and human borders; he was the only dwarren Aeren had ever dealt with. He'd only heard of Harticur.

Harticur bowed his head, and the shaman placed one

hand on it in a strangely formal and somehow powerful gesture. Aeren could feel it. He couldn't tell if any words were spoken, but Harticur looked up when the shaman removed his hand, and the shaman nodded.

Harticur stalked forward, the others following, and entered the tents, their pace subdued compared to the dramatic ride around the tents. They left their gaezels on the flat, a few of the Riders staying behind to watch over them.

When all the dwarren had entered the meeting tent behind Harticur, the shaman turned toward the Alvritshai gathered on the rise and motioned them forward.

Thaedoren's shoulders tensed, and his horse side-stepped, picking up on his unease. Aeren felt his own stomach clench in apprehension.

"Let's get this over with," Thaedoren said, and nudged his horse forward.

"Not the best attitude," Eraeth muttered, low enough only Aeren could hear, as he and Aeren started forward on their own mounts. The rest of the Alvritshai escort followed suit.

The Alvritshai didn't circle the tent with their horses. Instead, they approached the shaman without a sound except the jangle of harness, the creak of leather, and the snorting of the animals. Thaedoren halted twenty paces from the shaman, and even though, mounted, the Alvritshai loomed over the much smaller dwarren, he stared up at them without a trace of fear. Thaedoren met the shaman's eyes with a challenge, his posture edged in contempt, but when the shaman merely straightened, his expression hardening, Thaedoren relaxed and nodded with a hint of respect.

"Well met," the Tamaell Presumptive said formally in dwarren. "I am Thaedoren Ormae Resue, Tamaell Presumptive of the Alvritshai. I have come to speak to the Gathering, on behalf of my father, the Tamaell Fedorem Arl Resue."

The shaman registered brief surprise at his use of dwarren, but he recovered quickly, eyes narrowing as if he thought Thaedoren had offered some sort of verbal challenge with the gesture. "Harticur, Chief of the Red Sea Clan and Cochen of this Gathering, welcomes you." Then, in the silence that followed, the shaman gave all those in the group a hard look, met each with his own eyes and held the gaze, passing swiftly from person to person.

When his gaze fell on Aeren, the lord felt something deep inside him shiver, for the shaman's eyes were depthless and cold and powerful. He found he couldn't look away, and he drew in a sharp breath and held it. For a moment, the shaman's expression seemed strained, the wrinkles around his eyes tightening—

And then he let Aeren go, turning to look at Eraeth, before finally returning to Thaedoren. Aeren gasped, uncertain exactly what had happened. He wasn't given time to think about it.

"Harticur waits for you inside the meeting hall," the shaman said gruffly. "Enter."

He motioned abruptly with the spear, as if he'd asked them to enter ages ago and didn't understand why they hadn't moved yet. Thaedoren dismounted, although Aeren saw him hesitate, as if he'd taken offense and had considered ending the meeting right there. As soon as he started moving, Aeren followed suit.

They left the horses with two Phalanx and entered the shade of the tent, the wind ruffling the edges of the entrance. Aeren could smell the dampness of the distant storm in the gust, bitter with cold, tasting like metal.

Then he ducked through the interior entrance behind Thaedoren, stepping into the meeting room. The seven dwarren clan chiefs and their escorts—two dwarren each—were already seated on the pillows around the large table. The hint of the winter storm was subsumed by the sweet incense of the dwarren lanterns, the interior already cloudy with drifting smoke. The room was warm but not yet stifling. Thaedoren had halted just inside the entrance, but before Aeren could adjust his breathing enough to speak, the Tamaell Presumptive moved stiffly forward and sat on the empty cushions near the entrance.

Aeren settled to Thaedoren's right, Eraeth beside him. As he shifted to find a comfortable position, Aeren noted that the table would have seated many more, but the dwarren had spread everyone out evenly, a large space between each of the dwarren and their escorts, a larger separation between the dwarren and the Alvritshai. He also noted that the dwarren had unsheathed their swords—no longer than Alvritshai daggers—and set the naked blades before them on the table, the metal catching the occasional flicker of the lantern light.

Beside him, Thaedoren frowned at the swords. His gaze swept through the rest of the dwarren, most sitting with their backs rigid, arms crossed over their chests, watching the three Alvritshai with stern expressions.

Then, slowly, keeping his eyes on Harticur, seated directly across from him, he drew his own cattan, the blade coming free silently, and held it out before him.

The dwarren tensed. Aeren felt sweat break out in the palms of his hands, felt it begin to trickle down his back. Eraeth eased his own hand toward his blade.

Thaedoren twisted his wrist, so that the lantern light gleamed along his sword's length . . . and then he set the blade down before him, mimicking what the dwarren had done.

"Do as I did," Thaedoren said softly, never taking his eyes off Harticur's scarred, angular face. The Cochen had obviously seen many battles, his nose broken at least twice.

Eraeth frowned, but when Aeren removed his blade—slowly, as Thaedoren had done—Eraeth did so as well, his reluctance clear. He shot the dwarren a warning glance as he withdrew his hand.

When all three Alvritshai blades rested on the table, Harticur inclined his head.

"Where," he said in a rough, thickly accented but understandable Alvritshai, "is the Tamaell?"

Aeren closed his eyes, bowed his head, and prayed to Aielan.

Thaedoren straightened where he sat, drew in a deep breath, and began formally, "I have been sent—"

Harticur's hand slammed down onto the thick wood of the table, making all of the swords rattle, the sound like a crack of thunder in the confines of the tent. A few of the dwarren escort flinched, but none of the chiefs moved a muscle.

"Where is the Tamaell?" Harticur repeated into the silence, his voice rising, losing some of its fluency as his anger grew. "Where are the Alvritshai? The Lords of the Evant, the White Phalanx, the wagons and horses that have desecrated our Lands? Where is the Tamaell!"

Thaedoren pulled back slightly from the tirade and regarded Harticur's flushed face, his brow knit into a tight frown, his lips pulled thin. When it became clear that Harticur had finished, he shifted forward, and Aeren's shoulders tensed.

"I have been sent," Thaedoren began again, speaking slowly, his words biting, laced with anger, "by my father, the Tamaell, to extend to you his regrets. His intention was to meet with you here, to speak to you about the possibility of reconciliation. On the way here, a situation on the border with the human Provinces forced him to halt and reassess. He could not ignore the threat the Legion presents, so he has gone to meet it.

"He has sent me here to talk to you of reconciliation in his stead."

Eraeth shot a glance at Aeren, but Aeren didn't move; he kept his gaze locked on the table before him, on the glints of light on his own blade. He could feel the stress in the room, heavy and thick, like the lowering of clouds before a storm, as one of the other dwarren translated everything Thaedoren had said for the clan chiefs who did not speak Alvritshai. When the translator fell silent, the air trembled, stretched. The Tamaell had told him Thaedoren was here to voice his regrets. Aeren had not known that the Tamaell Presumptive intended to initiate the talks. He wondered briefly if that had been the Tamaell's plan all along.

And then, imperceptibly, Harticur relaxed. The dwarren clan chiefs' arms uncrossed as they leaned to whisper to each other. They spoke too low for Aeren to hear—he caught only a word or phrase here and there, all in dwarren. No one spoke to Harticur.

The Cochen broke his locked gaze with Thaedoren and turned to Aeren.

"Is this true?"

Aeren stiffened. Garius must have informed Harticur that he was the one who had initiated the contact, although he didn't risk turning to Garius for confirmation. "Yes. A force of Legion gathered near the border days after the Tamaell and the rest of the Evant departed from Caercaern. The Tamaell halted nine day's hard ride north of here to assess the situation."

"Did you feel the threat was significant enough to draw the Tamaell away?" Garius asked.

Aeren considered, recalling the map in the Tamaell's council tent. "The threat is significant. We estimated there were five thousand Legion on the border."

New conversations broke out among the dwarren as soon as the translator finished, louder than before, and more ominous. Eraeth shifted uncomfortably in his seat at the dwarren's tone, although Aeren was relieved to see he did not reach for his cattan, even though his hand twitched in that direction as two of the dwarren began arguing heatedly, one standing, fist raised as he punctuated his words. The other spat a response, both glaring at each other—

And then Harticur said a single word in dwarren, one Aeren knew. "Silence."

All the clan chiefs fell silent, although neither of the two arguing turned from the other. The tension in the air increased as their expressions darkened, the hand of the one standing clenching and unclenching . . .

But with a sudden snort of disgust, he turned and sat.

None of the dwarren had reached for their blades, had even looked in their direction, and yet Aeren felt sweat running down his arms, felt his shirt sticking to his neck. With effort, he forced his hands, hidden in his lap beneath the table, to unclench.

Leaning forward, his brows drawn close together, Harticur motioned to one of his aides with a sharp word. As the dwarren slapped a roll of thin leather out on the table before them and snapped it open, Harticur said, "Show us where."

Thaedoren leaned forward, face carefully blank, to look at the map, along with Aeren. It had been worked into the leather itself, giving the mountains to the north sharp texture, the plains a wide open region with small impressions of tufts of grass, the forests stained a dark green. A few circles with dwarren symbols pocked the plains in what appeared to be random locations.

Aeren tensed, eyes widening, as he realized what the circles represented: the entrances to the dwarren underground cities, their warrens. The dwarren had, for the most part, kept them hidden for the last two hundred years.

He also noticed something else, something that sent a

shiver of shock through his arms. The plains themselves were interrupted by four straight lines. The westernmost line he recognized as the location of the underground river, which emerged as a huge waterfall at the Escarpment at the human city named Tappinger's Falls. The Alvritshai hadn't ranged far enough south or east to find the others.

But the four lines—the four rivers, he assumed, by the markings on the map, all perfectly straight—converged at a point near the base of the eastern mountains, well east of the forest, deep within dwarren lands. And those lands—the lands that the dwarren claimed according to the map—were far more extensive than the Alvritshai thought.

He would have searched longer, but Harticur repeated, "Show us!"

Thaedoren glanced up, then pointed to a position on the map. "The Legion was amassing here when Lord Aeren and I left my father's convoy. We estimated that he would intercept the human forces here," he shifted his finger slightly to the south, without dropping his gaze from Harticur's, "at the Escarpment."

Harticur blinked once, and even as the translator began to translate for the other dwarren, his face filled with rage. He leaped to his feet with an anguished roar, face red, and in one smooth motion he snatched up his sword from the table and pointed it toward Thaedoren, the length of the blade trembling with his fury. With cries of shock and hisses of anger, most of the rest of the dwarren clan chiefs grabbed their own swords as they lurched back from the table and brandished them, but none of them advanced, leaving Harticur at the front. Only Garius remained seated, his head bowed.

Thaedoren's hand shot out and latched onto Aeren's arm, holding him in place as he instinctively reached for his own sword, but the Tamaell Presumptive could do nothing to stop Eraeth. The Protector's cattan was in hand and trained on Harticur in the space of a breath, before most of the other dwarren had managed to grab their own swords. Eraeth's cattan remained steady, pointed toward Harticur's throat, nearly touching it across the length of the table. Harticur's reach wasn't so long; his sword fell nearly a foot short of Thaedoren's chest.

Harticur didn't notice. His nostrils flared as he breathed

in huge lungfuls of air, chest heaving. "You," he yelled, and his blade wavered. He paused a moment to steady it. "You insult us!"

"No," Thaedoren said, voice utterly calm. "No insult is meant."

Harticur snorted. "You seek to trick us, as you and the humans did before! You expect us to rush to the Escarpment, to protect our borders, and then you and the human army will kill us all."

"This is no trick. Send your scouts on their fleet gaezels to the Escarpment, have them report, if you haven't sent them already. They'll confirm the location of the Legion and the Alvritshai forces. But I have no intention of asking you to go to the Escarpment. That confrontation is between the Alvritshai and the humans; it does not concern the dwarren. If you are interested in talking, we can talk here. If not, then we will leave, and you can return home."

Aeren knew at least three of the Lords of the Evant who would not have been able to act so calmly in the presence of so much rage and with nearly twenty dwarren swords trained on them. But those lords had not been trained in the Phalanx. Aeren's estimation of Thaedoren rose as the Tamaell Presumptive eased back in his seat. His grip on Aeren's arm tightened once—in reassurance or warning, Aeren wasn't certain—and then released, falling to his lap. His own cattan still rested, untouched, on the table.

To either side of Harticur, the dwarren clan chiefs who'd stood began grumbling, muttering to each other, voices steadily rising into heated arguments. Harticur listened intently for a long moment, his eyes fixed on Thaedoren, measuring him, but slowly some of the rage that suffused his face seeped away.

He lowered his sword, and after a suitable interval, Eraeth withdrew his own blade. Aeren wasn't certain Harticur had even noticed the Protector's cattan.

The arguing dwarren quieted, focusing on Harticur.

Voice still rough with anger, the head clan chief said shortly, "The Gathering must discuss this."

Thaedoren nodded, and Harticur stepped back, away from the table, the rest of the dwarren—including Garius—retreating with him. One of the aides rolled the map up with smooth precision and spread it out again on the floor where the dwarren gathered, all of the clan chiefs leaning forward over it. The discussion began immediately, the dwarren speaking far too fast and too low for Aeren to follow.

Thaedoren touched his shoulder, and the three Alvritshai moved farther back, toward the edge of the tent, near one of the tables with burning incense and a tray of fresh fruit. The Tamaell Presumptive picked up something small, brown, and fuzzy with a frown, sniffed it, then broke the skin with one finger. Peeling the skin back, he bit into the greenish-yellow interior, grunting in surprise before peeling the rest of the skin off and eating everything but the pit.

When he reached for a second, Aeren said, "Neither you nor the Tamaell mentioned that you intended to hold the talks in his absence."

"I didn't intend to hold the talks."

"Any particular reason why?"

Thaedoren frowned. Aeren had let his irritation creep into his voice. "I didn't believe the dwarren intended to take the talks seriously, didn't even think that the dwarren would be here to meet us." He glanced toward the Gathering, now hunched so far over the map that their heads were practically touching. "I assumed that they'd send a token force, that at most I'd have to placate them with the Tamaell's absence, and then we'd be on our way."

"But?" Eraeth prompted.

Thaedoren shifted his gaze to the Protector. It narrowed, as if he'd suddenly realized that he was speaking to a member of the Phalanx, not a lord. But then his stance shifted, and Aeren was again reminded that Thaedoren was not Fedorem. "My father did not intend for me to hold the talks either, only to offer his regrets in the hopes that they could be renewed later. Yet his intent in coming here was honorable. He sought peace. I did not believe peace would be possible because of the massacre at the Escarpment. But then the dwarren arrived, and I realized they were serious. I've seen what the tension on the border between Alvritshai lands and dwarren lands is like firsthand. If there is a chance, however slim, to end it . . ."

When Thaedoren turned back to look at the huddled dwarren, Aeren shared a glance with Eraeth, eyebrows raised.

This was not the impression he'd gotten of Thaedoren in the council tent with the army.

"My father and I have had our differences," Thaedoren said a moment later. "In fact, we have not agreed on anything for the past thirty years. But we are as one in this. We want the conflict with the dwarren to end. It is the only reason I returned from the border and the Phalanx at my father's request."

The dwarren's voices suddenly rose, Harticur and Garius arguing viciously with two other clan chiefs. The fight escalated, until Harticur cut everyone off with a half growl, half shout. One of the dwarren sat back with a snort and gesture, the other spat to the side, and the remaining clan chiefs grumbled. Harticur silenced them all with a glare, then turned his attention to the Alvritshai.

He stood and motioned to the table, stepping forward as the other dwarren rose, some reluctantly.

"Let's see what they have to say," Thaedoren said, his voice neutral.

As soon as the Alvritshai were settled again, Harticur drew his sword and set it formally, meaningfully, on the table. The rest of the dwarren followed his lead, although the two who had argued the most slammed their blades down. At a nudge from Aeren, Eraeth laid his cattan in front of him as well, although he kept his eyes on the two dissenting dwarren.

"What of the urannen?" Harticur waved to one side, toward the east. "The darkness, the night."

Aeren frowned, knew that Thaedoren had done the same by the shift in his posture.

"What do you mean?" the Tamaell Presumptive asked.

Harticur scowled. "The urannen! The ones who guard! The ones who rage! The darkness and the lights!"

Aeren sucked in a sharp breath, and something cold and bitter stole into his chest, squeezing it tight. "He means the sukrael," he said.

Beside him, Thaedoren tensed. "What about the sukrael?"

"Did you set them free?

Thaedoren drew himself upright, his eyes going dark in defiant affront . . . but not in shock, Aeren noticed. "The Alvritshai would never set the sukrael free. They are a desecration to Aielan's Light, to everything living. They consume it, destroy it!" Thaedoren seemed to catch himself. He exhaled in a long sigh. "But we have noticed that the sukrael have become more active."

Harticur studied Thaedoren's face intently, then nodded slowly as he leaned back. He said something to the other dwarren, received a few grudging nods and grunts of assent in return.

"The urannen—the sukrael," he said the Alvritshai word carefully, "have left the forest. They've begun to attack the dwarren. They've invaded our cities, our tunnels, our sacred grounds."

Thaedoren nodded. "They have attacked our easternmost House lands as well. Entire villages have been found dead."

Harticur growled, a low rumble from the chest. "The same for us. It is why we have Gathered, why we have chosen a Cochen. Something must be done. It is why we are here, why we came. If the urannen have begun to move, if the world is Turning, we cannot fight among ourselves. We cannot fight with you. We must fight the urannen, fight the terren, the gruen and the kell."

All the dwarren stirred at the mention of the Turning, shifting uncomfortably in their seats as Harticur named each of the creatures. Aeren had no idea what the terren, gruen, and kell were, but he felt a shiver course through him as their names were spoken.

Drawing himself upright, Harticur glanced around at his fellow clan chiefs, received sharp nods from all of them, including those who'd dissented earlier, then turned to Thaedoren.

"The Gathering wishes to discuss a formal treaty with the Alvritshai." Aeren felt relief flood through him, more powerful than the unease he'd felt as the dwarren mentioned the Turning and the other creatures. His hands, chest, and arms tingled with the release of tension, and he exhaled sharply.

But Harticur was not finished.

"But we cannot do so here, with you," he said gravely. "We must speak to the Tamaell, with all of the Alvritshai lords. We have been promised a formal apology for the desecration to our Lands, to appease Ilacqua, and an agreement to honor those Lands. So it is the agreement of the Gathering that we will travel with you to the Tamaell's side. We will come to the Escarpment to meet with the Tamaell."

"The Tamaell didn't inform the entire Evant of the attacks of the sukrael."

Thaedoren turned to Aeren as they watched the dwarren encampment break down in a mad rush of short dwarren figures. Close by, the ancient shaman directed a large group of dwarren as they tore down the meeting tent, chanting the entire time in a frenzy, with an occasional disapproving shake of his head and a black frown. The meeting with the clan chiefs had barely ended, and the remnants of the storm were still on the southern horizon. Harticur hadn't given any of them, Alvritshai or dwarren, time to react. Within a heartbeat of his pronouncement, he'd stood and ordered the dwarren to prepare for the march.

"It was decided that until we knew more, the attacks would be kept secret," Thaedoren said.

"Decided by whom?"

"Be my father and Lord Vaersoom. And Lotaern. My father has been working closely with him regarding these attacks, since the sukrael fall under Aielan's purview."

Aeren nodded. "Then there's something you should know."

And Aeren told him of what he and Lotaern had discovered regarding Lord Khalack. Thaedoren's attention was still fixed on the dwarren encampment at first, but by the end, it was centered on Aeren.

"You should have warned us sooner," he said at the end, his voice edged with anger.

"I have no evidence to support my suspicions about Lord Khalaek, and our rivalry within the Evant is well known. Any accusation I made would have been seen as a personal attack, nothing more. Would you or Fedorem have believed the word of a human?"

"That was for us to decide!" Thaedoren snapped, and Aeren drew himself upright defensively. But Thaedoren suddenly turned away, looking down toward the Alvritshai

camp, which was nearly packed up. Aeren felt new tension
radiating from him, a palpable force, evident in his stance,
in his clenched jaw, in the hardness of his features.

"Someone has to get back to the convoy," he said suddenly, tightly. "As fast as possible."

"Why?"

"Because having the dwarren join us at the Escarpment
was never part of the plan. Someone has to warn my father.
And someone needs to tell him about the possibility that
the sukrael and these Wraiths may be working with Lord
Khalaek."

19

NEITHER AEREN, ERAETH, nor any of the other four members of House Rhyssal's Phalanx guard saw Colin until he blurred into existence twenty paces in front of their charging horses, staff canted to one side. At least two members of the escort cried out in surprise, and Eraeth barked a sharp warning, but Aeren had already pulled back on his mount's reins. Dirt churned up from the ground as the horses on all sides were jerked to a halt, the guards cursing. One had to back away, nearly trampling Colin where he stood.

Colin didn't flinch, his face grim as the escort regrouped, milling about around Aeren and Eraeth. "We're too late," he said.

"What do you mean—" Eraeth began, but Aeren cut him off with a sharp gesture.

Everyone fell silent. Aeren listened to the heaving breath of the horses, caught the whistle of the wind over the dead autumn grasses—

And then he heard it, in a gust from the north, the unmistakable sound of swords striking armor, almost buried beneath a lower rumble that he could mistake for the wind but knew with a sick heart was the sound of men bellowing, screaming, and dying.

Aeren felt the Phalanx's mood change, felt the air pull taut as they shifted positions in their saddles, could almost taste the metal of the cattans as if they'd already drawn them.

"What do we do?" Eraeth asked, although it sounded as if he already knew the answer.

"Thaedoren ordered us to warn the Tamaell of the dwarren's arrival," Aeren said; he caught Eraeth's nod of agreement, then turned to Colin. "Show us."

Colin pointed toward the north and east with his staff. "There." And then he blurred and was gone, a black smear, an afterimage on the eye—

And within the space of an indrawn breath, he reappeared over a hundred yards beyond.

"Move!" Eraeth commanded, and Aeren and the Phalanx kicked their horses forward, heading toward Colin. As soon as they neared the human's location, he blurred again, reappearing farther along, leaping ahead as the horses charged across the flattened dead grass, churning up clods of dirt and roots and brittle grass behind them. The sounds of the battle built until Aeren could hear them over the pounding of his own horse's hooves, over his own harsh breath, and he tensed. He'd seen such battles before, fought in them, grown to hate them. A wash of grief filled him, unwanted and unexpected, and he could feel his brother's blood on his hands, warm and thick and drying in the sunlight. Tears burned in his eyes and phlegm clogged the back of his throat.

But then they crested a low rise, not even high enough to be called a hill, and the current battle came into view, a dark spill of horses, Alvritshai, and men across the battered and beaten grass.

The breadth of it sucked Aeren's breath away and he lurched back unexpectedly, pulling his horse up short again, the animal snorting and stamping its foot. At a shout from Eraeth, the rest of the Phalanx halted as well, returning to Aeren's side. Colin saw them halt and vanished, blurring into place so close to Aeren's horse that he skittered to one side with a jerk.

"What's wrong?" Eraeth asked, voice tense. He scanned the battle, eyes flickering left and right.

"We can't charge into that," Aeren said shortly. "There are only seven of us. We need to find the Tamaell, or the Tamaea. Or Lotaern."

Eraeth nearly protested, straightening where he sat, but as the Protector watched the battle, the tide of men and Alvritshai flowing back and forth, he grudgingly sat back in the saddle.

The Phalanx fidgeted on their horses, a few pacing their mounts closer to the fighting. Aeren watched in silence. Screams rose into the air, tattered and torn by the wind, coming in gusts, along with the familiar coppery taste of blood. Alvritshai fell upon a human contingent, the cries of the men muted at first, then suddenly loud as the wind shifted, as if the fight were happening twenty paces away instead of over two thousand. A group of Alvritshai on horseback were repulsed by a human charge, the horses banking away, circling around, one body dragged behind, a foot trapped in a stirrup. The horse trampled two more bodies already lying on the ground as it panicked at the unfamiliar weight pulling at it, and the body jerked free, falling loosely among the dozens of corpses already littering the ground.

Aeren grimaced, bile rising at the back of his throat. He swallowed as he watched the rest of the Alvritshai group rejoin the fray at the rear.

"House Licaeta," Eraeth said. At Aeren's raised eyebrow, he added, "I recognize the style of the riding . . . and the colors on the saddle."

Aeren frowned, focusing on the battle again, trying to pick out colors. He hadn't looked too closely at first, too sickened by the ferocity and the deaths. "Do you see the Tamaell's colors?"

"There," one of the Phalanx guards said, pointing, "to the left of center, where the fighting is thickest. You can see the House Resue banner."

Eraeth asked. "Do you see it?"

Aeren stood up higher in the saddle, then caught the red and white flare of the Tamaell's pennant. "I see it." He settled back with a frown. "We'll never reach him."

"Not with only an escort of six," Eraeth agreed.

His gaze fell on Colin and remained there for a long moment.

"No," Aeren said. When Eraeth looked up, a protest on his lips, he repeated more firmly, "No." He knew what Eraeth was thinking, and he wouldn't allow it. Not for something as trivial as this. They could wait. The dwarren wouldn't be arriving for at least another two days.

Eraeth sat back, disgruntled. "Then what will we do?"

"We'll find the Alvritshai camp and report to the Tamaea instead."

Eraeth shot him a surprised look, but Aeren had already begun searching the plains, drawing upon old memories of the Escarpment. Old, bloody, dark memories. He tried to push those memories away, focusing on what he remembered of the land around the Escarpment before the fighting had started. If the Tamaell had been coming from the south, and the Legion had already arrived, then the most likely place for the Tamaell to set up his encampment would be ...

"There," Eraeth said, pointing toward the east.

Aeren had already turned. He could see figures on a rise watching the battle, one of the Lords of the Evant who'd been left behind to guard the camp. On the battlefield, the lords were subordinate to the Tamaell, their individual House Phalanxes subject to the Tamaell's orders first, then their lord's. The tents and wagons and the rest of the support were mostly hidden behind the rise, although a few banners and the tops of a few tents could be seen.

"Let's go." Aeren nudged his horse into motion, picking up speed. He banked wide, keeping his distance from the battle, approaching the camp and the Phalanx on guard from the south. The Phalanx saw them approaching, and a sortie of twenty headed toward them along the top of the ridge.

Aeren swore when they rode close enough to see their colors: black and gold.

The sortie spread out, and Aeren slowed, motioning the rest of his escort to fall back slightly. He could see the rest of the encampment now, and the plains beyond, but his attention remained fixed on the Alvritshai lord who stood at the front of the sortie where it had halted, waiting.

"Lord Khalaek," he said as he pulled his mount to a stop. He did not nod formally, and his voice was cold and stiff.

"So," Khalaek said, looking past him toward his escort. "Have you managed to get the Tamaell Presumptive killed? Is this all that remains of the entourage sent to meet with the dwarren?" He paused for a moment, then added blandly, "Were they even there?"

Aeren gripped the reins tightly, but he refused to be baited. "The Tamaell Presumptive is following behind us, with the rest of the escort. We were sent ahead to speak to the Tamaell."

Khalaek's eyes narrowed in suspicion, his previous mild amusement gone. "About what?"

"That is for the Tamaell alone."

Khalaek said nothing, but Aeren could see him considering options. His dark eyes flicked toward Colin, standing far back in the group, as unobtrusive as possible, then toward the south and east, the direction he knew they'd come from, but the plains were empty there.

Not satisified, Khalaek motioned toward the battle. "As you can see, the Tamaell is currently occupied."

"And he left you behind," Aeren said. "Interesting."

Khalaek twitched the reins he held in one hand, his horse shuffling at the movement. "Someone needs to protect the Tamaea. We wouldn't want anything to happen to her, now would we?"

Eraeth shifted forward at the underlying threat, but Aeren didn't react.

To the west, battlehorns cried out, distantly. A gust of wind pushed past them and sent the pennant that Khalaek's sortie carried flapping. Aeren and Khalaek held each other's gazes, the hatred between them palpable. Aeren could taste it.

But a ripple of strange but familiar movement caught his attention out of the corner of his eye.

He turned to the east with a frown—

And the bitterness and hatred bled out of him in one shocked breath. "Aielan's Light," he said, voice filled with a terrified awe.

"What is it?" Khalaek demanded, voice tinged with anger and doubt, as if he thought Aeren's gasp some kind of trick. But then he turned.

Aeren saw him stiffen in his saddle, then spit a curse under his breath. On all sides, the sortie and Aeren's escort gasped, Eraeth edging his horse out in front of Aeren reflexively.

On the plains, still distant but approaching fast, one of the occamaen—what Lotaern would call a "breath of heaven," and what Colin called a Drifter—slid toward them. It was beautiful in a way, its rippled distortions stretching high into the sky and even farther to either side, its center clear, like an eye. Through that eye, Aeren could see the plains beyond . . . but altered. Sunlight glowed on the horizon there, the clouds in the sky suffused with a purple-orange haze, the grass on the ridges a vibrant, spring green, waving in a contrary wind.

Aeren glanced up at the sun that glared down on the autumn-dead grass at his feet and shuddered. The juxtaposition—two suns, one setting, one angled an hour after midday; early spring grass against late autumn—twisted in his stomach.

"It's huge," Eraeth said.

"And it's headed straight for the camp," Khalaek hollered. He spun his mount and roared out orders, his sortie breaking into two groups, one headed toward where the occumaen bore down on the camp from the east, the other, including Khalaek, headed toward the rest of Khalaek's men on the ridge behind them, both groups shouting and pointing as they charged their horses across the grass. The men on the ridge hadn't seen the danger yet, were watching either the battle below or the confrontation with Aeren. After a moment of confusion, they turned . . . and then broke into sudden motion as Khalaek arrived. Horns sounded, piercing the air, frantic and warbly. In the camp below, men and women turned from whatever task they were doing in confusion, but they couldn't see the occumaen, not within the confines of the tents and wagons.

Aeren swore. They weren't reacting fast enough. The occumaen bore down with silent, deadly grace. And with sudden dawning horror, Aeren realized Eraeth had been right. It was huge, large enough and wide enough to encompass at least half the camp, if not more.

"What do we do?" Eraeth asked, and Aeren latched onto his strangely calm voice.

Thinking furiously, cursing the small number of Phalanx he'd brought with him, he scanned the growing chaos in the camp below as Khalaek's men fanned out, charging into the tents still mounted, shoving and herding people outward, away from the occumaen's path.

And then his gaze fell on the white and red banners near the center of the camp. The Tamaell's banners.

His eyes widened. "The Tamaea."

Eraeth reacted faster than he did, spinning and shouting, "Colin!"

Without any hesitation, Colin shifted and blurred.

~

Colin raced down the slope toward the camp, time slowed around him but not stopped. Glancing back over his shoulder, he saw Aeren, Eraeth, and the rest kicking their mounts into motion, heading down toward the camp itself, but then he shoved the Alvritshai lord from his mind and focused on reaching the Tamaea.

The Drifter loomed large to the east, a coruscating array of light, mostly white but with iridescent shadings, its arms reaching out like antennae, tasting the air on all sides. The scent of the Well, of new earth and pine and dry leaves, crashed into him, so strong he felt his body shuddering in reaction, the craving for the Well almost overwhelming. He shoved that craving aside and forced himself not to look at the black mark on his arm, the black mark that had expanded each time he'd been within reach of the Well's power and now throbbed with pain.

He slowed as he reached the outskirts of the camp, slid among the tents, around the Alvritshai who were now scattering as Lord Khalaek's Phalanx warned them of the Drifter. Some of them had already seen it and were fleeing into the grass, their faces etched with terror. Colin didn't stop, slipping through their mad rush caught in slow motion, brushing by their outstretched arms and bodies, keeping the white and red banners of the Tamaell's tents in sight. He passed Khalaek, the lord caught in mid-shout, his face contorted and ugly with panic. Two of his Phalanx in black and gold were shoving people toward the edge of camp; one woman overbalanced, crashing into the folds of the tent behind her. The scene was eerie with no sound to accompany it, but he didn't pause, didn't stop to help.

There wasn't time. The taste of the Drifter had grown stronger.

He burst through a section of tents and found the White Phalanx guards of the Tamaell standing alert and on edge. But they hadn't seen the Drifter yet, were reacting to the chaos created by Khalaek and his own Phalanx, hands on their swords. Colin moved past them, searched through the Tamaell's tents until he saw the Tamaea's to one side, more guards stationed in front of it. He squeezed through the half-open tent flap, praying to Diermani and Aielan that the Tamaea would be there, but he was drawn up short by the closed tent flaps on the inner rooms.

Spitting a curse, he let the world return to normal.

Sound crashed into the silence: screams, bellowing horns, the harsh rasp of the canvas tent thrashing in an unnatural wind. Colin sucked in a sharp breath—the wind must be coming from the Drifter—then filtered the raucous noise out and focused in on the sounds from inside the tent as he shoved the nearest flap aside. The room inside was empty, so he dodged down to the next, pushing it aside with his staff.

And then he heard someone snap in a troubled, impatient voice, "Oh, stop it, Faeren. If there's something to worry about, the Phalanx will tell us!"

Colin let the flap fall and crossed the corridor to where the voices had come from, throwing the flap back more roughly than he'd intended. Inside, the Tamaea's personal servant shrieked, drawing back at the sudden movement, her eyes wide with fright. The Tamaea turned, eyes narrowing. Her hand slid to something concealed in her sleeve.

In a cold voice, she said, "Who are you?" in Alvritshai. But then recognition flickered across her face. Tension in her shoulders—what Colin had at first taken to be regal composure—softened, although her hand did not move from its place inside her sleeve. "You're the human Aeren brought with him." Hope flared in her eyes, as Colin struggled to piece together the Alvritshai words. Eraeth had taught him much of the language, and he'd learned some during his time at the Well, but everyone still spoke too fast. "Has Aeren returned? Is Thaedoren here?"

Colin stepped into the room, spoke slowly in broken Alvritshai. He could understand it much better than he could speak it. "No time. A Drifter—an occumaen—is coming. Leave now."

The Tamaea shifted uncertainly. The tent shuddered again in the unnatural wind, and behind her, the servant sobbed slightly, looking upward.

"How did you get past the Phalanx?" the Tamaea asked suspiciously.

"No time!" Colin barked, and reached out to grab her arm, to physically force her to follow him.

With a flick of her hand, the Tamaea withdrew a knife from her sleeve, holding the blade before her.

Colin froze, hand half extended. The tent shuddered again, more violently. Outside, they could now hear screams and shouts beneath the wind, closer than before. He could *feel* the Drifter, a pressure against his skin, tingling in the hairs on the back of his neck.

Slowly, he drew back. His eyes were locked with the Tamaea's, pleading with her. He nearly growled in frustration, but he forced himself to remain calm. He gave up on Alvritshai and used Andovan instead. "Aeren sent me. To get you out of the Drifter's path. Come outside and you'll see."

Then he turned and slipped through the opening, moving down the short corridor toward the tent's entrance. He waited a moment there, watching for the Tamaea, for the servant, Faeren.

What seemed an eternity later, Faeren slid out into the corridor, stilled as she caught sight of him, then murmured something to the Tamaea inside. As Faeren held the flap open, the Tamaea stepped into the corridor, straightening slowly.

Colin could barely contain himself. The pressure of the Drifter now felt like a heavy blanket, smothering him from all sides, settling in his gut. The fine hairs on his arms stirred, prickling as they stood upright.

Before any of them could move, one of the Phalanx guardsmen burst through the main entrance with a desperate, "Tamaea! Tamaea, we have to leave here now!"

He pulled up short as he saw the Tamaea and Faeren in the corridor, saw the knife in the Tamaea's hand.

And then he sensed Colin.

His cattan flashed from its sheath, the blade out and passing through the space where Colin had stood an instant before in less than a heartbeat. But Colin had already shifted, slowed time enough to see the swing of the blade, the bead of sweat that flicked from the Alvritshai guardsman's nose as he turned, the shift in expression on the guard's face—from panic to a grim, deadly determination.

When he let time return, he stood halfway between the guard and the Tamaea.

Faeren gasped. The guard recovered quickly, turning to where Colin now stood with a cold intensity . . . and a much more guarded and wary stance.

"Grae!" the Tamaea snapped over the increasing roar of the wind. "Leave him. He came to warn me of the occumaen. He's part of Lord Aeren's party."

Grae didn't relax, the look in his eyes easy enough to read. He didn't believe her, but he didn't want to defy her either. Colin held his gaze, ready to shift again if necessary—

But then the Tamaea intervened, stepping between them. Colin noticed her knife had vanished back into her sleeve as she passed. Grae was forced to lower his blade. He took his eyes off of Colin reluctantly to face her.

"Faeren, come," the Tamaea said, stooping to brush her way out of the tent. As she did so, a gust of frigid air shook the tent, threatening to rip the stakes from the ground. Colin saw the Tamaea's dress and hair whipped to the side as she raised one hand to protect her face and glanced upward.

And then her eyes widened, and she swore, although Colin couldn't hear the words. They were lost to the wind.

Faeren slid past Grae and Colin and joined the Tamaea. Grae glared at Colin, turning his back only as he ducked outside. Colin followed.

The wind stole Colin's breath away, slamming into him with a violence and force he'd never felt before. Men and women were screaming and running on all sides, dodging debris in the air as tents shivered and shuddered. Before he could turn, one of those nearest collapsed with a sudden *whoomph,* stakes and ropes flailing, chunks of dirt thrown into the air and whipped away. The tough canvas snapped and cracked, a few stakes still holding it in place, and then those gave and it tore free of the earth, carried up and away. Horses reared, men desperately trying to control them, a few riderless mounts tearing through the encampment as they fled.

Colin turned into the wind, dust and grit stinging his skin, his eyes tearing up . . . and felt his heart shudder in his chest.

The Drifter was almost upon them. He could see the setting sun through its eye, and that eye stretched up and up, higher than most of the trees on the plains. It stretched to the left and right even more, larger than the Well.

It would swallow them all.

He turned toward the Tamaea, toward Faeren and Grae and the rest of the Phalanx who'd been waiting outside for the Tamaea to join them, and bellowed at the top of his voice in Alvritshai, "RUN!"

His roar broke the Tamaea's paralysis. Without waiting for her Phalanx, without waiting for Faeren or Grae, she spun and headed away from the Drifter, angling toward its nearest edge, her dress thrashing in the winds, slowing her down.

They ran, the pressure of the Drifter threatening to crush Colin to the ground, the scent of the forest, of loam and leaves, choking him. The taste of the Well filled his mouth, his body clenched with longing. He fled without looking back, could feel the Drifter rushing forward, the howl of the winds increasing even more, the earth seeming to tremble beneath his feet. Splinters of wood and stalks of dried grass sliced across his exposed skin, and small pebbles pelted him. A tent torn free from the ground caught one of the guards ahead and he fell, thrashing as it bore him to the ground, but none of the Phalanx stopped. None even slowed. Terror clutched at Colin's heart, pulsed in his blood, the same terror he saw on all their faces, even the Tamaea's. The facade of her rank had been completely stripped away, leaving nothing behind but raw panic and unadulterated fear.

Then, out of the corner of his eye, he saw the edge of the Drifter sweeping across the tents and grass beside them, sucking them into the eye, into its heart, and he felt a single moment of clarity through the pounding of his heart.

"We aren't going to make it," he whispered.

There, in the infinite space between one heartbeat and the next, without any conscious thought, his hand snapped out and caught the Tamaea's arm—

And he shifted and *pushed*.

He cried out as something inside threatened to tear apart, something vital, wrenched in two different directions at once. His body tried to slow, but the Tamaea's body held him back, like a weight, anchoring him to the real world, to real time. He'd never tried to draw anything along with him larger than a flower, a lock of hair, or his staff, never anything as large as another person. He dragged the Tamaea toward him, shoved against the pull of time harder, tried to envelope her with the throbbing pulse of the Well he could feel inside himself, which was echoed in the Drifter itself, and felt the world twisting around him, pulling taut, the muscles of his body screaming at the resistance.

Then, with a wrench, time gave, the wind halted, and the Tamaea lurched into his body. He wrapped the arm carrying his staff around her, drew her in tight, heard her scream in panicked terror as she fell, her other arm thrashing. She clawed him across the face, her fingernails sinking in deep, and then they were rolling on the ground, Colin gasping, but holding onto the Tamaea with a death grip, knowing that if he let her go, she'd be lost, caught back up in the tide of time, and the Drifter would have her.

They rolled to a stop, the Tamaea still struggling, tangled up in her dress, in the staff, until Colin cried out, "Stop!"

She halted immediately, trembling in his embrace, and with an effort that Colin felt shudder through her body, she stilled.

"What's happened?" she heaved, her breath coming in ragged hitches. "What have you done?"

She tried to pull away from him, a new horror crossing her face, directed at him.

"Don't," he barked, and he heard the weakness in his voice. He could feel himself trembling as well, shudders running through his body. In a halting voice, in Alvritshai, he said, "Don't let go . . . or you'll end up . . . back there." He swallowed, the tremors in his arms increasing. His grip on time slid slightly, not enough for the Tamaea to notice, but enough to make him gasp.

He wouldn't be able to hold them here long. Not both of them.

"We have . . . to move," he managed, stirring.

"You're shuddering," the Tamaea said. Now that he'd told her not to let go, she seemed determined not to move at all. "Are you hurt?"

"No. But we have . . . to move . . . Must move." He glanced significantly at the Drifter.

The Tamaea looked in its direction, and he felt her stiffen. It hovered over the tents, the chaos caught and held, debris in the air, Faeren, Grae, and the Phalanx suspended in midcharge, their terror clear. The iridescent arms of the

Drifter, invisible except for here, swept back and forth greedily, as if tasting everything before it gathered it into its eye. One of those arms flickered past overhead, and the Tamaea flinched.

"It's so beautiful," she whispered, but her voice was layered with dread.

Colin pushed her away slightly. "We have to move."

She responded to the urgency in his voice, wincing as she shifted away, his grip on her arm so tight her skin had turned white with the pressure. He tried to relax it, but he was afraid to let her go.

They climbed to their feet, Colin stumbling, his legs giving way beneath him, using the staff for support. The Tamaea caught him, held him upright. "What's wrong?"

"My legs," Colin gasped. "Weak. Holding you here is—"

He cried out as he stumbled again, and the Tamaea shrugged his arm over her shoulder, supporting his weight.

"Then let's move," she said, and she began half-dragging, half-pulling him forward. She'd regained some of her composure and drew the mantle of the Tamaea around her like a shield.

They staggered out of the tents, past men and women, horses and guardsmen. The farther they moved, the looser Colin's grasp on time grew, and slowly the Tamaea began to notice as first they felt the breath of the wind, then gusts, and on all sides the people and debris began to take on visible motion. She lurched forward at a faster pace, the world picking up speed around them.

"Can't—" Colin gasped, swallowing hard. "Can't hold it."

And then he lost his grip completely.

Both of them cried out as they fell to the ground, Colin releasing his hold on her arm. The wind howled overhead, spattering them both with debris, and Colin rolled to his side.

To catch the verge of the Drifter sweeping past overhead, the ripples of the distortion no more than six feet away. Every hair on his body prickled and stood on end, energy pouring over him, filled with the taste of the Well, the loam and leaves so thick on his tongue he thought he'd swallowed dirt. His body shuddered with the ecstasy of the Well, with its blatant potency, and he felt tears streaming down his face.

Then it passed by, the sensations fading, the roar of the wind dying, and he collapsed onto the grass on his back.

Beside him, he felt the Tamaea stir, sit upright—

And then she screamed, "Faeren!" A tortured scream, choked with tears.

He felt the Tamaea scrambling to her feet and, body shaking with weakness, a strange lethargy stealing through him, he managed to roll back onto his side. He couldn't lift his head. The effort was too great.

He watched, dead grass pricking his cheek, as the Tamaea stumbled out into the remains of the camp. Where the Tamaell's tents had stood, there was nothing but a swath of exposed earth. To either side, the ground was littered with collapsed tents, tattered canvas still fluttering to the ground. And bodies. Most were beginning to stir, moans and groans replacing the fading winds. The Tamaea worked her way through the detritus, took a few steps out into the empty earth, and then halted.

Faeren, Grae, and the rest of the Phalanx who had run with them from the Tamaea's tent were gone, swallowed by the Drifter, along with a significant chunk of the camp itself.

And the Drifter hadn't faded.

Colin fell onto his back again.

No, the Drifter wasn't finished. He could still feel it.

～

"Look!"

Aeren shifted his attention from trying to control his frenzied mount out toward the plains, in the direction the Phalanx member had pointed. The group of Phalanx—from both House Rhyssal and House Duvoraen—had gathered on the ridge above the camp, other Phalanx members and servants scattered among them. All of them had expressions of exhaustion and horror on their faces as they watched the huge occumaen wreak havoc among the tents. It pushed its way westward, tents flailing in its winds like birds, debris whirling in a deadly storm. People ran in all directions as it plowed its way forward, swallowing tents and earth whole. Those caught at the edges were sliced in half. Aeren could see at least two crawling away from it, a woman without an arm and a man without legs.

Those closer to the eye simply . . . vanished. Once the occumaen passed by, they were gone, nothing left behind,
simply gone.

Breath of Heaven. They'd been called to Aielan.

He felt an overwhelming horror creep through him, his
body going numb with shock. His heart still pounded from
the mad dash into the camp, yelling and bellowing, trying
to goad people up and away before the occumaen hit, followed by the scramble to get out of its way himself. One of
his own Phalanx hadn't made it, he and his horse caught in
its eddies as they tried to flee.

Now, body still numbed and shaking, he saw what the
Phalanx guard had pointed out.

There, on the edge of the occumaen, he saw a smear of
motion, a shadow drawing away from the distortion that
lurched and solidified into Colin and the Tamaea. His heart
leaped with hope, and then the two stumbled and fell to
the ground.

The arm of the occumaen—the Breath of Heaven—
passed above them. Their bodies rippled with its distortions, as if they were trapped beneath heat waves . . . and
then it slid by, leaving them unscathed.

An uncertain cheer spread through the group, led by his
own Phalanx, who understood what the smeared shadow
had been. The rest picked up on it when the Tamaea
lurched to her feet and staggered toward the remains of
the camp. He thought she'd fall to her knees in the churned
up dirt where tents had stood mere moments ago, but he
saw her shoulders stoop instead.

"Berec, Larren, take a contingent down to get the
Tamaea, immediately!"

Aeren turned toward Lord Khalaek as his men broke
into swift action, bellowing orders as they went. "That
man—that human—saved the Tamaea's life," he said.

Khalaek looked at him in disdain, then glanced around
at all of those closest, who'd heard what Aeren had said,
who'd witnessed what Colin had done. He stiffened at
some of the looks he got. "He'll be treated . . . well."

Khalaek practically growled it, but Aeren nodded.

Eraeth suddenly appeared at Aeren's side. "The occumaen," he said, but didn't finish.

"What?" Aeren and Khalaek snapped at the same time.

Eraeth grew suddenly formal, face blank, body rigid. "It's headed directly toward the battle."

Both Aeren and Khalaek spun, saw the occumaen churning over the ridge. From this side, there was no eye, no glimpse into another stretch of plains, no second sun and spring grass. From this side, it appeared to be nothing more than a ripple of heat waves.

"Sound the horns!" Khalaek roared. "Sound them for retreat!" Then he kicked his horse into motion, the rest of the House Duvoraen Phalanx charging after him. They hadn't been gone two breaths when the sound of a horn pierced the air, joined a moment later by two others, all pealing out the long note for retreat.

"Come on," Aeren said, motioning to Eraeth.

They followed Khalaek's men to the crest of the rise and stared down into the flat beyond, where the Legion and the Alvritshai armies still fought. Khalaek continued to sound the retreat, even as he and his men raced across the flat. Dust rose behind them as they banked wide around the occumaen.

On the field, the mass of men surged back and forth, oblivious to the distortion. As Aeren watched, the sounds of Khalaek's horns finally caught the attention of those at the back of the Alvritshai army. He saw the ripples in the army spread as word was passed, new horns joining Khalaek's, and Alvritshai began to break away from the rear, men and horses fleeing. Khalaek altered course, swinging his group wide and circling the army to the left. But still the conflict raged in the middle, swords flashing in the afternoon sunlight, blood flying, men falling.

The occumaen drifted closer, its distortion obscuring part of the army to the north. Aeren saw the first men in the Legion break away as they spotted the danger, practically stumbling over each other in their haste to retreat. The horns grew more frantic, the smooth notes blatty and warbled.

Eraeth edged forward, his hands tight on the reins of his mount. "They aren't going to see it in time."

Aeren pressed his lips together, but said nothing.

Then, when it seemed that the occumaen would plow through the edge of the two locked armies, three short blasts sounded, the single horn piercing through the cacophony of all the rest.

The Alvritshai army abruptly turned and broke away from the lead group of Legion. Aeren saw the Tamaell's flags pulling back from the center, saw the Legion spilling into the gap, a few men chasing after the retreating Alvritshai.

But not the King. His banners remained behind. Banners flashed back and forth among all of King Stephan's groups. Aeren couldn't read the signals, but when the men began pulling back, he knew they'd also called a retreat. The men charging after the Alvritshai either hadn't seen the orders, or were blatantly disobeying them.

It cost them their lives.

The occumaen plowed into the edges of both armies, its arms catching those who'd stayed to fight a little too long and those who'd been unable to retreat fast enough. Banners on both sides were caught in the occumaen's winds, thrashing as dust churned upward. Closest to the occumaen, bodies of horses and men were lifted from the ground where they'd fallen earlier, and Aeren would have sworn the winds were tinged a black-red from the blood already spilled on the battlefield.

It sliced cleanly through the two armies, and when it passed, it left behind a scar of churned earth, as it had in the Alvritshai encampment. When Aeren saw the Tamaell's banners still raised, he released the breath he hadn't realized he was holding in a harsh sigh. The two armies, separated by the scarred earth, milled about for a long moment, long enough that Aeren thought they might engage each other again. He felt the old, bitter anger building inside him. The occumaen drifted out past the flat, to the edge of the Escarpment that could barely be seen in the distance, and then beyond. It hovered in thin air, still drifting, and then wavered as it began to dissipate.

Both sides of the battle turned from the field. Aeren relaxed back into his saddle and watched as the Alvritshai moved wearily up the slope toward them, the Tamaell's escort edging to the front ranks. The Legion withdrew to the north, where Aeren could make out their own encampment, untouched by the occumaen.

As the Tamaell's escort approached, Aeren stepped forward, Eraeth at his side. The Tamaell sat in the saddle, back rigid, his armor coated with dust and blood, his face smeared with sweat and grit. He carried himself stiffly, yet with a deadly grace, the exhaustion from the day's battle apparent only around the edges of his eyes and in the angry creases in his brow. All the men around him appeared the same—except Lord Khalaek—although their fatigue was easier to see in their slumped shoulders and hunched backs.

Fedorem saw Aeren's approach and slowed. The army began to slow as well, until an order was passed back. The Phalanx—the Tamaell's and the rest of the Houses of the Evant—began spilling around them toward the camp. Groans escaped most men as they saw the destruction the occumaen had caused, some of shock, others of worry.

Khalaek must have already informed Fedorem, for he didn't react to the state of their camp at all. Instead, he scanned Aeren's group and called, "Where is the Tamaea? Where is Moiran?"

"She is—" Aeren began.

"Here, my Tamaell."

Aeren's escort parted, and the Tamaea stepped through, her clothes stained with mud and grass, her hair in disarray. A smudge of dirt marked her forehead, as if she'd wiped at it with her arm.

She halted a step away from the Tamaell's horse, and for a moment it appeared that Fedorem would not react. He sat, staring at her, his face unreadable, although Aeren thought he trembled.

Then he swung down from his mount and drew Moiran to him in a hard embrace. He murmured something to her, his face pressed into her hair, and tears shone in Moiran's eyes as she hesitated and then held Fedorem in return, clutching his battered and bloody armor to her, uncaring.

Aeren and the rest of the escort that surrounded them shuffled and looked elsewhere. Such displays were not generally shown in public, especially not among those in the Evant.

They clung to each other a moment longer, until the Tamaell pushed Moiran back. The Tamaea regained her composure immediately and said, her voice rough, "It was the human, Colin, who saved me from the occumaen. I would not have survived otherwise."

Surprise flashed across Fedorem's face, replaced with

a solemn expression as he searched among the Alvritshai faces. Not finding Colin, his gaze settled on Aeren. "Where is he? I wish to thank him personally."

"He is with Lotaern and the acolytes, recovering. The Order has already begun tending to the wounded, at the Tamaea's request."

"I see. Then I will attend him later." His stance shifted, and he stepped away from Moiran toward Aeren. "Lord Khalaek informs me you've come with a message from my son."

"I have."

"What is it?"

Aeren looked toward Khalaek and narrowed his gaze. He couldn't tell the Tamaell about the sukrael, not with Khalaek standing there.

"Out with it!" Fedorem barked, startling everyone.

Aeren straightened where he sat and met the Tamaell's angry, brooding gaze. "The Tamaell Presumptive has met and spoken with the dwarren Gathering, as you requested, and they've refused to deal with the Tamaell Presumptive."

Khalaek snorted in derision, as if he'd expected no less.

But Aeren wasn't finished.

"Instead, they wish to speak to you directly, Tamaell. They're coming here, to the Escarpment. And they're bringing their army with them."

· { 20 } ·

"I TOLD HIM *NOT* TO BRING the dwarren here!"
the Tamaell snarled, flinging the last sweaty article
of clothing he'd worn beneath his armor to one side
of the lantern-lit room as he emerged from a secondary
room where he'd recently washed. He wore loose, clean
clothes now, simple breeches and shirt, not the stylized
outfits Aeren was used to seeing him in. The informality
felt strange and uncomfortable.

He tried not to react as the Tamaell began pacing, his
hands clasped behind his back, ignoring the look Eraeth
shot him from one side. Colin, seated on the other side,
simply watched silently, not quite recovered from saving
the Tamaea.

The Tamaell had controlled himself while they reached the
tattered remains of the camp, had marshaled all of the Lords
of the Evant into action to clean up and salvage what they
could of the tents and supply wagons, over half of which were
unscathed, including the wagon that Aeren had left with the
contingent. He'd spent a long moment alone with the Tamaea
before she took control of the medical teams tending to the
wounded, paying close attention to those like the man who'd
lost both legs to the occumaen and the woman who'd lost her
arm. But during all of this, Aeren could tell the Tamaell had
been fuming.

It had only been a matter of time. And privacy.

"I don't believe the Tamaell Presumptive was given
much choice," Aeren ventured.

"Thaedoren and I discussed this at length. He was to

meet with the dwarren, placate them, act humble or defiant, but he was to *keep them away from the Escarpment*! It should have been a simple task, after what happened to them the last time all three races met here!"

Aeren frowned. "It might have been simple, except for one thing."

"What?" Fedorem growled, but it caught his attention. He stopped pacing, his black gaze leveled at Aeren.

"The sukrael."

It surprised him. His eyes widened, then narrowed in suspicion. "What do the sukrael have to do with this?"

Aeren shifted where he sat, aware of the Tamaell's eyes boring into him. He felt Colin stir to one side.

"The Tamaell Presumptive—"

"Thaedoren," Fedorem said gruffly. "Call him Thaedoren here."

Aeren nodded, although it made him even more uncomfortable. "Thaedoren informed them of the attacks in Licaeta. It appears there have been similar attacks on the dwarren, to the south and the east in particular. These attacks are more serious than those in Licaeta, to the extent that the dwarren have been forced to turn their attention toward protecting themselves from the sukrael."

Fedorem had bowed his head in thought. "So when you approached them with the possibility of peace—"

"It came at an auspicious time for them, yes."

"So they actually intended to form some type of agreement with us? A treaty of some sort?"

Aeren nodded. "Yes."

Fedorem continued pacing, mumbling to himself. "Thaedoren didn't believe it. He thought it was a trick."

Aeren thought about Thaedoren standing on the rise before the meeting tent, frowning down at the dwarren encampment in consternation. "I believe the dwarren convinced him otherwise."

Fedorem drew in a deep breath through his nose and let it out in a sigh, one hand pinching the bridge of his nose. "Do the dwarren know why the sukrael can suddenly move beyond their usual boundaries? Those boundaries have remained stable for generations, hundreds of years at least. Lotaern has told me of your claims that the sukrael have begun reawakening sarenavriell."

Aeren felt sweat break out along his shoulders and in the palms of his hands. "The dwarren have no idea. They believe this may be a sign that the world is Turning. But what Lotaern told you was correct: the sukrael are reawakening the Wells."

Fedorem nodded, as if he'd expected that answer.

Aeren hesitated, glancing once toward Colin; the human's face was drained, leeched of color, the skin beneath his eyes bruised with exhaustion. Then Aeren said, "However, there is something more that we have discovered about the sukrael and the sarenavriell."

Fedorem turned toward him with a questioning look.

"It has to do with the Wraiths, the creatures created by the sukrael. And with Lord Khalaek."

And he told the Tamaell all that he'd told Thaedoren and had learned from the dwarren in turn. He told him of Colin's powers, of Benedine, of how Colin had followed Benedine as he'd met with one of Khalaek's aides, how that aide had reported back to Khalaek, and Benedine's subsequent horrific death by the Wraith.

Fedorem remained silent the entire time he spoke, nodding or grimacing, but never once looking at Aeren, Colin, or Eraeth.

When Aeren finished, he said stiffly, "And you did not feel the need to inform me or the Evant of your suspicions regarding Khalaek?"

"As I told Thaedoren, I have mere suspicions, no proof. The Lords of the Evant would not accept the word of a human, not with the power that Khalaek wields."

Fedorem nodded, whether in agreement or simple acknowledgment of the explanation, Aeren couldn't tell. Then the Tamaell turned to Colin.

"It seems the Alvritshai—that I—am in your debt," he said, in perfect, uninflected Andovan. "The Tamaea explained that without your intervention, the occumaen would have claimed her."

Colin seemed taken aback, although it was hard to tell through his exhaustion. His mouth opened, then closed, then opened again. Finally, in a rough, weary voice, he managed to say, "There is no debt, Tamaell."

"So you say, but what you have done will not be forgotten." Fedorem drew breath, as if he'd say more, but then turned toward Aeren instead. "When do you expect my son and the dwarren to arrive?"

Aeren could hear the change in the Tamaell's voice—a shift toward action, the discussion nearly over. "No more than two days from now. The dwarren are moving fast. The clan chiefs agreed to march ahead of the supply wagons, so the army will be arriving first, with the entire Gathering, and Thaedoren as escort."

"Then we have little time to prepare," Fedorem said, motioning for Aeren and the others to rise. "Wait here for a moment while I change."

Aeren and Eraeth exchanged a glance as the Tamaell ducked back into the room beyond. "That went better than I expected," Aeren said.

"It isn't over yet," Eraeth muttered.

Aeren frowned. "No, it isn't."

Colin wavered where he stood, and Aeren reached out to steady him. "You look pale."

Colin smiled, but it didn't reach his eyes. "I'll be fine. I just need to rest."

"Then rest. As soon as we leave the tent. The Tamaell and I will not need you."

Colin nodded.

And then Fedorem returned, dressed now in the formal white and red of the Tamaell.

"Where are we going?" Aeren asked as Fedorem led them out of the tent, into the section of the camp that had not been torn apart by the occumaen.

"I want to speak to Lotaern about the sukrael and the sarenavriell," the Tamaell said tightly.

~

"You should have come forward with this information," the Tamaell said.

Aeren, Eraeth, the Tamaell, and Lotaern stood outside one of Lotaern's tents as he watched the members of his Order picking through the debris left by the occumaen by torch and lantern light. Darkness had fallen, but the camp was still full of movement, fires scattered to either side of the occumaen's path. A much larger blaze burned to the south, where the dead had been taken to be honored, blessed, and burned in order to return their souls to Aielan's Light under the direction of the Order of the Flame's acolytes. The black, oily smoke blotted out the stars as it drifted south, carried away from the camp by the faint breeze.

"And you would have listened?" Lotaern growled. His arms were crossed over his chest, his body turned slightly away from the Tamaell. "Listened to the word of a human, brought to you by one of the lords of the Evant, a known rival of Lord Khalaek?"

Aeren stiffened at the tension he felt between the two—Lotaern and the Tamaell—but forced himself to relax. The leader of the Order and the ruler of the Alvritshai had opposed each other since Fedorem had ascended within the Evant. Lotaern wanted more power, for himself and for the Order. Fedorem felt the Order had no place in the Evant. The argument was old and had lasted for decades.

"I would have listened to the Chosen of the Order!" Fedorem spat. "Especially regarding the sarenavriell and the sukrael. You are the holder of the Scripts. This is your domain."

For the first time since they'd arrived, Lotaern turned and faced the Tamaell directly, one eyebrow raised. "The sarenavriell, the ruanavriell—all of the five powers—are under the mantle of Aielan's Light and as such are the Order's concern, not the Evant's. Unless I have reason to believe they will somehow affect the Alvritshai directly, there is no need for me to report to you."

"The Order does not consider the involvement of one of the Lords of the Evant a direct assault on the Alvritshai?"

Lotaern's eyes narrowed. "I did not realize until recently that Lord Khalaek was involved," he hissed. "If I had known . . ."

He trailed off in furious indignation.

The Tamaell straightened. "And what of these men?" Fedorem demanded, motioning toward the members of the Order working to clean up the damage done by the occumaen. "This Order of the Flame? The creation of an army within the Order, trained in secret? What is the Evant to make of that?"

His voice had gone dangerously quiet. Lotaern met the challenge silently, the two glaring at each other in the firelit darkness.

"You have overstepped the bounds of the Order," Fedorem said quietly.

"We shall see," Lotaern growled.

Aeren stepped between the two, catching their attention. "Right now—" he nodded to where Lotaern's men were lifting up a collapsed tent, one of the men crying out and bending over a limp body "—it's unimportant."

Both Lotaern and Fedorem watched in silence as one of the members of the Order of the Flame grabbed the body beneath the arms and lifted, another taking the legs. They carried the man's corpse to one side, out of the reach of the torchlight, murmuring the litany for the dead, their words fading into the night.

The animosity between the Chosen and the Tamaell lessened, Lotaern bowing his head a moment, eyes closed.

When he looked back up, he said to Aeren, "What have you told him?"

"Everything that Colin has told us."

"Then there isn't much more I can explain." His voice was still cold. "The sarenavriell have existed since the Scripts were written, have existed since before the last time the world Turned, even before that."

"And the sukrael?" Fedorem asked.

Lotaern hesitated. "It was thought that the sukrael and the Faelehgre had existed as long as the sarenavriell, that they had been established as guardians and protectors. That is how they are depicted in the Scripts." He drew in a deep breath, let it out in a long sigh. "But since then I've spoken to Shaevaren at length about his time in the forest, his time among the Faelehgre and near the sarenavriell. It seems that the sukrael and the Faelehgre are more prisoners than guardians. And now they've found a way to escape, in a limited way. I'm afraid there isn't much more I can tell you than that. I do not know how they are awakening the sarenavriell. I do not know how they created the Wraiths."

Fedorem frowned. "And what about the occumaen? Is there a connection between it and the sukrael?"

Lotaern grimaced, but then he paused, brow creasing in concentration. Almost reluctantly, he said, "It's possible. The sukrael have been awakening powers long left dormant. It may be having unintended or unexpected consequences. But if there is a connection, I think it's just that: unintended. I don't think the sukrael are creating the occumaen on purpose. They have a different agenda."

"It would explain why they've become so much larger," Eraeth said from his place a step behind them all.

"And stronger," Lotaern agreed. "It might also explain the increase in the number of unnatural storms on the plains as well." He mulled the new idea over in his head, considering the possibilities.

Fedorem fell silent for a long moment. On the far horizon, purplish-blue lightning flickered in the darkness, although there were no clouds obscuring the sky yet.

Finally, Fedorem turned. "Why? What does Lord Khalaek hope to gain from an alliance with these ... Wraiths?"

No one spoke. Lotaern looked at the ground. Fedorem eyed both the Chosen and Aeren, until Aeren finally said, "We don't know."

Fedorem considered this, mouth downturned. "Then it's all speculation. With Benedine dead, there's no way to link Khalaek to the Wraiths. It would be your word against his, one lord against another. There's nothing I can do."

~

"Do you believe them?" Moiran asked as she used shears to slice blankets and cloth into thin strips for bandages by lamplight, the tent draped in shadows. Most of the material had been scavenged from the camp, from all the Lords of the Evant and what remained of her own supplies.

On the far side of the small tent—much smaller than the one they'd been using—Fedorem halted his slow pace and settled into a small chair. "Do I believe that Khalaek would infiltrate the Order with a member from his own House? Yes. Do I believe that he'd use that to help him undermine my hold on the Evant, to extend his influence? Yes. Do I believe he'd work with these Wraiths, creatures that Aeren and Lotaern claim were created by the sukrael, creatures that no one has seen or heard of except for this Shaeveran, this human named Colin?" He shook his head, brow creased, but said nothing, one hand pinching his lower lip in thought, elbow resting on the arm of the chair.

Moiran frowned. "That human ... is no longer human. He saved me from the occumaen."

"So you said."

"No, you don't understand," she said sharply, and she stopped cutting, placing the shears in her lap so she could catch Fedorem's eyes and hold them. "He didn't simply drag me to safety. *He halted time*. He somehow stopped everything and gave us the chance to escape." Something hot and hard rose up into her throat, and she felt tears burning at the corners of her eyes. In a choked voice, she added, "I thought the occumaen would claim me. I could feel its breath upon me, the Breath of Heaven—"

She bowed her head, fought down the heated pressure in her chest. She'd avoided the thought of the occumaen all day by burying herself in the tending of the wounded, in their pain.

She heard Fedorem rise from his seat and approach, felt his hand on her shoulder.

"You're saying he is one of the Aielan-aein, that he has been Touched by Aielan."

Moiran gave a snorting laugh, the sound thick and phlegmy. "He is more than simply Touched. He has been gifted. None of the Aielan-aein within the Order could have done what he did. None of them have shown that kind of power, that kind of strength." She paused, thinking of the terror she'd felt as the occumaen bore down on her. "I only wish he'd been able to save Faeren and the others."

Fedorem squeezed her shoulder once, and then his hand slipped free. Moiran noted that he looked more troubled than before as he settled back into his chair.

"That changes nothing. Even if I did believe Lord Aeren and the Chosen, it is still one lord accusing another. And in the confines of the Evant, I cannot choose between the two unless the Evant demands it."

"Then Aeren should present his claim to the Evant."

Fedorem shook his head again. "He won't. Aeren knows his place in the Evant. House Rhyssal has descended in the ranks these past hundred years. It is now one of the lesser Houses. Aeren would not find the support within the Evant to even bring his accusation to the floor for serious consideration, let alone get them to hand the decision over to me. The rivalry between House Rhyssal and House Duvoraen is too well known."

Moiran's frown deepened as she picked up the shears again and began cutting.

"No," Fedorem said, mostly to himself, as he rose again
and moved toward the entrance to the tent. He stood before the opening, although he didn't stoop to go outside
into the night. It was late, but Moiran could still hear the
sounds of the Phalanx and servants picking through the
destruction caused by the occumaen, guardsmen calling
out as more bodies were found. "There's nothing I can do
about Khalaek."

Moiran was happy to hear a trace of venom in Fedorem's voice at the lord's name. "Then why are you so
restless? You should sleep."

"I can't," Fedorem murmured. "There's too much death,
too much—"

Moiran glanced up as he broke off, saw the sudden stiffness in his shoulders, in his back, saw the shift from Tamaell
to Phalanx guardsman in his stance, wary now, dangerous.

Before she could react, he ducked and shoved his way
out of the tent into the darkness.

"Fedorem!"

She tossed the shears aside and scrambled to her feet,
her heart quickening. She slid out of the tent, one hand
checking to make certain she still carried her knife, but she
found Fedorem standing with a group of Phalanx immediately outside, all facing in the same direction, all almost
preternaturally still.

She moved up beside her husband and whispered,
"What is it?"

He glanced toward her, eyes hard, jaw tight. "Listen."

She frowned and grew still. All she could hear were the
calls of the workers, coming from all sides. She'd drawn
breath to ask what she should be listening for when she
heard it.

Drums. The faintest echo of drums.

"From the south," one of the Phalanx members said.

Fedorem nodded. "Yes." Without another word, he
headed toward the northern part of the camp. A breath
later, the rest of the Phalanx followed.

Moiran hesitated, then straightened and trailed after.

They moved through the camp as the sounds of the
drums grew louder, loud enough that the rest of the camp
began to notice. By the time they reached the ridge to
the northwest, they'd been joined by at least twenty other

Phalanx and a few of the servants. Others had already gathered there, including members of the Evant. Moiran saw Lord Aeren and the Chosen of the Order on one side, Lords Waerren and Jydell on the other.

And waiting to meet them was Lord Khalaek.

"Tamaell," Khalaek said with a deferential nod as Fedorem approached.

"Lord Khalaek. What news?"

Khalaek smiled slightly. "See for yourself."

As she reached the ridge, Moiran halted, drawn up short by the sight.

On the plains to the south, still distant but drawing closer with every resounding thud of the drums, were the pinprick reddish flames of torches and lanterns, stretching away into the darkness in a thick but ragged column.

"It would appear," Khalaek said, his voice soft but filled with satisfaction, "that Lord Aeren was misinformed." He turned to Fedorem, the smile still touching his eyes.

"The dwarren have arrived."

~

Aeren squinted into the early morning sunlight and felt his stomach roil sickeningly. His mount shifted beneath him and snorted, stamping one foot. He reached down to calm it and said, voice tight, "It's just like before."

To his left, Eraeth grunted.

Before them on the flat, the three armies had gathered.

The Tamaell and all of the Lords of the Evant were present at the base of the small rise east of the battlefield, the Phalanx from each of the Houses gathered in close formation behind them. Banners for all of the Houses flapped in the stiff breeze, and armor clanked as the Alvritshai and their mounts shifted fitfully beneath the glare of the sun. The Tamaell stood at the forefront, the lords arrayed to either side, all except Aeren, who stood within the Tamaell's escort, a few paces back.

On the plains below, the Legion stood to the north. Aeren could just see the banners of the King, surrounded by those of the Provinces. It appeared that all of the Governors stood with the King. Most of the Legion were on foot, those mounted grouped behind the King himself.

The dwarren Riders had gathered to the south. They'd

set up their camp during the night, their drums a continu-
ous thundering presence until nearly dawn, when they'd
suddenly fallen silent. That silence had been almost worse
than the constant sounding of the drums. Those still awake
in the Alvritshai camp had looked up from whatever they
were doing, then returned to their tasks, unsettled.

Now, there were no drums. The dwarren were mounted
on their gaezels in a loose formation, nothing like the ordered ranks of the Legion, or even the Alvritshai. A few
pennants marked the general location of each of the clans,
but unlike the Legion, the clan chiefs appeared to be scattered among their own men.

The large gash the occumaen had left in the plains separated the dwarren and human armies, a dark line that cut
diagonally from the Alvritshai armies toward the cliffs of
the Escarpment to the west.

The plains were eerily silent. There were no storms on
the horizon, only a few scudding clouds. The air felt hollow
and empty, yet tight with anticipation, with expectation.

Aeren felt dread eating away at his stomach. He'd felt
this same tension over thirty years before, on this very
ground. Only back then he'd been filled with the hope that
the battle would end all the fighting, all the conflict, all the
bloodshed. An alliance had been formed, and with it the
first tentative ties between the Alvritshai and human races.

Except that those ties had been torn to shreds during
the battle that followed, destroyed and thrown to the
ground by Khalaek and then, shockingly, by Fedorem
himself.

Aeren resisted glancing toward Khalaek's position, his
hand gripping the reins so hard his fingers had gone white.
His horse stirred again and tossed its head, picking up on
his tension.

The Tamaell turned, sought him out. Aeren straightened
in his saddle and shoved the sickening roil in his gut aside.

No words were spoken. They'd discussed what Aeren
would do long into the night, after the dwarren's arrival.
The Tamaell simply nodded.

Aeren kicked his horse forward, Eraeth and two other
Rhyssal Phalanx—Dharel and Auvant—accompanying
him. The Tamaell's escort parted before them, then closed
ranks behind as Aeren picked up speed, racing out onto

the flat, toward a point midway between all three of the gathered armies, in the center of the occumaen's path. He listened to the snap of the truce banners carried by Dharel and Auvant beneath the thundering of his horse's hooves and his own heart, heard that thunder change tenor as he reached the edge of the exposed dirt left behind by the occumaen. Out of the corner of his eye, he caught movement and saw a small party of Legion break away from the human army and move to intercept them at the center of the field, carrying the same banners of truce. He turned toward the south, to where the dwarren army waited, but saw nothing.

He clenched his jaw grimly. This wouldn't work unless the dwarren sent out representatives as well.

When he reached position, he pulled his mount up sharply, then waited, his horse prancing slightly. Eraeth and the others brought their mounts to a halt as well, ranging out behind him. To the right, the members of the Legion party were already halfway there.

To the south, the dwarren had still not moved, although Aeren noticed new activity. He muttered a small curse, then turned his attention to the approaching human representatives.

There were five of them, all members of the Legion, fighting men. They halted their mounts nearly twenty paces away, and as the two groups sized each other up, Aeren realized he recognized their leader: the commander who'd been in the meeting hall in Corsair.

Nodding grimly, Aeren said, "Commander."

The Legionnaire smiled without any trace of humor. "Lord Aeren. I see you've brought reinforcements."

Aeren frowned at the coldness in the man's voice. "The dwarren weren't invited."

The commander held himself loosely in the saddle, but Aeren wasn't deceived; his horse wouldn't stop fidgeting. He regarded Aeren with a blatant stare, brow slightly creased, jaw clenched. A fresh cut marred his forehead over his right eye. "We'll find out soon enough," he finally said, and jutted his chin out toward the dwarren army.

Aeren turned to look.

A group had broken away from the dwarren, streaking toward them on gaezels and a single horse. Aeren tensed on seeing the horse, then realized it belonged to the Tamaell Presumptive, who hadn't returned to the camp the night before.

He allowed himself to relax slightly, although having Thaedoren arrive with the dwarren wouldn't help alleviate the commander's suspicions. But perhaps he could use those suspicions to his advantage.

"Did you call the Drifter?" the commander asked suddenly. "It's said you can control the elements—the wind, the water, the very earth."

Eraeth snorted and rolled his eyes.

"No," Aeren said, ignoring his Protector. "We did not call the Drifter. As your scouts have probably already reported, the occumaen destroyed a large portion of our own camp and killed at least fifty Alvritshai. Another thirty are missing. Why would we call something so destructive and unleash it on ourselves?"

"Perhaps it got out of control," the Legionnaire muttered.

Aeren didn't bother to respond, but he saw a fleeting expression of doubt cross the commander's face.

Then he heard the pounding of the gaezels' hooves as Thaedoren and the group of dwarren arrived. They banked away, then turned and swept past the group, curling around into a position the same distance from both Aeren's and the Legion's groups, all except Thaedoren, who rode up into position behind them on his horse. Thaedoren nodded at Aeren, his expression unreadable. He was obviously deferring to the dwarren.

Aeren was not surprised to find the dwarren led by Garius. The clan chief's nose and ear chains glinted in the sunlight, the beads woven into his beard clicking against each other as he nudged his gaezel out in front of the rest of his group. He'd brought six other dwarren with him, plus Thaedoren.

Garius glared at Aeren, then at the Legionnaire, before returning his gaze to Aeren. "What is the meaning of this?" he asked in dwarren. He motioned toward the two groups.

Aeren straightened in his saddle. "The Tamaell of the Alvritshai, Fedorem Arl Resue, wishes to end the bloodshed on the plains. He proposes that all three leaders of the three races—King Stephan Werall, Cochen

Harticur of the Red Sea Clan, and himself, along with a suitable escort—gather here, on this ground to discuss a treaty among our peoples." Aeren waited while someone from each party translated from Alvritshai to their own language.

A silence settled, held for a long moment—

And then was broken by a harsh laugh from the Legionnaire. "You want to talk peace? After what happened here over thirty years ago?" His voice lowered dangerously. "You would dare suggest peace on *this* ground, at *this* place."

"It is precisely because of what happened here, at this place thirty years ago that Tamaell Fedorem suggests we talk," Aeren said. "A mistake was made, one that he wishes to rectify."

"A mistake!"

Aeren winced at Garius' deep-chested, enraged roar. The clan chief had edged his gaezel closer, and for the first time Aeren noticed that he brandished a sword, the weapon laid across his lap.

"A mistake!" Garius' gaze was scathing. "You slaughtered us. You cut us down and then drove us off of the Escarpment. You call that a mistake? It was butchery!"

Behind him, Garius' men grumbled, and Thaedoren shot Aeren a warning glance.

Waiting until the muttering had died down, Aeren looked directly at Garius and said, "No. That was not a mistake. That was planned."

The outrage was instantaneous, the dwarren erupting in curses, swords raised for emphasis. Thaedoren stiffened in his saddle behind the group, his jaw set, his gaze black. But the dwarren didn't move to attack; Garius hadn't even raised his weapon.

Instead, he simply glared at Aeren past his lowered brow. "So you intend to speak the truth here as well?"

"Yes."

Garius nodded.

"And was the betrayal of Maarten, our King, planned?" the Legionnaire demanded bitterly.

Aeren turned toward the commander, looked into his enraged eyes. He hesitated, but he realized he'd grown tired. Of the lies, the half-lies. Of veiled suspicions and secrets.

He drew in a deep breath, aware that Thaedoren stood to one side, aware that he'd already stepped over his bounds by admitting to the dwarren that there had been an alliance between the Alvritshai and the humans to the dwarren. But he no longer cared.

"The betrayal at the Escarpment was planned," he said bluntly.

The commander jerked back as if he'd been struck, his eyes going wide in surprise, his hand falling to the hilt of his sword. Behind him, his men gasped or cried out, those not carrying the banners of truce edging their mounts forward. But they did not draw their weapons.

Because the commander hadn't drawn his.

Aeren could see the rage, pent up for thirty years, feeding on suspicion, on his lord's blatant hatred, fostered by the constant struggle on the borders among all of the races. His teeth ground together, and his breathing came harsh and ragged. The hand holding the hilt of his sword clenched and unclenched as he fought himself, the urge to draw and vent his rage on Aeren and the Alvritshai clear in his eyes, in the strained lines of his face.

Aeren didn't know what held the commander's hand, but in the end he calmed himself, enough to release his blade, enough to wave his men back, the gesture sharp, barely controlled. The muscles in his face contracted as he drew a short breath. "And yet you come here expecting us to discuss peace."

"The betrayal was planned," Aeren said, "but not by all of the Evant. I was not aware of it, nor was my brother, the Lord of House Rhyssal at the time. I know of at least two other lords who were dragged into it after your King had been killed."

The Legionnaire spat, "And what of Fedorem? What of your precious Tamaell? Was he aware?"

Aeren winced. "That is what the Tamaell wishes to discuss."

"Ha!" The commander shook his head in disgust. He leaned forward in his saddle, leather creaking. "It matters little if the Tamaell was aware. He kept his mouth shut afterward, didn't he? He became complicit the moment he allowed it to happen, the moment he allowed it to go unpunished."

The commander took the reins of his horse in one hand, nudged his horse around, turning it back toward the human armies. "There will be no talks," he said coldly. "We learned a harsh lesson here at the Escarpment thirty years ago, one we have not forgotten: The Alvritshai cannot be trusted."

Then he turned his back on them all, motioning with one hand toward the others in his escort.

Aeren felt a moment of panic, even though he'd expected this response. He'd seen their resistance, their human stubbornness, in Corsair. He'd seen the hatred and pain that still lay on the surface, both there and in Portstown, in all the other cities he'd visited in the Provinces.

But circumstances had changed. The world had changed.

The world was Turning.

"How goes the war with Andovan?" he asked loudly, before the Legionnaire and his men could move beyond earshot.

The commander halted, his back stiffening, his men pulling up short around him. One of them looking back with a glare.

Aeren edged his horse forward. "It doesn't appear to be going well," he said casually. "They've attacked nearly every port on your coast, in nearly every Province. We know that they're hounding your shipping fleets, interrupting your trade, sinking what they cannot take. We were surprised you could send so many of the Legion here, especially since we weren't posing an imminent threat at the time."

The Legionnaire shifted slightly, so that Aeren could see his profile. But he did not turn around. "What is your point?" he said, voice still heated.

He knew the point. Aeren could hear it in his voice. He answered anyway.

"You can't afford to have your forces divided. This conflict on the plains is useless and only distracts you from a more pressing threat: the Andovans. They've been distracted by their internal conflict these long years, by their Feud. But that's ended. They have their sights set on their lost colonies, on their lost lands. And their attacks are escalating.

"You need this peace. You need it more than we do."

Which wasn't exactly true. The Alvritshai couldn't afford to lose many more lives. There were fewer than eighty thousand Alvritshai left, when once there were two hundred thousand. And he knew the dwarren were in a similar situation. He'd seen the decrease in dwarren on the plains, although the dwarren would recover much more quickly than the Alvritshai. In that respect, the dwarren were like the humans. They bred like rabbits.

But the attacks by the Andovans were more immediate and more pressing.

Aeren saw the commander frown, his chin dropping slightly.

Then he turned away again. But before he kicked his horse forward, he said bitterly, "I'll inform King Stephan of your request."

Aeren watched him and his escort gallop back across the plains to their ranks for a moment before turning to Garius.

The dwarren clan chief eyed Aeren shrewdly. He'd been listening to the conversation intently, and he now fingered the hilt of his sword as he stared Aeren down.

"You already know why we must talk of peace," he finally said.

Aeren nodded. "The sukrael."

Garius glanced in the direction of the forest, too distant to actually see on the horizon. "The urannen." His lip twitched as he said the name, and he spat to one side.

When he turned back, he said, "I will tell the Cochen of your talk."

Then he spun his gaezel around, calling an order to the rest of the dwarren. Their gaezels leaped forward, leaving Thaedoren behind on his horse.

He cantered forward, to face Aeren. "You risk much for this peace."

"I risk everything," Aeren said darkly.

Thaedoren measured him with a glance, then nodded. "I'll remain with the dwarren until the meeting can be arranged."

"I'll inform the Tamaell."

Thaedoren pulled his horse around and charged out after the dwarren.

Aeren met Eraeth's gaze.

"That could have gone better," his Protector said

blandly as they headed back toward the Tamaell and the rest of the Alvritshai army.

"It gives us a chance. Let's hope the talk itself is less anger fueled."

It wasn't.

Aeren could already feel the tension radiating from the men, dwarren, and Alvritshai gathered about the tent that had been erected in the center of the battlefield. All of those assembled were glaring at the other two contingents, even as each party sent a single member into the tent to verify that everything had been set up as established during the two days of negotiations. The dwarren had demanded that their own meeting tent be used, but King Stephan had refused on the grounds that he was unfamiliar with their setup and layout. An argument had ensued, with Tamaell Fedorem finally offering the compromise that they use a human tent, with the stipulation that one of the dwarren shamans be allowed to sanctify it. Both sides had grudgingly agreed.

Then the question of how many men each leader would be allowed to bring with them into the tent. Tamaell Fedorem had requested fourteen, intending to bring the seven Lords of the Evant, with one aide each. The dwarren had immediately demanded twenty. Aeren suspected that the number itself didn't matter to them, it only had to be higher than the Tamaell's choice. Stephan had scoffed and said he would only need seven.

They'd finally agreed on ten additional men each.

After that, they'd argued about how the tent would be set up, how they'd verify that the tent was safe before the other leaders entered, how the guards would be positioned outside, what food and drink would be available, whether weapons would be allowed, and how many weapons each guard would be able to carry.

As soon as all of these matters were settled, the argument within the Evant began over who would accompany the Tamaell. The dwarren had demanded that both Thaedoren and Fedorem be present. Moiran had protested. Thaedoren was the Tamaell Presumptive—it made no sense to risk both Fedorem and Thaedoren at the meeting. Her voice had been quiet and controlled, but Aeren had heard the tremor beneath it, had seen the fear in her eyes. A mother's fear. But Fedorem had overruled her. Daedalen, their second son, still remained in Alvritshai hands, ready to take Thaedoren's and Fedorem's place if something should happen to them both.

Moiran had pursed her lips, but she said nothing.

That left nine places to be filled. Some would have to be reserved for the Phalanx. Fedorem didn't intend to enter the tent without some guardsmen. He allocated three places for his own personal guard, leaving six at the disposal of the Evant.

In the end, after nearly an entire day of exhausting discussion, of tirades and brittle conversation, of anger and heated words, it was decided that Aeren and Khalaek would accompany the Tamaell. Each would be allowed two others of their own chosing.

Aeren's brow furrowed as he glanced toward Khalaek, the lord dressed in formal black and gold. He caught Aeren's stare and held it . . . then smiled before turning away, back toward the two aides he'd chosen to bring along with him.

Eraeth leaned forward and murmured, "The one on the right is the man Benedine met with in the courtyard."

Aeren faced Colin questioningly and received a nod in return.

He frowned, considering the man. He could see the training of the Phalanx in the way the man held himself. When he sensed Aeren's attention, he looked over, met Aeren's gaze, held it a long moment without moving, then returned to waiting, without a second look back.

Then the scouts—all three—emerged from the tent, giving an all-clear signal as they retreated back to their respective groups.

Aeren drew in a deep breath, glancing around at the rest of the escort gathered, including those who would wait outside the tent. They held the banners of those present— the black and gold talon of House Duvoraen; the white and red eagle rampant of House Resue, the Tamaell's colors; and the blue and red wings of Aeren's own House Ryhssal. The dwarren shaman stepped forward, chanting as he gestured with the feathered spear he carried and spread what Aeren had verified were tiny grass seeds into the wind. Aeren caught King Stephan muttering impatiently to his commander, both of their expressions dark. Aeren had learned the commander's name was Tanner Dain.

And then the shaman stepped back, his chant dying.

Tamaell Fedorem turned to Aeren and nodded.

Drawing in a deep breath, Aeren stepped toward the tent, Eraeth and Colin following in his wake. He saw representatives from each of the other two races doing the same.

The tent had four entrances, each one leading to a small room sectioned off from the large interior where the same wide, low table the dwarren had used in the previous meeting tent had been set up. There were no chairs on the dwarren's side of the table, and none on the Alvritshai side, but when Aeren stepped past the fold separating the entrance chamber to the main room, he noticed the human King had brought in three wooden seats. Pillows had been positioned for the Tamaell and the Cochen of the dwarren, with a few set to either side for those that accompanied them. In the center of the table sat a shallow bowl containing a sheaf of grain, a few eagle feathers, and assorted fruits. Otherwise, the tent and table were bare.

Even as Eraeth and Colin emerged from the outer room, Colin using his staff to push the tent flap aside, Aeren caught the whiff of smoke, followed by the incense the dwarren used. But the braziers he'd seen in the dwarren's meeting tent were absent.

"They must have lit one inside their own chamber," Eraeth murmured, nodding toward the southern side of the tent.

Even as he spoke, a clan chief Aeren was unfamiliar with stepped into the room, followed by three others. He glared at Aeren, arms crossed over his chest, then scanned the room.

The entire tent shook as the Legionnaire Tanner Dain shoved through. He rested his hand on the hilt of his sword meaningfully, frowning as he caught sight of Aeren, his stance shifting slightly, more on guard. When two other Legionnaires entered behind him, he motioned toward the table.

They inspected the room, even though they'd already sent in one person to look things over, then fell back to

Tanner's side without comment. He spoke to one in a whisper; the man ducked back outside, but Tanner kept his attention fixed on Aeren and the dwarren clan chief.

"Tell the Tamaell that everything is ready," Aeren said.

Eraeth grunted, gave Tanner one last dark glance, then slipped through to the outer room.

The dwarren clan chief simply nodded. He hadn't moved since he'd entered.

King Stephan arrived first. He wore a yellow shirt, a sheaf of wheat—like the one in the bowl in the center of the table, Aeren noted—embroidered in black on the front, the contrast stark. The shirt was formal, but plain, with no frills around the cuffs or neck and nothing adorning the shoulders, as Aeren knew the Andovans favored. This was practical, and with a shiver Aeren realized that the King wore armor beneath.

Stephan straightened, his gray eyes taking in Aeren, Colin, and the dwarren with one casual sweep, while one of the guardsmen held the tent flap back as what Aeren guessed was one of the Governors followed in the King's wake, six other Legionnaires coming in after him. The King moved to the central chair and sat, Tanner and the Governor taking the other two seats. The rest of the Legion spaced themselves out behind them.

Even with eight guardsmen behind him, Aeren knew that Stephan posed the biggest threat. Each of the humans carried a sword, and they all radiated a cold, wary hostility.

Harticur entered next, followed by Thaedoren, Garius, and two other clan chiefs. Three other Riders joined the two dwarren already present, as Thaedoren nodded at Harticur and moved around to the Alvritshai side. Stephan watched the interaction with a suspicious glare, his hands clenched where they rested on the arms of his chair, but Thaedoren ignored him. The rest of the clan chiefs moved to the edge of the table and sat, but Harticur remained standing.

"Lord Aeren," Thaedoren murmured in greeting. His gaze flicked toward Colin, brows rising in slight surprise. "Was bringing him here a wise choice?" He nodded minutely toward Stephan and the Legion. "We could have used one more of the Phalanx, if things go bad."

"One more member of the Phalanx would mean little."

"Perhaps. Or it could mean the difference between life and death."

Aeren was spared a response as Eraeth returned, holding the tent flap aside as the Tamaell, Khalaek, and the rest of the escort arrived. Khalaek seemed unnaturally nervous, his gaze darting about the room as if he were searching for something, his hand never far from his cattan. The casual smile he'd given Aeren outside had vanished, replaced by a hard expression, grim and apprehensive.

The Tamaell appeared grim as well. He wore a simple red and white shirt over light armor, his cattan strapped to his side. He took his place at the eastern end of the table, the western edge remaining empty.

Nodding formally to both Stephan and Harticur, he said, "I thank you both for coming—"

Before he could finish, Aeren caught movement out of the corner of his eye, a flicker, a blur of shadow. He frowned, a coldness lancing into his gut, a frisson of warning. Behind him, he heard Colin shift forward, heard the human say, "Wait," in startled confusion—

And then something splattered across his face, across his chest, something hot and fluid, soaking instantly through his clothing to his skin.

He jerked back, blinked, one hand already rising to touch whatever had struck his cheek—

And then he froze in mid-motion, eyes locked on the black-cloaked figure that stood before the Tamaell, one gloved hand fisted in the Tamaell's shirt over his chest, holding him upright and close, the other finishing the sweep of the blade across Fedorem's neck. The figure's face was hidden beneath a cowl, the hood drawn down, but Aeren caught the impression of human clothing beneath, a shirt styled like the Provinces, the glitter of a belt buckle, a sword's sheath.

He saw it all in the space of a heartbeat. Then the shadowed figure released the Tamaell, almost disdainfully, and with a smeared blur he vanished.

In the shocked, confused silence that followed, there was no sound except the patter of blood as it flew from a blade that was no longer there, as it gushed from the Tamaell's throat, coating the front of his shirt, his head thrown slightly back. It struck the table, hit the shallow bowl in the center, staining the sheaf of wheat, the eagle's feathers, the fruit.

Aeren felt his entire body go numb, his hands tingling, his heart stilled in his chest. He couldn't breathe. A roar filled his ears, like the wind of the plains, harsh and hollow and constant, a howl that drowned out everything.

And then the Tamaell dropped to his knees and toppled forward. His torso struck the table with a sickening, meaty thunk, his head cracking into the side of the wooden bowl. It flipped, the wheat and feathers and fruit scattering.

The clatter of the bowl coming to rest broke the silence.

Khalaek leaped forward, cattan sliding from its sheath in one smooth motion. "We've been betrayed!"

His roar filled the tent and sent a shudder through Aeren's chest, down into his gut. He heaved in a broken gasp even as the Phalanx who stood at the back of the tent surged forward with answering roars, charging onto the table toward the dwarren and the Legion. Blades snicked from sheaths as both the human guardsmen and the dwarren Riders sprang forward to protect their rulers. Aeren stepped back from the sudden din of shouts, of battle cries, of blades striking blades and hatred being unleashed.

Then a hand latched onto his arm and jerked him around. He cursed, one hand going automatically to his cattan, half drawing it before he recognized Eraeth's face. "Get back!" his Protector bellowed. He thrust Aeren against the side of the tent, where Colin stood, wide-eyed with horror, then stepped in front of them both, cattan already readied.

The blur, the figure, the Tamaell . . .

Aeren sucked in shocked breath and murmured, "A Wraith." He reached forward and grabbed Eraeth's arm. "Thaedoren! We have to protect Thaedoren!" But before he finished, he realized that neither he nor Eraeth could protect the Tamaell Presumptive. Not from what had killed Fedorem, not against a Wraith.

Only one of them had a chance.

He spun and yelled, "Colin!"

The human caught his gaze, and Aeren saw the realization sink in through the shock, the same realization he'd come to.

Then Colin blurred . . .

And vanished.

~

A moment before the Wraith appeared and slit the
Tamaell's throat, Colin had felt a disturbance in the air,
like a breeze. The hairs on his arms had prickled and risen.
Something stabbed into his left arm, where the black mark
from the Well swirled beneath his skin, pain searing up
from his wrist to his elbow. He'd hissed, clutched at the arm
with his other hand, turned to the side—

And then he'd smelled the Lifeblood: earth and leaves
and snow.

One of the Phalanx behind them met his gaze. He stood
near the entrance to the inner room where the three races
were meeting, one hand holding the flap of the tent to one
side, and as their eyes met, Colin felt a shock of recognition
pierce through him.

Khalaek's aide. The one who'd met Benedine in the
courtyard.

He heard the Tamaell begin to speak, heard his voice
cut off. "Wait," he muttered, as a stunned silence settled
over the room, broken by another sound, the sound of rain,
of droplets hitting wood and grass and cloth.

He caught a glimpse of the Wraith . . . and then it
vanished.

His hand tightened on his staff, his eyes going wide.

He'd known the Wraiths had left the forest, but the
sight of the Wraith there, in the tent, cloaked in shadows—

His chest squeezed tight, so tight he couldn't breathe, a
strange, queasy, fluid warmth settling in his gut, making his
legs tremble with weakness.

The Tamaell's body fell. He heard Khalaek shout, felt
the Phalanx around him charge forward, but everything
was removed and muted. Eraeth pulled Aeren back from
the escalating fray, blades and shouts filling the tent, and
still the warm, tingling weakness filled him.

And then he heard Aeren cry out, "Thaedoren! We
have to protect Thaedoren!" The Lord of House Rhyssal paused, one hand still clutching Eraeth's arm . . . and
then he spun, eyes intense with fear, with determination.
"Colin!"

It wasn't a question, it was an order.

With a sickening sensation, Colin felt the numbness

break. No one here had any hope of stopping the Wraith. No one *could* stop it.

Except him.

And Khalaek wanted to Ascend. He wanted the Evant. It wouldn't be enough to kill the Tamaell. He'd need to kill the Tamaell Presumptive as well.

Colin's jaw clenched, and without even a nod in Aeren's direction, he *pushed*.

The world slowed instantly, so fast Colin gasped. He'd shoved harder than he'd intended, but he didn't pause to steady himself, didn't even twitch at the sharp pain that shot through his side like a runner's cramp. The mark on his arm flared with pain again as he spun, centering on Thaedoren, the Tamaell Presumptive frozen in mid-motion, sword drawn, rising to strike at one of the Legion, the man's face twisted with rage, Thaedoren's face cold. The Wraith stood directly behind Thaedoren. Even as Colin watched, it brought its sword around to strike. A pressure built, prickling along Colin's skin, as the Wraith prepared to slip back into real time, the tip of its sword angled now toward Thaedoren's back.

Colin reacted without thought. His staff swung in a wide arc, whirring through the tight confines of the tent and cracking into the Wraith's neck.

The Wraith staggered, lurched to one side, then spun, sword flicking out to parry Colin's second swing. Metal met wood with a solid thwack, and a chunk of Colin's staff broke free. It slowed as it lost contact with the heartwood of the staff, froze in midair, returning to real time, but the Wraith didn't give Colin enough time to recover. It lashed out, sword nothing but a blur, going for his stomach.

Colin sucked in a breath as he stumbled backward, his staff whipping around to shunt the Wraith's blade aside. He cried out as he felt metal slicing through his clothing and into the skin at his side, but he ignored the flare of pain, bringing his staff up and around, trying to fling the sword from the Wraith's grip so it would return to real time like the chunk torn from his staff, but the Wraith merely grunted and turned into the staff's motion. Shifting his grip, Colin brought the bottom down toward the Wraith's feet.

Heartwood shuddered as it struck flesh, and the Wraith

shouted in pain as its leg folded and it fell to one knee, half-turned away. Colin threw himself backward as it pivoted, swinging its entire body around with a low growl, sword flashing through where Colin had stood a moment before, its cloak flaring.

The two faced each other, both breathing heavily, Colin with the staff angled before him, the Wraith on one knee, sword leveled, the world stilled around them.

And then the Wraith chuckled. A deep sound, unpleasant, rumbling from its chest, laced with hatred and contempt.

"What's the matter, Colin?" the Wraith sneered. "Don't you recognize me?"

Colin frowned, but before he had a chance to think, the Wraith swept the cowl from its face.

It took Colin a moment. The thin forty-year-old face beneath the cowl was mottled with swirling blackness, like oil, the darkness beneath the man's skin, like the mark that had slowly begun taking hold of Colin's forearm. But this darkness, this shadow was more complete, had reached a point where there was more darkness than there was skin. The face was scarred because of that darkness, age lines marring the flesh, as if the man beneath had suffered for long years, had been forced to suffer. The hair was a dirty blond but streaked with gray—at the temples, on the sides—long and unruly, tangled and mussed, with leaves caught in it, small twigs. The mouth was twisted in a sardonic smile, edged with vicious anger. And the eyes . . .

The eyes were not those of a forty-year-old man. They were the eyes of someone much older, someone who had experienced far more . . . and yet they were the eyes of a younger man as well, one who didn't know his place in the world, who desperately wanted a place but, however hard he tried, could not find it. Gray-green, those eyes regarded him with heated, deep-seated anger.

An anger Colin recognized.

The eyes, the face, the hair, the rage—

Colin sucked in a ragged breath. "Walter."

Walter's smile broadened even as his eyes narrowed, and Colin could see the fifteen-year-old boy who had beaten him in the back alleys of Portstown, could see the slightly older boy who had pissed on him while he was locked into the pillory and had choked him against the side of the wagon on the plains. "So good to know I haven't been forgotten," Walter murmured.

And now Colin recognized his voice, the younger Walter still hidden in the undertone, in the contempt. As all of the memories of his time in Portstown—the harassment and vicious bullying, the times that bullying had crossed over the line into something more deadly, more dangerous—as all of that and more returned, Colin found himself hardening. His chest tightened, the warmth of rage burning deep, sliding down into his gut, into his arms and legs. The coldness on seeing the Wraith vanished, subsumed by the anger, and he found himself slipping into a more solid stance, his jaw set in quiet resolve.

"I thought you'd died with all of the others in the wagon train, there at the edge of the forest," he said, his voice like stone. "I thought the Shadows got you."

Walter chuckled again. "Oh, the Shadows did. Only, unlike the rest, they didn't kill me. They took me to the Well. They made me drink, and then they fed off of my soul. They made me into *this*."

Walter leaped forward. Colin hadn't noticed him shifting his weight onto his bent leg, but he dodged to the left as Walter thrust upward. He brought the staff down hard toward Walter's exposed back, but Walter rolled, the heartwood thudding into the earth. Colin bit out a curse, already moving, Walter doing the same. He swung at Walter's retreating figure, the two dodging in and out among the static figures of the dwarren, the humans, and the Alvritshai. Blade met staff, both shoved aside as they parried, struck again, spun and twisted. Walter's sword sliced through Colin's shirt, nicked him in the arm, across the cheek, along the thigh, each cut stinging, blood flowing, soaking into his clothes, trailing down his leg. He hissed each time metal kissed flesh, but he struck back, using all the skills he'd mastered hunting the sukrael in the forests surrounding the Well, calling on everything he'd learned. The staff thudded into flesh with bruising force, catching Walter on the upper arm, the thigh, in a glancing blow across his back. Walter shouted with each touch, but he didn't slow. His attacks grew less precise, more haphazard, as they both began to tire. Sweat ran down into Colin's eyes, blurred his vision and stuck his clothes to his back, his sides. Weight settled into his arms, weariness and exhaustion setting in. He saw the same weariness lining Walter's face with every swing, but Walter wasn't tiring as fast. Colin thought about his time in the forest, fighting the sukrael, hunting the Wraiths, the Faelehgre at his side. He suddenly realized that nearly all the attacks he'd suffered from had come from one Wraith, from Walter. His hatred of Colin had never died, even after suffering at the hands of the Shadows. Walter had been the Wraith at the Well his last day in the forest, the bait for the trap that had lured him into the Shadows' grasp. Walter had been the one to hunt him throughout the years, even as Colin hunted the Shadows.

Which meant Walter had more practice with the power of the Well.

Even as he thought it, Colin felt his grasp of time slipping, as it had when he'd dragged Moiran outside the reach of the occumaen. He realized Walter would win. The Wraith could hold himself suspended longer.

And then Walter stumbled, tripped over the rough, trampled grass, falling to his side, his free hand reaching out to catch himself. He cried out, began scrambling away, sword clutched tight, feet digging into the earth. Colin slammed the staff into his back and he collapsed to the ground, sword arm beneath him; Colin struck him again as he tried to rise, and this time Walter stayed down, heaving, face pressed into the earth.

Colin stood over him, rage burning in his chest, through his blood, pounding in his ears. He could hear it, a rush of wind that throbbed with every pulse, that filled his mind, that bled from his fingers and seeped from his skin like sweat. He trembled with it, felt the urge to strike Walter again and again and again, once for every kick that he'd landed in the alley of Portstown, for every blow he'd suffered, every time he'd been spat upon by the townspeople while in the pillory. He wanted to see Walter bleed—for his father, his mother, for Karen and all that they had suffered at the hands of Walter and his father. He wanted Walter to bleed for Benedine, for the Tamaell Fedorem and the shattered chance of peace, for all of those who'd died at the hands of the sukrael.

He'd raised his staff to strike again when Walter rolled, a growl rumbling from his throat. His sword arm came free and he swung, even as Colin reacted, his shoulders tensing, the staff descending.

Walter's sword hit the staff between Colin's hands, and with a sharp crack, the staff broke.

Pain shivered up into his hands, numbed them. Colin gasped as he felt the shock tremble up through his arms, as he felt the power of the staff, gifted to him by the forest, release, a pulse that shuddered through him in a wave. The staff tumbled from his grasp, the two pieces returning to real time.

And then Walter's foot drove into his stomach, shoving him up and back.

He struck someone as he fell, tumbled over the immobile form, then struck the table where the Tamaell's body lay. His breath exploded from him, and he felt his hold on time loosen. Gasping, he snatched at it, the world lurching for a moment with motion, a roar of sound swelling, then dropping as he firmed up his grip. He tasted blood in his mouth, realized he'd bitten down on his tongue as he fell—

And then Walter loomed above him.

He saw one of Walter's booted feet rise and he rolled away.

But not fast enough. Walter's heel slammed into his side, dug into his back as he twisted, pinning him to the table. Something hard gouged into his stomach, trapped beneath him and the table and he hissed at the pain, Walter's weight digging it in deeper as he leaned into his foot.

And then he remembered what it was: the knife. The knife he'd used to try to kill himself in the forest. The knife Eraeth had begun training him with weeks before at the same time he started to teach him the Alvritshai language.

"All those years," Walter said, grinding his heel in harder, his teeth clenched with the effort. His breath came in haggard gasps. "All those years in the forest, near the Well, learning from the sukrael, learning how to speak to them, learning to manipulate them. All those years trying to hurt you, trying to catch you away from the Well, away from the cursed white stone of the city, so that I could make you suffer as I had suffered. All those years learning to live with myself! All because of you and your damned father, because of that stupid expedition."

The weight pressed into Colin's back released, and he shifted, rocked far enough that his hand could scrabble in the loose folds of his shirt, reaching for the handle of the knife. The tip of Walter's sword appeared in his line of vision, digging into the wood of the table a few inches in front of his face, and he stilled, fingers curled tight around the knife's handle, hidden from Walter's view by his body.

"If it hadn't been for you," Walter said, his voice close, leaning forward, weight on his sword, "I would have been the Proprietor of Portstown in my father's stead."

"No," Colin said, voice calm. He tensed, hand tightening its grip on the knife. "Your father only thought of you in one way." He turned slightly, so he could see Walter's face, the half-Shadow, half-man bent slightly forward, brow creased in consternation. "As his *bastard* son."

As he spat the last word, Colin flipped onto his back and brought the hand holding the knife out from under his body and up, inside the curve of Walter's arm. Walter lurched back, but he was too late.

The knife drove into Walter's chest with enough force to sink to the handle. Colin felt the blade strike bone, felt it scrape across it, shunted to one side, before puncturing deeper.

Walter screamed, pulling away with enough force to rip the knife from Colin's hands. His sword tore free of the table. Before he'd taken two steps, the scream turned into a liquid gargle as blood from his lungs filled his throat. Colin swore as he scrambled away, to the opposite side of the table. He'd missed the heart. And now he had no weapons at all.

On the far side of the table, Walter's scream gurgled out into a harsh cough as he leaned forward, spitting blood. He reached toward the dagger's handle protruding from his side, and with a wrench, he yanked the blade free. He screamed again, staggering to one side, nearly collapsing. Using his sword as a brace, tip dug into the earth, he steadied himself, still coughing, still spitting blood, although not as much as before.

Then he raised his head.

The lower half of his face was covered in blood, and when he grinned—a snarling, vicious grin—his teeth were stained with it. His face had gone pale, the swirling, mottled blackness more vivid in contrast. His hand, still holding the knife, clutched at his side, blood pouring over his fingers, saturating his black shirt.

"I—" he began, then broke into another fit of coughing. More blood—a dark, red, heart's blood—snaked from the corners of his mouth.

When he recovered, he was no longer grinning. His face was harsh, caught between rage and a grimace.

He'd hurt him. Hurt him more than Walter had thought possible. Colin could see it in Walter's eyes.

"I don't have time for this," Walter said, low and pained, but clear.

He drew himself up, wincing with effort, and considered Colin for a long moment, seething. Colin searched frantically for another weapon, but the only weapons available were being used by the Alvritshai, the Legion, and the dwarren surrounding them, and he couldn't touch them, couldn't drag them into his time frame. Not without restoring time first.

"I don't have time," Walter repeated.

And then he drew his hand away from his side, fresh blood spilling out as he released the pressure there and adjusted his grip on Colin's knife. Turning it, he flicked his wrist and threw the blade.

But not in Colin's direction, Colin realized in horror, even as the knife slowed in midair, returned to real time, no longer under the influence of Walter's or Colin's grip. Walter hadn't thrown the knife at him because he'd known Colin could move out of its way after it returned to real time.

Instead, he'd thrown it at one of the only other people in the tent that Colin cared about:

"Aeren," Colin said, eyes widening in horror.

Walter smiled grimly—

And then he blurred . . . and vanished.

21

A WAVE OF WEARINESS washed over Colin the moment Walter Traveled. He raised a hand to his face, his arms trembling, tremors coursing through his legs, wincing at the small cuts that riddled his body. When he tried to take a step forward, he stumbled, nearly fell—

And his grip on time slipped again.

Sound rushed back, motion, the sharp tincture of spilled blood.

Colin cried out, seizing hold again, his hands closing into tight fists in reaction.

It had only been a moment, but it was long enough for him to see the knife Walter had thrown fly toward Aeren, enough for him to see that it would hit the Lord of the Evant in the chest.

Breath hissing out through his teeth, Colin staggered to where the knife shivered in midair. Walter had been close to Aeren when he threw it. There wasn't much space between the blade and Aeren himself, barely enough for Colin to slip between the two.

Colin reached out with both hands and grabbed the handle of the knife and pulled, trying to move it, to make it budge.

Nothing.

He growled in frustration, even though he'd known the gesture would be useless. He'd never been able to change anything once it had happened. He hadn't even been able to brush the strands of hair from Karen's eyes. He'd never be able to move the dagger.

But perhaps he could shift it if he just loosened his hold on time.

Steadying himself, hands wrapped firmly around the handle, he let the part of his mind that held time relax, just a little, like letting a contracted muscle release.

The blade slipped forward, slowly, the sound of the fight in the tent surrounding Colin like a low, muted murmur. He began pulling on the knife, applying a steady pressure, even as it edged toward Aeren. Sweat broke out on his face, and he gritted his teeth, the muscles in his hands and fingers cramping. The knife shifted forward an inch, then two, and Colin felt his hold on time growing tenuous.

He began to growl, the sound rising as he exerted more effort, until—the growl escalating into a roar—he released the blade and fell back, halting time again.

Panting, one hand rising to wipe the sweat from his face, he inspected the blade, its angle, its path.

Nothing had changed.

He spat a curse. Because now the blade was a handspan closer to Aeren. He could barely squeeze between the two.

Still cursing, he began to pace. "Think, Diermani damn you, think!"

He paused in front of Aeren. The lord was looking toward where Colin had stood, one hand still gripping Eraeth's arm, hard, his grim, determined expression beginning to shift toward hope, the transformations subtle. He'd begun to turn, toward Eraeth, or perhaps Thaedoren. Colin could see it in the musculature of his neck, in the angle of his body. He had no idea the knife hung two handspans from his chest.

Colin couldn't tell the precise location where it would strike him, but he could see that it would likely be fatal. It might miss the heart, if he turned fast enough, if the blade struck bone, if . . .

Colin sighed.

He couldn't stop the blade. He couldn't move it, and there wasn't enough room left for him to deflect it once he restored time. The blade would hit Aeren in less than a breath, less than a heartbeat.

But he could let the knife hit something else.

Straightening grimly, steadying himself, he slid between the blade and Aeren, felt the tip of the knife catch on his

shirt, then dig into flesh. The height put it near the level of
his heart and he grimaced, thinking back to the time he'd
used this same knife in an attempt to kill himself.

It had hurt like all hells.

But it hadn't killed him.

He drew in a deep breath, felt the tip dig a little deeper
into his chest. He shifted slightly, so that the blade was centered over the right side, so that it wouldn't hit his heart.
For a moment, he considered letting it strike his arm, but
he needed to make certain it stopped, that it didn't simply
tear through flesh and muscle and hit Aeren anyway.

"And I can't die," he whispered to himself. He looked toward the heavens, raised one hand to grip Karen's pendant
around his neck, felt the sharp edges of the vow that he'd
never been able to fulfill digging into his hand. "I can't die."

And then he released time. No slight relaxation like before. He didn't need to feel the knife sinking into his flesh
inch by inch, didn't need to feel it cutting through muscle,
scraping across bone.

He just wanted it to be over. So he let time go.

The knife punched into his chest with enough force to
throw him backward, directly into Aeren. He screamed,
the sound filling the tent, blending with the cacophony
of blades clashing, lost among the blur of shouts, of commands, of battle cries that had been bellowed only moments before. White-hot pain shattered through Colin's
chest, exploded outward, so intense it muffled the noise,
dampened his own scream in his ears. He felt himself falling backward, felt tears streaming from the corners of his
eyes, heard Aeren shout as hands scrambled at his body,
caught him and lowered him to the ground. His scream
died down into a low moan, punctuated by sharper cries as
the hands holding him jostled the knife before he felt the
prickling sensation of dead, dried grass pressing through
his shirt as they lay him on the ground.

"Colin," Aeren said, his voice calm, but urgent. "Colin,
can you hear me?" Hands tugged at his shirt, jogged the
knife, and Colin hissed. Blood began to bubble up into his
throat, choking him, and he realized it had become difficult
to breathe.

In a voice barely above a whisper, Aeren muttered,
"Aielan's Light, what happened?" Then, harshly, "Eraeth!"

Colin opened his eyes, the light in the tent, the sun that glared down on the canvas above, too bright. So bright he felt his eyes watering. A shadowy figure moved into view, and with effort he focused, recognized Aeren, the lord joined a moment later by Eraeth.

"What's he saying?" Eraeth asked.

"It sounds like 'I can't die, I can't die.' He just keeps repeating it over and over."

"What happened?"

"I don't know. I told him to protect Thaedoren and he vanished, but before I could turn he fell into me, and—" Aeren broke off, then said, "Thaedoren!"

Aeren's face slid out of view and he felt the lord moving away. The sounds of the fight intensified, the voices of everyone blurring into a senseless mess of Alvritshai, dwarren, and Andovan.

Colin swallowed the blood in his mouth, fresh pain tearing through his chest. He could feel the knife where it had lodged against his rib cage, could feel it scraping against one of his ribs. His entire right side throbbed, and he felt the blood soaking his shirt, felt it pooling beneath his back. His right side felt hollow, yet leaden with weight.

He swallowed again, his mouth strangely dry even though it continued to fill with blood, and he tried to speak.

Eraeth leaned forward, close enough Colin could feel his breath, could smell his sweat, dark and musky, like turned earth. "What, Colin? What are you trying to say?"

"Lift," Colin gasped. He motioned feebly with one hand. "Lift."

Eraeth's lips pressed into a thin line, his expression one of doubt, as if he'd refuse—

But then he grunted, shifted to Colin's shoulders, and with more gentleness than Colin would have expected, lifted his torso up so that Colin could see.

He sought out Thaedoren first. Walter had vanished, but he had no doubt that the Wraith would try to kill Thaedoren again if he could. But Thaedoren stood surrounded by Aeren and at least three of the Phalanx, the group already beginning to retreat from the table, one of the Phalanx members dragging the Tamaell's body with him. Colin choked, tasted still more blood in the back of his throat, swallowed it down.

The look on the Tamaell Presumptive's face was terrifying.

Colin waved his hand, and Eraeth set him back down on the ground. Waves of heat washed through his body, and darkness had begun to edge his vision, a darkness tinged with a deep yellow. He fought it, not wanting to pass out, knowing that it was inevitable. It was how he'd healed when he'd stabbed himself in the heart in the forest, knew that's how he'd heal from this.

But then Aeren knelt down next to him, Thaedoren standing above, looking down, the rest of the Phalanx surrounding them on all sides.

"Colin," Aeren said, "what happened to the Wraith?"

"Walter," Colin breathed. The darkness had begun to converge, the heated ache in his chest throbbing outward.

Aeren frowned in confusion. "No, the Wraith, Colin. What happened to the Wraith?"

Thaedoren sank down beside Aeren in a crouch. "We don't have time for this, Lord Aeren. The dwarren are retreating, and the Legion is pushing us hard. I don't know how long we can hold them here. And once they reach the field . . ."

He trailed off, but neither Colin nor Aeren needed him to continue.

Once they reached the field, it wouldn't be a conflict between a select group from each race. It would be an outright battle.

Just like before. Everything that Aeren had feared, everything that he'd attempted to forestall, would happen again.

"Colin," Aeren began—

But a spasm rocked through Colin's chest. He gagged on blood, his chest rising from the ground as he rolled and choked and spat the blood to the side. Hands held him in place, kept him from thrashing around as he coughed up the blood.

When he settled back, his tongue sliding over his teeth, slick and coppery tasting, he saw a flicker of shadow.

Ten steps distant, Walter blurred into view at Lord Khalaek's back as the lord and his men pressed the Legion forces back. Walter looked as bad off as Colin felt, perhaps worse, his hand clutching at the wound in his side, beneath his armpit. But he didn't notice Colin, didn't even glance to the side. His face—eyes sheathed in darkness, mouth drawn down in rage—never wavered from Khalaek's back.

With his free hand, his sword now sheathed at his waist, he reached out, grabbed Khalaek by the shoulders—

And then the two vanished.

Colin held his breath, eyes going wide . . .

Then he rolled onto his back, stared up into Aeren's face, caught Thaedoren's hard expression, and said, "Proof. Need proof."

"What are you talking about?" Aeren said.

Colin's hands reached out, caught hold of Aeren's arm and Thaedoren's hand in a death grip. He didn't know if he could take them both, or how long he could hold them there, not after the great effort it had taken to save Moiran, not with the knife digging into his chest, but he had to try. "Proof," he breathed, then squeezed his hands tight, made certain he had their attention. "Don't move. Don't speak."

And then he *pushed*.

It felt as if someone had taken the knife in his chest and ripped it out by dragging it down and to the side, tearing through bone, through lungs and muscle and gut, opening him wide. He wanted to scream, to shriek until his throat tore, but he knew he couldn't, knew he had to be quiet, hoped and prayed that both Aeren and Thaedoren would remain silent as well, and so he clamped down on the scream, bit down hard on his tongue; he tasted fresh blood, but he focused on that small pain to take his mind away from the agony that his chest had become. And through that agony, through the exquisite pain, he felt the world slow and settle.

And he heard Walter's voice, black and deadly.

"That wasn't the original deal," Walter said.

"No, it wasn't," Khalaek spat, contemptuous. "That was before my esteemed colleague, Lord Aeren, brought forth this preposterous treaty, before the Tamaell Presumptive was brought back from his banishment, before this foolhardy envoy left Caercaern and came to the plains!"

"None of that is my concern. I only care about the Well. I've done what you asked—done more by killing the acolyte. The Tamaell is dead. Now give me the location of the Well."

Colin felt the muscles in Thaedoren's arms tense, heard the Tamaell Presumptive draw in a ragged breath, but he squeezed hard, warning him to keep silent. Thaedoren's blood pulsed beneath Colin's fingers, a quickened throb, but he restrained himself. Colin stared up into Aeren's widened eyes, saw the lord relax, saw Thaedoren's face beyond, the Tamaell Presumptive's eyes locked on the two figures Colin could not see, the muscles in his jaw clenching.

Colin heard someone shift.

"You're bleeding," Khalaek said, his voice low.

"I'll heal."

"What happened?"

"I ran into an old acquaintance."

Khalaek drew in a deep breath. "Perhaps I made a mistake in dealing with you. Perhaps you aren't as strong as I thought."

Silence. And then Khalaek gasped. At the same time, Colin heard the faint scrape of metal against metal as a sword was drawn.

"You," Walter said, his voice deadly, "are simply a convenience. The Well will be found, whether you help us find it or not. The Lifeblood will be restored. All of it. Every last node. You provided a way for us to shorten that task, nothing more." The rustle of clothes, followed by a gasp from Khalaek. "Now, tell me where the Well is."

Colin couldn't see what was happening, but he didn't need to. He'd begun trembling, his hold growing more and more tenuous. His vision had narrowed down to a thin tunnel, the darkness creeping inexorably closer. The effort to hold himself, Aeren, and Thaedoren here had escalated it.

As he struggled to hold it a moment longer, he heard movement, something swift, followed by a meaty thud. Khalaek gasped—

And then Walter yelled. A sound of pain and fury, a sound that consumed the tent, that reverberated in Colin's ears. He winced, heard Thaedoren swear, the words bitten off, and then felt the Tamaell Presumptive leap forward, jerking out of Colin's grasp. He brushed the handle of the knife still protruding from Colin's chest—

And the white-hot pain wrenched at Colin's hold on time. He couldn't hold the scream in this time. But even through that pain he felt the world slide back into place, heard Thaedoren barking orders, heard the clash of blades return yet again as Aeren shouted a command to Eraeth, the Protector blinking, looking confused, but reacting to the urgency in Aeren's voice. He bellowed orders, the escort of Phalanx breaking away from the Legion forces, drawing back. At a look from Aeren, Eraeth grunted, reached down, slid one arm beneath Colin's armpit, the other beneath his knees, and without warning heaved him up and ran for the back of the tent.

The pain filled him. Eraeth hadn't had time to be gentle. What had been isolated to Colin's chest now pummeled his entire body. He gagged as fresh blood filled his mouth again, spat to one side, the yellowed blackness of his vision closing in entirely. He hung on to consciousness long enough to feel the breeze as they exited the tent, long enough to hear the horns being sounded, the drums pounding, calling the dwarren to battle. He hung on long enough to feel Eraeth's dash away from the tent toward the safety of the Alvritshai army juddering through his body, his free arm flailing, the other trapped between his body and Eraeth's chest. He hung on long enough to listen to Eraeth's blistering curses.

And then all sensation faded—all sight and sound, the smell of Eraeth's sweat, the silky texture of his blood-stained shirt where it pressed against his face.

All of that died, and the darkness closed in.

Eraeth didn't stop running after leaving the tent. He didn't pause to throw Colin's sagging body over the back of a horse, didn't even halt when Thaedoren shouted, "The Tamaell is dead! Sound the horns! Sound them for battle!" the Tamaell Presumptive—the Tamaell now—swinging up into his saddle. Appalled gasps ran through the Phalanx who had waited outside the tents as the Tamaell's body was dragged into view, but Eraeth ignored it all, ignored the mournful blare of the horns as the entire group mounted, horses whickering and dancing as they picked up on the escalating tension. He locked his gaze on the line of the Alvritshai army in the distance and ran.

Drums began to pound to his right, ragged at first, then slipping into a steady, inexorable rhythm. He heard the thunder of gaezels charging across the grassland and ground his teeth together. To his left, a battle cry erupted from the waiting Legion, and he risked a glance to the side, saw the King's entourage galloping toward the human lines, flags already flashing, the men there mobilizing.

And then Thaedoren's escort charged past him, dirt thrown by their passage pattering against his legs. The Tamaell's body bounced on the back of an unmanned horse being led by the Phalanx, and Lord Khalaek had been lashed to his own horse, the Tamaell's men surrounding him. Khalaek rode with an arrogant pride, back rigid, shoulders set, but with a wild look in his eyes.

"Moiran!" Aeren shouted as he passed, motioning toward Colin. "Take him to Moiran!"

Eraeth nodded and slowed, Colin's weight beginning to wear him down, the adrenalin rush fading, the pounding of his heart lessening. Thaedoren reached the Alvritshai army, and an instant later the White Phalanx roared in outrage, the sound spreading outward in a wave as word of what had happened in the tent spread to the other House Phalanx, a gasp of shock at the Tamaell's death, followed by a roar of escalating rage. The Tamaell Presumptive was surrounded by the Lords of the Evant. At a sharp, dismissive gesture from Thaedoren the escort surrounding Khalaek jerked the lord's horse toward the camp, Khalaek rocking in the saddle. The horse carrying Fedorem's body followed, both heading back toward the camp beyond the ridge.

And then Thaedoren turned to face the field. He took a moment to survey the two other armies, his gaze flickering left and right . . . and then he began issuing orders.

Eraeth entered the edge of the army as the first horns began to blow, each a different tenor, each with a different pattern as the orders were spread. He fought through the ranks as the men of the Phalanx began to move, Colin's legs catching on one guardsman until Eraeth turned sideways. He stumbled down the back of the ridge as the army broke away into the flat beyond and nearly collapsed, but he caught himself, hitching Colin's body into a higher position in his arms. His muscles ached, but he staggered forward, passing through the tents, past servants and Phalanx warriors scrambling to prepare, the reserve already assembling near the front of the camp.

And then he was there, at the Tamaea's tents.

He shoved through the interior tent flap and stood, breath coming in gasps, to find the Tamaea leaning over the Tamaell's body. Tears streaked her face, although she was not sobbing. Her hands were adjusting the Tamaell's shirt, tugging it back into place, unmindful of the blood that stained her fingers, but the motions were abstract, fumbling, her hands shaking slightly. The Phalanx who had brought the body stood to either side, backs to the tent walls, shifting uncomfortably.

Moiran finally seemed to realize that her ministrations were useless. Her hands paused, hovering over Fedorem's body . . . and then they dropped into her lap. Blood from her fingers smudged her dress in brushlike patterns, but Moiran didn't notice.

"Oh, Fedorem," she murmured, her voice hoarse, thick with phlegm.

She sensed Eraeth's presence and glanced to the side.

Eraeth flinched at the stricken look in her eyes. But even as he did so, the blankness faded as Moiran focused on what Eraeth carried. Her eyes narrowed, and her lips pressed into a thin line.

"Lord Aeren told me to bring him to you, Tamaea," Eraeth said.

Moiran hesitated, her body trembling. Then her stooped shoulders straightened. She glanced down at Fedorem and smiled bitterly, painfully. "There's nothing I can do for you." She leaned forward and kissed Fedorem's forehead. As she straightened, she wiped fresh tears from her face, leaving a smear of Fedorem's blood behind.

Then she stood, her eyes hardening. "Not here. The next room. We'll leave my husband to Aielan's Light in peace."

Eraeth didn't argue, even though his arms were straining to hold Colin's body aloft. He followed Moiran into the next room, where she began moving chairs and blankets and a platter of fruit aside to clear room around a low table. "Set him here."

As Eraeth laid Colin down on the table, the Tamaea snapped to the two guardsmen who'd followed them, "Get me fresh linen and a bowl of warm water, and fetch one of the healers."

One of the guards dashed out of the tent, but Moiran

didn't wait for him to return. She knelt down beside Colin, checked his eyes, felt for his pulse. "What happened?"

"He saved Lord Aeren," Eraeth said, but he hesitated. "Or that's how it appeared. It was hard to tell. It happened too fast to follow."

Moiran nodded, her hands moving over Colin's body, searching for more wounds, for bruising, for broken bones. She frowned as she came across a cut along his upper arm, at another, deeper slash along his side, but in the end, her gaze returned to the handle of the knife protruding from the right side of Colin's chest.

They both looked up as horns sounded in the distance, followed by the clash of weapons.

Moiran winced but turned back to face Eraeth. "And Fedorem?"

Eraeth shifted uncomfortably. "One of the Wraiths."

"And Khalaek? Why was Khalaek brought back under guard?"

Eraeth thought back to the tent, to when Colin had reached out and grabbed both Aeren and Thaedoren, had told them not to move, not to speak . . . and then all three had vanished.

He didn't know where they'd gone, had barely had time to react before they'd returned, Thaedoren already leaping over Colin's prone figure, face contorted in rage, heading toward Khalaek, the Lord of the Evant inexplicably stumbling backward, as if he'd been thrust away by someone, although no one was there.

He'd been facing away from the fight with the Legion, when a second before he'd been fighting alongside his own Phalanx.

"I'm not certain," Eraeth said. "But I think Lord Khalaek helped the Wraith kill the Tamaell." He looked down at Colin, the human barely breathing. "I think Colin stopped the Wraith from killing the Tamaell Presumptive and showed Thaedoren that Khalaek and the Wraith were allied in some way."

Moiran's face lightened at the mention of Thaedoren. "Then Thaedoren is safe?"

When Eraeth nodded, she sighed in relief. But within moments, her eyes darkened again, with hatred. "Khalaek

will be dealt with," she said flatly, and Eraeth found himself
stiffening at her tone.

The healer arrived, carrying bandages. "Tamaea, the
White Phalanx said—"

He halted, sucking in a deep breath as he caught sight
of Colin, of the blood, the knife jutting from his chest. "Aielan's merciful Light," he whispered.

Then he shook himself, face turning serious. He shoved
Eraeth aside, moving into position on the opposite side
of the table from the Tamaea, motioning the guardsman
who'd returned with him to bring the bowl of water he
carried closer. After a quick survey of Colin's body, similar
to what Moiran had done, he sat back.

"I don't think he'll survive. The knife wound . . ." he
shook his head. "If he were Alvritshai, it would be a mortal
wound. The damage on impact was extensive, but he appears to have been jostled around. The blade has moved,
causing more extensive damage to the surrounding areas.
He should be dead already."

Moiran sat back. "He's still breathing."

"And he shouldn't be. I don't understand it."

Eraeth edged forward, caught their attention. "He's not
Alvritshai."

"Even for a human—" the healer began, but Eraeth cut
him off.

"He's not human either." At the perplexed look on the
healer's face, Eraeth turned toward Moiran. "In the tent,
after being struck, he kept repeating, 'I can't die, I can't
die.' He didn't pass out until after we'd left the tent. He's
been touched by the sarenavriell."

They sat in silence a long moment, Colin between them,
his chest rising and falling, slower than normal, but still
moving.

"Take it out," Moiran said. When the healer began to
protest, she insisted, "Take it out! And if you have any of
the water of the ruanavriell, use it on him. I don't care how
rare it is, or that he's human."

The healer shot her a black look, but he set about ar-
ranging his bandages, removing needle and gut and a small
vial of the precious pink-tinged water of the ruanavriell.
He wet a cloth in the bowl and passed it to Moiran, then
ripped Colin's shirt down the middle, exposing his chest.

Moiran began wiping the blood clear, the cloth instantly stained a dark red. The skin beneath was a pasty white, bruised in a few places, and more blood seeped from the wound around the knife, sluggish and thick. She frowned but continued her work as the healer prepared.

The healer, gut threaded and in hand, hesitated, looking at the handle of the knife.

"What's wrong?" Moiran asked.

"Taking the knife out may kill him."

"I thought you said he should already be dead," Eraeth muttered.

The healer replied. "Twice over if you dragged him all the way here from the tent."

Moiran snorted in disgust. But before she could say anything, Eraeth crouched down, grabbed the handle of the knife, and jerked it out of Colin's body.

Colin spasmed, chest heaving upward, his eyes flying wide as he coughed up more blood while rocking over onto his side. His eyes caught Eraeth's, held them for a moment. Eraeth couldn't tell if the human was conscious, if he knew what Eraeth had done.

But the healer did. Cursing, he pushed Eraeth out of the way, rolled Colin onto his back once he stopped coughing, tilting his head to the side so the blood could drain, then turned back to the chest wound.

When he leaned forward, vial ready and needle poised, Moiran glaring as she fought the dark flow of heart's blood, Eraeth nodded to the two Phalanx and stepped out into the tent's corridor.

He stood for a long moment, hand clutching the bloody knife in one hand, trying to control the tremors caused by the thought of Colin's death, the nausea that burned like acid in the back of his throat. He swallowed, steadied himself, then let his hand fall back to his side.

Moving to the front of the tent, he stepped out into the afternoon sunlight and stared up at the cloudless sky. Distantly, he heard the low rumble of fighting and he turned, his ear automatically picking out the direction of the disturbance.

The urge to ride into battle made his hands twitch. He crossed his arms over his chest to control them, forced himself to wait, even though he knew Aeren had ridden into battle with the Rhyssal House Phalanx.

Aeren had ordered him to take care of Colin. Not in so many words, but he knew his lord.

And Colin was Rhyssal-aein.

A short time later, Moiran emerged from the tent, wiping her hands free of blood with a wet cloth. She squinted into the sunlight and turned toward the sounds of battle.

After a long moment of silence, she said, "He's still alive, although barely. The water of the ruanavriell—the Blood of Aielan—it helped to stanch the flow of blood, but the healer says Colin is still bleeding inside, that the damage there is . . . extensive. He's sealed the wound, but he does not expect him to survive. The ruanavriell is not enough."

"Colin was given into my care by Lord Aeren himself."

She faced him, hands on her hips, her eyes intent. "I owe him a debt myself," she said. "For Thaedoren's life, if you are correct, as well as my own. There's nothing more to be done here."

Eraeth hesitated. The knife he'd drawn from Colin's chest weighed heavily in his hand, the blood already drying.

"Go," Moiran said, her voice gentle. "I will take care of him. You need to protect your lord."

Eraeth handed Moiran Colin's knife, pressing it into the soiled cloth she still held, even though she still wore the bloodstained dress and had a smear of dried blood on her cheek. "Return this," he said, and then he dug into the pocket hidden in the folds of cloth of his shirt beneath the hardened leather of his armor and removed the cloth-wrapped vial Colin had given him on the plains, the vial that contained the Lifeblood.

He held it before him a long moment, staring at the clear liquid through the glass. He could see Colin's pained expression, heated with anger, as he handed it over, still hunched in the grass from the seizure. Those seizures had decreased after that, until he'd begun returning to the forest to converse with the Faelehgre about the Wraiths and the sukrael.

The Lifeblood hurt him, but Eraeth knew it could save him as well.

"Take this," he said gruffly, handing the vial to Moiran, catching her confused gaze and holding it. "If he asks for me, give this to him. But only if he asks."

Moiran nodded.

And then Eraeth stepped away, letting his concern over Colin fall behind, resting it on Moiran's shoulders. He motioned to one of the nearest Phalanx. "A horse! Now!"

Ten minutes later, he dug in his heels, the horse leaping forward, charging out of the camp and over the ridge, toward the battlefield below.

~

Aeren's cattan met the Legionnaire's blade with a clash, metal scraping against metal as it slid down toward the hilt. The grizzled, bearded man howled and jerked his blade away, thrusting Aeren's cattan to the side, swinging wide. Sweat drenched the man's face, droplets flung from his hair as he twisted, bringing his sword around for another strike—

But Aeren was quicker. His cattan sank into the break in the man's armor beneath the armpit, in and out in the space of a breath.

The man's roar choked off and he staggered backward, the momentum he'd built up for the swing faltering and dragging him off-balance. He tripped over the body of a fellow Legionnaire and went down, but Aeren barely saw him, spinning where he stood, searching for Thaedoren.

The Tamaell Presumptive was still astride his horse, surrounded by at least twenty members of the Phalanx, all from House Resue, and as Aeren's gaze picked him out of the mass of men and Alvritshai fighting on the open battlefield before the Escarpment, the leader of House Resue and the Evant bellowed a challenge and charged toward the thickest group of Legionnaires, his mount plowing into the morass without hesitation. His Phalanx roared after him, cattans already bloody.

Aeren moved toward the group, his own escort—slightly scattered and dealing with the last of the men who'd hit them hard an hour before, as the three armies collided on the plains—falling in around him with a sharp order.

"What now?" Dharel asked, trotting alongside him. His face was dark, a trail of blood down one side of his neck from a cut near his ear.

"Back to the Tamaell Presumptive's side," Aeren said.

"That last wave spread us out too far. We need to regroup."
He didn't mention the loss of his horse, cut from beneath
him when the humans had first struck, their front line so
overwhelming it had split their forces nearly in two. Thaedoren had divided the army into two fronts, had struck
the field at the head of a vee, each side ready to face
the two opposing forces, the left—consisting of Houses
Nuant, Licaeta, and Baene—confronting the dwarren, the
right—Houses Redlien, Ionaen, and Duvoraen—facing
the Legion. After careful consideration, he'd ordered Lord
Khalaek's men to follow Khalaek's caitan, not trusting
Khalaek's men to follow any other lord's directions on
the field. House loyalty was fierce, and most of Khalaek's
men were already grumbling over the seizure of their lord.
Thaedoren then ordered Aeren to stay close, leaving Lords
Jydell and Peloroun in charge of the southern flank.

The strongest Houses were facing the Legion. They
were the greatest threat. The Legion were better trained,
had better armor and longer reaches, and there were more
of them. And the Legion had the greater conviction, the
most hatred. Aeren could sense it on the field, had seen
it in each of the men's eyes as they attacked him. A good
portion of the Legion here on the field were older. Old
enough to remember the previous battle on this land, when
the Alvritshai had turned on their allies and assassinated
their King.

The memories of that battle crowded forward. Not the
fighting, but the final stages of the attack, when they'd pressed
the dwarren to the lip of the Escarpment . . . and then over.

The screams as they'd fallen—both dwarren and the
higher, more piercing shrieks of the gaezels—haunted his
dreams still.

"Look!"

Aeren slowed and spun, caught sight of Auvant, then
turned to look in the direction his House guardsman had
pointed.

The northern edge of the line, near where Lord Peloroun stood, had begun to crumble. Legion poured
through the breaks.

"Signal House Duvoraen!" Aeren snapped, his horn-
bearer scrambling to pull the curved horn from its place
at his side.

The short peals of the horn rang out, ordering House Duvoraen to aide Peloroun. Aeren watched, breath held, as Peloroun fought to keep his line intact. Lord Jydell attempted to send some of his own force, but his men were already locked in desperate battle with the Legion.

As Peloroun's line finally sagged and gave way completely, House Duvoraen, led by its Phalanx caitan instead of its lord, charged into the middle of the fray in a tight arc around Lord Jydell's men. Aeren expelled a held breath in relief.

For a long moment, the Legion that had broken through held. Alvritshai fell to human swords. Horses stumbled and sank beneath the crushing waves of men, killing more men and Alvritshai as they panicked. The caitan's mount reared, and Aeren heard Dharel suck air between his teeth as it wavered, threatening to tumble backward and crush the Duvoraen's temporary leader. But then he regained control, and the horse dropped, hooves kicking, one crushing the head of a Legionnaire, the man falling like a sack of grain.

The caitan roared, so loud Aeren could hear it through the chaos of the battle on all sides, the sound flat with distance. The Alvritshai responded, both Duvoraen and Ionaen. They surged forward, gaining momentum as they charged, like an ocean's wave approaching the shore. They crashed into the rough line the Legion had formed and shoved it back, hard, enough that the Alvritshai line rejoined with Lord Jydell.

Aeren allowed himself to breathe, grimacing at the stench of the battlefield. The smell of blood was sharp, permeated with death, an undertone of churned earth and trampled grass beneath that and, faintly, from somewhere close, smoke. Satisfied that the line would hold, Aeren turned back toward the Tamaell Presumptive. He hadn't been certain how the caitan of House Duvoraen would react to his lord being supplanted, but it appeared that his fears were unjustified. "Call House Rhyssal to me."

The horn-bearer nodded, raising the silvered horn to his lips. As the call to regroup faded, Aeren heard the pounding of hooves, close, and turned to see Eraeth pulling to a halt on the outside of the assembling group.

"Lord Aeren," Eraeth said. "You called?"

Aeren grinned, Dharel and Auvant doing the same to either side. "It's good to see you. While Dharel and Auvant are more than competent, it's been strange not having you fighting by my side." But then his grin faltered. "Shaeveran?"

All of the surrounding guardsmen shifted. Word of what Colin had done in the tent had been passed among them almost instantly, and nearly all of them had seen Eraeth carrying him from the field, had seen the knife in his chest, the blood that even now soaked the front of Eraeth's shirt.

Eraeth's expression darkened, and when he spoke there was apprehension in his voice. "I left him in the Tamaea's care. A healer tended him, but he couldn't say whether he'd survive. I left the Tamaea the vial Shaeveran gave into my care on the plains."

Aeren nodded, as those of House Rhyssal who'd continued to gather to the call murmured, passing the word. "Her debt to him is as great as ours," he said, and saw Eraeth relax slightly. Then the edge of his grin returned. "And Shaeveran has a habit of surviving longer than he has any right to."

A few of the men chuckled. Aeren felt the moment of dread, of depression and despair, slip away and thanked Aielan's Light, sending a prayer for Colin along with the thanks. He had his doubts about Colin's survival—he'd seen the wound, seen the blood and the paleness of Colin's face as Eraeth gathered him into his arms—but he'd be damned if he let his men see them.

"What now?" Eraeth said. He scanned the field, gazing at the line to the north. The southern line against the dwarren had held, but that was because the dwarren had kept half of their force in reserve and were only fighting defensively. They'd made no push to take ground or break the Alvritshai line, focusing most of their attention on the more aggressive Legion forces trying to break through their ranks to the west.

As Eraeth eyed the dwarren lines, his brow furrowing, Aeren said, "They're waiting. To see how the battle plays out."

"Or to see if this is some type of trick," Eraeth said. "Like the last time they were on this field. They're wary it may happen again."

Aeren nodded. But before he could respond, Dharel said, "Movement in the Legion ranks."

Both Aeren and his Protector turned toward the north, but Eraeth had the advantage of height, still astride his horse.

"Two groups, a hundred men each," he reported. "Reserve units. They're heading toward the Tamaell Presumptive's position."

"Dharel, left flank, Auvant, take the right, we'll support the Tamaell Presumptive."

"Until he sounds a retreat or we're all dead," Eraeth threw in with a feral grin.

Both Dharel and Auvant chuckled, then spun and began shouting orders, the House Rhyssal Phalanx falling into line behind them. Eraeth stood down from the horse and handed the reins to Aeren. After a moment's hesitation, Aeren swung up into the saddle. Eraeth took position to his left, the horn-bearer to his right. Someone had salvaged the Rhyssal banner—a deep blue field with the red wings of the eagle flaring to both sides—and carried it a few paces behind.

Eraeth tugged at his arm, and he glanced downward. "The Wraith?"

Aeren frowned, thought back to what he'd seen of the Wraith when Colin had pulled Thaedoren and himself back so they could witness Khalaek's betrayal.

The Wraith had been wounded as badly as Colin, if not worse. He'd been clutching the side of his chest at first, blood pouring out of him, more blood than Aeren thought a human could possess.

And then Khalaek—with the Wraith's sword leveled at his throat, touching it with enough pressure to draw blood—had punched the wound hard.

Aeren had seen a flare of metal in Khalaek's hand a moment before it struck, some type of dagger or knife jutting out between the fingers of the clenched fist.

"I don't think the Wraith will be an issue," Aeren said. "Not right now."

When Dharel and Auvant signaled ready, Aeren turned toward the Tamaell Presumptive's line, less than a hundred paces distant. He could see Thaedoren in the center of the mass of men and Alvritshai, could see the House Resue

colors as the line shifted back and forth, undulating like a
river. And beyond them, the Legion reserves, thundering
forward on horses, coming from both sides.

He raised his cattan, readied it. He felt the exhaustion
from the battle already fought, felt the weariness in his
arms, in his legs.

Then he signaled the horn-bearer.

As the first clear note sounded, he kicked his horse into
motion, eyes forward, locked on Thaedoren, the Tamaell
Presumptive who would become the Tamaell once the
battle ended ... if he survived.

And Aeren intended him to survive.

With that thought he cried out, his men breaking into
battle cries to either side.

And then they struck.

Aeren felt the impact through his entire body, juddering
up from his horse as it plowed into the Legion's ranks, the
Alvritshai that had held them back opening up before them
as they heard the roar of their approach. Aeren brought his
cattan down, slashing through the throat of the Legionnaire
in front, letting the blade's momentum carry it to the side
before adjusting its motion and punching it down through
the chest of another man. He planted his foot on the man's
shoulder as blood fountained from his mouth, the man's
scream drowned out in his own blood, then shoved, his cattan slipping free. He nudged his horse forward, caught Eraeth's blade flickering with the dying sunlight to the left, saw
the horn-bearer, horn now at his side, cattan free, scream as
a Legionnaire's blade took him in the side. Another Alvritshai in Rhyssal colors took the horn-bearer's place.

And then time slipped, became a blur of parry and feint,
his blade flicking across throats, cutting into arms and legs.
He brought the hilt down on top of exposed heads, kicked
with his feet to dislodge helms and shove his horse forward, heading toward Thaedoren.

He felt the Legion's reinforcement join the fray more
than saw it. A ripple spread through the mass of men,
packed so tightly together they could barely move, a surge
that shuddered through his legs. He glanced up in time
to see resurgent hope spread through the Legion before
the entire Alvritshai line was physically shoved backward.
His horse screamed as it stumbled, fought for footing on

ground already churned to mud, soaked with blood and riddled with the bodies of those that had fallen. He struggled to bring it around, stabbed down into a man's face, his cattan slicing along the man's nose before he jerked back with a shriek, his cheek sliced open and hanging, the bone of his jaw exposed—

And then his horse regained its footing. The Alvritshai line steadied as well, and it continued to hold, on all sides, against the dwarren and the Legion, to the north and the south. Lines shifted, wavering back and forth across the blood-drenched plains, no one force gaining any appreciable ground, no one race making any headway. It continued for hours, the sun sinking into the horizon to the west, over the edge of the Escarpment.

Before it had half vanished, a shudder ran through the entire ranks of the Legion. Glancing up, the position of the sun only now registering, Aeren saw a group of Legionnaires standing two hundred paces back from the line, men with flags racing back and forth on either side of the main group. King Stephan stood at the front of the group, surrounded by two of the Governors of the Provinces, glowering at the Alvritshai position, at where Thaedoren had withdrawn slightly.

The two stared at each other as the Legion began to retreat, breaking away and withdrawing back toward their camp to the north.

The Alvritshai forces pursued them, until Thaedoren motioned to his own horn-bearer, and the call to retreat echoed across to the plains, joined by the long, drawn-out beats of the dwarren drums.

As all sides pulled back, dragging wounded with them, Aeren surveyed the dead they left behind, counted the Legion on the field and those they'd kept back, then turned to Eraeth, his Protector covered in sweat and dirt and blood, some of it his own.

"We cannot win this battle," he said grimly.

And then he signaled House Rhyssal to retreat.

22

AEREN STOOD INSIDE THE TENT, at the head of the gathering of the Evant—only Lord Khalaek was missing—with the Tamaell Presumptive sitting to his right, Lotaern to his left, Eraeth and a few Phalanx from House Rhyssal and Resue behind them. Servants had brought trays of food, platters of cheese and fruit, and jugs of wine, passing them among the lords as they marched in from the field. Others eased their lords out of armor, while healers dabbed at wounds. Lord Waerren had taken a vicious cut to his upper arm and winced as it was stitched closed. Barak ran fingers through hair matted with blood, taking a proffered towel so he could wipe the grit and dust from his face. Each was surrounded by his House Phalanx, nearly everyone being tended, all of them grumbling or grimacing as they were poked and prodded. Moiran moved among them, helping where she could.

The day's fighting settled over Aeren like a mantle, heavy and encompassing. Exhaustion dragged down on his arms, threatening to pull him to the floor. Weariness lay thick on his shoulders. He ached in places he hadn't felt in thirty years, since the last time they'd fought on these plains. He wanted merely to retreat to his tents, tend to his wounds, as minor as they were, and sleep.

But the Tamaell Presumptive had called a meeting of the Evant.

As soon as the healers had finished and the servants had retreated, Thaedoren ordered everyone but the Evant out, including his mother, then turned and nodded at Aeren.

Aeren didn't wait for silence, didn't even wait until he had the lords' attention. He simply said again, quietly, "We cannot win this battle."

The reaction was instantaneous and explosive. The lords spluttered or growled, would have stood had they not been as exhausted as Aeren himself. Their protests escalated, until Lord Peloroun leaned forward and shouted, "Preposturous! How can you say this at this stage? We have only been on the field for a few days!"

"And how were you faring during those few days? How much ground did you gain before the dwarren arrived?" Aeren shot back.

The rest of the lords fell silent at the vehemence in Aeren's tone, surprised. Aeren had never been quick to anger, but he was furious now. "We didn't come here to fight," Aeren growled. "We came here to *end* the fighting, to negotiate a peace with the dwarren. There was never any intention to stage a prolonged battle, especially against two separate armies on the same battlefield!"

"That was not the intent," Peloroun said, voice hard, "but some of us knew that forging peace was merely a weak lord's—a *diplomat's*—dream, nothing more."

Aeren ignored the slight. "And so you brought your Phalanx, nearly five hundred strong from your House alone by the time we'd reached the borders."

"Two thousand more joined us while you and the Tamaell Presumptive went off to meet with the dwarren," Peloroun said. "Or were you not aware of the reinforcements the Tamaell had arranged?"

"I was aware of them. And it is still not enough. Not when you factor in the loss of over two hundred Alvritshai on the battlefield today. Two hundred Alvritshai sent to Aielan's Light!"

"Ha!" Peloroun spat to one side. "What does a diplomat know of war?"

Aeren drew in a deep breath to calm himself, glanced around at the other lords, saw some of them with skeptical expressions, clearly siding with Peloroun.

But a few were frowning.

He focused on Peloroun. "Think back to the field today, Lord Peloroun. Think back to the battle."

Peloroun grunted and sat back grudgingly. "Our lines held."

"Barely. The dwarren lines held as well, and the Legion provided a serious threat. They nearly broke through your own ranks on the northern flank. If not for House Duvoraen in reserve to bolster it, the Legion would have overrun Lord Jydell's forces." Some of Jydell's men nodded in agreement.

"But it isn't House Ionaen's weakness that I wish to emphasize," Aeren continued, and Peloroun's eyes sharpened. "What I want to point out is that neither the dwarren nor the humans committed their entire force. Harticur—Cochen of the dwarren Gathering and commander of its Riders—sent only half of them to the front lines—"

"He was acting in defense only!" Peloroun protested.

But Aeren overrode him. "—and King Stephan kept over a third of the Legion in reserve. He sent a mere two hundred men to bolster his line near the end of the fighting today, and it nearly broke us!"

More grumbling and nodding from the rest of the lords and their caitans. Most were frowning now, at least two in whispered conversations, comparing notes and observations on the battle. They'd had little time to talk since it had ended.

Aeren wasn't finished. With a sharp look at Thaedoren, the Tamaell Presumptive giving an almost imperceptible nod, he said, "And then there's the matter of supplies."

Peloroun practically leaped forward. "Supplies are on their way as we speak. Arrangements were made before the convoy even left Caercaern."

"We couldn't have accounted for the occumaen. It plowed its way through the heart of our camp and nearly wiped out our current resources. According to the latest inventory, we have enough supplies with rationing to last for five more days. The next load of supplies isn't scheduled to arrive for at least ten days.

"We're outnumbered, and in another few days, we'll be out of food."

The silence that followed slowly gave way to muted murmurs. He caught fragments of a few of the conversations, lords verifying their own supplies after the occumaen's passage with their caitans. Lord Peloroun leaned to one side, not taking his eyes off Aeren, to listen to his own caitan, and his frown deepened.

Finally, the mood in the tent now black and apprehensive, Peloroun said, "If what you say is true—and from what my caitan tells me, it is—then what do you propose we do?"

He already knew what Aeren was going to say, Aeren could hear it in his voice, but he answered anyway. "Withdraw."

For the first time since the meeting had started, Peloroun surged to his feet, his face contorted with rage, with indignation, his hands clenched into fists at his sides, barely restraining himself from crossing the short distance separating them. "You expect us to retreat after the bastards killed the Tamaell?" he spat through clenched teeth.

Aeren opened his mouth to respond, but Thaedoren was the one who answered, his low voice filling the room, cutting everyone's protests short.

"The humans didn't kill my father," he said. "Lord Khalaek did."

Aeren counted three breaths before the shocked silence broke into a tumultuous uproar. The only Alvritshai in the room who didn't react were Aeren, Eraeth, Lotaern, Thaedoren, and the Phalanx behind Aeren and the Tamaell Presumptive. After a closer look, Aeren realized that all of the White Phalanx with Thaedoren had been in the parley tent, had seen the Tamaell die. Each of them had tensed at the Tamaell Presumptive's words, their stance rigid.

The group didn't quiet until Lord Barak announced loudly, "I heard that a human killed him, that it was an assassin."

"It was, but Lord Khalaek is the one who hired that assassin," Thaedoren said.

"How do you know this?" Lord Peloroun barked.

"I learned of Khalaek's plans from Lord Aeren."

"Ha! The Duvoraen and the Rhyssal have always been rival Houses! That proves nothing."

Thaedoren's gaze fell on Peloroun, narrowed slightly. "I thought so as well, Lord Peloroun. And it's true that Aeren and Khalaek despise each other. It was for that reason that I ignored Lord Aeren's warning. And now," he said, standing slowly, so that he was on the same level as

Lord Peloroun, taking a step forward so he stood directly before him, "my father is dead. But it wasn't Lord Aeren who convinced me Khalaek was involved, it was Khalaek himself. I heard him speak to the assassin, I heard him order my death."

The lords glanced toward each other, uncertain.

"Where is Lord Khalaek now?" Peloroun asked. "We should ask him what he thinks of these . . . allegations."

"These *truths*," Thaedoren spat.

"So you say."

"You would doubt the Tamaell Presumptive? Over a question regarding his father's death?"

Everyone turned toward the new voice, toward Lotaern. The Chosen of the Order had said nothing since the Lords of the Evant had arrived, had weathered the few searching looks he'd received. Most of the lords had shrugged his presence aside, effectively ignoring it, assuming that Lotaern was here at the Tamaell Presumptive's request.

Now, they regarded him with mixed curiosity, confusion, and subdued dissension.

Speaking carefully, Peloroun said, "I would question the word of one of Khalaek's greatest rivals."

"And yet, moments ago, you called Lord Aeren a 'weak lordling' and nothing but a diplomat."

Peloroun sneered. "Oldest rivals, then." He turned back to Thaedoren. "I would still like to speak with Khalaek."

Thaedoren turned away, moving back to his original position, although he did not sit down. "Khalaek will be dealt with," he said.

Everyone in the room heard death in the soft words.

"By the Evant," Lord Barak interjected, a warning note in his voice. "He will be dealt with by the Evant, after this . . . altercation with the Legion and dwarren is resolved."

Thaedoren stilled, but he said nothing.

"As for this altercation," Lotaern said, as if the matter of Khalaek had already been agreed upon, "I believe that Lord Aeren has left out one important factor. Two actually."

Peloroun's gaze narrowed suspiciously. "And what would those be, Chosen."

"The first is another reason that the Legion poses a serious threat. They have more men, yes, and their supplies were not affected by the occumaen as ours were . . . but those by themselves would not be enough to sway me into the belief that we cannot win without something else."

Impatient, Lord Waerren said, "Which is?"

"The reason King Stephan and the Legion are here, the reason they came to the plains in the first place: the death of his father and their King, Maarten." He paused to let the words sink in, then added, "Stephan isn't here to keep the Alvritshai and dwarren from forming an alliance. That's a pretext. They have their own problems with the Andovans attacking their coastline. And yet, with no provocation, King Stephan came out here to the plains. He—and all of his men—are here for revenge. That is why they will be next to impossible to defeat. They came to fight because they have something to fight for."

The lords sat back, exchanging troubled glances. Aeren closed his eyes and bowed his head, images of the previous battle at the Escarpment running through his mind. When he finally glanced back up, he saw similar pained expressions on most of the lords in the room, some tinged with guilt.

But that was the past. Nothing could change it.

Aeren turned to Lotaern, brow creased. "You said there were two factors I neglected to mention. What's the second?"

Lotaern smiled . . . and yet Aeren felt himself shiver. "The second you could not have known about. You forgot to factor in the men I brought with me, the acolytes, the Order of the Flame."

Peloroun snorted. "And what good will acolytes do us?"

"They're more than mere acolytes," Lotaern said, voice laden with a satisfaction. "They are warriors of Aielan."

~

"You led us here, Cochen. We should fight! My Riders are willing, even if others are not."

Sipa, clan chief of Silver Grass, sneered in Garius' direction as the other clan chiefs grunted in agreement. Garius tried not to react, even though the yetope smoke in the meeting tent was thick and heady. Shea bristled beside him at the insult, made to stand, but Garius held him back. His son's scathing look shifted to him.

"The Thousand Spring Riders are ready to fight," Shea growled.

"We did not come here to fight," Garius rumbled. He turned his attention to Harticur, the Cochen, who was the only clan chief standing, and repeated, more harshly, "We did not come here to fight the humans or the Alvritshai."

"We did not intend to come here, to the Cut, at all!" Harticur retorted. His face was flushed from the heat of the tent and the fight to hold the dwarren line after the brutal death of the Alvritshai Tamaell. "But we are here now. We should seize the opportunity. The humans are not interested in us. It was clear on the battlefield. They lust for Alvritshai blood."

"Let the Alvritshai wear them down," Sipa said, and most of the other clan chiefs nodded and stroked their beards. "Then strike when they are weakened."

"We came here to speak to the Tamaell," Garius countered.

"And the Tamaell is dead! Murdered by the humans in front of our eyes! The humans cannot be trusted."

A thread of doubt slid through Garius. Sipa was correct. The Tamaell had been killed by a human, although how it was done he had no idea. Even there, in the parley tent, the conflict had centered on the Alvritshai and the humans. Harticur, Garius, and the rest of the dwarren had been forgotten, were able to escape the tent and retreat to their Riders unmolested. Harticur had fought only to keep the human and Alvritshai conflict from overrunning the dwarren, nothing more.

But now, Sipa's words were causing the Cochen to reconsider. He could see it in Harticur's eyes as he stared down at the brazier taking up the center of the tent, mimicking the central fire pit of the keeva in each of their warrens. His hands were resting on his knees where he sat cross-legged before the burning coals.

No one spoke for a long moment, everyone inhaling the smoke and contemplating the humans' treachery and the Tamaell's death. And then:

"The death was not natural."

All of the clan chiefs turned toward the gravelly, wizened voice of Harticur's shaman, Corteq. Wreathed in tendrils of smoke, his hard eyes latched onto each of the clan chiefs for a moment as he scanned the room before returning to the Cochen.

"The gods are troubled. The death was not natural, the events cloudy and obscured. Much turmoil there, much that I do not understand." He waved his hand through the smoke, appearing to be staring at the patterns it made before him.

"What do you see?" Harticur asked.

"The world is Turning, and the Four Winds have begun to blow. Nothing is clear." Corteq stared at the tendrils a moment longer, his eyes slightly dilated, then grunted and leaned back. "Tread carefully, Cochen. Your choice will determine the fate of the People of the Lands."

Harticur frowned, the rest of the clan chiefs stirring uneasily.

"We should attack the humans. It is a chance to avenge our unsettled ancenstors' spirits," Sipa said, and Garius saw at least three of the dwarren nodding in agreement, including Shea.

Harticur's brow furrowed, and he looked up at Garius.

Garius thought for a long moment. This was his last chance to convince Harticur, the last chance to sway him toward peace. "We are at the Cut. If you attack and the humans rally, if the Alvritshai join them . . ."

Tension tightened the corners of Harticur's mouth and he nodded.

"Do you think they will make a difference?" Eraeth asked, nodding toward the ranks of the Order of the Flame behind them.

Aeren shifted in his saddle, turning from his perusal of the churned plains to look back, squinting into the light of the rising sun. "I don't know," he said carefully. "Lotaern wasn't forthcoming about what they could do. But he claims that they are more than simple warriors."

The acolytes had formed up into lines, four deep. Dressed in armor similar to what most of the House Phalanx wore, they could have blended into any of the surrounding Houses and been indistinguishable from the rest of the Alvritshai . . . except for their white tabards. Those tabards blazed in the morning sunlight, the stylized flames on their front picked out in gold. He recalled seeing these acolytes emerging from the Sanctuary in Caercaern, felt the same sickening twist of dread in his stomach as he had then.

"The Order was never meant to have a Phalanx," he murmured, even as Lotaern rode to the front of his acolytes on his white horse, a standard-bearer with the blue and white flame emblem on his banner a step behind.

"It appears he has one now," Eraeth said.

Aeren glanced toward his Protector. "We'll see for how long."

Eraeth merely grunted.

During the meeting of the Evant the night before, Aeren had seen the deepening lines of concern on the Tamaell Presumptive's face as they planned, as Lotaern revealed more and more about his warriors, his Order of the Flame.

But the Order and its army could wait. He turned his attention back to the ranks of the Alvritshai and the field.

The Houses of the Evant were set up the same as the day before, spread out in a wide v-shape, Thaedoren and House Resue at its point, where it would intersect both the dwarren and human forces. The Duvoraen Phalanx had been kept back as a reserve at Lord Barak's and Vaersoom's insistence; they were even more concerned over their loyalties after the allegations of Khalaek's involvement in the Tamaell's death, though they had fought well. In fact, they demanded that the caitan be relieved of command and the force given over to one of the Lords of the Evant instead. Peloroun opposed the action, supported by Aeren, much to the Lord of House Ionaen's surprise. After much argument, Thaedoren settled the matter by pointing out that the Duvoraen had already proven themselves as reserve units and that Khalaek's men had proved they would follow the caitan of House Duvoraen's commands.

Everyone else had claimed the same positions along the line and now stood waiting as the sky lightened, the sun finally emerging completely above the horizon behind them. Aeren fidgeted in his saddle, unable to find a position that didn't aggravate the aches and bruises from yesterday's battle. The parley tent had collapsed and been ground into the earth, one stake with a fold of cloth still attached jutting upward toward the sky. He stared at it a long moment, a different ache building in his chest. To either side, he could see the dwarren and human lines, too distant to discern faces but close enough to see movement among the men. Banners flapped in a gusting wind. Horses stamped and huffed, jangling their bridles.

He glanced at his own men and met Dharel's eyes, Auvant's, a few others. Dharel gave him a short nod, his expression tense, set and ready. All of House Rhyssal was ready. The breeze smelled of anticipation, of sweat and fear, of grass.

Drums sounded, and Aeren spun to see Harticur and a string of Riders sweeping down the length of the dwarren line. To the north, runners scattered from King Stephan's escort, set a hundred paces in front of his own army. The throbbing pulse of the drums escalated, and the dwarren broke into a roar. The runners for the human army halted, unfurled their flags—red and black, cut diagonally across the rectangular field—and all along the line men voiced a battle cry.

And through it all, the Alvritshai horns sounded.

"So it begins," Aeren said, so softly only Eraeth could hear. "Again."

All three lines began to advance, the dwarren on their gaezels streaking forward, their drums a frenzy of sound now, pounding as the thunder of the gaezels' hooves grew. The Alvritshai and humans advanced more slowly, but as the lines drew closer together, the pace increased. The humans broke from their march to a trot. Their front line grew ragged as a few men surged forward, ahead of the rest.

"Steady!" Eraeth bellowed. "Hold!"

Aeren heard Thaedoren barking the same orders to his left, yet he found himself nudging his horse forward a little more, a little faster. He could feel the tension boiling in his blood, could feel it building.

On the field, the dwarren's far edge swung inward, its center slowing. It struck the end of the human line—

And as if that contact had been a command, the rest of the humans surged forward. No longer contained, no longer making an attempt at control, they simply charged.

The two armies—dwarren and human—converged,

crushing into each other, the connection speeding toward
him. Sound filled Aeren's head, a roaring of wind, a crash
of thunder, and without thought he released his horse,
released the sound inside his mind in a bellow. The lines
folded in upon each other, closer and closer, until they
struck the point of the vee, until there was nothing in
Aeren's field of vision except the human army, rushing
toward him, eating up the churned mud and grass as they
sprinted forward—

And then they struck, Alvritshai and human lines merg-
ing into one, and Aeren felt nothing but the wind and the
clash of his cattan.

~

Moiran glanced up from where she knelt in her tent,
needle poised, as the first of the Alvritshai horns cried out.

A shudder ran through her. She held still for a long
moment, listening to the pealing notes, so calm and clear
at first, then breaking, becoming more scattered, somehow more desperate, as the armies met. She imagined
she could feel the earth trembling beneath her from the
tread of thousands of feet. Or perhaps it trembled at the
senselessness of it all, a shudder at the spill of blood, at
the death.

Her heart quickened, its beat hard for a moment as she
thought of Fedorem, of his body lying nearby, in another
room. But she seized the threatening emotion, grasped
it tight even as the tears began to burn at the corners of
her eyes. She'd allowed herself to cry the night before,
after tending the Lords of the Evant before their meeting
and seeing to the needs of the wounded. She'd cried until
her ribs ached, until she felt hollow and empty, until she
thought there were no more tears, and then she'd cried
more. All in solitude, in the confines of her tent, the White
Phalanx Thaedoren had set to guard her dismissed. They
hadn't wanted to leave. She'd had to shout at them, nearly
breaking at that point, her hands knotted in her dress. She
thought it was her hands that had convinced them. Or perhaps it had been the pain in her voice.

She'd fallen into an exhausted sleep, so deep she hadn't
dreamed. But she'd woken early, dawn still an hour away.

Now the horns scattered even farther, no longer an-nouncing orders to the entire army, focusing on their own Houses. She let her gaze drop to the pile of clothes she had begun to mend, to the shirt she held in her lap.

One of Fedorem's shirts.

A hot liquid sensation filled her chest, and she let the hand with the needle drop to her lap, leaning her head forward, the pressure building in the back of her throat.

She'd almost given in to it when someone moaned.

Her head snapped up, breath caught, the grief lodging with a sharp pain in her chest. For a moment, hope flared as she thought the sound had come from Fedorem—even though she'd seen Fedorem's body, had seen the gaping wound across his throat, knew that Fedorem lay too far away for her to hear him even if he weren't already dead—

And then she realized it was the human. Colin. Shaeveran.

She tossed the shirt aside and lurched to her feet, moving to the human's side.

She hovered uncertainly above him as his head rolled from one side to the other, his features etched in pain. When his eyelids began to flutter though, she knelt, reached for the wet rag sitting on a table nearby, next to a shallow basin and a stack of clean bandages. She dabbed at his sweaty forehead with the cool cloth.

His eyes flared open, the pupils dilating. He focused on her, one hand shooting upward to grab her wrist, his grip tight.

Then he lurched upright—

Except he didn't make it. He tried, but a spasm of pain tore across his face and he gasped, collapsing back onto the pallet. His entire face went a grayish-white, and fresh sweat broke out on his skin, his hair already matted to his forehead.

The grip on Moiran's arm relaxed, although he didn't let go.

Sucking in a ragged breath, he murmured, "Aeren?"

Moiran shifted, took his hand from her wrist and laid it across his chest, noticing a blossom of blood seeping through the bandage with a frown. The water of the rua-navriell had stopped the flow of blood the day before, but its power had waned . . . or been neutralized somehow. "On the battlefield at the Escarpment," she said quietly, wetting the cloth again and drawing it across his face. "Can't you hear it?"

He stilled. Moiran sat back, let the distant echoes of the battle wash over her, until she saw a subtle change in Colin's eyes, a deepening, a hint of regret. "He couldn't stop it," he whispered.

It wasn't a question, but Moiran answered anyway. "Nothing could stop it, not after Fedorem's death."

Colin looked up at her, somehow exposed. She could see everything in his eyes: his compassion, his fear, his pain. Not the wound he'd suffered to save Aeren and Thaedoren. She saw a deeper wound, one that had scarred him, the loss of a loved one.

And she saw something else as well. She saw his humanness, his darker skin, his rounded face, the brown of his hair and the darkness of his eyes.

Yet he was not human. She had only to look down at his arm, at the exposed darkness that swirled beneath his skin. She need only recall the knife that had been driven into his chest, a wound that should have killed him.

"I have to help him," he said.

She frowned. "Why?"

The question seemed to surprise him. "Because . . ."

When he didn't continue, she leaned forward. "Why do you need to help him? Why *have* you helped him, helped us? He is Alvritshai; you are human. There has always been a rift between us."

"Not . . . always." He winced as he tried to move.

Moiran snorted and wet her rag again, frowning as she noted the seepage of blood on his bandage had spread, no longer a few spots, but a circle the size of her thumb, its center a deep, dark red. "Always," she said.

He shook his head. "Not at first. Not on the plains." His voice was soft, his thoughts elsewhere.

She let him reminisce for a moment, then returned to the original question. "Why are you with him? Why do you follow him?"

He drew himself out of memory, stared at her a long moment, then said simply, "He's all that I have left."

She paused in her ministrations, pulled back. His answer was unexpected, and she found she didn't know what to say, didn't even really understand it.

He sensed it, and his eyes went hard. Struggling to sit up again, he repeated, "I need to help him."

She set her hand firmly against his chest and pushed him down. "No, you don't. Both sides want blood—for the death of Maarten and for Fedorem. They intend to get it, no matter the cost. There's nothing you can do."

"But—"

"No! One man—one human—will not affect the outcome of the battle! There's nothing you can do to help!" They glared at each other, her hand still pressed into his chest.

When Colin's gaze didn't waver, she leaned forward. "You're hurt. You can barely lift yourself off of the pallet, let alone rush off into a fight."

Resignation flickered through the intent in his eyes.

But within the space of a breath, the determination returned.

"Find Eraeth," he said.

"What?"

"Find Eraeth, Lord Aeren's Protector," he growled.

Moiran leaned back, suspicious. But when she removed her hand and he didn't move, didn't try to roll onto his side or lift his chest, she stood and walked toward the tent's entrance.

The White Phalanx set to guard her and the Tamaell's body turned the moment she stepped outside. "Tamaea?"

She shook her head and went to the chamber where she'd slept the night before, to her satchel. The cloth-wrapped vial Eraeth had given her, along with the knife that had been pulled from Colin's chest, rested on top.

She unwrapped the vial and stared down at the clear liquid inside.

The sound of battle raged outside, louder here, more distinct. And harsh.

~

The first thing Aeren noticed, within moments of the three armies colliding, was that the Legion had changed.

The day before, he'd seen the cold desire in their faces, the need to kill, to take revenge against the Alvritshai demons that had broken their alliance with their King and then slaughtered him on this very land. He'd seen the intent in their eyes, had seen the rage. But it had all been leashed then.

It wasn't leashed now.

The Legion struck in a frenzy of hatred, the men breaking ranks, throwing themselves upon the Alvritshai, screaming, howling, blades flashing downward, a hint of madness in their eyes. Aeren saw the first of his own House Phalanx fall, saw the first blood spray outward from a severed arm, the Alvritshai shrieking, hand clamped to the wound, even as the man who'd loped the limb off bowled past him, sword already cutting across another Alvritshai's chest. Aeren fixated on him, on his silvered beard, on the scars cutting down along his cheek, etched in white, on the glint of gold in one ear, on the crazed green eyes. As more Alvritshai fell—to this man, to the hundred others behind him—Aeren kicked his horse forward, brought it sideways into the space left by another of the fallen, and stabbed the man through the neck.

He met the man's gaze. He saw the madness, the whites of the eyes, as blood poured from his neck. And underneath the madness he saw the haunted soul beneath, a soul tortured by what had happened here over thirty years before, what he had seen on this battlefield when he had been barely old enough to shave.

Then the life in those eyes faded.

What he'd seen sent a shock through Aeren's heart. He'd discounted the emotions of the Legion, the emotions of those that had been here before. He'd thought those emotions would have dulled over time. That was why he'd approached their King in the first place, why he'd gone to Corsair and the Needle and proposed a peace treaty.

But Lotaern was right. The humans hadn't come to the plains to protect their lands from a threat that didn't exist. They'd come to provoke a fight, to draw the Alvritshai here.

They'd come for revenge.

King Stephan had reined that rage in, had controlled it. But not anymore.

Aeren glanced toward where the King fought against the Tamaell Presumptive's forces, the Legion and his own Phalanx jostling around him. His horse snorted and shifted away. All along the line, north and south, he saw the hatred,

felt it, the raw emotion sending the Legion into the Alvritshai forces with reckless abandon. Men were dying on
Alvirtshai blades due to that recklessness, but the Legion
had men to spare.

The humans were going to overwhelm them, it was only
a matter of time.

He glanced up at the sun, then back down to the Legion
immediately before him, to their faces, to their eyes, to
their contorted features and gritted teeth as they surged
forward, meeting the Alvritshai resistance—

And Aeren felt his own anger building. These were the
men who had killed his brother. He'd held his brother's
head in his hands on these fields, had listened to his brother
choke out his last words, the hilt of a cattan pressed unwill-
ingly into his bloody palm.

Aeren let the image grow in his mind, let it consume
him, then drove forward.

And the world faded into a collage of images, of bloody,
screaming faces, of bodies pressing against the flanks of his
horse, hands scrabbling at his legs, trying to pull him down,
swords and daggers flashing in the sunlight. The outside
world faded, everything centered on this one stretch of
land, on this one struggle. He stabbed down at those hands
trying to pull him free, drew blood, kicked at the bodies
with his boots, slapped armor with the flat of his cattan
and sank it deep into flesh at every opportunity. At one
point, a man drove a dagger into his thigh. Aeren hissed air
between his teeth at the pain, punched the hilt of his sword
into the man's face, felt bones crunch, blood and snot coating his fingers before the man stumbled back howling, his
face nearly unrecognizable. Reaching down, Aeren yanked
the dagger free, gasping as the pain flared, then drove the
dagger into another man's back, Eraeth skewering him
from the front as he arched backward.

He met Eraeth's eyes, saw the question there, but shook
his head and turned, already shoving the pain back, knowing he couldn't stop, not for such a wound. And without
thought he cried out Aielan's name, Eraeth joining him,
the battle cry spreading down the Alvritshai lines. They'd
been driven back by the fierceness of the Legion's attack,
had given ground, but with that cry the Alvritshai pressed
forward, the lines shifting. Aeren's group surged forward,

ahead of the Tamaell Presumptive's line to the left and Lord Jydell's to the right, bulging outward. Jydell's House rallied, keeping the lines connected, but with a collective cry of triumph, the Legion on the Tamaell Presumptive's side broke through, creating a gap.

Legion poured into the gap, fanning out, hitting Aeren's and Thaedoren's lines from behind.

"Fall back!" Aeren shouted. "Fall back and close the gap!"

Horns blared—from the left, from behind, from two paces away—shattering the cacophony of the battle that had sunk into the background of Aeren's mind. He winced as orders clashed on the air, but he couldn't turn to look, to see whether anyone was reacting. He was too close to the front, nearly surrounded by the Legion, the men packed too closely together to effectively use their swords. They were howling, spit flecking their beards, and their free hands reached upward, caught hold of Aeren's legs, his horse's bridle, snagged the reins and his shirt, yanking him downward. He beat at them, dug his heels into his horse's flank, felt the animal try to leap forward, felt the muscles flexing beneath him, felt the animal beginning to panic. It screamed, eyes wide, head tossing, but there were too many men, too many hands tugging, pulling, pushing. Slashing out in desperation, he felt his sword clang against armor, snag in cloth, sink into flesh, but he felt himself tip, the saddle loose beneath him. He began to fall. The world skewed, raving faces replaced by wide open sky. Hands grappled with him, drawing him down. He tasted bile, felt his heart shuddering in his chest, felt armor dig into his side as he tried to kick his feet free of the stirrups.

In a vividly clear moment, he found himself marveling at the position of the sun. Hours had passed. It was early afternoon.

And then his horse reared, feet kicking, mane flaring in that afternoon sun as it threw Aeren from its back. He felt one foot tangle in the stirrup, wrenching his leg—the one that had been stabbed earlier—upward and to the side as he fell. New pain seared through his hip, and then he struck the ground, the breath knocked from him. He twisted, foot still caught, slammed his cattan into the muddy ground for balance, tried to bring himself onto his elbows. As his body turned, he saw a sword drive upward into his horse's chest, sink in deep.

The horse screamed—a raw, tortured sound that pierced Aeren's gut.

Then the animal sagged to the side, began to collapse.

Aeren's foot wrenched free, and he lost his precarious balance, his face slamming down into the mud. A bootheel pressed into the ground beside him and he rolled, caught someone else behind the knees, felt that person stumble, but he couldn't see, half blinded by mud caked to his face.

The earth beneath him shuddered as the horse's body hit. Men screamed, one or two voices cut off as they were crushed. Aeren scrambled backward on his ass, kicking his feet, using his elbows, trying to escape being trampled—

And then a hand—half-glimpsed—reached down, fingers digging into his shirt, into the edge of his armor, and hauled him up.

He staggered into Eraeth, his Protector's face a contorted mix of fear, determination, and anger. He dragged Aeren back, plowing through the press of men, Rhyssal House Phalanx breaking to let them through when they saw who Eraeth led. Aeren's leg twisted, and he hissed, tried to keep his weight off it, and then they broke through the back of the main force. Eraeth hauled him twenty paces farther across the churned mud of the flat and halted.

Aeren pulled himself upright, using Eraeth for support, then spat mud from his mouth, fingers pulling a clump of mud from his right eye. "Eraeth." Eraeth's eyes narrowed, but before he could say anything, Aeren asked, "What's happened?"

"Our line is crumbling."

Aeren swore.

He'd broken formation. He'd called on Aielan's Light.

Eraeth must have seen the despair in Aeren's eyes. "Not just here. It's broken in at least three places. Stephan called in more men, fresh men."

"The Duvoraen?"

"They're split, trying to hold in two places, here and near Lord Waerren."

"Waerren! He was on the dwarren front! Have the dwarren broken through?"

Eraeth shook his head. "They've realized the Legion is

out for Alvritshai blood, not dwarren. They withdrew, back
to a defensive line, nearly two hours ago."

Aeren swore again. Clearing the last of the mud from
his eye, he spun, oriented himself in the general chaos, saw
the Alvritshai line in tatters, the Legion swarming over
them all—

And then his gaze fell on the blazing white tabards of
the Order of the Flame, still standing in tight formation in
reserve.

"Lotaern," Aeren whispered. He watched the Order
silently for a moment, then added, "Why doesn't he do
anything?"

And at that moment, he saw Lotaern, Chosen of the
Order, raise both hands to the sky.

Colin lay in the dim light of the Tamaell's tent and tried not
to writhe in agony. His entire chest hurt, an ache that went
deep inside his lungs, deeper still, and it throbbed with
every slow pulse of his blood. Each breath, no matter how
shallow, brought the pain to the fore, so that it felt as if he
were lying on waves on the ocean, the pain swelling, then
fading, rising and falling, like a ship at sea.

But the pain never fell far.

He knew he shouldn't be awake. When he'd tried to kill
himself in the forest, when he'd driven the knife into his
heart, he hadn't woken for days. Something had drawn him
up out of sleep. He just didn't know what.

He frowned up at the ceiling of the tent, undulating in
the wind, and tried to focus, to pull his mind away from
the pain. But it was too intense. He couldn't shove it aside,
couldn't ignore it. Yet even through the pain he could
sense something. A shift, a tingling in his skin, not the
prickling sensation he'd felt before Walter had appeared
and slit the Tamaell's throat, but close. That had felt like a
breeze, as if someone had just walked past him, someone
he couldn't see.

This tingling came from everywhere, seemed to be seeping up from the earth beneath him.

He concentrated, let the sensation course over him,
hoping it would dull the pain, but then Moiran returned.
Alone.

She carried something in her hand, her face fixed in a bleak frown.

"Where's Eraeth?" he asked, still shocked at how weak his voice sounded. Exhaustion lay just beneath the pain. He'd felt it when he'd tried to lift himself upright, when he'd tried to leave.

Moiran hesitated, then moved closer. "He's on the field, with Lord Aeren, acting as his Protector. It is his place. It's where he should be." She stood over him, watched his face intently. "Why?"

Colin tried not to grimace. "He has something that I need."

"What?"

He turned toward her, searched her face. "A vial. It . . . would help heal me."

"Is it the Blood of Aielan?" When Colin frowned in confusion, she added, "The water of the ruanavriell."

Settling back, Colin shook his head. "No. This is . . . more powerful. More dangerous. I'm not even certain Eraeth would agree to give it to me."

Moiran watched him a long moment, then sighed and put what was in her hand on his chest. "He said that if you asked, I was to give you this."

Colin breathed in deep, could smell the Lifeblood now: wet earth and dead leaves, musky and sharp. He should have noticed it earlier, when Moiran arrived, but its scent had mingled with the strange prickling sensation coursing upward from the ground. But now the scent hung heavy, dug deep into his gut.

He raised his left arm, halted when he saw the swirl of darkness beneath the bared skin, the marks darker than bruises. He shuddered, recalling the thick swirl of black on Walter's face. His lips pressed together as he pulled the protective cloth away to reveal the tiny flask within.

Moving slowly, carefully, he held the flask up to the light, peered into the clear liquid within, at what looked like water.

He could *feel* it, could sense the power behind it, the *presence*.

And as it always did, that presence woke a depthless ache in him, sent tremors of pain coursing down his arm. Need filled him, a need he'd fought in the long weeks after leaving the forest, a need that he thought he'd finally conquered when he handed the flask over to Eraeth to protect.

He knew now that the need, the ache, would never go away, that he could bury it, but it would return as soon as he drew near the Lifeblood.

"What is it?" Moiran asked.

Colin turned, surprised to find her kneeling beside him. He hadn't heard her move, too absorbed with the flask, with the power coursing through his arm, through his chest.

Through his blood.

"Open it," he said, handing her the flask. He couldn't open it himself, not with how tightly he'd sealed it, and not with one arm. He'd tried to lift the other, but the pain in his chest had been too harsh. "Open it carefully. Don't spill any of it on yourself."

"Why not?" Moiran asked.

"Because I don't know what it will do to you."

She stared into his eyes, her own narrowing.

Then she unsealed the cap. "What will it do to you?"

"Heal me." Which was a lie. It wouldn't heal him, wouldn't close the wound that bled in his chest, wouldn't stitch skin and muscle and bone back together. That wasn't the Lifeblood's power.

But it would take care of the pain . . . for a price.

Moiran glared at him. "You can't stop this. You can't halt the fighting. One man—"

"You're right," he interrupted. "I can't end the battle . . . but there's one man who can. And I can convince him. But I can't do it from here."

Her glare intensified—

And then, in a low, curt, bitter tone, she said, "Men."

She removed the cap.

The scent of the Lifeblood flooded the tent, a hundred times stronger than before, and Colin gasped, his entire body trembling now, the ache in his stomach almost as strong as the pain in his chest.

"Let me have it."

Moiran handed the flask to him reluctantly. He held it reverentially before him, let its power wash over him, soothe him.

Then, with one quick gesture, he tipped it into his

mouth, felt its coolness against his tongue, tasted its sweetness, its pureness—

And then he swallowed.

~

Nothing happened.

Aeren watched, tension bleeding down his arms, tightening across his shoulders, as Lotaern kept his arms raised.

And then the acolytes behind him began to move.

They fanned out, each group of four heading out from Lotaern's position, radiating outward, like the rays of the sun. When they were fifty paces from the edge of the fighting, the groups of four broke apart, each acolyte facing the chaos of the lines. Each drew his cattan, nearly in unison, and Aeren realized that Lotaern was issuing orders. He could see the Chosen's mouth moving, but the battle itself drowned out his words.

The acolytes held their cattans to the sky, then reversed them and drove their points into the ground with both hands on the hilts, kneeling as they did so, heads bowed.

"What are they doing?" Eraeth asked.

Aeren shook his head, lips pursed.

Lotaern was still speaking. Aeren strained, tried to make out what was being said, but it was Eraeth who answered his own question.

"He's chanting."

"What?"

Eraeth stilled, drew and held a breath, concentrating. "Part of the Scripts."

"They're all chanting," Aeren said abruptly. "They're all chanting the same thing."

Aeren felt it on the air first. A cessation of the winds, a silence beneath the rumbling roar of the fighting still taking place on all sides. Then the air . . . thickened. It pressed in around him, made it harder to breathe.

But even as this began to register, the ground trembled. Tremors coursed up through Aeren's boots, shuddered through his feet into his legs, low at first, increasing steadily, until they couldn't be ignored. On all sides, those at the edges of the fighting halted, stepped back, glanced around in confusion—

And the earth in front of the kneeling acolytes suddenly

exploded skyward. Mud boiled, spewing up chunks of sod, clumps of dirt and roots and trampled grass, seething upward in a huge arc, as if something were trying to emerge from the ground itself, trying to shove its way free. Aeren caught glimpses of what lay beneath the churning surface: a white glow, vibrant and intense, so pure it hurt his eyes. The earth continued to fountain for a breath, two—

Then it began to push outward, away from the acolytes who still knelt, still chanted, heads bent. It plowed forward, mud and dirt erupting like geysers, shooting ten feet into the air, like spume from the ocean as it struck the rocky shore. It surged forward like the swell of a wave, rumbling through Aeren's legs and up into his chest, juddering in his teeth.

The human men who had broken through the Alvritshai lines were caught by surprise, too stunned and confused to move. The boiling earth knocked them off of their feet, buried most beneath heaps of dirt, their screams cut short. Before each of them vanished, Aeren saw a tongue of that brilliant whiteness beneath the ground lick out, touch the person an instant before he was engulfed, as if tasting them. Then the arcing wave of moving earth reached the first Alvritshai. It flung them to the ground, but didn't bury them, leaving them behind, shaken, struggling to rise.

"It's Aielan's Light," Eraeth said suddenly. "The whiteness beneath the earth—it's Aielan's Light."

Aeren's brow creased skeptically—

But those Alvritshai near them had already heard. They whispered it beneath their breath, muttered prayers, gestured in awe, the reaction spreading outward.

On the field, the raging earth hit the most crowded parts of the battle, and at the same moment the acolytes rose from where they knelt, jerked their cattans free from the earth and pointed them toward the sky, and roared, "For Aielan! For the Order! For the Flame!"

Everyone in Aeren's vicinity gasped.

The acolytes' blades were limned with white light.

They rushed into the earth's wake, pausing to kill any of the human forces who hadn't been buried, their motions quick, merciless, hitting throat or heart before sprinting onward, into the heart of the fighting.

But the fighting had lurched to a halt, both Alvritshai

and human forces stunned, even as the disturbed earth bore down on them. Some shook the shock off and began to run, fleeing toward their own lines or simply fleeing before the earth and the white light beneath. Many of the Alvritshai heard the acolytes' war cry. To either side, Aeren felt his own men rallying, saw hands tightening on hilts, eyes hardening from shock to anger.

Thrusting his own cattan into the air, he bellowed, "For Aielan! For Rhyssal!"

And then he charged toward the nearest group of the Legion, whose attention was fixed on the approaching ridge of earth. His leg burned with pain from the knife wound and being twisted in the death of his horse, but Aeren killed two of the Legionnaires before they began to react, a few bringing swords to bear, still others breaking away toward the west. Aeren felt the writhing earth bearing down on him, felt the Legion he fought growing desperate—

And then it struck.

He was lifted off the ground, thrown by the force of the earth. Dirt pummeled him from all sides, flung so high and with such force that he could taste it. He breathed it in, choked and coughed on it, felt something lick up along his leg, felt its cold touch, felt it burning against his skin, recognized it as Aielan's Light, as the same fire he had passed through to earn his pendant in the Order. Visions of that moment, of descending into the heart of the mountain beneath Caercaern, of traversing the empty halls and corridors, of marveling at the massive pillars, the carved stonework, the delicate stone stairs, flashed through his mind. But this was merely a taste of what he'd endured when he'd reached the final chamber, deeper even than the halls, hidden within the rough hewn catacombs below the ancient city where the pool of white fire blazed. There, he had submerged himself in the fire, allowed it to consume him, allowed himself to be exposed completely to Aielan and her judgment—

Then he was falling. He struck the ground hard, tumbled onto his side, spitting grit from his mouth, scrubbing it from his face. Alvritshai were coughing and hacking on all sides, a few groaning, holding their arms or legs where they'd twisted them on landing. Aeren dragged himself to his feet, wincing at the renewed pain in his leg, fresh blood staining his breeches, but he stumbled toward where a young human boy lay half buried in the sod, blood trickling from one corner of his mouth.

He never saw Aeren coming. His eyes were wide, staring off into the distance, tears streaming down his face, as he murmured, "I shouldn't have taken the coin from Codger. I shouldn't have taken the cart."

Aeren hesitated.

A blade sank into the boy's chest and Aeren spun.

Eraeth withdrew his cattan and met Aeren's accusing glare stoically. "The battle isn't over." He motioned toward the plains behind them.

The wave of earth and white light had diminished. As Aeren watched, it threw up a few fitful geysers, as if it were gasping a last breath, and then it rumbled into stillness.

He glanced back at Lotaern in time to see the Chosen, arms still lifted, stagger, then fall, body crumpling.

Turning back, he gazed beyond where the earth had finally settled ... and saw the remains of the Legion reserve. Hundreds of men, on foot and in the saddle, waiting for the order to attack. To the side, from the Tamaell Presumptive's position, Alvritshai and Legion were picking themselves up and dusting themselves off.

Including King Stephan.

The leader of the coastline Provinces spat to one side, wiped his mouth on his sleeve, sword still clutched tight in his other hand ... and then he gestured.

A lone runner raised a single flag and began waving it back and forth.

And the reserve unit began to move.

~

Colin stood on the ridge above the Alvritshai encampment overlooking the field of battle. The dwarren stood to one side, their lines withdrawn, disengaged, although they were riled. The Legion and Alvritshai forces were in disarray, no clear lines on either side, men and Alvritshai pulling themselves up from the ground, horns beginning to sound, everyone beginning to regroup even as the Legion reserves charged toward the battle.

He'd arrived in time to witness the wave of earth, had

seen it toss the Alvritshai and the Legion aside like stones as it rippled across the plains, then dissipated. He'd felt the power the acolytes had called thrumming through his feet, had felt it tingling in his skin and vibrating through him, in counterpoint to the pure ecstasy of the Lifeblood throbbing in his veins. The pain from the knife wound in his chest had receded, had become nothing more than a minor nuisance, an occasional tug that made him wince if he twisted or turned too fast or too sharply. The exhaustion that lay underneath the pain had also vanished, replaced by euphoria. He breathed in the plains air, tasted it, savored it, felt the coppery taste of blood against his tongue from the death below. He touched the desperation, the sweat, and the terror of the men who fought there, soft as silk, and reveled in the sounds of the horns, the shouts, the thunder of running feet, each distinct and brittle in his ears. Each breath, each heartbeat, each movement pricked his skin, tickling in the hairs at the base of his neck and along his arms. He bathed in the sensation, knowing it would cost him in the end, in the darkness of the mark on his arm, in the claiming of his soul by the Well, but he didn't care.

The price was small. Nearly infinitesimal.

With the battlefield wrapped around him, he focused, picked out the banners of the Tamaell Presumptive, the pennants of the King of the Provinces, and then he reached out—

And halted time.

Picking his way down from the slope, he crossed the stilled battlefield, slid past individuals fighting to the death, around groups no more organized than a brawl, past horses in mid-rear, men falling, hands outstretched to catch themselves, unaware that they were already dead. He wound through splashes of blood frozen in midair, ducked beneath swords in full swing. He made his way through it all.

Until he stood before a single individual, the man he'd come to speak to, the man he'd come to convince:

King Stephan.

He peered into the King's face, into his gray-green eyes, locked on his opponent, expression fierce as he prepared to drive his sword through an Alvritshai's heart. He could feel the man beneath, could feel the vibrant energy of his life, even though everything was still, motionless.

Then he caught sight of another man, the King's commander, Tanner Dain. The Legion commander fought beside the King, was in the act of stepping back, an Alvritshai's body falling away from his blade.

Colin hesitated, then drew the mantle of the Lifeblood's power around himself, like a cloak. He positioned himself so that Tanner Dain would see him the moment time resumed, but close enough so he could touch Stephan.

Then he let his grasp on time fall away.

Stephan roared as his blade plunged into the Alvritshai's chest, blood flying as he drew back, half turned—

Then halted as he caught sight of Colin, dressed in an Alvritshai shirt, open at the front to keep it from getting soaked in the blood seeping through the bandages across his chest. As a frown creased his brow, as recognition began to flare in Tanner Dain's eyes and he began to lurch forward, Colin turned to the commander of the King's guard and said, "I'll return him in a moment."

Then he reached out and snagged the King by the arm, gathering the Well's power around himself and Stephan—

And Traveled.

23

"DON'T LET GO," COLIN SAID.

The tenor of Colin's voice brought Stephan to a halt, his instinctive response to pull away from the hand that held him in a viselike grip, even as the world around them shuddered, slowed, then halted. Colin watched Stephan's face intently, saw the man lurch as he enveloped him with the Lifeblood. It was easier to pull Stephan back with the Lifeblood flowing so cleanly, so recently, through his body. There was no wrench as there had been with Moiran as they fled the occumaen, no anchor trying to hold him in place, as with Aeren and Thaedoren in the parley tent.

But the transition wasn't completely smooth either. Stephan gasped, his eyes going wild, darting around, seeing the entire battle in mid-motion, a battle he'd been part of only a moment before, adrenaline racing through his blood.

His gaze fell on Tanner Dain, his commander already leaning forward, foot poised to take a step in Colin's direction, expression caught in transition, hardening into rage.

He turned to Colin. His terror had died. He'd already begun collecting himself. "What have you done?"

"I've halted time."

"Why?"

"Because there's something you need to see."

"And what if I don't want to see it?"

Colin shrugged. "I can't force you to go, can't force you to watch. All you have to do is break contact with me, free yourself from my grip, and you'll return."

Stephan's mouth twitched into a sneer. "What is it that you think I need to see?"

Colin looked into his eyes, into the derision he saw reflected there, and said, "Your father."

The sneer faltered, a look of horror, of hope filling the void that it left. For a startling moment that felt like eternity, Stephan lay exposed, the mask of rage and hatred and despair that he'd worn for the past thirty years gone, torn away, the man beneath—the boy who'd been transformed on these fields, who'd been murdered by Khalaek and the Alvritshai just as his father had been—peering through, vulnerable and young.

But then the mask slammed back into place, rage twisting Stephan's face. "My father is dead," he growled, then tensed to break free.

"He's dead, but you can still see him. You can see how he died. You can see what really happened, who really killed him."

"I've already seen how he died. I was there! I saw it with my own eyes!" He began pulling away from Colin, struggling, although half-heartedly. Perhaps he'd grown weary from the fight. He made no move to shift his sword to his free hand, to threaten Colin with it when it was obvious Colin himself held no weapon.

"But you saw it at a distance," Colin said. "You don't know what really happened. You've lived the last thirty years not knowing the truth, told one thing and another, until not even those who were there know what they saw and what they've learned to see, what they came to see based on rumor, not on fact." Colin's voice had deepened as Stephan's struggles increased, his teeth clamped together. But Stephan suddenly let out a harsh cry and stopped trying to shake his arm free.

They glared at each other, both breathing hard.

"I can show you what truly happened," Colin said, voice hoarse. "I can show you who turned against your father first, who followed and who didn't."

Stephan still didn't believe him. Colin could see it in his tortured expression, as he squeezed his eyes shut and bent his head, his shoulders.

He remained in that bowed position a long moment, mostly still, jaw clenched.

When he lifted his head, he'd calmed himself, although his eyes shone with hatred. "How? I've been told a hundred stories, heard a thousand songs. How can you show me the truth?"

Something deep inside Colin relaxed. "I can take you there."

He reached out with the Lifeblood, still pulsing through him, still strong, and then he pushed. Pushed against time. Not halting it, not slowing it. No. Those were simpler tasks. Instead—as he'd done so many times before on the outskirts of the forest, where his mother and father and the rest of the wagon train had stood and faced the Shadows—he pushed back, pushed through the barrier and against the force trying to shove him into his proper place in time's flow.

Stephan sucked in a sharp breath as the figures around him began to move, edging backward, swords pulling out of punctured chests, unslicing throats, uncutting arms and legs. Colin saw the image of Stephan himself, howling in reverse, but before the real Stephan could turn and see himself Colin concentrated and shoved, the reversal picking up speed, until all motion was smeared, then blurred, and yet still he pushed harder. Sweat broke out on his forehead, and Stephan took an unconscious step closer to him as time slid back even faster. The armies retreated, the sun set in the east, rose in the west, the field suddenly enveloped again in warfare, until they retreated again, the parley tent popping up from its collapse. Colin saw his body being carried in Eraeth's arms as the Protector raced backward into the tent, caught a glimpse of Eraeth's stricken face a moment before he vanished back inside. He staggered, surprised by that glimpse—

And in that moment, as the reversal of time lurched and slowed, he saw how the Wraith—how Walter—had gotten into the tent without being seen.

Khalaek's men had held the tent flaps aside.

In a flash, he recalled seeing Khalaek's aide standing beside the inside flap. A second had stood outside, guarding the tent with the others.

It would only have taken a simple signal—a whistle, a hummed refrain. Both men could lift the flap at the same moment, keep it open only a moment. With time slowed, or halted, Walter wouldn't even need a single breath to slip inside, wouldn't have even needed to appear at all with the tent flaps already pushed aside—

And even as he thought it, Walter flickered into view, ducked down between the opening and into the darkness within.

All to bring about the Tamaell's death. Thaedoren's as well. All so that Khalaek could ascend in the Evant, seize control and become Tamaell himself. An assassination within Caercaern would have been harder to manipulate, harder to explain. There would be no one to blame except an Alvritshai.

But here, on the battlefield, with an assassin so obviously human if he was seen at all . . .

Colin felt his rage boiling higher, his breath quickening, his heart thundering. He wanted to reach out and kill Walter as he slid into that darkness, wanted to strangle him—

But he couldn't. This wasn't the real Walter, the real Wraith. This was the Walter that was. This Walter couldn't be stopped. He'd already assassinated the Tamaell, nearly killed the Tamaell Presumptive and Aeren as well. This Wraith had already set Lord Khalaek's plans in motion.

But neither Khalaek nor Walter had planned on Colin. He'd stopped the Tamaell Presumptive's death and had implicated Khalaek in Fedorem's.

Now he intended to halt the conflict with Stephan.

Straightening with purpose, he caught Stephan staring at him in confusion. His gaze flicked toward the tent flap, toward where Walter had vanished. "Who was that?"

"The man who killed the Tamaell."

"I don't know him. He wasn't part of the Legion, he wasn't one of my men."

"I know, and the Tamaell Presumptive knows, but they don't." He motioned toward the Alvritshai army grimly. "The White Phalanx within the tent saw a human kill their ruler. And what one member of the army sees—"

"They all see," Stephan finished curtly. His gaze rested on the Alvritshai banners. "They all think the Legion is behind the Tamaell's death."

"Not all. The lords of the Evant thought so at first, as did the Tamaell Presumptive. I showed them that one of the lords himself was behind the attack. The man you saw entering the tent . . . is like me. He's tasted the sarenavriell, drunk from the Well of Sorrows. He's no longer human."

"One of the Lords of the Evant?" Stephan asked. His nostrils flared, chin lifting.

"Yes."

"Which one?"

Colin hesitated. "Lord Khalaek."

Stephan's eyes narrowed. "The lord inside the tent. The one who rushed to attack."

"Yes."

Colin allowed Stephan a moment to absorb the information, saw it settling into place in Stephan's mind. He relaxed his grip on the King's arm, no longer afraid Stephan would bolt at the first opportunity.

But he couldn't wait long. He could feel the power of the Lifeblood draining from him, absorbed by the effort it took to hold them here, in this moment. He still had to push them back thirty years, back to the first battle here at the Escarpment, back to where all of this had begun, at least for Stephan.

So as soon as he saw Stephan's gaze shift from internal thoughts to him, he shoved hard.

They leaped backward, the world blurring, moving so fast that Colin could only catch glimpses of images as they passed. Most were of the flat, sometimes sunlit, the sky wide and open, sometimes black as pitch, the night sky clouded over. He saw suns set and rise, stars glitter, seasons pass. The moon flickered, full and gibbous, a sickle, new, all at different positions in the sky. Snow blanketed the flat, a rarity, although becoming more common; grass waved in gusty winds, yellow one instant, young green the next; a herd of gaezels grazed, then scattered; rain poured down in sheets as blue-purple lightning scored the heavens.

And then Colin caught the first glimpses of the aftermath of a battle: columns of smoke for the dead, flocks of carrion birds so thick they darkened the sky.

He eased up on the flow of time, the blur settling down to a smear. The black smoke vanished, the dead rose, sunlight poured down to glitter on spears, on swords, on armor and banners, pennants and flags. It bathed the horses and men of three armies, fell on a dusty expanse of flat land at the edge of the Escarpment, the deadly cliffs plummeting to the west.

The armies were positioned differently from the current battle. The Legion, led by King Maarten, by the Governors of the Provinces, a young Stephan—not yet eighteen years of age—among the ranks, held the south. They were already lined up in groups of forty, spread out, reserves fidgeting in the back and on the eastern flank, all of them facing the Alvritshai's White Phalanx and the other House Phalanx to the north, on the far side of the flat. Colin could see the now familiar banners of the Houses of the Evant, could pick them out against the clear sky as the summer sun rose. He could feel the heat, could smell the grass, not yet trampled into the earth by thousands of gaezels.

With a start, he realized that he and Stephan stood on the field in the same position where Stephan had been battling the Alvritshai when Colin had stolen him away. But here, in this time, it was where the dwarren would be arriving at any moment. "We need to move," he said.

"Why?" Stephan murmured. His eyes were locked on his own forces to the south, were centered on the highest banners.

On his father.

His expression was profound, yet unreadable, too full of scattered emotions.

"Because we're standing where the dwarren Riders will be in another ten minutes."

Stephan looked at him, and at the same moment the sound of more than a thousand gaezels thundered out of the distance as the dwarren force rose over a far-off ridge.

"Move," Stephan said, and began to run. South, toward his own ranks.

Colin was dragged along behind. He knew they couldn't be trampled by the gaezels, but he'd already been in the midst of one of their stampedes and didn't want to experience that again. Heart bursting, he stumbled after the King, his shorter legs threatening to give out beneath him as he tried to keep up with Stephan's pace, the sound of the dwarren's approach rising behind them.

Then the roar of the gaezels shifted. Glancing over his shoulder, he saw them swerve, banking away from the Alvritshai to the north, arcing around toward the Legion to the south, toward Stephan and Colin's position. But Colin had seen the dwarren perform this maneuver before, and he knew that the arc wouldn't reach them, would cut in sharply at the edge as they regrouped and re-formed, so he slowed, dragging Stephan back with him.

They watched as the dwarren reassembled, the thunder of their passage dying down, their drums silent. Their line was curved, facing both the Alvritshai's White Phalanx and the Legion.

Colored flags began waving among the Legion, men readying, shouts rising into the stillness. Horns blew from the Alvritshai line. Tensions grew, almost tangible, roiling on the air between the three armies.

And then a signal was passed. Colin didn't see it—they were too distant—but he felt it on the air, felt it shift.

The Legion charged with a hoarse battle cry, the Alvritshai as well, the dwarren surging forward on their gaezels as their drums began pounding. Stephan took a step forward, his hand tightening on the hilt of his sword, as if he yearned to join the battle, as if the battle cry had pulled him forward, but Colin held him in check.

"I remember this," he said, his eyes darting over the field. The Legion and Phalanx were rushing toward each other, the dwarren coming in from the side—

But then the human and Alvritshai ranks pivoted. Instead of heading directly toward each other, those nearest the cliffs of the Escarpment began turning inward, those closest to the dwarren slowing down, until the two forces merged . . . and fell upon the dwarren.

"I remember this," Stephan said, louder. He turned toward Colin. "What have you done? Is it real?"

"It's real," Colin murmured. "I've brought you back to the battlefield, so you can witness what really happened."

"Then I have to stop it," Stephan growled. He began moving toward the fighting, the battle playing out before them both, the dwarren Riders shoving hard against the Legion, pushing them back, the Alvritshai doing the same, the three races eddying back and forth, the tension Colin had felt on the air broken, shattered, replaced now by desperation. The tension had encompassed the entire field; the desperation was focused on individual battles, the clash of swords and weapons between men. "I have to warn my father!"

"You can't," Colin said, and when Stephan ignored him, continued toward the battle, plowing stubbornly through the grass, he dug in his heels and jerked Stephan back. "You can't!"

Stephan turned on him, fist clenched so hard Colin could feel the muscles in his arm contract. He raised his sword threateningly, but Colin met his gaze steadily, saw the raw pain there.

He sighed, let his own pain over Karen's death at the hands of the Shadows and his inability to go back and warn her bleed into his voice. "It doesn't work that way, Stephan. I can bring you here, I can show you, but neither of us can change anything. It's already happened. It can't be altered." He swallowed but heard the roughness creep into his voice nonetheless. "Trust me, I've tried."

Stephan shoulders tensed . . . then drooped.

He lowered the sword, his entire body sagging. "So what do we do?" he asked, bitterness edging the resignation.

"We watch."

He closed his eyes, then drew in a deep breath and let it out in a slow, emotion-riddled sigh.

And they watched. The battle ebbed and flowed, fluid and violent. Colin found himself thinking back to the storyteller at the inn in Portstown, to when he'd first heard of the battle at the Escarpment. But that had been a story, told after the fact, tweaked and twisted to manipulate the teller's audience, colored by the emotions and half-memories of those who were here.

The battle itself was different. It wasn't as smooth, as concise or coordinated. It wasn't as honorable. Men were torn from their horses and crushed underfoot. Gaezels skewered others with their lethal horns. Groups were separated from the lines as dwarren broke through, were surrounded, then slaughtered. And when the battle shifted, it left behind the dead and wounded, men and Alvritshai and dwarren crawling on elbows to escape, or dragging themselves with one arm as their life's blood soaked into the grasses beneath them.

It was vicious, and cruel, and merciless.

And as the sun shifted overhead, the tide turned. The dwarren Riders had held the Legion and the Phalanx off, had fought fiercely, but they'd been unprepared for the combined forces, for the alliance between the humans and the Alvritshai. As morning bled into afternoon, the dwarren forces grew weary. Their responses slowed, reinforcements called to block breaks in the line didn't arrive on time, and men and Alvritshai spilled through the holes in the defenses.

An hour after midday, the tenor of the dwarren drums changed, and the dwarren began to retreat.

Colin recalled what the storyteller said happened next and looked toward Stephan. He'd cleaned and sheathed his sword as they watched, had relaxed, his eyes intent on the field, analyzing, shaking his head occasionally as something significant happened.

Now, though, he took an involuntary step forward.

On the flat below, signals were passed, flags flashing in the sunlight. A large force broke away from the rear of the human ranks, led by a single man on horseback.

Led by Stephan.

Colin could hear the young Stephan's battle cry as he charged toward the dwarren flanks. Men broke away from the army in answer to his cry, until a hundred men trailed him.

He struck the retreating dwarren's flank first, at least ten strides ahead of those that followed him. He drove into the ranks, sword flying, was almost absorbed by the dwarren's reaction before the rest of his contingent arrived.

On the ridge where they stood watching, Stephan shook his head. "Stupid. Stupid and foolish."

Colin said nothing.

On the flat, the Alvritshai surged around the dwarren's other flank, joining forces with Stephan and the Legion, so that the dwarren were encircled. They pushed hard, the dwarren shoving back, but there were too many against them. They were hemmed in on all sides, with no escape.

Except the one the Legion and Phalanx offered them. To the west, the two lines parted, as if crumbling beneath the dwarren onslaught. And the dwarren seized the opening, surging through the break—

Only to find themselves at the edge of the Escarpment. They turned back, Alvritshai blocking them to the north, the Legion to the south, the combined forces—led by Stephan—pressing them from the east.

The dwarren closest to the edge milled about, dashed to the north, to the south, their own line pushing them from the east. Their motions became frantic as the space between the Riders and the cliff decreased, as the realization of what was to come spread through their ranks. But the humans and Alvritshai didn't slow, didn't waver. They continued to advance, inexorably, dead falling in the hundreds as the dwarren became more and more frenzied, more and more desperate.

When the first few dwarren, still astride their gaezels, tumbled over the edge of the cliff, Colin stirred. Sickened, he turned away, unable to watch as the human and Alvritshai ranks closed, the knot of dwarren dwindling. But he couldn't block out the screams of the dwarren, the inhuman shrieks of the gaezels.

He paused at the look of horror on Stephan's face. He'd expected to see triumph, or vindication.

He met Colin's gaze. "I don't remember the screams," he said. "All I remember is a blood-rush of noise, filling my head. All I remember is heat and sweat and a trembling, as if my entire body were vibrating. And exhaustion. I remember feeling exhausted."

"We need to move," Colin said. "If you want to know the truth, we need to move to the cliff's edge."

He nodded, lips pressing tight together.

They walked through the grass, to the edge of the dry and dusty flat, to the edge of the battle. They moved among the dead and dying, scattered at first, the bodies piled thicker as they passed the central part of the battlefield. The stench was overpowering, the death ghastly. Colin stared at the faces as he passed—Alvritshai, dwarren, and human—saw heads crushed in, faces shattered, throats slit and limbs severed. He saw bodies cut from shoulder to shoulder, throat to groin. He saw horses impaled on spears, gaezels riddled with arrows.

And then the death became too much. He fixed his eyes on the armies milling around the edge of the cliff, Alvritshai and Legion mixed together as the last of the dwarren died. They moved among them, weaving in and out through the crush of bodies, through the reek of a day's worth of drenching sweat and spilled blood.

They were halfway to the Escarpment when a ragged cheer broke out.

Stephan pushed forward faster, and Colin followed, keeping up. Stephan knew when the Alvritshai had turned on his father; he'd been here.

They broke through the combined army into an open area, King Maarten and his escort on the left, staring across the expanse at Tamaell Fedorem and the Lords of the Evant on the right. Stephan—the boy, not yet eighteen—stood back, behind the Governors of the Provinces who were present, behind their escorts, everyone in the Legion cheering, clapping each other on the back. Someone ruffled the young Stephan's hair, and he grinned uncontrollably, ducking out of the way.

Maarten was grinning as well, shaking hands with a few of his Governors. One of them leaned forward and shouted something over the noise, and Maarten burst out in laughter, the sound rolling over the general noise.

And then the King turned toward the Alvritshai, toward where Tamaell Fedorem waited, his lords arrayed behind him.

The Alvritshai were more subdued. They did not shout or cheer, although most of those behind the Tamaell, behind the Evant, were exultant, grinning in weariness and exhaustion. Those mixed in with the Legion endured the slaps of their allies with tight smiles.

But the Lords of the Evant and the Tamaell himself stood formally. Khalaek stood to the Tamaell's left, a few paces away, another between them. He had not yet risen high enough in the Evant to stand beside the Tamaell. Colin did not see Aeren, but then he realized that Aeren had not been part of the Evant yet, that his brother had ruled the House at the time of the battle . . . and that his brother had died here, on these fields.

And one of the Lords of the Evant was missing. Aeren must have been away when this had happened. He must have been with his brother.

Seeing the Alvritshai waiting, King Maarten quieted, the silence spreading outward in a wave, not quite dying on the outskirts of the army.

But here, at its center, at the edge of the Escarpment, the celebration stilled.

Maarten and Fedorem regarded each other over that stillness. Maarten sheathed his sword, Fedorem doing the same, and they both stepped forward.

"It is done," Tamaell Fedorem said in Andovan.

Maarten chuckled. "It is done."

Maarten extended his hand. Fedorem smiled, reached forward to shake it.

The moment trembled. Colin felt it, its weight bearing down upon him. All of the fighting, all of the conflict between the two races, between them and the dwarren—all of it would end here. An accord had been reached, an alliance struck. Everything would change.

Except that at that moment, Khalaek, Peloroun, and a lord Colin did not recognize but who wore the colors of House Baene, leaped forward, knives gleaming.

Maarten had enough time to lurch back before Khalaek's blade buried itself in his neck, above his armor. The Lord of House Baene sank his own blade in Maarten's side, even as Khalaek jerked his free and struck again and again. Lord Peloroun grabbed Fedorem's shoulders, the Tamaell clearly stunned, and hauled him back. The rest of the Lords of the Evant looked as stunned as Fedorem, eyes wide in shock, Lord Barak appearing confused.

They weren't given time to recover. Someone in the Legion—one of the Governors, or perhaps one of the men who made up Maarten's personal guard—shouted, "Betrayal! They've murdered the King!"

Shock transformed to horror and rage in the space of a breath. The Legion, its Governors at the forefront, surged forward. Khalaek roared something in Alvritshai, something Colin didn't recognize, and suddenly the air was filled with hundreds of arrows, launched from the rear of the Alvritshai army. The Alvritshai at the front took a moment longer to recover, as if they couldn't quite believe what had happened, what *was* happening, even as the arrows cut into the Legion itself, dozens dying in an instant.

Then the human army overwhelmed them.

In its midst, Colin saw the lord he didn't recognize cut down, even as he drew his knife from Maarten's body. Khalaek drew his cattan, pierced the first enraged Legionnaire to make it to him, then thrust the body into those behind as he retreated. Through the chaos, he saw the young Stephan screaming, his voice lost among the crash of weapons, the roaring outcry. He tried to press forward, but the Legionnaires around the young heir were dragging him back, the rest of the Legion surging around him, protecting him, all of their faces locked in rage.

The elder Stephan watched in silence, even as the battle began anew around them. He watched as he was pulled away, drawn to safety, watched as the Legion surrounded his fallen father's body, watched as the two armies fell upon each other, the moment of accord shredding before his eyes.

"Stop it," he said, his voice dull. When Colin didn't react fast enough, he spun, eyes blazing, and shouted, "Stop it! I don't want to see any more!"

Reaching out, Colin seized the moment and halted it.

He waited, giving Stephan time to think, time to adjust to what he'd seen. He hadn't been certain what he would find here. Aeren hadn't been able to tell him, because he hadn't witnessed it himself. He'd only known what Aeren suspected, what Aeren had learned from those lords who had been here and were willing to speak to him.

But what had happened seemed clear.

Stephan finally stirred.

Without turning, he said softly, "Take me back."

And Colin did.

"To me!" Eraeth roared at Aeren's side. "House Rhyssal to its lord!"

To either side, the remains of Aeren's Phalanx pulled back desperately toward Eraeth's voice as he continued to shout. Aeren didn't have time to count how many still survived, too intent on keeping the Legion from overrunning his position completely.

Lotaern and the Order of the Flames' flaming swords and the churning earth might have worked if the Legion hadn't had fresh reinforcements waiting.

Now, the Alvritshai lines had shattered completely, pockets of Alvritshai fighting desperately all across the field, all of them trying to retreat toward the Tamaell Presumptive's center, his horns blaring the retreat, issuing no other orders except to fall back, the direction of the retreat changing every moment as Thaedoren withdrew as well. They'd already been driven beyond where the acolytes had called forth Aielan's Light from the earth. They were approaching the ridge overlooking the flat, beyond which stood the Alvritshai camp.

And the Legion would not stop. Aeren could feel it. With a sinking sensation, Aeren realized that the Alvritshai could not win, that they might not even survive the battle, as the dwarren Riders had not survived thirty years before.

And then shouts rang out, spreading through the mass of Legion before him. He couldn't see past the crush of men, but he felt the pressure pushing the Alvritshai back decrease, the faces of the men before him turning to look back, exclaiming in anger, in disbelief. Those at the front didn't stop fighting until they realized that those behind were retreating, backing off step by careful step.

When the men Aeren grappled with finally withdrew, Aeren gasped and sagged, one hand going to his side, coming away black with blood. His own blood. He hadn't even felt the cut, hadn't seen the blade that had scored there, opening the flesh beneath the edge of his armor. It wasn't a mortal wound, but he placed his hand over it and pressed, trying to halt the blood flow. His armor weighed down on him, his cattan heavy, but he remained upright as Eraeth staggered to his side, his own face covered in blood from a wound to his head.

To either side, the Legion were retreating, leaving the decimated Alvritshai behind. Aeren picked out Thaedoren and closed his eyes in relief, began counting up the rest of the Lords of the Evant. He saw Peloroun and Jydell, Waerren and Vaersoom, Waerren's forces cut down to fewer than fifty men. None of Lord Barak's House remained, and he didn't see Barak either. Altogether, he estimated there were fewer than fifteen hundred Alvritshai remaining on the field.

Over four thousand had arrived at the flat.

The loss of life sickened him. It would take decades for the Alvritshai to recoup such death.

If they recouped at all.

"What . . ." Aeren heaved; he couldn't seem to catch his breath, ". . . happened?"

"Look," Eraeth said, and pointed.

Turning, Aeren saw where the main bulk of the Legion's forces had regrouped. He saw the flags of the King, but not the King himself, saw those flags break away and head toward two figures walking toward them, a small group of Legion slightly behind.

Aeren frowned. "That's Colin."

"With the King."

They shared a look. Then: "I thought Colin was with Moiran in the Tamaell's tents."

Eraeth's frown deepened. He nearly growled. "He was."

On the flat, the King and Colin merged with the approaching contingent of banners and horsemen. After a pause, the King led the group back to the main army as ragged cheers broke out.

"Gather the House," Aeren said. "Regroup with Thaedoren."

"What's going on?" Eraeth asked.

Aeren shook his head. "I don't know."

As Eraeth gathered what was left of House Rhyssal's Phalanx, Aeren moved toward Thaedoren's pennants, wincing as pain flared in his side. Halfway there his House arrived, Eraeth leading all two hundred of them, a horse in tow. With help, Aeren made it into the saddle, someone cinching a makeshift bandage around his waist. His Phalanx behind him, he rode through the White Phalanx's ranks to Thaedoren.

"What's happening?" he asked.

Thaedoren shot him a look, nodded in acknowledgment then turned his attention back to the Legion. "The Legion has withdrawn. It appears to be on the order of King Stephan."

"How did the King get to the far side of the battle?" Lord Jydell asked as he trotted toward them.

Thaedoren frowned. "I . . . don't know."

"He had Colin with him," Aeren said abruptly, as he suddenly understood.

The Tamaell Presumptive's eyes narrowed thoughtfully.

They waited, the surviving lords joining them, each asking the same questions, no one coming up with any answers.

Then flags were waved at the edge of the Legion's forces, asking for a parley.

Thaedoren straightened in his saddle, brow furrowed.

"He'll want our surrender," Peloroun said tightly.

Thaedoren glanced toward him, let his gaze wander

over all the lords present. "Aeren and Jydell, you're with me."

Aeren caught Eraeth's gaze, and his Protector fell in beside him as they moved out onto the flat, stepping over bodies. Jydell had brought his own Protector, and two of the White Phalanx accompanied Thaedoren. Across the field, King Stephan, Tanner Dain, and Colin matched their progress, the King surrounded by two Governors and a contingent of seven Legionnaires.

They met halfway between the two armies, each group halting when they were ten paces apart. The Governors, Tanner, and the Legionnaires glared at the Alvritshai, on edge, their hands close to their swords. Stephan regarded them with a cold eye, frowning, as if he didn't know what to think of the Alvritshai lords, of Thaedoren. Colin appeared pale, unfocused. His face was pallid, his eyes bleary, and the bandage over his chest was black with blood, the Alvritshai shirt he wore matted to it.

The Tamaell Presumptive nudged his horse forward a step. "What is it you wished to say?"

Stephan stiffened, lifted his chin. "The fighting needs to end."

Thaedoren nodded, face neutral. "You wish us to surrender."

Stephan shook his head. "No. I want a truce. Between us. With the dwarren. A truce among all of us."

His Governors and a few of the Legion instantly protested, their voices loud, hands gesturing, until one voice broke through the others.

"You can't be serious!" the Governor exclaimed. "We have them on their knees. We can crush their resistance here, now! We can crush *them*—"

"No!" Stephan barked, cutting the Governor off with a look.

The Governor's anger narrowed as he drew himself up in his saddle. "At least require their surrender. Take hostages to ensure their behavior."

Stephan considered for a moment, then shook his head again. "No. They didn't come here to fight this battle. We did. That's the only reason we've managed to subdue them."

Tanner Dain sidled closer and said in a low voice that

could nevertheless be heard by everyone, "Remember what happened here thirty years ago. Remember your father. These pale-skinned bastards don't deserve any mercy."

Stephan shifted and glanced at Colin, who was looking even worse now. "But I do remember, Tanner. Better than you might imagine. And yes, some of them deserve no mercy—" his voice hardened. "—and they will get none. But not all of them."

Tanner clenched his jaw. "Then you believe their lies?"

"I didn't," Stephan said, an edge of warning creeping into his tone, "but I do now."

Tanner's gaze shot toward Colin in suspicion, but he listened to the unspoken warning and said nothing.

As soon as his commander backed off and the grumbling of the Governors had subsided, he turned back to Thaedoren. "There are conditions."

Cautious, Thaedoren asked, "What conditions?"

"Lord Aeren, when he came to see me in Corsair to suggest an accord, claimed that not all the Lords of the Evant were involved in my father's murder. I didn't believe it then because of everything I'd been told since the battle, everything that I'd come to see as true. But I've been shown the truth, and I realize that he was correct. Only three lords were involved. One of them was killed almost immediately. And one did not actually raise a weapon against my father that day, he simply pulled the Tamaell—your father—to safety." Stephan's eyes darkened, his voice deepened. "But the other, this Lord Khalaek . . . I want him."

Thaedoren's shoulders squared. "He has already been sequestered for murdering the Tamaell—"

"If you want this treaty—if you want this peace—*then you will give him to me.*"

It was said softly, between clenched teeth, but the anger, the rage, came through clearly.

Aeren adjusted his position in the saddle, but didn't dare look at the Tamaell Presumptive. There were too many emotions involved, too many political implications regarding Khalaek and the Evant, Thaedoren and Stephan, the Alvritshai and the Provinces.

"Very well," Thaedoren said. "But Lord Khalaek must face the Evant first."

Stephan shrugged. "As long as I get him alive."

Thaedoren nodded. "I'll make certain of that. What are your other conditions?"

"That the dwarren be included in the treaty, that Lord Aeren be there for the talks, that we meet on this field, in the open, just you, me, the Cochen, and one adviser each, along with him." He motioned toward Colin, who didn't react. The human's head had dropped, hair falling over his face so that Aeren could no longer see his eyes.

Aeren shifted forward. "Speaking of Colin," he began, but paused when both Thaedoren and Stephan turned their gazes on him. Both had frowned at the interruption, but they were too focused on each other, on the discussion. Neither had even looked at Colin. "Speaking of Colin," he began again, "I'd ask that you allow my Protector to take him to our healers. He's obviously wounded."

Their attention shifted toward Colin sharply, even as he began to list in his saddle. Stephan swore and caught him before he could fall, holding him upright. "Of course," he said. "Take him."

Eraeth moved forward immediately, bringing his mount alongside Colin's. With Stephan's help, Eraeth pulled Colin's body into the saddle in front of him and headed back toward the Alvritshai camp.

Stephan watched them for a moment, then turned back to Thaedoren. "We can discuss everything else once we've had a chance to recover. Tend to your wounded. I'll send an emissary to the dwarren and arrange matters with them, as well as discuss them with my Governors."

"As will I with the Evant."

"Very well."

The two leaders nodded at each other, then turned and headed back to their own armies.

"That was ... unexpected," Lord Jydell muttered.

"Yes," Thaedoren said tightly, "but welcome. Assemble the Evant, and order everyone else to begin searching for the wounded on the field. And collecting the dead."

"And what will the Evant be discussing?"

Thaedoren's face tightened with anger. "Lord Khalaek."

～

When Colin woke the first time, he never opened his eyes.

He could sense someone leaning over him. And then,

as if through a dense fog, he heard someone say, "Will he survive?"

He recognized Stephan's voice, could feel the King withdraw slightly.

"He should never have survived the knife to his chest," Aeren answered. "I don't understand how he had enough strength to take you to the battle thirty years ago. But yes, we think he will survive."

A long silence. "Who is he?"

Someone snorted, and Colin smiled. Eraeth. He could imagine Aeren's glare.

"He came from Portstown."

"That wasn't what I asked."

"That's all I can say," Aeren answered. "Other than to say that he is Rhyssal-aein, a friend."

"He's more," Eraeth said gruffly. "More than Rhyssal-aein. He is a member of the House. He is Colin Harten, Colin Shaeveran. He is touched by Aielan and touched by shadow."

A significant pause, and then Aeren said, "Indeed."

Colin heard movement, people shifting. Stephan sighed. "I suppose we should start the talks without him then. I'd hoped he would have recovered by now."

"The wound was deep," Aeren answered carefully. "Deeper than perhaps we know."

"Then let him rest," Stephan said, his voice already retreating. Colin listened as Aeren and Eraeth followed. "We'll begin at midday, on the field. Is everything prepared?"

"I believe so . . ."

And then the voices faded, and Colin faded with them.

When he woke the second time, he opened his eyes to find Moiran and Aeren talking quietly on one side. He listened to the soft murmur of their words, not trying to understand, simply staring up at the undulating canvas of the tent above. The room was lit with a soft lamp, shadows flickering on the walls.

He stirred, his stomach growling, and the conversation halted.

Moiran appeared first, frowning down at him, Aeren a moment later, both concerned.

"How do you feel?" Moiran asked. It took a moment for Colin to piece together the Alvritshai.

"Hungry," Colin rasped, his voice sticking in his throat. He coughed, winced at the pain. He dug his chin into his chest, trying to see the bandage that bound him. He picked at it, Moiran gently slapping his hand away.

"Leave it," she said, then glanced toward Aeren. "Watch him while I go find something for him to eat."

As soon as Moiran left, Colin asked, "How long have I been asleep?"

"Ten days."

Colin sighed, raised his left arm to scrub at his face, but paused.

The black mark, what had begun as only a freckle on the inside of his wrist, had now spread to his entire arm, the darkness swirling and eddying beneath his skin like a living tattoo.

He stared at it a long moment, the same dread that had seized him in the forest deep in his stomach . . . and then he let his arm drop.

"Is that the price you paid?" Aeren asked. "Is that what it cost to take Stephan back to the first battle to witness his father's death?"

Colin couldn't look at Aeren as he answered. "Yes."

He expected Aeren to protest, to say the cost was too high, that they would have found another way.

Instead, the lord said, "Then the Evant and all of the Alvritshai thank you."

Colin turned, met Aeren's gaze directly, and in his eyes he saw what Aeren could not say, saw the gratitude that could not be expressed in words.

Shifting uncomfortably, he asked, "What happened?" then began struggling up into a seated position. Aeren frowned but helped him, propping pillows up behind him. His chest ached—his entire body ached—but not to the extent it had immediately after the fight in the tent with Walter.

"Stephan has asked for an accord, a treaty among all three races. We've been discussing the terms for the last eight days, after seeing to our wounded and burning the dead, including Tamaell Fedorem. Thaedoren has met with the dwarren shamans and chiefs and made a formal apology for desecrating the Lands. He has pledged the Evant and the Alvritshai to the preservation of the Lands, as they requested, which is the main reason the dwarren are talking at all. I was there. It was ... an interesting ceremony. And I believe Thaedoren actually intends to enforce the pledge." He sat back, having gotten Colin settled. "Stephan would have waited longer to start the talks—he wanted you to be there—but we convinced him that you needed time to recover."

"Why would he want me there?"

"Perhaps because of what you did. But also, I think, because of what happened in the parley tent with Fedorem. He wanted you there in case the Wraith returned." He held Colin's gaze a long moment. "Could the Wraith return? Or is it dead?"

Colin thought about Walter, about the wound he'd inflicted, about the fact that Walter had drunk from the Well in the forest, and grimaced. "He's not dead. He's like me. He'll heal."

"And where is he now?"

Colin shook his head. "I don't know. But I think he'd head back to the Well, back to the forest. The Faelehgre will know. I'll find out from them as soon as I can. He was wounded as badly as I was."

"Worse. Khalaek stabbed him as well in order to escape."

Colin's eyebrows rose in surprise. He hadn't seen what transpired between the two. "What's happened to Khalaek?"

Aeren looked away, troubled and angry. He stood, began pacing. "The Evant has declared him a traitor. If it had been anyone but a lord of the Evant, anyone but him, he would have been executed immediately. But he is a lord, and as one of the conditions of the treaty, Stephan has required that we hand him over to the Provinces for justice. So the Evant has decided to exile Khalaek from the Evant, from all of Alvritshai lands, forever. He'll be banished after the treaty has been completed and then immediately given over to Stephan."

"When will that happen?"

"Tomorrow ... or perhaps the day after, depending on when the final minor details of the treaty are agreed upon." Aeren stopped pacing and faced Colin. "Will you be well enough to attend?"

"Yes," Colin said. "Whether Moiran agrees with me or not."

Aeren smiled, the expression vanishing the instant Moiran ducked beneath the tent flap with a tray of food held carefully before her.

As she rose from her stooped position, she froze and shot Aeren a glare. "You let him sit up?"

When Aeren said nothing, she sniffed and moved to Colin's side. The smell of hot soup filled the tent as she settled down beside him and checked his bandage, and his stomach rumbled loudly. Satisfied he'd come to no harm, she spooned up some of the soup and brought it to his lips, murmuring, "I leave you alone for five minutes . . ."

Colin nearly moaned as the soup filled his mouth with flavor.

Aeren grinned. "I'll return tomorrow," he said, moving toward the door flap.

"I'll be ready."

"Ready for what?" Moiran snapped.

Colin sent Aeren a wordless plea for help, but the lord ducked out of the tent with a low chuckle.

~

The next night, as the sun set, the Lords of the Evant gathered with their guardsmen and a few of their aides in the center of the flat. To the north, east, and south, sounds of celebration could be heard, muted by distance. The treaty had been agreed upon and signed. Official borders had been established and terms worked out regarding trade, politics, and aid. It was still tentative, still a little too new, no side quite trusting the others.

But it was a beginning.

Aeren stood at the front of the Alvritshai contingent along with Thaedoren. The rest of the lords hung back, their guards surrounding Khalaek, his hands secured behind his back. The Lord of House Duvoraen had suffered at the hands of the White Phalanx. Bruises covered his face, his arms, his chest. Aeren expected there would be more bruising beneath his clothes. His lip had been split and was crusted now with dried blood, but he stood rigid, back straight, head high, an arrogant sneer touching those lips. He kept his gaze forward, not looking at any of the

Lords of the Evant, not reacting, even when one of the guards spat on the ground at his feet.

On the horizon, the sun vanished, the orange of the sky darkening and fading, the light withdrawing. Darkness bled westward, stars slipping into existence. Scattered fires appeared throughout all three armies.

And a single fire wound its way onto the flat from the direction of the human forces.

"Here they come," Thaedoren said.

The lords waiting behind fidgeted, and in the light of the lanterns they'd brought with them, Aeren saw fear flit across Khalaek's face, there and then gone, the arrogance returning.

They waited, the night cooling around them. A breeze gusted past, bringing with it smoke and the smell of roasted meat. Aeren glanced at Eraeth, at Colin on his Protector's far side, the human looking healthier than he had any right to be, then turned back.

King Stephan and his Legion had arrived.

They came out of the darkness and into the Alvritshai lights like shadows, halted on the far reaches of that light. Aeren saw one of the Governors, Tanner Dain, and a few Legionnaires . . . but that was all. No escort of guardsmen to lead Khalaek back to the human army, no tribunal. Just Stephan and what Aeren would consider a minimal escort.

Ice slid down into his gut, and he grimaced.

Stephan meant to take care of Khalaek here.

"Do you have him?" Stephan asked.

Thaedoren stepped forward. "We do. But first we need to formally banish him."

Stephan nodded.

Turning, Thaedoren motioned to the White Phalanx, who shoved Khalaek out into the space before the Tamaell Presumptive . . . the Tamaell in truth now, Aeren realized. There, they forced him to his knees in the churned up earth so that Thaedoren looked down on him.

"Khalaek," Thaedoren said, and for a moment he let his own pain and hatred of the lord seep into his voice, "the Evant has ruled that you are a traitor to the Alvritshai people, that you conspired to murder the Tamaell of the Evant, and that you have betrayed the trust and loyalty given to you as Lord of House Duvoraen. As such, your life is forfeit. Your House has fallen, and a new House will ascend in its stead. Your lands, your properties, and all that is yours, will be given to the rising lord."

No one within the Alvritshai ranks stirred, not even Lord Peloroun.

"However," Thaedoren said, drawing a dagger from its sheath at his waist as he spoke. Khalaek flinched back, the White Phalanx around him grabbing his shoulders, holding him in place. "You were a Lord of the Evant. Because of this, and because of the newly established treaty with the Provinces, the sentence of death is rescinded. Instead, you will be branded a traitor and exiled from Alvritshai lands forever. Any who harbor you, any who give you aid, will be deemed traitors to the Alvritshai as well and punished accordingly."

With that, Thaedoren stepped forward, grasped Khalaek by the hair and thrust his head back, turning it so that his cheek was exposed. He struggled, the Phalanx bearing down on him, but he stilled as soon as the blade touched his skin.

Thaedoren brought the dagger down slowly, slicing deep, cutting from near the corner of his eye, down along the cheek, to the base of the jaw. Khalaek hissed as blood welled, lantern light dancing on his face, the blood appearing black. As it dripped onto Khalaek's shirt, Thaedoren twisted the lord's head in the other direction and cut again on the opposite side, the same mark, taking his time, savoring the pain he inflicted.

When he was done, he pushed Khalaek's head back roughly and spat into the lord's face. "From now on, you are Khalaek-khai. You are nothing. Less than nothing."

Khalaek fought the White Phalanx as they held him in check, blood flying as he thrashed his head back and forth.

But Thaedoren ignored him. Turning to face Stephan, he said, "He's all yours."

Then he turned, motioned to his Phalanx, to the lords, and moved away from Khalaek. The White Phalanx thrust Khalaek to the ground, where he writhed in the dirt, trying to rise, to gain his feet, his arms still trussed behind him.

But Stephan and the humans moved in, taking Thaedoren's place.

Before Khalaek could gain his knees, the Legionnaires grabbed him, jerked him to his feet, spun him so he stood facing Stephan. His breath came in ragged gasps, and dirt now smeared his face, mixing with the blood.

Stephan drew his own dagger. Without preamble, he growled, "This is for my father."

He shoved the dagger into Khalaek's stomach, beneath the rib cage, one hand reaching up almost gently to cup the back of Khalaek's head and bend him over the blade. He held it there a long moment, Khalaek gasping. Blood drooled from Khalaek's mouth in a sickening, wet stream.

Then Stephan's hand shifted. His fingers tangled in Khalaek's hair, pulled him upright, and with a vicious wrench he tore the dagger from Khalaek's gut.

He let Khalaek fall. The Legionnaires had stepped back, so that now he faced Thaedoren and the Alvritshai over Khalaek's body.

"Are the final terms of the treaty now satisfied?" Thaedoren asked, his voice expressionless.

"Yes."

"Good."

And without another word, the two rulers turned and headed back toward their respective armies in the darkness, their escorts trailing behind them.

~

The shadow waited until darkness had reclaimed the flat . . . and then it waited a moment longer.

When night had settled again, the songs and dancing of the celebration thinning, it moved forward to the body left in the middle of the field. It gazed down at the crumpled shape a long moment, barely visible in the starlight, in the faint luminescence of the partial moon.

Then it crouched. Placing a hand on the body's shoulder, it rolled Khalaek over onto his back.

The ex-lord moaned and coughed up a gout of blood. His guts lay partially exposed, blood bathing his entire front, drenching the earth beneath where he'd lain, but the figure ignored all the gore, moving so it could look into Khalaek's glazed eyes.

There wasn't much life left in those eyes, but there was enough.

The shadow smiled. "Ah, Khalaek-khai. If I didn't have a use for you, I'd sit here and watch you die."

Walter pulled a vial from his coat, held it up to the star-light a moment so he could peer through the clear liquid within then pulled the stopper.

Leaning close, he whispered, "Drink this," then dribbled some of the liquid onto Khalaek's lips.

And the scent of wet earth and dried leaves filled Khalaek's senses.

S.L. Farrell

The Nessantico Cycle

"[Farrell's] best yet, a delicious melange of politics, war,
sorcery, and religion in a richly imagined world."
—George R. R. Martin,
New York Times bestselling author

"Readers who appreciate intricate world building,
intrigue and action will immerse themselves effortlessly
in this rich and complex story."
—*Publishers Weekly*

A MAGIC OF TWILIGHT
978-0-7564-0536-6

A MAGIC OF NIGHTFALL
978-0-7564-0599-1

A MAGIC OF DAWN
978-0-7564-0646-2

To Order Call: 1-800-788-6262
www.dawboks.com